I0822848

BROKEN ALLIANCES SERIES

Alliances are broken and hearts stolen.

SADIE WINCHESTER

Cover art by Artista Gráfico Cover Design.

Editing by Baldwin Editing Services. Second Round Editing by Nikki Clark PA (Oct. 2024).

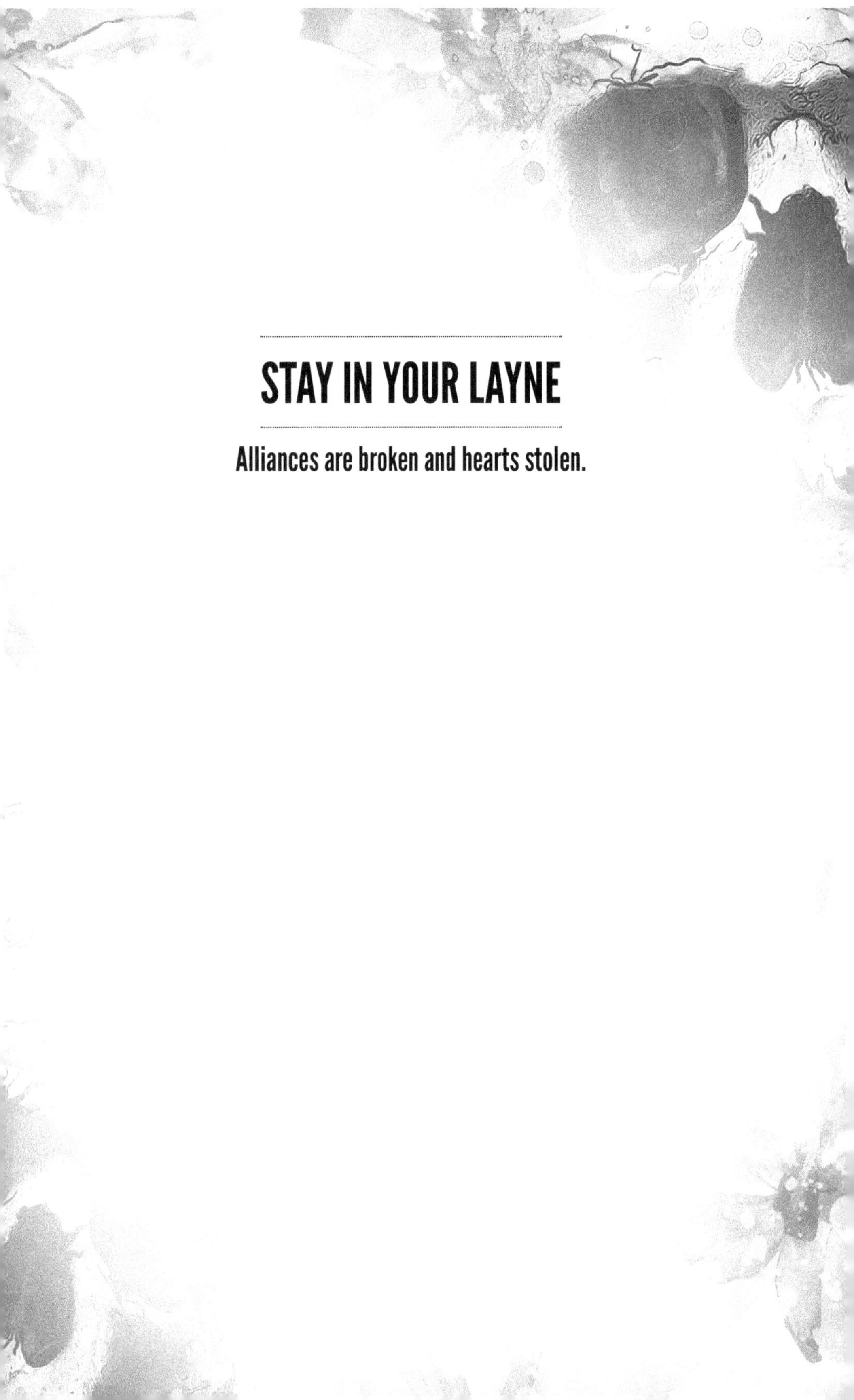

STAY IN YOUR LAYNE

Alliances are broken and hearts stolen.

For all those who never thought they could:

Life is short. Do the thing.

OFFICIAL PLAYLIST

Blow (ft. Spencer Charnas) - Eva Under Fire
Breathe Underwater - Bullet For My Valentine
Coming Undone - Korn
Contemptress (ft. Maria Brink) - Motionless In White
Harder To Breathe - Letdown.
Just Pretend - Bad Omens
Little Fight Left - Tommee Profitt, Fleurie, Jung Youth
Love the Way You Hate Me - Like A Storm
One For The Money - Escape The Fate
Popular Monster - Falling In Reverse
Save Yourself - My Darkest Days
Snuff - Slipknot
Take Me Back To Eden - Sleep Token
THE DEATH OF PEACE OF MIND - Bad Omens
The Very Last Time - Bullet For My Valentine
Voices In My Head - Falling In Reverse
When The Darkness Comes - Jeris Johnson
You're Going Down - Sick Puppies
Your Betrayal - Bullet For My Valentine

The official playlist can be found on Spotify.

CONTENT & TRIGGER WARNINGS

All trigger and content warnings can be found on www. sadiewinchester.com.

CHAPTER ONE

Three years ago

She had been away from home for the past four years. Had it been Layne's choice? Hell the fuck no. She would have preferred to stay in the Upper East Side, where she had been born and raised in New York.

According to her father, going to school for an education and degree was far more valuable than deep diving into the family business. Insert Layne's aggressive eye roll here. However, she had a solid hunch that he had sent her away to get her off his back about getting more heavily involved in his business dealings of the organized crime persuasion.

You see, her family was at the pinnacle of power in the city's criminal underworld, and her father sat at the top of his organization as the kingpin.

Another reason to send her away to the other side of the country? So she would stop picking fights and inserting herself into legitimately dangerous situations.

Layne couldn't help herself. She had always had an attitude the size of the Hudson, and an even bigger right hook. Just ask Rob Holmes, her first (ex) boyfriend from when she was in the tenth grade. Nothing topped getting your clock rung by a girl in front of the entire gym class.

Living out on the West Coast at UCLA for the last four years didn't change any of those pesky personality traits. The only thing going out west got her was an expensive piece of paper and time to polish her fighting technique with a few high-end trainers. Daddy didn't even realize what his money was paying for. The one thing she didn't come home with? A tan. Damn her Irish genetics.

Most people knew her father as Scott O'Reilly—Scotty to his closest confidants. When questions were asked about the details of the family business? It was always don't ask, don't tell. The criminal underworld they operated in was a carefully crafted web of a few legitimate business transactions, under-the-table negotiations, and outright violence and intimidation tactics.

Her dad took pride in his heritage, having been born in a small town just south of Limerick, his mother and father moved themselves over to the U.S. when he was a wee lad of just two years old. Any traces of an accent were non-existent, but the Irish tricolor ran through every fiber of his being.

The hired associates who took orders from Mr. O'Reilly were part of a local network of men of mostly Irish-Catholic descent throughout the footprint of Manhattan. Most of them were well-versed in the sketched-out operations within the shadows of the underworld. There was no sense in hiring rebellious kids who were looking to make a quick buck and potentially get a stint behind bars due to their irresponsible fuckups.

Any women that were part of the network of employees merely had the archaic supporting role of either popping out all the babies or being the friendly entertainment for all those hardworking men her father employed.

From a young age, Layne knew that she was not like the other ladies she saw coming and going from O'Reilly Manor at all hours of the night. By contrast, there was her mother who embodied the epitome of the finest maternal attributes and had played the role of a perfectly doting wife and homemaker. Shannon O'Reilly had embraced her position within the family structure, invested in maintaining the public-facing image of a well-adjusted family unit.

Iron-willed, stubborn women looking to make waves were not welcome in this particular enterprise.

As for little Miss Layne O'Reilly? She had wanted to be involved in business operations for as long as she could recall. However, her father had always discouraged her or outright prayed she'd grow out of such a silly aspiration. Scott insisted on telling her that a beautiful young lady need not be worried about these sorts of matters. Insert yet another heavily used eye roll here.

Instead, when it came to business, her father favored his youngest child, Liam, who was only eleven months younger than Layne. Liam was going to be the big man in charge one day, and it showed in the opportunities he was given as a means to get his hands dirty.

Meanwhile, Layne was only given almost anything and everything an uptown girl could have asked for. Yet, Liam was going to be handed the O'Reilly legacy. It pissed her off.

The driver pulled up in front of the multi-million dollar townhome that belonged to the O'Reilly family—O'Reilly Manor as it was frequently referred to. She had grown up inside of this house with some fond and some not-so-fond memories.

When the driver promptly rounded the Escalade and opened the door for her, Layne tossed her phone back into her jacket pocket and stepped out onto the sidewalk.

"Thanks, Artie." She offered him a polite smile as she stood right outside the expansive residence, taking in the view and mentally preparing for yet another drawn-out conversation about her future and role in this family. Artie gave a nod of his head and stood there at full attention, in the event she needed anything further from him.

Drawing one more deep breath, she gathered a little more courage inside of her to take the first step. Confidence was going to be key here.

Layne approached the stone steps that led up to two wrought iron gated doors protectively situated ahead of the front door, and let herself through both entranceways into the interior of the excessively opulent residence. Everything was as she recalled it; polished floors, sparkling chandeliers, high-end artwork, and cold. It was not physically cold, but nothing inside the house made it feel like a home. Not anymore anyway. Even burning a damn Yankee Candle would have helped.

She had arrived wearing a dark pair of blue jeans and a cream-colored blouse under a fitted cargo-styled jacket. Layne's favorite pair of heeled boots gave the ensemble a pop of her grittier personality. Her lengthy locks of dark chestnut hair were gently pulled back away from her face into a simplistic ponytail. The depths of her stunning emerald eyes scanned the foyer for any signs of activity. That's when she heard it.

"I don't give a damn! You go back and tell that motherfucker that if there is so much as a whisper about his people stepping foot in my territory, I will personally deliver each one back piece-by-piece in shoeboxes!" The familiar thunderous male voice boomed from down the hall where a mahogany door had been left ajar. There was a pause, followed by some quieter voices discussing something or other.

Layne approached, keeping her ears open to see if she could garner additional context on what her father had been shouting about. Right as she got to the door to the office, it swung open as Mick, her father's second in command, was on his way out.

"Oh!" Taken by surprise, Layne stopped in her tracks to avoid running right into the tired-looking man who had short, salt-and-pepper hair, though it was more pepper than salt. If he had been surprised to see her standing there, it didn't show. Mick gave her a warm smile and opened his arms, "Ah, there she is! Layne, I heard you were back. You look radiant."

"Thanks, Uncle Mickey; it's nice to see you, too." She leaned forward and gave him a big ol' hug. Even well into his fifties, Mick Flannigan was built like a tank, making it difficult to fully wrap her arms around him. By that same token, his arms engulfed her all too easily.

He wasn't truly her uncle, but he may as well have been. Mick had been working for her father since before she was born. Every birthday, every holiday, every heartbreak, and every blow-out argument with her parents, he had been there.

He returned her hug with a big squeeze and a quick peck on the cheek. Before they could catch up, another more slender figure appeared beside them.

"Hey, sis." Her brother, despite being almost a year younger than she was, looked like he had aged twice as much in the four years she had been gone. It was all in his eyes—he had seen some serious shit. The type of shit that saturates your soul with an inconceivable darkness.

Mick patted the back of Layne's shoulder as he walked off down the hall.

Liam didn't offer a hug and instead kept his hands inside the pockets of his black dress slacks. "Surprised to see you so soon. Figured you'd want to settle in and catch up with your friends first." The tone of his voice said it all; he wasn't going to be the one throwing her a homecoming celebration. That was fine by her.

Getting on the defensive, she crossed her arms in front of her chest and gave an indifferent shrug. "Family first, right?" Her tone was dry and unamused to match the tension between her and her little bro.

Before things stewed much longer, a large hand grasped Liam's shoulder. Her father appeared beside his son, "Go help Mick with the arrangements for our meeting this evening."

As usual, there were no requests from her father—only orders. Liam nodded, but then tossed Layne a smirk, "Sure, glad to do my part to keep the family business running smoothly." He had to make that final jab before he followed Mick down the hall. Layne shook her head in utter annoyance before turning her attention back to her father.

Just shy of six feet, he was an average-looking man. The beginnings of grey hairs were fading in right near his ears, contrasting with the rest of his light auburn hair. His custom grey suit didn't hold a single wrinkle and had probably cost more money than most cars.

"Layne, sweetheart, I can't tell you how much I missed you." His arms surrounded her in a loving and affectionate hug.

"Hi Dad, I missed you too. I've been looking forward to coming home and doing my part to help around here." She offered him an excited smile and he matched it with a smile of his own. He wrapped a single arm around her shoulders and guided her into his office, shutting the door behind them.

"It makes me so happy to hear you say that, Layne. I know you've wanted to be involved for a long time now. You've been incredibly patient, and for that I am grateful. After giving it a lot of thought," Scott finally parted from her and made his way around his massive wooden desk to ease into an oversized leather chair, "I have come up with the perfect fit for you."

Could she believe her ears? Was her father finally going to let her join in on the business dealings? Her thoughts were already racing to try and figure out what her role could be. Maybe it would involve managing some client relationships on her own, pulling in a commission of payments collected. Her thoughts were ricocheting all over the place inside her head at the potential.

Ultimately, it didn't matter which assignment he was going to give her, she was going to excel at it like the stubborn perfectionist she was. She may have been a petite young woman, but she knew not only how to defend herself, but how to physically get her point across to those who needed some 'convincing'. Layne wasn't above using violence where it was needed, that's for sure.

Her dad continued speaking while Layne's eyes lit up in anticipation of getting what she had always wanted, "With your degree in business administration, there's a lot I could use your help with, but not nearly as much as you can help Bryan Madigan."

Suddenly, she was very unclear about where this train was heading. Layne furrowed her brows and tilted her head slightly, "Ian's son?"

Scott nodded his head. "Yes. He's heading a large project for us and could use your skillset. After talking with Ian, it became clear that you and

Bryan would work together nicely. Once you two are legally married, you can help take charge of the assets in his family's name and keep it looking good as far as Uncle Sam is concerned."

"Wait. I'm sorry, what?" It was as if someone dropped the floor out from underneath her. Had he just said something about marriage?

"What do you mean married?" She hadn't escaped her family's affinity for having a short fuse and vicious temper and it showed, her voice escalating in volume.

"I didn't want to spring this on you as soon as you got here, but if we rush to get this done before year-end it would look spectacular during tax season. You know what I mean?"

It was the beginning of September, and he wanted her to marry some guy within the next four months? There he was, sitting in that massive chair, talking about her future as though it was just another business transaction. When she said she wanted to be involved, she hadn't meant getting married off to a guy she only knew by name. Layne had expected something a little more…illegal.

"No." It was a full sentence emphasized with a shake of her head.

"Now, Layne, I sent you to a damn good school, and you're telling me you don't understand how marriage and assets work? How this would benefit everybody's wallet?"

"No, as in I'm not marrying him. In fact, I'm not marrying anybody. I told you that when I got back here, I wanted a respectable role in this family," she emphasized the respectable part.

She continued, "Being hooked up with one of your lackey's kids was not and has never been what I meant!" She went from feeling like her heart had sunk into the basement, to feeling her rage erupting through the proverbial roof. Layne was allowing her temper to rear its fiery head. Scott looked at her without any visible emotion, as though he had expected this level of response.

"I missed the part where I asked whether or not you had an opinion on this. You wanted a role, and I am giving you one that is an appropriate fit for you. He will be over for dinner tonight. You can get to know him on more of a personal level."

Her hand angrily lashed out and swiped at the pencil holder on the corner of his desk, knocking it clear across the room with various writing utensils scattering through the air before dropping to the beige carpet.

She screamed at him, "This is bullshit!"

Layne's dad hadn't changed one bit. She stormed out of the office, swinging the door open so hard it gave a reverberated clatter against the stopper behind it.

Layne passed Liam on her way toward the front door. He had a shit-eating grin on his face, clearly knowing what their father had lined up for her.

"I hear congratulations are in order for the future Mrs. Madigan." He even snorted in amusement seeing her clear discontent at the situation.

"Fuck you, Li!" Harshly she shoved him, hoping to knock that snarky look off his face.

The shove had more strength behind it than he had been expecting, causing him to stumble a step back. In typical O'Reilly fashion, his ugly temper reared up and he stepped up to her, shouting in her face. "You're just pissed because you're more valuable as a hot piece of ass than—" She didn't let Liam finish that sentence.

Her fist connected and followed through with the side of his face. He dropped to the floor and before she could strike again, two barrels for arms encircled her waist and drew her back. Layne's legs kicked to squirm out of the lock hold.

"You're a piece of shit, Liam! You've been riding dad's coattails since we were kids! You've had it all handed to you because you're not man enough to do it on your own!" It may have been harsh, but from Layne's point of view, it was the solid truth.

She was getting pulled back further and further away from Liam, who was now sitting up groggily as his hand rubbed his temple. As for Layne, Mick had her off near the staircase a few feet away. Finally, he set her down on her feet and stood in front of her, blocking her path. "Alright, alright, knock it off."

Layne was fuming as she stood there, but she knew damn well she wasn't going to be able to get around Mick. That was, not without trying to throw a punch at him too.

After witnessing the entire situation unfold, Scott stood outside his office door rubbing the bridge of his nose as the impending headache descended upon him. "Mick, call Ian and cancel tonight's dinner."

Dinner wasn't the only thing that got canceled. Shortly thereafter, her father canned the engagement as well. It was painfully evident to the O'Reilly patriarch that his daughter had far too much of his spirit in her to be cast off to the side, all because he wanted to spare her from being exposed to the same life of organized crime that had robbed him of his wife.

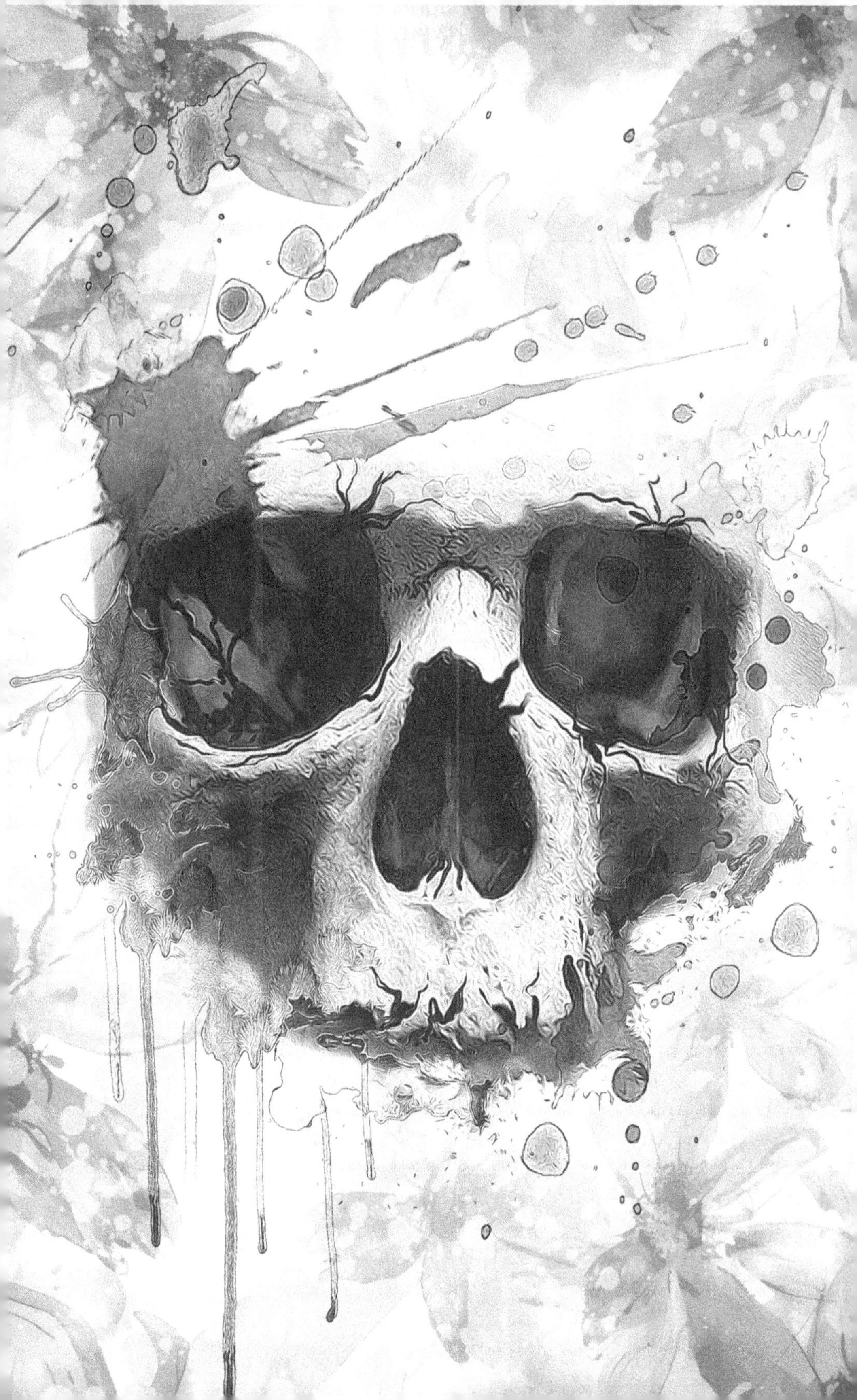

CHAPTER TWO

Present day

The past three years had been a whirlwind of highs and lows. Finally, Layne was getting her way and making a name for herself in the O'Reilly family business. It started with small tasks such as picking up and dropping off packages, graduated to being present during discussions with folks who were late on debts owed, and then slowly she was given the blessing to be free to negotiate terms and collect debts on her own. Recently, she began playing an integral role in strategic planning and advanced discussions in evolving their enterprise to the next level.

Scott had insisted that she continue to work with some of his top men to refine her ability to physically defend herself and fine-tune her expertise with various weapons. She hit the gym regularly and worked with weights to keep her strength up to par as well as cardio to ensure she had endurance worth a damn.

These days, Layne had her hands in a little bit of everything when it came to projects she managed. She was like a bit of honey with a killer bee sting: she could assist in negotiations by supplying that charming smile of hers or be the small but mighty strike.

A lot of her interactions had been mostly with weak, small-minded, white-collared businessmen that pissed their pants the second you brandished a gun in their presence. Of course, she had her own learning curve of understanding when to reign in her hot-headedness.

Liam was still being groomed to take the lead over the entire enterprise, which was fine by Layne as she had zero interest in being the head boss lady. Over time, the tension between her and her younger sibling eased up. He had done a lot of maturing, and Layne had been willing to give him the space to earn her respect while he worked on proving himself capable of his eventual promotion. There were still those days though when she wanted to smack the crap out of him for his holier-than-thou attitude.

She had woken up to her phone buzzing on her nightstand. Wearily, she answered and immediately regretted it when she was informed that today was not going to go as she had planned. Layne expected to sit in her feelings today, drink heavily, and wallow in solitude. It was the one day of the year she allowed herself to come undone. Instead, she had to get herself up out of bed and take care of a small matter down in Chelsea.

Layne ended up paying a visit to one of her more problematic clients, George Sallakis, who was about as shady as they came. He was a small-time attorney with a big-time ego problem. Surprising for a lawyer, huh? However, he was conveniently useful when it came to handling any run-ins with the law. The number of times charges were dropped thanks to his connections was invaluable, and her family richly compensated him for it.

There was the expectation per their agreement that he was on retainer solely for the O'Reillys and keeping the details of their delicate matters to himself. Yet, intel was drifting in that he was passing highly sensitive information freely between the two biggest factions of the criminal underworld in the city: the O'Reillys and the Franzettis.

The Franzettis were headed up by one supremely arrogant Michael Franzetti. Michael, by comparison to Scott, was less old-school about how he operated his business. He got his hands dirty, occasionally using outside resources that weren't in his circle of trust, and as long as those hired resources got things done, he didn't give a shit how they accomplished it.

Sometimes these hands Michael hired were some thug-wannabe that was sloppy as fuck. Why did the O'Reillys care about the way Franzetti handled his business? It put all the city's factions at risk thanks to these punk kids having no loyalty, no respect, drawing far too much attention to themselves, and having no ability to intelligently execute a simple assignment without collateral damage.

As for poor little Georgie, he had made the mistake of getting drunk and bragging to a hooker about how he was raking in all the dough from double-crossing the two largest elite factions in the city. That particular hooker just so happened to be on the O'Reilly books for exclusive entertainment for extraordinarily important clientele. More importantly, she was Liam's own personal booty call. When Liam got the word from his favorite piece of ass, she was rewarded very generously for her contribution.

Layne found herself leaning forward, her hands on the edge of George's cheap metal desk in his musty-smelling office. Files were scattered haphazardly across the top of the desk, the computer monitor collecting a layer of dust on the back of it, and a half-drunk cup of coffee sitting on top of a pile of papers. Framed certifications and licensures hung crookedly on the wall. It was amazing this man had any level of competency, based on the state of affairs of where he spent his time working.

"George, I am having a *really* bad start to my day. Do you want to know why?"

He was held down by his shoulders in the creaky office chair on the other side of the desk by two of Layne's muscled helpers. He shook his head, a bead of sweat slowly rolling down his temple.

"Let me tell you. I was supposed to have today off for some critically important self-care. I even had a spa day scheduled that I booked for myself six months ago, but I had to cancel because I received some very troubling information. I heard that you might have been running your mouth to the wrong fuckin' people. A slutty little bird told me that you've been sharing with some friends over in Franzetti's camp."

Immediately, he tried to interject with his defense, "That's not true, I—"

"Don't interrupt me with your bullshit, Sallakis." She could feel her blood pressure rising at the thought of how this was how she was spending *today* of all days, dealing with this asshat.

"I thought to myself when I was told this little piece of information that no, you couldn't possibly be that much of a moron. So, naturally, I looked into it. Imagine my surprise when I came to realize that you've been helping Franzetti's goons with get-out-of-jail-free cards. It did not give me the warm and fuzzies, George."

She frowned at him and straightened up, walking around the desk so she was now on the same side as him. She perched her ass up on the edge of the desk, resting her hands on top of her thigh.

"You've been working for us for a very long time, and you know we reward loyalty. But this?" Layne shook her head with a sigh of straight-up disappointment. George sat there, getting antsy in his seat like he had roaches crawling up his legs.

"You don't understand," he responded in a panic, quick to plead his case to her. "They were threatening my sister and her family. I didn't have a choice."

"You're right, I don't understand. But that's the easy part of my job here, George. I don't have to understand. You could have come to us first and let us handle things. Instead, you run off and stab us in the back after all we've done for you. The Benz you have out front? Wasn't that a generous Christmas bonus last year?"

"It-it was, and I am beyond g-grateful," he stuttered.

This was the part of her job that never got any easier, but the message they had to send was crystal clear. Double-crossing Layne's family resulted in swift and severe punishment. A few years ago, she might have let it bother her, but now? Layne had become numb to ridding the world of a little evil on occasion.

"I wish I could say this will hurt me more than it will hurt you." Layne dug around in her pocket, pulled out a silver lighter, and tossed it to the bulky man to the right of the traitor. "Let it burn," she ordered as she slid off the edge of the desk.

"W-wait! No! It's a big misunderstanding! I can fix this! I can make it right!" George shouted at her while the two men began to forcibly restrain him to the office chair at the wrists and feet. As for Layne? She had given her command, and her two lackeys were following it. There was nothing left for her to do other than make her exit.

Moments later, her associates joined her outside the quaint office building while she leaned back against the side of George's freshly washed Benz and stared. Within minutes, smoke was beginning to seep out of the building, followed by flames licking at the curtains in the windows.

Such a shame, Layne thought. One less scumbag lawyer in the world.

CHAPTER THREE

This morning's unexpected meeting hadn't changed the fact that she still had been looking forward to this much-needed day to herself. It was a day where booze of any type was a requirement, not just thanks to George's demise.

Every year on this particular day was reserved for mind-numbing drinking until all the feelings folded in on themselves. All of this meant she was going to spend her evening at McGregor's Pub until the owner, Sean, ceremoniously kicked her out.

The dive joint resided in the heart of the O'Reilly territory, making it a safe getaway for all the associates and underlings that worked for them. Layne assisted the bar with keeping the books clear of any red flags, and in return, there was a no-questions-asked policy when there were business discussions taking place.

McGregor's was said to be one of the oldest bars in Manhattan, established in 1854. The exterior had a green sign above the door with its name written in a Gaelic-styled font, the façade was black with massive glass windows on either side of the two black doors of the entrance. To the right of the door flew the Irish flag, and to the left was the proud Star-Spangled Banner.

Once inside, the ragged and run-down charm was plastered from floor to ceiling. The walls had nearly no bare space due to the plethora of framed photos taken of patrons over the years. The front half of the establishment had a handful of wooden tables to the left, a narrow walkway in the center, and a well-used wooden bar to the right. Past the bar, into the back half of the pub was a second room that held a few more tables and allowed for more privacy and discretion.

Part of the innate appeal of McGregor's was that it also did not install any televisions, didn't have WiFi, was dimly lit, and was thoroughly stuck in its ways.

Sitting at the bar as far back from the doors as possible, Layne stared into the depths of the dark ruby liquid in her pint glass that most people mistook for a thick black beer. Her sparkling emerald-colored eyes were locked on the heady stout as the reflections of the lights above shifted into a daydream of memories. One memory in particular ravaged her brain.

"Layney, which snack would you like? I have chocolate chip cookies or vanilla pudding," both were homemade by her mother, Shannon, who had a knack for finding her way around the kitchen.

Her mother was to thank for the green eyes Layne inherited. Shannon had been a very attractive and classy woman. Even knowing what Scott did for a living, she brought out the best in him where she could. Everything Layne's brain could recall about her mother was the epitome of pure innocence and overwhelming love.

She could remember her mom standing there by the kitchen counter, ready to dish up whichever snack a then five-year-old Layne desired.

"I want the peanut butter cookies you always buy."

"Honey, we don't have any more. You have to wait until I go to the store to get some."

"But I want some now!" Even back then, that trademark temper and hard-headedness flared up. Of course, her mom knew the best way to do damage control before the waterworks started pouring out of little Layne's eyes.

Shannon drew in a calming breath and placed her hands lightly on Layne's shoulders as she lovingly looked at her daughter. "How about this? I will go to the store and pick up cookies, but you need to go upstairs to your room and have it spotless by the time I get back. Sound like a fair deal?"

Little Layne sniffled and was quick to nod her head. Her mother came in closer and wrapped her arms around Layne, drawing her into a warm embrace, and pressed a kiss to her forehead.

That moment likely only lasted a second or two, but in Layne's mind, it had lasted for an eternity.

"Sweetheart," the voice was no longer the delicate and feminine one of her mother. Instead, it was deeper and raspy. "Hey, sweetheart."

Layne snapped out of her head and was back there sitting at the bar in McGregor's. She blinked a few times and noticed the owner and current bartender, Sean, was staring at her from behind the bar. He must have been in his seventies and was the one trying to flag her attention.

Slowly her lips curved into a weakly held smile, "Sorry, it's been a long week."

"I gotta go in the back and fix a tap line. Shout if you need something, eh?"

Layne nodded. "Got it," as she lifted her glass to her lips and took a hefty sip to help diminish the pain of the past, the pain that started fifteen years ago today.

The gruff and shaggy-haired man made his way into the back, disappearing from sight.

It was a quiet Tuesday night inside the pub. The music playing from the speakers in the ceiling was only at a volume loud enough to blend into background noise, a few businessmen were at the circular four-top in the back corner with their ties hanging loose around their necks while they talked shop amongst themselves, and the ceiling fan's pull chain lightly tapped against the bare light bulb as the fan blades slowly spun round and round. It may not have been a fancy spot, but nobody bothered her here.

The soft ring of a bell sounded off as the front door was pushed open, allowing a caressing breeze of fresh air to slip inside. A man who looked rough around the edges, who easily was in his mid-to late thirties stepped inside the establishment. Layne didn't bother taking her eyes off the pint in front of her.

She picked up on the sound of the stool next to her being dragged across the floor a few inches and felt the new presence perch on it right beside her. Didn't people have common decency anymore? The entire rest of the bar had seating available, and this person couldn't at least sit one more seat over as a courtesy as to not encroach on her personal bubble?

Not too long after the newcomer settled in, the husky scent of sage and leather drifted her way. It was pleasant on the senses, not aggressively applied, and for a brief moment, made her want to lean in a little closer.

"Who do you have to kill to get a drink 'round here?" The stranger next to her spoke up. His voice bore a tone that prickled at her most intimate desires. It wasn't clear who he was speaking to. One thing was painfully clear, he had never stepped foot inside this place before.

Here's the thing about McGregor's; it was always the same damn crowd, which had its pluses and minuses. It was rare to have new faces finding themselves coming in here. Not only was it off the beaten path and had an aesthetic that looked worse for wear, but it also had an ill-conceived reputation. Her family may or may not have had something to do with all that.

Tiredly, Layne set her pint down on the counter and drew in a breath, transforming it into a forced smile as she looked over the guy next to her, "First time?"

The moment her eyes focused on him, the air in her lungs vanished as she temporarily forgot how to breathe. Across his square jaw was a light layer of scruff, dirty blonde hair haphazardly styled longer on top and shorter on the sides, eyes the color of bitter dark chocolate, and a body that screamed either prison time or professional model.

It was just a hunch, but from the look of the tattoo creeping up the side of his neck, it was likely the former. The inked wings on the side of his neck wasn't the only tattoo either. The tops of his hands and fingers also had various images and symbols etched into his flesh. Without leaning over and appearing as intrigued as she truly was, the only piece of art she could make out was a thorny stem and the bottom half of a toothy grin of a skull before the sleeve of his jacket concealed the rest of it.

Her very core immediately reacted to the easy-on-the-eyes stranger situated next to her. A sense of excitement was building as she realized that he wasn't part of the typical clientele that came to this spot.

The man was dressed in a pair of work boots, rugged jeans, a black tank, and a silver chain draped around his neck that disappeared into his shirt. To top it all off was a black leather jacket that looked well-worn in multiple aspects. The day may have suddenly started looking up.

Layne internally appreciated the fresh face but avoided entanglements with random men she met at shady, rundown bars - even here at McGregor's. Those types of guys were the ones that were more trouble than they were worth. This one looked like a hell of a lot more trouble than average, that's for sure. The temptation to break her own rule was already beginning to taint her thoughts.

He didn't even try to hide the fact he gave her a solid once-over from head to toe. All he did was smirk. "It hasn't been my first time since I was fourteen." There was the not-so-subtle insinuation that he wasn't talking about his first visit to McGregor's anymore. Oh, yes, this one had epically bad news written all over him. Layne wondered how many hearts he had broken in the last month alone. If she had a heart to break, she would love to see him try.

"Oh, be still my heart. I bet that type of charm gets all the girls dropping their panties for you," she mockingly replied, a hand coming to her chest for a dramatic gesture.

Amused, he leaned in a little closer to her so she could inhale a little more of that intoxicating cologne, "You offering?"

Cocky son of a bitch. Attempting to keep her head on straight, Layne quickly changed the topic before it devolved any further. "If you want a drink, rest assured that you won't need to commit a felony. Sean is in the back, he'll be out in a minute."

"In that case," the stranger leaned over the bar and reached into the well, lifting up a bottle of whiskey and grabbing a rocks glass on the nearby drying plate. Layne perked an eyebrow as she stared in disbelief, wondering if this guy was for real as he began pouring the amber liquid into the glass for himself.

"You can't just..." she initially struggled to pull together a coherent thought as he thought he could just help himself to a drink here.

"What do you think you're doing?" She snatched the bottle out of his hand and set it down on the other side of her. "You don't just walk in here and serve yourself." Given her family's oversight of McGregor's books and business, she felt duty-bound to protect their asset. Layne scoffed that he had the balls to think he could do as he saw fit.

All she got back in response from him was an entertained grin, and he raised the glass of whiskey in the air slightly, "Cheers." He downed the mouthful of booze followed by extending his hand out towards her, "Joey. Joey De Luca."

With his hand outstretched towards her she blinked a few times, skeptically looking it over. So, the skull tattoo on his hand indeed continued up towards his wrist. Across its head were deep red petals of a rose sitting there like a floral crown. Finally, she extended her hand to him, but before she could give it a shake, he embraced it and drew it to his lips where a delicate kiss was laid on her knuckles.

Was he trying to be some sort of knight in shining armor pulling out all the moves in an attempt to woo her? It may have been just a little effective as her cheeks fostered a slight warmth. Men didn't go to such lengths to get her attention, nor did she go around looking for those that did. Typically, it was just a catcall or in some cases a decision to lay a smack on her ass. Both instances always ended poorly for the guy. Dating apps were so much easier for weeding out some of the assholes.

"I'm Layne." Her skin was still tingling where he had kissed her, and she was trying her damnedest not to pay any attention to it. She was utterly failing at the latter.

"It's a pleasure to meet you, Layney." The way he uttered the word 'pleasure' felt intentionally intimate, especially as his hand was still embracing hers. His thumb rubbed over her fingers idly.

Layne pulled back her hand from his before her hormones got any more bright ideas, more so than they already were. Today was not about getting laid, but damn if the universe wasn't trying to make it happen.

"Don't call me 'Layney'." That nickname was what her mother had always called her, and now it was just too painful to let anyone else have the privilege.

"Why not? I think it suits you." Joey ran his tongue over his lips as those inviting brown eyes took in the sight of her again.

"Because, then I'd have to kick your ass out of here. I wouldn't want you to suffer that embarrassment." She smirked at him, knowing that she had bruised a metric ton of male egos. Joey wouldn't be the first, and he wouldn't be the last.

He chuckled. "I'd like to see a little thing like you try. You're what? Five-foot?"

"Five-one." She rolled her eyes after correcting him. "You're what? Like six-foot with three inches below the belt?"

Apparently, his ego wasn't easily bruised. Instead of taking offense, he bantered back. "Six-two and I will let you check what's below the belt right now." His hand moved down to the waist of his pants, tugging on the tail of his belt, willing to prove her assessment of his other measurements wrong.

Layne's hand nearly knocked over her pint glass in an effort to brace herself as he seemed ready to just whip himself out right then and there. Quickly, she stabilized the drink and moved it off to the side to prevent any other potential spills.

Before she could come back with a snarky comment, her cell phone in her pocket began going off. Taking it out of her pocket, she looked at the caller's name and cursed underneath her breath. She placed the phone up to her ear as she answered in the sweetest voice she could muster. "Hey."

But before she could get another word out, the caller on the other end immediately began to go off on her, leaving it difficult to get a word in edgewise. "No, I—Yes, but—If you'd let me—" She pressed her lips together in a hard line, attempting to restrain herself from lashing back verbally.

Finally, after a few more minutes that dragged on she was able to speak up. "I understand. I will take care of it. Bye, Liam." Layne hung up and returned the phone to where it came from.

"Ouch, somebody out past curfew?" This guy just thought he was so funny, didn't he?

"Haven't you heard of staying in your lane?" She retorted. There was no time wasted in finishing off the last of her pint. Pulling out a twenty-dollar bill, she left it next to the now barren glass. Meanwhile, she could feel Joey's eyes still locked on her. She was already agitated from that unpleasant phone call and not so politely reacted to his stares. "What are you looking at?"

He casually shrugged and shook his head. "Nothing. Just observing."

"Well, don't. There's nothing to observe." She took off towards the exit, but before she reached the door a set of strong hands wrapped around her waist and spun her around, taking her by surprise. Layne found herself staring up into Joey's eyes as he towered over her figure by over a foot.

There was a burning heat in the way he looked at her that caused an ache that she didn't expect between her legs. It was unclear how long it was that both of them stood there looking at one another, saying nothing at all. Finally, she broke the silence, and her words managed to only sound slightly breathless. "I have to go."

It wasn't her most profound statement of the night, but it was the truth.

"Before you run outta here, how about you at least give me the chance to buy your next round another night?"

She stared up at that incredibly handsome face, searching for a reason not to take him up on his offer. "Leave your number with Sean, and I will call you the next time I'm looking for a guy to make bad decisions with."

Amusement in his grin, his face lowered down closer to her, prompting Layne to squirm out of his grasp at the very last second before he had the opportunity to make any big mistakes.

Without looking back, she hurriedly left the pub, mentally reassuring herself that it was the best course of action. Guys like Joey may have been good for a one-time romp, but they often came with a shit ton of baggage. Layne had enough of her own baggage to carry around, she didn't need complications from someone else's.

Once the cool night air hit her face, Layne focused on putting one foot in front of the other. Why was she so stirred up? It was one guy. One stupid, annoying guy. She shook her head, mentally scolding herself for being so caught up in this.

Despite the temptation, Joey didn't follow after her and instead hung back at McGregor's to order another round of firewater after Sean returned from fixing the equipment. He wrote his number down as instructed, pushing the slip of paper over towards the bartender.

Any other night he would have shot his chance and followed after Layne, but he had other obligations on his agenda for the evening. He had only come in here to piss away some time because it had been conveniently located on the way to his next appointment. That appointment was a particularly important job he had to get to in an hour's time, and he didn't want to be late. He really hated being late.

CHAPTER FOUR

Layne arrived at the parking garage one block down from the pub and pulled out her keys from her jacket pocket to her vehicle which was parked there on the ground floor. It didn't take long to realize that her steps weren't the only ones tapping against the concrete. There was a light shuffle following behind her.

Giving a huff and a sigh she stopped in her tracks. "Look, I don't have time for this."

She turned around ready to give Joey a piece of her mind. That's when she felt the heavy palms slam into the front of her chest in a violent shove, causing her to stumble backward. Instead of falling straight onto her ass, a set of bulging arms locked around her, pinning her arms down to her sides.

Instantly her body triggered its fight or flight mode, and she was sure as hell ready to get into a fight. The edgy feeling was very familiar to her. Adrenaline caused her heartbeat to pound like a war drum inside of her ears while her thoughts raced frantically to assess the threat.

"Get the fuck off of me!" Her foot stomped down onto the stranger's foot followed by an elbow thrusted back into his squishy stomach. Layne found temporary freedom from Squishy Guts, only to have the first attacker grab her by the throat and toss her down onto the ground.

Her body fell onto the unforgiving surface with enough momentum that she rolled over once. As she was rolling onto her back, she was able to free her 9mm Shield from the inside of her jacket holster. These days, she didn't leave home without it.

Before she could steady the aim of the pistol it was kicked right out of her grasp. It skittered across the concrete underneath a nearby Corolla parked several yards away. Now she found herself lying there on the ground, weaponless, staring at two very pissed-off men. They both had guns drawn, pointed directly at her.

Layne kept her hands out in front of her and didn't make any sudden movements. Who knew how itchy their trigger fingers were? She sure as hell didn't want to find out.

"What the hell do you want?"

Ignoring her question, the averagely-built bald one barked at her while keeping his weapon's sight locked on her. "Get up, bitch."

When she didn't move right away, his partner who looked like he had eaten one too many creme puffs leaned down, and with his free hand, snatched her arm with a painful squeeze before jerking her up onto her feet.

What happened after that she didn't know, but she felt the impact on the back of her head right before everything went dark.

Ouch. Her head was killing her, and there was the dull ache of what was going to grow into a bruise, if it hadn't already started. Layne attempted to assess how much of a bruise she was going to have with her fingers, but immediately came to the realization her hands were bound at the wrists in front of her by some standard zip ties. Fucking fabulous.

She gave a quiet groan in response to the pain while her eyes slowly opened. Swallowing hard, Layne tried to focus her vision. Things were moving, and it wasn't immediately clear if it was a byproduct of getting struck on the back of her head or if the movement was legitimately occurring. As her eyes began to adjust and process the surroundings, it was evident that much time couldn't have passed since she had been jumped in the parking garage.

Things were still cloaked in darkness, but now she was noticing the coming and going of street lamps to her right. Warm glows that approached and then passed by at semi-regular intervals. She was in a car. The scent of cigarettes, cheap air fresheners, and old takeout containers filled the air around her. It was nauseating to breathe in, or maybe that was due to a potential concussion.

When she began to shift in her seat, something jabbed into her side. Looking down, it was a gun being held by one of the men who had attacked her. Baldy to be precise. The other man, Squishmallow, was at the steering wheel transporting them all to their next destination, wherever that was.

She thought about the speed they were going and how likely it was she could jump out of a moving vehicle without getting killed.

"Don't even think about it you stupid cunt." Just to be a brat she thought about it again anyhow, not that they had to know that. After assessing the precarious situation, there were too many unknowns for her to attempt to flee. So, Layne sat still and didn't say a word. It was a rare occasion indeed.

After what may have been the longest five minutes of her life, the sedan slowed and pulled in behind a small grey building by some docks. Once it came to a complete halt, her backseat chaperone tugged her out of the car with him. Her feet stumbled on the gravel while trying to keep up in whichever direction he was heading.

All three of them approached the dimly lit building that looked like it was some sort of administrative office that was no longer actively used. The one with the big belly opened the door. "Ladies first."

Once inside, it was confirmed this place wasn't currently being used and required some dire repairs. The walls had water stains, the carpet was fraying and torn in multiple places, what little furnishings were in there looked like they were from forty years ago, and the musty smell was overpowering to the senses.

The driver of the car followed inside just a few steps behind them, shutting the door and looking out through the window to make sure they had all the privacy they required. Mr. Clean gave her a shove towards a metal folding chair facing away from the door they had just come in from. "Sit."

"Where's your 'please'?" Layne remained standing.

That was the wrong question. The back of his hand went flying across her face. Layne stumbled and lifted her hands to feel her cheek, which was now on fire. Her eyes began to water involuntarily, and she did her best to blink the tears back. She didn't want to look weak and rattled. When in fact, it was quite the opposite, the pain was only adding fuel to her fire that was flickering in her murderous glare.

Defiantly, she remained standing there refusing to take a seat just because he told her to.

"Sit, or else I will give you something better to do with that smartass mouth," he sneered lecherously at her.

Layne begrudgingly sat while she thought about which battles she wanted to pick right now with the position she was in. The driver was still standing by the door peering out the window. "Where is he? Shouldn't he be here by now?"

The bald one didn't take his gaze off her when he answered his partner. "I say we give it two more minutes before we take the lead on the job, Victor." So, the fat one had a name, wonderful. Layne now had at least one piece of useless information that she didn't have before. She wasn't sure what he meant by finishing the job but was certain she did not want to find out.

The silence in the room wasn't just uncomfortable but felt like it was growing louder with each second that passed.

Even though she didn't have any visibility of the window behind her, she knew a car had just pulled up in front of the building. There was the crunch and roll of gravel sounding off underneath the tires, and then it came to a stop.

An authoritative pound came against the door. Victor looked at Mr. Magoo with a curt nod, confirming their expected guest had arrived before opening the door for the newcomer.

The door swung open, and a seemingly lofty figure stepped inside. With her back to the entrance, all she could rely on was the dancing of shadows against the floor and walls. The sound of heavy-duty boots thudded against the floor; Layne was willing to bet it was the man of the hour.

Conflicted on whether she should have felt a sense of relief that this third individual had arrived to join the party or not, Layne found minimal comfort that at least she didn't have to worry about whatever sick thoughts Baldy was having. Or maybe she was just being delusional.

After she assessed what was around her, and knowing her hands were mostly unavailable, the options were very limited. The upside was she still had her feet. The downside was right now it was three against one.

She heard a few husky whispers going back and forth behind her. Then, the heavy footsteps drew nearer. The sound stopped directly behind her, creating an overwhelming sensation of dread spilling over her.

A new voice broke the silence. "Is this the girl the boss was talking about?"

"Yeah. A real pain in the ass, too."

Layne couldn't help but scoff at her attacker's personality assessment of her.

"You think something's funny?" The hairless man began to step forward to make another move at her. Before he could jump on the opportunity, the newcomer reached out and stopped him with a hand bracing against his chest.

"Go get some fresh air with Victor." There was a long pause before the man at her side reluctantly left. Then, there was a light click of the door latching shut moments later.

Layne sat in the cold and rigid folding chair willing herself not to show any signs of frayed nerves. She had been in some shit before, but never on her own and never at this level of seriousness. She took another hard swallow when she felt the man's hands settle on top of her shoulders from behind and squeeze them firmly. Now it was just the two of them there.

She jerked her shoulders to attempt shrugging off his grip. It was a failed attempt as he pulled her to sit back in the chair. He didn't have to say any words, instead, it was clear that he was trying to ensure she was intimidated. Knowing all about the effective use of intimidation tactics, she knew that he was doing a decent job of using them.

There was something familiar lingering in the air, but she couldn't quite pinpoint it. Not to mention, now didn't seem like the time to assess the minor details when bigger problems were going on here, like survival. Survival would be good.

The large pair of hands eventually released her shoulders, and the man circled 'round from the back of her seat to stand in front of her. He was decked out in all-black tactical clothing from his boots, up to the cargo pants that hugged his muscular thighs, a long-sleeved shirt with black gloves on his hands, up to the mask covering the lower half of his face from right under his eyes downward past his chin, and a knit cap over the top of his head. The only exception to the all-black ensemble was that the mask had white markings on it to mimic the bottom half of a skull's nose, jaw, and teeth.

When this new threat came to stand in front of her, his body went rigid for a split moment. It was indiscernible as to why.

Layne stubbornly refused to show any fear and coldly locked her gaze right on him. He leaned over with one gloved hand roughly grabbing her jaw as he gave a hard stare right back at her. "It's just you and me now, princess. I'm only going to ask my questions one time, and you're going to be a good girl and answer them."

His voice rang low on the register with a dark undercurrent that suggested he was going to make good on any threats he made.

"Good luck with that." Layne wasn't going to give this theatric creep the time of day.

He chuckled in amusement at her confidence. "Now, tell me your name." The strength of his hand prevented her from turning her face away from him, though she tried. His fingers digging into her cheeks were starting to become uncomfortable, even with her tolerance for discomfort.

"Betty White."

He growled under his breath, releasing her jaw only to pull her up onto her feet by her upper arm. The masked man spun her around, wrapping one thick muscled arm around her waist, pinning her arms against her, and forcing her back against his chest. That's when she felt the cold of a steel blade up against the bare skin of her throat. This man was a different breed than the other two individuals standing guard outside.

Her chest rose and fell heavily with her labored breaths as her fear spiked. Layne's body tensed and she strained to keep her neck away from the sharp edge of the knife. She didn't manage to get very farm except leaning further back against the brick wall of his torso.

The coarse fabric of the mask brushed up against her ear and through the mask's material, she could feel the warmth of his breath and smell the light scent of really cheap whiskey. "Do you want to reconsider your answer? I would be a good little girl if I were you."

He dropped his voice down to a whisper, "You don't want to find out what I do to bad girls."

"And you don't want to find out what I do to deranged psychopaths." Her retorts were one of the few things that kept her from giving in to straight-up panic.

He tsked at her response, the knife now starting to apply more pressure against her throat, prompting her to wince and draw in a sharp breath. The acknowledgment of defeat began to creep in, and she took a second to steady her voice. Still, it didn't come out as strong as she would have liked. "It's Layne."

The masked man lightly dragged the tip of the blade along the length of her neck, the weapon threatening to break her skin if she so much as thought of speaking too loudly. "Mm, thank you. What's your last name, Layne?"

The way he spoke her name made her feel something deep inside of her that should have been illegal. She hesitated to respond to him, knowing damn well her family name could be a toss-up in either getting her out of trouble or catapulting her into a shit ton of it.

He wasn't feeling very patient with her. The blade was removed for a split second, only for him to turn her to face him. His left hand grabbed a handful of the back of her silky strands of chestnut hair, tugging harshly so her throat was more exposed to him. The knife returned to its spot against the delicate skin covering her carotid artery.

"I can see your pulse in your neck. Do you know how excited that makes me?" If Layne hadn't figured it out before now, it was confirmed that this man was definitely on another level of unhinged, unpredictable, and dangerous. Perhaps even as much as she was.

"O'Reilly. My last name is O'Reilly." She didn't need an unstable individual getting too antsy to spill her blood before she could strategize an escape.

"That's a good girl. Let's continue behaving, Layney, and this will be more enjoyable for us both." He didn't release her or lower the knife. Instead, he remained in his current position, and unless he was packing a lot more distinct weapons, it was clear he was getting plenty of enjoyment out of this from what she could feel.

The interrogation continued. "What is the 227 project?" He dragged the knife down over her collarbone in a slow and intentional movement.

Genuinely confused, she wrinkled her brows, "The 227 project? I have no fucking clue. Sounds like a terrible band name." The masked assailant was silent for what felt like an eternity, so Layne decided now would be the time to try and stall to buy herself more time for a miracle opportunity to make a move.

"I swear, I have no idea what it is. Please, don't hurt me." She dialed up the emotions that danced over the words she spoke to appeal to any sliver of humanity he had. "I can get you money - however much you need."

Her father's words of wisdom to her, etched into her brain from a young age, were on repeat in her head; exhaust every option to escape from a bad situation, it is better to risk potential death than to do nothing and make it definite.

"Shut up." His words weren't yelled but they held a commanding tone to them. He needed to reassess if it was possibly true that she had zero knowledge of the project. His intuition told him that she wasn't lying, not about this anyway.

The blade was taken away from her throat and rehomed back into a sheath at his hip. During that brief window of an opportunity where he didn't have the knife readily available, Layne willed herself to make her move. She thrusted her foot in a front kick directly at his belt buckle, driving the force from her hips. The angle wasn't ideal, but it was better than nothing.

Taken off guard by the impact of her kick, his footing yielded, and he grunted upon contact. His hand released her as he bent over, drawing in a sharp breath while his hand held the temporary discomfort of his stomach.

She turned and burst into a sprint for the only way out of this hellhole. Running with your hands bound together in front of you isn't as efficient as one would like, but she had to go with what things were. No, she didn't have a plan for what she'd have to deal with on the other side of the door, but she had to handle one problem at a time.

Her fingertips had just grazed the stainless steel door handle before her body was lifted by the waist, feet coming off the ground. Her legs kicked wildly as she yelled like a banshee. "Let me go!"

The struggling and thrashing seemed to have little impact as the skull-masked man utilized his strength to carry her back to where she had been previously seated. He harshly exhaled as he dropped her onto the ground in front of the folding chair.

"Stay!" He yelled at her. "Goddamn, woman!" He groaned, making it clear he was still feeling quite uncomfortable from the unexpected shot she made and pissed off about it.

Layne tried to steady her breath as she now found herself on her ass on the cold and damp floor looking up at him. "What are you going to do to me? I don't know shit about your stupid project."

She expected an answer involving torture and death, but he said nothing as he looked down at her. Something switched in his demeanor, and what came out of his mouth next was not what she expected.

"...Fuck." A sigh followed.

"I'm...sorry?" Layne was confused as to what part of her question had given him this pause. As much as she wanted to take credit for whatever crisis he was having, she wasn't sure that she could.

He yanked his mask down away from his face to around his neck and knelt on one knee in front of her. Revealing his face was never something he did while working his assignments, it was part of the many protective measures he took to keep an added layer of safety for himself. Even those who hired him went through an intermediary and didn't get to see him without the getup.

One look at that face underneath the mask and she found herself with her jaw hanging open and in a wordless stupor.

CHAPTER FIVE

"Joey? You've got to be fucking kidding me." The stupid, annoyingly hot as fuck guy from McGregor's Pub. Joey. Joey motherfucking De Luca. She should have known. The scent of cheap whiskey, the boots, the eyes, and the way he called her Layney. She should have picked up on it all, but then again, she wouldn't have ever pegged him for being involved in this level of shit.

Layne felt played like a naive little fiddle. It wasn't a feeling she was accustomed to, but hell if she was going to let it happen again.

After her brain processed the sheer confusion of how they both ended up here, her speechlessness no longer became a problem. "Oh, you asshole, motherfucker, son of a bitch jackass!" There weren't enough curse words in the Merriam-Webster for her to spew at him. She swung her bound hands in his direction, but he easily captured them in his grasp and held them still.

"Stop being a little heathen! Just let me explain."

Her heart was palpitating even harder than it had been moments ago, but now it was because she was fuming. Who the hell did he think he was? Was his conversation with her in the bar all part of some scheme? There were a million questions and scenarios zipping through her mind.

Each attempt to physically lash out at him was a failure as he expertly kept her hands still.

"Layne, give me a minute, will ya?" His eyes darted over towards the door, confirming they were still alone before looking back at her. "I didn't know it was going to be you here. Franzetti hired me, told me to come here to take care of some business, and get some answers out of you." He decidedly left out the part where he had been instructed to dump her body off the docks afterward. "Jesus, why didn't you say something at the bar earlier, huh?"

She was not going to take any fault for this. "Are you kidding me right now? What was I supposed to say? 'Oh, hey, in case you might be involved in a kidnapping later, you should know who my dad is'?"

He grumbled and rubbed his forehead while he tried to process this unforeseen complication.

"Look at me." He reached out to gently take her chin in his grasp so he could convey his intentions. "We can fix this." Joey stood up on his feet. When he tried to assist Layne up onto her own as well, she pulled back from him and did it on her own.

"We? I missed the part where this was a team effort." Her hands still clinched together via the uncomfortably hard plastic, managed to brush off the front of her pants of dirt they picked up from the likely unsanitary floor.

"Stay here." He pulled his mask back up over his face and walked away. The door creaked as it opened and shut. Not more than two minutes later, the sound repeated as he came back to her with his knife in his hand. Joey grabbed her wrists and yanked her closer to him. The tension in her body made her stiff as a board.

"Relax, I'm not going to hurt you as long as you keep your hands to yourself." Yeah, famous last words before a lot of serial killers did indeed hurt people, Layne thought.

"Don't move." She wasn't sure if it was his tone or the look in his eyes, but she fought every urge to distance herself from him as much as possible. With wary eyes, she watched as he expertly maneuvered the blade with one precise motion, slicing through the zip tie that bound her wrists together. The piece of plastic fell to the ground, and he let go of her.

She rubbed each one of her wrists now that they were experiencing freedom. Perhaps he actually was trying to help her. "Thanks." Her voice was calmer now but that didn't mean she wasn't still irritated. There may also still have been some skepticism, but she was willing to at least wait to see what was going to happen next in this grand plan of his.

"I sent Marco and Victor to the hardware store to grab a few things to buy us a little time. Here's what's going to happen; you're going to get in the Challenger out front and get the fuck out of here." Joey dug around inside his pocket and pulled out a set of keys.

She looked at the set of keys in front of her and took them. "Fine, but there's one problem."

"What's the problem?"

POP!

Layne's fist swung and made contact with Joey's jaw. It was clear it caught him off guard and left him stunned slightly. Deep down there was a bit of satisfaction of getting that out of her system after what he had put her through.

His hand rubbed his jaw. "Christ! What the hell? I'm trying to help you!"

"I figured if the story is that I got away, it should look half believable. That is, unless you're really shitty at what you do even on a good day."

Joey took Layne by the arm and escorted her to the door. "Get out of here before I realize how stupid of an idea this is."

She started to make a move to open the door, and then paused and turned to look back at him. "Why are you let—"

"Just go!" He barked at her and gave her a firm shove in the direction of the exit.

Moments later, she was in the black Challenger with tinted windows all around, the engine turning over with a roar, and the tires kicking up gravel as she got the hell out of dodge. All that was left was Joey standing there inside the building wondering how much he just fucked up.

When she was gone, he slammed his fist into the door in front of him multiple times as he yelled out in a fury of emotions. His hands then grabbed the metal chair she had been sitting in and threw it across the room. It gave a loud clatter as it crashed into the dusty desk in the corner. "Son of a bitch!"

His chest heaved up and down as the internal conflicts raged through his system. When he took jobs, he always completed them. There were never any complications, and Layne was one hell of a complication that resulted in him thinking with his dick instead of his head.

When Marco and Victor returned a little while later, he told them the fabrication of what had transpired in their absence. Joey reassured them that he would smooth things over with the big boss.

She sat in the driver's seat of the Challenger, focused on the road in front of her and constantly checked all her mirrors in a stroke of paranoia that somebody was following her. Layne's knuckles were turning white from gripping the leather-wrapped steering wheel so tightly. When she finally arrived in a safer part of town, she parked the vehicle around the corner from her townhome.

Her house was such a sight for sore eyes after the culmination of events that had transpired that evening. This had not been on her top ten list of how she pictured spending the anniversary of her mother's death.

Layne swiftly made it inside using the electronic pin pad to unlock the entrance, then immediately shut and locked the door behind her. Everything was quiet, except her mind. An overwhelming onslaught of thoughts and questions had been plaguing her mind the second she left the docks. Most importantly, why had he decided to let her go?

If what Joey had told her was true, those were Michael Franzetti's men who attacked her in the parking garage. Franzetti and her father had never been able to see eye-to-eye. Everything her father did, Franzetti either wanted to destroy it or one-up it.

It had only been in the past two years that things had settled down enough that they were able to come to some sort of arrangement to coexist. Franzetti had his defined territories in the city, and her father had his. Those boundaries were always respected by everyone on each side. McGregor's Pub and the parking garage should have been off-limits to them. Based on tonight's turn of events, the respect for the O'Reilly territory had gone dry.

Layne was tapped out - physically and mentally. Her head was banged up, a small bruise was beginning to bloom on her cheekbone where Marco had struck her, and the adrenaline rush had left her feeling entirely depleted.

Leaving the foyer, she began the slow ascent up to the second floor. After a quick shower to rinse off all the sweat and ick from her, she crawled into bed in nothing but a red camisole and panties.

There was just something about her bed that was sedative, feeling the pillow cradle her head and the blanket envelop her, it wasn't long before her eyes fluttered closed.

CHAPTER SIX

She rolled over onto her back, her room cast into pitch darkness. There was a heavy weight on her bed and a presence above her. Layne's eyes opened groggily, and she saw a male figure looming over her on all fours, hands on either side of her head and his knees between her bare thighs spreading them apart. The familiar and intoxicating scent of musky leather mixed with woodsy sage overwhelmed her senses.

A dark skull mask was concealing the man's identity, but she had no doubts about whose identity it was attempting to conceal. Her hand reached up to touch his face and tug at the disguise, but his hand firmly took her wrist and pinned it above her head. His hips lowered between her legs and pressed against her center.

Layne's lips parted slightly, and a breathy moan slipped out as she felt his erection straining against his pants and pushing against her. His other hand ran up the front of her camisole, slowly grazing over her breast and right up to her throat where she hoped maybe it was going to stop. Instead, his hand continued to travel off to the side and under her head where he grabbed a handful of her thick tresses. The masked man tugged dominantly to force her head to tilt back and in turn caused the rest of her to arch up towards his body.

"Are you going to be a good girl and give me what I want?"

A swirling of desire and temptation rampaged deep down inside of her as he spoke with that dominating voice of his. Her body trembling with need under his touch. "Always."

"Don't lie to me, Layney." His hips began to grind up against her with purpose and sinful intentions. The thin fabric of her panties was already damp with excitement.

She whimpered and moaned out in approval with each distinct movement he made. Her pleasure was swelling, her heart was racing, and her alarm clock was buzzing.

Everything faded from the deep recesses of her subconscious and soon she was staring up at her ceiling illuminated by the sunshine pouring in from the window off to her left.

Layne groaned in despair as she smacked the alarm clock until it shut up. She didn't give a shit that it was almost ten in the morning. With conflicted feelings between her body and head, her hands covered up her face and tried to come to terms with all the feelings her dream had stirred up.

After a long, steamy shower with some desperately needed self-love, compliments of her favorite rose-shaped toy to relieve the nagging desire between her legs, Layne got dressed and went downstairs to make herself a cup of coffee.

She opted for comfort today with just a pair of black leggings and an oversized long-sleeved shirt that sloped off her shoulder. Pouring the life-saving freshly brewed caffeine into a mug with a splash of half-and-half, she attempted to clear her mind of everything and anything related to the night before.

She stood at the kitchen sink and slowly drank the piping hot goodness while gazing out the window in front of her to focus on what her next steps were today. Keeping herself busy was going to be key to easing back into routine.

"Did you really have to park the car on the street?" A voice unexpectedly broke the silence and caused her to nearly jump out of her skin.

The mug fell from her hand, crashing into the stainless steel sink and shattering into pieces. Layne spun around to see Joey standing there at the entranceway of her kitchen, leaning against the frame with both hands in his pockets. He was dressed in a pair of well-worn jeans and a grey t-shirt that emphasized just how much effort he put into working out.

The short sleeves allowed a series of tattoos crawling up his arms to be on full display. On the side with the skull on the back of his hand, the collage of roses, vines, and more skulls intertwined before the edge of his sleeve covered up the imagery. On the other arm, he had what appeared to be a sleeve of ravens, various clock faces, and tombstones.

"Shit!" An exasperated sigh was released as she glared over at Joey. "How did you even get in here?"

He chuckled, pushed off from the frame, and stepped further into the kitchen. "Practice."

"Wait, how long have you been here?" Suspicion rose in her voice. Layne had never been one for holding back her sounds of pleasure, especially when she thought she was home alone.

"Not long. Only came to have a chat about last night. We have some loose ends to tie up." However, there was an amusement in his eyes that indicated he might have been lying about how long he had been snooping around.

Layne raised a hand to get him to cease his talking right there. "No. There's nothing to chat about." Nothing at all. Nope. Not a thing. "You found your car, so there's no need for you to be here. Not to mention that if anyone sees you here, we'd both have hell to pay."

Joey rolled his eyes at the bossy attitude. "Look, it's not all about you, sweetheart. I risked my ass last night letting you go. So, maybe it wouldn't kill you to be a little nice and say 'thank you'."

"Thank you? That's what you came here for?" Layne scoffed in disbelief of where in the hell he got off on thinking she was going to be bowing down to him in gratitude after he just admitted to breaking and entering her house. Sure, she was grateful that things didn't get messier last night, but she wasn't about to forget that he had taken the job in the first place either.

"You're delusional. Get out." She pointed to the door.

"Not until I get what I came here for." He now stood directly in front of her. She took a step backward, feeling the edge of the center island press against her lower back. What had he come here for? Her heart skipped a beat as her mind hopped between two strikingly different scenarios; one, he came here to finish the job; or two, he was here to finish the job he had started in her dreams.

Her eyes tracked him while she held still, watching as he lessened the space between them. His hand reached past her and grabbed the keys from the countertop, then raised them in front of her face. "My mail key is on here." He gave a slight jingle of the keys in the air before dropping them into his pocket, remaining all up in her personal space - a trend that she was fairly certain she shouldn't be welcoming.

"Great, you've got your keys. Are we done here? I don't need rumors flying all over the city that I've got one of Franzetti's goons hanging around."

That made Joey outright laugh and shake his head. "One of Franzetti's goons? I'm hurt." A hand went to his chest feigning some level of offense to her assumption of who he was and what he did. "Clearly, you don't know my reputation."

Layne let out a scoff with enough attitude for ten divas. "Is that supposed to be some flex? You're some big ol' baddie and I got off easy?" He inched in closer to her, his hips just barely pressed up against her own. Holding her ground she didn't lean backwards in this little standoff they had going on in her kitchen.

"Let's get one thing straight, you got lucky. Don't expect to have it happen again. I'm the guy they call in when the bad guys are too chicken-shit to get the real dirty jobs done. I don't make mistakes, I don't get involved, and I don't leave loose ends." His tone was painfully serious.

Those deep brown eyes pierced into her like daggers. Was it just Layne, or was it a little warm in here? Nobody had to tell her how bad things could have been last night. Joey had been hired to take care of the dirty work for her dad's biggest rival in this city. No matter how self-sufficient she was with handling herself, she would always be someone of value to her father and ultimately a target for enemies like Franzetti to take aim at.

"I can handle myself; don't you worry your pretty little face." Her eyes narrowed at him, and she placed her hands on the edge of the counter behind her so that she could make sure she kept them to herself.

"Is that right? Didn't look that way last night." His voice lowered as an entertained grin curved across that perfectly shaped mouth. Something dark and tempting slid into his gaze.

Layne was not going to be intimidated by anybody, especially not him. She adamantly stood her ground and maintained eye contact with him, which was starting to feel overly intimate. "I got away, didn't I?"

"You want to hear about my reputation? The ugly shit I've done? It's not pretty. You want to know how easily you got off?"

"But, did I? Get off…easily?" A teasing sparkle shone in her eyes as the air between them began to grow heavier.

His hands grasped her sides, hoisting her up as though she weighed nothing at all, and set her ass down on the edge of the granite counter behind her. Stepping forward, he forced himself to stand between her legs, his hips making contact at the apex of her thighs.

Layne's heart was racing a mile a minute like a racehorse. Joey's face was now nearly nose-to-nose with hers. Inside her core, something else was stirring at having the warmth of his body radiating against her.

Despite the clothing separating them, she could feel how hard he was. It was delightfully head swirling. Her hands rested on top of his chest, fingers curling into the fabric of his shirt.

"Don't tempt me, Layne," he demanded. "You're not a good girl, and I'm not a good guy. I'm not the nice guy next door. I'm not your knight in shining armor. I'm not a country club twit that your dad wants you to marry." His voice came down to a whisper, his lips brushing against her own while he spoke.

Barely being able to gather her own intelligent words in response, she was proud of herself when she was able to say something semi-coherent. "Then, what type of guy are you? Hm?"

Joey may not have been the type that played golf every weekend at the local country club, but Layne saw something in him far more worthy than anything pompous asshats at the golf course could offer.

His hands ran down over the sides of her stomach and curved down over her ass, each hand taking a handful of it possessively.

As he squeezed her sweet cheeks roughly, he positioned his mouth over to the side of her throat, laying a trail of light kisses up it until he reached her ear. The heat of his breath was promising sweet, delicious, and wicked things before he finally spoke into her ear. "I'm the guy that gives you the best fuck of your life then you never see me again."

Her breath hitched and arousal was pooling between her legs. Layne's hands were grasping onto his shirt for dear life now as she prompted him. "Prove it." That was all the green light Joey needed as he gave a rumbling growl of anticipation at what he was going to do to her.

Knock, knock.

Damnit. Whatever sexual anticipation was in the air between them quickly dissipated.

Pound, pound, pound.

It wasn't Layne's heart; it was someone at her front door.

"Shit," she shoved Joey away from her, hopping off the counter and down onto her feet. Luckily, he had already read the situation and recognized he couldn't be seen there. Joey didn't hesitate to give Layne the space she needed. If anyone recognized him, it would be a major shit-storm. Being seen co-horting with his target that he had reported back as having escaped under some extraordinary circumstances would be a massive blow to his business and reputation.

"Stay here, I will go take care of it." Now she was the one giving orders, and assuming he'd have the sense to listen.

Layne went to her front door where the pounding was increasing in frequency and strength. As she drew in a deep breath to gather her composure, her hand twisted the doorknob and pulled the door open. On the front stoop was her brother, Liam. His cropped auburn hair which mirrored the same shade as their dad's, was uncharacteristically a tussled mess.

Before she got the opportunity to say anything, he pushed his way inside.

"Where the hell have you been? Are you okay?" The unpredictable level of crazy in his eyes was off the charts, even for him. He looked like he just needed to be told who had to die and he was going to send an army.

Liam stepped up to her and threw his arms around her in a suffocating hug. "Nobody has been able to get a hold of you, and given yesterday I didn't know if…" His voice trailed off, refusing to even speak the assumption out into the universe.

"I'm okay, relax." She let him practically cut off her oxygen during that hug, her hand lightly patting his back in reassurance. "I ran into some trouble and my phone got lost in the process. It was a bitch of a day, so I just wanted to pour myself a drink and pass out in bed before processing everything."

Liam's relief was quickly replaced by anger. He pulled back and now began inspecting her for any injuries, noticing the bruise on her cheek which prompted his eyes to narrow. "What in the blessed fuck happened? Who did this?"

He didn't even wait for her account of events as he pulled out his phone to begin rallying the troops. Layne gently placed her hand on his to stop him and shook her head. "Stop Li. I never saw them before, they were looking for information on something we're not even involved in, but the important thing is that I got away and I'm fine. You know that I can handle myself." She could have given him the information that it was Franzetti's men, but she wasn't trying to rock that particular boat just yet.

Liam didn't look convinced. However, after pause and consideration, he conceded for right now. Out came an exasperated huff before he slid his phone back into his pants. "I'm going to have one of the guys keep a closer eye on you for a little bit. Just precautionary and all that. I'm sure dad would agree."

Her eyes widened slightly. "You're overreacting."

"Deal with it." Right now, he had the clout and standing in the organization to make this decision. While Layne had made progress in securing her standing, she still had to battle a lot of misogynistic attitudes.

A babysitter was the last thing she wanted, but unless she could convince Uncle Mick to side with her, it would always be Liam and her father taking the same side when it came down to it.

Now wasn't the time she wanted to bother putting up the fight, especially since she just wanted Liam on his way so she could go back and pick back up where she left off with Joey.

Finally, she convinced Liam to leave after reassuring him no less than one thousand times that she would keep every nook and cranny locked up in the house. To avoid situations like a man supercharging her sensual needs after breaking and entering into her home.

After he left, she walked into the back of the house towards the kitchen to give Joey the all-clear.

"Joey? It was just my brother, he's gone now." Then, as she found herself in a now empty kitchen, she saw the note left on the counter.

I'm not the knight in shining armor. You got off easy. -J

Layne wasn't sure why, but she felt a pang of disappointment as it was clear he had left through the back door. Glancing one more time at the handwritten note, she released a soft sigh and dropped it into the trash can. Now, all she was left with was a frown on her face at the lost opportunity and a lost chance at an orgasm or three.

Go figure that he was now the one to take off on her. Maybe it was just better off that way and it wasn't meant to be. After all, everything about him was bad news, as she had accurately predicted in McGregor's. They would be a hot mess of a match together.

The O'Reilly family highly valued loyalty and allegiances, and with Joey taking jobs from the highest bidder, his ties were only to himself. Not to mention, as he said himself, he wasn't the polo-wearing country club type her dad was set on her aligning herself with. The best-case scenario is he would never be accepted or tolerated, and the worst-case scenario? He would have a bounty hanging over his head that she couldn't protect him from.

It begged the question, why couldn't she stop thinking about him? His cocky entrance into McGregor's, the way he had ensnared her in the empty building at the docks, and the way his eyes tracked her every move.

Layne shook her head to erase the addictive thoughts of him right out of her mind.

CHAPTER SEVEN

Later in the evening, she found herself sitting at the oversized dining room table inside her father's house about a ten-minute drive north of where she resided on the Upper East Side. The formal dining room was large enough to handle fourteen guests, maybe sixteen if you squeezed some extra chairs in there. Tonight, there were only three of them occupying seats.

Her father was in the very same seat at the head of the table he was always in for as long as she could remember. Layne was sitting to his left, and across from her was Liam to the right of their dad.

Scott had invited both his children over for dinner after hearing Liam's overly dramatic briefing of what he had witnessed and heard from Layne.

He thanked the plump, black-haired maid who took away his empty dinner plate, and then sat back in his chair and looked over at Layne while swirling what was left of his Old Fashioned in the glass he held.

"You want to tell me anything?" His hand motioned to her cheek where the makeup only managed to lighten the bruise on her face.

Layne fiddled with the fork in her hand, twirling it this way and that, and then pushing around some leftover potatoes on her plate. "I already know that I don't have to. I'm sure Liam already filled you in." He always was good at tattling on her.

Liam was already about to defend his stance on all of this, but silently

Scott lifted a hand to stop his son before he even started down that road. "I want to hear it from you. All of it."

She dropped her fork down onto her plate, causing a clatter that echoed in the air of the expansive room that seemed far too large for just three people to be eating in. Layne looked over at her father, letting the unspoken words build the tension.

Her father didn't move an inch while he waited for her to go ahead and respond to his initial question. She wasn't even sure he blinked.

After it was clear he wasn't going to let the subject change, she acquiesced. "Fine." Layne went ahead and gave the bare bones of her version of events, leaving everything out that had to do with Joey, and didn't drop any names of anyone else involved.

"Interesting." Her father nodded before continuing. "Nothing else to add?"

"No, I told you all that I know." She sat back in her seat, trying to find a comfortable spot in the hard wooden chair.

Mulling over everything his daughter said, Scott kept his gaze directed at her. "You mean to tell me, you don't know anything about anyone who was involved, they got the jump on you, and then you just… got away? Can you understand why I'm skeptical, Layne? You are better than this. I've taught you better than this. So, either you're lying or you're getting reckless."

She winced slightly at the tone of disappointment weighing on his words.

"Which is it, Layne? Because I can't imagine that you'd be stupid enough to lie."

Sitting there in silence, she wasn't sure what to tell him that would still keep the truth protected. Scott shook his head in disbelief that he was even having this conversation with her.

"I'm assigning a guard to keep an eye on you."

It didn't come as a surprise to her. "For how long?"

He snapped back at her with a roar. "For as long as it fucking takes for you to get some sense!" He smacked a fist onto the table, prompting a rattle out of the place settings.

Layne flinched as he lashed out. She looked at Liam across from her, he looked all smug that Dad once again took his side. Oh, how she wanted to wipe that look off his face with a handful of rusty nails, but all she could do was stare daggers at her brother before giving a pleading look to their father.

"Dad, please…"

"No, don't 'please' me. You're getting a security detail, and you're not getting any more jobs until I know you aren't going to compromise yourself or this entire damn family." Her eyes widened slightly as he tacked on that last bit that she wasn't going to be able to do any work for the organization at all.

She popped up from her seat. "What? What the hell am I supposed to do, then?"

Scott gave a tired sigh. "Layne, go out, have fun, go meet people."

"You mean go meet my future husband? Go make the rounds at all the luxury clubs, bat my eyelashes, and pretend that I want a life being cared for and providing offspring in exchange?" It sounded more like a prison sentence than any type of life she ever wanted to live.

When he didn't say anything in response to her question, she took it as confirmation that it had crossed his mind.

"Unbelievable." She gathered her belongings.

"It was a life your mother enjoyed and embraced, Layne." His attempt to make it sound more of an appealing option failed.

"No! You don't get to say that!" She pointed her finger at him. "She tolerated it! She tolerated all of this, and how was she repaid for it?" Years worth of tears filled with anger pricked at her eyes. "She got burned anyway, so don't sit there and tell me that I need to go be some damn trophy wife because it's for the better good!"

Liam tried to do his best to de-escalate the situation seeing the pain in their father's eyes at his sister's outburst. "Layne, that's not a fair comparison."

She choked back a few tears with a laugh. "The hell it isn't, Liam." Layne yanked her arms into the sleeves of her jacket and walked away from the dinner table. Both of the O'Reilly men had the sense not to agitate her further by following.

Going into the main hall, already waiting there for her was her newly assigned guard. He was going to be the first of many in the rotation of shift to shift. This one, in particular, looked like he took life way too seriously, and not the type that made having fun easy. She did her best to tell herself that all of this would blow over in a few days after everybody cooled down.

The cranky-looking guard escorted her to his car where he drove her back home, making sure to walk her inside once they got there. Mr. Uptight made himself comfortable in the living room, planning on staying in the house with her. It should have made her feel safe, but all it did was make her more aggravated.

Layne silently left him be, going into her small office and shutting the door to find some privacy inside her own house, where she could focus on anything other than the past twenty-four hours.

CHAPTER EIGHT

The next few weeks were inarguably painful from Layne's perspective. If there was anything that made her top ten list of things she hated, it was having a bodyguard hovering over her day and night. There was no opportunity to have privacy aside from hiding inside her own house.

One silver lining was that she had convinced her dad that taking away her work would result in allowing her skills to get rusty, and her contacts would have a lot of questions about where she had gone. Scott was in agreement that Layne had a valid point and reinstated her duties after two weeks off. However, she was still stuck with around-the-clock eyes on her.

The guard currently on watch was James. He was only a couple of years older than she was, but he had years of experience doing a bunch of the grunt jobs for Scott and Mick. He also had a personality that was far too serious.

They were in the back kitchen of a local pizza joint, the owner trembling as he sat in a wooden chair that threatened to snap underneath his weight. Kevin Beal, the proud proprietor of "Slices of Heaven Pizzeria," had been late on a payment due to one Scott O'Reilly. Let's just say that her family did not appreciate not getting what was owed to them in a timely manner.

Layne was standing in front of him, eyes analyzing the look on his face. James hung back by the door with a grumpy expression on his face but was ready to spring into action if needed. God, the way he hovered though, it was so damn distracting.

"You know, Kevin, my heart bleeds for you. It totally does. These are tough times." Layne gave him a pouty frown that insinuated she was sympathetic to his troubles. Her hand pulled out a baby Glock from the back of her snugly fitted black pants and casually held it in her hand just so he could see where this was going.

His eyes widened at the sight of her firearm. "I swear, I can get the money next week. Please, just give me a chance." His pleas were pathetic. Did this guy have zero backbone?

Layne looked back at James who hadn't changed the expression on his face for the past ten minutes. "He sounds like he regrets not having our payment ready on time. What do you think?"

James didn't so much as blink at her. What a damn killjoy. Layne shook her head and turned her attention back to Kevin. She stepped closer to him, crouched down in front of him, resting one hand on his knee while she casually waved the semi-automatic pistol around as she spoke.

"Next week doesn't help us when the money was due this week. But, I tell you what, I like you, Kevin. You make really shitty pizza, but I like you. You get the money to us next week, and for our troubles, go ahead and double it. Deal?" Layne was in strict business mode as her eyes stared at Kevin's face which had several lines of sweat coming down it.

He was very quick to nod, "Y-Yeah, that's a deal. I promise I will have the money. Ok? I swear."

Layne stood up and leaned over, pecking a quick kiss on his cheek. "That makes me so happy to hear. Thank you, Kevin. It's a date for next week." She backed up and turned to approach James, before recalling she had one more thing to add. Turning to look back at Kevin who had just been filled with relief, "Oh, and just so you remember this time." She aimed the Glock and fired a single round at his leg. The sound of the shot echoed against the walls of the tiny kitchen.

The poor sap screamed out as the bullet entered his thigh, his hands grabbing onto it. Layne looked to James and patted him on the arm. "Let's go." She tucked the Glock back into the back of her pants, making sure her shirt draped over it to keep it concealed.

They left the pizza place, walking out onto the street into broad daylight. Layne flinched at the sun shining so harshly today. Slipping some shades over her eyes she looked up at James who was at her side, barely giving her space to breathe. "Can you at least pretend like you're trying to give me space?" Her brow arched questioningly, but James just shook his head.

"No." That was all he had to say. He was a man of many words it appeared. She sighed. This was just painful dealing with an unnecessary and unwanted protector. Pulling out her secured cellphone, she made a brief call to Liam letting him know that Kevin would be paying them double next week and had been incentivized to keep his word. That was the last of the business matters she had on her plate for the day. She walked with James back to the car where he drove her back to her house.

Trying to think of a way to strike up a conversation he would actually engage in, Layne sat in the passenger seat, opening a bag of dill pickle-flavored potato chips. Crunching into the first one was utter bliss.

Working always stirred up an appetite for her. "You want one?" She extended the bag to James while he kept a watch on the road like a hawk.

"No, thank you." His voice was flat and monotone.

Layne shrugged and continued to snack on the chips, basking in the tangy and salty flavor.

"Aren't you bored of this whole gig? I would be." He didn't respond to her, leaving them in more awkward silence. She decided that if he was going to be as dull as a Fisher-Price butter knife, then it presented a challenge for her to overcome.

"For shits and giggles, what would happen if I happened to ditch you? On a scale of one to dead, how much trouble would you be in?"

James glanced over at her, before averting his eyes back onto the road and resigning himself to the small talk. "It would depend on if anything happened to you and how long before we tracked you back down."

"So, let me take a guess. If I get hurt on your watch, you're basically a dead man walking? If you only happened to lose track of me for a short period of time, you would be less dead?" Layne sucked the potato chip flavor off her pointer finger.

"Depends on the type of day your father was having."

Layne gave a little chuckle. "Ain't that the damn truth. The moody son of a bitch."

James cracked a subtle smile, but she caught it out of the corner of her eye. "So, you do have a personality somewhere in there. Good to know."

After they both arrived back at her safe haven and settled inside, James still didn't leave. It had been weeks of this bullshit and she was getting sick and tired of it to the point of considering straight-up violence just to put an end to the nonsense. He took a seat in her living room and began to read a magazine.

"I'm going upstairs to try and catch a quick nap. Feel free to help yourself to whatever food is in the fridge." Layne jogged up the stairs, walking down the hall to the master bedroom. She shut the door behind her, stripped her jacket off, and flung it onto the bed.

From behind, a gloved hand clamped down over her mouth to stifle any screams. Layne instinctively went for the gun still tucked in the waistline of her pants. Her attacker's free hand snatched her wrist and twisted her arm behind her, limiting her movements.

"Shhh," a husky voice hushed into her ear. Seamlessly, as he spun her around, he disarmed her of her pistol while releasing her. Layne was ready to lunge at the intruder until she saw a very familiar sight. He had on the same black tactical attire and the same black skull mask concealing his face that she had seen down at the docks weeks ago.

Her muscles relaxed as she recognized it was Joey, her heart rate slowly recovering. She approached him, expectantly holding out her hand palm face up.

"My gun." She kept her voice quiet so James didn't hear anything from downstairs.

Joey gave a playful grin, feeling proud of himself. "You promise not to shoot me?"

"You will just have to take your chances. Right now, you're looking at a fifty/fifty shot."

"Ouch, I would have thought it would have been at least forty/sixty."

"You should be so lucky." She waited until he finally passed it back to her. Layne walked over to her dresser, ensured her Glock was unloaded and no longer live, and laid the weapon right on top to be cleaned later. "What are you doing here?"

"You're a hard woman to get alone these days."

Wasn't that the damn truth? "I'm working on that."

He followed her over to her dresser and plucked a bright pink thong that was hanging out of the top drawer. "I didn't peg you for a fan of the color pink."

Layne pulled the panties off his finger and flung them back into the drawer, shutting it tightly.

Joey suddenly went quiet, shifting his stance in a way that was unnerving to her. She looked over at him while she took her hair tie out of the ponytail it had been in all day, allowing her dark hair to drop down behind her shoulders.

"You haven't come back here to finish the job, have you?" Only partially teasing him.

He shook his head, but his demeanor screamed that he was all business now. "No, but I found out some information that you need to know. I don't have all the details yet, but it's not looking good."

Confused about what type of information he could have she crossed her arms in front of her chest. "Usually any information in our line of work isn't good. What is it?"

Joey stepped up to her, his hands gently sliding up onto her arms, "The 227 project I asked you about at the docks. It's you. You're the project."

He wasn't making any sense, and it prompted her to wrinkle her brows together and shake her head. "That doesn't make any sense, I have never even heard about it. I would know if I was working on something."

He corrected her. "No, Layne, it's about disposing of you."

Downplaying the scenario, she shrugged. "I pissed someone off, what else is new?" She had heard all these things before. All it took was one whisper to get the criminal rumor mill lit up in a frenzy.

Frustrated, he let out a short sigh at how little she was taking seriously. "Layne, you're not listening to me. This isn't a Franzetti project, we don't know where it is coming from. Initially, we thought that you were working on something that was going to be a massive blow to the Franzetti family, that's why Michael needed answers to see what you knew. But that's not the case, Layne."

"As much as I would love to give Michael a run for his money, I'm not that stupid." It had been a long day and Layne couldn't wrap her brain around what Joey was telling her. It didn't even make sense. Sure, she had been increasing her footprint in the organization, but she still wasn't making the big decisions in the family.

Why would she be considered a big enough threat to anybody? As a pawn, she could see that scenario, and as a target to leverage that would even make sense, but what he was insinuating didn't.

"Your intel is wrong, Joey. That doesn't even make sense."

"My sources are always right, don't you just brush this off as nothing."

Layne stepped back from him as she battled all the feelings inside of her right now, trying to come to terms with whether he was telling the truth and what if he was right. What did that truly mean for her?

"I will take it under advisement. You need to leave before someone realizes you're here." After their last encounter, he had made it clear he wasn't going to play the role of Prince Charming and be her gallant knight, not that she wanted him to.

The puppy dog brown eyes of his had a softer look than normal in them. "I'm not going to leave and put you at risk."

"That's funny coming from you. Look, you can't—" starting to have raised her voice she caught herself and lowered it again, "—you can't stay here. Looking all," she waved her hand around to wildly motion at his attire, "like this. It's creepy as shit."

He tilted his head and leaned in closer to her. "You didn't seem to mind it down at the docks."

She chuckled. "You and I have two very different recollections of what went on that night."

His gloved hands latched onto her hips as he pulled her up against him. "I could tell by the look in your eyes." One hand slid behind her onto her lower back and then settled onto one side of her ass. "It's the same look you have in your eyes right now. I bet you're just dying to be a good girl for me, Layney."

She inhaled sharply trying not to lose her train of thought as his touch caused electrifying reactions deep inside of her body. If he kept talking like that, her legs were going to melt into a puddle on the floor. Looking up at him, her hands slid up over his sculpted biceps. "I told you not to call me that."

"I'm going to call you whatever I want, and you're going to like it."

Lightly she bit her lower lip, her body craving more of him like a sexual designer drug. "I thought you weren't a knight in shining armor?"

"I'm not. I told you, you get a one-time deal."

"In that case." Her hand dropped down to feel over the front of his crotch, rubbing over the sizeable erection that strained against the zipper of his pants. "We are going to compromise. You take me out on a proper date, and then you get one night of me being a *very* good girl for you. How's that sound?"

As her hand fondled him, his cock throbbed and Joey groaned in excitement. "How do you propose that I do that with your little entourage?" His hand took hold of her wrist to keep her hand right where it was.

Layne smiled up at him and tugged down the front of his mask briefly just enough to expose those perfect lips, she gave them the lightest of kisses. "You're smart, you'll figure out a way." Her hand gave two pats to his chest reassuringly and slipped her hand out of his hold.

He took a moment to adjust himself in his pants before walking over to the bedroom window that overlooked the back patio. He stared at her with a thirst in his eyes. "Be careful, Layne. Don't get yourself into any more trouble."

She couldn't help but smirk when he said that. "I think trouble has already found me, and if trouble doesn't get the hell out of here, he's going to risk causing an all-out war. Go." Her hand shooed him to leave.

He left, and Layne flopped onto her bed wondering what the hell was wrong with her. She was putting so many aspects of her life at risk, for what? A one-time fling with a dick that already had her charged up and ready to go?

Before she could honestly answer that question, she felt something underneath her vibrate and buzz. Confusion set in, and she reached underneath her, feeling an item that was thin and hard in her back pocket. When she pulled it free, she took a look at the phone that didn't belong to her. The screen lit up with a text message from an unknown number.

UNKNOWN

Be ready for me Friday night at 5:30.

I'm never late.

That sneaky bastard had managed to leave her with a clean and secured phone. She smiled to herself, impressed that he had successfully distracted her enough to slide it into her back pocket.

CHAPTER NINE

The week had crawled by at a snail's pace. The more Layne attempted not to think about her and Joey's official outing on Friday, the more it kept creeping into her mind at the most inconvenient times.

It was Friday morning, and she had purposely made sure her work schedule was cleared for the latter half of the day. She had told Joey that he was going to have to figure out a way they could get together even with eyes constantly on her, and she wasn't sure that he was going to be able to pull off a plan.

When she had texted him throughout the week, she hadn't received any return messages. Being left out of the loop and not having details was a pet peeve of hers. Call her crazy, but she liked to have a solid plan in advance for everything and anything. She was a bit of a control freak like that. How was she even supposed to know what attire to pick out if she didn't know what the plan was?

With the lack of communication from him, she had her doubts as to whether or not he would even show. Worst case, he stood her up and she found a quick date at a corner bar to spend the night with. She wasn't going to let some bad news guy chase her back home into pajamas and a pint of ice cream, all because he didn't know a good thing when he saw it.

That thought spiraled into an even worse worst-case scenario, what if this was all a setup and he was just going to deliver her head on a silver platter to Franzetti? Cue the paranoia. That's why she was going to be prepared with safety measures. One could never be too careful these days, especially if somehow, they were going to ditch the bodyguard of the day, Lenny.

She unwrapped the piping hot curling iron from her dark chestnut strands and watched as the last section of hair was freed and bounced into a loose curl. Layne stood there in front of the bathroom mirror analyzing what she saw in her reflection.

Her outfit was one of her more casual looks, but she figured he wasn't an uptown trust-fund baby expecting her to pull out the finest threads for this little get-together. Her favorite pair of dark blue skinny jeans flattered the shape of her legs and fed into her favorite pair of thigh-high black boots with laces up the back. For a top she had opted for something that screamed innocent and flirty, a white cropped blouse with thin straps that criss-crossed over her back, leaving her flat stomach exposed. To polish it all off, she grabbed a black jacket so that her favorite pew-pew could remain concealed in the back waistline of her pants.

Glancing at the smartwatch on her wrist, it was 5:02 p.m. Seeing how quickly the half-hour mark was approaching, a series of figuratively squirmy butterflies bounced inside of her stomach. It had been a long time since she could recall getting this worked up over a date, and not just any date, a date that she wasn't even sure was going to happen.

A knock came at her bedroom door which had been left open. Layne left the bathroom to see who was at the door, color her disappointed that it was Lenny standing there.

"Just got a call from Liam, he wants to debrief you on a situation."

Talk about shit timing. "Right now?"

Lenny nodded. "Said it was critical."

The irritation and frustration set in. "Crap, okay. I will be down in a minute."

The tall and lanky guard left without another word to return downstairs. This was going to be such a letdown after going through all the effort to dress herself up for this.

"Liam with the perfect fucking timing," she muttered quietly to herself as she snatched the phone Joey had left her and tucked it into her pocket so she could text him in the car to cancel.

By 5:07 p.m., she was sitting in the back of the town car and Lenny was pulling away from the front of her house to bring her to midtown to meet up with Liam on whatever it was that he decided was so incredibly urgent to discuss. Retrieving the phone from her jacket pocket her fingers tapped away at the screen to give Joey the bad news.

5:11 P.M.

LAYNE

Got called to a meeting, on my way there now.
Not looking good for tonight.

5:12 P.M.
UNKNOWN NUMBER

I'm never late.

Well, kudos to him for being punctual, but she was stuck in traffic heading towards midtown. Layne sighed and leaned back in her seat, staring out the window. She was going to be royally pissed off if this debriefing ended up being a waste of time.

Lenny cursed at the other cars also sitting in the traffic, occasionally laying on the horn to make his displeasure loud and clear.

Another text came in on the phone at 5:29 p.m.

UNKNOWN NUMBER

Better be ready.

Staring at the screen of the phone, she found herself questioning if she had been clear in the prior messages to him. He did realize she wasn't even home, right?

"Oh, you son of a bitch! You could have gone through that light!" Lenny yelled from the driver's seat, waving his hand around angrily during his fit of road rage. The offense? The car in front of them stopped at a yellow traffic light.

Layne's eyes looked at the clock on the front dash which ticked over from 5:29 p.m. to 5:30 p.m. "Never late, my ass."

Lenny looked up into the rearview mirror at her. "What was that?"

She shook her head. "Nothing."

The purr of a sports bike drew closer, moving in and out of the stopped cars on the avenue. A bike rolled up right next to Layne's passenger side door, the rider putting his feet on the ground to steady the ride between his legs.

When she noticed the biker stopped right there, she raised a brow questioningly at the odd decision to come to a stop on the marked dashes between the lanes. The man on the bike turned his head to look over at her while he sat there. That's when she saw on the black helmet, white decals designed into a skull mouth on the front of it. There was a spare helmet right behind him on the back of the seat.

"What the hell is this asshole doing?" Lenny had noticed the bike situated there on the dashed lines dividing the lanes. Layne grinned like a giddy schoolgirl and seized the moment.

She swung open her passenger side door and hopped out. Not wasting any time, she pulled the helmet down over her head and mounted the back of the sports bike, scooting herself close to the man's back as she wrapped her arms around his waist.

"Shit!" Lenny exclaimed as he scrambled to get out of the car and run around the front as Layne made her exit.

The bike's engine revved several times before taking off, accelerating down between the cluster of vehicles. He maneuvered it through the intersection expertly to avoid getting taken out by oncoming traffic.

Lenny got left behind at the car, running his hands through his hair as he realized that he just somehow managed to lose the boss's daughter. He kicked a front tire. "Damnit!" Even if he had gotten back in the car, there was no way he would have been able to get through the congestion and catch up with the stranger Layne took off with.

He got back into the car, immediately making the phone call to Scott to alert him of the situation.

"Hi, sir. I—" he cleared his throat to muster up the balls to admit what he had allowed to happen on his watch, "—I, have some news about Layne. She took off with some guy on a crotch rocket."

After the initial escape, Joey drove at a more reasonable speed. He didn't take the time to tell her where they were going, but she noticed that they were going over the Brooklyn Bridge right as the sun was dipping down below the horizon.

Layne kept herself securely situated on the back of the motorcycle. There wasn't much talking to be done while they were traveling. At least not verbal communication anyway. While it couldn't be seen underneath her full coverage helmet, she smiled mischievously as one hand slid down to Joey's upper thigh, giving it a firm squeeze. Her thumb stroked over the inside of his leg suggestively as her hand glided up over his zipper to the top of his pants.

His body tensed as Layne's touch continued, feeling her fingers slip under the front of his shirt and begin to travel south inside the front of his pants, but before she could execute her bright idea, he moved her hand back up to the front of his flexed stomach.

It seemed someone didn't like being distracted. She chuckled in light entertainment and behaved herself as she watched all the sights around them pass by.

It was incredibly liberating to know that she had successfully ditched her security detail. They may not have known it, but she knew that Joey was far more capable of keeping her safe than the recruits who worked trying to make a name for themselves in the O'Reilly family operations.

CHAPTER TEN

Finally, they eased to a stop and the engine cut off. When Layne looked past Joey's shoulder, she saw a narrow and battered boardwalk separating them from a sandy beach where the water was lapping at the shore.

He stepped off the bike and removed his helmet. Layne remained there on the back seat, taking off her complimentary head protection.

"Oh good, it really is you. I was concerned that maybe I had just hitched a ride with some random guy." She smirked as she set the helmet down on the seat between her legs.

Joey held out a hand for her to take, assisting her off the back of the bike. Layne didn't decline in taking the assistance.

"And if it had been a stranger, he would have been one lucky son of a bitch with the way you were providing quite the distraction."

"You're welcome." She winked at him.

"C'mon." He kept a hold of her hand and led her towards the quiet and unoccupied beach.

It was a welcome reprieve from the constant noise pollution of Manhattan. Joey released her hand so he could hide both his hands in his pockets as he stared at the last bit of sun reflecting off the water as it sunk lower in the sky.

"It's not much, but I like to come here when things get too heavy."

She stopped right next to him, linking her arm through his. "I can see why. It's like a mini-escape from reality."

Layne rested her head against the side of his arm as her eyes drank in the scenery of the ripples of the water caressing the shoreline. She could have stood there with him, getting lost in the serenity of this spot for days. What she really should have been thinking about was the chain reaction of events her taking off was going to cause, but instead, she found herself wondering why she had never felt this level of ease with any other man.

When she eventually took her eyes off the mesmerizing waters and looked up at Joey, she was surprised to see him looking right back at her. Turning to face her, his finger gently moved underneath her chin and tilted it upwards. Her breaths seized in her chest in anticipation as his mouth approached her rose-stained lips.

Layne pressed an index finger to his lips before they were able to connect with hers, giving him a sweet smile.

"Sir, our date has only just started. What kind of girl do you think I am?" Joey eased her finger away from his mouth, drawing it to the side.

"You're going to be in so much trouble later." The glimmer in his eyes showed he had every intention of following through on that. He dropped his finger from underneath her chin and took a peek at the time showing on a silver watch on his wrist. "If we don't get going, we are going to be late."

"Late for what?"

"For someone who comes off like she knows everything, you ask a lot of questions. Just trust me, eh?" He led her back to his bike, but instead of mounting it, he walked right on by.

It was several minutes of walking along the sidewalk before they arrived at their destination, a cozy brick building with no discernable signage indicating if it was a business or residence. Once he escorted her in through the front door, it was clear it was a homey little restaurant. There were not very many tables in there, and the ones that were appeared to barely fit in the room.

"Are you sure they're open?" Layne noticed there wasn't a single soul to be seen.

"For us they are." Joey grinned at her with a mischievous wink. His fingers slipped between hers as he took them into the kitchen, where it was clear they were no longer by themselves.

An elderly woman stood in front of the commercial stove, stirring a metal pot of red sauce with a wooden spoon. She was a frail-looking thing, but what she lacked in height and bulk she made up for in an aura of warmth and kindness. Her soft blue eyes were set behind a pair of thick glasses that were a little too large for her face and her pure white hair was kept in short but voluminous soft curls. The well-aged woman banged the wooden spoon on the edge of the pot to rid it of excess sauce before setting it down on a ceramic spoon rest.

"Ah! You made it, finally." She wiped her hands off on the front of the vintage-looking apron wrapped around the floral fabric of her dress. The woman turned and gave them both a larger-than-life smile.

Approaching Joey, she reached out her wrinkled hands and cupped his face. Her hands had a minor shake to them that one could venture came naturally with age. She pulled Joey's face down and greeted him with a kiss on each cheek.

Then, she turned to Layne, still emitting an extraordinary level of happiness despite being strangers to one another. "So, this is the one, huh? What a beautiful young lady!"

Layne was surprised to then be welcomed so affectionately by the woman when she released Joey and embraced her in a warm hug. It reminded Layne how long it had been since she felt such a motherly gesture. Layne gave a light squeeze back to the woman and smiled sweetly. "Thank you."

Joey spoke up, "Layne, this is Marie, but everyone calls her Nonna."

Marie nodded in agreement. "Everyone who comes through that door is family here. Especially this one right here." She hooked a thumb at Joey. "Now, the sauce is on the stove." She wagged her finger at Joey. "And don't you go messing it up by adding anything else to it now. It is absolutely perfect the way it is." Her words were firm with him, though not nearly as threatening as they should have sounded.

Joey's finger crossed over his chest. "Cross my heart."

"Mm-hmm." She eyed him skeptically. "You two have fun," she stated as she pulled her apron off and hung it up on a hook near a narrow set of stairs that led to an upstairs apartment.

After Marie retired upstairs, Joey removed his leather jacket, hanging it up next to Marie's well-used apron. He went to work setting up a pot of water on the stove.

Layne watched, unclear of what to do with herself. It wasn't often she found herself in a kitchen with someone else. "Do you need help?"

"You can help by taking a seat right there." He pointed at a stool by a center island where he set two plates down.

She tried to reassure him of her competence. “Believe it or not, I can reasonably find my way around a kitchen.”

“Sit your pretty little ass down, Layne.”

“Yes, sir.” She stripped off her jacket, adding it next to Joey’s before taking her assigned seat.

He continued to work his way around the spotless kitchen, preparing them a meal complete with freshly made garlic bread, a side salad, and a dish prepared with al dente spaghetti covered with Nonna’s sauce and meatballs. All made with love. The final touch was the two wine glasses filled with a rich chianti wine.

“I didn’t take you for the type to cook for a girl or…” she examined the label on the bottle of wine. “Know your wines.”

He settled onto the stool next to her. “I didn’t take you for the type to be so easily impressed.” Joey smirked at her as he took a sip from his glass of wine.

They both chit-chatted over the meal. Talking about everything from his upbringing to her time out west. Layne felt like she could have eaten five more pounds of the meatballs alone they had been so delicious. Joey’s hand rested on top of her thigh while he listened to her speak.

“Rebecca is my best friend, but she doesn’t get my life, not truly anyway. She’s been around long enough to know enough about how dangerous it is, but not how far down the rabbit hole it goes. Some days it’s a relief that she is in the dark about it, and other days…” Layne’s voice trailed off, leaving the thought incomplete. She shook her head and finished off her glass of wine. “Now it’s your turn, Mr. Big and Bad. How is it that you got into this life?”

“I’m not sure there’s enough wine for all of that.” He chuckled, pouring Layne another serving before topping off his own.

“My mom got locked up when I was young, busted on drug charges. When she got out, instead of thinking about seeing her kid, she went straight to her dealer to get high. The cops found her with the needle still stuck in her arm in an alley. My old man barely knew I existed except when his bottle was empty and needed a refill.” He gave a shrug of his shoulders as though it was a story that had been spoken a hundred times.

“Nonna has been the only one who ever showed she gave a shit since I was a kid. She made sure I never went hungry, she tried to make sure I stayed out of trouble, but I had a mind of my own there. Got sent to Rikers a few times, met a few guys who showed me a few things, and here I am.”

It sounded like such a simple explanation, but there was far more to it than that.

Joey had come to terms with his life never having been happy-go-lucky and had even embraced it so that he was comfortable with the man he had become as a result of the unfortunate circumstances.

She listened to how rough his upbringing had been in comparison to her own. Layne didn't have it all easy though, pain and death had been splattered across her life like an arterial spray. "And what about the whole mask thing? Is that just some kinky shit that gets you all ramped up when you go in for a kill?"

"No, but I think it gets you ramped up though." His hand squeezed her thigh suggestively before sliding to the top of it, inching up closer to her center, seemingly going to repay her for her distraction on the ride here.

She bit her lower lip in response to his touch. "You didn't answer the question."

"I will answer it if you answer mine."

Layne shook her head. "That's not how this works, but fine, I will play."

"The morning after we met, were you thinking about me while you were touching yourself in the shower?" His fingers brushed over the crotch of her jeans, prompting her cheeks to burn red hot and her hips to twitch in excitement.

So, he had been in her house long enough to overhear her pleasuring herself after that vividly hot dream she had. Layne should have been embarrassed and perhaps even mad about the invasion of her privacy, but she wasn't.

"Maybe you should have come up there and joined me instead of lurking." Her hand drifted between her legs to meet his, intertwining her fingers with his and guiding him away from her aching core.

He smirked as she could see him imagining what could have transpired if he had. "Now who's not answering the question?"

"It's a first date, a girl has to keep some secrets."

"In that case, we have one more stop to make." Joey winked at her as he rose from his seat, pulling her up out of her seat onto her feet with him.

After they both cleaned up their dishes so as not to leave Nonna a mess, they retrieved their belongings, and Joey guided her outside.

"What's next in your playbook?" Playfully she grinned at him, wondering what other tricks he was going to pull out of his bag for the rest of their time together. He struck her as the type of guy that always had a plan.

"I had to ditch my playbook for you. I didn't think you'd go for the flowers and a five-star restaurant."

The smile on her face hadn't faltered since they left Nonna's. "You're not wrong."

He led them back to the sports bike they arrived on, handing the spare helmet over to her. "One last stop." Layne pulled the bulky helmet on and got on the bike behind him making sure she was scooted all the way up against his firm backside.

They took off, the headlight on the front of the bike cutting through the dark of the open road ahead of them now that evening had fully descended on the city. The cool air whipping around them made her grateful for his body providing a shield against it and giving off some residual heat.

When he turned the engine off in front of an older apartment building, it was hard to fully see its historical charm at this time of night. It only rose to maybe seven floors tall, a short building by New York's standards. The reddish-brown bricks looked mismatched as if they had replacements throughout the years resulting in uneven fading. The street lights reflected off the glass entryway doors. A callbox mounted to the right of the doors was only one of a few features that gave away an indication of more modern amenities.

Joey helped Layne off the back of the bike, taking both helmets and locking them in place onto the bike. Leading her by the hand, he took her inside the double set of doors and to the elevator. Once they were in the confined space of the metal box, he stood behind her resting his hands on her hips. The button for the seventh floor was lit up as their destination.

"Lucky number seven, hm? Seems fitting." She observed.

"Why's that?" His mouth was closer to her ear than she had realized when the warmth of his voice fell against her neck.

She leaned into him, her ass teasingly pushing back against him as her hand reached out to pull the bright red stop switch on the elevator's control panel. They were roughly five floors up when the car ceased its movement between floors.

Layne twirled around to look at him face-to-face, not hesitating to pull herself up to the front of his chest, her lips crashing onto his. All her needs funneling into that passionate moment full of heat and desire.

Joey's hand came to hold onto her face while the other drew her even nearer at her lower back. The searing kiss intensified as their bodies pressed into one another. He guided her back until she was up against the wall. She was unable to escape the feeling of the strength of his hard body on her—in every regard.

Layne devoured his taste, consuming all of it and willing to drown her very soul in it. After fantasizing about this night after night, she was now getting exactly what she had been pining for.

Even when she should have come up for air, she couldn't bring herself to do it. She couldn't tell whose breath was in either of their airways. Joey's mouth was the most addictive drug she had ever experienced. His tongue possessively claimed hers inside of her mouth while her figure rubbed up against him in a suggestive fashion.

His hand slid onto the top of her breast, roughly kneading it in his hand, indicating she hadn't been the only one thinking about this moment. Her pert nipples were poking at the light fabric of her crop top in a delighted reaction to his touch.

Assertively she pushed him back to the wall opposite her with a smile on her face, breathless. "We're going to need more time than this elevator is going to stay held up for."

Joey's hand gave a smack to the red stop switch, popping the button back in, causing a jolt of the lift as it continued its ascension once more.

As far as she was concerned, she had an itch, and Joey was the only one that was going to be able to scratch it. Her hand reached out and grabbed him by the belt of his pants, pulling him back towards her. He responded by nipping at her throat, hungrily speaking with the deep gravel of his voice rumbling against her skin. "Hope you cleared your schedule. I'm going to take my damn sweet time enjoying all of you."

The doors opened and she backed up out of the elevator, already in the process of unlatching his belt. Feverishly she captured his lips again while he fumbled for the keys to his apartment. Layne spoke between breaths and sporadic kisses. "I'd be disappointed if you didn't. I hate being disappointed." Her playful smirk promised an array of all the sinful delights ahead of them.

Joey reached behind her as they came to unit 701, twisting his key in the lock and swinging the door open as he prepared to begin the ravaging.

Layne shrugged off her jacket, tossing it to the floor as they both stumbled inside. Using his foot, Joey kicked the door shut directly behind them. The unit was blanketed in darkness, causing them to bump into a side table knocking some unopened mail onto the floor.

The clearing of a throat interrupted what should have been nothing but silence in the apartment. The light in the living area flickered on. Joey and Layne weren't the only ones there in that apartment.

CHAPTER ELEVEN

It took a moment for Layne's eyes to adjust when the darkness in the apartment was cast away by the sudden light. Standing there in the living room were two men, one of whom she would recognize any day of the week; Michael Franzetti.

The thinning raven hair was long enough to pull into a small bob of a ponytail. A patchy goatee on his face, and one of those flesh-colored moles on the side of his nose the size of a shirt button. He was dressed in a gaudy-looking suit with a mixture of patterns and colors that were abrasive to the eyes.

Shit. That was the first thought that fired off inside Layne's head.

Standing next to Michael was a heaping giant of a man, whom she didn't recognize, with a scowl on his face. Layne could only assume that he was hired muscle to keep Franzetti safe and protected.

It was challenging to get a good read of Franzetti's expression, if he was surprised to see Layne there with Joey it was well concealed. The strap of her top hung off the side of her shoulder. Layne immediately pulled it back up into its place as she swallowed down her anxieties while trying to process the gravity of the situation that had just presented itself.

On the other hand, Joey's demeanor immediately went ice cold, his hands casually relatched the belt of his pants as though they hadn't been about to be yanked off just a few seconds ago.

"Go home, Layne." Joey sternly told her.

"Ah, ah, ah. The evening is still early, and the party has only just begun. Take a seat." Franzetti motioned to one of several open spots to sit there in the living room.

Layne glanced at Joey, looking for any indication of his thoughts on the next action he was going to take, but he didn't take his eyes off Franzetti. She stood there silently begging for some signal they were on the same page here.

"SIT!" Michael roared like a petulant and impatient child as he showed signs of running out of patience. The sudden outburst caused her to flinch.

Getting any closer to Franzetti wasn't anywhere on her top ten list of things she wanted to do, ever. Layne ran a quick calculation and risk assessment in her mind. Normally, her fight-or-flight instincts erred towards fighting. This was one time she knew that staying not only put herself at risk but her family and everyone else who worked for the O'Reillys.

She pivoted on her heel and ran to the door, flung it open, and dashed out as Joey had originally told her to do. Bursting into a sprint down the hall towards the fire exit stairwell, she glanced behind her to see if Joey was going to follow.

Crash.

Layne collided with another ape of a man built solidly and towering over her. His arms locked around her like a vise, lifting her off her feet and easily carrying her back to apartment number 701. She bucked, trying to break his hold on her at least enough to get her arms free.

"Let go, asshole!"

She was taken right back into the apartment, and now Joey stood in front of Franzetti in mid-conversation in the living room. His attention was drawn from his employer to Layne being brought back into the apartment.

"I told you; she doesn't know shit. Just let her go run back to daddy."

The hulkbeast of a man restraining her didn't loosen up his hold until he flung Layne like a ragdoll onto the sofa with enough force to cause it to rock back and bang against the wall. The momentum and movement of her body caused her gun to unknowingly slide out from the back of her pants, sinking between the cushions.

Franzetti stood there, holding his hands together in front of him. "See, that's the dilemma. Is it that she really doesn't know anything, or are you just letting your dick do all the thinking for you? I would like to think I'm a good judge of character. All I'm going to do is ask her a few questions."

A vein popped up in the side of Joey's neck as his blood pressure rose.

Layne sat up on the couch, murderously glaring at the man who had tossed her there. Michael approached her, sitting on the edge of the coffee table in front of her, his arms resting on top of his knees as he tried to come off as friendly and approachable. She knew better. He was about as friendly as a pissed-off hornet nest.

"Layne, I would like to think that we have mutual respect for one another, given our lines of work. Call it professional courtesy."

She shifted her gaze onto Michael's scumbag face, the glare not altering one bit. Keeping her mouth shut she waited for him to get to his point of what he wanted.

"All this buzz about this 227 project just isn't going away, and I feel like I wasn't invited to the party. That hurts my feelings."

"Boo-fucking-hoo, that makes two of us. You're operating off of bad intel." She finally spoke up, unsympathetic to his concerns.

Franzetti sighed. "Such a fresh mouth on such a beautiful face." He looked back over his shoulder at Joey while chuckling in twisted amusement. "I can see the appeal."

He looked back at Layne. "I really would like to believe you, dear. Yet, you've managed to compromise one of my best contractors here with your wits and charm. Let's make a deal that benefits everybody." He reached out to place a hand on her knee, his thumb stroking the inside of it.

"If it doesn't involve putting a hole between your beady eyes, I'm not interested." Layne shoved his hand off her.

He took the hint and kept his hands to himself but leaned over, dropping his voice down to a whisper. "Just wait until your poor father hears about all of this. I need to know if you're telling the truth, so you will just have to forgive me." Without any hesitation, he snatched a handful of her hair, yanking her up onto her feet as he stood.

Joey lunged, only to be pulled back by the two hired hands as he yelled out viciously. "You touch her and I will fucking kill you!" One of the men slammed a fist into Joey's stomach in an effort to subdue him, causing him to double over.

Michael dragged Layne out of the living room, harshly yanking on her shiny chestnut locks close to the roots. He took her into the glaringly bright white bathroom located down the hall where the tub was pre-filled with water. The bastard had planned on someone taking a swim tonight.

"I dislike getting my hands dirty Layne, but having the opportunity to dish some karma back at Scott O'Reilly… Mm, it's just too good of an opportunity to pass up. Now is your last chance to be a helpful little flower."

Her fingers scratched and pried at Michael's hand tangled in her hair, beginning to solidly plant her feet into the ground upon seeing the still and eerily calm body of water in front of her.

"Go to hell."

Franzetti smiled, seemingly delighted that she chose noncompliance. He kicked the back of her knees, causing them to buckle under her. Layne's body fell into a kneel in front of the tub and as she yelled out, he shoved her forward over the edge of the tub plunging her head into the cold water.

It was a shock to her system as the air disappeared around her. Layne's hands pushed and shoved against the edge of the tub while her feet scrambled to push herself up. Franzetti's other hand pinned her down against her back with his weight against her.

She tried not to panic, but the struggle of her body was quickly diminishing what little air she had left in her lungs. Just when she thought that she was nearly out of oxygen, he pulled her head back up. An involuntarily loud gasp as she drew in much-needed air came out of her mouth. Her heart was beating so hard that she was pretty sure it was about to burst through her chest walls.

Michael leaned down to the side of her face, giving her an emotionless look. "The 227 project?"

"I don't kn—" and before she could complete her response, he thrust her head back under the surface of the water. Being a little more prepared for it this go around only helped marginally. Water was splashing out of the tub onto the floor and the walls. Once again, she felt the slow depletion of life in her lungs before being greeted by the cool air in the bathroom as she was drawn back up again.

"Last chance, sweetheart."

Her lungs were on fire as she sucked in heaps of air. "I… I swear, if Joey doesn't kill you, I will."

"Unlikely. Say hello to your mother for me." He pressed his slimy lips to her temple.

This time when he shoved her back down into the tub, he used all his weight to keep her under, minimizing the amount of flailing about she was able to do. With all the water getting splashed on the floor, her feet were slipping against the tiles. Her hands scratched at the smooth sides of the tub for anything to grab onto. It seemed like hours with her head fully submersed, and everything began to feel light as a floating sensation took over her senses.

She remembered the smell of her mom's homemade chocolate chip cookies.

She could feel her mom's loving embrace and the light fragrance of peonies in her perfume.

She could hear her dad's voice and see the beaming smile on his face as he told her how proud he was of her when she stood up to the bullies on the playground.

She could hear Uncle Mick's laughter as Liam and she tackled him to the ground during a snowball fight.

She could feel a heat deep inside aflame as Joey looked into her eyes and how he had kissed her like she was the only woman on the planet.

That was the last thought she had. Joey had been her last thought.

Franzetti left Layne's soaked body, void of any movement, slumped over the edge of the tub. The strands of her hair were in a wet and tangled mess.

He grabbed a hand towel off the rack, wiping his hands dry as he came back out into the living room to see that his two right-hand men were taking turns pitching shots at Joey. He gestured to them both, prompting them to drop Joey onto the floor in a heap. Michael stood there feeling tall and mighty as he tossed the damp hand towel down onto Joey.

"I'm going to make myself crystal clear. The only reason you're not dead is because of all the work you have done for me in the past. Let this be a lesson to you that if you ever fuck up a job this badly again, I won't be nearly as kind."

Joey groaned as the back of his hand wiped some blood from his mouth, struggling to get up on all fours. Franzetti turned to leave, then paused. "Send my condolences to her family for me, will you?" The asshole even made an attempt at sounding half-sincere when he said it before he left with his two goons.

As for Joey, the realization of the words Michael parted with sparked a surge of adrenaline. He scrambled onto his feet and ran to the other side of the apartment, through his bedroom, and into the master bath. His heart sank into his stomach at the sight of Layne's body hanging there over the side of the tub.

His body moved before his mind could catch up, in an instant he was pulling her back to lay her down on the floor. "Layne! Layne! Wake up!"

His hands checked her over frantically, cupping her face and shaking it hoping she would just awaken and open those mesmerizing green eyes. Joey brushed her hair away from her face, "Fuck, no, no, no." Coupling his hands one on top of the other, he began chest compressions on her. His arms locked and steady as he stared down at the peaceful-looking Layne lying there on his bathroom floor.

"You stubborn bitch, c'mon!" He shouted at her in frustration with each compression that felt useless and ineffective. "Layney, please. Please, Layney." His voice cracked with raw emotion.

She sputtered up the first wet cough, followed by several more as she expelled water out through her nose and mouth. He rolled her onto her side quickly to ease the coughing fits as she gasped a few times. Layne groaned as her entire chest, inside and out, felt like she had been run over by a freight train, twice. Slowly she sat herself up, Joey's hands assisting.

"Take it easy." He stared at her, relief overwhelming him as she gazed up at him with those entrancing doe eyes he had fallen for the very first day they met.

Joey's hands held her face. Overwhelmed with gratitude that she escaped death's cold grasp, he kissed her with gentle affection. Her hand ran over the side of his face as she weakly returned his kiss as she tried to gather her wits.

Drawing away slightly, she winced as her entire body screamed at her in pain.

With a light rasp to her voice, she offered up a light curve of a smile. "Ten out of ten do not recommend drowning." Layne went to chuckle, but immediately whimpered and rubbed a hand against her chest at the fresh round of aches and pains. Joey kissed her forehead with a sigh. "You have no idea how much you had me worried."

As she tried to get up onto her feet, Joey shook his head. "Oh, no you don't." He scooped her up into his arms, holding her securely to the front of his chest. Normally, she would have protested at being carried anywhere, but he felt warm and safe. Not to mention she wasn't confident her legs would have had the strength in them.

Layne rested her head against his chest, closing her eyes and focusing on how the air felt, moving freely in and out of her lungs. He carried her out of the bathroom and over to the edge of his bed where he sat her down.

"Stay here." Joey left and returned with a dry towel, wrapping it around her. His hands rubbed her arms to help dry her off and generate warmth through her body.

Layne should have been feeling an unholy rage inside of her toward

Franzetti, but instead, all she could do was keep looking at Joey in awe that she wasn't robbed of ever seeing him again.

"I should have had things handled, but-"

"Shh." He pressed a tattooed finger to her mouth to stop her right there. "We aren't doing this. We aren't doing the blame game. What is going to happen is you are staying here tonight. I'm not letting you out of my sight. Everything else will get dealt with tomorrow."

She let out a quiet sigh as she gently moved his finger away from her lips. "I'm okay, Joey. Really. I don't need to stay here."

"It's not up for debate, so shut that gorgeous mouth and deal. I will go get you some dry clothes."

Her energy was entirely spent after the evening, and arguing with him was looking less and less like a priority. Allowing Joey to get the final say this time, she let him take care of her just this once. One time couldn't hurt anything.

After getting her his old Slipknot t-shirt, he gave her privacy to change while he walked around his apartment securing every possible entry. He came back into the room to see that the size of the shirt swallowed her up. Even in that oversized shirt, she made it look hot as hell.

He got Layne tucked into his bed, lying next to her until she fell asleep. His hand rubbed up and down her back soothingly while he studied each of the features of her face. Joey vowed that he was never going to let anyone try and take her from him again, he couldn't let that happen

CHAPTER TWELVE

Morning rolled around and Layne rolled right into Joey's side as she began to feel her slumber fade away. Half-asleep, she curled up against him and draped an arm over the smoothness of his bare stomach. He lay there on his back, shirtless with the top sheet loosely draped over his lower half.

Protectively, Joey drew his arm around her shoulders, pulling her in even closer. When she opened her eyes and lifted her head to take a look at him, his soft brown eyes were already open and staring at her.

The tattoos inked across his skin were now on full display before her. Various designs and images sprawled in a sleeve over his left arm, onto the back of his shoulder out of sight, across his toned chest with one-offs branching off down his ribs and up his neck. Of the splashing of multiple images across his skin's canvas that stood out the most, she saw various scenes of bloody skulls and roses, birds, and the words 'Chaos Addict.'

Joey smiled in amusement; his other arm tucked behind his head. "Good morning."

Layne cracked a smile. "What's so funny?"

He shook his head. "Nothing."

"Tell me!" She gave a shove to his side, prompting a laugh from him.

"You have the cutest little snores I've ever heard."

"I don't snore!" She propped herself up on one arm, hoping it would help solidify her defense.

"Whatever you say. I know what I heard."

Her eyes looked him over, becoming suddenly aware of his lack of clothes. Layne appreciated the sight of each of the muscles on display in front of her like a heavenly buffet. Joey didn't interrupt her as her eyes drank in the view, but he did pull her up on top of him.

Her legs spread to straddle over his hips as she got comfortable in the new position, her hands resting on top of the chest she had just been admiring seconds ago. He reached up and tucked a section of her hair back behind her ear. "You know, this is not what I expected for your first time spending the night with me."

Layne tilted her head. "Oh?"

"I imagined a lot less clothes." His smirk oozed with charm.

Leaning over onto her forearms as she sat atop of him. "Don't worry, you wouldn't have gotten that lucky last night."

"I find that very hard to believe by the way you were trying to climb me in the elevator."

She smirked back at him and rubbed herself teasingly over his hips where she could already feel the growth of his morning wood pressed up against her, begging for attention. "I don't give it up on the first date, too many bad apples to waste the effort on."

His hands latched onto her hips as he pulled her down harder against him with a groan of approval. "Good thing I'm counting this morning as our second date."

"Mmm." Layne bit her lower lip as the sensation of grinding against him had her panties soaked with her own arousal.

Her hands slid down over the tanned skin of his stomach, fighting every urge inside of her to just give in. Leaning down onto him, she lightly kissed his lips, feeling the stubble around his mouth scratch at her face with a bit of a tickle.

"I don't give it up on the second date either, but a third date? That might be the charm." The glimmer of playfulness shone in her green eyes.

Joey rolled over, pinning her underneath him as his hand slid to the front of her panties. The hem gave away as his fingers invited themselves into the poor excuse for a layer of clothing. His fingers found her excitedly wet clit, stroking it with slow intentional movements. Layne whimpered as her legs spread enough to allow his hand to go to work between them.

"Such a good girl, already all wet for me. You want to revise your stance on waiting for a third date?" His finger circled her nub again, causing her to bite back a moan at the sensation. Layne pulled her upper half up to him, burying her face in the side of his neck to muffle the sweet sounds he was causing her to make.

The sounds she made against his skin only encouraged him further as she squirmed beneath him, her hand clenching onto the sheets underneath her.

"What was that, Layney? I didn't get that." He smirked as he pinched her wet little button.

Her voice was heavy with desire as she looked up at him as his fingers relentlessly teased her sensitive bundle of nerves. "I can't think when you do that."

Joey knowingly grinned as his fingers continued to explore and tease her body. "All you have to do is say it, Layney. Tell me you want it."

He slid a finger down her slit and pressed it inside of her to drive his point home. He leaned down, his stubbly cheek scratching against her neck as he gave it a nip followed by a press of his lips against the sensitive skin. "I will fuck this tight pussy of yours until you scream loud enough for the entire damn city to hear."

Her hands gripped onto him desperately, one burying into his shortly cropped hair while the other clutched onto his back, her nails digging into his flesh.

Layne's hips pushed against that one finger sliding in and out of her. God, she needed him more than life itself at that moment. She had been telling herself since the moment she had laid eyes on him that he was bad news, and maybe she was right, but damn it all to hell if she didn't care right now.

"God, Joey, please…" her breathy voice was laced with wanton disregard for anything but him.

He looked at her with a devilish grin. "That's my good girl." He didn't hesitate to crush his mouth to hers, claiming it with the eagerness of a starving hellhound. His hands were quick to get to work on yanking her panties off. Their mouths explored one another, sparking an electrifying sensation throughout Layne's entire body.

With a hand on the back of her neck, he sat back, pulling her upright. "I need to see all of you." His hands stripped his well-worn t-shirt off her, revealing the supple curves of her bare breasts. Carelessly, the shirt was tossed aside to join her thong on the other side of the room.

Layne dropped her hands onto his sides as she sat there fully exposed to him. She gave a small grin as his eyes lit up. "You see something you like?" She watched as his eyes slowly roamed and appreciated every detail of her body.

"I'm never going to let anyone else ever touch you again like I'm about to. You're fuckin' stunning, and every part of you is going to be all mine." He pulled off his black boxer briefs, exposing his long and thick length which was fully engaged and ready.

Layne was glad that her three-inch assessment in McGregor's was far off base. On a scale of one to ten for Layne, by comparison to any other man she had been with, Joey was so far off the charts he was halfway to Mars.

Her hand didn't hesitate to reach out and wrap around his massively hard cock while she looked up at him with a need and desire unlike anything else she had felt in her lifetime. As she stroked him, it elicited a groan of approval from Joey.

He guided her back down onto her back. "Uh-ah, there's going to be plenty of time for that. Right now, I'm dying to taste you." There was something alit in his eyes that made her stomach fill with glorious anticipation. It then magnified when he firmly took her by her wrists and pinned them above her head with one hand easily. She squirmed against his hold, the feeling of helplessness and vulnerability prompted even more excitement from her body.

His mouth came down onto one of her breasts, taking one of her stiff nipples hostage, sucking on it nice and slow. She arched her back, pushing her breast further up against him. His hand, which wasn't forcing her to keep her hands to herself, latched onto Layne's other breast. A delightful whimper escaped her as he ran his tongue around the tip of her nipple before his teeth gave a teasing nibble to it.

After getting a taste of both of her bountiful breasts, he released her wrists so he could run his hand down along the front of her body where both hands settled on her hips. His lips traveled their way down her stomach, journeying lower inch by inch. The further down her body he got, the more she felt like her desire was going to explode.

Layne dropped her hands down from above her head to get her fingers lost in his hair. He slid down to right above her center, the strength of his hands now rubbing over her skin from her hips over onto her inner thighs. His hands grabbed her thighs as if he owned them and spread her legs wide to fully expose the sight of her pussy that was throbbing and aching for his attention.

"Layney, you're already making a mess of the sheets with how wet you are. I bet you're just aching for me to bury my cock in you." His mouth hovered over her inner thigh, his tongue escaping and drawing a long line over her skin.

Feeling the warmth of his breath against her body, her hips rocked forward, trying to make contact with his mouth, but he made sure to stay just out of reach. With a yearning in her eyes, she looked down at him. "I want it. I want all of it. Your mouth, your hands, your cock." She pushed her hips forward again, still not getting what she wanted as she made a small sound of frustration.

Joey smirked at her, enjoying seeing her struggle without control. "Such an eager little girl. Don't worry, you're going to get all of me."

Without another word, his tongue gave one long lap against her slit causing a jolt from her body as she moaned out at first contact. Joey savored the taste of her body, already becoming a slave to how addictive she was going to be for him.

His mouth captured her now highly-sensitive clit, sucking intently on it. Asserting his control over her body, his hands held her by her thighs as she wriggled underneath him while the strokes of pleasure zipped through her body like lightning.

Her hands squeezed tightly onto his head as she cried out, feeling a quick and furious escalation deep within her. With every sound she made, it prompted him to take more of her and explore all the sweet tastes of her pussy.

Just when she thought her body couldn't take much more and it teetered on the edge of falling into the depths of ecstasy, he pulled back and looked at her mischievously.

His tongue ran over his lips, gathering the remnants of her most intimate flavor from them. "Did I tell you to come yet?"

With her climax having been so damn close and now receding from the edge it had been so close to spilling over, she whined in desperation. "Joey, please, I was so close. That felt so good, I need more of you."

"You didn't answer my question, Layney." He let go of her thighs and moved up higher on her, meeting her mouth with his. The taste of her arousal still lingered on his tongue as a reminder of how he had used it to bring her to the edge of release. The head of his shaft teased against her opening as he briefly lost himself in the taste of her mouth before pulling back.

"I want the first time you come for me to be all over my cock while screaming my name. You're going to be a good girl and do that for me, aren't you Layney?" His words made it clear he was in total control of the situation in his bed. It wasn't like her to let a man call the shots. But, for Joey? She already knew that she didn't want anything else but to have him take full control over her.

She nodded in response to his question. He could have asked her to rob a bank, and she would have done it. It had made her nearly lose her mind, feeling the tip of his shaft so close and he still hadn't given it to her. Her hand reached down, attempting to coax him to push himself a little closer to her opening, but he promptly removed her hand, pressing it down into the mattress at her side.

His fingers grabbed her face. "Don't be a brat, I will give it to you when I think you deserve it."

"I need to feel all of you inside me." Layne was used to getting what she wanted, and it was clear that Joey wasn't going to let that fly. "Fuck my brains out, Joey. Take all of me."

He sat back and flipped her onto her stomach, pinning her upper body down while propping her ass up in the air, drawing a gasp of surprise from her. "Oh, that was always in the cards. I just need to hear you say one more thing for me." His hips were up against her ass, the tip of his erection teasing as it rubbed against the tight entrance to her sex.

"Tell me you're mine, only mine."

Feeling a primal heat overcoming her, her hands balled up the sheets. "I swear, I'll be a good girl. I'm all yours."

Hearing her promising to be a good girl and give herself to him, Joey growled as he sank himself deep inside of her in one smooth push. Layne's body forcibly stretched and wrapped around him as she moaned out as a mixture of sensations swam over her. A little bit of pain and a whole lot of pleasure as her tightness was forced to accommodate him. Her hips pushed back against him as she felt herself filled with the hard length of his shaft.

"Fuck, Layney, you're so goddamn tight." His hands ran down the length of her back and over the curves of her ass where he squeezed them while he drew himself back before pumping back into her again. Joey took his time, enjoying each languid movement inside of her.

Layne's heart was pounding inside of her chest as she maintained her position on her knees with her chest pushed down onto the mattress. It felt akin to being a lioness in heat while the king of the jungle claimed her body. Repeatedly. Over and over again. Nothing else could have made her feel more alive than being there in his bed with him driving himself into her.

As his tip stroked over her body's deepest sensitive spot, she felt a trembling threatening to take hold of her. Barely being able to catch her breath as her sexual high drew nearer, she clawed at the headboard in front of her, tensing up her entire body.

Joey groaned, feeling her bear down around him. "That's it. You're taking my cock like such a good girl. Now, fuckin' come for me, Layney." His words were strained between each of his thrusts as his own swell of pleasure was drawing closer to its peak.

Hearing both his praise and his demand triggered her vision to explode into stars as her release violently took control, and her body was wracked with ecstasy. She screamed out his name as her climax rushed over every part of her from head to toe.

Joey didn't slow his movements, eliciting a steady stream of pleasurable cries from her, extending the high he had given her while the inside of her pussy spasmed around him.

The next thing she knew as the fog in her head cleared, he had paused briefly to turn her onto her back where she was staring up into the depths of his brown eyes as he held himself over her.

Each of his muscles flexed while his hips mercilessly pushed himself back into the wet mess of her cunt. "I'm not done with you yet," he said while his hand held onto the side of her face, his thumb trailing down over her bottom lip.

Layne was in such a haze from her first orgasm that she could have died an extraordinarily happy death right then and there. Lightly she sucked on the tip of his thumb as it passed by her mouth. "Mm, you have me feeling so good right now, you could do anything you want with me."

A sinful smirk crossed his face. "Don't tempt me more than I already am." His face closed the gap between them, capturing her mouth with his own as he continued to build a second swell of warm pleasure within her. Her fingernails dragged across his upper back, her hips meeting his as their bodies repeatedly joined together.

His movements were getting less and less smooth as he groaned out while trying to keep a grasp on his self-control. She wrapped her legs around his waist, locking them at her ankles. Her body felt so conflicted as her back arched pushing her up against him trying to escape the intensity of feelings that were quick to build back up once more and craving another dive off the precipice of divine release.

"You're gonna make me come again." Her words were forced out through her panting and heavy breaths. No sooner than she said it, the orgasm ricocheted throughout her. Layne screamed out, clutching onto everything and anything within her reach. Her fingernails left scratches along his back.

Joey's body stiffened as he rammed himself as deep inside of her as she would take him, holding himself still as he gave a feral groan. The throbbing of his cock finally maxed out as his sticky seed erupted into her depths before he collapsed down on top of her into a sweaty pile of entangled body parts.

Thank God for birth control.

Layne's head was swimming in a glow of hormones and emotions that she had no business feeling. She kissed the top of his head as he basked in his own post-release euphoria.

"Fuck," she muttered still in a state of absolute bliss. "That was worth breaking all of my rules for." She'd had her share of decent one-night stands, but this one topped the charts.

He lazily lifted his head up off her chest with a satisfied smile. "Just wait until round two." He pulled her face in for an affectionate kiss as he rolled them both over so that Layne ended up back on top of him. His dick still felt quite at home inside of her.

"What makes you think you'll be lucky enough?" Her head rested on top of his chest, while she listened to the thudding of his heart.

His hand playfully came smacking down on her ass cheek. "Call it intuition."

"Well, Mr. Intuition, you're going to have to wait. I have to get back home and see what hell has broken loose since I ditched Lenny yesterday."

It was a sobering thought that she had to go back to reality and likely some highly pissed-off people, particularly Liam and her dad. Though, it was worth it. So incredibly worth it.

CHAPTER THIRTEEN

Despite her protests, Joey was adamant that he bring her back home. After the incident with Franzetti, there was a whole new level of complication in Layne's life. He made sure to leave her a few doors down where they exchanged goodbyes.

"Thanks for everything," she wanted to avoid any awkward discussions with him and leave things in a good spot between them. "Take care of yourself."

All the talk back in his apartment during their morning romp she chalked up to mere words in the searing heat of the moment. Neither of them needed any long-term entanglements, not when they both led very chaotic lives.

She stepped away from the sports bike before he could try to say words they would both regret, and half jogged up to the steps leading up to her home.

He sat watching her until she reached her front door and then took off. The sound of the exhaust fading the further away he got.

After letting herself inside, when the door shut behind her, she had captured the attention of several unexpected house guests; a few associates who worked for the O'Reilly family, Uncle Mick, and Liam who was paused halfway down the stairs.

Everybody was staring at her and the silence was deafening. It was her Uncle Mick who spoke the first words. "Thank Jesus, Joseph, and Mary."

He let out an exhale like he had been holding his breath for hours before coming over to her and pulling her into the biggest of bear hugs. Layne blinked a few times and gave a small squeeze in return.

"Um, hi. What is everyone doing here?"

Liam came down the steps, if he had been relieved to see her it wasn't obvious given the level of heated emotions rolling through him. "What the hell, Layne?"

Mick released her but stayed nearby in case a mediator was required between her and her sibling. Her brother looked like he was barely holding onto the last straw of restraint he had ever been given. "Tell me what the fuck happened!"

She held her hands up in front of her defensively. "Whoa, calm down. Look, I ditched the babysitting patrol, I take full responsibility for that, but that's all because you couldn't keep out of my business. But this," she gestured to the number of people currently standing around her home looking through her belongings, "this is excessively overreacting!"

"Overreacting?" Liam's voice raised another decibel. He pulled his phone from his pocket, shoving it into her hands. "How else do you think we should be reacting when we get this note from Franzetti, huh, Layne? What the fuck happened?"

She fumbled with the phone that was thrust into her palm. Turning it right side up, she saw a photograph of a bouquet of white roses and a note attached to them that read, 'Condolences on the loss of your daughter. - M.F.'

Layne winced a bit, there wasn't a whole lot she could do to smooth this one over.

"I need answers, Layne!" Liam's barking voice startled her slightly as she tried to figure out the best way to give him an explanation. He snatched the phone right back out of her hand. "You know what this did to dad? I'm surprised the man didn't have a fuckin' stroke!"

She ran her fingers through her hair taking a deep breath in. "It's complicated, Liam."

"Un-fucking-complicate it!"

Mick stepped forward, lightly placing a hand on Liam's chest to try to get him to ease up. "Alright, let's all just take a moment here. Layne is alive, and someone should let your father know as much before he outright wages a war on everyone in the entire damn state."

Layne shook her head, guilt starting to weigh on her about how the situation escalated beyond even what she had anticipated for a rebellious night out.

"Look, I went on a date. It was a fluke that I ran into Franzetti, one thing led to another, and he may have tried to drown me. But look," she motioned to herself, "I'm fine." Sure, she was understating the turn of events last night, but just like anyone else there, she didn't want a war breaking loose.

"Goddamnit!" Liam turned and violently crashed his fist into the nearest wall.

Mick turned to look at Layne, rubbing the side of her arm. "Let's get you back to headquarters so we can straighten this all out. You know your dad is going to need more than the Cliff's Notes version, Layne." She knew that he was absolutely right about that.

Everyone wrapped up what they were doing, and Liam refused to utter another word to her. She got into the passenger's side of Mick's vehicle where it was just the two of them. He looked over at her empathetically. "You want a piece of advice?"

"You're going to give it anyway, you always do."

He nodded. "That's true. Well, here's my advice; be honest. We can't help if we don't have all the facts."

She leaned back in the seat, glancing up at the roof of the car, and shook her head. "You know, I always appreciate your advice, right? Ever since I can remember, you've always been the best shoulder to lean on when things seemed unbearable. But this? It's different."

Mick frowned, mulling over her response before he reached over and patted her leg. "It may seem that way, but whatever it is that has you spiraling, Layne? You're more levelheaded than this. Whoever the guy is, he's not worth it. He *will* get you killed."

She looked over at him, furrowing her eyebrows as he pinpointed it down to being a guy issue.

"I'm smarter than I look." He flashed a smile at her as he pulled away from the curb.

Joey was going to get her killed. She couldn't exactly argue that given she barely survived last night.

When they arrived at O'Reilly Manor, she was led into Scott's office where Liam was already seated in one of the two chairs positioned across from the glossy mahogany desk their dad sat behind.

"Sit," was all Scott had to say to her. There was no grand family reunion and rejoicing she was alive. No emotion was present at all in his voice, just a simple one-word command.

Today was not the day she was going to push buttons, so she went ahead and situated herself in the vacant seat.

He only gave a brief look to his son. “Liam, you can go.”

From the change of Liam’s face, he had expected to be a part of this conversation and wasn’t pleased that he was being excluded. But, like the good little soldier, he up and left, slamming the door shut behind him for extra measure on how he felt about it.

Now that it was just the two of them there in his office, Layne almost wished that Liam had stayed. Almost. The tension and unspoken awkwardness in the air was stifling. Her dad peered at her from across his desk, his hands lightly folded in front of him.

“I thought I lost you like I lost your mother. Do you understand what level of excruciating pain that has been? I don’t know what the hell happened, Layne, but I need to know. And, so help me, if you lie to me about any of it.”

Each time she thought of a way to start off her explanation, it never seemed to be the right thing to say, so she sat there for a solid five minutes under the weight of her dad’s gaze as he waited patiently for her.

“I know I messed up. I met someone, and apparently, he has a history with Franzetti. It was all a series of bad coincidences. Franzetti is going on a bender about some project he’s heard about in the grapevine, and when I didn’t have the answers, he got doubly ticked off.”

Her father leaned forward as this was all news to him. “What project?”

“Some project 227, that’s all I know.” She shook her head.

“227?” He repeated the number back to her.

Layne nodded, affirming he had heard correctly. “He thinks it’s something we’re doing that impacts him, but I have a source saying otherwise.”

“We don’t have anything we are working on with that name, Layne. He’s barking up the wrong tree.”

“I know that, but…” she hesitated to even say anything further given the sensitive nature of it and what her dad’s reaction potentially would be.

“But, what?” Her dad prompted her to continue.

“My source said the project is about me. I mean, it’s not clear how, but that’s all the info I was able to get.”

It was one of the few times she ever saw her dad get taken back in surprise when he wasn’t expecting something.

“Who else here knows about this?”

She shook her head. "Just me."

"Let's keep it that way. Where did you get the information from?"

Her teeth lightly bit into her lower lip. "I-I can't tell you that."

"You can, and you will, Layne. I'm not going to play games here, not with something like this. If something is going on related to anything or anyone in my organization, there is going to be hell to pay. Especially, if this all turns out to be true, it will make this whole Franzetti situation look as inconsequential as an incorrect weather forecast."

"He does contract work, and Franzetti was just the last person who hired him."

"Layne, that doesn't even make sense. If he works for Mike, then why would Mike be willing to go to these lengths to determine if it has something to do with him?"

She shrugged her shoulders. "I don't know, that's why I didn't say anything because I'm not even sure it's good intel."

Scott stood up and circled his desk so he was standing in front of Layne, taking her hands, and easing her up out of her seat. "I will get to the bottom of this. Until I do, this chaotic behavior has to stop. You don't talk to anyone having anything to do with Franzetti. He's already going to be livid you made a fool out of him by not actually dying. You got it?"

She nodded in agreement. "Got it."

"Second, for appearance's sake, all your jobs are going to be reassigned for now. Once we sort this all out, things will go back to the way they were."

"And the security detail?" Call it wishful thinking, but she had hoped that she would get a response different than she knew it was likely to be.

"I will tell them to give you a little more space, but I'm not calling them off entirely. If you try to ditch them again, I will lock you away in a tower and throw away the key."

While he may have only been joking about the tower, it wouldn't be far off from what lengths he would go to if it was to keep her safe. Layne felt it was at least a fair compromise, and she wasn't going to push back on it.

"And, one more thing," he drew in a steadying breath as he pulled her in against his chest and kissed the top of her head. "Don't ever give me a scare like that again. Understand?"

Layne hugged her dad back, nodding against his dress shirt during the rare moment he showed any emotion at all. Scott held her for a few moments, refusing to let her go before he was ready.

"What are you going to do about Franzetti?" She lifted her head to look up at her father, curious how he was going to handle this political shitshow of an attempt to snuff out her life.

"I have a few connections that are telling me that there's someone who is particularly adept at handling sensitive situations like this and looking for new work."

She raised a brow, curious enough to want more information and potentially be involved. If they were going to make a move on Michael Franzetti, she wanted her sweet revenge. After all, she was the one who had almost been drowned here.

"You have to let me get involved."

Her dad immediately released her and shook his head. "No, absolutely not, Layne. That's not an option."

"I'm the one he tried to kill, Dad! I should get my chance to serve him up a big dose of karma."

"We hire specialists for jobs like this, it needs white glove treatment - not emotionally driven revenge."

She rolled her eyes in annoyance as she crossed her arms in front of her chest. "Getting drowned is pretty fuckin' emotional."

"And we didn't see it coming. Franzetti is smart, and he's already prepared for the shit to hit the fan." Scott rubbed her arms reassuringly to try and persuade her that this was the best course of action.

"Please, dad. Let me at least vet the specialist, let me have some hand in it. I think I deserve that much."

Contemplating the minor ask, her dad finally gave in. "Alright, but you listen when I tell you to back off."

"I promise, I will." She criss-crossed her finger over her heart.

"I'm serious, Layne. When I tell you to leave it alone, you have to leave it alone."

"I told you, I promise I will back off if things get out of hand." She tried to reassure him by offering up a sweet-as-pie smile and giving his hands a light squeeze. Something told her that he wasn't thoroughly convinced. Hell, she wasn't even fully convinced she could just let this go.

CHAPTER FOURTEEN

Things didn't progress as quickly as she would have preferred. A few weeks had gone by, and she found herself attempting not to think about Joey and their one night together. The exceedingly great parts of when they had been together, and then the not-so-good parts such as the whole brush-with-death thing.

He had made it clear when they first met that he was the one-and-done type, and she was comfortable with that. Layne didn't need attachments and complex relationships in her already complicated life. The phone he had given her ended up shoved into the bottom of a drawer until its battery ran out of juice.

As much as it irked her, she had been doing her best to avoid work at her dad's request and to tolerate the security detail that was still hanging around. Only this time, instead of them hanging out inside her house, they generally stuck to exterior watches. Nobody came or went without them knowing, and if she went somewhere, they followed in a separate vehicle versus needing to be attached at her hip.

Scott had been working to put the word out there that he required a specialist who could handle the very delicate Franzetti situation. So far, everything had been radio silent.

Word on the street was that Franzetti had blown a gasket when he realized that Layne hadn't actually drowned. There was nothing like bruising the man's ego that he couldn't even do a job right himself.

It was a mild autumn day, and since she had nothing better to do than be an uptown girl, she spent the morning on her back patio curled up in a cushy chair reading a book. The story itself was nothing but pure smut, making it difficult to keep her mind clear of anything related to one delectable Joey De Luca. Out of frustration, she closed the book and tossed it onto the small glass table in front of her.

What else was a poor little rich girl supposed to do with her day when it didn't involve beat-downs, debt collections, and illegal bookkeeping? She picked up her cell from the seat next to her and scrolled through until she brought up her favorite contacts. One name in particular; Rebecca.

Her bestie since childhood, Rebecca was probably the only one who tolerated Layne's idiosyncrasies and lifestyle choices when it came to the family business. She lived a much more clean-cut life, and Layne lived vicariously through her when she needed to imagine an escape from her current insanity.

She selected the call button and waited for the familiar voice on the other end to pick up.

"Girl! It's about damn time you called!" Rebecca's perky voice was a ray of sunshine on the other end of the line. It brought forth a smile from Layne and immediately lifted her mood. However, she could tell from the background noise on the other end of the line that Rebecca was still in Cancun soaking up the sun and tequila. Lots of tequila.

"I know, sorry, it's been an eventful few weeks." Layne quietly sighed, and yet even with all the music and drunken shenanigans happening around Rebecca, she still managed to pick up on the tone Layne used when she was stressing over things.

"Oh, no. Alright, spill it. Do I need to hop on a plane right now and beat the crap out of someone? Well, do I need to tell you to beat the crap out of someone? You're much better at it than I am." Rebecca giggled on the other end of the line while a series of cheers of "Shots! Shots! Shots! Shots!" raged on in the background.

"No, nothing like that. It's just forced downtime, and you know how well I do with that. My dad throws me some extra cash and expects me to happily go spend it on Fifth Avenue like it's therapy."

Her friend scoffed. "It *is* therapy. I've told you, I will make the sacrifice and go spend the money for you any time you need."

Layne grinned and made a mental note to at least snag a new pair of ridiculously expensive designer workout leggings for Rebecca this week so when she returned, they both could hit spin class together with fabulous-looking asses.

"You're right, as usual. I won't keep you from all the fun any longer. I just needed to feel a bit more grounded."

"That's my job, I will see you when I get back and we will have a girl's night and catch up, okay?"

Layne agreed and they said their goodbyes. The talk was everything she needed to get a kick in the ass to go and do something like a normal twenty-something-year-old. She gathered her things and was out the door less than thirty minutes later.

She drove down to the fashion district where she could waste her time hopping from store to store. A few of the clerks at the concierge desks at several stores recognized her and were sure to give her the VIP treatment, champagne and all. If there was one thing that Layne knew about high-end shopping it was that champagne never hurt.

Selecting a few items to try on, she headed back to the dressing room while her assigned security guard stuck to his post right outside the store's front entrance.

She finished off the flute of champagne as she stepped into the excessively large fitting room. It was large enough to be considered a bedroom by comparison to places like Old Navy or Macy's. In the center of the square-shaped room was a round pedestal with mirrors coming from all angles on the walls to ensure one could give themselves a complete visual inspection.

Layne peeled away her shirt, exposing the black lace racerback bra she had on underneath. Before she could slip on one of the three tops she had gathered, there was a knock on the door of the dressing room.

"Thank God, this is going to need more champagne." She muttered quietly to herself. When she opened the door, instead of it being the female sales associate she had been working with, it was a familiar face that she hadn't realized how much she missed.

"Joey?" She blinked a few times as he slipped into the room with her. His gaze slowly looked over her as his hands slid onto her hips. Before he could attempt to dial up the charm, she stepped back and snatched one of the shirts from a hanger.

Layne may have missed him, but she sure as hell didn't miss the fact that they were supposed to be a short and hot fling. He was supposed to go back to his life and she hers.

"Don't get dressed on account of me," he slyly remarked.

She shot him a slight glare as she yanked the shirt down over her head and pulled her hair out from underneath it afterward. "What are you doing here?" Then, the more she thought about it she changed her question. "How did you know I was here?"

He shrugged but gave her the space she had created for herself. "I have my methods." Joey leaned his shoulder against one of the walls casually as he kept his eyes on her with his hands tucked in his pockets.

"Fine, whatever. Why are you here then? I figured you'd be off to find your next conquest." Layne defaulted to her defensive mode when she needed to stomp down on any nagging feelings that were going to cause complications in her life.

He placed a hand over his heart. "Ouch. That's what you think of me?"

"That's what you made clear to me when you broke into my house."

"That's because," he pushed away from the wall and stepped up behind her, his hand traveling over her shoulder and up onto the side of her neck before sliding over the front of her throat, "I didn't realize how addictive you were going to be." His breath tickled over the delicate skin of her neck, while he left a steamy trail of kisses in his wake.

Not realizing how long she had been holding her breath, she slowly released it. "Knock it off."

Joey straightened. "What's the problem?"

"Nothing, I just figured you'd be elsewhere and with someone else." She looked at her reflection in the mirror, trying to gauge whether or not she liked the shirt. She was leaning towards not.

He took her arm and spun her around to face him. "It's more than that." His fingers came up to hold her chin. "Tell me what it is."

Layne tried to turn from him, but his hold on her kept her in one spot unless she wanted to choose violence. While it was still on the table, she opted to be civil for the time being. "I have obligations to my family, and you're a distraction from that."

He had the audacity to slap an amused grin on his face. "Hm, how much of a distraction?"

She let out a flustered sigh. "Joey, I don't have time for this."

"Bullshit, your boy out front is paid by the hour and daddy's credit limit is wide open. Don't make me ask twice, Layney." His tone grew impatient with her responses.

Her legs just wanted to melt from the way he called her that little pet name, and that right there was a reminder of how effective of a distraction he was.

"I need to be able to focus on my job, and with you doing work for Franzetti, that makes it a conflict of interest. I think we already learned that lesson the hard way, didn't we?" Drowning was a hard fucking lesson.

He tilted his head to the side slightly as he mulled over her response, trying to determine if she was being fully honest with him. "I'm taking care of that."

Layne wasn't fully convinced. "Oh, is that right? Well, so am I."

He dropped his hand from her chin, but still kept her close. "I haven't been able to stop thinking about you. About us." It was a rare moment of truth and honesty in Joey's thirty-seven years.

"There isn't an 'us'." Layne corrected him. She shook her head, side-stepped around him, and began to spout off one difficult truth after another.

"You're the one who said you aren't a country club and caviar guy. You're the one who said you were going to get your rocks off and then I'd never see you again."

"I know what I said. That was before."

"Before what? Hm?" She pulled the blouse up and over her head and hastily tossed it onto a hanger inside out. Her hands began digging through the rest of the clothes, searching for the shirt she had arrived in. When she looked over at Joey, he had it hanging off the tip of his finger. She reached over and snagged it from him.

"Before I realized how much—"

Layne cut him off, "—of a good fuck I was?"

Exasperated, he began to lose what little patience he was clinging to. "Damnit, Layne! Yes, but it's more than that! It's the way you look at me, even when you're pissed off. It's the way you think you own a room even when the odds are stacked against you. It's everything you do. To think that I would never get the chance to experience all that again would either drive me insane or send me into a homicidal rage."

As he explained himself, she found herself forgetting how to handle just the basics of getting her shirt on, fumbling it in her hands. Mick's words echoed in her head about being distracted, this mysterious project no one knew anything about, Franzetti's move to eliminate her, and then there were just the basic day-to-day things in her life.

When she looked up, Joey had moved closer to her and cupped her face in his hands. The warmth of his skin on her cheeks made her want to tell him she could ignore everything inside of her head.

Layne shut her eyes trying to find the words she should say and not the ones she wanted to say. "I don't do commitments, Joey. My life is too sticky for that."

His voice was gentle. "Not asking you to."

She opened her eyes back up, hoping for a little more clarity to come to her on if she should listen to her head, her heart, or her carnal desires. "You're a stubborn ass." A small chuckle passed through her lips as she fought back the smile tugging at the corners of her mouth.

His boyish grin spread across his face before capturing her mouth in a feral kiss. His hands dropped away from her face as he wrapped his muscular arms around her waist, lifting her up from her feet.

Layne's legs wrapped around his waist while her tongue intertwined with his. Joey backed Layne up against a wall as the heat between them began to simmer.

A couple of text messages dinged on her wrist. Capturing a peek at them pop up on her smartwatch, she groaned at the inconvenience of timing. Trying her best to break the seal of the kiss for more than a quick breath, Layne managed only a word or two at a time.

"I have…to leave…to get ready…for…a meeting."

His arms pulled her up against him tighter at the thought of her leaving so soon. Pulling his mouth back, he gave her a wanton gaze. "Skip it."

"It's my dad, I can't just not go."

He pressed his forehead against hers. "In that case, guess you'll owe me one."

She indulged in a few more kisses from him before regaining some self-control over her actions and dropping her legs down from around him. Once he settled her back on her feet, she slowly got her top back on.

"Come find me when you're ready to cash in that favor." Her hand lightly patted his chest, trailing her fingertips down across his stomach as her smile lit up her face.

Layne left the privacy of the dressing room before she risked losing all her damn senses.

CHAPTER FIFTEEN

When she arrived at O'Reilly Manor later that evening, Liam walked in through the front door moments after her. Their dad had summoned them both here but hadn't disclosed the nature of what he wanted to talk about.

"Aren't you supposed to be out getting your nails done or something?" Liam quipped.

"Aren't you supposed to be out getting laid by a hoe or something?" She fired back.

"At least I'm getting some."

Layne rolled her eyes, regretting her life choices this afternoon when she could have gotten wrecked by Joey in that dressing room. She could have fired a kill shot about Liam paying to get his kicks, but she was working on self-improvement and all that crap.

Before their bickering could devolve any further, Scott calmly came down the primary staircase that led into the front foyer. He was dressed in a dark grey suit with a dress shirt in an even darker shade of grey underneath. Layne noted that he appeared to be ready for a meeting, not just with his children, but he must have been expecting to meet with someone else tonight.

"Good, you're both here. Let's have a talk."

Liam glanced over at Layne, clearly coming to the same conclusion as she had. This wasn't going to be just any typical discussion. Not saying another word, they both followed after the head of the family.

He walked past his office until he came to a door painted in the same greige as the walls. He pulled on the handle, swung the door open, and began the descent into the wine cellar down below.

Liam made sure he cut ahead of Layne, following behind their dad like a loyal puppy. She was sure to pull the door shut behind her before she took up the rear.

One would expect the wine cellar to look like something out of the French countryside, perhaps musty and reminiscent of what you might find in a medieval castle. That wasn't the case. The glass cases housed bottles upon bottles of a multitude of fine vintages. The lighting was designed to focus all the attention on the extensive collection that spanned across all four walls. In the center of the cellar was a narrow island that housed glassware underneath.

The cellar made an ideal location when one wanted isolated privacy and confidentiality. All the walls were buffered, no cameras were installed down there, and there was precisely one way in and one way out.

Scott decisively grabbed a bottle of Cabernet Franc, easily valued at a cool grand. "I wanted to speak with you both before Liam and I go take care of some business." He selected three glasses and began to pour each of them a serving of vino.

Layne selected the glass nearest to her, taking a preliminary sip. She wasn't a huge wine snob, beer was more her drink of choice, but she could appreciate the notes and flavors dancing across her palette.

Scott continued, "As the two of you know, I've been looking for a specialist to handle the very delicate situation that we have with Franzetti. It hasn't been easy tracking down someone with both the skillset and the discretion. The last thing I want is for Franzetti to see it coming more than he already does." He paused to taste the bold flavors from his glass.

"With that said, I believe I've finally found the right person. We have a meeting with his coordinator in an hour to talk specifics, then if all goes well, we will do a final vet with the specialist next week."

"Great." Layne swirled the red liquid around in her glass. "That gives me enough time to run back home and change."

Scott looked at Layne, his expression apologetic. "It's just Liam and I going tonight, Layne."

"What? Why? I have every right to know who is going to be doing the dirty work on my behalf." Her temper began to ignite due to the fact that he was already trying to exclude her from this.

"You don't need to be put at any more risk than you already are." He attempted to explain his reasoning.

She wasn't buying it. "That's a bunch of bullshit! I should have a say in this."

Liam cleared his throat lightly. "I agree with Layne."

She paused, looking over at Liam in a bit of surprise. "Not that I'm complaining, but since when do you agree with me on anything?"

Liam shrugged. "I just think that if I were in your shoes, and I wasn't going to be taking care of business myself, I'd want to evaluate the person who is."

Layne's hand motioned at her brother. "See? Even he gets it."

With her father silently staring down into his wine glass he donned a calculating expression, taking into consideration what they both had told him. It was obvious he was hesitant to backtrack on his initial decision, but once he lifted his eyes to Layne, she knew she had won on this matter.

"If the meeting tonight goes well and we get to the final stage of the hiring process, then you can join us next week. To be clear though, if we get to next week and there is even the slightest indication that shit is going to hit the fan, you are to leave without so much as an eye roll. Got it?"

She tried to contain the smile of victory by hiding it behind taking another sip of her beverage. "Mm-hm."

He muttered under his breath. "God help me."

Scott finished off what was left in his glass. "The meeting will be at Death's Door in an hour. Liam, do what you need to prepare, and then meet me there. Do not be late." He set his glass down on the center island and left the two of them there alone.

Layne could have picked the battle about Liam going tonight to discuss the administrative minutiae, and she should have also been involved but instead, she was more concerned about who was going to be the one getting their hands dirty. It was a strategic decision to give up one less important meeting to get what she ultimately wanted.

Giddy that she was finally getting looped back into business operations again if all went well tonight, Layne was going to be chomping at the bit waiting for next week to arrive. Until then, she would have to find a way to occupy her time.

Before she stepped away from the table to leave, Liam stopped her with a hand on her elbow. "Just because I agreed with you this once, doesn't mean that you're going to be in charge of the final negotiations next week."

She turned to look at him with annoyance written all over her face, shoving his hand off her. "Say that to me after you get nearly drowned. You may be Dad's first choice when it comes to taking over operations, but it doesn't make you his favorite."

Not waiting around to see the look on his face, she jogged upstairs. Liam was left there with a scowl on his face that he had been cursed with a sister who didn't know her place in the family. He picked up his empty glass and flung it at the wall of wine bottles, causing it to break into a cluster of glass shards.

CHAPTER SIXTEEN

Still stuck on the equivalent of desk duty, Layne tried to take the time to enjoy life a little bit more. It wasn't easy, as she often lost herself in her work.

After several shopping trips, mostly to supply Rebecca with some hot finds, she grew bored of those outings. How her father had ever expected her to take on the role of a true uptown girl was insane to Layne. She needed something with a little more purpose than running up credit card statements.

The meeting Liam and her dad held with the administrative coordinator for the specialist in the lead spot for the job had gone extraordinarily well from everything she had heard. She wasn't given much in terms of details other than there was mutual interest on both sides of the transaction.

The last step was to meet the harbinger of doom himself to ensure an appropriate fit for the job at hand. If you were going to hire someone to take out a significant player in this game, you wanted to let your gut do the judging when meeting them in person.

Until then, she was stuck trying to live the life of any other twenty-five-year-old on a mandatory staycation. Her music was blaring throughout her living room, feet dancing her around the various pieces of furniture in an impromptu dance party. If only her clients could see her now, taking the time to let loose a little bit instead of being so uptight all the time.

Her hair wildly left down, the natural dark waves indicating she hadn't taken a blow dryer to them after her shower this morning.

Her phone dinged with a new notification, causing her to pause. When she grabbed the phone off its charger, she unlocked the screen to see a message waiting in one of her dating apps. A girl had particular needs from time to time, and Layne was no exception to that.

The message was from a guy she had been speaking with back and forth over a few weeks. His name was Cole, he supposedly worked as a trader for one of the top banks in the Financial District, owned a Golden Retriever puppy, and lived out on eastern Long Island. He had invited her out to his place to take a trip out on his boat several times, but she hadn't yet taken him up on anything.

COLE

Hey, beautiful. Want to save me from having dinner alone tonight?

LAYNE

Depends. What's for dessert?

COLE

Lady's choice.

She stared at the message for a few minutes while having an internal debate with herself. Layne desperately needed to get out of the house and find a distraction that wasn't online shopping.

"Fuck it," she whispered to herself as she sent a reply back in the chat.

LAYNE

Consider me your savior.

Cole was quick to send over the details of the time and place, leaving Layne wondering if her night out was going to be a major bomb or if things were going to be smooth sailing.

He had chosen a place called Annie & Cain's for dinner. It was a swanky place that a lot of the banker types frequented to toss around their excess funds. The restaurant was a little too stuffy for her likes, but she wasn't going to turn down her original plans this evening of Netflix surfing over it.

Checking the time, she had a little over two hours to get ready and head out to the Financial District where the restaurant was located. Turning her music down to a less deafening level, she poked her head into the kitchen where her guard of the week was sitting on a stool by the counter playing a color-matching game on his phone to pass the time. He had come inside to freeload some food and never left to go back out to his car.

"I'm going out for dinner."

He perked up, immediately straightening in his seat. "Where?"

"Annie & Cain's in two hours, it's in the Financial District off of Pearl Street."

Her security guard seemed to think he had a say in this as he sat there thinking it over. "I guess that's okay."

"I wasn't asking permission." Layne may have been under watchful eyes these days, but she sure as hell wasn't under any disillusion that her status in the O'Reilly family hierarchy had changed. The chain of command still operated as it had been, with her still only being outranked by a small handful of people. Those people were essentially family, and she had no desire to try and challenge those ranks.

Her new security detail was evidently annoyed as he abruptly locked his phone and pocketed it. "Do you want me to get the car ready, or are you going to insist on making me follow you down to the subway?"

It seemed her social life was going to be an inconvenience to him, or maybe it was because he still had to take orders from a woman as long as it didn't contradict what her father expected out of him.

"You keep that attitude up I may just go on a five-mile run in Central Park tomorrow morning." Layne gave the light warning she could make his job here even more painful than he already found it. She knew damn well that this man couldn't run fifty yards, let alone five miles. With that parting comment, she left him to go get herself ready for a night out.

It didn't take long for Layne to get ready for the dinner outing. She straightened out her hair so it wasn't a wild wavy wreck, opted for a smoky evening look for her makeup, and a tiny dark purple dress that clung to her curves and had a sexy little cut up the right leg. Layne slipped her feet into a pair of silver strappy heels.

Thanks to some rush hour traffic and her bodyguard's foul mood, she arrived about ten minutes late to Annie & Cain's. Her security detail followed her inside the high-class restaurant and opted to stand off to the side near the coat room, out of sight.

The entire vibe of the inside of Annie & Cain's screamed New York's elite. There wasn't one thing in there that didn't look like it cost a small fortune, right down to the light switches.

It didn't take long before she made eye contact with Cole after she approached the host stand. As stated in his message, he was at the two-top underneath the framed black and white photo of the cross-street signs for Wall Street and Broad Street about mid-way back into the dining room. She was pleasantly surprised that he looked like his profile picture, maybe even better considering how well he could wear a suit.

When she approached the table, he immediately stood up to greet her with excitement in his eyes to see her in the flesh. "Sorry I'm late, there was construction around Central Park."

"Don't worry about it, I'm not in a rush to go anywhere. Not to mention," his eyes soaked in the sight of her, "you're worth the wait. Just, wow, I knew you were gorgeous, but this..." He took a longer gander at her from head to toe, giving a light whistle of approval and a million-dollar smile.

"Don't let the lighting fool you, I had to do a lot of magic tricks to make sure I lived up to expectations." Layne gave him a flirty wink before taking her seat across from him.

Cole was decked out in a crisp white dress shirt, left unbuttoned at the collar, no tie, and a sleek tailored black suit jacket and pants. He had the type of slender physique that said he maintained a minimal fitness routine, but it didn't scream gym rat. His Norse blonde hair expertly coifed over to one side. Everything about him screamed pretty boy, and one with excess cash to spare.

"I hope you don't mind, I ordered drinks already." As if on cue, the college-aged waitress brought over two martinis each with a corkscrew of lemon peel in them.

"You're either feeling very confident or arrogant. So, which is it?" She grinned at him as she picked up her glass and let the warmth of the cocktail coat her mouth during that initial sip.

"Perhaps, a little of both." He sat back in his chair, martini in hand while grinning like a fool ear-to-ear.

The two of them made some small talk while he ordered a charcuterie board filled with various cured meats, pickled vegetables, crackers and breads, and a variety of fine cheeses for them both to pick at occasionally while indulging in another round of martinis.

Setting her half-drank martini on the table, she smiled at him. "I'm surprised you were so persistent over the past few weeks; most guys would have just moved on to the next girl in line."

Cole didn't miss a beat, which had been a theme all evening with him. "I know what I like." He was proving to be Mr. Charming indeed.

"And, let me guess, I'm just ticking off all the boxes for you?" Layne grinned while perking up an eyebrow.

"So far." His eyes dropped to the neckline of her dress suggestively.

"Well, we'll see how many more boxes I can tick off when I get back. I just need to take care of a few things." Layne stood from her chair with a playful smile at him and left to go find the restroom.

Snagging directions from one of the waitresses, she went to the back where there were the two marked doors indicating Gents or Ladies. Before she even got the chance to step inside the ladies' room on her own accord, a firm hand grabbed onto hers and pulled her inside the New York-standard cramped restroom that was only set up with two stalls.

Layne stumbled inside and immediately found herself pushed back against the bathroom door, a gasp escaping past her lips as she came face-to-face with Joey.

She had never seen him wearing anything but casual clothing, but he must have changed things up to blend in inside the swanky restaurant. The black dress shirt fit his upper body like a glove and was tucked into an equally flattering pair of black pants. The sleeves of his shirt rolled up to his elbows, leaving his marked skin on display. This look on him had her ready to drop to her knees.

His hands were on either side of her against the door, caging her in. Something dark and brooding settled in his eyes. His hand reached down to click the lock on the door to ensure their privacy.

Momentarily she felt relief with a familiar face, but it was quickly followed by shock. "What are you doing here?"

His voice kept low, seeming to have other thoughts on his mind that ranked more than answering her question. "Keeping an eye on you, since your current guard would rather become king of Candy Crush."

Layne knew that he wasn't wrong that her current babysitter would rather be doing almost anything else but his job duties. "It's not your job to keep tabs on me."

Joey leaned in closer to her, their bodies barely touching and her back still up against the door. His hand ran down her side slowly, over the swell of her hip, and inched down towards the hem of her dress.

His eyes lingered over the visual of all her exposed skin that wasn't covered by the tight-fitted cocktail dress. "Not officially."

As his hand slid onto the bare skin of her thigh, it was then she realized she was holding her breath in anticipation.

"I'm here on a date." It was stated more for herself as a reminder than for him.

Joey gave a reserved kiss to her mouth, picking up the remnants of her martini off them. "I saw." His other hand moved away from the door and wrapped around her throat, his thumb caressing the silky skin.

Feeling the possessive hold on her, her nipples tightened and pushed against the fabric of her dress. Awareness of her own body beginning to crave his touch left Layne squirming in his hold while a chill ran over her body. "I need to get back to him."

"You will after I'm done with you." The purr of Joey's stern words made her insides tighten. His hand still holding onto her throat, his other slid up between her thighs, finding the thin strip of fabric of her thong already damp from the sight of him.

She quietly moaned at the feeling of his touch so close to her center, her hands rubbed up the front of his chest as she used him to steady herself. Her legs felt as though they were just going to drop out from underneath her. In an unexpected and aggressive yank, it didn't take much for Joey to snap the fabric of her panties and he tossed them down onto the floor.

His mouth nipped at the bottom of her ear between words. "I'm going to make sure you know how much you have been driving me crazy, Layney." The edge of a growl hung on his words before two fingers slid along her crease and pushed their way inside of her roughly.

She sucked in a sharp breath before she moaned, one hand balled up in the fabric of his shirt while the other clung to the back of his neck. Her back arched resulting in pushing her breasts against the solidness of his chest. Coated in the warmth of her arousal, Joey's fingers easily slid in and out of her with dominating movements.

His hand kept her pinned to the door by her throat while she moaned out his name repeatedly in absolute pleasure. His gaze drank in the sight of her squirming in the small space he kept her confined to. As his thumb rubbed over the already sensitive bud of her clit, Layne looked at him longingly as the waves of sensual heat grew more intense throughout her body.

"Yes, please don't stop, Joey..." The urgency of need was clear in her voice as his fingers continued to fuck her pussy. His fingers curled deep inside of her to find just the right spot to tease.

"You want to be a good girl and come for me?"

"God, yes." Her hips rolled against him.

"Tell me how bad you want it." His hand applied more pressure around her throat prompting the walls of her pussy to squeeze around his fingers.

Her body was beginning to tremble as she approached the cusp of release. "So bad." Absolute neediness filled her voice.

He then stopped his movements, his fingers buried deep inside of her, the momentum of pleasure her body had been building coming to a slow halt.

"No, please, Joey… I'm so close." Her hand dropped down to his, trying to urge him to keep going.

He smirked at her deviously. "Uh-uh. That's not how this is going to work, Layney."

She whimpered in desperation, her body needing to spill over the edge he worked her up to.

His thumb gave another circle over her delicate bundle of nerves, causing her to curse and beg for more. Her heavy breaths resulted in her breasts struggling against the neckline of her dress, which was threatening to give way.

"You're absolutely soaked right now and believe me when I say that I want to taste every last drop of you, but," he slid his fingers out of her, raising them to his mouth where he slowly sucked the taste of her body off, one finger at a time, "this will have to do for now."

Layne swore her body was going to crumple down to the floor of the bathroom as he left her there teetering on the edge of what had been shaping up to be an explosive climax. He released his hold on her neck and smoothed out the fabric of the snug dress she had on so that everything was back to where it should have been.

"Are you fuckin' kidding me? No, come on, you can't do this." She groaned at having not gotten her firework ending stepping away from the door towards him.

"When you go back to your date, let this be a reminder of who owns your sweet cunt." He leaned in, claiming her mouth for a hot moment before unlocking the door and seeing himself out. Layne stood there with her body aching for satisfaction that only one person was going to be able to give to her, and he just left.

She took a few minutes to gather herself and freshen up, trying hard to ignore her screaming carnal desires that had been riled up to a full roar only minutes prior. When she rejoined Cole at the table, there was still a light flush on her cheeks.

Cole seemed surprised to see her back there sitting across from him. "I was beginning to think maybe you had ditched me."

"No, sorry, I got a work call that I had to take." She shifted in her seat, trying to find a new sensation of comfortable where your brain wasn't in the gutter. Her eyes glanced around to see if she could spot Joey, but if he was still lingering, he was expertly blending into the background.

Layne immediately downed what remained of her drink to attempt to wash away the sinful memories of the feel of Joey's hand nearly melting her into a useless puddle. She apologetically looked over at Cole. "I'm sorry to do this, but I have to cut our night short."

He seemed a bit taken back with slight disappointment painted over his face. "We haven't even gotten to talk about your choice of dessert yet."

She stood up, and he joined her. "I know, it's this issue at work that is going to be a problem if I don't go take care of it." Layne definitely had a problem that needed tending to, and Cole was not going to get the job done for her.

Layne said her goodbyes to Cole and rounded up her bodyguard still standing up front near the coat room. When she got a peek at his phone before he pocketed it, sure enough, she saw the brightly colored shapes of Candy Crush. Damnit, she hated that Joey was right.

CHAPTER SEVENTEEN

The establishment with the sign above it bearing the words "The Beacon" was known as Death's Door to everyone else in the criminal underground. There was a ton of speculation and urban legends on how it earned that nickname. Some people thought it was because of the eerie appearance of the exterior with its rotted door that had been the victim of one too many shoddy repairs. Others suggested it was because the clientele who frequented the joint met their fate by death more often than not. Layne's theory was that some kid probably thought it sounded cool.

The windows out front were painted over with streaks of black paint. During the day you could tell how poor of a job was done, but on a night like tonight it was effective in providing privacy from nosey outsiders. The burly-looking man standing at the door took one look at her and gave her a courteous nod, allowing her to pass him and enter the establishment. Bearing the O'Reilly name had its perks, one of which was not being questioned in seedy establishments like this one.

As soon as the door opened, she was smacked by the smell of rancid cigars, over-applied cologne, and stale booze. There would be no getting the scent out of her clothes for several washes after this. The knowledge that her dad wore his high-end suits here was mind-boggling.

Given the importance of appearances for a meeting of this caliber, Layne was sure to twist and overlap her hair into a neat braid. She opted for a pair of black pants, a hunter-green tank with a black military cut jacket, and a pair of practical and solid boots.

She also brought a girl's best accessories with her into Death's Door: a mini arsenal. There was never any telling when this level of negotiations could go poorly, and you never wanted to be stuck without the appropriate tools. Layne made sure she had at least two different knives, her baby Glock, and a spare clip.

Now that she was inside, she noted they had done some renovations and changes to the layout since she had last visited. There was a dimly lit bar in the left corner, booths lining the opposite wall, and a hall with maybe five or six doors from what she could see from where she stood.

Each of those doors led to a private room where business could be conducted. Sometimes that business was some exchange of goods, sometimes it was political games, and sometimes it was just delving into carnal pleasures. Layne shuddered at the thought of what diseases were likely left behind in such cases.

Liam stood outside the second room, flagging her down with one raised hand. The place wasn't too busy tonight, making it easy to take the straightest path to where he was. "Is our guest of honor here yet?"

"Not yet." He held the door open to the reserved room they were going to be using for the discussions. When she stepped inside, there were two mounted lamps on the wall ahead of her using red light bulbs to provide minimal illumination. Her father was sitting in an upholstered armchair in the corner across from the doorway. Two other chairs were set up, one next to him, and one near the door.

"Layne, Liam is going to sit here." Her father motioned to the chair to his right. "And I want you standing right behind him."

She had been doing this long enough to realize he wanted her to be behind Liam not only for purposes of hierarchical structure but for safety reasons as well. Layne may not have agreed with it, but being caught arguing amongst themselves would be bad for business if anyone witnessed it.

She went ahead and leaned back against the wall behind Liam's assigned seat. Her brother remained waiting outside for this specialist her dad had searched high and low for. Her nerves were starting to tingle with anxiety while they waited.

Liam's voice spoke up from directly outside the room's entrance. "Right on time."

A tall figure appeared in the doorway, bordering just over six feet from what she could guess based on the height of the door frame. Slowly he stepped foot inside and assessed the layout of their meeting space.

Liam followed close behind and closed the door to avoid any lurking eyes or prying ears.

"Take a seat. Please." Her father gestured at the chair across from them, separated by a rickety-looking coffee table with unknown stains and gouges marring its finish.

The specialist took a few steps forward to take his seat where the lights could provide a better look at his appearance.

With her arms casually crossed in front of her chest while she remained back against the wall, the first thing she saw was the white crooked smile of the skull-faced mask. Her poker face faltered while her heart flip-flopped in her chest and knocked an entire garden of butterflies down low into her stomach. She shifted on her feet, her eyes watching as Liam crossed the room and took his seat in front of her.

Logically, Layne attempted to rationalize that just because it was a masked man didn't mean it was Joey.

He cocked his head to one side curiously. "I didn't realize this would be such a family affair."

The depths of his gravelly voice sent the hair on the back of Layne's neck up on end. She would know that voice anywhere. She knew exactly how the mouth that spoke those words would feel against her skin. Her thoughts further strayed to the heated memories of his tongue doing things to her before she had to painfully bring herself back to the present.

Joey lounged back in his chair, giving off a vibe of comfortability despite being outnumbered in this small space. His eyes met hers with a gaze that sent her reeling back into thoughts of the number he did to her at Annie & Cain's the other night. She still hadn't recovered from how he had left her.

Scott rested his elbows on the armrests of his chair, folding his hands in front of him, "This is as much their business as it is mine. Now, before we talk terms, given the delicacy of this matter, I need assurance that you will use the utmost discretion in carrying out the task."

Joey's eyes shifted back to Scott with all seriousness. "I have a personal interest in this case, so believe me when I tell you that discretion is my top priority."

Liam chimed in. "A personal interest? That sounds like a recipe for you to get too tied up in your own shit." There Liam went, trying to insert himself into things like he was already in charge. Layne was thankful that he wouldn't catch a glimpse of the unimpressed look on her face.

This masked specialist her dad was on the verge of hiring leaned forward, perching his elbows on top of his knees while locking eyes with Liam. "C'mon over here, little boy, and let me show you what happens when someone gives me a reason to spread around some pain and suffering."

Scott shot a hard glare over at Liam the second he moved an inch in his seat. Liam slowly let out a measured count of an exhale to avoid embarrassing the family by lashing out at this guy, but the temptation had been there. Meanwhile, Layne was pushing her teeth into her tongue to prevent herself from giving even the tiniest of smirks.

When Liam didn't make a move, Joey sat back again and motioned with his gloved hand over at Layne. "So, is she the one who took a swim?" He posed the question to Scott.

Layne straightened up, stepping away from the wall she had been leaning back against. "Don't look at him, I'm standing right here."

"Sweetheart, you're not the one hiring me." Joey didn't even glance at her.

"The hell I'm not."

"*Layne*." Her father sternly warned her with the weight of his voice to mind her place.

"No, I am the one who got the shit end of the stick here. I should get the final say in who gets to handle this on my behalf. This guy comes rolling up here like he's celebrating Halloween, and you're going to trust him to handle this situation?" The problem wasn't that she didn't trust him to handle the job, it was what would happen if he didn't succeed in doing it.

A flash of anger lit up Scott's face that Layne was interfering with things, and it caused a strain in his voice. "You'll have to excuse my daughter; she can get a little opinionated."

The shine of amusement in Joey's eyes was accompanied by a chuckle. "You can say that again."

She was fuming that he found this amusing, and even more so that her father was trying to save face by minimizing her role in the decision-making process.

Meanwhile, Liam was doing his best to stay out of the crossfire. "Let's talk terms. You get a quarter million upfront, and when the job is done you get another half million."

Joey let out a whistle at the numbers Liam pitched to him. "That is a pretty penny, but I have some conditions."

"Name them." Scott leaned forward in his seat, willing to hear what else this was going to cost him.

He nodded over at Layne with a shit-eating grin underneath his mask that no one could see. "Drop her security detail."

No one had expected that caveat, and Liam in particular outright laughed. "You're kidding, right?"

"Do I look like I'm trying to be funny? I've done my research and seen the guys you have posted. I could have dropped each one of them before they had time to shit their pants."

Her eyes settled on her dad's face, trying to gauge what was potentially going through his mind. Not having her security detail would be a godsend in terms of having privacy.

"I can make sure she will be safe, but I can't have your crew getting in my way if I'm going to do the job and do it my way."

"Done. Anything else you want to add?" Hearing that, Liam rose up and saw himself out of the room before he did or said something stupid that he would regret.

"I'm going to need a moment of privacy with her, so I can set some ground rules and expectations."

Scott looked over at Layne. "I will be right outside."

"I will be fine, I can handle Mr. Theatrics over here." She reassured him.

Her father was a little hesitant but was willing to play ball with this particular man's terms if it meant removing a major player from the field and keeping his family safe.

After the door shut behind her father, Joey rose to his feet, his look enough to leave Layne feeling her body temperature rising. He crooked his finger, motioning her over to him. She obliged, and once she got over to him, she shook her head. "You can't take this job."

"Shut your sexy mouth." He yanked on his belt, pulling it in one slick motion from the loops dropping it to the floor. "I'm calling in that favor you owe me." He made quick work of the button and zipper of his pants as his swollen erection sprang forth.

She looked down at his thick length which was rearing and ready to go. Coyly she looked back up at him. "I don't know, this seems like a conflict of interest."

His hand grabbed her by the back of the neck dragging her in a little closer as he lowered the volume of his voice. "So help me, Layney, you've had me so fuckin' hard all week. If you don't get on your knees like a good girl, I will make sure that you can't walk straight for a month."

Layne tugged down his mask and locked her lips onto his, then pulled back as she lowered herself down in front of him, maintaining sultry eye contact the entire descent. "Get on my knees, just like this?" Oh, she knew she was being a tease and was enjoying every moment. Her hand wrapped around his stiff member, guiding him into her mouth one delicious inch at a time.

One of Joey's hands tightly clamped onto the back of a chair while the other held onto the back of her head. "Ah, yes." He hissed as her mouth slowly slid over him. Layne relished the taste of his flesh, feeling him press deeper into the back of her mouth. Moving her head back, she dragged her tongue along the underside of his cock.

He groaned. "That's it, Layney. Damn, you suck cock like such a good girl." She bobbed her head back and forth on him.

Joey's breaths grew heavier. "I have two simple rules. Rule one, I set the rules and you're going to follow them. Rule two, you don't go anywhere without me knowing." Her hand came up between his legs, gently cradling his sack while her mouth worked its way up and down his size, drawing a whimper from him.

There was a sense of danger and urgency in the air around them knowing that Scott and Liam were both just in the hallway right outside the door.

She eagerly continued to suck on him, his sounds of approval encouraging her even more. His hand began to push against the back of her head to control her movements on him, forcing himself even deeper so that his tip was prodding into the back of her throat.

Joey moaned as the tightness of her mouth sent him spiraling. Each time he felt her gag reflex on the edge of being triggered around the head of his dick, he held himself deeply in her throat for a moment before continuing to thrust.

Gasping for breath, he glanced down at her face, seeing her looking right back up at him while taking all of him in her mouth. He shuddered and shoved himself fully forward. "Fuck, yes!" His hips jerked as his thick ropes of cum erupted out of his dick and straight into her throat. Layne swallowed it down as her hand ran up over his tensed abs.

After the spasms slowed down and eventually ceased, she withdrew her mouth off him, giving a playful lick to his tip causing it to twitch before she stood back up. Layne smiled proudly at him, seeing how unraveled he was after finally getting his release.

She slowly ran her tongue over her lips, collecting the last tastes of him. "Feel better?"

He pulled himself back into his pants and began closing up shop. "Your mouth is a hell of a weapon."

A knock came to the door before it popped open, Liam partially stepped inside. "Are we done here?"

She looked at Joey with satisfaction in her own emerald eyes at a job well done. "Yeah, I'd say so." Layne stepped around Joey, pausing, and whispering to him, "Good luck with Rule One." She approached the door and left into the hallway.

Liam stood there for a moment eyeing up the masked stranger. "We will drop off the deposit at our previously agreed upon location." His eyes turned cold. "Oh, and don't forget your belt." Then he stepped back outside.

CHAPTER EIGHTEEN

As Layne stood outside the entrance to Death's Door, her father leaned down and gave a quick peck to her cheek. "You let me know if you run into any problems with this guy, ok?"

"I'm sure I can handle it." She gave him a reassuring smile to help him be put at ease.

Scott didn't look entirely convinced, but he was doing his best to give Layne enough space to make more decisions.

Liam stepped outside, immediately drawing a cigarette from the pack tucked in the inside pocket of his suit jacket. While he flicked open a black metal lighter, he stared at Layne with something in his eyes that she didn't quite understand.

"I'll drive you home." He said while the cigarette was wedged between his lips. The flame quickly lit the tip of it as he took a drag.

"I can get myself home just fine." Once again here she was being treated like someone who had no voice.

"Liam will drive you home," Scott interjected, making it a firm decision with the tone of his voice.

She made the effort to not make a mountain out of a molehill by sucking in a breath of cool air. "Fine." It was as polite of a response that she could muster.

Her brother removed the cigarette, holding it between his pointer and middle fingers as he exhaled a stream of smoke. He pointed over at the dark blue sedan parked underneath the sole street light on the block.

Layne got herself into the passenger side, leaning back with a sigh while she waited for Liam to join her. He stood out on the sidewalk speaking with their father another minute or two before parting ways.

When he took his seat behind the wheel, a half-smoked cigarette still in his hand, Layne glanced over at him. "I could have just taken the subway like a normal person. It's right on the corner."

He took one long and final drag from the cancer stick before pitching it out his window. "Just what the hell are you doing?" The white stream of smoke escaped from his mouth as he spoke.

She motioned to what she thought was obvious by making a gesture at the gear shifter. "Waiting for you to drive me home."

His hand smacked the top of the steering wheel. "That's not what I'm talking about!"

She sat there blinking a few times at his sudden outburst, unclear what was triggering him.

He didn't make her ask for more clarification. "With *him*. What the fuck, Layne?! Do you think I'm stupid?" Liam pointed to his temple for emphasis.

Still in a state of shock that Liam was this riled up, she sat there silently trying to even come up with an explanation.

"Li, I don't know wh—"

He turned in his seat to face her. "You just go around sucking any dick that presents itself like a fucking whore?!" His sudden outburst startled even her, having never seen him this bent out of shape before.

"Fuck you! You're one to talk when you chase anything with two legs and a set of fake tits!" Her hand yanked the door handle and swung the door open.

Liam's hand latched onto her upper arm, squeezing painfully hard. "No, you don't get to embarrass our family."

Layne winced as his hand prevented her from getting out of the car. "Ow! Let go, Liam!"

His fingers dug into her even more when she strained to pull away. "Close the damn door, Layne, we're not done here!" An intensity was in his eyes that sent chills down her spine.

When his driver's side door suddenly opened up, his grip loosened up inadvertently. A pair of hands gripped onto his suit lapels and extracted him out of the car.

Layne stepped out of her door to look across the roof of the vehicle to see one livid, masked Joey standing there with Liam in his grasp. Joey's hands harshly shoved her brother back against the side of his car, pinning him there with an unmatched rage in his gaze.

"You put your hands on her again, and I will break them," he growled through gritted teeth. "One bone at a time. Do you understand me?"

Liam was breathing heavily as his rage was going from a rolling boil and coming down to a mild simmer. "Only if the same applies to you."

She shoved herself between the two of them to break up the pissing match. "Enough!" She placed her hands on the front of Joey's chest, looking up at him. "I'm fine. Okay?" Then she half-turned to look at Liam who was brushing himself off and straightening out his clothes, "Go home."

The two boys were still staring at each other with chests puffed out.

"Jesus, just go home, Li." She urged so that the testosterone in the air could at least be brought down by half.

He shook his head, clearly annoyed and he got back into his car. He pulled out of the parking spot, tires squealing as he took off down the street.

Once he was gone, she looked at Joey with a sigh at this mess that was now on their hands. Crossing her arms in front of her as the night air began to bite at her skin she stepped up onto the sidewalk. "I don't think you understand, I don't need you hovering over me, waiting to fight my battles for me."

"I don't think *you* understand," he stepped up to her, "it's now my job to fight your battles."

She dropped her arms down to her sides tiredly. "Don't give me that macho bullshit." Layne turned and began walking past the Death's Door entrance towards the other end of the block where there was a sign for stairs leading down into the subway.

"Where are you going?" He didn't move from where he was standing.

"Home!" She called back to him without so much as looking over her shoulder.

He squeezed his hands into fists. This woman was going to be the death of him. She was driving him crazy with her fiercely stubborn temperament. Joey finally gave in and broke into a light jog after her. "Hey, I will take you home. Will you just stop?" He ran down a few steps ahead of her so he could stop her from going any further down the stairs.

Layne stopped short as he blocked her path. "I don't need you to take me home."

He moved one more step closer to her, his height still towering down over her despite the six-inch difference in where he was standing.

"Don't make me ask twice." His hands cradled both of hers.

"And if I do make you ask twice?" He often said it, but now she was ready to call his bluff.

His eyes shimmered with excitement, snaking an arm around her waist and pulling her up against him. "Try me and find out."

Her hands settled on top of his shoulders as she bit into her lower lip and felt her heart skipping every other beat. Layne tried to ignore the fluttering sensation dipping into her lower stomach, but all her senses tended to fly out the window the second he pulled stunts like this.

Before Layne could test him to find out exactly what he would do, his attention shifted to the quarter-dome mirror posted to the top corner of where they were standing, allowing him to see a few MTA police officers approaching the stairway.

"We have to go." He dropped his hold on one of her hands and led her back up the stairs. Instantly picking up on the change in his demeanor and seeing exactly what he saw, Layne didn't ask questions as she followed him back up to street level.

With his hand firmly holding onto hers, Joey led her around the corner to the next block. He cut down the wide alley between two industrial-looking buildings. About halfway down, she recognized the Challenger she had driven the night they both met.

The proximity sensors unlocked the doors as Joey got within a few feet. Without being told, she got into the passenger seat. Joey got behind the wheel, pulling his mask down around his neck now that they were behind illegally tinted glass.

"Friends of yours?" Layne strapped herself in.

"As much as they are yours."

"I'm not the one walking around in a mask like I'm on my way to a Call of Duty convention."

He grinned as he pulled out of the alley onto the street. "Maybe I will use that the next time I get questioned."

Layne giggled at the absurdity of anyone believing that, although in this city you saw a lot of strange characters that nobody batted an eye at. The Naked Cowboy, need anyone say anything else?

When they arrived back at her house, she pulled her arms out of her jacket, tossing it onto the coat rack near the front door. Joey carried a small black bag inside with him, slinging it over his shoulder.

"What's that?" She nodded over at the bag he was carrying.

"A change of clothes."

She put a hand on her hip. "And just why would you need those?"

"Did you think I was going to tell your dad I was going to keep an eye on you and leave you home by yourself on day one of the job?" He set the bag down on the floor at the bottom of the stairs with a light thud.

"First, no one told you to volunteer for this. Second, you can't possibly watch me every second of the day."

"But trying is half the fun." He gave her a sly wink. "Besides, did you already forget the rules?"

Layne rolled her eyes while walking into the kitchen to take a gander at what she had in her fridge. Beer, condiments, her weekly bag of salad mix that she never actually used and needed to be trashed, and a leftover slice of cherry cheesecake Rebecca had dropped off yesterday.

Opting for the decadent dessert, she pulled out the small plastic container and shut the fridge, only to see Joey standing there leaning back against the counter with his arms crossed in front of his muscular chest and his legs comfortably crossed at the ankles while watching her every move.

There was a calculating look in his eyes. She tried to reach around him to the drawer he was blocking, but he didn't move. "You're blocking my silverware drawer."

"You look a little agitated." A real Sherlock Holmes here picking up on her irritation, wasn't he?

"Agitated? No, I'm frustrated. I'm frustrated because somehow you have managed to work your way into my business. I don't mix my personal life with my business dealings, and yet here you are. I'm frustrated that you have me *frustrated*, when this," she motioned back and forth between the two of them, "should have been a one-time casual encounter."

He had the audacity to smirk at her while he stood there listening to her rant about her frustrations. Joey reached out, took the cheesecake container from her hand, and set it on the counter next to him. Without a word, he snatched her up and flung her over his shoulder with ease.

She found herself very suddenly staring down at his nice-looking cargo-clad ass. "Joey! I'm being serious!" He carried her upstairs to her bedroom, dropping her down onto her bed like a ragdoll. She bounced against the mattress with a squeak. "What are you doing?!"

"Going to take care of your frustration." He pulled the bottom of his shirt up and over his head, exposing the hard physique of his upper body decorated with all of the tattooed artwork.

He didn't need to say it to her twice. Layne quickly disposed of her clothes, wildly flinging them off to the side. Not a second after Joey dropped his pants, he pinned her down underneath him. She buried her fingers in his hair as she pulled herself up to latch her mouth onto his out of raw lust.

His hands ran up her legs, pushing them apart to expose her sex, glistening with her excitement. While his tongue forced its way into her mouth to explore her addictive taste, he lined up the head of his shaft with her opening.

Breaking herself away from his mouth, she showered his face with several more hasty kisses. "Don't you dare make me wait. I need you."

As soon as she said those last three words, he sheathed himself deeply into her. "Fuck, Layney, you have been waiting for my cock, haven't you?"

She cried out as he pushed himself into her in one go, welcoming the sensation of pleasure and the way her body was forced to take him. His hips began pumping his dick into her, losing himself in the moment. His hand slid between them, his thumb circling over her aching clit. The second he made contact, her hips bucked at the intense sensation as she yelled out a series of unintelligible words.

In a few firm strokes of her swollen clit, Layne's body shook to her core with an otherworldly orgasm that had her vision hazy as her pleasure-filled screams filled the air. He continued to grind himself deep into her, groaning out loudly as her pussy locked down around him.

Staying buried deep inside of her, his arm slid around her back and pulled her upright with him as he sat back on his heels, so she was straddling him. His hands ran down her back and possessively grabbed a handful of her firm ass with each hand and began rolling her hips against him.

Layne was still trembling like a leaf from her explosive release moments ago, her arms wrapped around his neck, keeping their bare bodies in contact. She rode his cock at a slow and steady pace as she recovered from the intensity that had surged through her body. However, she quickly unleashed the hunger that was still gnawing at her for more of him.

"I need more of you." The intimate position had her staring right into his eyes as she panted from the intensity of the sensations her body was experiencing.

"I've got all night planned to take care of my good girl." He nuzzled his face into the side of her neck, trailing hot kisses along her throat as he handled her ass to encourage her to ride him more vigorously.

Joey kept good on his promise and used the rest of the night making sure Layne had her fill of him, until she was left with a mess between her legs, a sheen of sweat slowly drying on her skin, and pure satisfied bliss overcoming every inch of her body.

CHAPTER NINETEEN

The next several days were spent trying to assess what type of normal there was going to be between Layne and Joey. He had two tasks on his plate: keeping her safe while simultaneously plotting out how to fulfill his obligations to the head of the O'Reilly family on repaying Michael Franzetti for his unfortunate decision to try and snuff out Layne's life.

It wasn't going to be a quick process getting a plan of action in order if he was going to do this the right way. Layne had been sending her resources out to gather some information from Franzetti's weakest links to assist Joey in making his plans. He wasn't thrilled about her trying to insert herself into the process, but he was losing that battle with the fiercely determined woman he had chosen to put his life and reputation on the line for.

Joey came downstairs freshly showered, wearing nothing but a pair of jeans belted around his waist. His dirty blonde hair looked darker than normal thanks to it still being damp. He grabbed the cup of coffee Layne had set aside on the center island for him and carefully sipped the dark roast.

Partially seated at the kitchen table, Layne had one knee on the chair and the other foot on the floor while she leaned over the table. She was already dressed and ready to start her day in a pair of lightly distressed blue jeans and a snug long-sleeved shirt with a low-cut neckline. Layne flipped through a few texts and emails on her phone.

Noticing the way her curves fit into those jeans, he smiled. "Coming downstairs to this view every morning is something I could get used to."

"I think you've seen enough of my ass to last a lifetime," she said not even looking up from her phone.

He approached her, pulling her phone from her hands. "And I will continue to appreciate it for at least two more lifetimes."

She finally looked over at him as he confiscated her phone, and whatever she was about to say was replaced with a silent stare at the fine-looking shirtless specimen standing next to her. A smile tugged at the corner of her mouth before she plucked the phone right back out of his hands. "I have work to take care of today, some things have come up."

"We can talk about it after I get something to eat. I'm starving." He patted a hand to his defined abdominal muscles.

She rested a hand on her hip. "There isn't anything to talk about. I have business to take care of."

"Not without me you don't."

She silently said a prayer for more patience with this man. "I thought that when you convinced my dad to drop the security detail on me, I would have more leeway. Instead, you're…"

"Up your ass?" He chuckled.

"For lack of a better phrase, yes. And stop looking so smug about it!" Her hand smacked against the center of his bare chest, where he caught her wrist and tugged her up against him.

He nodded his head down to her ear and whispered. "I will quit looking so smug about it when you tell me that you don't enjoy it." With that, he gave a quick peck to her cheek and released her wrist.

It had been a lost cause convincing Joey that she didn't need his over-protective services while she took care of some routine business matters. The best she got out of him was a promise he would stay out of sight, and she wouldn't even know he was there. Layne found that hard to believe, but it was all she could negotiate for now.

She sat in the closed-off backroom of McGregor's Pub, straddling a backward chair at the wooden table that was unbalanced on one of its four legs. Joey was out front sitting at the bar in the same seat he had chosen the night he met her. He was at least allowing her to conduct her check-in meeting with family associates in private.

Two of her men, or more accurately her dad's employees who reported to her, were seated across the table. Standing off to the side, there was one tall and leggy redheaded woman examining her cheap manicure.

"Gary, explain to me one more time what's going on with Thursday nights at the Brass Mirror." Layne lifted her glass of golden ale and took a long, therapeutic sip as this meeting wasn't inspiring her that the minions were holding down the fort. Brass Mirror was one of a few of their back-room sites in the O'Reilly underground gambling circuit, only the elite received invitations, and even then, those memberships were reviewed and scrutinized quite frequently.

"Diego wants a bigger cut. He said that things have been getting a bit wild and he's had to hire more personnel to keep things civil." Gary was in his seat, bouncing both of his knees like he was sending erratic Morse code. He was close to Layne's age, and yet he was struggling to keep up with the pace of the job.

"Jesus, Gary, could you pop a pill and stop with the damn jittering?" She let out an exasperated sigh. "Tell Diego, he needs to hire better help to replace who he has. He's not getting a bigger cut just because he's a shitty judge of character."

Gary smoothed his hands over the tops of his knees trying to slow the movements.

Layne looked over to his partner in literal crime. "Update, Darin?"

He dug around in his jacket pocket, pulled out a few folded pieces of paper, and slid them across the table toward her.

Layne reached out and took the documents, unfolding them and reading the contents. Doing her best to control the expression on her face, she immediately finished off the rest of the beer in her glass. "Alright, go ahead and follow up on this, and let me know what you find out." She waved the papers at him before shoving them into her back pocket for safekeeping.

"It may take a while, it's been like casting pearls before swine."

Layne raised both her eyebrows at the idiom, but promptly shook her head. "I don't even want to know what the hell that means. Just find out what you can."

"Are we done here, yet?" The shrill voice of the woman interrupted as she crossed her arms over her stomach, impatiently waiting. God, Layne hated dealing with Kristill, and she hated how she spelled her name even more.

Layne motioned for Gary and Darin to be on their way. "Take a seat."

"I'm fine standing," Kristill replied with boredom hanging in her voice.

"I said fuckin' sit, Kristill." Layne's tone getting kicked up a notch at the attitude she was getting.

"I'm fine." She slowly emphasized each word.

Layne pushed away from her seat, stood up, and walked over to the woman with a really bad box-dye hair job. Going toe-to-toe with her, she lowered her voice, letting the seriousness of her voice edge each syllable. "Take a seat, or I will put you in one."

Her eyes looked Layne up and down, appearing unimpressed and unthreatened. "Oh, whatever, Layne. I don't take orders from you."

If Layne hadn't already been in work mode, perhaps she would have backed down from a mouthy hoe, but Kristill was on their payroll and sure as shit knew better. Her hand snatched Kristill's throat, shoving her back against the wall, harshly pinning her there.

"The hell you don't. Just because you fuck Liam when he's bored doesn't make you indispensable. Now, I have a need for your services and there's a nice little bonus attached to it. So, sit your damn ass in the chair." Layne released the girl's throat and backed off allowing her the space and opportunity to comply.

Kristill rubbed her throat, glaring at Layne with a catty snarl, but finally put herself in a chair.

Layne pulled her phone out and brought up a photo, showing it to her. "Have you seen him before?"

After a look at the face on the screen, Kristill shook her head. "No, I would have remembered a hot piece of ass like that for sure."

"Well, today is your lucky day." Layne grinned mischievously. "I'm going to need you to make him a hell of an enticing proposition. He's out sitting at the bar, do you think you can do that?"

She looked up at Layne with a smile of disbelief. "Shit, I'd do that one for free."

"Good, give it five minutes, and then go out there and work your magic." She put her phone away.

Kristill nodded in agreement and immediately pulled out a compact mirror and a tube of lipstick to jazz up her look. Layne used the floor access to step down into the storage area underneath McGregor's where all the kegs were stored. At the far end of the cramped storage room was a set of BILCO doors where deliveries could be easily made from the alley.

Unlatching the cold metal doors, she pushed one door up to step out onto the street level of the alley adjacent to the pub. She walked down the alley towards the bordering backstreet that ran behind the rundown Irish pub, figuring she was in the clear. Kristill knew how to keep a man distracted for at least fifteen minutes, maybe five minutes depending on the guy.

She rounded the corner of the building and collided with Joey's solid chest, nearly bouncing right off it. Saving her from falling on her ass, his hands gripped her arms and pulled her back to him with a smirk. "You didn't think that was going to work, did you?"

He pressed her back against the back of the building there in the isolated backstreet. She felt the cool brick against her backside as she looked up at him. "I've heard Kristill has impressive flexibility, you probably should have taken her up on her offer."

His hand came up underneath her chin, gently grasping it. "Afraid I will bend you until you break?"

Just hearing the way he spoke those words, the imagery in her head caused a heat between her legs. "I don't break easily."

"Good." Joey tilted her chin up so he could slowly adhere his mouth to hers in a drawn-out and surprisingly gentle kiss. It was simultaneously sensual and delicate as it stirred up feelings inside of her that prickled along her skin.

Her lips caressed his, reciprocating the energy between them as it seemed that time itself stood still. Maybe it did.

CHAPTER TWENTY

The sweat was dripping down the back of her neck, rolling between her shoulder blades in a slow tickle against her skin. Layne groaned while trying to catch her breath. "I hate you right now."

Rebecca laughed after setting down her kettlebell on the mat between her feet, her own skin dewy from perspiration after a killer workout. After brushing a rogue strand of sunny blonde hair away from her face she shrugged. "That's fine, but you'll love me when you feel how sore your ass is tomorrow after a solid workout."

Layne lay there on the mat, pushing up into cobra pose to feel the stretch all the way through to her stomach. Drawing in several deep breaths, she worked on completing a few more stretches alongside her bestie.

It had been a hectic few weeks, and she hadn't had the opportunity to catch up with Rebecca the way she typically did. Joey had stuck to his word about trying to give her space, so he wasn't breathing down her neck every second of every day. She often wondered if he really was keeping tabs on her or not given how well he blended into the background.

When it was suggested by Rebecca that they meet up at the gym for a much-needed workout sesh and grab a bite afterward, Layne figured it was as good of a plan as any.

"Still on for margs and tacos? A little protein, a little booze, and we'll call it balanced eating."

Layne laughed. "Is there an option just for tequila?"

"Oh boy," Rebecca chuckled. "I didn't realize that you needed girl time that badly."

After they both hit the showers and got changed, they left the gym and headed down to a small Mexican joint that always had late-night specials for bottomless chips and salsa with two-dollar watered-down margaritas.

After dunking another chip into the salsa bowl, Layne shoved it into her mouth as she waited for Rebecca's reaction.

"I knew it, I knew there was a guy." Clearly, feeling vindicated that her best friend Spidey senses had been spot on. "You have been far less chatty, which usually means you don't want to give anything away."

Washing the saltiness of the chip down with the tang of the margarita, Layne winced that Rebecca could read into things that easily. "Look, all I said was there has been a guy. There are always guys, Rebecca, a girl has needs."

"No, no, no. You have specifically avoided talking about this one, and I want all the details." She leaned forward, ready to take in all the salacious particulars.

Layne took pause trying to gather her words, and before she got the first word out Rebecca interrupted her. "Oh God, he works for your dad, doesn't he? Is he older? Tattooed?" The barrage of scarily accurate line of questioning was fired off quickly.

She blinked several times at Rebecca's sudden conclusions. "No! I mean, yes, he does but… It's complicated. Yes, he's twelve years older, and yes, he's got some tattoos." Layne eyed her bestie warily while pouring her next round of margarita into her glass from the pitcher sitting on the table. She was left wondering if she was that easy to read, and if so, she was going to need to work on that.

"Oo, nice. It's exactly what I've always pictured for you. Does your dad know? Crap, he would flip his lid." Rebecca pondered all the potential fallouts that would transpire if Scott got wind of anyone working for him fooling around with Layne. It had always been a non-negotiable for as long as Rebecca had been around.

"I don't think so, not unless Liam has gone tattling." Layne grimaced thinking about how Liam would be holding this over her head in the future.

Rebecca raised her eyebrows, looking for more information on that little nugget of information.

A little bit of pink flushed over her cheeks. "He may have overheard some things. Either way, it's not a big deal everything has been very casual"

"Liar." It was an aggressive calling-out, even coming from Rebecca.

"What?"

"You did that thing with your left eyebrow when you lie. Plain as day." She attempted to mimic the little twitch that had given Layne away.

Layne rolled her eyes. "It's casual, Rebecca, you're reading too much into this. You know how I feel about getting too far into the weeds with guys."

Her bestie rolled her eyes having heard this story before. "Yeah, yeah, yeah, I know. Commitments aren't your thing."

"Exactly." Just when Rebecca was going to try and push the issue, Layne gave her a rare look, pleading her to drop it. Being the good and sensible friend that she was, Rebecca didn't press it any further.

After a change to a lighter subject involving Rebecca's adventures in nannying, they wrapped up the chit-chat after a not-so-subtle hint from the workers in the restaurant that they were closing up for the night.

Right outside the cantina, Layne gave Rebecca a huge hug. "I'm still going to hate you when my ass is sore tomorrow and I can't get up the stairs." She teased before letting Rebecca go from the embrace. "Do you need me to walk you back to your apartment?" The apartment building was only four blocks from there, but Layne was willing to keep her friend company to ensure she made it back safely.

"Nah, I'm fine. I will text you when I get in." She waved off any concern that Layne had.

Layne knew better than to offer up a second time and let Rebecca take off to head home. Being that she was all the way downtown, it was going to be a long trip back to the other end of the city. She hoped maybe she could catch the next 4-5-6 train uptown. The station was only a half block away.

When she got there, she heard the train pulling away as she ran down the stairs of the station, watching the train leave just as she made her way onto the platform.

"Shit." Now she was going to have to wait for whenever the next one decided to show up. She leaned up against one of the pillars in the center of the platform as she waited impatiently by herself—just her and the rats that moved between the tracks. Fifteen minutes passed and there still was no train to be found.

"Screw this." She said out loud to herself, figuring at this point it was easier to hail a cab. Just as she got to the bottom of the steps to leave the platform, a train finally pulled in. Layne changed course and boarded it as soon as the doors opened up.

She took a seat in the empty car, relieved to finally be on her way back home. After indulging in several margaritas and an embarrassing amount of chips, she could use some sleep.

Before the doors shut, a small group of men were laughing amongst themselves as they just barely made it onto the train. The doors shut and the train pulled away from the station beginning the long journey uptown.

One of them locked eyes with her and gave an eerie smile, his hand hitting the chest of his closest buddy lightly. "Looky-look at what we got here. I know you."

His two friends leered at her, and then one spoke up. "You're that chick that got the slip on the masked freak." That wasn't oddly specific at all.

Layne stood up from her seat, holding onto the pole in the middle of the aisle for balance as the train jostled along the tracks. "Wow, I've got a reputation now? I'm impressed."

Three of them and one of her—this was going to be fun. She made sure that her feet were planted firmly in a wider stance given the dynamics of the train movement being a challenging variable.

The guys snickered amongst themselves before the leader of the pack took a few steps closer to her. Layne stood her ground, her eyes locked on his as she evaluated his every movement. When he stopped a few inches from her, she gave him his one warning. "Think carefully about what you do next. I would hate for you to end up limping away with your tail between your legs."

"I also heard that the boss got you all," he ran his tongue along his bottom lip, "wet." Internally, Layne cringed at how gross he just made that sound.

One of her eyebrows perked up, and as one of his hands reached out for her, she grabbed his wrist, pulling him off-balance as her other hand pushed on the back of his shoulder to send him face-first into the pole in the middle of the aisle, causing a fracture of his nasal bone, resulting in a gush of fresh blood pouring from his nostrils. He stumbled onto the floor behind her as his two friends were quick to charge at her.

Her hand latched onto one of the straps hanging from the bar to the left and with her hand on the pole to the right, she kangaroo kicked at the two jackasses while Mr. Broken Nose was shouting a string of profanities behind her. Tweedle-Dee and Tweedle-Dum stumbled back.

The connecting door to the next car back slid open. Joey stepped in, his eyes lit up with a wrathful vengeance as his fists flexed at his sides. He grabbed one of the two men closest to him, pounding a fist to his face, which caused him to immediately drop to the floor like a sack of bricks.

The second thug charged at him, and Joey stumbled back against the now-closed door. He struggled with the man for a hot minute before gaining the upper hand and propelling him towards the glass case that contained the emergency fire extinguisher. The glass shattered and the man was rendered unconscious with several lacerations to the face.

Momentarily distracted, she witnessed one pissed-off Joey show up to the party, a bloody hand wrapped around and seized her throat. A sharp and pointy blade pressed below the bottom of her ribcage. Before there was any time to react, the train made a sudden turn around a bend in the subway tunnel, causing a massive shift in the movement of the car.

She and the lead thug both stumbled, and it was Layne who took advantage of the well-timed opportunity. Her body snaked away from him; his hand smearing a bloody handprint across her throat.

Joey was on top of him before he re-established his footing. The leader's dominant hand was grabbed and twisted until the bones cracked, resulting in the knife dropping to the ground and sliding under a set of seats.

Protective instincts drove Joey's fist into the guy's face, beating him down repeatedly. The fresh blood splattered in various directions with each impact Joey made. Even when the man lost consciousness, Joey's bloody knuckles continued the vicious assault.

"Joey! *JOEY*!" Layne's hand grabbed his shoulder, forcefully tugging on it to pull him back. The train began to slow as it approached its next stop. "We need to go."

He gave one final strike to the man's face before dropping the body down onto the floor of the subway car. His chest heaving with adrenaline-fueled breaths. The tattoos on his right hand were now covered in the sticky mixture of the man's blood and nasal fluids.

Joey looked at Layne and then the doors as the platform came into view. His bruised hand wrapped around hers, tugging her along with him to the doors that popped open shortly after the train came to a complete stop.

Fortunately, at this time of night, stations outside of tourist areas had very few people. Joey guided her off the train, leaving the three men behind to lick their wounds. After they both got up to street level, he finally paused to turn and face her. His hand softly took her chin, turning her face to inspect for any injuries.

"I'm fine." She fought a wince, feeling the burn along her side now that the adrenaline was fading.

His hand dropped away from her face as he looked over the rest of her, noticing the tear in her shirt. When he went to lift it to take a look, her hands shoved his away. "Let's just get home, it's a scratch."

The fact he hadn't spoken a word since they stepped off the subway train wasn't reassuring her that he was going to be a happy camper for the remainder of the evening.

Layne would have been nominated the world's biggest liar if she had said that by the time they did make it back to her townhome, she wasn't in a little more pain than she had been willing to admit for a mere scratch on her side.

Once the front door shut behind them, Layne attempted to lighten the mood. "Didn't expect you to run late to the fun back there in the subway."

That was the wrong fucking choice of levity.

Joey glared at her. "I went to take a damn leak, Layne, and just barely boarded the last car before the doors shut."

Getting defensive at his tone, she deflected it right back at him. "And I would have had everything under control until you came and caused a distraction."

"Yeah, you really had things under control." The sarcasm and anger heated his words.

"Don't get pissed at me, I didn't invite the jackasses to come tango." She yanked off her coat, tossing it over the banister. Layne then turned to look at the mirror mounted on the wall, lifting her shirt to reveal a cut where she must have gotten nicked during the scuffle. Examining the wound in her reflection, she tried not to grimace. She wasn't so successful.

Joey took notice and exhaled his frustrations at what had transpired, he was more concerned about making sure Layne was okay. He came up to her, placing a hand on her lower back and motioning at the living room. "Go, sit. That needs to be cleaned up."

Stubbornly she responded. "I can do it."

"It wasn't a suggestion, Layne."

She looked at his eyes in the reflection. Not having it in her to die on this hill, she lowered her shirt and went into the living room. Layne eased herself into one of the armchairs. Joey disappeared briefly, only to return with a first aid kit.

"Shirt off." He commanded.

Layne pulled her arms through the sleeves and eased the fabric up and over her head, dropping the shirt to the floor leaving her sitting there in just her navy lace bra. He pulled up an ottoman and took a seat in front of her as he began sorting the materials he required.

His typically rough hands were surprisingly gentle as he began to clean the three-inch cut on her side. Layne had gotten lucky that it wasn't deep and only needed minimal attention.

"That kick you gave to the two guys though." A bit of pride tugging at the smile settling across his face.

"Impressive, right?" She grinned, only to flinch as he applied pressure to the sorest part of the injury.

"Just about done." He took a few more minutes to fix her up before applying a bandage over it. His hand motioned to the dried blood smeared across her fair skin. "Go get yourself cleaned up. I don't want to keep looking at the reminder that another man's hand was on that pretty little throat of yours."

CHAPTER TWENTY-ONE

Scott O'Reilly stood there peering into the massive fish tank taking up most of one wall of his office. The vivid combination of colors among the various species provided a calming visual. He had several orangey-red Discus, a school of Cardinal tetras, and his favorite: the German Blue Ram. The entire community of fish swam peacefully in the tank.

Behind him stood Joey, hands in his pockets comfortably as he waited for his current employer to explain the purpose behind the meeting he had called. As per his standard protocol, his mask stretched across the bottom half of his face. Also present was Layne, relegated to leaning back against the office door merely for observation. A few feet to her left, Mick stood there with a sour look on his face as he disapprovingly stared the masked contractor down.

Scott finally spoke up. "Beautiful creatures, aren't they? Living their lives to the fullest, blissfully unaware of what exists outside of this ecosystem. At any point, I could play God and drain the water from the tank, leaving them all unable to survive. Yet, they don't fear that. It must be nice."

Unclear where this line of conversation was leading, Joey chose not to interrupt. Scott turned to face him, locking him in his gaze. "I'm not fond of the idea that Layne is as close to this entire Franzetti ordeal as she is. Where are we with resolving everything?"

Layne rolled her eyes at the overprotective sentiment her dad had.

"I don't disclose my methods but rest assured that things are very close. Your daughter is in good hands, and it will stay that way. I have no intention of allowing her to get caught in the crossfire." Joey maintained a professional demeanor in responding to Scott's inquiries on the status of things.

"I'm going to need more assurance than just your word. There's a lot of talk going on in the shadows and tensions are coming to a snapping point. When can I expect you to deliver what has been promised?" The typical O'Reilly impatience that ran in their blood started to present itself.

Joey spoke matter-of-factly. "For everyone's safety, I can't give you that information. You hired me for my methods and discretion, not for a sloppy rush job."

"I didn't expect you to wait until he keels over from old age either." Scott's irritation weighed on his words. He approached his desk, perching on the corner of it. "Let's make sure we don't have a conversation about timeframes again, understood?"

"There will be no need for it, but let me be clear, I will not be pressured into making a move before the time is right. He will be dealt with. Until then, I'm not going to answer summonses to explain my methods." Not too many men presented a backbone to Scott, but Joey was standing tall.

Scott chuckled with amusement. "You've got some stones, I will give you that."

Finally deciding to interject, Layne spoke up as she pushed away from the door. "It will be done when it's done. I want this wrapped up as much as anybody else. I want to see karma smack Franzetti in the face so hard that he is reduced to a groveling wreck."

Her father gave her a disapproving look, opening his mouth to correct her, but she put her hands up. "I know, I know. You want me to stay out of it."

He pinched the bridge of his nose tiredly. "There are days I wish you were still on the other side of the country, away from all of this." Scott sighed and looked at the two of them. "I want this finalized as soon as possible. I'm not getting a good feel from all the talk around the city."

Joey nodded in agreement that the pulse throughout the criminal underworld was uneasy. "It won't be much longer."

"Good. Now, I have an appointment to get to. Keep me apprised if anything changes." Scott stood up from the corner of his desk.

They all said their goodbyes with Scott wrapping his arms around Layne in a protective bear hug. He pulled back to look down at his daughter. "I meant what I said. It is too big of a risk to have you poking around." He pressed a kiss to the top of her head.

Scott walked both Layne and Joey to the door, opening it up for them. Once they saw their way out, Mick stopped at the doorway looking at Scott. "I don't like this. I don't like him. I wish you would have brought me in on this sooner."

Scott shook his head. "I couldn't."

Not liking the response he was getting, Mick pressed on. "What makes this different than anything else?"

Scott chose each of his words carefully, "I needed to be sure. It's a delicate situation that could drastically change the dynamics of power as we know it." He didn't expound upon what he had needed to be sure of.

"I've never known you to hold back. You aren't going soft now are you, old man?" He gave a playful jab to Scott's arm. Mick looked at his lifelong friend, seeing a man who once had the vicious tenacity of a bull in the ring. Now? He saw this life wearing him down little by little.

Joey pulled away from O'Reilly Manor in his car, with Layne taking up shotgun.

"Why didn't you just tell him?" Layne's eyes were full of curiosity.

"Tell him what?" He kept his eyes straight ahead, focusing on the road.

"That you have a plan." Her hand reached over and rested on top of his thigh.

"Because the fewer people that know the better. The only reason you know as much as you do is because you have this knack for not leaving things alone." As he felt her hand touch him, it caused him to think about other things that she wouldn't leave alone, and he definitely didn't mind it in the least.

"And here I thought you were going to say it was my unparalleled charms."

He cracked a smile, glancing over at her.

Layne put her other hand in her coat pocket, only to find it empty. "Oh, hell." She frowned.

"What?" Joey raised a questioning brow.

"My phone is missing. It must have fallen out of my pocket back at the house. Can you turn around real quick so I can grab it?" She couldn't believe that she hadn't noticed it fall, but it was the only conclusion that was reasonably logical.

Joey already began the process of backtracking. "Are you sure you had it?"

She nodded. "Positive. Liam texted right after we got there saying he couldn't make the meeting today and would just get an update later. He's probably with Kristill." Whatever her brother saw in the paid piece of ass, she would never know.

Minutes later, they were right back at her dad's house. Leaving Joey in the car, Layne hopped out and jogged up the front steps. Once inside, she ran into Mick pulling his arms through the sleeves of his coat by the door.

"Back so soon?" He grinned as he adjusted the collar of the grey coat.

"Hey, yeah. You didn't happen to see my phone lying around here, did you?" Layne was already looking down at the floor to trace back her path.

"You mean this phone?" He pulled the device out of his pocket and held it up for her to see.

Relief flooded her face. "Yes, thank you."

Mick handed it over to her. "Your dad found it on his way out. I was just about to bring it to your place, but you beat me to it."

Layne stood on her tiptoes to wrap her arms around Mick's neck in a quick hug. "You're a lifesaver, I appreciate it." She smiled at him, and he returned the same.

Layne turned to head right back out until she heard Mick speak up. "Layne?"

Her hand still on the door handle she looked back over her shoulder. "Yeah?"

His hand rested on her shoulder in a caring gesture. "I spoke with Liam, and he told me everything. You know how much I care about you, but this guy is the worst type of scum. I haven't said anything to your dad, but you need to quit fooling around. You're going to end up getting burned, and I hate to think what the fallout will be."

Her face fell hearing how much the man she considered an uncle was concerned about her and Joey. Of course, he had heard it from Liam to boot. "I know what I'm doing."

"Do you? Because from what I'm seeing, you are being careless. You have worked so hard to get where you're at, are you so quick to put it at risk? I'm only saying something because I'm concerned." His hand gave her shoulder a squeeze before he continued. "If your dad found out, you and I both know it would be game over. All the progress you've made wouldn't mean anything. It would be back to square one where you were three years ago and there would be no coming back from that."

She shook her head. "I know you're trying to look out for me, but there's nothing to be worried about."

Mick's forehead was all wrinkled up in concern. "Just give it some thought, 'kay?"

She nodded before slipping out the front door. Layne knew he was coming from a place of concern for her, but she wasn't the same girl she was three years ago. She wasn't going to let her father dictate every aspect of her life to shield her from the grit and grime of a life in this business of organized crime.

When she returned to the car, she shut her door roughly, prompting a look from Joey. "Everything okay?"

"Liam is an ass determined to undermine everything I do."

"What else is new?" He put the car back in drive, pulling back into the roadway.

CHAPTER TWENTY-TWO

With Liam being extra ornery, Mick voicing his concerns, and plans being slow to come into place after the not-so-peppy pep talk her dad had with Joey, she was beginning to burn out from all the stressors taking a toll on her life.

Tonight, Joey insisted on taking her to one of her favorite restaurants, a low-key burger spot that had the best bacon cheeseburger she had ever tasted. As much as she argued about going out and wanted to sit and stew at home, he had been right to drag her out. A good meal and change of scenery had helped tremendously. Not to mention the company hadn't been half bad either.

Having Joey around all the time had naturally become an expectation. Things between them were growing more and more complicated in some ways and in other ways? To put it simply, Layne hadn't opened any of her dating apps in weeks.

Leaving the restaurant, they stepped out onto the sidewalk together. The holiday lights had just gone up last week on most of the storefronts indicating the approach of the very merry season. She didn't like to admit it, but the city this time of year was always capable of lifting Layne's mood.

Her fingers slid between his as she held onto his hand for warmth. "I definitely enjoyed that."

A proud smile slid across his face. "Which part? The food or the way I had you squirming in your seat?"

Layne nudged a shoulder up into his side as the heat crept up onto her cheeks and let out a soft laugh. "Both."

With Joey's Challenger currently in the shop until tomorrow for upgrades, they had opted to take one of her two cars. It was parked about a half block down from the gastropub they had just eaten at. She pulled her keys out of her jacket pocket and hit the remote start to get the engine rolling to warm up the interior of the car.

Next, what sounded like a loud crack of thunder filled the air, followed by a rumbling of the ground underneath their feet and a sudden flash of heat. In the vicinity of where her car was parked, an explosion rocked the area with a furious mix of metal, glass, fumes, and flames. Lucky for them, they were far enough from the blast that they were barely outside the edge of potential harm. A few people who had been too close to the blast were not so lucky.

The bomb that went off was strong enough to take her off guard and Layne stumbled into Joey. Protectively he wrapped his arms around her, drawing her closer into his chest and turning in case of any flying debris. Her ears were ringing, dulling the sounds of people screaming and yelling at the violent scene that had just unfolded in front of them.

Once Joey was sure that everything was in the clear, he pulled Layne away from his chest and held her face in his hands as he looked at her. "Layne? Are you hurt?"

The typically unshakeable Layne O'Reilly was visibly trembling. Her eyes were still focused on the remnants of that burning vehicle that used to sit in her garage. Deep inside her brain, her memories rushed back to vividly relive one of the worst days of her life…

A young Layne at barely ten years old shouted back at her mother. "Why can't I go to Rebecca's?! It's not fair! You and dad never let me go hang out with my friends!"

Shannon O'Reilly, with her hands resting on her hips, sighed as she was about to repeat herself for the fortieth time in the last hour.

"I told you Layney, not tonight. Things are very hectic for your dad at work right now. I have already repeated myself multiple times, you can spend the night with Rebecca another day, okay?"

Layne stomped her foot in anger. "Why are you being so mean?!"

Her mother frowned at her slightly, feeling terrible that her daughter was too young to understand. "Layney, it's for your own good. Now, go upstairs and start getting ready for bed."

To continue putting on a display of how displeased she was, she stomped off past her mom to hide away in her frilly pink room upstairs. Once she was slowly calming down from her outburst, she sat in the reading nook set into her bedroom window. Drawing her knees to her chest and resting her chin on top of them, she watched what was going on outside in front of the house.

Her mom stood a few feet out from the front door, leaning in to press a kiss to her dad's mouth briefly. Shannon's hand patted the side of his arm, and she gave him that sweet smile that could warm a million souls. Layne's mom followed the walkway to where her car was parked right out front. When she got inside, she sat there for a minute, and then that's when the explosion happened. Layne bore witness to that great flash of fire blossoming, felt the rattle of the windows of the house, and experienced a sudden onset of fear seizing her heart.

Her mother was in that car. If Layne had gotten her way, she would have been in there with her to be brought over to Rebecca's house. It was the darkest day of Layne's life riddled with grief and guilt, accompanied by a gruesome visual of the personal attack that robbed her of her mom.

Joey shook her by her shoulders. "Layne! Layney, look at me!" Suddenly, she was mentally back there in the present, on the sidewalk with him. She blinked her eyes several times, trying to refocus on what had just transpired. Smelling the distinct burning of various fluids and metal it caused her chest to seize up. She felt like she was beginning to suffocate, and she couldn't get enough air into her lungs which felt constricted, not helped by the shakiness of her body.

"Oh, God, I… I… I… Can't breathe. I can't…" Her hand went to her chest, searching for any sign that her heart was still beating in there. The more she thought she couldn't breathe, the faster and shorter her breaths were as she heaved in response to the traumatic memories that were physically overcoming her.

"Yes. You can." Joey kissed the top of her forehead, clutching onto her and bringing his face up close in front of hers to force her to come eye-to-eye with him. "Look at me! We have to get out of here. You're fine, I've got you." Holding her close to his side, he was quick to hurriedly walk her away from the burning heap of metal.

Joey's eyes were on the lookout for their surroundings as he escorted her off to some place further away and safer than their current location.

After several minutes he sat her down on a bench. He squatted down in front of her, placing his hands on top of her knees as the concern flooded his eyes. "Just try to breathe."

Tears were stinging her eyes as she shook her head with certainty. "I… can't."

His hands began to gently rub up and down over her legs to provide reassurance. "Yes, you can. Focus on me."

Layne's lower lip quivered as she shut her eyes tightly, forcing the tears to trickle down her cheeks. After a few minutes of keeping her eyes closed like that, slowly she was finding a bit of ease in her chest. "It's happening again."

"What's happening again?" He inquired, keeping his words soft.

"My mom… She…" Layne couldn't even bring herself to speak the words as to what transpired over fifteen years ago to her mother. Thankfully, Joey didn't make her say it either.

He stood, wrapping his arms around her as a cloak of protection. "Shh, it's okay. Nothing is going to happen to you, I won't let it."

Layne felt him kiss the top of her head, while the strength of his arms remained locked around her. He continued to hush into her ear. It felt like an eternity that he sat there while he let her work through the emotions that had overtaken her. Gradually her trembling ceased, and she felt calm enough to open her eyes.

Joey hooked a finger under her chin and lifted it to face him. "We will figure this out. Someone wanted to scare you. I will find whoever it is, and I guarantee you, that fucker will regret the day he was born."

Normally, Layne would have argued that she didn't need a man to go off and fight battles on her behalf, but she was too emotionally wrecked to argue with him. She also trusted that he would do just as he promised her: this person would pay dearly.

CHAPTER TWENTY-THREE

Once Layne was settled down enough, Joey took her back to his apartment. She sat down on the cushy sofa, leaning back. Joey brought her over a heavy pour of straight Jameson in a rocks glass. "Drink this, it will help."

He didn't have to tell her twice. She took a small sip at first but then parted her lips more to suck down more of the liquid gold. It didn't take long for the alcohol to take the edge off. Layne offered him up a light smile. "Thank you."

"Thank me when I pull the spine out of the asshole that set off that explosion." His words promised a whole new level of violence to keep her safe.

For a moment she questioned if he actually was capable of going to those lengths, but then she reminded herself of all the things he confessed to her on their first official date together.

Joey continued, "You're not getting more than an arm's length away from me until we get this all sorted."

"What?" Her brain was still struggling to cope with the night's events and even more so as the booze muddled everything so she could avoid an even bigger and epic emotional meltdown.

"You heard me." He leaned over, placing two hands on the back of the sofa on either side of her as he intensely looked at her. "You don't so much as open the door without me. You got that?"

"Don't start with this, Joey. I've got one too many overprotective males in my life as it is." Her hand rubbed her forehead, trying to fend off a headache.

His voice lowered, unwavering in his stance there in front of her. "Then, you have one more to deal with. I'm not fucking around."

She shook her head as she ducked under his arms to get up off the couch. Layne finished the last of the whiskey and set the empty glass on the side table. "The hell I do, I don't need you going all macho man because you think you have something to prove. If I wanted to be controlled, I would have let my dad marry me off years ago."

Joey straightened up, taking his hands off the couch now that she was no longer sitting there. As for Layne, she walked over to the door to his apartment.

"What are you doing?" He asked even though it was obvious.

"What does it look like I'm doing? Leaving. I am not dealing with this bullshit." Her hand slid the chain lock off and twisted the door handle.

Joey's hand shoved the door shut, leaving her unable to jerk it open under his strength. "Did you ever think you're in over your head and actually need to let someone help you, huh? Instead, you're being a stubborn bitch."

That caught Layne's attention, and she turned to look at him, her hands violently shoving his chest, but he didn't budge an inch. "You're one to talk about being stubborn!" She gave him another useless push against the muscles of his broad chest. "Now, stop getting in my way."

"No." His response may have been short, but it carried a heavy weight.

"Argh! See how stubborn you are?!" All of her emotions were bubbling up and now being taken out on him.

Joey wrapped an arm around her waist and hoisted her up, tossing her over his shoulder and walking her away from the door. Layne sharply gasped as she was suddenly flung over his shoulder like his own personal ragdoll to do with as he pleased. Her hands pushed against his back as she squirmed against him.

Dodging her feet kicking up near his face, he carried her into his bedroom and tossed her down onto his bed without any effort to ease the drop. "You're not leaving."

"Oh, fuck you, Joey." Exasperated, she sat up from where she had landed in the center of the mattress.

"Promise?" He tugged his shirt off over his head, dropping it to the floor to be laundered later. His mouth curved into a devilish smile as his bare chest was exposed now, his tattoos that crawled up over his flesh on full display. He knew damn well what effect he had on her when he gave her something to look at.

Layne scoffed but couldn't look away now that he was standing there half-naked. Damn him. She pressed her hands against the bed behind her. Her own body started to betray her as she felt desire pulsing between her thighs. "I'm not gonna stay here and be watched over like a prisoner."

Joey didn't respond. His hands moved down to the belt around his hips, yanking it open and slowly sliding it out from the loops of his pants. He proceeded to fold the leather belt in thirds, licking his lips as he kept his gaze on her.

Layne's heart began pumping blood a little harder, distracting her from her original intent to leave. Damn her insatiable hormones, they were getting out of control.

"You know what, Layney? You're right." Both of his hands wrapped around the leather belt in front of him.

Was this a trap? Did he really just say she was right?

He approached the bed slowly, continuing, "maybe you're not going to stay here, but you are going to have to make a choice."

"And what choice is that?" Her tongue licked over her lips that suddenly felt dry as her eyes settled on the way he held the belt in his hands.

Joey tossed the belt onto the bed next to her. "Whether or not you can live with walking out that door."

Her eyes softened as she mulled over what he had to say. Joey's hands suddenly took hold of her legs and pulled her so her ass came right to the edge of the bed. He stood there in front of her, the front of his pants eye level with her.

"You either stay and accept that you're mine, and I *always* fight for what belongs to me, or you can walk out that door. If you walk out that door, then this," he unbuttoned his pants as he spoke, "is over. Your choice, Layne."

Her eyes looked up at Joey while he stared down at her, waiting for her to make up her mind. Her brain was telling her to walk out that door if she ever wanted to live life the way she had before he interjected himself into it. Every other part of her was screaming to live in the moment and damn the consequences.

"Nothing good can come of this." And she was likely right whether he wanted to admit to it or not. Layne stood up from the edge of his bed, her body brushing up against his. It was a struggle to resist wanting to lay her hands on him, even just for a split second. Catching herself about to do it anyway, she closed her hands into small fists and shook her head.

"We were *never* supposed to get to this point, Joey." All the unspoken apologies were evident in her eyes. Her lips pressed together firmly to avoid spilling out words that would only convince herself to stay.

She walked away from him and made her way towards the exit of the bedroom. Looking back at him would be a huge mistake if she wanted to get further than fifteen steps past the threshold.

Joey kept his eyes on her, keeping a straight face while Layne seemingly made her decision. He didn't make any effort to keep her there.

She placed a hand on the doorframe while pausing her footsteps and did exactly what she told herself not to, she looked back at him.

Cursing under her breath, she couldn't bring herself to walk away from him, no matter what his faults were. Despite the consequences of both of their lives colliding with one another, she tossed it all out the damn window.

She ran back to him, throwing herself at him with her arms wrapping around his neck as she ferally kissed him. There was no hesitation from Joey, he welcomed her mouth as his arms pulled her in against him possessively.

He walked her back until she felt the dresser knobs pressed against her back. Breathlessly she devoured the taste of his mouth. His hands impatiently pulled her shirt up over her head, tossing it off to the side.

"That's my girl." He grinned between feverish kisses as she made her choice to stay. His hands shoved her pants down, taking her panties down with them. "Now, you're gonna show me how much you want to stay."

Her hands unclasped her bra with a single flick of her fingers, letting it slip down her arms and drop to the floor. She smiled as her hands grabbed the waist of his pants, yanking his hips forward closer to her. "In that case, you better be prepared for a long night."

Her full lips were already slightly swollen from the aggressive kisses, and now they were taking a tour of the designs inked over the flesh of his shoulder and down onto his chest. Layne's hands made quick work of his pants while her mouth took things nice and slow.

She lowered herself down in front of him while her lips drifted further south on his body. Her fingers played with the waistline of his underwear, and just as she laid one more kiss on his lower stomach right where the thin line of hair began to lead down into his boxer briefs, she rose back up with a look of hunger in her eyes. Layne playfully pushed him back, until she got Joey onto his back on the bed. She stripped him of the last piece of clothing between the two of them.

Layne crawled onto the bed, sliding her bare body against his. The hardness of his erection pressed against her lower belly.

"You're so fuckin' beautiful, even when you're a pain in my ass." He stared at her in awe that he had her all to himself. Joey's hands tangled themselves into her hair, pulling her up to capture her lips with his. The slickness of the lips between her hips teasingly brushed against his cock, eliciting an excited groan from him.

Pulling back from him just enough to keep their mouths lightly caressing one another as she spoke. "You sure that you're willing to put up with me?"

"Only if you're going to be a good girl for me." The sparkle in his eyes made her all the promises in the world, and she was going to believe in all of them.

Layne smirked as she whispered into his ear. "You mean, like this?" She guided her body down onto his cock, feeling him sink deep into her hot and ready pussy. He moaned, his hands leaving her hair and firmly grabbing her hips.

Sitting up on him with her body capturing exactly what it was craving, she drove her body against him, riding the length of his shaft with slow and purposeful movements. Layne moaned at the sensation of him stroking her from the inside. Joey growled as he allowed her to set the pace. "I want to see how hard you can ride my cock. Show me how much of a good girl you are, Layney."

"Oh, I'm not going to be your good girl tonight." The look in her eyes held a sinful motive. It captured his attention, especially when she paused the rolling of her hips against him.

"In fact," her hands ran up the series of muscles flexing on his stomach, "I'm going to be a very, *very* bad girl." She could feel his hips pressing up into her and the grip of his hands on her hips trying to get back what she had stopped a few seconds ago.

"Mmm, you know what happens when you're not good for me." He looked up at her, his breathing on edge in anticipation of her next move. Of course, Layne smiled knowingly at exactly what she was doing to him.

As she took up her rhythm again, taking him into her repeatedly, she reached down to where they were connected. Her fingers found her clit, stroking it, causing herself to increase the already intense pleasure she was feeling. Her body squeezed around him even tighter as she circled her sensitive bud. Joey's eyes were saturated with desire as he watched Layne touch herself and make those moans of excitement.

Unable to hold back any further, he flipped them over so he was now in control over her. "You still want to be a bad girl?" He gave a hard pound of his throbbing member into her to make sure he captured her attention.

She pushed her hips up against him to feel him as deep in her as she could, a bratty smile dancing across her lips. "You're just mad that I was in charge, and you actually enjoyed it."

He gave a hard nip to the side of her neck before licking the red mark he left on her skin. "Oh, Layney, you have never been the one in charge."

He wasn't wrong, they both knew it, and it scared the crap out of her that she was losing herself within the chaos they had created for themselves.

CHAPTER TWENTY-FOUR

Things with the car bomb had gotten far too close for comfort for both Layne and Joey. While it had been a run-of-the-mill scare tactic last night, it was doubtful that the next time they would be so lucky.

Hearing rummaging, Layne rolled over in bed, all tangled up in the sheets. She saw Joey leaning over a large trunk on the other side of the bedroom. He was wearing nothing but a pair of grey boxer briefs that clung over his firm ass providing quite a sight to wake up to. The muscles in his back flexed as he moved objects around inside the trunk.

"What are you doing?" Still trying to shake off the slumber from her voice.

He straightened up and looked over at her, immediately smiling. "I didn't expect you to be up for another couple of hours after last night." Joey came to the bed, crawling across it to greet her with a kiss that felt criminal for this early in the morning.

Her hand ran over the thick stubble on his face as she matched the intensity of his lips working over hers. The fresh scent of soap was clear on his skin indicating he had already taken a shower while she had been catching up on beauty rest. Last night's activities had left her requiring a little extra time to recover. The soreness was already setting in reminding her of each deliciously intense moment they had shared.

When they both came back for air, she sank back into bed with a satisfied smile and a sparkle in her eyes. "You still haven't told me what you were doing."

"Checking my stock in case I need to do some shopping." He got off the bed and retrieved a tee and jeans from his dresser drawer. Layne was mildly disappointed as he pulled the shirt down over his upper body, covering up many of the tattoos she enjoyed memorizing line by line. His jeans and boots were quick to follow as he expanded on his initial response. "I'm going to have to take care of a few things later on tonight."

She frowned. "What do you mean take care of a few things?" Layne had grown adept at reading people, and Joey was no exception.

"Don't worry about it." He pulled his jacket off the hook on the back of the closet door.

Immediately, she tossed the sheets off herself and got out of bed. "Try again." She pulled on some clothes that she tracked down off the floor. Arguing with him while she was naked was about as effective as baking a cake in the bathtub.

He slid his arms into his jacket, still avoiding her question. "I have to go run a few errands, that's it."

She walked right up to him, her finger firmly poked him in the chest. "No, you're not telling me something."

He placed his hands on her arms, kissing her on her forehead to placate her. "I can't sit back anymore and risk that Franzetti is going to slither through the cracks like the snake he is. You and I both know that this entire shitshow needs to come to an end."

"And you were just going to leave me out of the loop, is that it?" She didn't even bother hiding the irritation behind her words.

"That's always been the plan, Layne. Your dad doesn't want you involved, and I don't want you involved. End of story."

He was being so calm about this, and it was only making Layne more irritable. "So, a bunch of alpha-minded men are trying to tell me what I can or can't do?"

He sighed seeing this go down an unproductive path. "You know that's not the case. Look, I know you can stand on your own two feet - I have never doubted that. Shit, I've been on the receiving end of your right hook. This has to be different though. I can't risk you being a distraction or liability and I sure as hell won't put you through the pain and suffering if things go poorly."

"You mean, if you fail and Franzetti sends you six feet under?" Her heart ached even imagining the dark hole of emotions she would go through if that were to happen.

If he was worried about that possibility, he didn't show it. "It's always a risk in what I do."

Her hands held onto his forearms, feeling the muscles flex underneath his skin. "I'm a big girl, why don't you just let me worry about my own sensibilities, hm?"

He moved his hands up to cup her face as he locked his sight on her nearly staring straight into her soul. "No." Then, he released her and grabbed his keys off the top of his dresser. "But if you want to come with me to get coffee and a bagel I won't stop you."

He didn't want to let her out of his sight, but now the tables were turning, and she wasn't going to let him out of hers. So, breakfast and caffeine it was.

It wasn't a difficult choice though, as there was just something about a freshly made bagel piled with an over-easy egg, grease-soaked bacon, and cheese that could lift Layne's mood. Joey took her to a mom-and-pop bagel shop for that delicious breakfast and a strong cup of coffee. But she never let his words leave the back of her mind.

Knowing damn well he had some dark intentions looming on the horizon, she had intentionally glued herself to his side all day long.

His arm was wrapped around her there on her sofa while she snuggled up against his side with the television on watching the New York Rangers get their asses handed to them by the Philadelphia Flyers. Things were looking ugly being down 3-0 before the end of the first period.

Joey's phone buzzed, and he took one glance at the message before lifting his arm off her. "I have to go make a phone call." He got up off the couch and began to dial a number on his phone as he left the room.

Layne sat there a few minutes before she straightened up in her seat, straining to hear his voice but she heard nothing at all, not even the pacing of his footsteps.

"Joey?" She got up off the couch and looked into the hallway, finding it empty. Layne walked to her front door, looking out the window only to see his car no longer parked in his typical spot in front of her house.

"Shit!" She ran back into the living room, rushing to jam her feet into the shoes she had left in front of the couch. Layne was hellbent on not being left behind just because everyone thought she needed an excessive level of protection.

When she went to her purse she dug around for the keys to her now only remaining vehicle, each second she didn't find them in the small bag, the more she panicked. Quickly, she realized that he had taken her damn car keys. "For fucks sake!" She hustled into the kitchen to grab her spare set.

Layne grabbed a few more necessities, unsure of what was going to await them and she wanted to be prepared. Once she sat in the driver's seat of her silver Beamer, she ran down the mental list of possibilities of where he was going.

"Think, Layne, think." She had zero care about the aesthetics of holding a conversation with herself out loud as she began narrowing down the most likely locations he would be at. Mentally preparing a preliminary list of spots, she pulled out of her garage speeding down the street.

She attempted several calls to him without any answer. Layne analyzed everything they had ever discussed about the way he ran his operations, Franzetti's patterns, and any minor detail about his vague commentary on how he was going to make his move when the time came. Joey had been careful with the details he shared with her, but not careful enough that she didn't have some guesses on his next moves.

The only question was if she was going to track him down before he took away her chance to serve up her sweet revenge.

CHAPTER TWENTY-FIVE

Things were coming full circle, and Joey decided it would be perfect justice that Franzetti would meet his end down at the very docks where Layne was supposed to meet her fate at Joey's hands. The shoddy building where he had briefly held her captive all those months ago was still situated across the gravel lot.

Thanks to some friendly flies on a wall, he had been able to intercept Franzetti during a small window of opportunity as he was leaving his mistress's home.

Masked up, Joey loomed over Franzetti while a dark and sinister shadow reflected in his eyes. Michael arrogantly held his head up high while he was forced down onto his knees there on the wooden boards at the end of the very same dock Layne should have been pitched off if Joey had done what Franzetti had hired him to do. It was nothing but them and the sound of the water lightly slapping against the supportive pilings of the dock.

"Your time's up, Mike." Joey's head was already in the grim mind space where he was able to calmly focus on the process of taking someone's life.

The sound of a car door slamming shut in the distance and a small pair of feet pounding against the gravel neared them both. The hell if Layne was going to allow Joey to do this without her there. She had every right to witness the end of this particular chapter of her life. It was going to be her own personal version of therapy.

After trying a few other locations, she had concluded this was the next logical spot to check. Fortune was shining upon her as it seemed she arrived in the nick of time.

Not removing his eyes from the man kneeling before him, Joey sternly spoke to her, "I told you I didn't want you here."

"And I told you…I wasn't going to listen." Her chest rose and fell from the quick sprint across the large lot from where her car was parked.

She took in the sight of Franzetti kneeling there, hands secured behind his back. It appeared Joey had already repaid a few debts to him from the fresh swelling around his eyes and the busted lip.

Franzetti laughed as he saw the two of them standing before him. "What a joke - the two of you. The stone-cold killer turned weak by an uptown bitch who doesn't know her place. Have you even told her? Does she know about your deepest, darkest secret?"

Layne's brows furrowed as confusion settled in as to what type of deep dark secret Michael was referring to. Joey had confessed to his lifetime of crime, and not once had she ever judged him for that. In return, Joey had never judged her for her own lifetime of sins.

A delighted grin popped across Franzetti's face. "She doesn't know, does she?"

Joey's hand grasped a handful of Michael's greasy dark hair, shoving the barrel of the pistol against Franzetti's temple. "Shut the fuck up, you sorry excuse for a human being!" His words seethed with anger.

Layne's fingers wrapped around Joey's arm to give him pause. "Wait! Stop!" She glared down at the man who had brought so much pain and mayhem into her life. If anyone was going to have the chance to eliminate him, she wanted to be the one to do it if she was ever going to sleep at night.

"Don't listen to him, Layne, he's trying to buy time I'm not going to give him." Joey cautioned her, but she ignored his warning.

Her hand remained on his arm which was flexed tight with tension. She wanted to try and make sure that Joey didn't pull the trigger. "No, I want him to think that whatever he says is going to make a difference."

Not even flinching, Franzetti continued to casually speak like his life wasn't about to end within minutes. "I've known Joseph here for a long while. The first job he ever did for me was a doozy. When was it? About fifteen years ago?"

Michael kept his eyes on Layne's face, ready to soak in her reaction as he continued to share the bombshell. "I couldn't risk one of my own men placing the explosive on your mother's car. I needed someone without any known ties to me. I needed someone just like Joseph here. He did such a good job, too. Don't you think?"

The world began spinning around her as she tried to reconcile what Franzetti said. Her hand fell from Joey's arm as she backed up a few steps, staring at the man who had promised her everything. The very same man she had been willing to risk her life, job, reputation, and heart for.

"Layne..." Joey's words to even begin explaining himself were lost. He glanced over at her, regret flooding his face.

Her chest grew heavy while her chin quivered as the vivid imagery of her mother's last moments flashed through her mind. Layne's green eyes —her mother's eyes—began to blur with a well of tears. The tears were packed full of anger, betrayal, pain, and sadness. Her heart was being squeezed by a vise until it released into an eruption of rage.

Her hand pulled her firearm from its holster underneath her jacket and without a second thought, she fired a chain of rounds.

Bang, bang, bang, bang, bang, bang. Click. Click. Click.

The entire contents of the clip were emptied, and even then, her finger still squeezed the trigger several more times.

All the bullets formed a cluster in the center of Franzetti's chest. His body jolted and jerked with each impact until lifelessness overcame him and his corpse slumped onto the boards. The scent of gunpowder, singed flesh, and blood tainted the night air.

There was a moment where Joey thought that she might have shot him as well, and he would have deserved it. He moved slowly, sliding his pistol into his thigh holster, not wanting to make any sudden movements that might startle Layne.

His hand pulled down the front of his mask, exposing his face to her. He placed one boot in front of the other towards her, keeping his palms open and in front of him. The last thing he wanted to do was come off as anything other than harmless.

Her arm was still extended out towards Franzetti's body with her baby Glock still tightly grasped in her hand, but steady it was not. Her entire body shivered from the adrenaline wracking through each of her muscles. Now, tears were freely flowing from her eyes, and when she finally noticed Joey making a slow approach.

"Why?!" Her voice screamed out with all the pain of unanswered questions. Her dominant arm lowered under the weight of the hunk of metal. "WHY?!" She repeated herself, simultaneously hurling the Glock right past him into the water of the depths of the Hudson behind him.

He flinched as the weapon was cast in his direction and barely wooshed past his head. "Layne, please, let's just talk about this." His words were calm and slow as he attempted to de-escalate the situation. Another step forward was taken.

"I don't want to talk about this! I want to know why!" She ran her fingers through her hair, as the tears burned her cheeks leaving a trail of red behind them. Layne closed the last few feet of distance. Her hands harshly shoved him back. "Were you ever going to tell me? Huh?!"

Joey let her create some space when she shoved him, but he didn't let it stay that way. "Was I going to tell you? No, because I knew you'd go fully unhinged before I could explain shit."

She half laughed through the tears in her voice. "Unhinged? That's putting it nicely. She was my *mother*! She was the one beacon of light and love in my life, and you robbed me of her!"

Layne lunged at him. Her fists swung wildly without any mental clarity to support a thoughtful or well-executed attack. The only thing that fueled her right now was erratic emotions.

Easily avoiding any blows, Joey grabbed her wrists stabilizing them. Layne dug her feet into the ground but unsuccessfully planted herself there. Her arms yanked back from his grasp but found herself unable to overcome his strength.

"Layney, I'm so sorry. If I could go back and change things, I would. If I could have seen you coming into my life, then I wouldn't hesitate to fix things. I can solve a lot of things, but going back in time isn't on the table here."

"Fuck your apology!" She flung her weight down to try and free herself from his restraint. He lowered himself down with her until they were both sitting on the ground. He tugged her into his chest and wrapped his arms around her in hopes that he could chase away the agony she was experiencing.

Squirming against him, she let out a scream against his chest that broke down into heavy sobs. Joey's chin rested on top of her head, his hands soothingly rubbing up and down her spine as she let out all her pain. It wasn't only the pain of knowing his past had violently collided with hers, but it was the pain that couldn't be healed even after taking Franzetti's life for his wrongdoings.

When the tears had slowed, and her sobs had quieted, Joey pulled her away from him slightly and looked down into the bloodshot eyes. "We can't stay here much longer. I need to clean things up. Go wait for me in my car, and I will take you home. I don't want you driving like this. Okay?"

All the emotions left her feeling drained and numb. Layne's face was blotchy from all the tears that had been shed, and her eyes were swollen from crying herself dry. She wanted to argue with him, but she didn't have it left in her, so she simply nodded.

While she went and sat in the passenger seat of the Challenger, Joey took care of the gory task of dumping the heaping corpse off into the churning waters of the river. Shell casings were collected. All evidence of what had transpired was erased.

Meanwhile, Layne sat there studying the mundane-looking dashboard as she tried not to think about the painful truths she had learned tonight. Insult to injury, Franzetti's death didn't even soothe her soul as she had hoped it would.

The driver's side door opened, and she looked over at Joey as he slid into the leather seat. "We should be good to go."

"Thanks." Her voice was quieter than a mouse.

The engine churned to life, and they left the dock behind them. During the ride home, the silence was beyond uncomfortable, yet she didn't care. What was she supposed to say to him? Layne looked out her window, taking in the scenery of passing by various buildings, parked cars, and pedestrians still walking about on the sidewalks and living their dull little lives.

The silence allowed her to begin rebuilding the wall inside of her that Joey had started disassembling from the first moment he had laid his eyes on her. He had effectively begun making a path inside of her heart to allow her to open up. Layne realized that it was her mistake in allowing him to do that.

CHAPTER TWENTY-SIX

Though not his typical parking spot, Joey pulled into the parking garage underneath his apartment building and found a space not far from the elevator.

After the engine quieted, he immediately got out of the car and opened her door for her. "Let's get you inside."

Finally paying attention to their location instead of escaping inside her head, she found herself not where she had expected to be. "You said you were taking me home."

"I will, but I'm not driving all the way uptown tonight. Besides, you look like you're ready to keel over." Was part of his reasoning selfish? Perhaps, but he still felt compelled to ensure her safety even if she currently wanted nothing to do with him.

He escorted her inside, and when she was in the comfort of his unit, she drew in a cleansing breath, trying to feel more at ease. Her body wanted nothing more than to render into relaxation mode, or perhaps a coma.

Joey stood by the front door, hands tucked into his pockets. "A bath will help."

She ignored his advice. "I'm just going to get some sleep on the couch." Her words were heavy with fatigue.

He shook his head. "Not happening. I'm not leaving you to your own devices."

"I'm not in a mood to argue, Joey. Just go into your damn room and leave me alone." She rubbed her hands over her face trying to push away the exhaustion and combined frustration. Yet, he remained right where he was standing without any indication that he was willing to budge.

She looked up at the heavens, at her wits end that he was being his typical stubborn self.

Giving up this particular battle after deciding it wasn't worthwhile, she tiredly looked at him. "Then, make yourself useful and get a bottle of booze." She left to see her way to his master bath, where she began drawing the steamy water for a soak.

Morbidly, she gave a quiet chuckle to herself. Here she was about to take a bath in the same tub that Michael Franzetti had tried to drown her in on the very night she blew him away down at the docks.

While the tub filled, she tossed in a selection of scented salts and aromatherapy bubbles she had stocked Joey's bathroom with over the past couple of months.

Her clothes fell to the cold tile floor piece after piece. Gradually, Layne lowered herself into the heat of the bathwater until she was submerged up to her shoulders.

Leaning her head back against the edge of the tub, she closed her eyes and tried to clear her mind of everything except the sensation of her muscles relaxing in response to the warmth surrounding her.

Joey appeared in the doorway, a bottle of Sagamore Rye in one hand and two glasses in the other. She cracked open one eye when she felt his presence and peeped over at him before closing her eye again. "I don't need a glass."

He used his foot to nudge a bamboo stool over to the edge of the tub and took a seat on it. Cracking open the bottle, he filled the two glasses. One was handed over to her.

She opened both eyes, and her soapy hand took the glass. "How long are you going to stay in here?"

"As long as it takes." Sincerity and honesty wrapped around his response.

"For what?" Her eyes got lost in looking at the amber liquid sitting still in the glass.

Joey hadn't touched his beverage yet, focusing all of his attention on her. "To know you will be okay."

Layne scoffed lightly. "You might be waiting a hell of a long time."

A small smile tugged at the corners of his mouth. "I know, but you're worth it."

She gulped the stiff liquid to try and squash down how those words made her feel. Fortunately, he didn't press her for small talk while she took some downtime for herself.

With the heat surrounding her in the tub, and the warmth of the rye inside of her, she finally felt a state of nothingness overcoming her. Her brain wasn't yapping in her ear, and her heart wasn't trying to fill her soul with sunshine and rainbows.

As for Joey, he just sat there on the stool next to her while indulging in the occasional sip from his drink.

When her beverage was gone, she handed him the empty glass. "Could you hand me that towel over there?"

Setting her glass on the counter next to the sink, Joey fetched the towel and handed it to her. Without asking, he gave her privacy and exited into the bedroom.

After drying herself off, she brushed her hair out, looking at herself in the mirror as she did so. She could still see the evidence of her emotional outburst all over her face, especially in her eyes. Layne wrapped the towel around her body, securing it in place before she came into his adjoining bedroom.

Joey wasn't anywhere to be seen, but on the bed laid out for her were a pair of royal blue silk pajama shorts and the matching camisole she kept here for overnight stays.

A few minutes later, she emerged from the bedroom in her pajamas to see Joey standing there in the hallway, leaning back against a wall as he scrolled through some messages on his phone. "Where are you planning on spending the night?"

He looked up to see her appear in the hallway, smiling as he admired how stunning she looked even after a hell of a night for both of them. "Where do you want me to?" There were no expectations set in his voice.

She was silent, unsure of what she wanted from him. Seeing her uncertainty, he approached and set his hands on the soft bare skin of her shoulders.

"Go get into bed." He nudged her back towards his room, encouraging her to do as he said. Layne trudged back to the bedroom, glancing back over her shoulder to see if he was following her.

Joey indeed followed, watching as she climbed into bed laying down in the middle with the sheet pulled up to her waist. He stopped at the edge of the mattress, tugged a blanket up over the sheet, and tucked it in around her.

Then, he joined her. Laying on top of the blanket, on his side facing her, he brushed a few rogue strands of her hair away from her face. "Try to get some sleep. I will be right here in the morning."

She looked up at him with eyes full of all her vulnerabilities. "I'm sorry."

Her apology took him by surprise. "For what?"

"That I lost my shit tonight." Layne frowned, hating that she let her emotions get the best of her. She was used to being more level-headed than that. Maybe Mick was right. Maybe Joey was responsible for clouding her thoughts and judgment.

He shook his head, a hand cupping the side of her face. "Shh, you don't have to apologize for being you, Layne. Never apologize for that. I signed up for this, and that includes you flying off the handle. It includes you being stubborn as fuck. But it also includes all the benefits of seeing the way you look at me when you think I won't notice, the way your nose has a cute little wrinkle when you laugh, and the way your voice sounds when you say my name."

Layne's lower lip quivered slightly as his words sank right down into her heart, past the partially crumbled emotional wall she had tried to reconstruct inside of her.

"Come here." He pulled her into him as he rolled onto his back, leaving an arm around her.

She curled up into his embrace, resting her head on his chest where she could listen to the sound of his heart steadily beating. Layne's eyes fluttered closed and allowed the rhythm of his breathing and the warmth of his body to lull her into a much needed deep slumber.

Unsure of how many hours of sleep she had gotten, she lay there in Joey's bed, staring up at the ceiling cast in the amber light from the street lamp right outside.

The sounds of car horns, emergency vehicles, and hollering from folks leaving the bar could all be heard despite the window being shut. It truly was the city that never slept, and tonight Layne wasn't getting much more sleep.

Her brain wouldn't shut off. It was processing all the scenarios of how all of this could go wrong, all the things she would need to address, who was going to cause problems, and an entire slew of other hypotheticals. Sure, some of these thoughts were warranted, but there was a large chunk that was turned into mountains from molehills - if the molehills even existed in the first place.

The top sheet was still draped over the top of her body, providing just enough comfort from the light air movement from the ceiling fan above the bed. She looked over at the clock on the night table next to her, nearly four in the morning. Joey was lying next to her on his back, his body sprawled out comfortably with an arm tucked underneath his pillow.

He must have gotten undressed after she had initially fallen asleep, as he was now in nothing but his boxer briefs. The sheet was just barely covering his hips. Staring at him, he looked so at ease while he slept.

Admiring his body, it brought her a fleeting moment of reprieve from her harrowing thoughts, but only for them to come barreling back into her mind with a vengeance when she thought about all the challenges he would also face for everything that had transpired to this point. Reality is such a bitch.

She may have pulled the trigger on Franzetti, but Joey would be guilty by association if the rest of the Franzetti clan found out. He had cleaned up her mess. Then, there was the concern that her father would lose his shit if he found out that Joey had been screwing his little girl when he should have been focused on the job.

The real kicker was if it ever came out that Joey had been responsible for installing the explosive device that took the life of her mother. It didn't matter if Franzetti had ordered the hit, it was Joey who executed it. It seemed that she was setting herself up for a life full of pain if she let this continue.

Cringing at the worst-case scenarios, she finally lifted the sheet off her body, moving slowly to not wake him. Layne felt certain she couldn't do this. She would get hurt. He would get hurt. It was all inevitable.

There was no way she could face her deepest feelings, and she couldn't risk things going to hell in a handbasket. She sure as fuck couldn't handle her feelings getting shattered if things did go poorly.

Gathering her clothes that were neatly folded on a chair near the window, Layne stealthily changed from her pajamas into what she had worn that night.

Once she was in Joey's living room, she found a scratchpad and pen.

Tearing off a piece of paper, she quickly wrote a message on it. Her eyes stung with unshed tears as she imagined how badly he would take this.

Thanks for being my best fling yet. Let's make a clean break while we can. ~ Layne

The tip of the pen hovered over the paper after signing the 'e' in her name, catching herself before she added a 'y' to the end. Abandoning the pen on the paper, she decided the note said all it needed to. Short and sweet.

Layne reminded herself that he wasn't the knight in shining armor, he had said so himself. It still didn't take the ache away from writing off their time together as a meaningless affair.

Leaving his apartment there on the seventh floor of the building felt like trying to pull away from gravity itself. She wiped her fingers underneath her eyes to catch any tears before they fell. Too many tears had already been shed. She scolded herself for being such a little bitch about all of this.

Suck it up, buttercup. There were plenty of other men out there that weren't nearly as much trouble as he was. A polo-wearing country club type from the Hamptons would be more acceptable, she tried to convince herself. Her leaving things where they were was easier on everybody and quieted the overwhelming thoughts and feelings deep inside of her.

She stepped into the elevator, allowing the doors to seal her decision to end this thing that Joey and her had going on between them.

CHAPTER TWENTY-SEVEN

The next week had been the most difficult for Layne. After the first twenty missed calls and nearly a hundred text messages, she outright blocked his number without so much as giving him any responses.

She should have expected that he would be so persistent despite her note to him, but she naively hoped otherwise for her own sanity. He had gone so far as to show up at her house several times from what she could tell from her security cameras, but she had been spending her time anywhere else except her own residence. Primarily, Layne had been at O'Reilly Manor pretending to sink her free time into work and also where it would be a death mission if Joey tried to show up here.

As far as her father was concerned, the job he had hired Joey for was complete and no one had seen Franzetti. People disappearing unexpectedly in this line of business typically only meant one grim conclusion. Scott wired the balance owed to Joey to the previously communicated offshore account.

The second week after breaking things off, things began to calm down, and by a month later she was considering trying to resume a normal existence again.

Sitting in the cozy reading nook by the third-floor window inside of her old bedroom, she heard her phone ding. When she took a look at the screen, it was a text from Rebecca.

Her best friend was the only person she had confided in, and even then, she only gave the bare-bones version of what happened. Layne had framed it as she determined Joey was bad news with a horrific past and she ended up cutting things off.

REBECCA

Where have you been?

FYI, being a recluse isn't healthy.

LAYNE

It's called soul-searching thank you very much.

REBECCA

Bullshit.

LAYNE

That's your opinion.

REBECCA

That's my statement of fact.

Let's go out tonight. Girl's night only. Eat too much food, drink too much, and dance our asses off somewhere. It would be good for the soul.

Layne cracked an ever so slight smile at the memory of their last girl's night out that had involved hitting up a club. They indeed ate too much, drank too much, and had an embarrassingly good time.

She hated to admit it, but Rebecca likely had a point here. Girl's nights weren't about going out on a hunt for men, but as Rebecca put it: it was good for the soul.

LAYNE

I hate you.

REBECCA

I know. I will meet you at six tonight by the Broadway-Lafayette Station.

Calling it a done deal, Layne sighed out loud knowing that it was time to shake it all off.

That night she met Rebecca right on the corner of Crosby and Houston Streets outside of the subway station. The first order of business was

Rebecca dragging Layne to her latest restaurant find. The menu had been all Asian inspired with a twist in the cooking method.

Layne had been hesitant at first, but once again Rebecca didn't lead her astray and the food had been phenomenal. She wasn't much of a foodie, but in New York, there were so many restaurants competing for business it created a demand for each establishment to up its A-game.

During dinner, the two caught up on life. Layne fielded the hard and heavy questions about this tumultuous relationship with Joey. As for Rebecca, she had recently gotten news that the family she nannied for was adding to their clan which meant a pay bump.

After dinner, it was a few blocks down to some club Layne hadn't ever visited before. It was unassuming on the outside, in fact, she probably would have walked right by if Rebecca hadn't said something.

Once they were inside, they were led down a dark hallway and a small flight of stairs before the hall opened up to a large open space, reminiscent of an industrial factory. The music was upbeat with the bass booming loud enough to feel it in your bones.

It was packed with people all looking to either grab drinks at the over-crowded bar or move their bodies in the centralized dance space. Along the perimeter of the room were private booths designated for VIPs with table service. If Layne had known ahead of time, she would have snagged a table for them. It's not like she didn't have money to burn.

As if reading her thoughts, Rebecca leaned in to shout over the thumping of the music. "We don't need a table! We are going to dance all night and have a damn good time!"

Rebecca grabbed Layne's hand and began weaving through the sea of folks towards the bar barely visible by all the people surrounding it. Thankfully, Layne's red heels were sturdy enough to handle the sudden changes in direction wherever an opening appeared between other patrons to squeeze through.

Leave it to her bestie when they got to the bar to bat her eyelashes and lean forward to flaunt the eye candy on her chest as a means of capturing the male bartender's attention. A few minutes later they both had a freshly made cocktail. After taking a sip, Layne knew there were at least two varieties of booze in it, but which ones were difficult to decipher from the mixer masking the taste of the alcohol making it easy going down.

After the first drink worked its magic, Layne was starting to feel more relaxed and starting to realize how much she needed this night out.

"You were right!" Layne shouted over the club-mixed pop tunes playing.

"Of course, I was!" Rebecca gave a massive smile as she continued moving her body to the beat of the music.

With all the people packed in the club putting off a metric ton of body heat, Layne was suddenly glad she had opted for a simple black dress with spaghetti straps. It hugged each curve of her fit figure, over the swell of her ass, and stopped shortly thereafter.

Her hair was down and free to fall over her shoulders and midway down her back. In one hand, Layne held yet another cocktail, she had lost count by now how many she had indulged in. She didn't come here to think about anything, including keeping count of beverages.

It didn't take long before they were both joined by the occasional guy looking to get in on a dance with them. Rebecca with her warm blonde hair and baby blues easily roped in attention. It wasn't to say that Layne didn't attract her own male fans, but she was used to keeping up a front that made her less approachable.

A younger guy came up to her, taking Layne's flash of a sweet smile as an invitation. He looked barely out of college, hardly five-eight, slim but not muscular, and had the whole clean-cut baby face thing going on. He wasn't her type, but that wasn't the point of going out tonight, now was it? She was here to forget all about her go-to type of man.

His hands settled on her hips as she moved them to the rhythm of the song that was currently on full blast. Gradually, the minimal space they had was fully eliminated when some drunk girl knocked into Layne, causing her to stumble forward right up against the guy's chest. "Oof!"

The buzz of the cocktails was kicking in full-time by this point, and she couldn't help but give off a giddy smile as she looked up into this guy's dull hazel eyes.

Once the song started to transition to the next, she looked around the guy's shoulder to see if she could lay eyes on Rebecca.

Not seeing her bestie, she leaned in a little closer to the guy so he could hear her. "I will be right back!" She patted his arm reassuringly before stepping away to navigate through the mobbed dance floor.

Layne considered texting her phone, but it was unlikely the shitty reception would allow it in here. What was likely was Rebecca was waiting in an insanely long line for the women's restroom, but she needed to make sure her friend was okay since she had gone off without saying anything. The only problem was she had no damn clue where the bathroom was in this place.

Layne finally shook her head. "Fuck this," and squeezed past a few more folks until she let herself into the VIP table area which was raised on a platform on the perimeter of the space. Her hands grabbed the railing designed to prevent the drunks from falling off the platform, and she leaned against it, straining to see across the crowd to see if she could spot the bathroom from here.

Some random girl at the table behind her stood up and tapped the back of Layne's shoulder. "Um, like, 'scuse me! Are you *supposed* to be up here?" The whiny voice matched what Layne saw when she turned her head back to answer the girl. She looked like she lived off seaweed and glitter, aggressive layers of makeup applied, and everything else that touched her body had a high-end designer label slapped on it.

"Piss off." Layne did not have time to deal with some nitwit thinking she could go on a power trip over a damn seating area.

The table right behind Layne where the girl had been seated was occupied by four other people. Two of the table occupants were nearly one entity by account of how close they were. The female was nearly mounted on the man's lap while heavily making out with him. She barely looked old enough to be legally allowed to drink. Her lengthy curls of black hair obscured the man's face all the while it looked like she was about to devour him whole.

The man's hands clutched the woman closer as she suggestively rubbed her body up against him. There was most definitely zero room for God between those two.

The other two individuals at the table were male and definitely out of their element in the club. They just looked stuffy and dressed like they were attending a business meeting instead of going out for a night full of debauchery.

"You can't be up here without a pass," the bratty voice interrupted Layne's observations.

Layne turned around to face the girl who looked like she would blow away with a strong gust of wind. "Oh? Gee, thanks. I will take that under consideration next time." Layne's words dripped with sarcasm.

You would have thought this chick would have gotten a clue that Layne didn't give a fuck and would have let it all go. But, no. She did not. She turned and looked at the two men who weren't engaged in the disgustingly aggressive display of affection, saying something to each of them.

While Layne couldn't hear over the loud lyrics of the music, she guessed it was something along the lines of 'She's being mean to me and I'm not getting my way, boo-hoo.' Layne shook her head in annoyance that anyone would be this territorial over the area around a damn table.

One of the men nudged the otherwise preoccupied man, not once but twice while relaying whatever was said to him by this broad. Finally, the preoccupied man peeled the woman off him enough to come up for air and investigate what was going on.

Layne had been ready to turn around and give up on locating the bathroom, but when she saw the man's face the second he pulled away from the maneater, Layne may as well have been knocked over the railing from the unsuspecting emotional assault.

How was it that Joey and she ended up at the same club in a city this big? It wasn't just her who was surprised by this, but it looked like he hadn't expected to see her here either. Oh, great.

Suddenly, the entire club felt incredibly tiny with the walls closing in on her. Layne's heart felt like shards of glass were stuck in it, and it took everything in her to not show any of this on her face. She had no right to be upset that he was moving on with some whore. That's right, now that girl was a whore who wasn't good enough for a guy Layne had ditched.

It wasn't clear when her feet started moving, but they did, and she just knew she needed to create distance between them. She rushed down the steps leading away from the VIP area down to where everybody else was gathered in the dance space.

Joey quickly shoved the girl off his lap as he slid out of the booth. "Layne, wait!"

She didn't even so much as look back behind her despite his call for her to hold up.

It might have been a few too many drinks that drove her brash reaction, but she eventually found the younger guy she had been dancing with a little bit ago. Like a good little Boy Scout, he had waited for her to return.

Layne snagged his hand, clutching onto it as she pulled him into the depths of the crowd on the dance floor. "Dance with me." The guy grinned, more than happy to oblige and yet so unsuspecting the motive behind her actions.

She pushed herself up against him, running her hands up the front of his torso and onto his chest while her body sensually moved to the rhythm of the music pulsing through the air. Layne spun around, pressing her ass right into his crotch and it was no surprise that this youngin' had a raging erection going on. She looked back over her shoulder at him with a smirk while she guided his hands down over her sides and the exposed flesh of her legs.

Joey hadn't given up on chasing her and was able to track her down even in this sea of people in a dark space with the strobe lights providing the only real means of lighting.

When he laid eyes on the guy dancing with Layne, his hands all over her, all he saw was red. Joey stepped up to them and gave a confrontational push to the guy. "Get your fuckin' hands off her!" He pulled Layne off to the side. "What the hell, Layne?"

"Don't touch me!" She shot him an icy glare.

The guy Joey shoved tried to intervene, "Look, man, she clearly doesn't want to talk to you." A-for-effort for the poor sap that was suddenly in the middle of this clusterfuck.

That sent Joey into a fury, he drew back and brutally punched the man in the face several times. Blood spattered from his mouth before he dropped to the ground, and now Joey's knuckles were smeared with the Boy Scout's blood.

Layne grabbed Joey by the arm and tugged with all her might. "Stop it! Jesus! What the hell is wrong with you?"

Joey turned to her. "You, Layne! You're what's wrong with me!" He was breathing heavily from the surge of anger that had just blown through his self-control.

She shook her head in disbelief that this was even happening. The two of them together were like absolute dynamite and C4 both going off in the same place at the same time.

"Leave me the hell alone!" She turned to leave the spot there on the dance floor that had attracted some attention to the guy who had gotten on Joey's bad side just by existing.

"No, you don't." He grabbed her wrist to prevent her from running off again.

Layne spun around, her hand flying and slapping him right across his face. Instantly, she regretted it. The hurt that washed over Joey's face showed that he hadn't expected it either, his hand dropped her wrist, so she was free to go.

She left and pushed through the crowd, even though it wasn't even clear which way the exit was. Her mind was too fuzzy to recall where they had entered. Pushing past a few groups of people close to the outskirts of the crowd, she finally got eyes on the exit and was hell-bent on making it there.

CHAPTER TWENTY-EIGHT

Once Layne was outside and the bite of the cold air hit her skin, she was feeling confident she had left Joey behind. Oh, how wrong she was.

He called her name again. "Layne, stop!"

Fuck. She quickly walked down the street as fast as the heels on her feet would allow. He repeated her name a few more times, getting nearer. Then, finally, he rushed around in front of her to stop her unless she wanted to run right into him.

"Dammit, you don't just get to run off like this again."

Layne tried to side-step him only to be blocked again. "You don't get to tell me what to do!"

Realizing that they were apt to draw even more attention to themselves standing out in the open, Joey maneuvered her a few feet back into the alley off to the side from the sidewalk.

His hands gently landed on her arms trying to persuade her to stay there with him. "You completely ghost me with nothing but a vague note full of bullshit, and you expect that I'm not gonna have something to say about it?"

Layne tapped into the only thing she had to work with as a defense - her temper. Her hands gave a firm shove to his chest to get him away from her. "It was never meant to be more than just a fling, take a fucking hint!"

He allowed her to shove him, but he soaked in the force and remained right where he was. Stepping forward, this time he firmly pressed her back up against a brick wall so she didn't have room to push him away. The front of his body connected with hers.

"That's the biggest bunch of cockshit I've ever heard. You and I were both on the same page, then you just took off. I get things got messy and complicated, but you could have grown a pair and given us a chance to talk it over and work through it. Just tell me what changed." His eyes pleaded for her to be straight with him, and potentially herself.

Layne squirmed while being pinned up against that wall, disliking where this conversation was heading. While she was capable of defending herself, there was little she could do when he was using his strength to overpower her and his words to disarm her.

"Get your hands off me. It's over! Get over it! Go fuck your date in the club!" Her heart was leaping inside of her chest being so close to him, making her frantic to either escape or cave into the lustful feelings she had shoved down inside of her weeks ago.

"I was trying, Layne. I tried to get over it, and you don't get to judge me for that! You didn't give me a choice!" He verbally lashed back at her. He brought both his hands up to her face, holding it affectionately as he peered into her green eyes full of hurt. His thumb stroked across her cheek.

Joey pressed his forehead to hers while the rest of his body kept her pressed up against the side of the building in the dark alley. "You know I don't ask questions twice, Layney," his words softer now. "What has you running scared?"

She licked her lips in an effort to distract herself from the ache in her heart that was prompting her eyes to betray how she felt. Big, fat, salty tears were welling up. The way he called her Layney felt like home and all she wanted to do was run home, not away from it.

Swallowing hard she shifted her eyes to glance away from him, "I'm not sca—"

Joey put a tattooed finger against her mouth to stop her mid-response. "Look at me when you say it." He dropped his finger down away from the softness of her lips.

Pressing her lips together in a hard line, she looked back at Joey's face which was intimately close to her own. The scent of his cologne full of sage and sweet leather contaminated the air around her. Her lower lip faltered and trembled involuntarily as she got lost in his eyes.

There was a long pause as time seemed to stop between them both.

When she finally spoke up, she couldn't say it any louder than a whisper. "Losing myself. Losing you." It was like sharing some deep dark secret she had never revealed to anyone else. Her biggest fear was giving all of herself to him only to have him torn away from her much like so many other times she had experienced in her life.

He took a moment to analyze her response before responding. "Never happening." Joey's mouth passionately claimed hers in a blindingly hot kiss.

It was then that Layne couldn't hold back anymore. She opened her mouth, welcoming his tongue to come intertwine with her own. Her hands went to the shirt he was wearing and slid up inside of it to feel the ripples of his abs straight up to the swell of his strong pec muscles on his chest. The familiar heat that he always made her feel between her legs was reignited with a demand to have every part of him.

He growled in excitement as Layne's hands made contact with his body, inciting him to claim her ass with his hands before dropping them down enough to lift her up. Joey forced her legs apart to wrap around his hips. The fabric of the dress gave away and rolled up to her waist, exposing the hot pink lace thong underneath.

His mouth pulled away from hers and moved down her neck towards the tops of her breasts on display above the daringly low neckline of her dress. His teeth bit into the fabric and tugged the dress down so her breasts popped free from their captivity. Joey's mouth took one of her stiff nipples hostage and assaulted it with his tongue.

She was already gasping for air as he worked over her nipples, his teeth nipping possessively at them. One of Layne's arms wrapped around the back of his neck for stability while the other dipped down between them to his belt. Her fingers unlatched it and yanked it open while she let out a light moan at the thought of what was already straining to get out of the front of his pants.

"My cock has been dying to fuck your sweet little pussy again, Layney. No amount of jerking off has helped how much the thought of you has had it aching." He gave another playful nip to the top of one of her breasts. His hand assisted in unbuttoning the top of his jeans and sliding the zipper down to allow his hardened length to spring out. "Are you going to scream for me like a good girl, hm?"

Layne now had both arms wrapped around his neck, one of her hands sliding up the back of his neck into the hair on the back of his head, gripping it hard. Her breathing grew more rapid out of eagerness.

She brought her mouth roughly back to his. Her teeth gave a bite and tug to his lower lip with a mischievous smile. "Only if you make me."

"Challenge accepted." His fingers pushed the thin strip of fabric away from her slick folds, and didn't hesitate to immediately sink his shaft into her. Layne gasped and then cried out in pleasure as she tilted her head back against the bricks behind her as her walls wrapped around him.

Joey let out a groan as he felt the tightness of her body welcoming him deep inside. Holding her up against the wall, he thrust his hips again this time with more force.

Layne's legs squeezed around his hips, moaning with each movement he made.

"That's right, Layney, you're doing such a good job of taking all of me. You're always so damn hot and ready for me to have you." He grunted as his pace began to pick up, letting feral instincts take over in pumping his cock in and out of her. There was no going easy after the high-strung emotions had played out between them. They both needed each other hard and fast.

After what felt like an eternity of them having been apart from one another, it was no surprise that an inferno of ecstasy was already intensifying at her core, nearly becoming unbearable. "Joey, yes, please. Don't stop!" It was becoming more and more challenging to get her words out now as all the lust and passion made her head delightfully light and foggy.

He possessively took her mouth with his once again out of need, like she was the last breath of fresh air on the planet. Afterward, his words were strained but demanding. "Beg me for it."

Her hips bucked against him, her body squirming as she neared the edge of absolute bliss. "Please." Her voice sounded so incredibly needy, even to her.

"Please, what?" He slowed his hips down to slow but intentional thrusts as he waited for her to respond.

"God, I want to cum all over you. Make me." Her body ached for him to push her over the edge while she locked her gaze on him.

"That's what I want to hear from my good girl," was all he said before he bucked his hips and pummeled himself back into her.

The tip of his length rammed into her at just the right spot deep inside her cunt over and over. Layne trembled and buried her face into the side of his neck as she gave out a long scream of absolute release.

Her warm arousal came all over his dick. As she climaxed, Joey grunted and shuddered as he unloaded deep inside of her as he found his own peak. His hands dug into her thighs hard as he cursed while yelling out fiercely. “Ugh, fuck!”

While her face was still buried up against the side of his neck, Layne’s body went limp around him as she tried to catch her frantic breaths.

Joey let out a sigh of contentment, lowering his lips to her throat and laying delicate little kisses on the skin there.

He whispered to her, “You will never lose me, and I will never let you lose yourself.”

CHAPTER TWENTY-NINE

Layne had been working on trying to not let her insecurities and fears get the better of her when it came to Joey. Hard discussions were constantly on the table, and Joey had been there to talk her down when she felt like the world was against them. She was a realist, and in both of their lines of work, neither one of them was guaranteed a happy ending.

He had been a saint, giving her all the space to be the hot mess that she was known to be. In a twisted way, things almost resembled a sense of normalcy of an average life - almost. Most weeks they saw each other three or four times depending on their schedules.

She still sure as hell wasn't about to broach the topic with her dad about her love life. He would have a coronary if he ever found out about Joey. Maybe someday she would raise it, but she was still trying to deal with one difficult step at a time while keeping her father in the dark.

Liam had been keeping his distance, burying himself in his work or a hooker - depending on the day. Layne considered that a win for everybody.

As far as anyone else knew, the skull-faced man who had been hired to eliminate Michael Franzetti from the playing board had moved on after the job was complete.

And today? Today was just another Tuesday, payday for the O'Reilly clan from all their clients.

Back at Slices of Heaven Pizzeria, the last stop on her collection route, Layne stood there counting a large sum of cash in her hands, "...forty-eight, forty-nine, five grand. I'm so proud of you, Kevin. You know how to count this week." She grinned at him as she tucked the wad of money into her bag. "If you keep this up, we may be able to start trusting you again."

Making quick work of this little check-in with Kevin to ensure he was keeping up with his payments to her family, she left to go back to her car. While sitting in the driver's seat, she texted Joey:

LAYNE

Working again tonight?

JOEY

Yeah, but it should be quick. In and out deal.

LAYNE

Good, because I have a job for you.

JOEY

If it involves burying my cock inside of you, I accept.

LAYNE

Show up by 9 or I'm starting without you.

JOEY

I'm never late.

A flurry of excitement settled deeply between her legs in anticipation of how this evening's plans were coming together. She dropped her phone into the cup holder of the center console and took off, heading uptown towards O'Reilly Manor to drop off the stack of cash in her possession from all the day's collections.

With an iced coffee in one hand and carrying a bag of cash in the other, she stepped inside her childhood home. Layne took another sip of the frigid brew, noting how unusually quiet it was inside the house. There was none of the typical hustle and bustle of workers coming and going and her father holding meeting after meeting.

She carried the bag upstairs into what was her old bedroom. She set her cup down on the Victorian-looking makeup vanity and entered the spacious walk-in closet where one of several safes in the house was located.

While spinning the dial on the safe she heard a voice break the silence. "I thought I heard someone come in."

Layne pulled open the safe's door after successfully unlocking it, she looked over and saw Mick standing there. "Hey." She smiled. "I was wondering where everybody was."

He stood there casually. "Your dad decided to take a trip up to Boston."

"Again? It's like the third time in the past two months." She glanced over at him with a perplexed look on her face that he had traveled north without saying a thing to her about it.

"Got me, you know how he is. No details until you need to know, and even then, it's the bare minimum." Mick shrugged, unbothered.

She unloaded the payments from the duffle into the safe one bundle at a time.

"Weekly collections go smoothly?" His hand motioned to all the money.

"Yeah. For once, everybody was on top of their shit." She grinned at him. Once the cold hard cash was all securely placed into the small vault, she locked things up.

Mick nodded. "That's good. We can't have people stepping out of line."

Layne approached the closet entrance where Mick's hulking form took up all the space. He stepped back, allowing her to get through the doorway back into the frilly pink bedroom.

Mere moments after passing him, she felt an iron grip yank her back by her shoulders and fling her into the wall roughly. Her body made contact with the unforgiving surface, and the force had her stumbling off to the side, her hands catching herself on a dresser.

Stunned, she looked over at Mick who had a look in his eyes she had never seen in all the years she knew him. She had heard stories of him from years ago, that he had been a violent and nearly psychotic force to be reckoned with, but she had never witnessed it first-hand. All she had ever known was the honorary uncle who had been full of nothing but support for her. "Mick, what the fuck?"

"Oh, Layne, you stupid little bitch." He stepped toward her, his words having disarmed her temporarily, she was slow to react when he grabbed for her. Barely ducking under his arm, she made a run for the door.

He was hot on her heels, and his hand latched onto her arm, giving a forceful tug as he spun her back around. The second the momentum spun her back to being face to face with him, the back of his massive hand made contact with her face. The impact sent her reeling down onto the floor with a thud.

The room was spinning as she lay there, willing it all to stop moving. Layne's watering eyes blurred her vision. Her heartbeat sounded louder than a fighter jet between her ears. It was unclear how long it was before she was rolled onto her back, looking up at the one person she never expected to betray her family like this.

Mick kneeled, his hand latched onto her throat and squeezed like a snake around its prey. Her fingers clawed at his grasp as stars began to prick at her consciousness. She yelled for help, but the words never came out.

"Don't fight it," he murmured to her.

She didn't have a lot to fight with, but she had enough. Her foot kicked against his chest with everything she had, which was enough to stagger him back after releasing his hold on her airway.

Layne rolled over with violent coughs wracking her body, pushed herself up onto her feet, and ran out of her bedroom. All the while, she was still fighting the wave of dizziness that was made worse by her movements.

Relying on basic survival instincts, she knew she had to get out of there. Get out, Layne. Escape when death is the inevitable outcome of staying - just like her dad had always told her.

The thunderous footsteps were getting closer to her, or was that the pounding of the blood pumping furiously through her body?

Clutching onto the railing, she descended the main staircase clumsily. When she made it to the bottom step, she felt a force plow into her from behind sending her plummeting to the floor. A cry of surprise erupted from her mouth and echoed in the acoustics of the foyer. Still summoning every ounce of stubborn fight in her, she pushed up onto her hands.

Mick's hands yanked her up the rest of the way onto her feet by her upper arm and a fistful of her hair. The hold on her arm was so tight she swore it would take him very little to crush her bones. "Stay awhile, sweetheart, we're going to have a little chat." With his hand ensnared in her hair, he gave a harsh tug, causing her head to tilt back uncomfortably.

His eyes met her own, full of sinister motives and a cruel grin stretched across his mouth. Fuck.

CHAPTER THIRTY

She sat there in the dining room, ropes biting into her delicate wrists as they restrained her from moving from the chair. Her ankles were equally indisposed to the legs of the chair.

Layne glared over at Mick, the betrayal that she felt was pale in comparison to the amount of anger and seething that she had for the man. "All these years, and this was your plan? Why?" He had spent over thirty years working for her father, and now he was making a play for more power? She just couldn't comprehend it.

"Oh, Layne, sweetheart, you never were good at seeing the bigger picture." His hand that wasn't holding his gun lightly patted the top of her thigh.

"Enlighten me." She needed to keep this conversation going. Every minute he was talking to her was a minute more to try and find a way out of this seemingly hopeless situation.

He squatted down in front of her so they could look at each other on the same level. Mick shook his head, either really impressed with himself or disappointed in her.

"Because it's not just about me. Project 227 is my big break in this industry. I have been at your father's side for years, and the moment he knocked up your mother, he decided that instead of rewarding all my hard work and loyalty he would mindlessly pass the torch onto a clump of cells. All he could talk about was how proud he would be to hand off this business to blood. For all his touting about loyalty, being the pinnacle of this business, loyalty has meant nothing but shit to him."

Layne was in disbelief that all of this was because he was butthurt. Typical men. "Well, you know what they say about loyalty? Blood ties strengthen the roots of loyalty. I guess, you didn't have what it took."

Mick's face twisted with rage as he used the pistol in his hand to strike her across the face. Her head harshly turned with the impact. A cut on her cheekbone where the cold and unforgiving metal had connected. The broken skin cried a crimson trail down the side of her face, falling from the edge of her jaw onto her jean-clad leg.

"Always with the fuckin' mouth, Layne. I can't tell you how many times I've told myself that someone needed to give it a good hard smack." He chuckled, "But that wouldn't have taught you a lesson though, would it? You just can't help yourself."

He placed the muzzle of the gun on the seat of her chair between her legs, slowly inching it to her apex so it was pushed up against the crotch of her pants. "Just like you couldn't help yourself chasing dick all over the city." He partially rose and leaned in, his lips harshly rubbing against her ear as he whispered into her ear. "Just like your whore of a mother."

Layne's arms tensed with all the anger continuing to escalate inside of her, but unable to lash out without the freedom of her arms or legs. She pulled her head to the side to strain away from his sickening breath as far as she was able. His hand promptly latched onto her face, fingers harshly dug into her cheeks as he turned her to look right at him. His fingers smeared her own blood across her face as he did so. "You're going to learn a lot of brutal real-world lessons today, and I can't wait."

His grip finally relinquished its hold on her as he stepped back, licking the coppery flavor of her blood clean from his fingers. Afterwards, he retrieved a phone from his pocket, dialing a number. Placing it on speaker, Layne shifted uncomfortably in her seat not getting any reprieve from the tightly bound ropes.

Ring. Ring. Ring. Ri—

"Mick, what's going on?" Her heart sank, hearing her father's familiar voice at the end of the other line. She squeezed her eyes shut for a second already foreseeing where this was going. He was on a business trip up in Boston - hours away and Mick knew that was to his advantage.

"Oh, just a little restructuring of this organization." His eyes never left Layne even though she had no opportunity to go anywhere.

"What are you talking about?" Scott's voice was wary and impatient with the lack of clarity of Mick's response.

"I'm sick and fuckin' tired of being put below your spoiled brats. There's going to be a lot of changes around here after I'm done dealing with them."

There was a silence so thick on the other end from her father processing the gravity of the situation from words alone. After a few seconds, her father's cautious tone came across, "Where's your head at, Mickey?"

He smiled like he had been envisioning this moment for some time. "I have Layne here with me, why don't you ask her?"

"Layne? Layne, tell me what's going on." A slight tick of panic in his voice as he asked for her.

Her eyes locked on Mick's, she refused to give him the satisfaction of confirming she was even present.

"She's almost as stubborn as you are." Mick sounded impressed.

Without warning, he lifted the pistol and fired off a shot. It left her ears ringing at first but was quickly followed by a searing pain in her left shoulder that tore a scream from her mouth. "Ahh! Fuck!"

On the phone, a series of expletives were given by her father, though she didn't hear exactly what they were as the sudden onslaught of pain throbbed across the upper left area of her body. A wet warmth followed as her light blue shirt began to soak up the blood escaping the small hole that was now in her shoulder.

"I'm sorry, what was that, Layne?" Mick inquired with an evil smirk across his face.

"Go to hell! Gah!" She screamed out again as it seemed to help nominally with the pain.

Mick's voice was oozing with confidence now. "As I'm sure you can tell, Scotty, she's not feeling too hot right now. Here is what is going to occur if you want her to have a quick and painless death, because let's be straight with one another, she's not leaving here in anything but a body bag. Don't worry about missing out on this though, I will be sure to leave enough of her blood around the house, so you'll be cleaning it up for months."

"I trusted and confided in you. You were treated as part of my family, and this is how you repay me?" Her father was gritting his teeth through his words.

Mick sighed with exhaustion evident in his voice. "All talk. Where was all my glory in this?! You coddled your kids, promising them riches and power, and what did my family get? Your eternal gratitude and a pat on the back?"

Layne drew in harsh and deep breaths as she tried to control the sensation of pain wracking her body.

Mick continued, "A pat on the back is just not going to be good enough. I want the offshore accounts all under my control. Then, you're going to turn yourself in to Boston PD while you're up there and confess to every scheme you've ever been involved in. The Feds will come in and will lock your ass up and throw away the key for the past two years alone, while I pick up the fractured pieces of business operations here."

"The accounts will take time, Mick, you know that," Scott warned.

"I guess you will need to hurry and do what you can to make them take less time. I already have people on the way to the Four Seasons Downtown to see to it that Liam is seen buckling under the pressure of the business, turning to a tragic encounter with a fatal dose of heroin. As for Layne, well, she and I will have to find a way to pass the time." The way he said the last few words made Layne's skin crawl and a wave of nausea rolled through her stomach.

"Son of a bi—"

Mick ended the call, cutting off her dad's words, and tossed the phone onto the table carelessly.

"You're a coward. You had to wait until my dad was out of town to make your move? You couldn't just face him directly like a man?" A sheen of sweat across her forehead from the nagging pain embedded in her shoulder. Her body involuntarily shook from a combination of adrenaline, anger, and agony.

His laughter abruptly burst out of him. "I'm ten times more of a man than your dad has ever been. Maybe I will show you before our time here is up." He walked behind her, a hand gripping onto her injured shoulder.

Layne writhed as the deep ache flipped back into an intense shooting pain. Biting her lower lip, she tried not to cry out.

"Don't hold back on my account." He gave her shoulder another squeeze. "I won't mind hearing you scream."

Things went dark.

For a moment even Layne wasn't sure if she had blacked out or not, but she blinked her eyes a few times and realized it was just the lights that cut out in the house.

Mick released her shoulder, and she could hear his footsteps as he moved away from her, murmuring to himself. "Damnit."

She tried to will her eyes to adjust quicker to the dark, but it wasn't happening fast enough. Her hands furiously tugged and pulled against the ropes holding her there to the chair. The burn of the ropes rubbing against her skin was nothing by comparison to what would happen if she didn't get free.

That's when she heard a thud come from the room above her. Instinctively, she looked up, wondering if she truly had heard anything at all or if it had been her imagination, or possibly delirium. While her heart continued pounding in her body, she continued to fight against her restraints.

Mick's footsteps were coming closer to her once more, she could feel his presence through the shadows. He stopped short, and suddenly all Layne heard were the sounds of two men grunting and Mick's strangled voice. The movement of air wisped around her, indicating there was a hell of a struggle going on.

The sound of a high-pitched shot pierced through the air. Layne flinched. No new pain that she could feel was reassuring that she hadn't been injured again.

A large thump occurred next to her, the thump of a lifeless body. Whose body? She couldn't be sure.

Hands settled on top of hers as the outline of a body appeared before her.

"Stop moving." The masculinity dripping from the voice in front of her was unmistakable.

She froze in her seat. "Joey?" Her voice broke with a sudden surge of relief.

The lights came flickering back on, and before her, he had a knife in hand that sliced through the ropes with ease. He was crouched in front of her, wearing his typical all-black ensemble except the infamous mask he normally wore while doing his dirty work was missing.

She leaped up from her seat, tossing her arms around his neck and immediately regretting it as her left shoulder protested, causing her to whimper. "How did you know I was in trouble?"

He frowned as he pulled back and inspected the blood-saturated shirt she was wearing and the marks on her face and throat. Anger flashed across his face at how extensively Mick had injured her. If Joey could have resurrected and killed the bastard again, he would have taken his time. "Your father's men up in Boston contacted me. I have some friends on the way to Liam right now."

She found herself stunned that he managed to coordinate all of this on a dime. When she looked down at the floor, she saw Mick's body lying face-down with a puddle of blood around his head that was gradually growing larger with each passing second.

Joey spoke in a hurry. "I only have a few minutes, let's get you outside."

"A few minutes for what?" Her attention was drawn back to him.

"You're hurt, Layne, you need to get checked out. C'mon." Stepping around the fresh corpse in the dining room, he led her outside with a supportive arm around her waist.

As her emotions began to come down from their heightened state, the blood that soaked into her shirt no longer felt warm but cool and tacky. Her head was beginning to float from the lack of adrenaline keeping her from succumbing to the unfortunate side effects of being shot.

Joey recognized the paleness in her face and coaxed her to sit down on the front stoop. "Hey, hang in there. Sit." Always giving orders this one.

She didn't have the strength in her to argue. Instead, she did as he ordered, and she plunked her ass down on the cold brick step. Her hand held onto her wounded shoulder, unclear if the pressure made it feel better or worse.

"I will be back." He took off back into the house, for what she wasn't sure but before she could ask questions he was already gone.

That's when the lights captured her attention, the reds and blues speeding down the street. Sirens wailed in the air. Once an entire herd of police cars were in front of the house, everything became a blur.

The city's finest immediately ushered her away from the house, asking her a series of questions until the paramedics arrived on the scene. She half paid attention to the flurry of activity around her, wondering if Joey was still inside the house.

As she sat on the back bumper of the ambulance, refusing to sit on a gurney like a wounded animal, one paramedic asked about her medical history while the other inspected her shoulder. Her head was thoroughly throbbing from the headache that had begun to take over. After medical personnel convinced her she needed to go to Mount Sinai, she began to climb into the back of the ambulance with the assistance of the medics.

Something caught her eye though, causing her to pause mid-step.

It was hard to tell from her limited view, but a man who looked like

Joey was standing across the street, talking to one of the officers. They grasped hands and pulled each other in for a hug, with Joey patting the cop on the back with a smile. Everything about the encounter appeared friendly, like they were long-time buddies just shooting the shit.

"Ma'am? We need to get you to the hospital." The sound of the female paramedic's voice interrupted her thoughts. She blinked a few times, conflicted with what she thought she was witnessing.

The paramedic spoke again, "Ma'am? We really have—"

"I know." Layne's words were impolitely short with the woman.

Up into the back of the ambulance Layne went, where she was transported to the hospital only a few miles away. Her thoughts nagged her as she over-analyzed everything in her head during the ride.

When she arrived at the hospital, she disconnected emotionally from the situation trying to clear her head of anything at all. A series of tests were run, imaging was taken, and so many questions were asked.

As it turns out, Layne had gotten lucky that the bullet had missed a series of arteries, nerves, and bones and only damaged her flesh as it passed through. It physically didn't feel lucky at the moment, but things were looking up when they began pumping painkillers in through her IV.

Feeling the tug of a drug-induced slumber on the horizon, Layne laid her head back on the uncomfortably shallow hospital pillow and let the meds pull her under.

CHAPTER THIRTY-ONE

Having been released from the hospital nearly ten days ago, Layne was still in recovery mode. The doctors sent her home with a series of medications and orders for physical therapy to restore full use of her left arm.

A bouquet of fresh flowers was neatly placed in a vase on her kitchen table. They were a simple and beautiful arrangement of white roses mixed with the rich purples of delphiniums, providing a light yet pleasant scent to the room. The get-well gift had been delivered without a name on the card, though she had her suspicions about who the sender was.

Joey had been M.I.A. since the entire ordeal with Mick leaving her even more cranky than her shoulder was already making her. Her thoughts about what she thought she had seen before getting into the ambulance had consumed her, and now with him being radio silent, she couldn't quiet her mind about it. She desperately wanted to be angry with him, but that was the thing about her relationship with Joey, she had problems standing and maintaining her ground. He was her Achilles' Heel, and she was his.

After speaking with the police, she learned that the house lights had been cut remotely through a phone app. Layne hadn't always been appreciative of new technology, but in this case, she was grateful. The cops had received an anonymous phone call reporting suspicious activity and shots fired at her father's residence which is what made for the swift arrival of the boys in blue. As for their investigation? It was an open and shut case based on Layne's recollection of events, sans Joey, and perhaps a little monetary incentive to those on the take thanks to the Scott O'Reilly bribery fund.

Liam had been railing his so-called date at the Four Seasons when a small crew of skull-masked men busted down the door of his suite. The men dragged her brother to a temporary safehouse, barely allowing him to collect his pants on the way out. Whether or not the crew had spooked Mick's hitman or if it had been a bluff all along wasn't known.

As for Scott O'Reilly? He hauled ass back from Boston and immediately sorted through the ranks to weed out any potential sympathizers of Mick's plight. It had been an ugly and violent process, but it sent a message loud and clear: no one is safe if you fuck with his family. As head of the organization, he set forth a new campaign to solidify his foothold in the city. With Franzetti's faction crumbling without their fearless leader, he was able to salvage a few good little soldiers and left the rest to their own devices.

The Flannigan family held a small funeral for Mick, in which her dad was in attendance. Despite the pisspoor ending to Mick's story, it still had been a lifelong friendship and Layne was sure that deep down her father had to mourn the tragedy in his own way.

Rebecca had summoned her natural inner caretaker, bringing Layne a series of homemade foods to help stock up a freezer stash. Layne was confident that she would never have to order takeout, like, ever again. Amongst the variety of foods, there was a particularly delicious-looking turkey tetrazzini she was looking forward to digging into tonight. In addition to all the meal prep, her bestie had left her very strict instructions pinned to the fridge:

1. Get rest.
2. Seriously. See #1 above.
3. Do your physical therapy.
4. Eat something.
5. Hydrate.
6. Binge-watch trashy TV.
7. Call me ASAP if you need anything.

XoXo, Rebecca

Layne had done her best to abide by the rules set forth for her, but listening to directions wasn't her strong suit. To make sure Layne didn't completely disregard her, Rebecca insisted on coming over for a taco night tomorrow.

After the ding of the microwave chimed, Layne grabbed the corner of the steamy hot bag of popcorn and brought it into the living room. The distinct aroma of the buttery snack filled the air as she took her seat on her sofa. She used her teeth to tug on one corner while pulling the other with her right hand to pry open the bag. Setting the bag in her lap, she grabbed the remote on the cushion next to her and un-paused an episode of *You*.

"Man, that guy is a freak." A husky voice that made her legs weak commented from behind her. Knocking her popcorn off her lap onto the floor, she spun around in her seat to look back at Joey. Layne's first instinct was to greet him with a smile, and she struggled to prevent it from tugging at her lips when she saw him standing there behind her couch.

"Says the guy who has made a habit of having never *not* broken into my house." She picked up a kernel of popcorn off the sofa and flicked it at him.

"If you want, I can go back outside and ring the doorbell if it would make you feel better." He had a smartass smirk on his face, but instead of making good on that offer, he leaned over onto the back of the couch on his forearms, a warm sparkle in his puppy dog brown eyes.

She turned back around in her seat doing her best to ignore the charm he was trying to pour on just by giving her that look. "So, what are you doing here?"

"Figured you could use some company." He spoke like he hadn't been invisible for the last week and a half.

"I could have used company the night I got shot." She fired right back at him casually.

He audibly sighed behind her, not with annoyance but with the knowledge that he had some damage control to do here. Layne kept her eyes focused on the television, but her brain wasn't focused enough to retain what was happening onscreen.

"Look, I know I haven't been around. I couldn't be." Kudos to him for sounding decently apologetic.

"Oh?" Not hiding the disinterest in her voice.

"Layne, don't be like that." He begged her.

"Like what?" Feigning ignorance at what he was possibly referring to.

"You know what. I get it, you're pissed, and you have every right to be."

She rose from the couch and walked over to a drawer on the far side of her coffee table. Using her uninjured arm, she pulled it open and retrieved a manilla folder with some papers in it. Going around the back of the couch, she shoved the file into his hands.

Joey took the folder, opened it up, and flipped through a few pages. His face fell at what was inside. Sheet after sheet of information on the very thing he had been avoiding telling her. Documents reflecting his assistance in police investigations as an informant.

"*Pissed*? I don't think that even begins to describe what I felt when my guy brought this to my attention. I saw you that night, acting like you and that cop were best bros. From there, I started to piece it all together. I had hoped I was wrong, Joey, I really did. You knew things about the 227 project that Franzetti didn't even know. The way you acted when we encountered those two officers in the subway. Not to mention all the other things I ignored because I have been so stupidly blinded by you."

"Layne," he reached out to touch her arm.

She pulled back from him. "Don't." She stared at him, searching for a sign of who he really was underneath the façade he put up. "How long have you been feeding information to the cops? The entire time I've known you?"

He stood there silently, confirming her assumption.

Layne scoffed at how she had been so blind to it all. "What about me? How much have you told them?" She was starting to downward spiral at all the things that could have been shared about her professional or even personal life.

He stepped up to her, his hands holding onto her face as he pressed his forehead to hers. "No, you stop right there. The only things I shared about you were irrelevant and only related to other cases. They've got nothing on you, I kept everything about you to myself."

Her eyes gazed up into his. "Liam? My dad?"

"Some stuff, but nothing solid they can stand on." He spoke like it was all no big deal.

"God, I trusted you! My dad trusted you!" Her temper rearing its vicious head. She pulled her face back from his hands, and he let her as his hands fell back down to his sides.

"Layney, I didn't have any other choice." His words were supposed to be reassuring, but they did little to settle Layne down.

Not to mention, his using her nickname suddenly did little to calm her. "Don't 'Layney' me, that's bullshit. There is always another choice!"

He ran his fingers through his sandy-colored hair in desperation, trying to find a way to make things right with her. She walked over to her front door and flung it open. "Leave." When he didn't immediately walk out the door she raised her voice. "Get out!"

A look of defeat washed over his face as he joined her at the front door. "I'm so sorry." He leaned in to give her one of the most tender kisses she had ever felt from him. It was full of bittersweet affection, and every fiber of her being was screaming at her to cave into the delicious addiction that he was.

It bordered on painful to pull her mouth back from his. "If I ever see you again, I will fucking shoot you myself. Get out and stay out." She averted her eyes from him as she waited for him to get the hell out of her home.

He backed away from her and took his sullen leave. Layne didn't hesitate to slam the door shut behind him. She pressed her back against the closed door and looked up at the ceiling trying to process the whirlwind of emotions flooding her body.

Layne pushed away from the door and screamed out in frustration, her hands swiping her purse and today's mail off the table in the foyer. Her purse's contents spilled out across the floor, scattering in various directions. Her hot tears relentlessly rolled down her cheeks at his betrayal, at seeing him leave, at him never knowing what else was going on behind the curtain.

She slid down to the floor onto her knees, sobs being choked out while she picked up the mess she created one item at a time. Her hands trembled as she pulled the last item up off the floor. Layne stared at the lab and biopsy results that one of her associates was able to hack from the hospital system before crumpling them up in her hand.

Life was going to get a hell of a lot messier.

EPILOGUE

Six months later

It seemed cruel that this was taking place on such a beautiful day, full of sunshine that beat down on the perfectly manicured lawn that seemed to expand off into the distance forever.

Headstones of various sizes and colors were planted every few feet around them. The vibrant colors of the flowers cluttering the ground in front of them were far too cheerful to be considered appropriate. The birds in the sky were even singing their cheerful songs without regard. All of it just seemed wrong. Today should have been as dark as her thoughts were.

Layne stood there, falling victim to the storm of her thoughts instead of listening to the priest standing over the gleaming red oak casket. A sea of people with tissues in their hands stood around the open plot. She wondered how many of them truly cared, and how many simply came to solicit some juicy gossip.

Being here was all about putting on a brave face and all that political bullshit. She felt nothing but fury and chaos deep within her soul. She wanted to cave to the darkness spreading throughout her. She was regretting every choice that led up to this point, right down to the shoes she had chosen this morning.

When she looked up once more, all the attendees were slowly dispersing to return to their vehicles. Murmurs of condolences spoken to her as they passed by.

If she never heard another "I'm sorry" in her lifetime, it still would be one too many. Each expression of sympathy added fuel to the fiery anger being pent up inside of her.

Her legs felt stiff from standing still for such a lengthy amount of time, the bottoms of her feet pleading for relief from the heels she had chosen, and all the muscles along the back of her spine up to the back of her head in knots from the tension in her body. Her eyes were dry and tired. Layne's jaw ached from being clenched so that she didn't unleash the venom she wanted to spew.

Time passed slowly while she stood there, and yet before she knew it, everyone had left to return to their regularly scheduled lives. Layne felt a hand rest on her lower back as a voice spoke to her the way you would speak to a predator who could strike to kill at any sudden sight or sound.

"There was nothing you could have done. You have to know that." He assured her.

She didn't buy that. "There was everything that I could have done."

"Let him go. He'd want that."

She squeezed her eyes shut again, finding darkness behind her closed lids.

Silently, she made a vow at that moment that things were going to change.

To be continued in ***Layne Closure Ahead****.*

LAYNE CLOSURE AHEAD

Alliances are broken and hearts stolen.

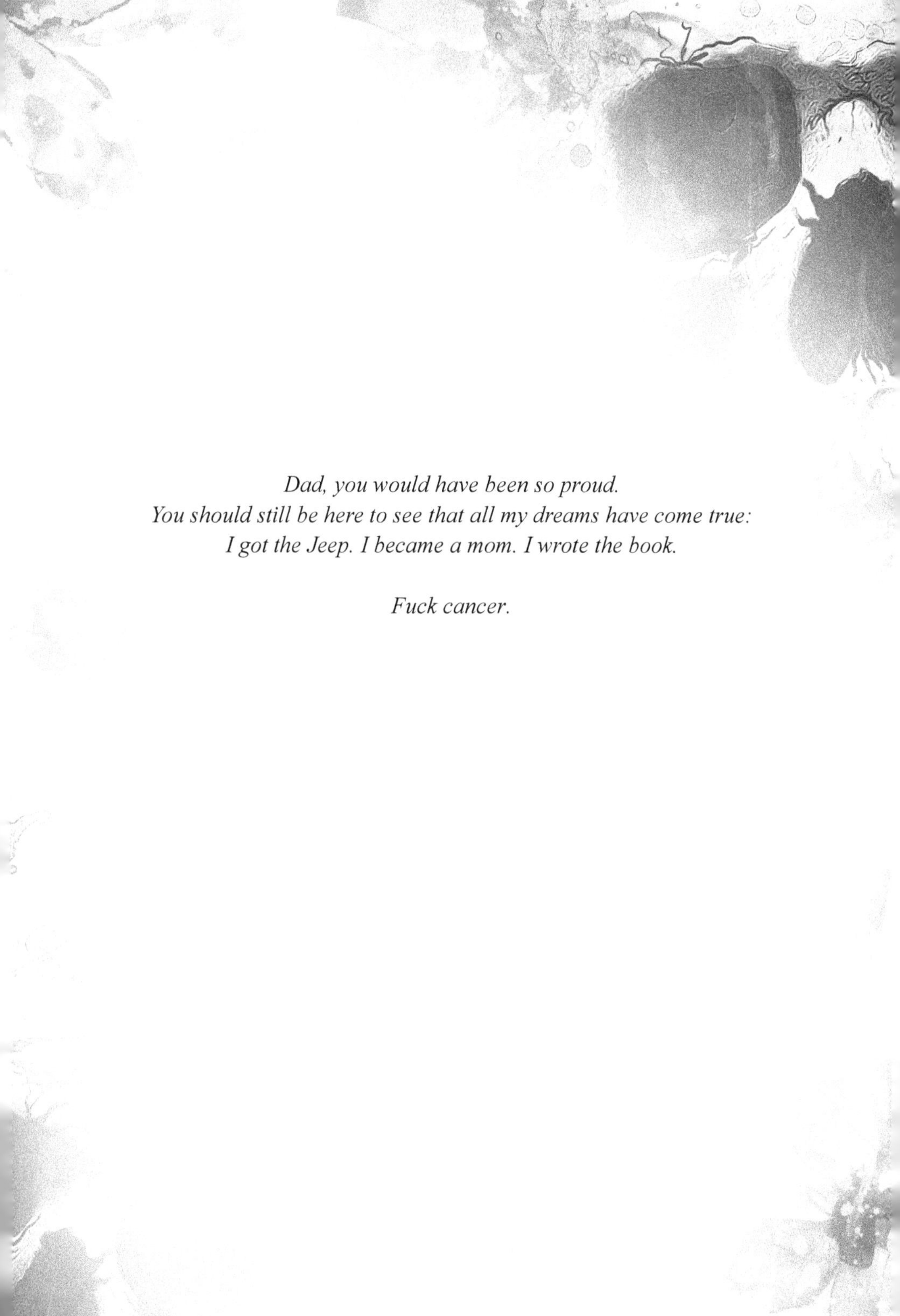

Dad, you would have been so proud.
You should still be here to see that all my dreams have come true:
I got the Jeep. I became a mom. I wrote the book.

Fuck cancer.

OFFICIAL PLAYLIST

Alkaline - Sleep Token
Bad Things - I Prevail
Battling My Demons - Jeris Johnson, BOI WHAT
Hostage - No Resolve
It Had to Be You (Dark Version) - Tommee Profitt, Tiffany Ashton
Joke's On You - Charlotte Lawrence
Judgment Day - Five Finger Death Punch
Kryptonite (Reloaded) - Jeris Johnson
Leave A Light On - Papa Roach
Let the Sparks Fly - Thousand Foot Krutch
Porn Star Dancing - My Darkest Days, Chad Kroeger, Zak Wylde
Ready or Not (I'm Coming) - OOMPH!
Saviour II - Black Veil Brides
Sugar - Sleep Token
Top O' the Mornin' to Ya - House of Pain
Welcome to the Chaos - Fame on Fire, Ice Nine Kills

The official playlist can be found on Spotify.

CONTENT & TRIGGER WARNINGS

All trigger and content warnings can be found on www. sadiewinchester.com.

PROLOGUE

Four months have passed

Had it really been four months since the funeral took place? Layne couldn't be sure, as everything had blurred together ever since. Since then, her life had taken a series of zig-zag turns, leaving her with whiplash. Instead of trying to juggle balls like a circus performer, she was juggling politics, sticks of dynamite, and her will to keep waking up to see another day.

Yet, here she fucking was again. Her annual self-sabotage party at McGregor's Pub had inevitably rolled around on the anniversary of her mother's death. Now, she just referred to it as the most cursed day of her life. It was the same damn day that Joey motherfucking De Luca had encountered and ultimately destroyed two O'Reilly women, only years apart.

She slung back another shot of whiskey, no longer feeling the burn down her throat as her intoxication numbed the pain.

With concerned eyes, the owner of the pub stood behind the bar watching the worst unraveling he had seen of Layne yet on this day over the years. "Layne," Sean gently tried to interject himself into the world of pain she was wallowing in. "Maybe it's time to call it a night."

Her eyes didn't even look up at him, the emerald hues remained staring blankly at the empty shot glass cradled in her hand.

"It's a pleasure to meet you, Layney."

The memory of *his* voice twisted the knife of betrayal a little deeper into her damaged heart. Her face winced briefly before the rage reared its ugly head. She forcefully pitched the glass at the wall as she screamed out. "Yeah, I bet it fuckin' was, motherfucker!"

Between her sudden outburst at seemingly no one in particular and the glass shattering against the wall, it elicited a flinch from Sean as he raised his arms to shield himself from any flying shards.

Layne got out of her seat, stumbling to find her drunken feet underneath her. The second she noticed Sean opening his mouth to speak, she tossed her hands up wildly. "I'm fuckin' leaving! Christ! You happy?! Because nobody else is!"

The smart man that Sean was promptly shut his mouth, standing there in silence. The remainder of the occupants inside the bar also had a hushed quiet come over them as eyes settled on the angry little Irish girl.

Thanks to copious amounts of booze, her body felt like it was floating as she left McGregor's. Once she made it outside, she began walking without a care for whichever direction she was heading while her mind wandered.

The same day she had kicked Joey out of her life ten months ago, she had an even bigger emotional bomb dropped on her. A cruel chain of events followed, each one popped off and struck her back down anytime she tried to get back up on her feet.

Her father, Scott O'Reilly, the kingpin of the family's criminal empire, had been taking business trips up to Boston quite frequently. As the head of the organization who had built things from the ground up, it wasn't out of the norm for him to travel across state lines on occasion, but this had been different.

During her investigation into the Project 227 rumors to assist Joey during that time, Layne found herself digging for answers as to what had captured her father's interest a few states away. When she got her answers, they hadn't been what she had pictured in her wildest nightmares.

It turned out that when her gut instincts were screaming at her that something wasn't right, she needed to listen. Through the use of her technologically inclined associates, she illegally obtained medical documentation from the top cancer center in Boston. At the top of those documents was her dad's name. Right underneath it? *Diagnosis: Stage IV Kidney Cancer*. The news had struck harder than a freight train squishing an empty beer can.

He had hidden his diagnosis from everyone, including both his children. Despite that, Liam was supposed to be the one eventually taking over the family business, and he hadn't even been told. When Layne brought the evidence to light, Liam refused to believe it. It wasn't until she had dropped the papers into her dad's lap that Scott O'Reilly finally revealed the full extent of his illness.

What a sick and twisted game fate was playing. Her dad's right-hand man, Mickey Flannigan, had betrayed them all, and then her dad ended up following him to the grave nearly six months later.

Sure, this business always had a high risk of death, but dying of a cancer that spread through your bones and left a path of destruction behind while it metastasized? Orthopedic surgeries to attempt to strengthen joints and damaged bones did little to stem the tide. At the end of the day? No one ever anticipated this gruesome end to the head of the O'Reilly family.

Outwardly, Liam had taken their dad's premature passing the hardest. Currently, with his mental state on the fringe, he was handling his new role as the new head honcho as well as Layne had expected. He wasn't handling it at all. Some days, he was all in on taking leadership, and other days, he was trying to issue everyone around him a death sentence. Then, there were weeks when he would abandon all responsibilities for a lick of his dick and a handle of booze.

As for Layne? She had been trying to pick up all the pieces falling around her, except those of her own. Buried in the deepest, darkest sea inside of her were all her unwanted emotions. If Layne had been capable of being honest with herself, she was holding herself together with a prayer and Elmer's glue.

Dealing with Liam as the official figurehead of the organization made for a political shitshow while attempting to clean up his messes. Often, she found herself pussyfooting around issues, coordinating cleanups to the side, and trying to plant ideas in Liam's head to think of as his own. Lord knew that if she tried to insert her opinion on anything business-wise, he would shut her out entirely. It was thoroughly exhausting.

Before all of this transpired, she had an anger problem. But now? Layne was permanently pissed off. She questioned everything she had ever done in this family, even after she said her goodbyes to the one parent she had left while he lay on his deathbed.

She should have been involved more. She should have asked more questions. She should have considered trying to play her role the way her dad had wanted her to. She shouldn't have had to suffer another loss in her life. She shouldn't have had to take on the weight of this world while the threat of the next loomed over them.

There was no fairness or logic to any of it. Her mother was gone. Mick was gone. Her father was gone. Liam was on a suicide mission and looking to bring everyone down with him. Joey was out of her life…

…or so she thought.

CHAPTER ONE

She had been in her silver Beamer sitting at a traffic light in midtown just a few blocks away from Times Square when Diego from the Brass Mirror called her in complete dismay.

He had been running the club on behalf of the O'Reilly family for the past seven years. For the most part, he knew his place, how to handle the elite clientele, and how to resolve any disruptions to the services rendered there.

So, when there was panic laced in his voice and his words stuttering, she was quick to believe him when he told her that shit was hitting the fan at the exclusive VIP underground gambling club. Also, a good indication was the sound of crashing and shattering glass in the background. Doesn't sound very lucky for a place named after a mirror, does it?

After hauling ass downtown, she parked in the underground garage. Layne got out of her car and rounded to the trunk, where she rummaged around for some tools of the trade. She opted for the wooden baseball bat that had rolled to the back of the compartment.

Layne could use a little stress relief today, and whatever was going on inside was likely going to give her the chance to find a healthier outlet by comparison to other available options. Relatively speaking, of course.

As she anxiously awaited inside the elevator to arrive at the designated floor, she texted Liam:

LAYNE

Handling business at the Mirror.

S.O.S. received from Diego.

Standby.

LIAM

Whatever, I'm busy.

Shut it all down if you have to.

I don't give a fuck.

She drew in an attempt at a therapeutically deep breath at Liam's indifference. Layne tucked her phone away and reassessed the grip on the wooden bat in her hand. She couldn't focus on Liam's inability to cope with problems right now; she needed to get her head in the game.

When the doors of the elevator slid open, the bland and undecorated hallway was quiet. She stalked to the end of the hall where a twin set of glossy black doors were. After punching in the master security code to allow her access, she cautiously pulled a door open to slip inside.

The Brass Mirror was just beyond the entrance. The walls were painted gold with black accents, and red velvet chairs should have been perfectly positioned at various table setups across the space. The decor was sickeningly pretentious, and it matched the filthy rich bastards that maintained membership here to carelessly sling their funds around.

When Layne walked in, tables and chairs were in utter disarray. Poker chips were spread on the floor like New Year's Eve confetti. Multiple mirrors were in pieces around the perimeter of the room, superstitiously racking up decades of bad luck.

Grown-ass men were wrangling with one another while some pieces of arm candy were shrieking incessantly. She cringed at the high-pitched wails adding to the soundtrack of violence and destruction.

"Here we go," Layne muttered to herself. She rotated her wrist, getting a feel for the weight of the bat in her hand with a single rotation, ready to wield it where necessary.

She stomped toward the first set of grappling men, doubled up her grip on the handle, and wound up. Unleashing her swing on the back of one man's knees, it instantly dropped him to the ground.

One for the money.

It left the other man in shock, only to be greeted with her backhanded swing connecting underneath his chin. The sickening cracking of bone and shattering teeth should have bothered her, but today was not that day.

Two for the show.

Layne saw the second man drop like a fly while howling in pain as blood poured from his mouth. She pointed the tip of the bat at the first man, who was already propping himself up on one knee. “Stay.” The threat of an additional strike loomed on that single word spoken.

She looked across the room and saw Diego in an altercation with a man wielding an empty beer bottle. “For fucks’ sake, Diego,” she cursed under her breath before navigating through the strewn-about furniture.

“Alan! Let’s talk this through!” Diego spinelessly raised his hands defensively, trying to avoid getting assaulted by an empty bottle.

It took Layne one swing to smack the bottle from the attacker’s grasp, sending the empty brown container towards the wall where the sound of its shattering echoed across the room. She didn’t hesitate to follow up with a second strike right to his gut and a final third to his back as he doubled over in pain. He fell flat onto the floor.

Three to get ready.

Resting the bat against the front of her shoulder, she let Diego feel the anger in her gaze that she had to come down here to clean this shit up. With one hand on her hip, she scolded him. “You told me you ramped up security. What the hell happened?”

Diego opened his mouth to spout some insufficient apology, but from behind her, a hand grabbed onto the top of her bloodied bat while a large bicep wrapped around her throat, snatching the midpoint of the piece of lumber and yanking her back.

The length of the bat pressed to her throat forced her back into the brick wall of a man behind her. Her hands latched back onto the bat, pushing forward and away to relieve the pressure against her neck. Layne swung her body to the side, pushing one end of the bat up, allowing enough of a gap to squeeze out of the tight space.

Spinning around, she pulled out the small but mighty Glock, pulling the trigger for the money shot between the eyes. The bang filled the air, and everything went still. Her victim dropped to the floor with a thud, and his hand released her bat.

Four, motherfucker, let’s go.

The pistol was tucked back into the holster in the back of her pants.

The wooden weapon rolled slowly across the floor towards her until she stopped it with the tip of her boot. She reached down and picked it up, only to hear a pair of hands giving slow and deliberate claps.

Clap.

Clap.

Clap.

Looking over her shoulder to see who was finding entertainment in the violent scene that had just unfolded, she was surprised to find a man who was clean-cut from head to toe. He had jet-black hair on the longer side but kept it a neat style away from his face. He had chillingly blue eyes that could either melt you down to your core or pierce straight through your heart. He stood at barely six feet tall, and his presence had an elegant command to it. If one had to guess, he appeared to be just over the cusp of forty.

The attire he had on indicated he had money—lots of it. The suit appeared to be custom and tailored to each cut of his sleek musculature.

She completed her turn to face him, noticing he was standing only three feet away. This stranger may have been amused, but she wasn't finding the situation nearly as captivating. "Enjoy the show?" Her voice was not the least bit friendly.

Ignoring her question, the man snapped his fingers. The first two men she encountered, Alan, and any pieces of arm candy that hadn't already fled for the exit, all nodded in acknowledgment of the silent instruction they were given. They scurried from the confines of the Brass Mirror.

Finally, the stranger spoke with a silky but firm tone. "Diego, you are also dismissed. See my man outside for your payment for your inconveniences here."

Diego shamefully avoided eye contact with Layne as he rushed out of the room. She gritted her teeth angrily that he had been manipulated by another party at play here.

"Don't blame him; I made an offer he couldn't—" the man chuckled. "Well, you know the saying."

Warily, she shifted her eyes onto the man, her hand still firmly latched onto the handle of the baseball bat.

"Forgive me, and allow me to introduce myself. I'm Eric Ellis. Your new neighbor, if you will." He extended his hand out to her.

The name sounded vaguely familiar to her, which should have been an enormous red flag, but new players were always coming and going in this line of work. Sometimes, they proved themselves worthy enough to be a force to be reckoned with. Other times? They tightened their own noose and jumped from the platform.

While there wasn't some sort of monthly criminal newsletter that got distributed, Layne had heard about the new guy in town. He had snatched up a swanky corner lot and fully renovated the industrial building to convert it into a residence. It was the Upper East Side's biggest topic of conversation amongst the wealthy. What she hadn't heard was what else he had his hands in.

Layne shoved his extended hand away with the tip of her bat. "I'm not your welcoming committee."

The strength of his hand grasped onto the bat and roughly tugged her forward towards him. When he snaked an arm around her, his hold was like a boa constrictor, ready to squeeze the life out of her lungs.

"Now, that's not being very friendly, is it?" He smirked as he let his eyes wander over the features of her face.

Not showing any signs of distress, she stared into the handsome face of her self-proclaimed new neighbor. "I'm not a very friendly type of girl."

He grinned, bringing his mouth lower to her ear so he could whisper his words. "So I've heard."

Before she could snap back, he released her and stepped away to give her space. Eric walked behind the unattended bar and lifted a bottle of Johnnie Walker Blue Label, inspecting it. "I'm not here to start any wars. Instead, I figured I'd get creative in capturing your attention. How did I do?"

Still not willing to part with her bat, she watched his every move, wondering what game he was playing. "If you were looking to piss me off, you're off to a great start."

He chuckled quietly to himself as he poured himself a drink from the expensive whiskey, he nodded at an empty chair on the other side of the bar. "Please, take a seat. I won't bite." He paused and, with a debonaire smile, said, "Unless you ask very nicely."

"I prefer to stand." Stepping over a broken chair, she approached the bar, still on high alert.

"Suit yourself." When he took the first sip from the glass, he reveled in the taste dancing across his taste buds, finishing with a slow moan of delight.

Using the bat, she laid it across the wrist of his hand, holding the glass, preventing him from taking another sip. "What is it that you're here for?"

Not making an effort to remove the baseball bat lying across his wrist, he chose to focus all of his attention on her. "A business proposition."

"I hate to burst your bubble, but I don't do business with people who come in and poach my employees and destroy my property."

Eric switched the short-statured glass into his other hand as he moved away from the threat of her current weapon of choice. "You'll have to forgive me, but I had to see for myself what I was potentially getting into. You didn't disappoint. Actually, I am rather impressed. The stories about you hardly do you any justice."

Growing tired of the banter, she contemplated just disposing of him entirely, but that's when he gave a click of his tongue and shook his head.

"Ah, if I were you, I wouldn't want to try and take my life just yet. You will want to hear what I'm going to lay out on the bargaining table."

She blinked a few times in surprise at how easily he just read her. "Then, make your point of why you're here and make it quickly, I don't have all damn day for this bullshit."

Resting one hand on the edge of the bar and leaning against it, he smiled as though he had been waiting for this very moment to answer her. "A merger. You and I. We combine our efforts and organizations, and it creates an unstoppable alliance. Right now, the O'Reilly business operations are struggling and are on the brink of collapse. After the passing of your father, which, by the way, you do have my deepest condolences, things have not been smooth sailing, have they? Your brother, Liam, is proving to be rather incapable of navigating the stressors of leadership and is leaving it all on your shoulders."

"We are getting by just fine, but thanks for the concern." Immediately, she was on the defensive as he began to verbally offend the way she and Liam had been handling things. Sure, it wasn't perfect, but Layne was working on coming up with ways to improve operations while Liam got his shit together.

Another sip of the whiskey had him licking the flavor from his lips. "Ah, ah, ah. Are you being honest with yourself, Layne? Don't you even know what I can offer you?"

She rolled her eyes, figuring he was going to try and tell her whether she wanted to know or not.

Taking her lack of protest as permission to proceed, he continued, "After Michael Franzetti did his vanishing act, I've been picking up pieces here and there and turning lumps of coal into diamonds. With the right training and mindset, I have been able to salvage a handful of Franzetti's little worker bees. Not to mention my growing collection of assets. If you and I were to unite, I could promise you a world where you would never have to worry about cleaning up others' messes. Including your brother's."

Gradually, she was lowering her bat as her arm got tired of being at full tension while listening to him pitch himself. "Yeah, no thanks. Now, get the fuck out."

Leaving his partially drunk glass of whiskey behind, he came up to her. "I'm not looking for an answer right now. All I'm asking is to keep this conversation going. That's all. I want to help you salvage what's left of your father's legacy and turn it into something greater. He'd want that, wouldn't he?"

"Don't talk like you knew him." Her jaw tensed as she thought about how her dad might be rolling over in his grave, seeing the state of affairs everything was in right now.

Eric slowly reached out to hold her chin gently with his thumb and forefinger. "I'm not looking to be the villain in your story. I'm just trying to help us both get what we want."

Layne jerked her face away from his subtle, intimate touch. "What's in it for you?"

His lips curved into a proud smile. "What a smart girl you are. I don't have the history and clout with some of the other major top dogs across the city to pull enough weight to successfully execute my vision for my home base of operations here. The O'Reilly name is well known. If everyone knows we are working hand-in-hand, it would make both of our lives much easier. If I had your support, I could provide for an extraordinarily comfortable existence in whichever way you would prefer it."

"Let me get this straight, you want me to help you by using my connections to get you in the door with other contacts while you iron out the wrinkles in the way we are currently doing things?" It sounded far too simple to Layne. Easy ways out just didn't fall from the sky.

He grinned. "Something like that."

"Something like that, or just like that?" She knew the devil was in the details.

Eric put on the same smile that all the politicians used to pitch their false promises. "Let's make a deal here, huh? We can discuss the details further, but in the meantime, let's see if this could be a happy little alliance, hm? You can still be the force that you've always been while fulfilling your father's final wishes to settle down with a man to provide for you, and your family's business will get the support and direction it requires to thrive."

It all sounded far too good to be true, except the settling down part. When anyone approaches you with a deal out of the blue, the chances of them being a snake oil salesman are almost always a certainty. "I'll think about it."

"That's all I ask. As a peace offering and show of good faith, I will send my crew here to clean up the mess. Things will be back to fully operational by tomorrow evening."

"If they're not, I will personally ensure that you will be wishing you were in his shoes." She warned as she motioned at the dead guy behind her.

He chuckled despite she had made it quite clear she was being serious. "My little harpy, I promise you that there will be no such need."

Eric's hand reached out to stroke the side of her cheek in an affectionate gesture. Layne snatched his wrist tightly, preventing him from touching her face again. Her emerald eyes were full of nothing but cold and emptiness.

He gave a sharp tug on his hand, causing Layne to stumble forward two steps closer to him. He ran his tongue over his lips before displaying a smirk across his mouth. "One day, you'll be begging for the soft touch of my hand."

Disgusted by the look in his eyes as he watched her, Layne released his wrist and backed away. "That's one bet I wouldn't make if I were you."

He gave a casual shrug and walked over to the two front doors, pulling one open to make his exit. Eric paused before he fully passed through it, he looked back over his shoulder at Layne. "The odds are better than you think."

He left Layne there alone in the disastrous-looking Brass Mirror.

Looking across the room at her reflection in one of the few remaining intact mirrors, a person was standing there that she didn't even recognize. Layne took hold of her bat and unleashed the bottled-up fury inside of her, taking it out on anything in her path.

A series of liquor bottles were smashed, leaving behind a river of mixed spirits along the back shelves. A framed abstract painting was another casualty of her rage-fueled assault. Layne continued to take swings at anything that pissed her off.

The final blow was tossing the entire baseball bat itself at a full-length mirror, shattering it into an infinite amount of shards. The asshole could pay for that, too.

Layne stood there alone with only the sounds of her heavy breaths, hating how tired she felt with the shit cards she was always being dealt these days.

CHAPTER TWO

A month later

"Oh yeah, baby, does that feel good? How do you like that? I bet you haven't had it this good ever." The scruffy-looking construction worker she had picked up at the bar panted against the back of her neck as he thrust into her from behind again. She hadn't even bothered to catch his name, or if he had given it, she had already forgotten.

"So good. Keep going." Layne didn't even attempt to fake it in her voice, let alone her expression. Her eyes gazed at the hand-written graffiti on the bathroom stall's partition in front of her, between her hands bracing against it. Things like phone numbers for a good time, random doodles, and names of people that were going to be together '4 Ever'.

Forever? Seemed like a pretty far-fetched concept to Layne. Nothing lasted forever in her life.

The whiny groans of the man pumping himself into her in the sole stall in the men's room distracted her from her thoughts momentarily. Layne wondered if he realized his thrusts were in sync with the tune of *Danny Boy*. How fuckin' depressing.

Her body jostled with each of the man's movements. Half of her clothes were still on, and his pants were stuck at his knees. When he came to an unimpressive finish into the condom he was wearing, she shoved him away from her, not feeling any sense of satisfaction.

Yanking her pants up and straightening out her shirt, Layne swung the stall door open.

While washing her hands in the sink, she wished she could just shower away the rest of the filth she felt elsewhere. "I've got a meeting to get to."

Reaching into her jacket pocket, she grabbed a prescription bottle partially filled with round white pills and popped one into her mouth, chasing it down with a swig of water from the palm of her hand out of the running faucet. The label on the plastic orange bottle noted to take it as needed for shoulder pain. The same shoulder pain that had subsided a few weeks after the man she had grown up calling uncle—Mick—had shot her. So much for family loyalty.

Layne needed something to dull the painful memory of the pitiful disaster that had just transpired in the dimly lit public restroom at McGregor's.

The man lingered, hoping maybe she would grace him with a more affectionate goodbye, but Layne shut it down by wiping her hands dry on the thighs of her pants and exiting the lavatory. Not so much as giving him a polite smile.

She waved a hand goodbye to Sean, who was filling drink orders as she made her way past the bar, which was currently half-full of inebriated patrons. He gave her a nod of his head in return.

Once outside, she involuntarily shivered from the chill cascading over her body as the air temperature had dropped drastically in anticipation of a hell of a nor'easter expected to hit the city in the next hour or two.

Walking down the sidewalk, she avoided colliding with other passersby as she began to send a few texts on her phone.

LAYNE

Got hung up on a few things. On my way.

LIAM

You better have good news when you get here.

LAYNE

Feeling hopeful?

LIAM

I'm as optimistic as a nun, hoping there are no sinners in prison.

Did Layne have good news for her brother? Not in the slightest.

When Layne arrived at the cemetery in Brooklyn, just slightly southwest of Prospect Park, she already saw Liam off in the distance across the sprawling terrain sprinkled with an assortment of headstones.

She had heard that Mick's family had buried him in this very same cemetery. Perhaps one day she would find out where just so she could piss on his grave. However, there were larger and much more real issues on their hands than insulting cemetery dirt.

After attempting not to trample over anyone's final resting place, she stepped up next to him and handed over a grease-soaked paper bag that had the aroma of freshly cooked french fries emanating from it. It was her attempt at a peace offering to help soften the blow of the news he wasn't going to want to hear.

Liam stood there, pulled out a fry, and bit into it. Not a gracious thank you. No words. Nothing.

He was decked out in a black pea coat, a crimson sweater, and a pair of new blue jeans. Continuing to not say a word, he just silently stared ahead, with the only sound being the crinkling of the bag each time another fry was pulled out.

In front of them was an ornate headstone with 'O'REILLY' in large letters spread across the top. Below it was the remainder of the epitaph detailing the life of a great man who had his life cut short prematurely.

"Layne, make me a promise." Her father's voice was weak from his failing body. "Promise me you'll do whatever you can to keep yourself safe. Don't make the same mistakes I've made with Liam." His hand, now frail from all the last-effort treatments he had received, reached over and latched onto her fingers. His eyes were full of sadness and regret as this lifetime was coming to a close. "Promise me."

Clearing her throat, she tried to push her final memories of their dad from her mind and blink away the heartache in her eyes. How gaunt he had looked, how weak his grasp was on her hand, how strained his voice was, and how painful his struggles were until the morphine eased him into his afterlife.

"The good news is that we only lost a few guys." She tried to keep the positivity in her voice, but that was a trait she had always been terrible at.

Liam refused to look at her as he spoke up, "Just say it."

Layne paused, trying to choose her next words carefully. There weren't many times when she tried to protect Liam's sensitivities, but this was a rare exception.

"There's a lot of whispers, Li. I mean...*a lot*. So many that I'm not even sure it's considered whispering anymore." She cringed during the emphasis on how much chatter there had been. "You have to start pulling on the reins and cracking the whip if we are going to salvage what's left of Dad's legacy. People are getting antsy and seeking out work elsewhere. It looks bad."

"Don't fuckin' tell me how bad it looks. You think I don't know that?" He snapped at her, the anger and frustration soaking his words and finally, his glare settling at her.

She released a breath she hadn't realized she was even holding. "I know you know that, but goddammit, Liam, the ship is sinking, and you're still waiting for the captain to show up. You're the fucking captain! Show up and fix it because if you don't, I will, and you won't like how I start handling things." Her own irritation was beginning to rise up from its cage.

His brooding and inability to take charge of business matters over the last few months had been a constant, and it wasn't getting any better. Layne was doing her best to pick up the pieces, but Liam wasn't making either of their lives any easier.

His hazel eyes burned as he glared at her. "You think you could do a better job, Layne? Is that what you think?" His tone turned accusatory.

Oh, Christ, here we go. "Hell, yes. Jesus, Li, a toddler could do a better job than you are right now. Who was the one who got shit fixed down at the Mirror last month, huh? Sure as hell wasn't you!" Layne was all out of patience with her brother, and she wasn't about to spare him her thoughts on how he was handling matters. Coddling was not in her nature, especially not when he wanted to pick fights.

She may have had some help fixing up that mess at the gambling club, but she hadn't divulged to Liam her encounter with Eric Ellis just yet. Before she was willing to bring it to his attention, she needed to know more about this latest player in the city's criminal underworld. Why set herself up for another shouting match with Liam because his ego once again got bruised when business matters fell into her lap?

She had been doing her research on their new neighbor residing not too far from O'Reilly Manor. However, there wasn't much to be found out about him. The contacts who were still willing to work with her were struggling to figure out his story.

Liam squared up with her, and even given the size differential; she wasn't intimidated into backing away as he stared down at her with darkness in his eyes. He didn't say a word to her for several minutes while waiting for her to budge or look away.

Speaking through clenched teeth, he dropped his voice down low. "You don't know shit about what it takes, and you don't get to sit there on your high horse judging me. If Dad thought you had *any* potential, he would have given you the chance. Instead, you've always needed a man to save your ass when you've gotten in over your head."

The words pierced her heart, and the venom seeped into her bloodstream as he spat his verbal attack at her. The worst part was that he wasn't wrong, and Layne saw that plain as day.

Walking off, Liam pushed past her and harshly bumped against her left shoulder to serve as a reminder of the last time she had needed help. She closed her eyes and pushed the fury back down her throat into a metaphorical box to be locked away until a day when it wouldn't be contained any longer.

Today wasn't going to be that day. She hoped tomorrow wouldn't be either. Was it too much to ask to never let that day come?

The thunder echoed in the distance, announcing the approach of the storm.

CHAPTER THREE

The rain had begun to fall on the drive back home, splashing across her windshield and triggering the sensors of the automatic wipers to clear them away.

Layne had done her best not to sink into her thoughts where she could drown trying to fix everything that was wrong with her life.

When she went to pull into her garage, some douchenozzle was blocking the driveway path that had plain as day signs that said, 'Do Not Block Drive.'

"You've got to be shittin' me," she drove past her house and ended up finding an open spot around the corner. However, the storm appeared to match her current mood and picked up in intensity by the time she got out of her vehicle.

The skies opened up and unleashed a furious amount of rain that came down by the bucketful. Each raindrop stung as it pelted her flesh. Layne ran along the sidewalk, splashing in puddles that had formed in a matter of seconds as the storm drains attempted to relieve the flooding on the street.

When she did get inside her house, she looked no better than a drowned rat. Her long brunette locks were plastered to her fair skin, and there wasn't a single dry spot on her clothes. She flipped on the lights now that her home was cast into darkness thanks to the powerful storm raging outside and had devoured any sunlight.

Layne peeled her jacket off her, dropping it to the floor with a heavy splat. She shook her arms off, her grey tee clung to her upper body's every curve and swell. The drops of rainwater rolled down along her skin between the layers of clothing. She kicked off her shoes, flinging them off to the side in the main entrance's foyer.

Lightning flashed outside her windows, followed by the crackle and boom of thunder shortly after. The increased pressure of the rain crashing against the windows indicated the strength of the storm was intensifying.

She sighed as she moved to her modestly sized laundry room, leaving a wet trail of footsteps behind her. Peering inside the top of the washer, she realized she had forgotten to move the laundry to the dryer yet again. Embracing a fuck it attitude, she figured she'd wash it all one more time with a few more articles of her clothing.

The first thing to get pitched in was her damp socks, followed by her shirt, tossing it straight into the partially full washing machine. Before she could remove anything else, the lights in her house flickered, and the sound of the power cutting out caused her to curse.

Layne's eyes fought to see through the darkness as her hands reached out in front of her to ensure she didn't trip over something like a broom and die in a freak accident. She needed to find her flashlight, which she thought was in one of the junk drawers in her kitchen, or maybe she had left one in the office. After a brief debate on where she had left it, she opted to check the kitchen first.

Before she reached the entrance to the kitchen, she stopped in the hallway when something caused her to freeze up. Her steps came to a halt when one of the floorboards at the other end of the hall creaked. Layne's senses were all raised to high alert as she strained to sense any other movement or presence there in the darkness of her home.

The adrenaline prompted her heart to beat faster, delivering more oxygen to the rest of her body as she stood as still as a statue. The second she heard the rustle of clothing from someone else moving closer to her, she didn't allow herself to think before she struck.

She lunged at the shadow, and when she made contact, she ended up shoving the large body harshly against a wall. The shadow's hands grabbed for her arms, but she defensively evaded them.

Grabbing the tall shoulder of the shadow, she pulled down while simultaneously driving her knee upwards into its stomach. A set of hands grabbed the knee of that same leg and pulled her off balance, dropping her down onto her back on the floor. The impact of her back hitting the ground smacked the air right out of her lungs, leaving her unable to even gasp for a brief moment.

The shadow's considerable weight was soon down on top of her, attempting to pin her down, but she squirmed, using the leverage of her feet against the floor to roll herself over on top of what was most certainly a male shadow.

Straddling her assailant, she threw an aggressive fist at the slight outline of his head as her eyes began to partially adjust to the darkness. Her knuckles made contact, but it was a grazing strike while the size and strength of the shadow's hands shielded himself.

He bucked her off him, which caused her to fall off to the side, crashing into a small decorative table where she typically kept little odds and ends. As her body crashed into it, the table wobbled on its spindly legs and scratched across the wooden floor before it toppled over altogether.

Layne scrambled to her feet to create distance between her and the ominous shadow that hadn't been invited into her home. A powerful hand grabbed her ankle, which caused her to fall forward. Her hands broke her fall, allowing her to continue the fight to escape the shadow's hold on her.

It felt like an eternity that she had yanked and tugged to break the grasp on her ankle, but when she finally did, she broke out into a full sprint down the hall. The sound of heavy boots quickly followed behind.

Her hands outstretched in front of her ensured she didn't run into a wall at full speed. The change of the floor underneath her bare feet from wood to an area rug as she rounded a corner indicated she had successfully made it into the living room.

The bad news? So did the shadow. Layne was jerked back by her waist against the steel body of the shadow that had been so persistent not to let her get away. She screamed out in a mixture of surprise and desperation.

The powerful arms fought with her as she made it challenging as hell to restrain her there. A hand finally clamped down over her mouth, muffling the screams tearing out of her throat. Unable to compete with strength alone, Layne got pulled across the living room and forced down into the softness of her sofa cushions.

A knee forcefully pressed into her back, pinning her underneath the shadow's weight as her hands were pulled behind her and a set of cold metal cuffs clicked shut around each of her wrists. With her hands now bound behind her, she was pulled upright to sit on the couch.

She tried to stand up, only to have the pair of hands give her enough of a shove that she lost her footing and plopped right back down onto her ass again.

Layne glared at the dark figure in front of her. She hoped that he could see the dirty look she was giving.

She should have been afraid, but she wasn't. Instead, she felt an odd sense of nothingness that if this was going to be her demise, then so be it. Everyone had their day.

"Just get it over with," Layne impatiently spat the order out.

The figure crouched down in front of her, a hand came up under her chin and took hold of her jaw. Finally, the shadow spoke his first words to her.

"I need a favor." Joey's voice immediately became recognizable.

Some of the tension in her body released, hearing the soothing sound of vocals she would recognize in any crowd. The relief was quickly replaced by anger as she attempted to lash out at him with her hands, only to have the cuffs working by design to prevent her from doing so.

"What in the actual fuck? Get the hell out of my house; I don't care what you need!" She tried to get up off of the couch only to be easily knocked back down onto her ass yet again with a soft bounce against the seat cushion.

"You need to hear me out, Layney." His voice reflected a sense of calm and was collected, something that Layne currently wasn't having any of.

She shook her head in disbelief as he called her by her nickname, which she used to be fond of hearing from him. "No! No, you do not get to call me that." Layne pulled on her wrists, trying to squeeze them out of the steel restraints. "I told you that if I ever saw you again, I would put a bullet between your eyes."

Joey had the nerve to let out a small chuckle. "That's why you've got a pretty new set of bracelets on right now."

The storm outside continued to progress with several flashes of light and booms of thunder. Briefly, she got a glimpse of Joey's face there in front of her, thanks to the lightning that caused a split second of illumination.

His hands settled on the tops of her knees. "I swear, I'm just here on business. If I had any other choice, believe me, I would have taken it. Just take a moment to stop being stubborn and listen."

It may have been a little dramatic the way that she let out a sigh and sank back into the couch, not having much of a choice other than to listen to what he had to say.

Taking her decision to relax a little bit as a green light to continue, Joey began to explain his predicament, "A job came up—"

Layne interrupted. "With your police pals?" The disdain etched over her words after recalling what had been the final straw that forced them apart a little less than a year ago. His total disregard for loyalty in assisting the boys in blue by providing them with valuable intel.

"No, I already told you that there were special circumstances with that, Layne. If you had given me the chance to explain, we could have moved beyond that."

She rolled her eyes, though she would have been surprised if he could see it in the dark.

Joey stood up and took a step back so he could sit on the edge of the coffee table in front of her. "You know what? I wasn't going to bring it up, but since I have you here, you're going to sit there and listen."

He rested his elbows on his knees as his eyes stared at her. "I was going to get pinned on some old charges that were teetering on the edge of the statute of limitations. My only options were to let them rake me over the coals for a lifetime or to find a way around it by scratching their backs. The information I fed to them when it came to anything even remotely tied to you was crafted to send them on a wild goose chase."

The volume of his voice elevated slightly as he made his final point. "I kept your ass from getting raided and diverted their interests elsewhere. I'm not going to sit here and apologize for not only saving my ass but saving yours, too. I did what I had to do."

"And I did what I had to do. I guess that makes us even." Layne hated that his explanation even held the littlest bit of weight. Even knowing she would have likely done the same thing if she had been in his shoes, she was still angry. She was always angry these days.

He stood back up and leaned over, getting in her face so she couldn't avoid what he was about to tell her. "Bullshit, you did what you always do. You shoved me away. You were the one who tossed in the towel and ran away like a scared little girl."

Swallowing the lump in her throat, she turned her face away from him only to have his hand take her by the jaw and turn her head back to face him. "What's the matter, Layne? Is the truth a little too fucking hard to hear?" His words brutally bore down on her, leaving her emotionally reeling in the downward spiral her fractured mental state was already in.

Joey had a way of making it feel impossible to hide behind her defenses and shut everything down inside of her. Layne squeezed her eyes shut, hoping to imagine he wasn't back here in her house again. What she couldn't escape was the telltale scent of the mixture of leather and sage cologne that lingered in the air between them.

Not willing to admit that he pegged the truth spot-on, she sat there silently, trying to shrink down into a mental hiding place.

It was unclear how long they both stubbornly and silently stood their ground. Eventually, she felt his hand ease up off of her face. When she opened her eyes back up, his shadow was no longer there in front of her.

There was a click and a pop, and suddenly, the power was flicking back on throughout her house. Layne squinted as the lights erased the darkness and startled her vision.

Joey walked back into the room, shaking his head to himself as he griped, "You keep so much damn crap in front of your breaker box."

Unsurprisingly, he was wearing his signature style of black cargo pants and a black shirt, but this time, he had added a black zip-up hoodie overtop of it. As she got a good look at him, she hated that she noticed her eyes drifting to the front of his pants first before roaming upward to visually consume the rest of him. Either she had *really* missed him, or he had added a few more pounds of solid bulk at the gym over the past year, and it did him damn good.

Not only did it appear he had been working out more, but there were other noticeable differences. Joey's dirty blonde hair had grown a little longer and shaggier. It suited him, and the way her body was beginning to react, it seemed it didn't disagree.

CHAPTER FOUR

The storm outside was gradually easing up, slowing to an entrancing drizzle. It was nearly reminiscent of one of those meditative sound machines.

As the evening approached, the sunshine never returned from behind the grey storm clouds. Instead, the sky sunk further into darkness.

Once Joey was comfortable that Layne wasn't going to make good on her promise to immediately shoot him, he eased her up off of the couch and spun her around. She was suddenly aware that as his hands touched her bare skin, she was still shirtless and standing there in her fuchsia bra, still damp from being caught in the rain. His fingers trailed down the backs of her arms until they met her restraints.

With a twist and a click, each of the cuffs unlatched from around her wrists.

She mindlessly rubbed each of them, easing away the slight discomfort she had created by overzealously tugging on them earlier.

"Were those necessary?" She turned around, finding herself now looking up into his chocolate-colored eyes that easily had melted her soul so many times before this.

He must have seen something in her face, which caused him to step back and create a healthy amount of space between them. "You tell me."

Joey looked her over and raised an eyebrow. It wasn't just the soaked-to-the-bone look, but other stressors taking a toll on her physically. "You look like shit."

Rude. She tried to give him an offended look, but after the day she had coupled with getting caught in the rain, she had experienced better days. "You really know how to flatter the ladies, don't you?"

He unzipped his sweatshirt, pulling his arms from the sleeves as his muscles flexed underneath his shirt. Joey tossed it over to her. "Here. We still need to talk about my favor."

Reacting quickly, her hands caught the hoodie, resisting the urge to wrap it around her and bask in its warmth and scent.

It had been all too easy to hate him while he had been gone. Now that he was standing there in front of her, looking like ten delicious sins worth committing, she struggled to keep her thoughts out of the gutter. While her dreams had made it difficult to forget how his hands felt against her body, having him standing right there in front of her was sending sparks straight down to her core.

Layne needed to stomp out the old flames of desire, trying to light back up. She couldn't let herself fall into this same old trap with him again.

She tossed the hoodie back to him. "I will go change. If you want to be useful, go make some coffee."

She ran upstairs to swap out her wet clothes for a pair of dry joggers and an old UCLA tee. While she brushed the wet tangles from her hair in front of her bathroom mirror, she tried to run herself through a mental pep talk. Layne was not going to let herself get caught up in Joey's charms, not after everything he had done. Recalling his betrayal, she couldn't put herself through any more pain, even if he had his reasons.

Her eyes drifted down to the unassuming bottle sitting on the counter. After ingesting one pill to take the edge off of this unexpected visit, her hand paused as she examined the container holding the whispered promise of comfort and escape. The internal debate didn't last long before she finally gave in to the temptation and swallowed one more little pill down.

When she came back downstairs, the aroma of freshly brewed coffee greeted her. Following the trail, she found Joey seated at her kitchen table, legs propped up on the seat of a chair across from him with his arms folded in front of his chest casually.

The tattoos of various images flexed across his skin. She knew each one of them well. The clocks, the ominous ravens, gloomy headstones, gothic-looking skulls, and the spread of gentle roses between all of them.

The least he could have done was cover himself up so they wouldn't be such a damn distraction.

His eyes grew darker as he nodded over at the vase full of fresh blossoms. "Who sent those?"

The stems situated on her center island had been sent from Eric Ellis earlier in the week. They had come with an over-the-top designed invitation to a formal soiree he was hosting. Layne had no intentions of going to a party where a bunch of people got all dressed up just to talk shit in a classy upper-crust type of way. Thanks, but no thanks.

She noticed the dark green mug on the table and approached, lifting it to take a careful sip so as to not burn her mouth. "Why do you care?"

He scoffed incredulously. "I don't."

"Well, you obviously do, or else you wouldn't have asked." He wasn't the only one that could call bullshit when they saw it.

Her emerald eyes stared at him while waiting for him to dare and try to tell her otherwise. She took her seat on a chair across from him, drawing her legs up underneath her comfortably criss-cross style. The mug assisted in warming up her hands and getting rid of the chill the rain had set into her bones.

Wisely and predictably, Joey changed the subject. "As I told you, I need a favor."

"Oh?" She didn't hide the fact that she was delighted she was in a position of having something he needed.

Ignoring her sass, he continued, "I have a contract that's a little outside of my typical job. Less physical confrontation and more gathering of information and surveillance. Then, depending on what I find, I suspect it will end as it always does."

Listening to him explain the reason for breaking his way back into her life and her house, she waved her hand at him.

"I get it, so what do you need from me?" Forcing him to cut to the chase as she took another sip from the dark brew that he still managed to get just right with the perfect amount of half-and-half.

"Access to Eric Ellis. I heard he's going to be throwing a party under the guise of charity or some bullshit like that."

Layne coughed as the coffee started to go down the wrong pipe, and she put her hand up to her mouth, wiping away the hot liquid.

He raised a brow, dropping his feet down from the chair, ready in the event she truly was going to suffer death via coffee.

Layne shook her head adamantly. "No way." She put her coffee mug down on the table as she got up to grab a napkin to wipe her hands off. "Figure it out on your own; I don't want any involvement with this. Absolutely none."

He got up and walked over to her, his presence still holding that aura of intimidation and dominance he had always been so good at asserting.

"You owe me, just get me in there." He stared down at her intently.

Layne stepped back, bumping into the pantry door. "Damnit, Joey, I said no! I don't owe you shit. I'm not getting involved with that arrogant, self-absorbed asshole. What makes you even think I could get you in any way? I don't just get social invitations to every party on the Upper East Side."

He smirked. "So, you *do* know about the event."

Exasperated, she tossed her hands in the air. "Yes, ok? I know about it, but I'm not going. I am not playing a delicate princess for a night and have to pretend to like these people just so you can go play secret agent and snoop around for whatever it is you are looking for."

When she went to move past him to go back to the table, his tattooed hands slid around her waist to stop her in her tracks. His hold pulled her in close to him so their bodies were flush up against one another.

"Just one favor, that's all I'm asking." His voice dropped to a low tone that still had the power to make her legs quiver.

Her breath was stolen away from her when she found herself in the comfort of his touch that she had been unwilling to admit she had missed. But damn, did she miss it. Simultaneously, she was beginning to feel the ease of the two pills she had taken upstairs seeping into her system.

Wrinkling up her forehead, her hands pushed down against the strength of his muscled forearms in a poor attempt to remove his hands from her sides. "I-I can't. I won't do this."

Things began to feel like they were moving too quickly around her or perhaps too slowly. The air was too warm, but there were chills dancing along her skin. The normally welcomed fog in her head was making it a challenge to think straight. Maybe she should have stuck to just that one pill after all.

He tilted his head as his eyes carefully assessed the way she was reacting to him. "Can't do what, Layney?"

Her hands left his arms to rub over her face trying to force her brain to pull its shit together and fight against the high that was taking over. "I'm just tired. Just leave, ok?"

Joey's hands grabbed hers and easily pulled them away from her face so he could look into her eyes. It may have been the torment and hell of her life over the past year, or maybe it was her pupils beginning to constrict, but his entire demeanor shifted into a softer one of genuine concern.

He bent down and scooped one arm under the back of her legs and the other under her back as he picked her up, cradling her close to his chest.

Layne rested her head against his chest, letting the warmth of his body sedate her soul while her brain should have been telling him to piss off. She wanted to tell him to put her back down, but the words were only spoken inside her mind.

Carrying her out of the kitchen, Joey brought her up to her bedroom on the second floor. Her fingers toyed with the fabric of his shirt as she let her mind wander to wherever the pills were taking it.

"You smell like sex. Great sex." Apparently, they were bringing her thoughts straight back to the gutter.

He shot her a confused look. Normally, it would have been a welcomed compliment, but it was a sharp turn from her mood moments ago down in the kitchen.

After he approached her bed, he gently laid her down on it, and Layne's hands clung to him. "Wait." She gave a lazy smile as she stared up at him with heavy eyes. "I didn't mean it."

Joey raised an eyebrow at her words. "Didn't mean what?"

"I don't know, but I didn't." Whatever she was trying to say wasn't making sense as her body began to feel like it was floating through a cloud. She blinked, and when her eyelids opened back up, Joey was next to her in bed with a tight hold on her with, his chin resting on top of her head.

Layne curled up against him, drawing in a full breath of his soothing scent, and when she exhaled, she murmured, "You asked twice."

Her eyes closed once more as she let the opiate ease her back into a slumber where she didn't have to feel or think about the broken pieces of her life.

Joey smoothed her dark tresses away from her face as he watched her soft breaths coming and going rhythmically throughout the rest of the night.

She stretched out her body, feeling the pull of her muscles lengthening from her fingertips down through her toes before she rolled over onto her stomach in her bed.

Hearing rustling coming from her adjoined bathroom, she lifted her head from her pillow and saw the light shining out from underneath the small crevice at the bottom of the door. A moment later, Joey stepped out, still wearing the clothes he had been in last night, sans his boots.

Layne propped herself up on her elbows as she had to mentally try and recall the sequence of events of the night prior. "I didn't expect to see you still here this morning."

His face was as serious as she had ever seen it. "What's going on with you?" He had his suspicions, but given how hard they were for him to believe, he was willing to give her the benefit of the doubt.

So, it seemed that this was going to be a morning about picking fights. She scooted to the edge of the bed and got out, nearly stumbling over the boots he had left there on the floor. "God." She glared at the footwear that nearly killed her, then back to Joey.

"Nothing is going on with me. You're the one who decided to show up without an invitation."

She walked towards her bathroom, but he stepped in front of her, blocking her path. Both her brows perked up as she stared at him. "Do you mind?"

"Layne, something is going on with you." He made it clear he wasn't going to let her by without some sort of explanation.

"Ok." She crossed her arms in front of her chest as both her offensive and defensive mechanisms began to come out. "What's going on with me? Let's see, the one guy I was willing to trust with my soul betrayed me and lied to my face. Then, after a year, he decides to waltz back into my life, asking me to do him a shitty favor."

The anger and frustration filled her voice as she vented to him about only a fraction of what she had on her plate right now.

His eyes drifted over her, trying to assess not only her words but her body language before he let the issue go for the time being. "So, are you going to do it?"

Briefly, she glanced up at the heavens as he renewed his request, and she prayed that whichever god was listening would grant her the patience to deal with his stubbornness that rivaled her own.

Layne sighed as she looked over at him. "You're so good at breaking into my house, why can't you just break into his?"

He shrugged unapologetically. "Not for nothing, Layney, but you don't exactly make it difficult for me. Besides, Ellis has his place built like a damn fortress. Nobody is getting in or out of there without him knowing. Not without enough time, energy, and distractions, anyway."

There he was, saying her name like that again. Growing weary of his insistence about fulfilling his request, her arms dropped to her sides, getting the feeling he wasn't going to let this go. She just didn't have the fight in her to argue with him for days, and knowing him, he would argue with her for weeks if he felt so inclined. "What's in it for me if I do?"

An amused grin appeared on his face. "Always about the bottom line, aren't you? What do you want?"

The way he asked that second question seemed to hold a lot more than what met the eye. Then, he took a step toward her, his hands running up along her shoulders and up the sides of her neck until his palms settled on either side of her face. "Hm?"

A dryness overcame her mouth as he peered down at her while embracing her face in his hands.

Days before Mick's ultimate betrayal, Layne was coming out of her bathroom after her morning shower. Joey had greeted her right outside the doorway as she exited. His hands cupped her face and pulled her in to steal a kiss from her.

After claiming her lips for a moment, he looked down into the sparkle of her green eyes. "Where was my invitation to join you?"

Layne grinned at him. "Since when has a lack of an invitation ever stopped you?"

Snapping back from the playback reel inside of her head, she found herself in the same place and looking up into the very same eyes as he held her face between his hands.

"Just… behave yourself. This isn't an open invitation for you to start hanging around all the time." Her hands came up to settle on top of each of his, trying to will herself to pull them away.

Joey chuckled at such a minimal request. "Is that all?"

"I mean it, Joey. This one favor changes nothing. I will get you into the party, but that's it. I'm washing my hands of all of this, including you. I've got enough shit going on without having to deal with yours, too." Layne had no idea why she was bothering to grant him this one favor, but if it meant that he would quickly be back out of her life afterward, then she was willing to bend a little.

He pressed his forehead against hers as his thumb stroked over her cheek. "Thank you."

She cleared her throat and finally managed to pull away from him before she made any more stupid decisions with her life. Layne hoped that he wouldn't make her regret this.

"There are going to be ground rules because I don't want to get dragged into this blindly. One," she raised a finger at him as she counted, "you need to see someone about a tux. I can't have you showing up like you rolled out of a Humvee. Two, I don't want to know what the hell you need or why you need it at the party. I want total plausible deniability. And three, all your favors are all used up after this. Every. Last. One."

Seemingly, Joey was in agreement with all of her rules as he nodded after each demand. "It's a done deal then. We can talk about specifics as it gets closer." The temptation to seal it with a kiss lingered in the air. A temptation that neither of them gave into.

After Joey got his boots back on, she shooed him off so she could go about her busy day of doing damage control around town, primarily trying to rein in Liam.

Layne did her best to convince herself that this wouldn't get messy and that it was strictly a one-time business deal. The problem was that this had all the hallmarks of going to hell in a handbasket. Wasn't that how everything in her life went?

CHAPTER FIVE

Finally, she felt like she could suck in some fresh air after Joey left her house. Fresh air that wasn't tainted by the head swirling scent of him. She made a note that if she wanted to erase evidence of his time there, she was going to need to toss all her bedding in the laundry unless she wanted him haunting any more of her dreams. Damn it, she had forgotten the laundry again, thanks to Joey's unexpected visit.

Layne was seriously questioning her mental state in agreeing to this batshit insane request from him. She shouldn't have agreed to it, but if there was anybody who wasn't going to give up, it would be Joey.

Right now's problem though? She had to deal with her brother, which was an entirely different fiasco. One that had immediate and more damning consequences.

First things first, she went downstairs and pulled the invitation to Eric's soiree out of a drawer filled with various other paperwork and takeout menus. The fancy script listed a phone number to RSVP. Well, there wasn't going to be a better time than the present.

After dialing the number from her cell, she held it to her ear while it rang. Deep down, she hoped it would go to voicemail. That was until the smooth male voice answered on the other end.

"Eric Ellis."

She mouthed the word 'fuck' and winced at the thought of actually having to have this conversation with him. Layne had been doing an expert job of avoiding talking to him after their encounter at the Brass Mirror, though it wasn't for lack of effort on his part.

"Hi, Eric, it's Layne O'Reilly."

Immediately, she could hear the smile reach his voice. "My little harpy, I've been waiting to hear from you."

She cringed at his pet name for her but swallowed her pride for a brief moment so she could get through this discussion without compromising the whole damn setup.

"Things have been hectic. Look, thank you for the flowers, but they aren't necessary."

"They were entirely necessary." He sounded far too sure of himself.

Biting her lip gently, she tried to assemble her words intelligently. "About the invitation, parties aren't my thing, but Liam thought it would be a good idea to be seen out and about rubbing elbows with the city's top-tier elite." Yes, she was lying out of her ass and may have added another item to her checklist to let Liam know what a good idea he had when she saw him later.

There was a pause on the other end of the line, leaving Layne wondering if the call had dropped. Finally, after the awkward pause, Eric responded, "You surprised me, Layne. I expected you to call to tell me where I could shove the invite."

"I very strongly considered it." At least that part was the God-honest truth.

His laugh echoed on the other end. "Nonetheless, I will make sure that you are my guest of honor. I have been looking forward to continuing our discussion about how we can help one another. How about I pick you up tomorrow morning, and we can talk about things during a walk around Central Park?"

She pressed her lips into a hard line, doing her best to remind herself that she needed to focus on the business side of things and see past her personal feelings. "Fine, I will see you tomorrow morning, but don't get your hopes up."

Eric set a time, and they said brief goodbyes before terminating the call. Layne was already regretting her decision, but with her back up against the proverbial wall, she needed to keep her options open. Not just for herself, but for the sake of the O'Reilly legacy.

That afternoon, she sat in her dad's former office in O'Reilly Manor, waiting for Liam to show up. She looked at her smartwatch for what felt like the fifth or sixth time. He was supposed to be here twenty minutes ago.

Liam had taken over the office since their dad had passed, but it was only in the past couple of months that he began changing up the decor to fit his personal and flashy style. The formerly glossy wooden desk no longer filled the room, and in its place was something more ultra-modern with metal and thick panes of glass.

She walked over to the window and peered out across the street, watching the cars that drove by. Seeing a sports bike across the street that looked familiar, she narrowed her eyes to focus on it. However, her focus was quickly interrupted when the office door swung open forcefully.

Spinning around, she saw Liam walking in, a scowl on his face as he stomped over to his desk. His auburn hair looked like he had been running his fingers through it repeatedly, leaving the short locks sticking up in various directions.

"What are you doing here?" he said grumpily, clearly in a foul ass mood. Today was looking like a bucket of sunshine, wasn't it?

"We had a meeting scheduled, remember?" She walked away from her spot at the window and sat down in one of the two chairs across from him.

Her brother took his seat and then motioned for her to continue. "Just tell me what the hell is wrong now, and let's get this over with."

Under normal circumstances, that would have been a fair assumption, but this time, she was aiming for a more positive discussion. "There's a few things, actually, so you might as well get comfortable."

The irritation written across his face was plain as day. "Layne, I don't have time for this. Give me the shortest possible version."

This was proving to be such a stark comparison to the way their dad ran things, even when he was pressed for time, he had made others wait while he set aside time to listen to whomever he was meeting with.

She dropped the biggest item of focus. "Eric Ellis wants to discuss us potentially helping each other out. A whole 'we scratch his back, he scratches ours' type of situation."

That caught Liam's attention. "Ellis? The bougie asshole that moved here six months ago?"

She nodded. "Yes, that one. I'm vetting the whole thing; it may end up being nothing at all. He invited me to this get-together he is having so we can talk things over."

Maybe she fudged that part a little bit, but there was no reason to make Liam think that it was anything more than just idle talks. Nor did he know about Joey coming back around, or as Liam only knew him as the masked freak hired to dispose of Michael Franzetti.

To his credit, he sat there mulling it over as he sat back in his chair. His fingers lightly scratched at his chin. "What the hell does he have going on that we would need him for? You know what? Never mind, just find out. Anything else?"

She shifted uncomfortably in her seat. "Li, we need to talk about the books and client debts going uncollected. People are noticing the cracks, and—"

A bunch of commotion was heard coming down the hall, a shrill voice shrieking out words as the click-clacking of heels stomped against the floor until Kristill appeared at the entrance of the office.

Layne groaned and rubbed her forehead, seeing Liam's favorite hookup fuming with daggers for eyes.

Pointing a bony finger all accusatory at Liam, Kristill shouted. "You are a fuckin' prick, ya know that?! I want the damn money you promised me!"

Her brother rose to his feet and grabbed a decorative glass paperweight, chucking it in the woman's direction. It flew far right and smashed into the door. "I told you that you'd get the money when you did your job, you dumb whore!"

It was incredibly clear to Layne that she was unlikely to finish her discussion with Liam, at least not without getting in his volatile path and being the next person he tossed something at.

Kristill was undeterred by the flying object and was bound and determined to get up in his face. She spat her words out at him, saliva sputtering out venomously. "You're a sick bastard! I ain't sticking any of that up in my p—"

As a sister, Layne did *not* want to hear Kristill finish that sentence and hear about any of her sibling's more peculiar proclivities. However, Liam didn't allow her to finish her shouting as the sound of the violent slap of his palm across the woman's face cut off the words.

Shit. Layne popped out of her seat and scurried over between the two of them right as Liam went to lash out at Kristill once more. His face was beet-red and eyes wild with a whole new level of temper she had never seen before.

Layne ended up soaking part of his shove meant for Kristill, which was probably for the better, considering she was likely less than one hundred pounds soaking wet. "Enough! What the fuck is wrong with you?!"

Kristill was still reeling from the strike, holding her face, which had blossomed in a bright red glow.

If Liam wanted to throw another hit, he was going to have to go through Layne. While Kristill was not on Layne's list of favorite people, she didn't deserve to be Liam's punching bag either. Fortunately, he decided to choose his battles wisely and left Layne unscathed for now.

Noticing that a couple of the guys that still worked for them were standing in the doorway to the office, staring dumbly at the scene unfolding, Layne got even more pissed off. Glaring at them, she pointed at them and then Kristill. "What the fuck are you staring at? Get her out of here!"

She shook her head as the two men finally snapped into gear and escorted Kristill out of the office and, hopefully, out of the house altogether.

Layne turned her head to look back at her brother. "Really? You've been blowing our money on *that*? Damnit, Li! I keep telling you we can't keep doing this!"

He backed up and kicked over a wastebasket that was to the side of his desk, sending it skittering across the floor into a bookshelf. "I don't need you chastising me, Layne! Learn to stay in your damn place! I've got this handled!"

"Handled?! The only thing that I can see that you've got handled is dismantling this entire damn operation!" She scoffed that he could believe that anything they had going on in their lives was being handled.

"Do us both a favor, huh?" He came up to her, his face still flushed with enough red rage that it could have passed for a volcanic eruption. "Keep your damn mouth shut until I ask for your opinion. I'm tired of hearing you yapping at me every other day."

She should have been the one to explode, but she bit her tongue as she heard him loud and clear. Shaking her head, she made her decision. "I told you if you didn't salvage operations that I would, and you wouldn't like the way I handle things. You've left me no choice, and that's something you're going to have to deal with. I'm not going to be held responsible for your inability to step up and be a damn man. The spoiled little brat who doesn't get to play for free act is getting real fuckin' old."

Layne walked away from him. She knew what she needed to do. If she was going to survive in a world where the other big bad criminals fed on the weak, she had to strengthen her position. She couldn't rely on Liam any longer. If her family name was ever going to command the respect it once had under Scott O'Reilly's leadership, Layne was going to have to be the one to step up and make the hard sacrifices.

CHAPTER SIX

In a rare instance of waking up before her alarm wailed, Layne had been trying to fend off the headache nagging at the inside of her skull all night. The events that transpired the day before with Joey, Eric, and Liam had left her mind unable to turn itself off.

When she did finally get out of bed, she got ready for her outing with Eric. She stared at her clothes hanging up inside of her walk-in closet. Layne internally debated as to what she should wear to meet with a potential ally who appeared to have the hots for her. She couldn't deny that at least he was a sight worth looking at in return.

After spending far too much thought on it, she opted for a pair of skin-tight jeans that flattered the shape of her legs and the curve of her ass. They had always been her favorite pair. Matching the jeans with a light blue sweater with a low-cut v-neck was a compromise between casual and flirty. Not to mention a little bit of warmth, given the shift into the crisp autumn air that was falling over the northeast.

Layne swept her hair up into a loose bun, only a few rogue strands falling away from the bundle of chestnut locks at the back of her head.

Once she was downstairs, while she was draping a black knit scarf around the back of her neck, the chime of the doorbell sounded. Unhooking her coat from a rack on the wall, she swiftly slid it on before answering the front door.

Standing there on the other side was her potential new business partner, Eric. His eyes lit up when he saw her, and he held out a cup of coffee for her. "A peace offering for springing this on you last minute yesterday."

Trying not to let on that she appreciated the coffee too much, she managed to only give him a polite smile before accepting the steaming cup of joe. "Thanks."

After locking up her house, they walked a few blocks over until they approached Central Park. People were casually walking along a paved path, some with their dogs, others with their strollers, and some training for their next big 5k.

Layne took a sip from her coffee, noting that it had notes of nutmeg and vanilla in it, a satisfying combination with the richness of the dark roast. It was fancy, much like Eric, but still appreciated for its caffeine content.

She looked over at the man who was determined to find mutual ground with her. "Well, you have me here. What's your proposal?"

Eric wasn't dressed nearly as formally as he had been when they first met. He was wearing a navy pullover sweater with a lighter blue shirt underneath and a pair of khaki pants that fit his lower body perfectly.

He smirked as Layne cut right to the point. "I hoped for us to get to know each other on a more personal level before diving right into business discussions."

Her eyebrows lifted briefly before she gave a partial laugh. "I don't bring my personal life into my business if I can help it." She walked off the path onto the lawn that had the beginnings of fallen leaves sprinkled indiscriminately across it. The blustery air carried nature's little messengers of the season change to and fro.

He followed beside her. "Your life is your business, and soon you're not going to have either if drastic changes aren't made."

She stopped and turned to face him, not appreciating the way he pointed out the seriousness of her situation. "Are you trying to intimidate me?"

He shook his head. "Not at all, but you know as well as I that the state of things will make you and everyone tied to you a weak and easy target. I don't want to see that happen."

Layne narrowed her eyes at him. "Why should you care?"

Eric leaned in and dropped the volume of his voice as though he was going to share highly confidential information. "Call me a bleeding heart." He smiled at her before he walked to a bench set underneath a line of trees and motioned for her to take a seat beside him.

Stupidity generally wasn't one of Layne's top traits, and it would be stupid of her not to be skeptical of his motives. After following him to the bench, she continued to stand.

"Alright, let's get personal then." Her eyes reflected her consideration of the next move she needed to make in this game of dangerous and violent real-world chess. "Bleeding heart or not, this isn't solely a business move for you. If it was, you'd be speaking with Liam. So, why me?"

Impressed with her assessment, he nodded.

"All due respect, your brother isn't cut of the same cloth as your father was. You, on the other hand, very much are."

Her expression shifted slightly, indicating she didn't quite believe him. "Says the man who hardly knows a thing about me."

Eric grinned and leaned back against the bench as he spread his arms along the backrest, and he locked arctic blue eyes on her.

"I know enough. Besides, I know that an alliance between us would send a strong message to the other factions. Together, we could be a force to be reckoned with. Isn't that the type of respect you deserve? Your father had it."

Layne hated that he was laying out a game plan that was not only beneficial but made sense. She finally opted to take a seat next to him but was sure to leave a comfortable amount of space between the two of them. There was no sense in letting him get the wrong idea that she was particularly keen on this. She drank from her coffee cup as she let the entire concept of both a personal and business merger soak in.

"Just spit it out. What are the terms?" She stared straight ahead, her eyes focusing on the scenery of buildings jutting into the skyline.

His hand reached over and rested on top of her leg, just above the knee. "For starters, we could make it clear to the public eye that we will be working together very closely. Then, we can discuss how you'd like to tie the knot."

His touch immediately snagged her attention and shook something up inside of her. When her head turned to look at him, he seemed to be positioned closer to her.

"Gee, you go all out on a proposal, don't you?"

Eric's hand slid up her leg gradually. "Are you saying 'no'?"

She grazed her teeth across her bottom lip as she brought her face in closer to his.

"I'm saying you're going to need a hell of a lot more than a two-minute elevator pitch and a cup of coffee to convince me to say 'yes'."

Layne straightened up and pulled back from him. When she decided to stand back up to distance his touch on her leg, his hand grabbed hers to encourage her not to leave. His hold was firm but not painful.

"Give me a chance to show you how you can have everything you've ever wanted and more than you've dreamed of. But, let's face it, you don't have much time left to make up your mind." He was pointing out what she had been trying to avoid thinking about. Time.

After her encounter with Liam yesterday, she had even less time than most people knew. The painful realization couldn't be hidden from her eyes, knowing she was running out of options and the train was running out of track.

Eric keenly picked up on it and stood up, releasing her hand and running his hands over the yarn of her scarf draped around her neck. He wrapped his hands up in the material and used it to tug her in closer to him.

Looking up into the devilish charm of his face, she knew he was more aware of how precarious her position was than he was letting on.

His face neared hers while his silky tone offered unspoken promises. "We can take the world by storm, my little harpy."

She wanted to choke on the air around her. Damn him. Damn her. Damn it all. Damn everything to hell.

"I will have an answer for you by the time I see you at the party at the end of the month." That at least seemed like a decent amount of a delay for her to figure her shit out. Miracles happen all the time, right?

He whispered into her ear with a purr. "I look forward to it." The softness of his lips left a light caress against the side of her face as he uttered his words to her. Layne's heartbeat quickened, and when she turned her head, his mouth was right there, hovering over hers.

"If I were you, I wouldn't disappoint me." His hold released from her scarf, letting the ends fall back down into place before giving her a little more room to breathe.

Eric had insisted on escorting her back to her house after they had carried a lighter topic of conversation. He told her about the renovations on his house and the way he was getting to know some of the other faction heads planted across the city.

As they left the park, Eric took ahold of her hand and quickly crossed the street to avoid getting run over by typical New York drivers. Walking by various parked vehicles along the street, Layne failed to notice that they walked by a black sports bike with a helmet resting on the seat. A helmet with decals representing a skull-like smile across the front of it.

After arriving back on her front steps, Eric managed to sneak in a quick peck on her cheek before he went on his way. Something in the way he had looked at her before he left indicated there was far more to his interests than he was divulging to her.

Layne was left wondering whether tying herself to Eric was grabbing onto a lifeline or was it an anchor that was going to pull her down into the depths of the ocean? There was only going to be one way to find out.

CHAPTER SEVEN

Each day following her outing with Eric, a new bouquet of fresh stems was delivered to her house. Today's delivery was a unique set of blossoms wrapped in black florist paper. It was a mixture of roses and lilies, but it was their coloring that made them so eye-catching.

The starburst-shaped lilies had deep violet hues on the edges of the petals that grew lighter in a gradient effect towards the pistil in the center. By contrast, the tightly wrapped rose petals were a lighter shade of purple on the outside that darkened with each layer until they were nearly black in the center.

A shining silver card was tucked inside with a handwritten note which simply read:

My little harpy.

With all these deliveries, it was making it difficult to take her mind off the choice she was going to have to make in a few weeks. Not to mention, her house was beginning to smell like a florist as she tried to find a spot for each new delivery.

Layne chose to put this newest set of flowers inside her home office, arranging them in a vase that was centered on one of the shelves of her bookcase.

As for the other man weighing heavily on her mind, if Joey had been snooping around and keeping tabs on her, she hadn't caught him in the act…yet. After catching a glimpse of a sports bike outside of O'Reilly Manor the other day when she met with Liam, it left her questioning if she was just being paranoid, hopeful, or maybe both.

He was particularly adept at lingering without making himself known, she had learned that very early on after their first encounter. However, she still hadn't been able to fully anticipate his next steps, and that's what drove her crazy the most. Joey was capable of living in her blind spot when he wanted, and she hated not being able to get ahead of his every move.

As far as she was aware, he was behaving himself and keeping his distance. He had left her a new number to reach him at so they could talk over some of the more mundane details of getting him into the Ellis residence on the night of the party.

Layne pulled out her phone and texted his contact number.

LAYNE

Did you get your tux?

JOEY

Just got back from the fitting.

LAYNE

Are you still set on meeting me at the party instead of picking me up like a gentleman?

JOEY

You know I don't do the knight in shining armor act.

I will leave that to Prince Charming.

Even though she hadn't heard his tone, it was clear he had some opinions on Eric's affections towards her in referring to him as a prince out of a fairy tale.

Word was making its way through the grapevines around that Ellis and Layne had some personally driven interactions. Undoubtedly, Joey's tap into the criminal underworld hadn't spared him that knowledge. Unbeknownst to her, he may just have been seeing more than he was letting on.

LAYNE

Well, if you're late, I'm going in without you.

JOEY

Layney, you should know by now I'm never late.

LAYNE

Yes, I know you're obsessed with punctuality.

JOEY

(. . .)

Layne saw the text bubble that indicated Joey was typing a response, but one never came. She waited a few minutes before giving up and determining he thought better about what he wanted to say to her.

Frustrated yet mildly curious, she contemplated calling him out on his unsent thoughts. However, knowing Joey, he would just ignore the inquisition. She sighed and decided she desperately needed a distraction from all of this before her thoughts drove her crazy.

Good thing she at least had plans to go dress shopping with Rebecca in an hour. Girl time always proved to be an escape from the wild chaos of her life.

After a long period of silence, there was finally a sign of life. "I look like a pumpkin that's been rotting on the porch for two months too long!" Layne shouted out to Rebecca from behind the curtain of the dressing room of the boutique dress shop.

She yanked the curtain to the side and stepped out to confirm that the dress she tried on did indeed make her look like a deflated pumpkin—from the aggressive shades of orange to the poofs in all the wrong places of the sleeves and the awkwardly shaped bustle.

With a glass of champagne in one hand and her phone snapping photographic evidence in the other, Rebecca was crying in a fit of laughter.

Dryly and unamused, Layne spoke, "I'm glad you find this amusing." Layne gave a huff and a sigh as she tugged at the itchy tulle of the gown. "I don't even know why I even care, I don't even want to go to this damn event."

Her best friend sat there on the velvet bench across from the dressing room and put her phone down for a moment to wipe a few tears away from underneath her eyes, attempting to speak coherently between her giggles.

"I-I… hope it's a—" Rebecca chuckled again before sputtering out her thought, "it's a H-Halloween party!" She deteriorated back into side-splitting laughter for a moment before making a more serious effort to compose herself.

Layne stood there, not finding the humor in this hideous gown, her arms crossed in front of her. "Ha-ha." She came over and took a seat next to the one person who had always been there to support her no matter the hopelessness of the situation.

She leaned over and rested her head on Rebecca's shoulder. It gave her bestie pause, and she sobered up from her amusement over the ridiculous gown.

Straightening up, she wrapped an arm around Layne's shoulders and drew her into a reassuring hug. "There are plenty of other stores, Layne. You'll find something. There's plenty of time; the party isn't until the end of the month."

"It's not the dress." She frowned while debating how much she was going to be a disappointment to her lifelong friend.

"What is it, then?" The concern was evident in Rebecca's voice as she tried to look at Layne's face to assess just how big whatever was plaguing her was.

Layne raised her head and shook her head as she looked at her hands in her lap. "Same shit it always is. My life is a mess, and I don't even know what to do with it anymore."

"Is Liam being an ass? More than normal anyway?" Rebecca moved her eyebrows questioningly.

Giving a partial crack of a smile at the lovely thought of if that had been the only thing weighing on her, how it would be so much more manageable. "Obviously that, but it's not just that. Everything keeps stacking up, and nothing seems like the right choice anymore. Meanwhile, for every one thing I patch up, three more things fall apart."

Rebecca handed off the rest of her bubbly to Layne, who didn't refuse to consume the dry beverage.

"Well, if I know anything about you at all, it's that you eventually figure out what it is that matters most to you. You're one tough cookie, and you'll figure out how to make it all work out the way it needs to in the end." Rebecca offered her up a hopeful smile, and her pale blue eyes still held concern for Layne's demeanor. "You can't expect to fix everything yourself. You're one person, Layne. A hell of a badass bitch, but you still only have two hands to work with. It's ok to accept help every now and then."

Layne was incredibly grateful that Rebecca knew how to give some of the best advice without prying too much for the details. Communicating the unique complications of her not-so-legal life had never come easy to her, and there were days when it hurt too much to say all the words out loud.

Not to mention, the less Rebecca knew about the business side of things, the better. There was no need to expose her to things that could potentially drag her into the same danger Layne wrangled with on a day-to-day basis.

"I can't tell you how much I appreciate you. You've always been the sister I never had." Her arms wrapped around Rebecca, giving a strong hug.

While her friend returned the gesture, she laughed in response. "Thank God for that, or else we both would be the queens of the insane asylum. I'm not sure the world would have been able to handle it if we had been born sisters." Her words teased in an effort to lighten the mood.

Layne chuckled, imagining just how fucked they both would have been had they grown up together in the same household. At least one of them deserved a chance at a typical life.

Drawing back, Rebecca patted Layne's hand. "Now, please, for the love of God, get out of this dress so I don't go blind."

In full agreement, Layne didn't need to be told twice. She returned to the dressing room and discarded the eyesore of a gown.

Finally, after a few more dresses were tried on and immediately pitched, Layne found the one worthy of wearing in public.

Rebecca whistled in a catcall as she stared in awe at the chosen grown. "If you don't buy this one, I will never speak to you again. The way it fits, you would even have the Pope worshipping the ground you walk on."

Layne stared at her reflection in the mirror, turning to capture each angle of the way the material fit her figure. It had been a while since she had felt this stunning and undeniably beautiful. She smiled confidently to herself, imagining the look on *his* face when he saw her the night of the swanky soiree.

After squaring away all the details for the dress to be tailored to fit her height and size, Layne and Rebecca got to enjoy some lunch out on the sidewalk in front of a small Italian spot. Despite the cooler air of the fall outside, the restaurant had set up heaters to allow diners to enjoy the fresh air a little longer.

Layne stabbed her fork into the oversized meatball, cutting away a bite-sized portion and dunking it in the extra sauce and the mound of burrata. "This place has the best damn meatballs." She shoved the fork into her mouth and gave a satisfied moan.

Rebecca grinned as she also helped herself to the meatball appetizer they were both sharing. "You know," her friend looked at her from across the table, "I'm proud of you."

Layne lifted a brow. "For what?"

Her bestie gave a warm smile. "Not that I need a reason, but the way you—"

Whatever it was that Rebecca was going to say was cut off by the sound of a man yelling from a passing car. "Your time is almost up, you Irish cunt!" Followed by shots ringing out, shattering the front glass window of the restaurant.

Before her brain had time to process the words, Layne heard the firing of bullets. Dropping everything in her hands, Layne reached over and grabbed Rebecca's arm, pulling her down onto the ground. Protectively, Layne lay on top of her, flinching at the sound of each pop.

When the only sounds left were people screaming in a panic, Layne pushed up onto her feet to try and get a look at the vehicle as it took off down the street. The only thing she could make out was the white, blue, and red stripes of the Russian flag on a sticker in the back window.

Now that the threat had passed, she leaned down and helped a shaken-up Rebecca to her feet. "Are you okay?" Her friend gave a slow nod.

Layne stood there breathing heavily as the harsh reminder of the O'Reilly family's standing in this city was plummeting. Today was just a warning, if they had meant to take her out, they could have. But, if she didn't do something soon, Liam and she were going to be at the top of every criminal organization's hit list.

CHAPTER EIGHT

"Mr. Ellis is right this way." The host led the way through the hall down to a private box suite there inside Madison Square Garden. The space could have easily hosted ten or twelve people, but instead, it would just be the two of them.

Eric had been insistent that they continue to be seen together for appearances' sake. It was always about appearances, wasn't it? Money and power, and what you did with it. This was especially true among people in their line of illegal dealings.

Originally, he had tried to convince her to go to the New York Ballet, which was a hard pass for Layne. She had nothing against seeing people in tights and tutus weightlessly glide across a stage, but it was far too stuffy of a way to spend a night out.

His alternative suggestion of seeing a rock music concert at the Garden seemed far more appealing, and it was a bonus that she wouldn't have to get dressed up. Instead, she opted for a set of flattering and snug jeans fashionably torn in a few places across her thighs and a small black tank that had multiple straps crossing over her back and a glimpse of her smooth stomach depending on which way she moved.

Layne's hair was styled into a few edgy braids that fed into a teased ponytail for additional volume and sass. The makeup she opted for matched the rest of her, dark and edgy. Since she didn't anticipate kicking anyone's ass tonight, she had put in a pair of gold hoop earrings in each ear. Under normal circumstances, they just weren't practical when there was a risk of getting them caught up and torn from her lobes. Not something she wanted to experience; she would rather take a bullet to the shoulder. Oh, wait…

When she arrived in the suite, every beverage she could order was available for consumption. Multiple hot trays of food were on display, along with various cold platters. She'd never have to worry about eating for the rest of the week, given the sheer amount of food laid out for just the two of them. If nothing else, Eric was excessive in everything he did.

Eric greeted her immediately, wrapping his arms around her in a hug before pulling back to take in the sight of her with a smile. His right hand gently drifted over her shoulder, his fingers caressing along the shiny scar from where Mick's bullet had entered her body last year.

Self-consciousness caused her to draw her shoulder back from his touch over that grim physical reminder that would never disappear.

He spoke with words filled with awe. "I will never stop being amazed at how much you take my breath away."

At least he was making an effort to stay in her good graces, or maybe he was just hoping that it would help sway her decision in his favor.

She noticed he was dressed down the most she had ever seen him, yet there was still an air of sophistication wrapped around him, from the designer jeans to the plain long-sleeved tee that was sure to cling to the fit outline of his upper body.

His hand dropped down to the small of her back as he guided her over to the bar. "I wasn't sure what you'd feel like drinking, so I made sure there would be a little of everything." If this was his definition of a 'little bit,' she was scared to see him go all out.

Setting her small black purse on the countertop, her eyes scanned the beverage collection before she selected the tall can of *Brooklyn Brewery* Brooklyn Lager from the mini-fridge. "I see that." Her finger popped the tab, prompting the smooth sound of the metal opening up and the quick fizz of the pressure release.

After taking an initial taste of the brewery's flagship beer, she offered him a light smile. She should have felt a sense of awkwardness, but instead, he somehow managed to keep things on the lighter side.

The lights dimmed inside the suite as the remainder of the venue darkened in anticipation of the opening act taking the stage.

Layne walked over to the two nearest seats, with Eric following behind her. Expectedly, he took the seat to her left after she sat down.

Continuing to indulge in a couple of beers over idle conversation, Layne propped her booted foot up against the empty seat in front of her while the band she hadn't ever heard of continued its opening set. What had started as light topics of conversation began to take a turn into more serious things she had been avoiding.

"Layne, I need to know how things are business-wise," he urged her.

"Until you're on a need-to-know basis, Eric, I can't get into it with you." She shook her head, hoping he would leave well enough alone.

"I can't help buy you time if you don't let me." The weight of his arctic blue eyes were on her, even though she was avoiding looking at them. His hand reached over and turned her face toward him. "Let me help as a show of good faith that I'm serious about investing in all of you."

Briefly, she met his eyes but was quick to find another reason to escape. "I need another drink." She left her seat, tossing the empty can into a trash bin on the way back to the fridge. After pulling out the next beverage for herself, she reached into her purse that had been sitting there on the counter since she arrived and pulled out her emotional support pill bottle.

Beer was not going to numb her nearly enough to deal with Eric's probing. Just like it was nothing more than popping an aspirin for a headache, she swallowed down the tablet, chasing it with the freshly opened lager.

Layne returned to her seat, knowing that he was still waiting for her to provide the necessary details he had asked for. She turned in her seat so she could face him as her hands focused on the cold of the beer can between her palms.

"Things are not great, but I'm sure you already knew that. Funds are getting tighter, and it's getting harder to rely on people to stay in line. The list of people working for us is getting shorter by the day. I can only do so much trying to clean up the messes." She slowly dragged in a breath as her thoughts jumped to the last mess she had tried to clean up, thanks to Liam running his mouth to one of their oldest clients on the books. Not to mention the warning she had been given by one of the Russian families.

With another long sip of the slightly hoppy beer, she made an effort to lock all those problems away for another day.

That's when she noticed that Eric's gaze had turned into something more serious as he took in the words she had spoken. His hand reached over and eased the can from her grasp and set it off to the side.

"All you have to do is give the word, little harpy, and I will make it all better." Eric placed his hand on the back of her neck and drew her in closely. "I promise. All you have to do is say 'yes.' I won't even ask you to add a 'please' with it."

Now that the main act had shown up, the inside of MSG was only lit up on the bottom floor where the stage itself had come to life, and fans were screaming in excitement as the first chord erupted across the speakers. The remaining notes of the song followed, but Layne barely noticed over the roar of her resulting self-medication taking hold from behind her eyes and spreading quickly like a violent invasion of her senses.

Not thinking clearly, let alone wanting to think at all, her senses and inhibitions were quickly fading. Instead of committing to one problem of giving him a definitive answer, she committed to another. She latched her mouth onto Eric's. Taken by surprise, Eric gave a pleased smile into the kiss as Layne made the first move, and he was more than happy to embrace the connection with her.

Quickly, he drew her into his lap while his mouth feverishly captured hers and wrangled for dominance. Layne straddled his lap, feeling the growing erection press up against her body.

His arm wrapped around her body, tightly pulling her slender figure up against him while his hips pushed up against her to feel their clothed bodies rubbing against one another.

The more she kissed him, the more her head swam, relying on his hold to keep her in one place. Her lips ran along the line of his jaw as she tried to focus on what she was doing here with him. His cologne filled her nostrils, reminding her of a forest just after the break of dawn, but what it was missing was the scent of sage that she craved the most.

Eric pushed her hips down on him forcefully, eliciting half a moan to be exhaled into his ear, which only encouraged him further. His mouth ventured down to the juncture where her neck met her shoulder, and his teeth sank into her flesh in a possessive bite intended to leave a red ring behind on her unbroken flesh.

Layne didn't feel a whole lot on so many levels, especially in that moment. The result was her poor choices, leading to exactly what she had been after an escape from all the stress and pain in her life that had nowhere else to go. Her hands held onto his shoulders for stability, her face pressed into the side of his neck as she succumbed to the high taking over.

He grasped onto her and stood to shift and swap their positions. He placed her back down on the seat in a way where she was on her knees and the front of her body was up against the backrest.

Layne latched her hands onto the top of the back of the seat, using it like a handlebar for support. Eric's hand slid around to the front of her stomach and down to the waist of her jeans. His fingers pushed the button free, and as he slid his hand directly down the front of her, the loose zipper slid down on its own.

His other hand wrapped itself in the length of her ponytail and tilted her head back enough so he could growl his words into her ear. "I can't wait to hear how you call my name."

Her eyes were barely focused; the ceiling looked hazy from this angle. Yet, she didn't care. She was getting the distraction away from the cruel whispers of her past and current traumas.

Eric's fingers dove deeper between her skin and the fabric of her thong until they slid against the wetness of her slit. Her mouth parted in a breathy moan. He didn't make her wait long before two of his thick fingers found her entrance and buried deep inside of her.

"That's it, baby. You're going to give yourself over to me."

A sensation of pleasure mixed with the sedative effects of her impromptu cocktail of pills and beer. Seeking an even further high, her hips moved her body against his hand.

The heel of his hand stroked over her clit every time he thrust his fingers back into her. At first, the rhythm was slow and predictable, but it quickly began to elevate to something more. His touch was claiming her wet pussy, and she was encouraging it as a means to her own unraveling.

Her sweet moans grew more intense, though overpowered by the loud music of the band blaring across the speakers throughout the building. Layne's body shivered from the escalation of pleasure marking the approach of her release. "Mm, I'm gonna… come…"

"Go ahead and come all over my fingers. Show me how much you like it when I make you squirm, my little harpy. And, when you're done, you're going to do it again for me until I'm all you can think about." The tips of his fingers curled and pressed against the spot deep inside of her, causing her body to bear down around him as she cried out in release.

The sticky, sweet arousal from her body coated his fingers that continued to massage against the sensitive spot they had found, extending the lustful ride she was getting.

The surge of oxytocin gave a brief reprieve from the haziness of her thoughts. As her chest rose and fell due to the breathlessness, she attempted to get up off the seat.

He withdrew the hand from inside of her, only to release her ponytail with his other hand and press down on her shoulder to keep her right where she was. "Not yet, I want to see what else your hot little pussy can take." Eric brought his fingers to his mouth, sucking the taste of her off of each one.

"I need a minute." Mentally or physically, she wasn't even sure.

That's when some prying eyes decided enough was enough, and a strip of light cut into the suite as the velvety privacy curtain slid to the side.

Layne's eyes tiredly looked at the intruding figure and saw Joey walking into the room. She questioned if she was seeing correctly. Maybe she was dreaming again, and things were going to get really hot in here.

He was wearing a white shirt with the black outline of a skull on it underneath, a thin black jacket with the sleeves pushed halfway up his forearms, and a pair of slim-fitted deep blue jeans on his muscled legs.

Eric stepped back from Layne as if he hadn't just been fingerfucking her moments ago. "Private suite, asshole."

Joey's jaw clenched tightly as he approached the two of them, his size and build overshadowing Eric easily. He glanced down at Layne, his brown eyes set in a stony, cold look. "I'm Miss O'Reilly's personal security, asshole."

An arrogant and judgmental scoff immediately came from Eric. "As you can see, she's fine." He leaned down and turned Layne's head to face him as he slowly assaulted her mouth with his lips for a moment. "Isn't that right?"

Images of snapping Eric's neck flashed through Joey's mind. "She's had enough fun for the night." He shoved himself between Layne and Eric.

A spark of anger rose in Eric's eyes. "That's not your call."

Now, Joey was imagining all the other creative ways he could send Eric to the grave in the most spectacularly gruesome way. If he didn't need Eric alive for his current job, he would have acted on his urges without hesitation.

Layne pushed up against the seat, underestimating just how woozy and uneasy on her feet she was. Her legs trembled underneath the weight of her body and caused her to stumble.

Joey's strong hand immediately caught her by the upper arm, ensuring that she remained upright. The first flicker of emotion reached his eyes in a fiery glare at Eric. "The fuck it's not. She's done here."

When her eyes finally found Joey's, she recognized the indication that a dangerous shift in his demeanor was quickly approaching. It was not something that would easily be quelled if pushed too far.

Still being supported by Joey's hold on her, she looked over at Eric. "It's fine. He takes his job a little too seriously." Her eyes tried to give an annoyed glare at Joey, but it fell flat when she didn't have enough energy to expend on it.

Eric stepped around Joey to come around in front of Layne. His hand touched her cheek, paired with a smile filled with future promises. "Next time, we will pick up where we left off." He leaned in to give her another kiss.

Before their lips made contact, Layne was pulled to the side as Joey's hands guided her away with a gentle firmness. "C'mon, you have a busy day tomorrow."

On her way toward the exit, Layne snagged her purse. The strength of Joey's hold never faltered as he led her out, keeping her supported on her own two feet.

He shook his head at her, but it was his lack of words that was the loudest.

CHAPTER NINE

The ride home in Joey's car was all a blur for Layne. She leaned on him as he walked her inside her house. After he got her upstairs into her bed, he took a seat in a chair in the corner of her room. Leaning over with his elbows on his knees, he buried his fingers in his dark blonde hair. A shaky breath escaped his lips as Layne lay there quietly breathing while she slept off the sedative mix she had ingested.

He dropped his hands down to hang between his legs as he lifted his gaze to watch Layne's chest rise and fall. A grim darkness of realization slid across his pupils while he clenched his teeth together, and a series of thoughts plagued his mind and conscience.

The hours passed, and soon, the sun chased away the night. Joey was still seated in that very same chair. His jacket draped over the arm of it.

Layne was beginning to stir, her feet kicking at the sheets wrapped around her legs. When she cracked a look and caught sight of him, she slowly sat up. "Have you been sitting there all night?" Her hand rubbed the sleep from her eyes.

He looked at her and blatantly ignored her question. "What the fuck are you doing?" A simple and direct question.

It was a hell of a rude way to be spoken to when you were just waking up.

Layne popped up an eyebrow at his question; confusion shifted across her face. "Waking up on the wrong side of the bed, apparently. Christ."

He rose from the chair and came to stand at the foot of her bed. Joey reached into his pocket and pulled out her prescription bottle that had been in her purse. "What. The. Fuck. Are. You. Doing?" Each of his words punched out with a level of irritated sternness and demanded an answer from her.

Deep down, she knew what he was asking, but hell, if she was going to make things personal between them. Layne was still set on trying to get him back out of her life as quickly as possible after their business together was over.

She scooted to the edge of the bed, stood, and reached out to take the bottle from his hand. He held it out of her reach.

"You went through my things?" She scowled at him. "You need to learn how to mind your own damn business." She attempted to grab the bottle from him once more, unsuccessfully.

"Layne, I don't know what the hell you are thinking, but this?" He shook the container, rattling the pills inside. "This ain't going to fix it."

"It seems to fix everything just fine." She glared at him, wondering what the hell he knew about what she needed fixed in her life. He had been God-knows-where for the past year, and now he wanted to act like he had a right to give his opinion on how she handled herself.

He then laid down a demand. "You're going to stop with this bullshit. It's not you."

She outright lifted both brows before she laughed. "That's hilarious coming from you. What would you know about me? A person can change a lot in a year. You're just pissed because I'm not tripping over myself and landing on your dick."

Suddenly, the prescription bottle went flying from his hand and crashed into the wall, where it popped open and the pills scattered across her bedroom floor. Joey reached over, grabbed her by both of her arms and pushed her up against the back of her closet door.

His eyes flashed with a mixture of unfamiliar emotions, even to Layne. Staring up at him in shock, she didn't even resist as he held her still.

"This isn't a fuckin' game, Layne! If I thought I could fuck some sense into you, I would already have you bent over and taking my cock until you couldn't remember your own goddamn name."

"Maybe you should try anyway." Her voice set on making it clear she was just trying to push his buttons.

He growled as he gripped her jaw with the strength of his hand and tilted her head up towards him as his mouth fought the temptation to consume her despite being a breath's distance away. "I'm not going to so much as put my mouth on you until you start listening to me like the good girl I know you can be." God knew he wanted to, though.

Stubbornly, she glowered at him. "Well, if you're not going to at least do that, then get your hands off of me."

He didn't budge as he silently stood there for a moment while his eyes gazed over her face while he struggled with his thoughts about the destructive path she was on.

There was a trickle of frustration as he murmured, "Were you just going to let him fuck you last night?"

A slap to her face would have been less of a surprise than this very personal inquiry. "So, that's what this is really about?" Her temper was already on a low simmer, but now he had just added fuel to her fire.

"You're all pissed because I'm giving someone else the time of day? Well, fuck you! If I want to go around screwing half of Manhattan, that's *my* business. You had your chance!" She jerked herself against his grasp.

He willingly let go of her but didn't back away. "Layne, this isn't you. None of this is." His tone softened as it was made clear that his brute force methods weren't working.

"Why? Because fucking a guy that isn't you is so hard to believe?" Layne rubbed her fingers against her temple as her head began to ache at the unexpected stress so soon after she had woken up.

Joey realized that she was going to dig her heels in on this, making it an uphill battle. He had made a promise to her once to never let her lose herself. He needed to make good on that promise. He took a moment to find a little more calm within himself before speaking again.

"Look, why don't you go downstairs and get yourself some coffee? Then, we can talk about next steps with Ellis." He wasn't going to apologize for confronting her, but he knew when things were going to be on an unproductive path. The last thing he needed was to push her further in that direction.

She looked skeptically at him as he began to backpedal on everything that had started this argument. Layne deeply questioned her sanity in not just telling him to shove this favor up his own ass without an ounce of lube.

Not saying another word, she spun on her heel and left her bedroom to head downstairs.

Once she was gone, Joey drew his hand back, ready to smash it into the wood of her closet door. Pulling back in restraint last minute before contact, he gently rested his fist against the hard surface and leaned forward, pressing his forehead to the door as he squeezed his eyes shut. Feelings of guilt, helplessness, and frustration weighing down on him.

A few minutes later, he picked up the mess of pills from her floor and flushed them down the toilet. He knew it would only be a temporary solution, but it was one band-aid on the dam that was about to burst. If there was going to be any hope of pulling her back from the ledge, that band-aid was going to have to be enough for now.

When he got downstairs, the smell of freshly brewed coffee filled the air. Not finding Layne in the kitchen, he wandered from room to room until he noticed her sitting on her back patio. Moments later, he arrived with his own mug and took a seat in the cushioned chair next to her.

Layne had her legs tucked up underneath her to the side as she cradled the steamy beverage between her hands. Her eyes didn't even lift from watching the curls of steam rise from the top of the hot liquid.

He cleared his throat, deciding to break the silence and push past the awkwardness hovering between them. "Once we get inside at the party—"

"He wants to merge our organizations." She cut him off with her matter-of-fact statement.

"What?" Joey blurted out at the tidbit she just dropped on him.

She felt the heavy air enter her lungs as she breathed it in, and the weight remained even after she exhaled. Swallowing down a small sip from her mug, she finally looked over at him. "It's a cutthroat business, you know that. So, why don't you start by telling me what you need to get in there for?"

After setting the mug down on the small table in front of him, he sat back in his seat. "Thought you didn't want to know?"

"Want and need are two very different things, Joey. I don't have the luxury anymore of choosing what I want." And it was slowly killing her from the inside out, one shitty situation at a time.

She sat back and thought about each time she had to take another hit to her sanity. Over the past year alone, she had been dealing with betrayals left and right, deaths, and escalating tensions not just between her and Liam but across business relationships as well. There had been no reprieve in sight and no way out as she felt her world closing in around her. Some days, she thought about how she wished someone would just hire a hitman to come find her.

Immediately, she pushed the morbid thought back into the deep recesses of her mind and tried to get her head back in the game. That's what her father would have expected, right?

His face grew solemn as he thought about what he had been hired to do. "Eric's into some epic shit. I mean, this goes beyond just the city limits. At best, it's statewide. At worst? Potentially international."

This was just turning out to be a spectacular fucking morning, wasn't it? "He's an overachiever? Not surprised." Making light of the situation was the only tool she had at the moment not to crumple in on herself.

"That's why I need to get in there; my client needs to know how widespread things are. The things that they're claiming he's done, and what he is doing…" Joey shook his head, visibly disgusted.

"I will get you in the door, but you keep things discreet. I don't want this coming back to haunt me in a week or even a year."

"Discretion is my middle name." In fact, they both knew it was not. It was Elliot.

Attempting to circle back to their discussion upstairs, his hand reached out to rest on her thigh. "Layne, I know a lot has happened since last year."

She looked at her watch, seeing that it was time to avoid getting into her mushy feelings. "I have work to do today. I don't have time to sit and talk about the weather." Layne stood, allowing his hand to fall away from her leg.

His dark brown eyes were still glued to her, trying to figure out how to get past any imperfections in the invisible wall she had constructed around herself. After a resigned sigh and running his hand over the back of his head, he rose from his seat.

"Call me if anything changes." He didn't mean just with Eric, either. "I'm never far away."

She simply nodded at him and watched as he walked back inside to see himself out. The second he was out of sight, she flopped right back down into her chair, trying to suppress the quiver tugging at her chin. Layne drew her knees up in front of her and buried her face into them as the tears began to leak from her eyes.

After taking a few minutes to coil back up her self-control, she firmly pressed her lips together to start locking her feelings back down. Lifting her head from her knees, pulled out her phone to see a few missed messages.

ERIC

Thought about you all last night.

I haven't been able to focus on anything else this morning except what you're doing to me.

I will see you again soon, little harpy.

She stared at the screen, her fingers hovering over the onscreen keyboard. She shook her head and locked the screen. That could be dealt with later, just like everything else in her life.

CHAPTER TEN

She blew out a breath harshly. "Bianca just put him on the phone." Layne's fuse was running short as she held the phone to her ear while sitting inside her office at home.

The polite yet stern voice of the woman on the other end repeated itself. "Mr. Corelli is unavailable. I can take a message if you'd like to leave one for him."

Layne gave a soft growl as she summoned the last of her patience. "Bianca, I swear on all that is holy, if you don't go get Andrew, I will come down there myself. We both know he's standing right there next to you. Tell him if he doesn't get on the phone with me, I will make a special delivery to the *New York Times* pointing out his inability to properly file taxes because he's too busy jacking off to underage girls."

There was a pause as the call was placed on hold. Just when Layne thought she had been disconnected, a male voice came on the phone.

"Hi, Layne." Andrew almost sounded like he was expecting a pleasant conversation. Oh, how wrong he was if that was what he thought.

She leaned back into her seat, feeling partial relief that he had finally grown a pair to talk to her. "Where's my money, Andrew? I'm all out of patience."

He began to rattle off the excuses. "There's been some unexpected business expenses, and I was going to send it to you."

"The fuck you were. I'm getting tired of the bullshit. If I don't get it today, I'm going to be pissed that I have to come down there and get it myself in whichever creative ways I come up with."

There was a long pause followed by a defeated sigh. "Look, I didn't want to say anything, but another, um, business partner approached me."

She sat up in her chair. "What do you mean someone approached you? When?" Layne didn't want to jump to any conclusions and needed him to spell it out to her as plain as day.

Andrew cleared his throat on the other end of the line. "I am working with Russell Spencer now. He said if you had any problems with it, to take it up with him."

Russ Spencer and his crew were one of a few factions that had been not so quiet about speculating on the end of the O'Reilly era. Once word had gotten out that the great Scott O'Reilly was on a massive health decline, Russell began making moves to take advantage of the shift in leadership. The bastard was playing with fire and beginning to pick off their income sources one by one. It seemed that Andrew was the latest acquisition.

Layne didn't even bother to try to hide her displeasure at this news. "Believe me, I'm going to take it up with him." She hung up on Andrew without a further word.

"FUCK!" She tossed her phone down onto her desk in front of her. Monetarily, this was a hit they couldn't afford to take. Layne leaned over, her elbows on the edge of her desk, as she put her head into her hands. Her fingers scrunched up and got lost in her silky locks of chestnut hair as she tried to wrap her brain around this devastating blow.

She shook her head and pulled open a drawer on her right, seeing a spare bottle of pills nestled inside. Her eyes stared down at the easy escape that was calling out to her. The image of Joey losing his shit on her was still fresh in her mind.

Layne grunted as she slammed the drawer shut, leaving the pills untouched.

Still riding the coattails of anger and frustration, she slammed her car's shift knob into park after coming to an abrupt stop in front of a large retail storefront. Layne got out of her car, slamming her door shut so hard it would have likely amputated any fingers that got caught in it.

She was not giving a shit that she should have done the political thing and called Russell Spencer first before showing up here. If he was going to underhandedly start stealing her business, then she was going to step foot in his territory without one fuck given.

Was it stupid? Yes. Did she care? No. She also should have gone to Liam first, but she wasn't in the mood to add to her long list of things that pissed her off today.

Layne walked into the retail storefront, ignoring the girl at the cash register scrolling through her phone. Layne stomped towards the back-room and past all the iconic New York heart-laden merchandise on the shelves, Statue of Liberty souvenirs, and Empire State Building toothpick holders.

She shoved the door open, walking through the stock area full of plain cardboard boxes. In front of her was another door, but this one required an electronic keycard access. One of her fists began to pound on it repeatedly. "Open the goddamn door!"

She looked up at the camera mounted right above the door with a deadly glare set in her eyes. "I'm not fuckin' around! Open the door!"

An audible click was heard as the electronic lock was remotely disabled. She didn't waste a single moment before swinging the door open and walking inside a long hallway until she came to one more door. This one was left wide open.

When she stormed into the office, she was greeted by three of Spencer's associates and Russ himself perched on the edge of his desk. Russ was a stocky middle-aged man who may have been averagely handsome in his prime, but these days, he carried a little extra weight around his midsection, and his hair was noticeably thinning despite being clipped close to his scalp.

A small screen on the far right wall had the black and white CCTV feed where they undoubtedly had seen her coming to unlock the door for her. The remainder of the room was set up as a small meeting space with a plain table and chairs designed to hold up to six people, a mini fridge off to the right corner, and Russell's desk centered along the back wall.

There was no stopping her; she approached the man responsible for her foul mood. Without hesitation, she grabbed a handful of his polo shirt in one hand and let the fist of her other hand propel toward his face. "You snakelike motherfucker!"

Her punch was a glancing blow as he realized that she was actually crazy enough to spring an attack on him physically, and he raised an arm to block it. Chaos immediately erupted inside the room, with lots of yelling filling the air.

When the first punch didn't land to her satisfaction, she wound up and threw as many more as she could muster in her fit of rage before two of the men struggled to pull her off of their fearless leader. Even as they grabbed her arms and dragged her back, she spat at Russ, the saliva making it onto his shirt.

The hands on her arms were gripping her tightly, but Layne's eyes never left Russ's face. He looked down at his shirt and shook his head before he got up off his desk and stepped in front of Layne.

After a call from Andrew, Russ had been expecting to hear from her. What he hadn't expected was this unhinged visit. "Did your father teach you nothing? No fuckin' respect." His words almost sounded like he pitied her.

Russell's hand grabbed a handful of her face, squishing her cheeks in his hand. A switchblade was pulled from his pocket and sprung open to expose the sharp edge of metal. He tapped the tip of the knife against her bottom lip.

Still trying to catch her ragged breaths from her outburst and the rush of adrenaline pulsing in her ears, she tried pulling her face back from the sharp threat, teasing the softness of her lip with whispers of violence and pain.

He pulled the blade away, compressing it back into the handle until the locking mechanism quietly clicked. "If you were anyone else, I'd be teaching you a little bit about respect. But, I'm going to give you a pass this one time only, Layne. You come into my damn territory again looking to start a war, I will make sure you get one, and you won't win. Do you understand me?" His hand still latched onto her face, digging into her skin uncomfortably.

"As long as you understand that if you ever approach any of my clients ever again, I won't only bring the war to you, but I will have half the city at my back when I do." Her arms jerked against the grip of Russ's men, holding her back.

"Those are big words coming from a little lady. You don't have the resources, everyone knows it. It's just a matter of time before what's left of Scott O'Reilly's grand enterprise is dismantled, right down to his two brats." His hand finally released her face, but the red marks of his hold remained on her skin.

Layne's eyes held all the warning they needed to. "Tread lightly, Russ. I'd hate to put you at the top of my list."

He shook his head in disbelief and waved his hands at his two men on either side of her. "Please escort Miss O'Reilly out before she makes any other brash decisions today."

The two goons pulled her out of the room, her feet barely able to keep up with their steps as they guided her out a back entrance that led to the alleyway behind the building. She was given a harsh shove, sending her stumbling and nearly losing her footing until she caught hold of a chain link fence dividing this property from the next. The steel door shut behind them as the two men retreated back inside.

Layne's fingers curled around the thin ropes of metal of the fence and pressed her forehead to the cool links as she shut her eyes briefly. Her world was on the brink of collapse, and she felt powerless to stop it. One more client ripped from the O'Reilly books today meant two more were likely to follow. At this rate, they were going to be lucky to hold their ground for another couple of months.

CHAPTER ELEVEN

After her encounter with Spencer, she had been trying to pull her head back inside the game. As brash as it had been, Layne didn't regret storming into Russell's office and letting him know that she wasn't going down without a fight.

The event at Eric's house was only a few days away, and Liam's lack of leadership was going to sign both of their death warrants. It was quickly becoming clear that she couldn't run this business on her own, especially not without Liam's aid.

Layne sat on the floor of her dad's old office, now having been taken over by Liam. The house was empty most of the time since he had refused to give up his studio down in Tribeca. However, business was still conducted here. Well, what little business they had these days.

Surrounded by boxes, Layne pulled out piles of papers that appeared to be just thrown haphazardly into each box. She guessed that Liam had been the culprit and hadn't wanted to deal with any of the paperwork. The least he could have done was to keep everything organized in the boxes. Instead, she had to figure out why her great-grandmother's recipes were in folders labeled bank accounts.

She sighed as she dug through each piece of paper, her eyes scanned for anything that might be useful. Layne didn't even know what would be useful at this point, but she wasn't going to leave any stone unturned. Her dad had been old-fashioned, and he may not have left a paper trail for the less-than-legal aspects of his business, but everything else was done in a cold hard copy.

Layne sighed as everything seemed to lead nowhere. No useful contacts, no strategies, and no words of wisdom. A recipe for soda bread was not going to be the lottery ticket she needed. She sat there staring blankly at everything laid out before her, waiting for the answers to leap out of their hiding spot.

Her thoughts were disrupted when she heard the sounds of the front door opening and quickly slamming shut. Lifting her head at the intrusion, she pushed herself up onto her feet and stepped over several piles of documents.

Liam nearly ran into her when she got to the door, neither of them expecting the other to be there. She extended her hands out to brace herself in the event of an actual collision. Fortunately, all that resulted was a small bump into one another.

"What the hell are you doing here, Layne?" Her little brother already had a tone in his voice, making it clear he didn't appreciate her presence. His eyes looked beyond her and saw all the boxes and papers in disarray on the office floor. "What the fuck is this?"

She shrugged. "I'm going through Dad's things, looking for anything that might be useful."

Liam pushed past her, going to the nearest box and peering inside of it. "This is all trash; I should have just burned it all after the funeral."

He stepped away from the cardboard banker box, carelessly walking over some papers left on the ground on his way over to the wet bar built into the bookcase along the back wall.

While his back was turned to her, she began to clean up the mess she had made. One knee on the floor while she packed the papers back up, a blue letter-sized envelope slipped out from between a few other pages. It was seeing her name sprawled across it in her dad's handwriting that truly caught her eye.

Glancing up, she saw that Liam was still busying himself and opening up a fresh bottle of booze. Layne took the envelope and slid it into her back pocket. Quickly, she wrapped up cleaning the floor of the remaining disaster.

"While you're here, I got a call this morning," Liam spoke up before turning around and sipping whichever high-proof liquor had called to him today.

Layne finished stacking a few boxes on top of each other off to the side of the room. "From the therapist you haven't hired yet because you don't think you need one?" Not that she should have been one to talk, given her own mess she was actively ignoring.

He ground his teeth together, biting back the urge to immediately lose his shit. No, he was biding his time on this. "It was from Russell Spencer."

Oh, *that* call. It had only been a matter of time before word got back to Liam, being that he was technically the O'Reilly man in charge. Out of professional courtesy, it wasn't unexpected that in events where another faction's associate stepped out of line, the big guys ended up hearing about it.

She crossed her arms in front of her chest. "Go ahead, Liam, say what you're going to say about it."

As he did, he waved his hands around in corresponding gestures with his words. "Who the hell do you think you are? Acting like you're the damn head of this family, making stupid as fuck decisions like you have the authority to do shit. Why can't you just leave everything alone and stay out of things?"

"Because I'm trying to clean up your inability to get shit done, Liam! How many times do we have to have this conversation? You want to sit back and let things roll. Do you know where that has gotten us? Our guys, the few we have left in our ranks, are coming to *me* to put out fires you should have made sure never existed. So, yeah, I may have made a stupid decision with Russ, but it's because I'm *tired* of playing this game with you."

He forced the glass in his hand down onto his desk with a loud clunk that threatened to put a crack in the bottom of the drinkware. "Get the hell out! I don't want to see your face in here again."

Layne goaded him. "Or what? What are you going to do, Li?" Her eyes locked on his every move.

He took the bait and stalked his way towards her. When there was little room between them, he forced his arms out in an explosive shove.

Fortunately, she had seen it coming a mile away and dodged to the side. She grabbed his non-dominant arm with both her hands and painfully twisted it behind his back while bending his wrist at an awkward angle. To further make her point, she shoved him forward face first into the door. Her foot came up and struck down on the back of his knee, causing him to automatically drop to the floor. Layne released his arm during his fall to his knees.

For extra measure, she grabbed a handful of his hair and drew his head back to look up at her. "I've learned how to play with the big boys, Liam. It's about damn time that you did, too." She thrust his face forward again, letting it collide with the door before she stepped back from him.

Liam howled out as he sat back on his ankles, his hands going up to his face where a superficial nosebleed had begun from the two collisions against the door.

She left him there, hoping he would have some sense come to him after that. Layne was doubtful, though. If Liam hadn't had his moment of grand enlightenment by now, she found it unlikely he ever would.

Once she was back in the driver's seat of her car, she sat there trying to focus on her several deep breaths after dealing with Liam's inability to do anything but manage to piss her off. She wanted nothing more right now than to take the edge off of things and lay in bed in a beautiful foggy haze to escape from the hell she was dealing with day in and day out. After Joey had verbally laid into her before disposing of most of the stash she had on hand, she had been trying to go without.

Reaching behind her into her back pocket, she retrieved the blue envelope she had discovered amongst the other papers. Her eyes looked over the curve of each letter of her name in her dad's elegant penmanship. A breath caught in her throat as thoughts about how much she needed him there right now crept into her mind.

"Layne, you will never have it easy in this business. All the odds are stacked against you." Her father solemnly looked at her as he sat up in his bed after yet another surgery.

She frowned, waiting for him to try and convince her to leave this lifestyle behind. Go get married, have a kid and all that bullshit.

He gave a reassuring smile instead. "But, that is what will be your greatest strength. Nobody pays attention to the team that has to overcome a fifty-point gap. Take advantage of that."

Hastily, she shoved the envelope into the center console between the two front seats. She needed to be anywhere else right now but here. She needed to be somewhere where she could clear her mind. Layne needed a place where all the noise of her thoughts weren't overwhelming her.

"C'mon." Joey kept a hold of her hand and led her towards the quiet and unoccupied beach.

It was a welcome reprieve from the constant noise pollution of Manhattan. Joey released her hand so he could hide both his hands in his pockets as he stared at the last bit of sun reflecting off the water as it sunk lower in the sky.

"It's not much, but I like to come here when things get too heavy."

Layne smiled at her memories replaying in her head. The recollection of their first date together stirred up a warmth deep inside of her chest. She started up the engine of her car and drove off. Maybe a trip over to that quiet little spot in Brooklyn would do her good.

CHAPTER TWELVE

The Saturday night of the party came a lot quicker than she wanted. A pit had been growing in her stomach since the moment she woke up that morning.

All day, she had been pacing her house, wondering what the hell to do with her time. She had tried everything from reading, streaming a bunch of shows she needed to catch up on, and even attempted cleaning the house. None of it lasted very long before she felt compelled to move on to the next thing.

She stared at herself in the mirror and murmured. "Get your shit together." Her father had always been able to sternly direct her to what she needed to do, even if she didn't listen all the time. Now, she was left without that looming guidance in her life. It was only the lingering memories that haunted her, serving as a reminder of whose daughter she was.

One of the silver linings of having a wide open schedule for the first half of the day was that she could take her time getting ready. It also served as a perfect storm to overthink everything right down to the most meaningless details.

Layne preferred her hair down but kept it styled so one side of the dark chestnut locks was pulled back away from her face with some strategically placed pins. She brushed on some makeup, going for an elegant evening look with a seductively smokey eye and a flirty shade of dusty pink on her lips.

Pulling her dress off its hanger, she shimmied into it. The silky fabric was unforgiving in how it adhered to the curves and lines of her body. The regal shade of purple complimented her fair skin, which there was plenty of it exposed to capture the attention of any wandering eyes.

The dress was a halter-style gown that left her back fully open, down until the material wrapped around the roundness of her ass. The strap around her neck was embroidered with tiny shimmering crystals that dove down into a steep neckline.

The remainder of the dress fell into a narrow skirt with a slit just high enough to be considered a classy display of the flesh of her leg and, more practically, allow for more ease of movement.

Lastly, the outfit wasn't going to be complete without a little bit of safety insurance. She latched a thin strap to her upper thigh where a dagger was slid into the sheath. If shit went south tonight, she refused to be playing a game of 'could this random item be used as a weapon'?

After picking out a small clutch and strapping on her heels, she met her driver outside of her house. He held the door to the back seat of the SUV open for her with a heartwarming smile. "You look radiant, Ms. O'Reilly."

The older man with silvery grey hair, Artie, had been working for her family for years. She didn't make a habit of using his services too often, but on a night like tonight, where appearances were everything, she opted for the car service.

From everything she had heard about the guests in attendance, there were going to be some of the most important names in criminal organizations across the city coming together under the guise of raising funds for charity. It wouldn't be all the big bad guys there, of course. Politicians, financiers, judiciaries, and others amongst New York's social elite would also be in attendance.

"Thanks, Art. You've always had the kindest things to say." Her hand gave his arm a gentle squeeze while she sweetly smiled at him before sliding into the back seat. The door shut behind her, and moments later, he was driving her to the Ellis residence not too far from where she lived. It was only about ten minutes further uptown. A little too close for Layne's tastes, but she wasn't about to pack up and move on Eric's account.

By the time Artie pulled up, where others were also unloading from their vehicles, she was a solid ten minutes late. Still socially acceptable in her mind and by elitist standards. Layne wasn't in a rush to kick off this evening, which she had been dreading ever since she agreed to it.

While she sat in the back seat, she wrestled with her nerves that refused to settle down. This should be like any other job she had ever had a hand in. Joey's presence should have been inconsequential. However, she still found herself spending far too much time thinking about his involvement in tonight's affairs instead of thinking about Eric's proposition to salvage the O'Reilly family business.

The back passenger door swung open, and instead of being greeted by her driver, she noticed Joey standing there with his hand reaching out to her.

Her breath caught in her chest as she saw him dressed in the sharp lines of a tux, a crisp white shirt underneath the black jacket, and a corresponding black vest and tie. The way it fit the muscles of his upper body reminded her of the delicious gift underneath all that packaging. The creep of his neck tattoos peeked up past the top of his collar, and the ink on his hands was easily visible. It was the only indication that he wasn't in the same class as the rest of the pompous assholes in attendance.

Layne did her best to remember to breathe and not appear as shell-shocked as she felt seeing him all cleaned up for once. But, damn, could that man wear a tux.

Stubbornly, she ignored his offer of assistance, gathering the lower half of her dress and stepping out onto the sidewalk on her own accord. The length of her dress fell around her legs down to her feet, which were set in a sparkling set of heels encrusted with shimmering crystals that matched the shine of the crystals on her halter straps.

He dropped his hand back to his side, but his eyes never left her. Joey didn't usually break the serious façade when it came to his work, but in this case, Layne did manage to pick up on the subtle shift in his brown eyes. A shift that told her she wasn't the only one with a view worth appreciating. His tongue subtly swiped across his lower lip, an act that one would expect while eyeing a particularly decadent dessert.

"You're late." A slight edge of frustration could be heard hanging off the end of his words.

Layne gave a nonchalant shrug with a smile, knowing how it was eating away at him and how she was not bothered in the least about her tardiness to this little affair. "I guess you should have come picked me up if you wanted me to be on time."

After she was out of the car, he shut the door and stepped up to join her at her side. His arm wrapped around her lower back, pulling her in close to his side as he leaned in and whispered, "Remember, I'm still here as part of your security detail. Which as I recall from the last time I kept my eyes on you full-time, you were extremely satisfied with my services." His charismatic smirk stretched across his face.

As people walked past them on their way up to the front door, Layne plastered an over-the-top saccharin smile on her face. Tonight was all about wearing an invisible mask that told a story that not only did she want to be here, but she belonged here. That included upkeeping the premise of Joey being part of her security.

She didn't even look at him as she quietly responded. "I'm in four-inch heels, a dress that wants me to be ten pounds lighter, and my escort is breathing down my neck. You're asking a hell of a lot right now for me to look satisfied with *any* of your services."

His voice dropped down to a dominant tone, with his words teasing along her skin. "You used to like it when I did things to your neck."

Uncontrollably, her cheeks flushed a delicate shade of pink before her hand slapped his chest, and she managed to slither away from his arm that wrapped around her. "Stop dicking around."

Joey smirked, noting that he had managed to get under her skin. "Interesting choice of words."

Layne shook her head while trying to keep things between them strictly business. After all, that was the agreement, wasn't it? She would help him tonight, and then he would be on his merry way.

Quickly ending the conversation and moving straight on to the matter at hand, she followed the rest of the guests dressed to the nines into the obscenely luxurious private home of Eric Ellis.

It was situated on a prized corner lot and was previously an old printing house that had undergone massive renovations that turned it into a residential space to be admired by the city's deepest pockets.

What most people failed to notice was the extensive security on the outside. Cameras were tucked into various corners at multiple angles, turning the home into a fortress. Nobody was coming or going from this place without it being captured on video. At least, mostly nobody.

When Layne and Joey both approached the entrance, there was a delay in movement as everyone was checking in with event planners to ensure no unwanted or uninvited party guests tried to sneak their way in.

Joey stuck close to her, only a step behind, and even then, she could still feel his gaze roaming over her body. Despite all of her conflicted feelings, she couldn't deny that having him here with her put a part of her soul at ease. Something she hadn't felt in some time.

When it was finally her turn to check in, she smiled pleasantly at the woman who looked like she was typically as quiet as a mouse. Her condensed facial features were speckled with a few light freckles, and her brunette locks of hair were tied back into a short but low ponytail.

"Name, please?" Yup, Layne was right, the woman's voice was soft as a whisper in a confessional booth.

"Layne O'Reilly." While the woman began scrolling through an iPad with names on it, Layne took a glance at the entryway. The gothic style decor was a little over the top for her tastes, but it was better than the same boring old-money style that most of uptown was accustomed to.

The woman looked up from the screen and looked at Layne and then over at Joey. "I'm sorry, Ms. O'Reilly, but I don't see a plus one next to your name."

Joey stepped forward to intervene, but Layne rested a hand on his bicep as a signal for him to back down.

"Oh, he's not my date, he's my security. I didn't realize I needed to register him; I thought it was already taken into consideration."

The poor girl looked like she was on the edge of tears as an apologetic look crossed her face. "I do apologize, but we can't allow anyone inside who hasn't been pre-cleared. Mr. Ellis' orders."

This wasn't off to a great start at all. Right as Layne was about to choose some stronger words to make her point to this delicate little rose, she heard Eric's familiar voice as he approached. "Laura, it's ok." His hand patted the woman's shoulder and motioned for her to continue checking in other guests.

The host himself was done up in a tailored tuxedo that was all black right down to the shirt. His hair was slicked back except for a small piece that was having no part of compliance with the rest of it. With all the darkness wrapped around him, the blue of his eyes particularly stood out more than normal.

He turned to Layne and stood there, taking his time drinking in the image of her all dolled up. An image that he surely thought was solely for his benefit.

Eric's eyes memorized every fine detail and curve that was on public display. His lips parted in awe, drawn in by the vision in front of him.

"My little harpy, you do not disappoint." He exhaled a breath while his gaze remained locked on the vision that stood before him.

His hand reached out to take hers, bringing it up to his mouth, where he pressed a lingering kiss to the back of it. The gesture got minutely more intimate when his eyes lifted to stare at her as he did so.

The presence standing at her back was getting restless as Joey cleared his throat loudly.

Hearing the grumpy disruption behind her, Layne slid her hand out of Eric's slowly. "Eric, I didn't realize that I needed to register my security for the evening. I hope it won't be a problem."

The icy hue of Eric's eyes looked past Layne at the familiar tall and well-built man accompanying Layne. Judgment and condescension settled across his face. Their prior standoff at the rock concert while he was enjoying Layne's company had left a sour taste in his mouth.

He was quick to shift back into a man full of incredible charm the second he returned his look to Layne. "Of course not. Though, I will say there was no need for it. You have my full protection while you are here."

Joey interrupted. "It's not your job to keep her protected."

Eric gave a light shrug. "No. I suppose you're right; it's not. Not yet, anyway."

Starting to suffocate with the tensions growing in the air and the amount of testosterone being pissed around, Layne awkwardly tried to change the subject and move things along.

"I'm sure you have other guests to greet, I don't want to keep you from your obligations." She preferred he kept busy with all the other guests for as long as possible.

Eric gave a nod of appreciation that she recognized he had other duties to see to. "I look forward to us picking up our conversation later on the arrangement we've been discussing."

Before anything more could be said, a rather heftily round man came up to Eric and slapped a hand on the back of his shoulder. A rowdy greeting followed before immediately diving into a conversation about the renovations that were done to the recently acquired building.

Layne took the window of opportunity to scurry further inside, heading towards the stairs that led up to the next floor. According to the signage, that's where the primary party spot was.

As for Joey, he didn't let her get too far ahead of him. "What did he mean by 'not yet,' Layne?"

She gave an irritable sigh as she began to conquer one step at a time without tripping over her dress. "How the hell should I know?"

Once they were on the second floor, he pulled her by her elbow off to the side to peer into her eyes, looking for a better response from her. "Tell me what he meant. I'm not asking twice."

She glanced around in paranoia that someone would overhear them, so she kept her voice down to a whisper, hoping that Joey would do the same. "Even if you did ask twice, I wouldn't have anything to tell you. Now, I got you in here, go do whatever it is you came here to do."

There was no sense in getting him worked up and involved in her business affairs. He was here to do a job, as was she. The only difference was that his job was hopefully short-lived, while hers had more permanent consequences.

As she pried her arm out of his hand, Layne saw Joey's hands squeeze into tight fists in either anger or frustration — she couldn't tell which it was.

"This conversation isn't over," he warned. Knowing how well Joey let go of things, she knew damn well that he was going to continue poking the bear until he got a response. "I won't be far," he added before walking off.

Layne watched as he stepped away from her, blending into the hustle and bustle of the other guests who were also making their way towards all the festivities.

After Joey's departure, the tension in her body eased up momentarily while her emerald hues relaxed. With her thoughts becoming less clouded by his presence, she realized she desperately needed to drink half the bar if she was ever going to survive this evening.

CHAPTER THIRTEEN

It had been a painful and tedious task of playing all the social elitist games of fake smiles, fake pleasantries, and fake laughter at terrible jokes. Layne had spent the last forty-five minutes fielding conversations with various other guests. Some of whom she knew and others who were introduced to her.

Did she care about any of the pretentious assholes? Not a single ounce of care was to be found within her. But she had put on a smile that left her cheeks sore and aching for the sake of keeping a strong front. The last thing she needed to show was weakness while surrounded by representatives of various criminal factions that were in attendance.

Servers were constantly coming around offering beverages, collecting empty glasses, and providing a variety of hors d'oeuvres for those needing something to soak up the freely flowing booze.

There was live music playing primarily classical tunes, and if the songs weren't Beethoven or Mozart, they were classical renditions of modern melodies. The room's vaulted ceilings that seemed to go on forever made for acoustics that would have any musician swooning.

Most of those chattering away with small talk or even more serious conversations stuck to the perimeter of the room, while others danced to whatever was being played at the moment.

Finally breaking free from a conversation with an elderly man that couldn't hear for shit, Layne found her way to the bar. She ordered another glass of wine from the swamped bartender and stood there thirstily drinking down the chardonnay.

From behind her, a hand slid down over her bare shoulder with fingertips that caressed the back of her arm. She spun around to see the man who had invited her there. Eric's face was full of excitement. "Here you are. Follow me; I have something I would like to show you."

Eric offered his arm to Layne, who reluctantly took it as he guided them to a pair of glass french doors. Opening one and allowing her to step outside first, she saw the balcony had an artist's dream view of the expansive Central Park.

As dusk was fading into evening, it was eating away at the sky in shades of oranges and reds before fading into darker hues.

Layne sipped from her wine glass as she placed a hand on the edge of the balcony's rail, taking in the sight.

With Eric at her back, his hands rested on her bare shoulders as he looked past her at the picturesque scene laid out before them. He whispered into her ear. "I will never grow tired of this view." The meaning behind his words was layered with more than just one view he was enjoying.

She tried to keep the tension at bay as it was clear he wasn't just talking about the beauty of nature doing its thing. Her head turned towards him. "Never is a strong word."

"Yes, it is." He didn't apologize for using it, though.

Finally, she fully turned to face him, noticing that they were the only ones enjoying the privacy of the balcony. "I figured you would be busy mingling with all your guests."

"I'm only concerned with spending time with one very important guest here tonight. I hope you don't mind." His grin held a touch of cockiness that it still wouldn't concern him, even if she did mind.

He continued, "I was hoping we could talk a little more, away from any nosey eavesdroppers."

Swallowing more of the expensive vintage in her glass, Layne prompted him with the obvious question. "About?"

Eric gave her a chiding look. "Don't be coy; you know exactly what I would like to talk about. I met with one of my associates downtown earlier, and there are a lot of unhappy folks with the way the O'Reilly Enterprise is handling things. I know you are doing your best to do damage control, but time is of the essence if you're going to make a move —if *we* are going to make a move."

She looked down into her wine glass, watching the small ripples of movement as she swirled the liquid around idly inside the glass. "I know."

"Tell me how to make this comfortable for you. I have already promised that you would never be without anything you ever need. We can rise together and establish a chokehold on the other factions who are threatening to overthrow your family and everything it's ever stood for." His hand moved under her chin and gently lifted it so he could remove her focus from her beverage.

Hesitation was not just in her voice but in her body language as well. "It's a big decision, and I don't want to make it lightly."

"I don't expect you to." He nodded and then decided to switch up his strategy. He eased the wine glass out of her hand and placed it on the ledge behind her. "Dance with me."

"I don't dance, Eric." Her heartbeat sped up with panic over the idea of sharing a close space with him on the dance floor in front of so many pairs of eyes.

Despite her reluctance, he took her hand and led her back inside and onto the dance floor. "I do, and I make a point to share at least one dance with a beautiful woman during these parties." He found a spot in the middle of the floor, turning to face her with a look meant for a predator to lure in its prey.

He slid his hand around her waist onto the bare skin on the small of her back and forcefully pulled her in toward him until the fronts of their bodies were touching. His other hand, by contrast, lightly held onto hers.

Intuitively, she rested a hand on top of his shoulder as she found the space between them entirely gone. The music playing in the room transitioned over to a slow and haunting tune. One that seemed to tell a sad yet dark love story with its minor notes and dramatic crescendos and decrescendos.

Eric took the lead by beginning to move them across the dance floor, never once easing up his hold on her. His captivating blue eyes bore down on her, intent on maintaining all of his focus on her. Seeing the way he seemingly ignored everything else around them, Layne never once thought about her feet.

He brought his mouth to her ear as he whispered, "You promised me an answer tonight."

Briefly, she closed her eyes as the moment she had been dreading finally arrived. Layne had to make her choice. A choice she had never wanted to make for herself. A choice the person she was years ago would have never considered.

Her mind recounted each struggle up until this point. Liam's incompetence. The lost ranks of employees. Financials circling the drain. Clients flocking to other organizations. The warning shots that had been fired. Everything was piling up. How much longer before it was game over?

When she opened her eyes back up, revealing the depths of her green hues, he granted a moment of air from their tight hold as he raised her arm and twirled her around in a slow and elegant circle before drawing her back up against him.

When she came back into his hold, she saw a familiar pair of eyes watching from the depths of the crowd. Eyes that tugged heavily on her heart. Eyes that were full of darkness at what they were witnessing. Joey stood back, but even from where Layne was, she could feel the heat radiating off his emotions.

"I know what I promised." That was all she could respond to Eric with, trying not to allow herself to get distracted.

His hand inched lower along her back until it reached where the smooth material of her dress began at the top curve of her ass. Boldly and without hesitation or permission, he continued his exploration with his fingers. His fingertips slipped down between her skin and the dress, grazing over the hem of her seamless thong just underneath.

His voice had a rasp to it as he spoke quietly to her. "That's not an answer."

With his fingers still lingering inside the back of her dress, her mind struggled to stay in the moment. Layne felt a warmth in her core begin to spread underneath his touch. Her nipples strained against the fabric of her dress as they stiffened into peaks.

She knew her world was crumbling, and she couldn't stop it on her own. It felt as though she was a frightened mare out in the wild, and a lasso was already tied around her throat.

Layne glanced past Eric's shoulder while they continued to move slowly together to the tender notes of the song. The invisible mask she attempted to maintain broke, and her eyes betrayed her as they filled with dread and panic. She searched for any sign of Joey in the crowd.

Whatever was reflected in her eyes, Joey didn't like it the moment he saw it. He abruptly began to push towards them, creating a path for himself through the crowd.

Not realizing that she and Eric had gradually come to a standstill as the song faded to the next, his hand released its hold on hers and turned her face to force her attention back to him. "Look at me and give me an answer. No more stalling."

His demand held something new in it, something laced with a promise of death. It was a tone she was very familiar with in all her years in this lifestyle. The promise may not have been a threat from him, but there was no mistake that death was knocking on the O'Reilly door. Eric was just the one offering her a way to chase away the nightmares.

Her words felt like they were choking her while getting lodged in her throat. "Yes."

Eric tilted his head inquisitively, looking for clarity. "Yes, what?" The man wasn't stupid; he just wanted to hear her say it in no uncertain terms.

The sinking feeling in her stomach grew heavier. "Yes, to the merger and this alliance." Layne swallowed down her stubborn pride. "I'll marry you."

A victorious smile curved over his mouth as he whispered against her lips. "You're all mine now, my little harpy." He leaned forward so his mouth could territorially claim her lips while his arm squeezed tighter around her.

Things were abruptly broken apart when an arm came between them, prying Layne and Eric away from one another. Joey protectively pulled Layne back, putting himself between her and Eric.

Joey held his ground there with his eyes filled with a level of possessiveness Layne had never seen before. Fury was simmering underneath the surface as he kept it aimed at Eric. His jaw was tightly clenched as he spoke through his teeth. "Miss O'Reilly, unfortunately, needs to leave for the evening. A business matter has come up requiring her attention."

As the reality of what she had just done sank in, she made a futile attempt to shake off all the feelings that were crashing like relentless waves into her. The room began to feel too crowded. Layne backed up a step, nearly knocking into another guest before she turned and quickly headed for the exit while Eric was otherwise distracted by Joey.

As for Joey, when he went to follow after her, Eric's hand clamped down on his arm. An equally vile look was directed at Joey. "Let's get one thing straight. As of right now, she's mine to handle as I see fit. What she does is my concern, not yours."

Instead of giving in to the temptation of physically demolishing Eric's face and devolving into a blind rage, Joey gave a dark smile in amusement. "I don't give a fuck what you think you're entitled to. Touch her again, and I'll kill you. I won't just kill you, but I will make sure that you suffer an unfathomable level of pain before you beg for me to end your life."

Roughly, he shoved Eric's hand away and left to follow Layne.

When he managed to get eyes on her, she was already at the front doors pushing against several people coming back inside from having a smoke.

"Layne!" He called for her, hoping to get her to at least wait for him.

She never heard him through the roaring of her inner monologue that was screaming inside of her head. Her thoughts told her how much she had to do this for survival while simultaneously berating herself for being so damn stupid in agreeing to be at a man's mercy.

When Joey caught up to her, he didn't immediately say a word. Instead, his hand dropped down to take hers and guide her to where his Challenger was parked in an empty church parking lot. Layne let him guide her to the lot across the street. The plan had always been for him to drop her off at home after the party, just that the night had ended much sooner than either of them planned for.

He opened the passenger door for her to get safely settled. Joey pulled his suit jacket off, balling it up and forcefully tossing it into the backseat before he got into the driver's seat. He slammed his door shut with a force that rattled components inside the dash.

Layne wasn't sure what to say to him or where to even begin to explain what she was doing, if he even cared. Her emerald eyes watched him as he backed out of the parking space, and the tires squealed against the pavement as he left the lot.

His hands yanked at his tie, loosening it around his neck enough to unbutton the top couple of buttons of his shirt. Joey's breathing was heavy and ragged as he replayed what he had just witnessed at the party. It wasn't just what he saw, but the reading of how her lips moved to speak words to Eric he would never understand the reasoning for.

"Joey—"

He cut off her words. "What the fuck are you thinking?! Do you even know what type of monster Eric Ellis is?" His eyes parted from the road for a second to shoot a glance at her.

Trying to keep her voice calm enough for the both of them, she spoke quietly. "You don't understand; my hands are tied here. It's the only option I have. I can't sit around and wait for a miracle that is never coming."

His hand squeezed onto the top of the steering wheel. "You're not doing this."

She reached over and put her hand on top of his while he held onto the gear shifter. "I am doing this. I have to. I don't know why the hell you're so bent out of shape about it. You came back for your one favor, which, by the way, you're welcome."

His eyes looked down at her hand that was touching his, covering up the sprawling tattoos etched into his flesh. Joey made a sharp turn and pulled into an empty parking garage. He accelerated up the ramp of each floor until they reached the top level on the roof.

"What are you doing?" She stared at him questioningly as he pulled into the cement structure.

He parked the car diagonally across several spaces and got out. Layne flung open her door and met him in front of the Challenger, the headlights left on and cutting through the darkness of the night.

Now, she was beginning to slip as her anger started to rear its head. "What is your problem, Joey?!" Her hands shoved his chest, only for him to stay solidly planted on his feet as his eyes were locked on her. The rage she had seen in his eyes earlier now had melted into a softer burn.

"It's you. It's always been you." His statement was calm, but the words had a storm brewing behind them. When she tried to shove him again, he wrapped his hands around her wrists. "He doesn't deserve you."

She knew better than to struggle against his grasp. "And you do?"

He took another step closer to her, still restraining her wrists in front of her. "I've made some mistakes, but I'm not going to let you fall further down this spiral."

Layne rolled her eyes that he thought she was having any sort of spiraling crisis in her life that she couldn't handle on her own without his help.

"Roll your eyes again at me and see what happens, Layney." A soft growl rolled over his words. A growl that prompted several goosebumps to flitter across her skin.

Her teeth scraped over her bottom lip as his taunt had her body reacting with a heavy sense of arousal between her thighs. No matter how long it had been, he had always managed to get her body to respond with the slightest of actions or words.

She rolled her eyes at him.

CHAPTER FOURTEEN

Unsure what caused her to instigate him, Layne didn't have long before he reacted. Joey's hands dropped their hold on her wrists and pulled her face to his. His lips crashed against her mouth with a blazing kiss filled with pent-up emotions.

As she released a small gasp, his tongue took advantage and slid into her mouth to devour her taste. The electricity between them felt incredibly familiar, but now there was an edge of something else in how he touched her, tasted her, and held her.

She couldn't tell who was breathing the air out of whose lungs as they stood there on the roof of the empty parking garage.

Each movement he made prompted a chain reaction of sensations throughout her body. His hands roamed down over the front of her dress, making a momentary stop as they settled over her breasts. The palms of his hands aggressively kneaded each of the supple swells on her chest. She leaned her body into him, encouraging him to continue.

Joey's lips broke away from hers. "I told you once before, I *always* fight for what's mine. I lied. I will bring the fires of hell earthside if it means keeping you in my arms." His eyes lit up with an inferno of need for the woman standing before him.

He dropped his hands down to her waist and guided her backward. When she felt the front bumper of his car against the back of her legs, he picked her up and laid her down on the hood. The metal pressed against her bare back was still warm from the engine underneath.

Still craving more of him, she grinned. "Do you really think hellfire is going to keep me here with you?"

His eyes assessed what was laid out in front of him. Joey took one of her feet and ran his hands down the length of her leg slowly. The slit of the dress fell away up until its stopping point a couple of inches above her knee. "I don't know, Layney, but I'm going to find out."

Grasping a hem on each side of the slit, he yanked in one forceful motion to tear the fabric further up until it ripped all the way up to her hip.

It took Layne by surprise, and she should have been angry about how he just ruined a dress that had cost a small fortune. Yet, all she could think of was how she had wished he had torn it right in two.

With the night air whispering over the freshly exposed skin of her thigh, her black sheath containing her blade was revealed on her upper thigh. Joey immediately took notice and gave a playful smirk. "Look what we have here."

"A girl has to be prepared for anything. You never know when a man in a mask might show up." She smirked right back at him.

His hand unsnapped the knife, removing it from its holding place. Expertly, he twirled it in his hand while examining it, the look on his face made it obvious he had more than just thoughts of admiration for her weapon.

Joey dragged the tip of the blade along the inside of her thigh, letting the sharp edge threaten to split her flesh with any wrong turn or too much pressure.

She held her breath as she watched the steel tip hover over her femoral artery before continuing to move further north. Carefully, he hooked the knife underneath the thin garment that was a poor excuse for panties. With one upward motion, her underwear was sliced at the perfect junctures to fall away from her body.

While he licked his lips in anticipation of what was laid out before him, Joey tossed the blade to the side; it clattered as it hit the concrete.

"Joey," she began to warn, "this—us, can't—"

He leaned over; his hands pressed against the hood on either side of her as he slid a hand up over her throat. He gripped it firmly without depriving her of anything as he stared down into her eyes. "I need you to stop thinking so much, Layney."

She lost her train of thought as his face hovered above hers, leaving her lips parted around stubborn words that never made it out.

His hand fell from her throat and buried into her hair along the back of her head; he pulled her head up so that she could meet him halfway. Their kiss connected and exploded like a busted dam of emotions. The more she tasted him, the less she cared about anything or anyone else in the world.

His free hand rubbed down over her side until it found the exposed flesh of her hip. Layne moved her hips in an effort to motivate his hand to move exactly where she needed it most.

Her hand grabbed the tail of his tie, pulling on it to keep him there, hovering over top of her as she deepened the kiss further into an abyss of passion. Their tongues danced with one another, reacquainting themselves with each other's sinful tastes.

Breaking the connection of their mouths briefly, Joey nibbled on her bottom lip. "Tell me this is what you want." His finger teasingly grazed along her slit, purposely avoiding her aching clit.

Moaning quietly, feeling his touch so close to the small bundle of nerves between her legs, she tried to capture his lips again, only this time, his grasp on her hair prevented her from closing the distance.

Joey knowingly smirked. "Tell me."

Her eyes gazed up at him, already feeling breathless with need and desperation. "I want all of this. I've always wanted all of you."

"There's my good girl that I've missed so much." He took her mouth against his again while his finger stroked over her sensitive arousal, rewarding her with a jolt of pleasure.

Her moan got lost against his mouth as her hips drove against his touch. Layne's hands furiously worked to loosen his tie entirely to get to the remaining buttons of his shirt and the corresponding vest. With each button coming undone, Joey's fingers worked over her sex more fervently, making her concentration on the menial task increasingly more difficult.

By the time she released the last button, it caused his shirt to fall open to expose the rippling muscles of his chest, which had collected several more tattoos since she had seen it last. It was difficult to make out the designs in the dark of the night, but the one that stood out the most was a shamrock drenched in blood located directly over his heart.

Layne's mind wandered with questions as her fingertips delicately drifted over the red and green that stood out on his pec.

Before she could expend any more thoughts on his additional ink, three fingers were shoved deeply inside of her. Her hands latched onto his open shirt, scrunching up the fabric in her fists. A sound of straight pleasure was ripped out of her mouth and swallowed up by the stars themselves.

Joey's fingers curled up to massage over the particular spot deep inside of her each time he thrust his digits into her body. Her hips bucked against his hand while his thumb continued to circle over her throbbing clit.

The promise of release was descending on her, but before she could get a taste of it, he withdrew his hand from between her thighs.

"No, no, no. I was so close." She groaned in frustration the moment her orgasm began to settle back down into her lower stomach.

He pulled back, and the sound of his belt unbuckling could be heard now that he wasn't coaxing moans out of her. Joey grinned. "I know, but I need my cock to feel how hard you're going to come for me."

Reaching into his boxer briefs, he pulled out his hard length. His chocolate-colored eyes were filled with raw desire as he saw her on the hood of his car, soaking wet with need. His tatted-up fist wrapped around his cock and stroked himself twice while enjoying the sight of her laid out before him, ready for the taking.

Lowering himself down on top of her, he taunted her with the tip of his hardness pressing against her swollen clit. Kissing her a little more gently this time, he ran his thumb down over her bottom lip.

"Are you going to run away from me this time, Layney? Or are you going to finally open yourself up to me?" Joey's voice was as soft as that kiss he had just laid on her.

She shook her head. "You know it's not that easy."

Sternly, he responded. "I asked a question." He rubbed his length against her, prompting her hips to press against him with a deep yearning and the sound of her whimper.

Trying to keep her thoughts straight was proving to be quite the challenge as he distracted her even more so with his mouth nibbling along her throat one possessive nip at a time.

"I can feel how wet your pussy is against my dick, how much you want me inside of you. How much it wants me back where I belong." His tongue teasingly licked along the hollow of her throat near her collarbone.

Layne's back arched slightly, pressing up against him as the warmth of his mouth worshiped her skin. She gave him the answer they both needed to hear. "I won't run from you."

A spark lit up in his eyes. "Damn right, you won't. After I'm done with you, you'll be lucky to walk." He rammed himself fully inside of her, unleashing any final bit of restraint he had been clinging onto.

Her body jolted against the hard metal of the Challenger's hood underneath her as a moan came straight from the depths of her center and was swallowed up by the night sky. The vehicle's suspension shifted with each shove of himself into her body.

Layne's fingers dug into his back as the ecstasy she had been pining for since he had been gone was now coming to her full force.

Clear as the evening sky, Joey had been craving this as much as she had. His breaths ran hard as her inner walls wrapped around his shaft, welcoming him deep inside of her.

As she locked her legs around his waist, the skirt of her dress fell away from her lower half, draping against the front of the car. Her body trembled against him, her mouth dragging kisses anywhere she could plant them between her pleasure-laden moans.

"Joey! You're going to—I'm going to—" Layne cried out as the swelling tidal wave began to break its crest.

"That's it, fuckin' come for me, Layney. I want your pussy to fuckin' welcome my dick back home." Pumping his thickness even harder into her, repeatedly hitting the sweet spot relentlessly, her words had only incited him to continue the deliciously sinful assault between her thighs.

New stars came into her vision aside from the ones speckling the blanket of the universe above them. Her release overcame her and spilled onto him, threatening to send her to a blissful existence not on this planet.

He clenched his teeth as his own body began to shudder, feeling Layne's tightness squeeze around him even tighter. Joey's movements began to grow less and less controlled before he groaned out in a feral roar as he gave one final shove of his cock into her as far as he could get. His peak was reached as he spilled himself deep into her body with several spasms of his cock.

Collapsing down on top of her, he laid his head against her chest, hearing both his own heartbeat pounding away inside of him alongside Layne's pulsing heart against his stubbled cheek.

As her body began to relax from the height of her climax, he lifted his head to stare at her lazily. "You still with me?"

Layne nodded with a smile, feeling nearly cross-eyed from the intensity of the orgasm. "Mmhmm, barely, but I'm here."

He smirked. "Such a good girl for me." His hand ran over the side of her face affectionately.

The cool breeze on the parking garage rooftop should have sent a chill through her body, but all she could feel was the heat and passion still burning in her veins.

Layne knew it had been far too long since he had been gone, and now that he was back, she wasn't sure she had the strength in her to ever set him free again. Consequences be damned.

CHAPTER FIFTEEN

After their mind-shattering romp on the hood of Joey's car underneath Manhattan's night sky, he drove her back to her house. Things stayed light conversationally between them, with zero mention of Eric and what all of this was truly going to mean, if anything at all.

Layne could have begged him to stay the night with her and make her forget all about her life's chaos, but he had to take care of a few things related to his adventures inside the Ellis residence. She tried to mask the disappointment on her face, and whether or not she had failed miserably at that, he hadn't let on.

While alone in her bathroom, she removed the last of her makeup and tossed the sullied cotton pad into a wastebasket. Layne stared at herself in the mirror as her dark thoughts began to creep back into her head. Why was it that her life had to always come with complications? Couldn't a girl just work for a criminal organization and eat her cake, too?

She promised she wouldn't run, but she also needed to keep the family business alive. Liam was useless. Eric was her only lifeline, and she had agreed to tie herself to him. Joey may have ordered her to stop thinking so much while he ravished her, but now that he wasn't there? She couldn't stop thinking about the harsh reality of life looming over her. One night with Joey didn't change her circumstances.

With a mixture of intense emotions trying to surface, she squashed them all down deep inside of her. To aid in that endeavor, she popped a pill to make her forget they existed and ensure she didn't toss and turn all night. Joey may have disposed of the stash she had on hand in her purse, but inside her medicine cabinet, she had another bottle with a few tablets still remaining.

The very next morning, she heard some loud voices and power tools outside of her bedroom window. It sounded like it was not just coming from the back of her house but the side and front as well. If this had been midtown, she wouldn't have thought anything of it, but it was typically far quieter this time of day in her neighborhood.

Her bare feet walked across the cool wooden floor of her bedroom as she pushed the sheer curtain to the side to see what the hell was going on out there.

Surprise didn't begin to cover what she saw, which led to her stumbling over her own feet as she ran downstairs to the front door. She swung it open wildly to begin raising all hell on earth.

The poor workers got a hell of a sight when she appeared in the doorway of her home. Her long locks were still a tangled disaster from sleep and leftover hairspray from the night before, and she was barefoot and wearing nothing but a pair of bright green boy shorts coupled with a black tank.

"What the fuck is going on here?!" She stared at the men on ladders by her windows and near her front stoop. They were all carrying electronic equipment, wires, and various tools.

Despite the brisk autumn air pulling a shiver from her scarcely clothed body, she stepped down onto the front stoop to get a better assessment of the work being done—work she hadn't requested.

The men all looked dumbfounded while sharing glances amongst themselves and not sharing any answers with her.

That's when Eric rounded the corner, waving with his hand to the men to continue their work.

"Layne, I'm so sorry, I tried calling but didn't get an answer." He didn't sound one bit of fucking sorry to her.

One man uninstalled one of her security cameras mounted near a window. Layne couldn't believe her eyes, and she pointed at the guy. "*Hey*! What the fuck?!"

Eric softly wrapped a hand around her arm. "Why don't we go inside and talk, hm? I will explain everything."

She looked down at his hand touching her and then up into those stark blue eyes he had. Sliding her arm out of his hold with a glare, she walked inside, not caring who saw the lower curve of her cheeks peeking out from the bottom of her panties.

The front door closed behind Eric as he began to dial up the charm, mistakenly thinking that it was going to make her ok with strangers doing work on her house, which she hadn't approved.

"You want to explain what the hell those guys are doing with my security cameras?" She crossed her arms in front of her chest, not particularly caring how little clothing she had on at the moment.

Eric softened his look while trying to reassure her. "The security system you have is inadequate. Now that we are coming together, your safety is my utmost concern."

Bullshit—an anosmic bloodhound would still be able to smell it a mile away.

He was wearing a black dress shirt left untucked; the sleeves rolled up to his elbows, and a pair of jeans that looked like they had never seen a day of wear and tear. Eric stepped up to her, placing his hands on the edges of her shoulders.

"After you left last night, I was made aware of a concerning incident that occurred in my private office upstairs."

Her face softened up as her curiosity was piqued. "An incident?"

A sigh passed through his lips. "Two of my men were killed."

Immediately, her mind was back on Joey, but this time, it was what had brought him to the party in the first place and his disappearance to take care of some business matters. That jackass was supposed to be discreet, and he left two bodies behind? The back of her brain was furious at him. Joey better have a damn good excuse.

"By who?" If he had any suspicions, she figured she would be dead by now. That's what she would have done in his shoes.

Trying to be reassuring, he offered up a smile. "I'm still looking into it. It appears whoever was responsible was looking for something. Until I know more, as a precaution, I am having my top-tier security system installed here."

She shook her head. "That's not necessary; I am more than capable of dealing with anyone that wants to break in here and start shit with me." Well, mostly anyone.

When she went to step back, his hands tightened their hold on her. "As my future wife, it is very much a necessity." His voice grew more stern with her.

Her nostrils flared slightly, seeing that he thought he was going to be the proverbial man of the house. "Eric, let's get one thing straight. We're not married yet, and when that day comes, let's get one thing very, very clear." Her voice mirrored the same level of rigidness as his. "You *will not* be making any decisions for me."

With a firm shove, she removed one of his hands and shook off the other as she stepped away with unfriendly eyes targeted at him. Eric watched as Layne distanced herself. Switching up his approach, he softened his face.

"You're right; I should have said something. I apologize for that. However, I will not apologize for doing my best to keep you safe from any potential threats. It's now my responsibility since we have come to our agreement to be bound to one another."

As much as she wanted to lay into him about protecting his assets, she swallowed it down into the base of her stomach. Layne reminded herself that she needed to be smart in handling this situation and her alliance with Eric. Personal feelings needed to be shoved aside.

He presented her with an offer. "How about I make it up to you? I will take you out for a night, and we will forget about work and just focus on getting to know one another."

Layne peeked out a window at the workers beginning their installation of new cameras on her property. Part of her wanted to scream out her annoyance and frustration. The other part? She wanted to just give up and sink into a deep, dark, black hole. He may as well have shoved a tracking device up her ass.

"How does that sound, my little harpy?" Eric stepped up behind her, his hands trailing down along her spine before pausing at the small of her back. He rested his chin on top of her shoulder so she could feel the light caresses of his breath as he waited for her response. His hands began to knead the tense muscles along the bottom of her spine.

Layne couldn't explain why the world felt so much smaller around him. Maybe it was the fact that she didn't have a better way out of the current predicament the O'Reilly organization was currently stuck in.

"Sure." She craned her neck so that she was able to discreetly maneuver away from the proximity of his touch. It did little to persuade him to back off. When she turned around, he stood there in front of her like a wolf assessing its latest meal.

His hand lifted and settled lightly on her cheek. Despite the light touch, it felt heavy with something else - something more ominous.

So many thoughts bounced around inside of her head like an erratic ping-pong ball, overwhelming her. How was Liam going to react? What did this mean for her and Joey? Was she doing the right thing?

All the unanswered questions tugged on her heart to a point where she wanted to reach into her chest and tear it out in a move of utter desperation and hopelessness.

Whether it was the conflicted expression on her face or merely an affectionate gesture, Eric leaned forward and brushed his lips against hers. The newest of conflicts went to war inside of her as she felt like a hostage in a cage she had helped build for herself.

Tilting her head down before pulling it to the side away from him, she stepped away. "I have some work to get done." It was absolutely a lie, but a necessary one if it meant ending this unexpected visit. Layne scraped her teeth over her bottom lip as she scrambled to quickly rebuild her typically tough exterior and abolish any displays of weakness.

Eric allowed Layne to pull away from him but maintained a careful eye on her. "Of course. My men should be wrapping up outside in the next hour."

Layne nodded, having nearly forgotten about the new shackles being set up on her life with Eric's men installing a brand new surveillance system on her home.

After he left, she trudged back upstairs, pulling herself up one step at a time by the railing while trying to bear the weight life was taking on her. She just needed something to make it more tolerable. She needed something to make the world stop spinning. She needed something and anything to make her stop feeling.

Once she was in her bathroom, she struggled with the child-resistant cap on the prescription bottle. Her lower lip was trembling as she fought back the feelings that were growing heavier on her conscience.

Finally, the cap popped loose, and the second the pills were washed down her throat with a handful of water from the bathroom faucet, there was a sense of relief. Something was on its way to help relieve the pressure valve.

Still in bed well past dinner time, she woke up under a heavy fog. Attempting to shove the duvet from her body felt equivalent to moving a stubborn elephant. It took well over another hour before she could gather enough functionality to check the messages on her phone.

Several missed calls. Missed text messages. Unread emails. Social media notifications. Before she could wrap her head around where to begin catching up, her phone began buzzing with an incoming call—Liam.

Wearily, she brought the phone to her ear as she answered. "Yeah?"

His voice was the most serious she had heard in some time. "We need to talk."

"What else is new?" She wasn't feeling up to putting up a front at the moment.

Her brother grumbled. "Meet me at McGregor's."

"Now isn't a good time." Her head was pounding.

"Fuck that shit, it's a good time for me. Meet me there in thirty minutes." He hung up on her.

Great, now she had to be a functional human being, all for the sake of trying to appease Liam.

Layne pushed through the sluggish feelings and managed to get out of bed, dragging herself to the shower in hopes that the steamy streams of water could melt away the remnants of her faded high.

Afterward, she slid into a comfortable pair of jeans and a loosely fitted sweater.

Liam would just have to cope with the fact that she would be arriving forty minutes later than he wanted her to.

CHAPTER SIXTEEN

To her surprise, McGregor's was hosting a slew of people when she arrived. She walked inside, pushing past the folks who were spilling into the main pathway while waiting at the bar for a beverage.

As she got to the backroom, she noticed a few familiar faces. In particular, Liam was chatting with a couple of his friends while Kristill was perched on his lap. Either she had forgiven Liam, or he had made it monetarily worth her while to crawl back to him. Layne didn't care for either of those scenarios, but there were bigger issues than her brother's volatile involvement with an escort.

With an arm around the hooker's waist, Liam polished off the last of his milk stout. Layne approached the table, and it didn't take long before Liam dismissed the rest of the crew surrounding him.

Kristill leaned over and whispered something undoubtedly dirty into his ear before rising off his lap with a salacious grin. "Don't take too long, baby." Her teeth nibbled Liam's ear and tugged on it before releasing the flesh and walking out into the main room.

"Well, if I needed a reason to feel like puking my brains out - that may have been it." Layne shook her head, still unclear of what Liam ever saw in that girl or what Kristill saw in him.

Liam raised his view to stare at her, remaining silent. Layne took it upon herself to occupy the seat across from him while waiting for him to say something. When he didn't immediately speak up, she took it upon herself to start the conversation. "You're the one who wanted to meet."

"Did you really do it?" It seemed like such a simple question, and yet she was unable to comprehend where it was stemming from.

"Do what?" She sat back in her seat, balancing the chair on the back two legs for a moment. A waitress brought her over a light ale that she typically ordered on days when it wasn't the date of her mother's death. Layne gave a brief and polite smile at her before taking a sip.

Liam finally cut to the chase. "Marry Eric Ellis?"

A small spray of beer exited from between her lips, followed by a cough as the back of her hand came up to wipe across her mouth. "What? Fuck no!"

The expression in Liam's eyes remained unchanged and full of judgment. She quickly gathered her senses and shook her head. "No, not yet, anyway. Li, look, you have to understand where I'm coming from—"

He interrupted her, "—you have my blessing."

Her words trailed off as she looked as shell-shocked as she felt. Layne sat there wondering if her hearing was possibly deceiving her. "Wait, what?"

He shrugged. "I think it's a good idea. You have my blessing."

"*Your blessing*?" She lifted a brow in confusion. "I don't need your damn blessing. Besides that, I'm not sure your blessing means a damn as of lately."

"Shit is going south, and Eric has the means and desire to fix things. If that means you have to finally pull your weight around here, then so be it. I expect I will get appropriately compensated." He made it sound so simple. So matter of fact. So businesslike. So… easy. Not to mention entirely archaic.

"Compensated? That's the part you're worried about?" She rose from her seat, resting her hands on the table as she glared at him. "I'm putting my ass on the line here to try and salvage what Dad built from the bottom up, and you're worried about getting *compensated* while you sit back and get your dick warmed by some two-bit hoe?"

Liam shrugged again, seemingly unbothered and unfazed.

Irritated didn't even begin to describe the feelings bubbling up inside of her. She tilted her head as she stared at him suspiciously. "Where did you hear this anyhow?"

"He hasn't exactly been keeping it a secret, Layne. He's already making it known that anyone that crosses us is crossing him." Her brother looked the most relieved he had looked in months. It rubbed her the wrong way that he could just so easily be ok with this arrangement where he didn't have to put in any effort.

"Great." She didn't hide the displeasure from her voice that word was making its way around in less than twenty-four hours. She rubbed her forehead as her tumultuous thoughts made it ache. Why did everything feel like it was moving far too fast?

Her phone began vibrating in her pocket, and when she pulled it out, she immediately recognized the number. A sensation of butterflies filled her stomach. "I have to take this."

Liam waved her off to go do as she needed. Layne answered the call, pressing the phone up to her ear as she began to walk away from the table. "Hey, give me a minute to step outside."

Before she passed by her sibling, his hand reached out and paused her. "Just don't fuck this up, Layne."

That was rich coming from him, the same person who had been fucking up his own shit since he was born. She glared at him before she pulled away to cut through the crowd toward the side exit into the alleyway.

Once the fresh air washed over her, she let out a sigh of relief.

"Are you still there?" Joey's voice on the other end of the line brought her thoughts back into the present. Feeling an overwhelming sense of pressure and loss of control of her life tugging at her soul, she blinked back some tears as she looked up at the dark sky. She pressed both of her lips together tightly as she worked on reigning in all the emotions threatening to spill over the ledge.

He spoke up again, this time more concern evident in his voice. "Layne?"

She leaned back against the side of the building, her hand clutching onto the phone in her hand tightly. Her exhale was a little shaky, but she managed to at least respond to him. "Yeah. I'm here." She swallowed past the knot in her throat.

His voice tried to lull answers out of her with its husky tone. "What's wrong?"

Not that he could see it, but she shook her head and cleared her throat, trying to shake off the emotions. "Nothing. It's just been a day."

"Layney—"

She cut him off. "Why did you call?"

After a sigh of resignation that she was going to avoid answering his question, he responded to her. "We need to talk. I will come pick you up."

"I'm not at home." She looked down at the ground and kicked an empty beer can across the alley.

"I know." He always seemed to find his way to her, no matter where she was.

Feeling like she could push past the swell of emotions she had felt moments ago that had threatened to swallow her up whole, she moved away from the wall and walked towards the sidewalk.

"Of course, you'd know that." Not hiding the lack of shock in her voice. "Meet me right outside the 50th Street Station." It wasn't too far from McGregor's, making it a convenient spot to have him meet her, only a block and a half away.

During that walk, she was able to mentally string herself together, desperately hoping it would stay that way. When she got to the end of the block where the subway station entrance was, she immediately recognized Joey straddling his black sports bike, patiently waiting for her.

One boot-clad foot pushed the kickstand down before he got off his ride and walked over to her. He was wearing a dark pair of jeans that hugged over his broad thighs and his black leather jacket that always mixed in with his cologne in a delightful and intoxicating combination of scents.

Despite her efforts to keep a mask over her feelings, what he saw when he looked at her prompted him to pull her into his chest and wrap his arms around her without hesitation. His arms squeezed around her firmly, encasing her in his warmth.

Layne wanted to push him away so she didn't lose herself to something she wasn't sure she could shut down once it started. Despite wrangling with the side of her that wanted to maintain a strong front, her hands squeezed onto him tighter, and she buried her face into his chest a little more.

All the pieces she had just tried gluing back together inside of her were starting to show indications of faltering. A shudder shook her upper body as a quiet sob broke through. Layne had tried to stop it before it came out, but his embrace provided a sense of safety more than any security system ever could. Another sob soon followed, and her body lightly trembled against him. The tension could be felt all over her body as it fought against this breakdown that was currently taking its toll on her.

His hands worked gentle rubs along her back to try and erase whatever torment she was suffering. Joey's hard exterior managed to provide her with a soft landing spot for the emotions that were at war inside of her.

With people passing them by and going about their lives, Joey stood there holding her for as long as she needed at that moment. He was going to try to soak up anything and everything that was weighing down on her by physical touch alone.

CHAPTER SEVENTEEN

Joey had the sense not to ask her any questions before they arrived back at his place.

His unit hadn't changed much since the last time she had been there. It still had the same minimalist decor representative of how little time he spent in the quaint apartment. There were no photographs or anything else that made it feel personal. It was clear that if he had to up and move, it wouldn't take long to pack it all up.

The bottle of whiskey was set down on the center island of the kitchen in front of her at her request.

Layne sat there on a kitchen stool, her head held in her hands with her fingers tucked into her hair. When she finally looked up, she saw his puppy-like brown hues locked on her and filled with concern.

"Stop staring at me like I'm a wounded animal." She hated it when her emotions got the best of her, except for anger. She was more than happy to embrace that one any day of the week.

Her hand reached out, pulled the bottle closer to her, and removed the cork. Taking a swig straight from the bottle, she let out a sigh as the smooth burn traveled down her throat.

Joey came around from the other side of the island and pulled out a seat for himself. Perching on the stool, he turned to face her.

"What did you want to talk about?" Her eyes drifted over the label of the whiskey bottle to avoid any more looks of pity in her direction.

Angel's Envy. The bottle had an outlined design of feathery wings down the backside of the clear glass container.

His hands reached over and grabbed her legs, pulling her so the stool swiveled to rotate her to face him.

"Last night." His hands remained latched onto her legs.

Her eyes reluctantly looked over at him. "The part where you left two bodies in Eric's house or the part where you railed into me on the hood of your car?"

From the draw of his deep breath, it was clear he was summoning as much patience as he could. "Layne, I get there is a lot of fucked up shit going on. You gave me your word last night that you weren't going to run from this, from us."

"I'm still here, aren't I?" It sounded bratty, even to herself. "You told me you just needed to get into Eric's house to go poke around and look for information. You dropping bodies was not part of the plan. Do you realize how stupid that was? If Eric knew that it was you or that I had any knowledge of what was going on, I'd be six feet in the ground by now or worse."

Her temper was beginning to roll, and it felt better to embrace it than some of the other feelings trying to resurface. Layne lifted the bottle of amber liquid, and before she was able to bring it to her mouth again, Joey's hand grabbed her wrist and stopped her.

"First off, I didn't have a choice." He pulled the whiskey from her grasp and set it to the side out of her reach. "Second, he's not going to lay a hand on you."

She gave a short laugh of disbelief at how delusional Joey was to think he was going to step in and be able to protect her. That may have been the case a year ago, but it sure as hell wasn't the same world she was living in now. "Good luck with that."

He perked a brow at her. Before he could comment, she continued her thoughts, "In case you missed the memo, we're going to tie the knot so that Liam and I aren't executed in a horrible and grotesque display of fucked up dominance across the city's factions. Eric's ready to charge full steam ahead on this little agreement we have. He was at my house this morning, fucking around with my security system, all in the name of ensuring my safety."

She stood up to walk away from him, but his hand curled around her wrist and tugged her back so she was standing between his legs while he sat there on his stool. Joey's other hand came up to hold onto her chin so she could stare at him while he spoke calmly to her. "What did I just tell you? That twisted motherfucker is not going to lay a goddamn hand on you."

Attempting to refrain from rolling her eyes at him, she shook her head in disbelief. "What makes you so sure of that?" Her eyes searched his face for any hint that he had a miracle stored away.

"Because, Layney, you're mine, and I'm not sharing. Now, sit your pretty ass down so I can tell you what I need to say."

"And if I don't?" She was being a challenging pain in the ass, but she didn't give a damn as her words began to come out hot. He had signed up for this the moment he stepped foot back inside her house, asking for a favor. "Are you going to come at me again like you did when you told me that I should stop taking pills? They're the only thing that is keeping me fuckin' sane right now as I deal with all of this bullshit. If I'm not dealing with Liam's unhinged ass, it's Eric or you, or maybe the fact that I have to worry about getting shot at in public on any given day. You haven't been around for the past year, so news flash, people change, and I'm doing what I can to cope."

Joey's gaze darkened as Layne indirectly admitted that her coping mechanism of using pills hadn't ceased. He stood up to his full six-foot-two height, towering over her. "Give me a reason to remind you that I don't ask twice."

Maybe it was the whiskey, or maybe it was the mounting pressures she was dealing with, but she straightened up, not willing to back down this time. "You talk a big game."

He nodded as he considered her response. Joey's hand came up along the back of her neck until he had a handful of her hair in his grasp. He tilted her head back so that she was looking up at him. "Suit yourself." He spun her around until she was bent over the top of the counter.

Stepping up behind her, he sealed his hips up against her ass. Even through the thick jeans, she could feel the swell of his cock begging to be freed. Leaning over and whispering into her ear, "We're going to have this conversation whether you want to be my good girl or not."

The next thing Layne felt after he took a step back was the sharp sting of his palm landing on her ass. It was his way of ensuring he had her undivided attention. It elicited a sudden squeak from her, and when she tried to stand back up straight, his hand slid down from her hair and firmly pressed between her shoulder blades so she remained bent over the counter for him.

He continued to explain himself to her. "As I was trying to tell you, I had no intention of taking out two of Ellis' men. They were unfortunate but required casualties. If I hadn't indisposed them, you and I both wouldn't be here right now."

She pushed back against his hand, but he kept her pinned there. "That still doesn't make up for—"

Joey's hand came smacking back down onto the same spot on her ass, this time a little more vigorously. "I'm not done yet."

His hand reached around and tugged hard enough on the button of her jeans that it popped off entirely. It caused the sound of a light dink against the floor when it landed and rolled away. Joey made quick work of her zipper before he shoved the jeans down over her ass, exposing the bare flesh of her cheeks and the thin strip of material between them. A light flush of pink on the one side from where his hand had made contact twice already.

Layne wiggled underneath his hold. Her teeth pressed into her lower lip, finding herself getting heated at her center despite wanting to take her anger out on him. She then parted her lips to say something, and before any sound came out, Joey cleared his throat as both a warning and a reminder.

"Now, about last night. There was a small snag in what I was able to get my hands on, and I'm going to need your help to get it." He dragged his hand down along her spine to join his other hand as they both slid down over the curve of her exposed rear until they settled between her legs. He applied pressure, spreading them open at his command.

He continued talking while his fingers toyed with the narrow and stretchy material of her thong. He ran two fingers along the soft material up to the waistline and down all the way to its midpoint, where he felt her arousal dampening the underwear. "However, before we get to that," he gave a tug on the strip of fabric, allowing it to tug against the more intimate parts of her, "I'm laying down my rules."

Layne felt his fingers so close to her body, which was already begging him to explore further. Her eyes looked back at him while her hips pressed into his touch, hoping to get more of his attention.

He pulled on the back of her thong before releasing it to lightly smack against her skin. It was followed by the sound of his belt coming undone and the zipper of his jeans sliding down.

When he leaned over, his hard cock teasingly pushed between her thighs. Joey placed one hand on either side of her bent-over body on the countertop and leaned against her back close enough that his breath wisped at the skin on the back of her neck. "Rule one," he rolled his hips so that his length rubbed against her. "No running. I don't care how hard things get. If you run away this time, I will hunt you down and drag you back a thousand times over until you realize I'm all in and I'm not going anywhere."

Layne swallowed hard, whimpering at the sensation of the heat of his body so close but not giving her the touch she wanted. The pace of her breathing ticked up a notch.

"Two," he slid his hands down over her arms until they rested on her wrists, putting pressure on her hands to stay where they were. "No more damn pills. If you want an escape, I will fuckin' worship your body in every way I know how until you can't even find it in you to scream out to God anymore."

She pressed her lips together, squirming underneath him at the discomfort of his second demand to knock off her reliance on the prescription drug to wash away her stress.

He pressed a kiss to the side of her neck. The sensation seemed to draw away her anxieties for a brief moment. "Finally, my favorite, rule three." He paused and smirked down at her. "No more of these." His hand traveled down to the side of her hip, his hand wrapped around the waist of her thong and forcefully tugged. The material easily gave away under the sudden onset of force.

Layne gave a light gasp followed by an excited smile.

He dropped the now useless article of clothing to the floor. "Any questions?"

She pushed her hips back against his thick length. "When does all the worshipping begin?"

He grinned, already knowing by the feel of the warmth of her soaked pussy rubbing over him that she was very much looking forward to being taken. For added measure, he rubbed his aching cock against her slit. Her arousal left a sheen of desire along the top of his shaft. "If you had been a good girl, I'd already have you riding my dick."

He pulled back and tucked himself back into his pants despite the way he wanted to get another hit from his addiction to her body. "Since you wanted to mouth off, you're going to have to wait."

As he pulled away from her, her body's anticipatory tension tanked. Every part of her felt lit up like a firework about to be launched toward space, only to have the fuse fail before the fun could even begin. At first, she frowned in frustrated disappointment; then, she furrowed her eyebrows at him for leading her on. "You can't be serious."

With a sigh, she tugged her jeans back up, only zipping them since the button suffered a glorious end to its functionality.

He walked over to the freezer and pulled the bottom drawer open. "As the grave."

Joey reached in and grabbed a pint of Baileys Irish Cream flavored Häagan-Dazs and lifted it for her to see. "Go sit on the couch, Layne." So demanding, wasn't he?

"Ice cream is not really what I'm in the mood for."

After retrieving a spoon, he walked up to her, capturing her chin with his fingers, and gently kissed her. "Next time, don't make me ask twice." He grinned unapologetically.

After she begrudgingly went and sat on the sofa, she tried to ignore the desire that was screaming at her between her legs. Layne drew her legs up onto the couch with her, criss-crossing them.

He joined her and handed her the pint of ice cream and the spoon before sitting down next to her. Comfortably, he leaned back and rested an arm along the back of the dark grey sectional. The dark brown of his eyes settled on her as she opened up the frozen dessert and began to dig in. Despite the dirty looks she was giving him, Joey could have watched her like this all damn day.

Layne moaned quietly on the first taste of the ice cream as it danced across her taste buds. It had been far too long since she had indulged in this particular sweet treat.

Discreetly, Joey adjusted himself at the sound of her approval. It was going to be a long evening if she kept that up. By making his point to her there by the kitchen counter, she wasn't the only one who was being left unsatisfied here.

After Layne finished her pint of ice cream, Joey internally questioned how the hell it was possible to be so painfully hard watching a woman enjoy something as innocuous as a little frozen dessert. The idea of jerking off to find relief didn't even appeal to him when she was sitting right there, so close to him.

With the television on some show about two brothers and the family business, Layne curled up into Joey's side. He dropped his arm around her shoulders, keeping her close. His fingers traced small and senseless patterns along her arm as they sat there, just enjoying one another's presence.

He looked down at Layne. He parted his lips to say something, but before the words came out, he shut his mouth after thinking better of it. A few more moments passed, and he finally spoke up. "I will raise all hell for you, always. Don't ever question that."

When she didn't respond, he shifted to lean over and take a peek at her face. Layne's eyes were shut as she was soundly asleep in his embrace. Joey kissed the top of her head and carefully maneuvered her, doing his best not to wake the little Irish beast in the process.

He shifted her into his arms and carried her into the bedroom, where he got her tucked in. He joined her moments later. His fingers tucked a strand of her hair behind her ear as he leaned over and whispered a few words to her, knowing she'd never know of his confession to her come morning.

CHAPTER EIGHTEEN

It had been a rare occasion that she hadn't needed to rely on a pill to sleep through the night. The only thing that had been nagging at her was the deep ache between her legs after Joey had withheld himself from her. Even then, she had just felt at peace and calm as she breathed in the natural scent of his body mixed in with the familiarity of the last remnants of his cologne with notes of sage.

That wasn't the only pleasant smell that had her feeling at ease as she began to wake, the scent of food cooking filled the unit. When she was finally ready to open her eyes for the day, she found herself alone in Joey's bed. First things first, she hit the bathroom, where she found one of his tees neatly folded on the counter for her. Opting for the comfort of an oversized cotton shirt versus her jeans and sweater, she made the quick wardrobe change. As expected, his shirt swallowed her petite body up.

After emerging from the bathroom, she breathed in the scent of freshly cooked bacon that was hanging heavily in the air as an indication of the promise of breakfast. Layne shuffled out of his bedroom, rubbing the sleep away from her eyes as she came into the kitchen. She was greeted by the view of Joey standing in front of the stove, wearing a pair of grey sweatpants barely hanging onto his body at the hips.

The display of tattoos spilled over his shoulders and upper back and down along the sides of his ribs. She stood there in awe, her eyes appreciating the view. Her core between her legs also appreciated it very much, especially as she observed where his exposed skin stopped at his lower back, and the waistband of the sweats began as they barely adhered to the curve of his muscled ass.

Joey moved some eggs around in the frying pan with a spatula, and without looking over at her, he spoke up, "See something you want?"

Her thighs pressed together, reminding her that she was without her pair of panties he had so politely disposed of last night. "Maybe. What's on the menu?"

She grinned and walked over to his side, taking a look at what he was preparing. The scrambled eggs were just finishing up in the frying pan; there was a plate full of bacon, and pancakes were stacked on another plate.

It pulled a smile onto her face, seeing that he had gone to the effort to cook for her. Typically, she got her breakfast from whichever bagel shop was convenient.

Joey set the spatula down and turned to face her, giving her a more complete view of his toned physique. The lean lines cut around each muscle group on his upper body. Each tattoo decorating his skin was on full display for her to appreciate, from the sprawling mosaic over his arms, across his chest, and down to the "Chaos Addict" words scripted along his side.

The newest addition to his ink collection was in plain sight. Placed directly above his heart, the curves of the shamrock graced his pec as the crimson blood dripped from the emblem of luck just past his nipple.

He captured her face in his hands and drew her mouth up into an adoring kiss. "How did you sleep?"

She couldn't help but keep smiling up at him. "I would have slept better if I had gotten what I wanted last night."

His smirk flicked onto his mouth.

Before he could respond, the sound of her phone vibrating and the corresponding high-pitched tone rang against the kitchen counter where she had left it the night before. Layne walked over and frowned, seeing the name on the screen. "Eric." Her eyes glanced over at Joey, who didn't seem to have a change in his demeanor.

She slid the answer button over and placed the phone to her ear. "Hi."

The smooth sound of Eric's voice was strained as he spoke on the other end of the call. "Good morning. I didn't see you get home last night."

Joey approached her and took her by the waist, lifting her onto the edge of the counter. Layne swatted at him for fucking around while she was trying to have a damn conversation. What was Joey's response? He gave a mischievous grin and placed a finger to his lips as an instruction for her to remain quiet.

At first, Layne was confused about his intentions, but then he pressed her to lay back on the counter. He pulled her by her legs to the edge before spreading her legs apart. The t-shirt got caught up underneath her and remained pushed up around her stomach. Her half-naked body was fully revealed to him, making her arousal quite obvious from his perspective.

"Layne, are you still there?" Eric's voice echoed in her ear.

Her attention was drawn back to the voice on the other end of her device. "Yeah, I'm still here." Layne's brain struggled to recall his initial commentary, thanks to her attention being drawn elsewhere.

Eric repeated himself. "You didn't come home last night when I checked the security footage."

Joey leaned over and hungrily lapped up her arousal along her folds, with his tongue flicking over her sensitive bundle of nerves. Her hips jolted at the sensation, and before she could squirm away, his hands clamped down onto her thighs to steady her.

Her heart was hammering away inside of her chest as she choked down a gasp.

"No, I didn't." Layne's words purposely remained short as she spit them out.

That vague response didn't seem to satisfy Eric as he continued talking. "Where are you? I want to make sure you're okay."

She pressed her lips together in a hard line as Joey began to assault her pussy with his mouth. His teeth nipped at her clit while the scruff on his face continually brushed against her. Layne placed a hand on her forehead, trying to focus and maintain her composure while her thoughts felt scattered.

"I'm fine. I stayed at a friend's."

At the mention of the word 'friend,' Joey raised an eyebrow, then snickered quietly to himself. He removed one hand from her thigh and pushed two fingers deep inside of her.

Layne slapped her hand over her mouth as she nearly cried out at the pleasureful intrusion of her body. Joey continued to lick and suck at her most intimate bits. Her hips were unable to stop themselves from grinding against his touch.

"Are you sure you're okay? Let me send someone to come pick you up," Eric pressed on.

Joey's fingers curled inside of her, stroking over the special spot that drove her insane. Her face was flushing while her heart felt like it was loud enough to drown out Times Square on New Year's Eve.

She removed her hand from her mouth briefly. "No, no. I'm already on my way." As much as she wanted to set him straight about checking in on her, she just wanted to get him off the call.

That's when she felt Joey's teeth bite at her swollen bud. A squeak squeezed past her throat before she was able to muffle herself. Her eyebrows furrowed together as it became a struggle to keep all the pleasure bottled up inside of her.

Joey's hand gave her inner thigh a slap as a warning to keep her sounds to herself. She looked down at him with a silent whimper.

Eric's voice was barely audible in her ear over the sound of the blood rushing in her ears as it all traveled south to her center. "I need you to tell me these things, my little harpy." While he explained the importance of him knowing where she was at all times for her safety, Joey didn't ease up on devouring her.

The tattoos on his fingers disappeared inside of her every time he pumped them into her body. His tongue drew circles over her delicate pleasure button, occasionally drawing it into his mouth and sucking harshly on it.

She writhed under the overwhelming weight of desire and ecstasy building up inside of her and was unable to be vocalized. Her voice was strained as she did her best to wrap up the call with Eric. "Can I call you back? You're breaking up."

Noting that Layne was trying her best to end the conversation, only encouraged Joey to ante up. He pulled his mouth from her and licked the flavor of her body from his lips. It gave Layne a small window of relief, but it wasn't long before his hand reached up and sealed down over her mouth.

That's when Layne felt him shove a third finger deep inside of her as he picked up the pace of penetrating her body there on his kitchen counter.

Her hand grabbed the wrist of Joey's hand that was pressed over her lips. She wasn't sure if she wanted to pull him away or keep it there as sensations began to quickly escalate inside of her.

She thought she heard Eric say goodbye after she promised to call him back, but she wasn't sure of anything at that moment. The several moans that managed to slip from her were muffled against Joey's hand while her body looked for its release.

Out of the corner of her eyes, she noticed the call ended on her cellphone. Her hand dropped it down onto the counter in relief. Her sounds of approval were still muffled as he coaxed her body closer to her climax.

His eyes flickered at the uptick of noise against his palm. "Did I tell you that you could make a sound yet, Layney?"

Her face looked at him pleadingly while her hips rode against his fingers with a strong need to hit the approaching peak. Layne's whimpers vibrated against his palm.

Just before she spilled over the edge of sensual release, he removed both hands from her and pulled her upright. She panted heavily as the wave of pleasure began to ebb.

The second she was face to face with him, he pushed his fingers into her mouth with her body's wet arousal coating them. Layne hungrily sucked on his fingers in the same way she wanted to put her mouth on other parts of him. She watched the lustfulness fire up in his eyes as she did so. Her tongue slid over every inch of each finger, being sure not to leave any part of her desire behind.

Joey growled as her mouth sucked the taste of her own body off his fingers. "That's a good girl, cleaning up after yourself." He then withdrew his fingers and snatched her up off the counter. Her hands grabbed onto his shoulders, and her legs wrapped around his waist.

Her mouth kissed along his jaw and down over the spread of his tattoo of raven wings along his neck. "You better finish what you started."

"Mm, and if I don't?" With his hands grasping her by the curves of her ass, he carried her over to the fridge, where he pressed her back up against it, letting the hard bulge straining against his sweats press up against her bare pussy.

Her teeth playfully nipped at his lower lip, tugging at it. "I may need to hire someone to abduct you and bring you to an abandoned building so that I can have my way with you."

His grin widened. His movements shifted to tug at the waist of his sweatpants, allowing his cock to spring out, already locked and loaded, ready for her. A drop of precum glistened at the tip. "As much as I would like to see you try," he lowered her hips so that his head pressed against the entrance of her pussy teasingly, "I'd rather be the one doing the abductions and having my way with you."

"Mmhmm. Just shut up and fuck me." Layne leaned over and locked her mouth onto his.

She didn't have to tell Joey twice; he pushed himself into her slowly to enjoy the way her body felt as it welcomed his cock's invasion. He groaned as Layne's moan vibrated against his mouth.

Layne immediately felt a wave of pleasure as he fully sank into her. Her hips pressed back against him while he filled her. She tilted her head back slightly as far as the fridge door behind her would allow as she let the sensations overcome her.

He took his time laying kiss after kiss along her skin, starting along her jaw and traveling toward her neck. His hips slowly pulled himself back from her body before reentering at the same speed. Joey wanted to enjoy each moment of savoring her body. The neck of his tee on her tiny frame sloped down to expose her left shoulder. Joey's mouth found the shiny bullet-sized scar on her shoulder. He swiped his tongue over it, lapping over the healed gunshot wound to try and erase the bad memories associated with it.

Her hands ran over the tops of his shoulders and down onto his upper back, where her nails dragged across his skin. The way his length paused up against her sweet spot had subtle chills of desire running over her body.

As he continued to press that slow and decadent assault on her body, it was more than skin-deep. The feelings welling up inside of Layne weren't anything that she was accustomed to. It was a slow burn of desire that wasn't just tugging deep and low in her core. No, it was a tugging of feelings and warmth inside of her chest.

"Joey…" Her breathy voice whispered as she brought her eyes to meet his.

Using one hand to support her, he lifted the other to take hold of her face and passionately kiss her. Their bodies continued to grind against one another. It was a much different pace and swirl of sensations than the other night on top of the parking garage. This was something far more intimate.

It was unclear how much time passed, but each push into her brought her right up to the edge of release. Joey's hands tightened up on her legs that remained locked around him. "Layne," his words were spoken against her lips. "I've missed everything about you."

She pressed her forehead up against his while her lips caressed over his between each heavy breath released. "I haven't been able to breathe without you." Her clutch on him tightened up as her body shook as it spilled over the edge and crashed into complete ecstasy.

When her body tightened down around him and her flood of desire coated his cock, he shuddered, and the apex of his pleasure was unleashed. Joey pushed himself deep within her, trying to plow past the physical limitations as his release filled the depths of her body.

They both remained there, heavily breathing in each other's embrace. Layne slumped forward, her face buried in the crook of his neck as she held onto him for dear life. With an arm underneath her ass for support and one around her back, he stepped back away from the fridge. He inhaled the scent of her dewy skin below her jaw, planting several more kisses on it as they both came down from their orgasms.

After they both were adequately recovered, Joey made sure to reheat the breakfast he had prepared for her. He carried a plate over to the modest kitchen table where Layne sat. Her plate was full of a little bit of everything for her to feast on after expending all their energy on one another. She smiled up at him, a smile that hadn't left her face since the second he had given her a hell of a way to wake up this morning.

"Can't have you leaving here hungry," he stated as he set the plate down before her.

Layne couldn't even imagine eating, given how satisfied she already was. "I don't think you have to worry about that."

CHAPTER NINETEEN

Layne hated it, but now she had confirmation that Eric was watching her every move a lot closer than she anticipated. It left her feeling paranoid about how far he was willing to take things. Not to mention that Joey was going to have to be extraordinarily careful about his visits to her house.

Yesterday's breakfast with Joey had left her feeling renewed and refreshed in so many ways. For a small amount of time, he had managed to melt all her worries away. However, there was still the unsolved complication of salvaging her family's floundering business operations.

Feeling more optimistic than she had felt in some time, she was ready to take on this new day. She tossed on a pair of dark leggings with her knee-high boots and a cozy sweater knit with loose stitches so one got glimpses of the ivy tank top underneath. Her hand grabbed her coat and keys on her way out the front door.

As she stepped outside, she was greeted by two men dressed in boring black suits coming up the walkway to her door. Layne hadn't been expecting company.

"Can I help you?" She hoped not. Layne was planning a pitstop at Rebecca's to borrow a book, *Warlock: A Strange Grove Novel*, that had been recommended to her before meeting with the skeleton crew that still worked for the O'Reilly organization. Now was not the time to be asked about her satisfaction with her cable service by some salesmen.

Both men stopped, blocking her pathway. The taller man with a dark olive complexion nodded at her without so much as a smile. "Yes, Mr. Ellis has requested you join him for lunch."

Layne tilted her head, unable to hold back the look of disbelief that he had actually sent his people for this. "You can tell him I already have plans."

When she went to sidestep them, they stepped along with her, maintaining an obstruction. She sighed and shook her head. "I don't have time for this. Get out of my way."

The slightly shorter of the two men reached out for her arm. "We must insist you come with us, miss."

Layne jerked her arm away before he could lay a finger on her. "This is fuckin' ridiculous." She pulled out her phone and dialed Eric's number.

As if he had been expecting her, he answered immediately, sounding far too cheerful. "Hello, Layne."

She glared at the two suits in front of her. "If you had called, I would have been more than happy to tell you I already have plans today." Her tone did not hide any of her annoyance at the absurdity of the situation.

"If you had bothered to call me back yesterday, we could have discussed this. I'm afraid today's lunch isn't optional."

Great, Eric was going to be pissy about not getting a phone call, and Layne didn't do well handling fragile feelings. She drew in a deep breath, trying to weigh her options. "It better be a quick lunch." She ended the call.

Again, the shorter one reached out to take her arm, and she fired a glare at him. "Unless you want to part ways with your damn hand, I would keep it to yourself."

He paused to consider if she was bluffing or not. It seemed he was a smart man when he extended his arm away from her to indicate for her to follow them both to a sleek black sedan. The engine was still running while being double-parked in front of her house.

After they escorted her to the vehicle, they let her into the back seat while they both took up seats in the front. The entire twenty-minute ride had been in complete silence. Not even the radio had been turned on.

When they parked the car in front of a tall office building and killed the engine, Layne pulled on the handle to let herself out. Nothing happened. The fuckers had the child door locks on, preventing her from getting out on her own accord. Bastards.

If she hadn't been pissed off about this change in plans already, this was the needle on the bitter Irish girl's back. The taller man opened the door for her, and after she exited the car, they led her inside the building with large glass windows reflecting the damn near blinding sunlight.

After a stroll through the lobby and an elevator ride to the forty-eighth floor in awkward silence, they brought her to a corner office with a picturesque city view. An L-shaped desk on one side of the room and a leather sofa on the other, with two chairs and a table opposite it.

She noticed a few silver carryout containers on the oval table in the seating area. At least he didn't plan a six-course meal like she had expected from him.

Layne stepped inside and noticed that she was all alone. The door shut behind her, allowing privacy from any prying eyes of anyone else potentially passing by.

She tossed her coat over the back of one of the chairs and walked over to the massive windows, crossing her arms in front of her chest as her eyes took in the view. Layne didn't want to admit how she could stare at the beauty of the city she had grown up in all day long.

The office door opened up again, prompting her to glance back over her shoulder to see Eric walking inside with a folder in one hand and a coffee mug in the other.

He was dressed in a grey suit with a black shirt and tie underneath the jacket. Eric offered her a polite smile, seeing she had arrived, as he set everything down on his desk. "Ah, there you are. Glad to see you came to your senses."

He walked over to her like he had given her a choice to be here. When he placed his hands on her arms and leaned over to place a kiss on her mouth, Layne turned her head so he got her cheek instead. There was one mouth she wanted on her right now, and it wasn't his.

Noticing her evasive turn, he seemed surprised. She stepped back from him, keeping her arms crossed in front of her. "I'm giving you the benefit of the doubt that you somehow had a temporary moment of insanity and thought I could be summoned like a pet."

"Is that what you think that was?" He inquisitively looked at her before shaking his head and immediately moved on. "There are some business items that need to be handled. I thought we could have lunch together while we finalized a few minor items."

Eric walked back to his desk and grabbed the folder he had walked in with. He brought it back to her and handed it over. "I need you to sign these."

Opening the folder, she saw page after page of legal documents. Eric circled her until he stopped at her back and looked over her shoulder. He was close enough that she could feel the heat of his body hovering at her backside.

"What are these?" Her eyes skimmed each page, looking for the keywords of what each page entailed.

He rubbed his hands over her upper arms while his mouth came up to her ear. "Those, my little harpy, are what is going to save your family's business."

As she got to the final page in the batch of documents, Eric's hands dropped down to her hips. "And that one there is where we make it all official." Boldly printed across the top of the page was the certified heading for all New York State Government documents, and underneath it were the cold black letters spelling out *Marriage License*.

Immediately, she shut the folder. "I need my attorney to look these over."

He reached over her to ease the folder out of her hands. "With what money are you going to pay a lawyer? Not only that, but time is going to be of the essence. I've heard that Russell Spencer isn't very happy after a little stunt you pulled. I'm not a miracle worker. These agreements are going to be the only thing that gives enough leverage to avoid a major catastrophe."

Word got around quickly, and she shouldn't have been surprised that Eric already got wind of it. Coming back to stand in front of her, he traced a finger down her cheek, and it dropped under her chin. "Sign the papers, Layne." The blue of his eyes shone a little brighter from all the natural light pouring in from the windows.

Layne gritted her teeth. The very thing she had been against all her life was staring her in the face. She had never wanted to marry a man for strategic financial and business purposes. "This is happening really fast; I don't feel comfortable with this."

Eric pushed the matter without hesitation. "My little harpy, I can't promise the second you leave here that someone won't try to erase the O'Reilly name from the map. I don't want to wake up to the front page running an article that the Upper East Side lost a young woman to a horrific random act of violence." The strength of his hand shifted to latch onto her chin. "If you give a shit about yourself and your family, sign the papers."

With her forehead wrinkled up in torment as he made the veiled threat that wasn't too far off of reality, she understood the looming harshness of reality ready to descend upon her. Her hand pulled the folder back from his possession. "Get me a pen."

After she had a pen in her hand, she began initialing some pages and signing others. Most of the documents were typical arrangements tied to assets and liabilities. When she arrived at the last page, she paused at the sensation of a heavy weight settling in her stomach.

All her personal information, alongside Eric's, was already listed there. There was just one last remaining field for the signature of the bride. Even the alleged officiant and witnesses had signed. Layne forced the pen to glide across the paper:

Layne Nicole O'Reilly

She dropped the pen and stepped away from the desk she had been using. This was what was going to be what kept Liam and her from being swallowed up whole by the city's criminal factions, all waiting to pounce on them. Layne should have felt a sense of relief. Instead, all she could feel was intense suffocation.

Eric looked over all the papers, double-checking that she hadn't missed anything. Afterward, he approached her with a delighted smile. His hands cupped her face and, without any hesitation, lowered his lips onto hers. He clutched her face there in his hands while he deeply kissed her, drawing it out far longer than it should have lasted.

When their mouths parted, he grinned at her. "Congratulations, Mrs. Ellis."

The post-nuptial lunch had been some sushi from a five-star restaurant that Eric had splurged on in celebration of the joyous event. While he had been in great spirits, Layne didn't have much of an appetite and merely picked at the rice of her spicy salmon roll.

"Now that everything is official, the process of fixing all the fractured pieces of the O'Reilly organization can begin. I will personally reach out to the heads of all the major entities to make sure it is clear that no one is to make a move against you. If they do, they will have hell to pay and me to answer to." Eric was making a lot of bold promises, and she only hoped that he could deliver on them and it wouldn't eat away at her spirit from the inside out.

Layne finally gave up on her lunch and rose from her seat across from him. "I told you I didn't have time for a long lunch."

He put his chopsticks down on his plate and quickly wiped his mouth with a napkin before rising from his seat. "I thought you'd be a little more eager to celebrate."

Eric came over to her and wrapped his arms around her waist. "Maybe even pick up where we left off at the concert before your security guard rudely interrupted us." The words he spoke were eager to try and manifest his desires.

Before she could knock him off track from his train of thought, he drew her in so their bodies were flush with one another. Her hands braced against the front of his chest. She should have had no problem blinking an eye at a potential good time, but something in her was holding her back. That 'something' had many tattoos and a voice that sank into her soul.

A delicate smile lifted her lips as she looked up at him. "I haven't been sleeping well, and all of this caught me by surprise. Maybe we can celebrate some other time."

There was tension in his hands that were resting on the top curvature of her ass, but it released quickly as he rebounded from his clear disappointment. "That sounds like a great idea. I would rather we have all the time in the world to enjoy the moment. We can make an evening out of it, or perhaps, an entire weekend."

Layne prayed that her face masked her true feelings on the idea of turning this into a celebration with him.

His hand came up to the back of her head as he dropped his head down and made sure to savor, sharing another kiss with her. When he released her, he grinned. "We'll talk soon about all the fun we're going to have together."

Before she left his office there on the forty-eighth floor, he had offered his men to drive her to where she needed. Layne adamantly declined, citing that she preferred to walk, given Rebecca's condo wasn't too far and she could use the fresh air and sunshine.

The elevator ride down to the ground floor felt like it had moved at a snail's pace. When the doors opened up, the anxiety that had been building up during the descent of all forty-something floors was quickly coming to an insurmountable peak.

She hurried through the lobby in hopes that the outside air would provide relief. Instead, what should have been a refreshing late autumn day felt too warm and muggy. Or, maybe, it was just her disgust with herself.

Her palms began to feel clammy while her face paled. The twisting and spasming of her stomach was the only warning she needed. Layne ran over to the nearest trash receptacle and wretched up the little amount of lunch she had consumed into it.

The very thing she had been fighting against most of her life just became her reality.

CHAPTER TWENTY

For better or for worse, things over the next week moved quickly. Eric wasted no time in meeting with various figureheads across the city. One of those meetings is what had her pacing back and forth inside the office at O'Reilly Manor.

To hammer out some final details on the business end of matters, Liam needed to be involved whether she liked it or not. She tried to convince her brain to settle down while she waited. She wiped her palms against the thighs of her jeans before adjusting the bottom hem of her burgundy blouse.

"The office is right in here." She heard Liam say on the other side of the door before it opened up, halting her pacing.

In walked Liam, followed by Eric close behind. While Liam had chosen comfort over business, wearing a pair of jeans and a hoodie, Eric had gone with a more polished and professional look. He wore a charcoal set of pants with a matching vest overtop a light blue dress shirt and a navy tie.

Eric's eyes immediately landed on her. "There she is." He walked to her, smiling in excitement at her presence. Layne allowed him to greet her with a gentle kiss that left her feeling a little on edge, given the discussions that were about to take place.

Noticing her apprehension, he moved his mouth to her ear, where he whispered. "It will be painless, I promise." He followed it with another kiss on her cheek before he left to take a seat across from Liam. She doubted that any business discussions between the three of them would be painless.

Liam was already behind his desk, firing up the computer. He looked over at Eric. "Let's talk about what I'm getting for allowing you to marry my sister?"

Layne did her best to stifle her snort that Liam had anything to do with this. He had no authority to claim he had allowed this whole damn order. Now, his only interest was what kickbacks he was going to get. Apparently, her sound of disagreement hadn't been quiet enough, seeing the way that Liam's glare was shot over at her.

Sitting back with an aura of collective ease around him, Eric laced his fingers in front of him. "I don't think I was very clear over the phone. You're getting my help in bolstering your team of men, which seems to have been dwindling in numbers over the last six months. Not to mention investing my money in fixing the financial woes it seems that you have gotten into. For me to do that, I'm going to need you to provide me with account information and get me authorized to manage funds."

Her brother's face faltered slightly as he realized that things were not as he had imagined. Liam's hand rubbed over his jaw as he pondered how he could twist this around selfishly.

Layne spoke up, interrupting her brother's slow turn of the cogs in his head. "Li, this isn't the fuckin' middle ages. You're not getting a lump sum payment for bringing a woman to market."

"Did I fuckin' ask you? You shouldn't even be here anyway," he snapped back at her.

Eric straightened up in his chair. "Look at it this way: she won't be spending a dime of your money, she will be spending mine on whatever she pleases. That's savings directly in your pocket. You'll even get to sell her house once she moves in with me or keep it for yourself, whatever you choose."

There was no hiding the immediate attitude change on Layne's face at the mention of moving in together and giving up the home she had earned through all her hard work. "What?"

She stepped over to Eric's side, staring him down. He looked up at her and grinned. "You look so surprised; I figured it was understood that eventually, you'd be living with me under the same roof. It would look a little strange living separately, don't you think?"

A partial laugh mixed with disbelief came bubbling out of her. Before she could verbally lay into him for the assumption on his part, he quickly reiterated himself.

"I said *eventually.*" As if that was supposed to soothe her temper.

Liam interjected, "Yeah, Layne, he said *eventually.* Don't get your panties in a twist."

"Shut the fuck up, Li." Besides, she didn't have any panties on to get in a twist.

Eric steered the conversation back to his original points of interest, discussing timeframes for getting him access to all that he required to sort things out.

While the boys discussed the finer details, Layne's thoughts wandered to Joey's role in all of this. He still needed Layne's help in gathering some key pieces of information out of Ellis for his contracted job. Based on everything he had told her, there were one too many skeletons hiding in Eric's closet.

When her mind lingered back to the present, Liam was talking very animatedly on the phone. "What the hell do you mean I'm not authorized on the account?!"

She blinked a few times, wondering if she had heard him correctly.

Liam continued to berate the poor representative on the other end of the line before he hung up in a fluster. "Bitch." He looked over at Eric with instant regret that he had lost his temper without thinking about how it would look.

Clearing his throat, Liam shifted in his seat. "They must be having some sort of shitty system error. I will get things sorted and everything to you."

"I hope, for your sake, it gets figured out quickly." Eric pushed himself up out of his chair after taking a peek at his watch. "Based on that, I think we've discussed everything we can for today. I will be in touch by the end of the week so we can finish wrapping up everything here."

Layne's eyes remained critical while assessing each of the expressions tugging at her brother's face. She only drew her eyes away when Eric took her hands in his. He lifted them both to his mouth, where he affectionately laid a kiss on each set of her knuckles. "We still need to schedule that celebration we talked about." He gave her a wink.

"Of course." She was too bothered by what she had heard from that phone call to argue. "I will see you to the door, and we can talk about it soon."

Layne left the office with Eric to accompany him back to the front door. A few minutes later, she returned to the office, closing the door behind her and staring at her brother, who was sitting there with his hands buried in his short, auburn hair.

"What the hell was that about?" She stared at him.

Liam looked up at her with the gravity of the situation finally hitting him and showing in his eyes. "How should I know? The dumb bitch said I wasn't authorized to discuss details on the account!" His words were getting defensive.

"Goddamnit," she sighed and tried to think through all the potential reasons for their access to be restricted. "Did you have the right account number?"

"Yes! Do you think I'm stupid, Layne?!"

"How are you even just now finding out that you aren't authorized on the account? Haven't you been using it?"

There was silence.

Her tone grew stern. "Liam?"

He finally responded in a hurry of words. "There hasn't been a reason! I've been busy. Besides, the money has been going out as fast as it's been coming in."

Layne threw her hands up in the air. "Are you kidding me? Busy fucking off?!"

She walked over to the desk and placed a hand on it while her other hand pointed at him. "You have to fix this! This is your screw-up, not mine. I don't give a damn how you do it, but make it right."

"What do you want me to do?!" He threw his hands up in the air.

She shouted back at him. "Dad showed you the ropes and put you in charge, Liam. You should know these things and at least have a clue what to do. You wanted me to stay out of this shit, and I have. I have sacrificed enough of myself for this family for one week!"

When her phone rang, her irritation was already on a warpath. She saw Joey's name pop up on the screen, and she answered. "Joey, it's not a good time. I will call you when I finish dealing with Liam's fuck up." She hung up abruptly, not waiting for his acknowledgment.

"Who the hell was that?" Liam's eyes narrowed at her.

She shook her head. "None of your business."

He stood up and walked over to her to yank the phone right out of her hand. Layne turned and clutched onto it while using her other hand to shove him away. He grabbed her arm, and they both wrestled with one another until the phone slipped from her hold.

"Liam, give it back!" She was unable to reach around him as he turned and began tapping on the screen.

"Really? Mom's birthday is your passcode?" He scoffed. "Predictable." He shook his head as he began sliding his finger across the screen and tapping away.

He pulled his shoulders back as he pulled up a picture from her albums. Liam turned and showed her what was on her screen. Layne pressed her lips together, immediately recognizing the picture she had taken with Joey after their breakfast together. The memory of it was clear as day.

After getting dressed, she noticed his skull mask hanging over the edge of his laundry basket. She picked it up and dangled it in front of him. "Maybe next time you could wear this." Her eyes sparkled with playful excitement.

"Be careful what you wish for. That mask comes with a lot of other conditions," Joey smirked at her.

"Oh? I think I will take my chances." Layne stretched the mask over her face and pulled her phone out on selfie mode to see how it suited her. "It almost looks better on me than it does on you."

Joey came up behind her, wrapping his arms around her waist while laying a kiss against her neck. Her thumb snapped the selfie of them together with her in his infamous mask.

The sound of Liam's harsh words brought her back to reality. "It seems like I'm not the only one who is fucking around."

She stood there quietly, not feeling that she owed him any sort of explanation.

"Is this who I think it is? The masked freak that dad hired to take out Franzetti, and you couldn't keep your whore mouth off of?"

Layne shrugged at him. "Does it matter if it is?"

"Yes! You want to sit here and criticize me while you're off fucking two guys, one of which I might remind you has our business by the balls!" Let Liam's throwing of figurative stones begin like he hadn't wet his dick in half of all of Manhattan.

Both of her brows lifted now that he wanted to step up to the plate. "Oh, now you want to be concerned about the state of things? Where was this attitude six months ago?"

He tossed her phone back at her. "I told you not to fuck this up with Eric, and this is your idea of playing it safe?"

Her hands fumbled for the phone that was carelessly returned to her.

"This is my idea of doing what I have to in order not to lose my shit. You can take this holier-than-thou crusade and shove it up Kristill's ass or whoever is the flavor of the week."

Deciding she wasn't going to stand there and listen to him bitch at her any longer, she turned for the door before she decided to shoot the last member of her blood relatives.

Before she stepped out of the office, she got her last words in. "Just fix the goddamn account, Liam."

After the door shut behind her, all she heard was his rage-filled roar as something smashed against the closed office door, shaking it upon impact.

"Stop!" Layne giggled as Joey leaned over and buried his face against her neck, playfully nipping at her skin. The short hairs of the dark blonde scruff on his face tickled against the delicate skin of her throat.

They sat inside his Challenger parked at their quiet little spot near the water in Brooklyn. He was leaning over the center console, unable to control himself from showering her with attention to try and erase the mood Liam had put her in. His hand slid up along her inner thigh toward the center of where her legs came together.

"I'm trying to have a serious conversation!" Trying to fight back the smile on her face as she squirmed in her seat.

Joey smirked as he muttered against her neck. "So am I."

"Bullshit." Her hips jolted as his hand finally found the apex of her jeans. Finally, she grabbed his hand to pause his efforts temporarily. "Liam was off his rocker level of pissed."

He finally drew his head back and looked at her unbothered. "Fuck him. He's a whiny piece of shit." Joey wasn't Liam's biggest fan, not many people were. What else was new?

Before he dove right back in for another taste of her, she turned in the passenger seat to look at him with all business in her eyes. "I don't need him doing something stupid and interfering."

He exhaled, trying to bring the blood flow back up to his brain as he sat back on his side of the vehicle. "He may be a selfish prick, but he's not completely stupid, Layne."

She nodded, still not feeling at ease. "Let's just say this plan works, and you can get what you need from Eric's house this time. Then, what?"

"You let me worry about that." Layne had heard that from one too many people before and hated hearing it out of his mouth. It felt like she was just being placated and kept out of the loop.

Before she could roll her eyes at him, his thumb and forefinger captured her chin so she could look into his eyes. His eyes shone a slightly lighter shade of brown with the sun beating in through the windshield.

She didn't bother hiding her concern weighing down her voice. "And you're okay with all of this? I've seen the way you look at Eric."

Joey smiled at her lightly. "I'd be more than okay if you just so happen to become a widow at the ripe old age of twenty-six." He leaned over and captured her lips to lull them into a slow and drawn-out kiss.

When he pulled away, he looked back into the stunning green eyes he had fallen for time after time again. "Look, Layney, it's a piece of paper. It doesn't mean shit."

"And you're not the least bit remorseful that you're putting your hands all over a married woman, are you?" She grinned at the thought of it.

He leaned in and growled into her ear. "I plan to use more than just my hands."

"Promise?" The question posed to him was full of hopefulness.

He grabbed her and pulled her to his side of the car and into his lap. Layne faced Joey as her legs straddled him. His hand ran up along her spine until he could grab a fistful of her soft locks of hair and tugged her head back. Joey leaned over and dragged his lips down the center of her exposed throat and over her chest. Each kiss was more sensual than the last as they reached the exposed swell of her cleavage. His other hand slid in the opposite direction down her back until his hand squeezed a handful of her ass.

She pushed her hips down over the quickly growing erection. Each seductive movement of her body against him caused him to groan against her. Her hands grasped onto his head, letting her fingers get lost in the newer and longer length of his hair.

Joey didn't take long to make good on his promise to use more than his hands on her. Hell, if he was going to let her enter the lion's den without knowing who the real king of her jungle was.

CHAPTER TWENTY-ONE

The first snowfall of the season had taken hold of Manhattan. It was a light coating that barely interfered with daily life, but it added an extra touch of wintry beauty across the city.

Powdery white flakes clung to parked cars, signage, and street lights. While it was a gorgeous sight tonight, she knew that it wouldn't take long to turn into a sullied mess of sloppy gray debris on the sidewalks. But for now? She could appreciate the view seated by the restaurant window. She was sitting at a table for two with the chair across from her temporarily empty.

Outside, people walked by, minding their own business like typical New Yorkers. Occasionally, a person or two would stop and take a look at the outdoor menu in the glass case by the front door. The restaurant had only been open a couple of months, but it was already capturing all the attention of the food critics and anyone willing to throw obscene amounts of money at a meal that was the size of a chicken nugget.

If her nerves were on edge, she didn't let it show. Layne turned her attention to the half-drunk glass of rosé in front of her that she was idly swirling in light circles. That certainly didn't hurt keeping her anxiety in check, either. It hadn't been her drink of choice, but it contained alcohol, and that was good enough for her. She needed to get through this evening in one piece.

Her neutrally-colored fingertips tucked a loose strand of her hair back behind her ear. A thin silver ring in the design of Celtic knots adorned her pointer finger. It had once belonged to her mother and was thought to have brought good luck. Layne had chosen to braid and twist her hair back into a contained bun at the back of her head for the evening.

She refused to fully dress up for the evening, despising the impracticality of dresses when she was engaged in work matters. As far as she was concerned, Eric was going to be all work in her book. Layne had already worn one dress this year, and one man had made it worth her while. Such high hopes for tonight were nowhere to be found.

Instead, she compromised with a flirty black lace top that left her shoulders fully exposed but covered the length of her arms. Matched with the top was a pair of fitted black pants. Around her waist was a satin sash mimicking a belt knotted at her hip in a bow.

A presence sat down across from her, stealing her attention away from the stretching of the wine legs down the inside of the glass. Eric took his seat with a delighted smile directed at her. It was no surprise he had dressed his finest when Layne suggested they finally take a night out to celebrate their union as business and life partners.

"Apologies, I had to take a business call." He tucked the cell into the inner pocket of his suit jacket.

Even in the dim lighting of the dining room, his frigid blue eyes stood out against everything else about him that was dark and brooding. His raven hair, his fully black ensemble, and probably his black heart, too. One of these days, she'd have to confirm that assumption.

"I thought maybe you were going to make a run for it," she grinned at him.

Eric shook his head. "From you? Wouldn't dream of it. Running towards you? Now, that's something else, little harpy."

When the waiter approached, Eric ordered himself an Old Fashioned with the unusual twist of a lemon peel instead of the more traditional orange peel. The hairs on the back of her neck briefly stood on end, and the scar on her heart ached. That was exactly how her dad always drank his Old Fashioneds, his signature drink. Something deep down told her that it was no coincidence that Eric had chosen it.

Layne swallowed down another mouthful of wine along with her feelings.

His hand reached across the table and took hold of hers. "I can't tell you how much I was looking forward to tonight. I know there have been a few bumps along the way, but I'm confident we can smooth things out." His thumb caressed over the tops of her knuckles reassuringly.

She offered him a light smile and then nodded to the waiter, who returned with Eric's drink and offered another pour of wine. "So, just what is your plan once Liam gathers the last pieces of information you requested?"

He sat back in his seat after releasing her hand. "I don't want to talk business tonight; I'd rather talk about us."

That sounded awfully personal, and she hated mixing her private life with business. Though, in Eric's case, he was shoring up to be a bit of both, wasn't he?

She lightly pulled in a deeper breath into her lungs before slowly exhaling. "Alright. Then, what did you want to talk about?"

A victorious smile appeared on his smug face. "You. I know all about the fiery Layne O'Reilly on paper, but I'm more curious about what's underneath the surface."

"What you see is what you get," she assured him as she sat back in her seat. "But, if you've got time on your hands, I'd be more than happy to share a few stories that may not have been told to you."

Eric couldn't pass up the offer as his lips made contact with the whiskey-heavy cocktail in his glass.

Some stories may have been slightly embellished for his listening pleasure, but Layne shared some of her biggest wins in the business and a few of her early mistakes. It kept the conversation rolling throughout dinner.

"What about you? I've been talking about myself all evening. I think it's only fair." She folded her arms across the edge of the table as she leaned forward, prepared to sit there and listen to him do a little sharing of his own. The emeralds of her eyes peeked down at the time on her watch discreetly to take note of the time. It was nearly a quarter to nine, and she would have preferred to stretch this time here with him out just a little longer.

He polished off the rest of his beverage, sliding the empty glass away from him. "Now, that is something I'd be happy to do, but I think it requires a little more privacy." Eric stood and came over to her side, offering his hand for her to take.

Scooting her chair back, Layne reluctantly took his hand and stood. Once she was on her feet, he released her hand and slid his arm around her lower back. Pulling her in closer to his side, he whispered in her ear, "Did you think I wouldn't know what you're doing?"

There came back the bit of paranoia that had been quieted by the wine. She tilted her head curiously as she looked at him. "And what am I doing?" Better to appear ignorant and unknowing than to reveal one's secrets unknowingly.

His lips found their way onto her cherry-glossed lips and coaxed a kiss from them. "Let's talk about it in the car on the way back home." Eric gave a nod to the restaurant's manager on duty, having previously arranged the bill to be taken care of.

Outside, waiting for them moments later, was a black SUV. Eric let her into the back seat first and joined her a moment later after saying something to the driver that she had been unable to hear.

Layne automatically crossed one leg over the other as she settled in. After the vehicle pulled away, Eric's hand patted her thigh. "I think you underestimate how well I can read you, Layne."

She doubted that very much. "What makes you say that?"

The warmth of his hand should have been welcomed in this freezing weather, but instead, the cold settled into her bones. His gaze seemed to analyze every movement she made. "You can tell me all your stories about your successes and your failures, but you still don't want to acknowledge one very important thing about yourself."

"That I don't like cryptic talk?" She didn't try to hide the disdain in her voice.

He chuckled, removed his hand from her leg, and settled it on the side of her face. "I scare you. You're not intimidated by me, but you do harbor fear inside of you when it comes to this—to us. You're worried that you're going to let yourself enjoy the life you are destined to have. You got a taste of it the night of the concert, and now you are doing your best to close yourself off."

She saw the street signs indicating they were approaching the corner lot where his residence was located. Layne looked back into Eric's eyes and gave him a playful smirk. "Maybe you'd get the girl from that night if you asked nicely."

"One thing I will share with you is I don't ask nicely." To prove his point, he crushed her lips under the weight of his mouth as he consumed the taste of her. Layne pulled herself up against him, letting him take his share for the time being, knowing their destination wasn't too far. His hands began to wander down over her body, and right as his tongue pushed past her lips, the car came to a stop inside the multi-car garage of his home.

He pulled away from her reluctantly. "I have more fun for us inside."

The way the word 'fun' rolled off his lips made her think that his idea of fun was quite different from hers.

A few moments later, they were inside the vaguely familiar home she had last seen the night of his party. As they made it up to the third floor, where all the numerous bedrooms were, Layne questioned how much house one man needed.

As if reading her thoughts, Eric spoke up. "I know that the house is exceptionally bigger than I need, but I couldn't resist all the possibilities of how, one day, each of these rooms would have a specific purpose."

Layne nodded before Eric stopped at the entrance to one of the many closed doors in the hall. His hand dropped to the brass handle and gently swung the door open to the dark room. "This one is my favorite." He gestured for her to step inside before he reached in to flip the lights on so she could take it all in for herself.

What she saw was not the master bedroom she had expected to see. No, the master bedroom would have been very much welcomed. Eric came behind her, his hands on her hips and breath on the back of her neck. "It gets me excited every time I come in here. Consider it part of my wedding gift to you."

It was rare for Layne to find herself in a state of shock, but what was waiting there for them had managed to leave her brain unable to reconcile what was happening.

CHAPTER TWENTY-TWO

The lights illuminated the room, exposing its dark secrets. Along the walls were all the tools of the trade of a sadist's dream torture chamber. Various sharp-edged weapons, blunt objects, bindings and restraints, pliers, thumbscrews, choke pears, stun batons, and some items that she couldn't fathom their use. The tiled floor even had a few drains installed for easy cleaning.

Despite the violent decor along the walls, it almost looked like he put enough effort into dressing it up with fancy blackout curtains, several framed pieces of artwork, and elegant light fixtures. Her brain tried to comprehend to what extent this man was so sick that he went from wanting to devour her to proudly showing off this macabre part of his life.

When she looked in the center of the room, her lungs stopped after a short gasp as she held her breath. A man with his back to her was on his knees, hands restrained behind his back and chained to the floor with his head hanging down. A black hood was over his head, keeping the man and his identity in the dark.

She pressed her teeth into her tongue in an attempt to control her facial reactions despite an overwhelming sense of dread washing over her.

"Well? Why don't you go take a look at what I got you?" Eric's voice startled her as he moved up directly behind her. His hand pressed lightly against her lower back to urge her to approach the man.

Swallowing down the saliva pooling in her mouth along with her greatest fears of who she should expect to see underneath that hood, she slowly approached. Her beige heels quietly tapped against the floor with each step.

Her eyes glanced down at the hands bound behind the man's back, and she slowly released the breath she had been terrified to let go of. There was not a single tattoo to be seen on his hands or fingers.

Layne stopped in front of the man, glancing up to see Eric waiting patiently for the big reveal. Looking down at the poor soul before her, she reached down and slowly lifted the hood from his head.

The man squinted at the light with weary eyes that had fresh bruises and swelling around them.

"Andrew?" Layne questioned as she saw her former income source on his knees before her. The very same Andrew Corelli that had been poached by Russ Spencer. She hadn't been able to hide her surprise from her face, and it prompted a wide grin beaming with pride from Eric.

"Since things are official now, I wanted to make it clear to everybody that disloyalty will not be tolerated. Andrew, here, has made very poor choices and now will be suffering the consequences." Eric gestured to the various wall decor at her disposal.

She dropped the black hood onto the floor and stepped away from the man who was now looking at her with eyes pleading for mercy and forgiveness. Layne walked back over to Eric, keeping her voice low to spare Andrew from overhearing. "Eric, this wasn't needed." It sure as hell wasn't wanted either.

The back of his finger stroked across her cheek. "This is just the beginning. After seeing the way you asserted yourself at the Brass Mirror, it is only fitting that we can consider this a little foreplay before we proceed with our evening." His finger trailed down over her skin beyond her jaw and dragged over the bare skin of her shoulder, skimming past the scar on her left shoulder and down her arm.

To further reiterate his point, his lips brushed against her ear as he whispered to her. "I'm getting hard just thinking about watching you work. Don't insult me by not accepting this gift I have given to you."

Her eyes closed to try and force her mind into a disconnected frame where she could get through this. Joey's words echoed in her mind as a reminder.

"Do you even know what type of monster Eric Ellis is?"

She recounted all the things she knew that Andrew was tied up in. The way he watched little girls with too keen of an eye and too evil of a hand.

She reminded herself that the world would be better off without him. Andrew was owed a world of pain and suffering. Eric wasn't wrong in pointing out that disloyalty couldn't be tolerated if her family's reputation were to be restored. All of these things could easily justify what needed to be done.

When she opened her eyes, she felt nothing but a dissociative numbness as she nodded at Eric. "This was very thoughtful, thank you."

She gave him a gentle kiss of appreciation before she stepped away to review her options on how to punish and execute the pervert on his knees before her. He didn't deserve a quick death, but she didn't want to have highlight reels of his torture on repeat in her head for the next year.

Layne opted for one aggressively serrated blade with one hand and a rusty hammer with the other. This was going to get messy, and she wished she had known to dress for a little torture with her fancy evening out.

As for Andrew, his eyes reflected the rising panic inside of him when she approached with both objects in her grasp. "Layne, please, I'm sorry." Here came the begging for his life, the part that she cared for the least and the reason why she kept torture short and sweet just to avoid listening to it.

She squatted down and leaned in to whisper to him. "Andrew, there is nothing more I would love to do than to shove one or both of these up your ass, knowing what you like to do in your free time. However, I'm going to need you to man up and be fucking grateful that it's me you're dealing with and not him." Her eyes flicked to Eric, who was watching with a smirk, tugging at his mouth in anticipation of what was to come.

Then, it was down to business. Using the hammer, she inflicted blows to fracture his ribs one at a time. The only reprieve she gave him was when she slid the razorlike edge of the blade across his body, leaving one shallow cut after another on his body. The forked nail-puller part of the hammer was used to dig into his open wounds every so often. Andrew's howls of pain echoed in her ears while he begged for death.

When her eyes tore away from the bloody, broken mess before her, she saw Eric enjoying the show. No, he wasn't just enjoying the show, he was *enjoying* the violence. He stood there with his pants undone and his stiff cock in his hand. Slow and long strokes over himself at the sight of her inflicting pain on Andrew. Fuck, she was going to need to stock up on more ways to mentally escape her nightmares after this.

Not breaking eye contact with Eric, she tossed the hammer to the side, leaving her with just the jagged and blood-stained knife at the ready. Her hand grabbed the back of the whimpering man's neck to steady his writhing body. She plunged the blade into his chest, giving it an extra twist to make sure she thoroughly ripped into his heart.

Eric moaned out, seeing how Layne put an abrupt stop to the man's suffering. "Mmm, that's my bad little harpy."

She let go of the knife along with Andrew and pushed down the urge to re-experience her dinner that briefly threatened to make a second showing. There may have been one less predator in the world, but the one left watching her wasn't going to make her rest any easier at night.

She walked over to Eric, glancing down at the blood on her hands and then up at him. "Where can I go clean up?"

He released his hold on his still throbbing dick. "Don't bother." Eric grabbed her by the arms and pinned her against the wall as his mouth latched onto her like a rabid dog. The unexpected advance left her struggling against him before she succumbed and grabbed onto his sides to keep him close.

His hands roughly grabbed at every part of her in a lust-filled frenzy. His erection jabbed at her lower stomach. Layne returned the rough play as her nails dug into his chest. She shoved his jacket from his upper body, balling it up before pitching it to the side, leaving it a little lighter in weight before she did so. While his affections smothered over her, the weight she removed from his jacket dropped down into the pocket of her pants.

Eric breathed into her ear with a dark growl on the cusp of his words, "I'm going to show you exactly how you should be fucked." His hand yanked on the fabric belt of her pants, the shape of the bow falling flat as it came undone.

Layne internally cringed while her thoughts continued to strategize her escape from this hellhole and the monster standing before her.

A nervous voice interrupted the beginning of what Eric likely wanted to be a thorough ravishing of her, and Layne couldn't have been more thankful for the reprieve. "Um, sorry, boss. We have a situation."

A barrel-chested man stood at the doorway of the torture chamber. He looked to be too skittish and meek for his size, indicating he had a healthy dose of fear for Eric's demeanor.

Eric tensed up as he snarled. "Later."

Layne slid away from between him and the wall, causing a flash of annoyance in Eric's eyes.

The nervous employee spoke again. "There might have been an intrusion downstairs earlier this evening."

The news didn't settle well with Eric as he shoved himself back into his pants and buttoned them back up in frustration. He walked over to the man, and they stepped outside out of earshot for a few minutes. It allowed Layne to take a breath or three while she retied her belt, giving it an extra-strong tug while knotting it back into the bow.

When Eric returned a few minutes later, he appeared a little more composed. "I'm sorry, but we will need to continue our celebration another night." His hands came to her face and drew her in for a brief kiss as an apology. It was an apology she was more than happy to accept.

A dark smirk appeared on his mouth. "I look forward to sharing the rest of my gifts with you. But, until then, I will have my driver take you back home for the night while I handle things here."

"I completely understand." She tried not to give too eager of a smile that she was going to be getting the hell out of this room of horrors.

Now, being such a true gentleman, Eric walked her out to the car, waiting to take her away. "See you soon, Layne."

CHAPTER TWENTY-THREE

Back home, she turned the shower faucet on to begin warming up the water in her bathroom. Layne felt a layer of grit all over herself that needed to be washed away. Perhaps there was a little bit of her soul that also required some cleansing, too.

While she waited for the steam to begin filling the room, she peeled away her clothes, dropping each article to the floor. A quiet sigh of relief escaped from her lips as she pulled her elastic tie from her tresses, relieving the tension of her hair on her scalp. Her fingers ran through the locks of her hair a few times to allow herself to ease into a more relaxed mood after the toll the evening had taken on her.

Her hand pulled open the glass door to the shower as she stepped inside, immediately feeling the heat of the streams of water pelt against her skin. The temperature was almost unbearably hot, just the way she liked it. The shower door lightly clinked as it came to a close behind her.

Layne tilted her head back underneath the water from the showerhead, letting her hair soak up all the moisture until it was fully saturated. As the water ran down over her body, she already began to feel more at ease. She closed her eyes and just stood there under the waterfall coming from above, relishing in the moment.

There was a small swirl of cool air that breezed through the bathroom briefly. She opened up her eyes and tilted her head forward at the unexpected air movement. Her hand pressed against the foggy glass wall as her ears strained to hear any unusual sounds.

Clink. Clink. Swish. Zip.

The sound of a belt being unlatched and pulled from its loops followed by a zipper sliding down. Her breathing sped up. Her eyes darted around at her surroundings; she was caged in here like an animal. There was nowhere to go, and her only weapons were hair products and soaps, a shitty razor that she forgot to replace last week, a vibrating rose for the days when she needed a little relief, and a purple loofah.

Given the options, she opted for the razor with the anti-nick guards on it. Silently, she cursed herself, wondering why she was even bothering.

She wished that if someone was going to attack her, it wasn't while she was naked in the shower. It takes a special kind of asshat to take this approach to violence. At least they could have the decency to wait until she was clothed and attempting to eat a balanced meal.

A pair of large hands grabbed onto the top of the shower's glass wall. Her eyes darted north to see the tips of the fingers curling over the top. Swallowing hard, she swiped her hand across the steamy glass to get a better view of the outline of whoever was standing right outside her shower.

Joey smirked as he stood there completely nude. All of his muscles stretched out on display from the lean lines of his arms, down over the front of his inked chest, the cuts of his abs, and right down to the main event.

It didn't matter how many times she had seen this man without his clothes on; it took her breath away every damn time. Layne stood there dumbfounded to the point she dropped the razor. The shallow movement of water at her feet carried it down to the drain, where it halted.

He dropped his arms down and opened up the door to invite himself into the shower with her. "Did you think after watching you with that asshole all night that I wasn't going to want to get a piece of you afterward?"

The white tiles of the wall were suddenly at her back, and she didn't even recall backing up. Her eyes had been so distracted by his raging hard-on that her head wasn't thinking clearly. "Are you admitting to stalking me?"

The water began to cascade over Joey's body, drenching every part of him before he stepped up to her. His hands latched onto her hips, squeezing them firmly while he pressed her back to the wall so she had nowhere to go. His face gave a sexy devil's grin as he leaned down and trailed his mouth over the side of her neck. "I'll admit to stalking when you admit to eye-fucking me every chance you get."

Layne's mouth curved into a sassy smile. "Are you sure you're not just imagining things?" Her hand slid across the front of his body until it moved over his shoulder to run up along the back of his neck. Her slender fingers grasped onto it to encourage his mouth to continue its path.

His length pressed up against her lower stomach as he leaned into her. Joey's hand ran up from her hip onto her breast, roughly kneading it with his palm as he began to stake his claim on her. His teeth lightly grazed over the spot where her neck met her shoulder. "The only thing I'm imagining right now is how tight your pussy is going to clench around my dick." His words rumbled into a growl as he emphasized who was going to be the man reaping the pleasures of her body tonight.

The thought alone had her thighs pressing together as the excited sensation was intensely building between them. "A little presumptuous, aren't you?" Her fingers slid through the hair on the back of his head, grasping a handful of it in her hand.

"Hm." That was all he said before he eased up off her for a moment. Joey leaned over and grabbed something off one of the built-in shelves. "We'll see."

He grabbed her arm and spun her around so the front of her body was pressed up against the slick tiles of the shower wall. Her hands had nothing to grasp onto on the flat surface. Layne started to push back, but Joey's hand tangled up in her hair, keeping her right where he wanted.

A familiar sound echoed behind her. The vibrations of the rose from her adult toy collection were humming at a low frequency. His hand reached around in front of her and down between her legs. "How confident are you feelin' now that I was being presumptuous?" He tilted her head back to look at him so he could watch her face.

Before she could respond, he connected the toy with her sensitive clit that had already been aching with need. Her body jolted with the onset of immediate pleasure that shot through her.

Layne gasped out. The sweet sound of her moan filled the small space of her shower. Joey didn't ease up on assaulting her body with the silicone toy against her bud. Her legs could have given out right then and there. "Mmm, that's not playing fair."

He pressed his chest along the back of her body, his cock nestled right up against her ass. She pushed her hips back into him, drawing out a moan of approval from him. "Playing fair is for nice guys. We both know what type of guy I am."

Vibrations continued to hum viciously against her clit, quickly bringing a tremble throughout her body. Layne writhed and squirmed between two immovable objects: the wall and Joey.

"I love the way you squirm against me," his gravelly voice purred into her ear. His hand pressed the toy against her harder, sending wave after wave of intense pleasure straight up into her core. The swollen head of his member dragged down along the crease of her ass until he was positioned right at the opening of her pussy.

Layne's hands furiously began slipping against the slick tiles as the divine sensations began to overwhelm her. "Oh, God!"

Seeing that she was barely hanging onto her sanity, Joey sank himself deep into her in one smooth motion. His eyes locked on her face as she instantly became undone for him.

Her release erupted in a magnificent display of pleasure that took her hostage. Her primal screams were unleashed as her body immediately took him in and tightened around him.

Loudly, he groaned at the pressure of her body. "Fuck, Layney. You're going to be the death of me."

Joey damn near lost it the way her walls squeezed and spasmed around him. Typically, he was a pinnacle of self-control. Tonight was different. Having seen the way Eric was pawing at her tonight, Joey needed to have her. He needed to feel her. He needed to know that she was all his.

Her legs could barely feel themselves after she came with such force. So, when Joey made his sudden movements, she was hardly in a spot to protest.

The toy was removed from her body and tossed to the side with a clang against the floor as it rolled over to the corner. He released her hair and grabbed her by the hips. Before she knew it, he pulled her away from the wall and had her completely bent over with her one hand planted on the shower floor and the other braced against the wall.

Hard, firm thrusts began railing into her body. His cock claimed her precious cunt for his own pleasure tonight. Joey's hands dug into her hips as their bodies smacked together. "That's it. Take *my* dick like a good girl." His movements were harsh as he slammed his length into her. The tip of him continued to pound away at that delightful spot deep inside of her.

Layne's world began spinning as she cursed out between her heavy pants. "Joey! I can't take... You're gonna make me...." Her climax wracked her entire being, nearly causing her to collapse as it shook throughout every fiber of her body.

Even with her orgasm strangling his cock, Joey didn't ease up as he rammed into her. He needed to feel her body taking him, even at its limits. His hands latched onto her body so tightly it was likely to leave bruising on her fair skin.

The water continued to rain down on them both, washing away the sweat and sins of their bodies. Layne gasped for air as the aftermath of her release was stretched out while he continued to own her body and the pleasures of it.

He withdrew from her and pulled her up straight. Joey turned her face to him, drunk with lust. Roughly, his mouth claimed her lips, forcing them open to allow his tongue entry. The kiss was short-lived when he pulled back and urged her down onto her knees. "Now, I'm gonna fuck that mouth, beautiful."

It was a perfect view from his angle, seeing her now below him with those full green eyes gazing up. Joey's hands buried themselves in her wet locks of hair, grabbing onto her head and drawing her forward.

Layne parted her lips and opened up her mouth for him. As Joey guided himself into her mouth, the sensation of her velvety tongue dragging along the underside of his dick caused him to quiver in a moment of bliss.

Joey's cock twitched in excitement as she took every inch he pushed into her. He drew back only to immediately push forward into her mouth, this time deeper. The tip of his cock pressed at the back of her throat. He repeated the motion until it formed a rhythm. His hands held her head exactly where he needed it.

The movement of his hips picked up as he glided in and out of the depths of her mouth. Layne hummed against his flesh, instigating a deep growl from him.

"Fuck, I'm not gonna last much... mmm, longer." His thrusts became less smooth. The moment he took another look at Layne's eyes, peering up at him under her wet eyelashes and the streams of water running down her face, he lost control of his release.

He shoved her mouth onto him as his thick cock pushed past her gag reflex that pulsed against him. Ropes of his hot seed burst out of him and down her throat as he roared out in ecstasy. Joey removed one hand from

Layne as he leaned forward, gasping for oxygen while he braced the hand against the wall behind her.

With each pulse of his dick still buried inside her mouth, he gave a quieter moan and eventually a whimper followed by a satisfied sigh.

Slowly, he pulled back and assisted her back up onto her feet. Joey laid light kisses on her swollen lips that were plastered with a euphoric smile. Layne returned each one of his kisses in reassurance that she only wanted him.

Her hand came up to rest on the side of his face while he slid his around her waist to hold her close. A strong feeling inside of her wanted to bubble up to the surface as she stared into the affectionately warm brown eyes she had come to rely on to make her feel safe. Layne's lips slightly parted to say something, but the words never made it off of her tongue.

CHAPTER TWENTY-FOUR

"I wish you had stayed home. I don't like the idea of you tagging along for this." Joey kept his voice low as they stood there waiting inside the small cafe.

Layne grinned and shook her head. "Since when do I ever listen to what you want?"

"Well," his hand slid up along her spine and began to possessively take hold of the back of her neck.

After her cheeks began to feel warm with a slight flush, she interrupted his response. "Don't answer that."

Joey smirked at her, leaving his hand gently massaging the tiny muscles on the back of her neck a few times before dropping his hand back down to his side.

The young barista at the *Every Day I'm Grindin'* coffee shop in Greenwich Village looked like she barely was in her twenties. She looked at Joey with wide eyes that damn near had hearts popping out of them. "Can I get you anything else?" She extended her arm out to hand him the coffee he ordered.

Layne reached over and gently took the coffee from the girl's hand. "He's fine." Not bothering to toss a smile at the girl. Helping herself to the piping hot beverage, she walked with Joey out of the cafe.

Joey chuckled as he looked over at Layne. "You weren't getting jealous, were you?"

Layne scoffed at how ridiculous that sounded. "Of a girl that looked like she should be the spokesperson for Squeaky Clean magazine? Please." She walked with him toward their destination, an unassuming brownstone at the end of the block that had a "FOR RENT" sign in the front window with an invalid telephone number listed on it.

She caught the amusement in Joey's face when he took her elbow with a gentle hand and paused her in her path. He leaned in and gave her the type of kiss that was slow but did powerful things low inside of her body. When he pulled back, she had almost forgotten all about the googly-eyed barista.

He smiled at her. "You're cute when you're jealous and don't want me to know it."

She wrinkled up her nose at him. "You're a pain in my ass."

His hand lightly patted said ass. "Maybe later if you ask me nicely for it."

She shot him a look that was an attempt to be irritated with him, but he made it difficult when he gave her a wink that promised dirty things. Layne finished off the coffee before dropping it into an empty trash can next to the front steps of the house in front of them.

Joey jogged up the front steps of the rental and knocked on the door. Layne followed, letting him take the lead since these were his people, not hers. A raspy and cranky male voice came over the intercom to the left of the door. "What do you want?"

Joey grinned. "Open up, jackass." He placed his hand on the doorknob, waiting for access inside.

With suspicion in his voice, the unknown guy's voice replied. "Who's the broad?"

Layne straightened and stepped forward to give the man an earful, but Joey put a hand out to get her to back down. "She's good. Stop fuckin' around and let us in."

There was a grunt on the other end of the line before the door audibly unlocked, and Joey opened the door and went in ahead of her.

When she got inside, she closed the door behind her and took a look around. It appeared to be a vacant home that hadn't yet been rented out. There was no furniture, no personal touches, and the wooden floors could use a good cleaning from the dust and dirt gradually collecting on them.

Joey waved for her to keep up as he went to the door that led down into the basement. Once they descended a level underneath the house, the air became musty from lack of air circulation, and the lights remained dim.

There was only the glow of an excessive number of computer monitors displaying lines of code on the wall above an oversized desk that sat two men with several keyboards in front of them.

The man to the right had scraggly grey hair that hung down to his shoulders. He had to be approaching sixty if he wasn't already there. When he turned, he huffed at the sight of Layne and then looked over at Joey. "Do you have it?"

Joey reached deep into his pocket, pulled out the thumb drive, and tossed it over to the gruff old man, who caught it in his hand and began to get to work extracting the data from it.

The man to the left had short and spiky brown hair and a set of wire-framed glasses over his eyes. He was considerably younger looking; Layne would have been surprised if he was even of legal drinking age.

When he turned around and saw Layne, he made a sound akin to a schoolboy giggle. His pale face turned a dark shade of red as he fumbled to get out of his chair. "Oh, um, hi. I'm Brandon, but my codename is Cowboy." The poor guy was barely able to avoid tripping over his feet as he approached Layne, extending a hand out to her.

"Cowboy? Somebody ought to save a horse. I'm Layne." She shook his hand with a smirk, teasing the poor kid who seemed like he had never spoken to a girl before in his life.

While the innuendo went over Brandon's head, leaving him looking confused, Joey caught onto it and rolled his eyes at her. She flashed a cheeky smile right back at him.

Brandon nervously chuckled while standing there staring at her and fidgeting in his spot. "Uh, do you have it? The phone?"

Layne pulled out Eric's phone from her jacket pocket and handed it over to him. She was more than happy to be relieved of it after what she had to endure to get it the other night in the makeshift torture chamber. "I powered it down as soon as I could after I got my hands on it."

Brandon took the phone and smiled crookedly at her before he shuffled back to his seat and began working some sort of techie magic on it. While the data may have been on the drive Joey had taken during his break-in to the Ellis residence while she and Eric had been at dinner, it was something on Eric's phone that was able to provide access to it.

Layne didn't pretend to even understand the level of nerdiness required to get the data Joey had been hired to acquire. She preferred a more brute-force approach of pulling information out of people.

The cranky old man looked over at Brandon. "You good?" When he got the nod from the youngin', they both began to type commands on their respective keyboards. After a few minutes, the monitors lit up and began processing data.

Layne leaned over and whispered to Joey. "What are we looking for?"

Before he could respond, images popped up on a few screens, driver's licenses on another, lists of names and addresses, receipts, videos, and other large amounts of information.

Something caught Layne's eye, and she abruptly spoke up. "Wait! Stop! Go back one." She stepped up to the desk and pointed to a monitor that had flickered with an image that had captured her attention.

Brandon clicked a few things, and when the image came up, she blinked. She stood there staring at the image with her brows furrowing together while she tried to process what was staring right back at her.

Joey came up behind her to take a look at what had her giving funny looks. "Is that…?"

"Andrew Correlli," she confirmed for Joey. Her eyes read the text accompanying the image, seeing the file path indicating he was in a folder dedicated to employee bios. Continuing to soak in the data, it appeared that he had started working for Eric almost two years ago, long before Eric moved to the city. It noted that he was in charge of a territory covering all of Staten Island but doing what it didn't say.

She shook her head. "This doesn't make any sense. If Correlli was working for Eric, why would he want him dead?"

"I-I think I found something," Brandon spoke up while he filtered down to some information on the central monitor.

An audio clip file appeared, and when it began to play, it was obvious it was a conversation between Andrew and Eric.

"How many times have I told you not to sample the product?" Eric's voice seethed with anger.

Andrew responded like a nervous wreck under Eric's threatening tone. "S-sorry. I just thought that it needed a quality check. To make sure it is up to standards, ya know?"

"Your goddamn job isn't to quality check. It's to make sure the packages move safely from point A to point B so they can be cleared to be distributed across the state line!" Eric's voice thundered back in response. "If you ever fuck up this bad again, I will make sure that you get the ending you deserve. Am I clear?"

"Absolutely. Very clear."

"Good. Now, make sure that you go make good on our arrangement and go make friends with Russell for me."

The clip ended. Layne grimaced while grinding her teeth as she bowed her head down. Her hands clutched the edge of the desk so tight it began to turn her knuckles white as the realization hit her.

"He played me." She spoke through her clenched jaw. "Fuck!" Layne pushed away from the desk only to run right into Joey's chest. His hands steadied her by her arms and made sure not to release her, even when she pulled against his grip.

Joey didn't allow her to squirm away from him. "Hey, hey. Hold up." He looked past her at the two men still running an analysis on all the data. "See what else is on there that's useful; I will be right back."

After she felt Joey's hands release her, she pushed past him and quickly went right back upstairs. He was quick on her heels, though, and once she was upstairs, she spun around to face him.

"He's been playing me like a goddamn fiddle! I knew he had motives to strengthen his power in the city, but God knows what else he's been doing to make sure that Liam and I were desperate!" She placed a hand on her forehead, struggling to keep up with the storm of scenarios crashing into her brain. If he coordinated Andrew getting in with Russ Spencer, the potential for other puppetry was limitless.

"Layney, calm down." Joey's voice tried to ease her down from her escalating temper.

She glared at him as he told her the one thing that most certainly was not going to bring her temper down a notch. "Don't tell me to calm the fuck down!"

When he reached out to hold onto her shoulders, she swiped his arms away. "I'm going to kill him, Joey. I don't care. I will hunt his ass down, make him suffer in his freakish torture room, and he can get off on his own demise on his way down to hell."

Joey's eyes settled on her, and he waited until she was finished. "Are you done?" When she didn't interrupt him, he continued to talk. "He will get what's coming to him, don't worry about that. There's enough data there that my client is going to want him wiped from the playing board. After a little more due diligence on the details of what he's peddling and how far he's peddling it, then this can be handled."

She tried to ease her anger down with a deep breath and think a little more rationally while Joey laid out what would hopefully be the next steps.

After making sure that she wasn't going to go off on him like an Irish car bomb, he wrapped his large arms around her and drew her in close. He kissed the top of her head reassuringly. "We will handle Eric *together* when the time comes. Until then, we keep the status quo. Okay?"

Layne desperately wanted to argue with Joey, but having him hold her so close managed to ease the flare of her irritability. She sighed quietly as the tension in her body melted away one breath at a time.

"I hate you right now," she murmured against his chest as her arms wrapped around his waist.

"Only because you know I'm right." A cocky smile appeared on his mouth.

After Joey was confident that Layne wasn't going to go on a mission to immediately hunt Eric down, he went back to the basement to wrap up discussions with his associates. It turned out that they hit a snag in the encryption of data that would take some time to bypass.

There was enough time for her to soak in everything he had said to her. When he came back upstairs, ready to leave, she stopped him. "Did you mean what you said?"

He lifted a brow at her. "Which part?"

"That we would handle this together. The way things went down with Franzetti—" Her words were interrupted by his finger pressing against her lips.

Joey's eyes met hers to make his intentions very clear. "You're stuck with me, Layney. Hell or high water. I just need you to be on the same page. And, until you are," his hands moved to embrace her face, "I'm going to slay any demons standing in your way to get you there."

Words were pretty things. Layne wondered if they would hold the course of time or if he would end up another chapter that abruptly closed in her life.

CHAPTER TWENTY-FIVE

Now that Layne knew how much Eric had taken up the role of puppet master in her life, she struggled to play her part now that the veil had been lifted from her eyes. Regardless, she pushed through her feelings, knowing there would be inevitable retribution if only she played the game intelligently.

Jocy had been keeping his distance while working diligently with his tech-savvy associates to uncover how far Eric's web stretched and exactly what secrets it held. He didn't want Layne's involvement in this to get any deeper or last any longer than necessary.

As a way to refocus her energy on something other than violence and sex, she found a healthier form of escape in running through Central Park. There was something cathartic about her feet against the ground, the brisk winter air against her face and in her lungs, and her muscles being pushed to move faster for longer.

She was three-and-a-half miles into the run and finally getting into a groove of things. Layne had her earbuds in, listening to *Let the Sparks Fly* by Thousand Foot Krutch to keep up her pace. With frigid winter temperatures in full swing, she was thankful she had decided to toss on ivory gloves to keep her fingers warm and a matching knit hat on her head before she had left the house.

As she began to feel a surge of energy to keep gunning for her planned five miles, the sound of an incoming call dulled the upbeat music inside her ears. She groaned as she slowed down to answer the call through her earbuds. She panted as she tried to gradually ease her legs down to a walk.

"Hello?" Her voice sounded as out of breath as she felt.

Eric greeted her on the other end warmly. "Little harpy, I've been trying to get a hold of you. It seems you have been quite busy."

She winced at the stupidity of not screening her call before answering. Layne stepped off to the side of the path as she kept walking so her muscles didn't seize up on her. "I've had a lot going on."

"Oh? You'll have to tell me all about it. I will come meet up with you, and we can catch up."

Layne suppressed a groan as she placed a hand on her hip. "I'm actually in the middle of a run. Now's not a great time."

His voice during the start of the call had sounded cordial, but now there was something darker lurking underneath the words. "I wasn't asking whether or not it was a good time for you. Would you prefer I send my men to pick you up instead?"

She shook her head as she glanced around the section of Central Park she was in. It wasn't the most populated section, but she could quickly remedy that. "No, that's okay. I'm in Central Park; I can meet you near the first-mile marker."

His tone was quick to switch back to that lighter tone he had started the call with. "That sounds better. I will be there in fifteen minutes."

The call ended, and all the inner peace and calm she had begun to achieve on this run was quickly dissipating.

It only took her ten minutes to sprint back to the mile marker she had told Eric to meet her at. When she arrived, he was just walking up to it a solid five minutes early.

She pulled her earbuds from her ears and tucked them into the pockets of her leggings. Her face was still flushed from the mixture of physical exertion and the burn of icy wind hitting it during her workout. The warmth of her labored exhales was visible as it hit the freezing air.

Eric gave her a light smile as he looked her over. He had on a navy winter coat with a pair of dark leather gloves to fend off the cold.

When he leaned in to greet her with a kiss, she leaned away from him. "I'm all sweaty from my run."

His eyes narrowed but seemed to brush it off. "I wanted to talk about expectations that I may not have made clear enough, Layne. Let's walk." Eric's hand didn't make it a suggestion as he linked his arm with hers and began to escort them both down the path toward the more scenic and wooded area of the park.

Layne walked with him, already calculating the odds of various things he wanted to talk with her about. Had he known she had taken his phone? Was he upset that Liam was still struggling to get access to the last of the primary bank accounts?

"What type of expectations did you want to talk about? Aside from a few minor items, I feel like this arrangement has been going fairly smoothly." She tried to keep things in a positive light and not immediately jump to doom and gloom.

Eric reached into his pocket and pulled out a turquoise jewelry box. "I realized that I may have been unfair in expecting you to take us seriously when I haven't held up all of my end of the bargain. If I want you to act like my wife, I should at least act like your husband." He drew back the top of the box to reveal a diamond ring nestled inside.

The surprise on Layne's face was authentic, if nothing else. This was one time she didn't have to pretend around him. Taking a look at the piece of jewelry before her, it definitely wouldn't have been the ring Layne would have chosen. It was a ring designed for show and status.

The ring held its own brand of beauty with its thick gold band with a large round diamond in the center and smaller diamonds inset around the entire band. While some woman somewhere would have been over the moon to be offered the ring, it couldn't have been further from Layne's tastes.

He stood there, letting her take in the sight of what he was offering to her. "I want everyone to see this ring on your finger and know that you're mine. When you see it on your finger when you wake up in the morning, let it be a reminder of all my promises to you."

After removing the ring from its box, he reached down for her hand. Not waiting for any type of response from her, he slid her glove off of her hand so he could slide the ring onto her finger. "There."

The ring felt heavy and cold on her hand. It felt more like a set of shackles than a romantic promise. Layne finally gathered some coherent thoughts together as she looked up at Eric. "This... This was not what I was expecting today."

Eric took her chin in his hand and pulled her into his kiss as though it was going to elevate the moment into something more meaningful. Afterward, he smiled at her. "Now that we have that taken care of, I wanted to let you know I have the movers coming in two weeks to pack up your things and move you into my house."

"What?" She blinked as her brain did a hard shift.

As with everything he said or did, it came off as non-negotiable. "I've done my part and given you more than sufficient time. Now, you need to show me you're willing to do yours."

Layne reminded herself that she needed to bide her time. She wanted nothing more than to strangle the life out of the man standing there before her. Patience was not at the top of her list of things she was great with, but she was stuck having to do her best.

While Eric seemingly was holding off the figurative underworld hyenas from attacking the remains of her family's business, it was at a cost. After learning how he had manipulated the entire Russ Spencer and Andrew Correlli situation, she didn't trust that anything he said or did was as it was being presented to her.

They continued their stroll around the park. Layne put her warm glove back on her hand, at least covering up the eyesore on her ring finger. Though, she could still feel the odd sensation of it shifting around on her hand.

Later on that evening, she was sitting in the driver's seat of her car with Rebecca in the passenger seat after picking her up.

"Holy Christ, woman!" Rebecca exclaimed as she stared at Layne's hand and the massive rock now adorning it.

Layne grimaced. "I know."

Her friend grabbed her hand to take a closer look at the ring on it. "I don't even want to know how much this is worth." Then, her face shifted into one of concern as she let go of Layne's hand.

Immediately, Layne was already ahead of her and was quick to speak up. "It's temporary and complicated. It's all for business purposes. I just didn't want you to be caught off guard."

"Too late for that!" Rebecca gave a small shove to Layne's shoulder of minor annoyance.

Layne released a breath of relief, now getting this heavy secret off her chest to the person who had been in her life since childhood and always treated her like blood.

"To make matters more complicated," Layne winced as she was about to drop another bomb on her bestie, "there's something else."

Rebecca's mouth dropped open. "Are you pregnant?"

"No!" Layne immediately responded, almost having a minor panic attack at the thought of how that would turn this entire situation into an even bigger shitshow. "Remember the guy? *The* guy?"

"Oh, you mean the one that did you dirty? That one? The one I would like to smack for what he put you through?" Rebecca huffed, recalling how much she wanted to lay into the man who managed to put Layne in such a dark spot. She hadn't gotten all the specifics, but as the best friend, it had been her duty to be pissed off on Layne's behalf.

"Well…" Layne struggled to fully come out and say it. Thankfully, she didn't need to when Rebecca made the leap that Joey was back in the picture.

Rebecca's eyes widened. "Girl!"

Layne gave a slightly apologetic smile. "I know, I know. It's different this time. I don't know how to explain it. Things are just… I don't know. It's different. Like, it's beyond not being able to breathe around him. All I want to do is breathe him in. God, he just has this ability to make me feel like I'm the only person that exists in his world."

Rebecca nodded as she listened, a smirk easing onto her face.

Layne picked up on the expression Rebecca had that said she had some thoughts on all of this. "What??"

"I'm not going to say it." She grinned as she picked her water bottle up from the cupholder and took a sip.

Staring at Rebecca, Layne picked up a random crumpled-up receipt from her last fill at the gas station and tossed it at her. "Tell me!"

Smugly, Rebecca sat there, knowing something that Layne wasn't even aware of. "No, I'm not going to say it because you're going to get all freaked out and spooked. I'm not going to be held responsible for that."

Layne sighed and shook her head. "You're lucky that I would be unable to function without you around. Otherwise, I would drop your ass off at Penn Station and ship you down to Baltimore to go visit your mom."

Rebecca laughed. "You wouldn't last a week."

"I know, that's why you're still here. You're the one piece of sanity and normalcy in my life." Layne smiled, knowing that without Rebecca, she likely would have taken an even darker path in her life.

CHAPTER TWENTY-SIX

There was still a week before Eric had stated he was sending movers over her direction to pack all her shit up and move it. Layne had been doing her best not to stress over it while Joey was pushing his team to work as fast as they could.

With the knowledge that Eric was manipulating the entire criminal ecosystem to fit his agenda, Layne needed to start planning on how to get it back under her control. What did that mean? Late nights figuring out which contacts were trustworthy, financial planning, and stressing over all the strategizing to avoid her family business becoming defunct.

By the time the evening rolled around, Layne was exhausted. While she sat on the couch, nearly dozing off with the television in the background, the doorbell chimed.

Layne lifted her head and stirred groggily. Another ring of the doorbell echoed throughout her home. Her hand rubbed across her face, trying to shake off the excess fatigue.

"I'm coming." She muttered out to the emptiness of her home.

Shoving herself off the sofa, she shuffled to the front door and took a peep outside to see who was there at—she glanced at her watch on her wrist—nearly eleven-thirty at night. When she saw the familiar face of Eric, she shook her head. Did nobody call anymore?

Layne pulled open the door as her hand brushed some hair away from her face. "Hey, I didn't expect you here this late at night. What are you doing here?"

Eric pushed his way inside without a word.

She shut the door behind him while the expression on her face turned sour. "Nice to see you, too." Something was off about his demeanor.

Eric reached into his pocket and pulled out his new phone. He opened it up and pulled up security footage from her house's camera system. She leaned in to take a look at one video in particular that he was pulling up.

Layne didn't recognize the angle of the camera as she never had a camera posted on that side of her house. She glanced at Eric in confusion. "What am I supposed to be looking at here?"

"Give it a second." He responded dryly.

As a body appeared on the screen, that's when she knew they had fucked up. The only thing on that side of the house was an egress window that led into her cellar. She forgot that it even existed because she never went down there unless she had to dig around for holiday decorations.

The silver lining was that she now knew how Joey had been getting in and out of her house. The big-ass dark thundercloud, who was Eric, unfortunately, had evidence of it.

"It looks like a visitor to me." She attempted to keep both her face and her tone neutral to avoid giving too much away.

After the video ended, Eric put the phone away and turned to face her, not having an ounce of pleasantness on his face. "I was concerned that there was a safety issue after seeing this, and I went back, and to my surprise, I found this wasn't the only incident."

"What do you want me to say, Eric? Did you think I was going to ditch my security detail the second we made this official? We run drills to make sure we both are on top of our game in the event someone does try to make a go at me." Damn, that sounded like some of the better bullshit she had come up with on the fly in a while. She was impressed with herself for it, especially given how tired she had been before his arrival. Her eyes stared directly at him, hoping to make him feel stupid for even questioning her.

As good as it was, it didn't settle with Eric as well as she had hoped. "I have been more than reasonable with you. I have been fending off all the vultures of the city from swooping down and feeding off of what's left of your pathetic empire. I've been doing my part in our agreement, and what have you done to repay me for it?"

She could see Eric's jaw twitching and his nostrils flaring. He turned his back to her while clenching his fists at his side.

Before she could attempt a response to his question, he spun around to face her, his hand going flying. Layne may have been half asleep, but thank God her muscle memory kicked in, and her arm shot up to defend against a direct blow.

Eric didn't wait for her to counter, he grabbed her by the forearm and propelled her toward the stairs. Layne stumbled, and her hands caught herself on a step several up on the staircase.

When she turned, she felt his body knock into her, the edge of the steps painfully pounding into her back on impact. His hands wrapped around her throat, squeezing with a force that could rival a boa constrictor.

Layne's initial cough and gasp were immediately cut off as her airway was closed off. Staring up into Eric's face, his eyes were wide and lit up with the psychosis of an entire mental ward. He pulled her by her neck upward, only to slam her back down onto those unforgiving wooden stairs that had her brain rattling inside her skull.

Her hands scratched at his hand, pulling at individual fingers and straining to get even a brief moment of air while her face began to pale from the lack of oxygen.

Eric's words were vile and bitter as he spit them out at her. "You thought you could hide it from me?! The way you look at each other? It all makes fucking sense as to why you were reluctant to whore yourself out to me!"

Layne used a foot against the wall that bordered the staircase to push off to rotate them both while she shoved his back into the iron-clad stair spindles. It was enough to loosen his grasp.

She gasped for air but didn't wait long to recover. Pushing off the stairs with her feet, she jetted up the steps toward the second floor. Her feet pounded against the floor as she flung herself around the ninety-degree angle at the top of the mid-floor landing before dashing up the rest of the way to the second floor.

His words shouted behind her. "Little harpy! Come back!"

He had to be out of his damn mind if he thought she was going to go anywhere near him. She reached her bedroom and slid down onto her knees toward her bed, where she reached underneath to where she had a partial arsenal stored. Her hands grabbed frantically for the first available weapon of choice.

She drew forth a semi-automatic pistol and flicked the safety off.

When she pulled back the slide to load the chamber, she didn't hesitate to aim it at the doorway as Eric came charging in. Her finger pressed against the trigger.

Click.

Her eyes glanced down and noticed the bullet jam from the top view of the chamber. *Fuck.* She popped up onto her feet, not having time to mess around with the mechanical failure. She spun the pistol around in her hand and swung the grip at him.

Eric caught her forearm while his other hand twisted her wrist painfully until she couldn't hold onto the firearm any longer. It fell to the floor with a clunk. "That's not being a good little bird, now is it?"

Layne winced at the painful angle of her wrist, but it didn't diminish the hatred raging behind her eyes. "I will never be your bird to keep in a cage." She gave a front kick towards his gut.

While his grasp on her wrist was released, it was only in exchange for capturing her foot's attack. Eric pushed back on her leg, changing her momentum against her to knock her off balance as she fell back, smashing into the area where her mattress met her nightstand.

Her arm knocked her lamp onto the ground with a shatter of porcelain while her other arm tried to brace her fall as her hand grasped at the down-filled comforter. The engagement ring he had forced on her had also been on top of the nightstand and was also knocked off onto the floor.

The anger in Eric's glare at her was reaching an all-time boil. "Did you think I wouldn't know? You could have had the best life has to offer with me." He loomed over her while she was cornered there. "It's a shame because I was looking forward to showing everyone how I could own and tame the wild Layne O'Reilly."

His hands reached down, grabbed Layne by her shirt, and yanked her up onto her feet. Eric pulled her in so she was face-to-face with him.

With ragged breaths, Layne didn't shy away from looking him in the eye. "Go fuck yourself. I was never going to be yours."

His fist slammed into her temple. Layne dropped to the floor as the impact sent her mind for a brief mental vacation riddled with darkness.

When her consciousness slowly came back to her, she lay there on the floor as her eyes squinted. A splitting headache loomed over her brain, and an unparalleled grogginess suffocated her thoughts. Layne groaned and placed her hands on the floor to push herself up. It felt like it took the effort of a thousand lifetimes.

When she lifted her hands, they stopped midway up to her face. That's when she noticed the cold rounds of metal handcuffs latched around her wrists. Her mind fought to recognize why they were there.

As her wits became about her, she tugged on the chain connecting each wrist to feel it did not give her much leeway. Between the joints of the cuffs was a length of a metal chain that connected directly to the underside of the bed frame in front of her.

The ringing in her ears was deafening. Glancing around, it seemed that she was alone, but the roaring in her ears wasn't easing up, it was only getting worse.

She coughed as she managed to shift onto her knees with her hands linked together. Her eyes burned each time she blinked. Her nostrils flared with each breath, taking in an overwhelming odor of burning wood.

Soon, she recognized the source of the ringing in her ears. It wasn't inside of her head; it was inside of her home. The smoke detectors were all sounding off. Their high-pitched sounds sliced through the air.

Layne looked over to her wide-open bedroom door. The sight had a panic rising inside her chest. The billowing smoke and visible flames at the end of the hallway were eating away at her home.

It was all like a vicious monster slowly creeping towards her bedroom, ready to consume her. Frantically, she pulled at her hands, and the connected chain prevented her from getting very far from her bed. Each pull was harder than the one before it. Layne grunted with each yank, feeling the pinch of metal biting into her skin.

She used her body weight to lean back and her foot against the edge of the bed to try and overcome the strength of steel. Continually, she glanced over at the open doorway to notice her time was running short as the smoke continued to edge towards her room.

She ferally screamed out in frustration. Tears leaked from her eyes as she choked on a sob. Layne couldn't let this be how her story ended. "God, please, just this once," she begged for the pity of her maker.

The fear and adrenaline left her uncontrollably shaking as the situation felt insurmountable. She leaned forward, pressed her head against her mattress, and shut her eyes tightly. The sheets soaked up her tears. "Please…"

She sank back to sit on her ankles. Her eyes hurt from dryness in the air, licking away her emotions. Feeling lost, she stared at the metal bracelets around her wrists, which were now painfully raw from all her frantic struggles.

A sensation came over her in that moment of hopelessness. One final renewed effort filled her. Layne laid herself on the floor and took a look under her bed to see where the chain connected. Her one shot at a miracle presented itself to her. There may not have been hope in breaking steel, but a long shot presented itself.

Her eyes caught sight of the box underneath her bed that stored all her kinky toys. What were the chances that the keys from one set of cuffs were likely to open another? Using her legs, she maneuvered the box of goodies closer to her until she could use her hands to open up the lid and begin digging for what she hoped was still in there.

Her fingertips finally tracked down the key. It belonged to a set of Smith & Wesson cuffs, and looking at the etching on the ones around her wrists, she frowned. It was another brand, Peerless. "Fuck."

Not having any other bright ideas, she tried the key in the assembly anyway. When the most beautiful clicking sound was heard, and she felt the loops loosen on her, she could have sat there and cried if she had enough time to do so, but she didn't.

She removed the restraints quickly and dropped them to the floor. She wasn't going to be burning in hell today, as luck would have it.

The panic tugged at her chest as the overwhelming surroundings became more urgent. The burning smell. The smoke alarms. The heat. Pushing through the fear, she ran over to her bedroom window. Sliding the window pane up, she popped the screen out and watched it gracefully flutter to the ground two stories below.

No part of her was willing to burn to death in her own home. She put one leg through the open window and straddled the frame as she peered outside, looking at the best options to get down in one piece.

Strategically, she lowered herself out of the window. Her hands grasped the ledge as her muscles strained under her weight to control her descent. Her legs dangled beneath her as her feet stretched to touch the motorized sun awning casing just below.

Layne was now thanking her lucky stars that Rebecca had talked her into getting one installed to stretch out over a portion of the back patio for the hot summer days when there was no shade to be found elsewhere in her backyard.

It wasn't a graceful descent after that point, but the rolled-up awning cover helped buffer her fall. She rolled against the ground, scraping her arms up in the process against the cement. It was better than going down in a fiery blaze.

She backed up to take a look at her house, seeing the extent of how much the fire had already spread. The luck of the Irish had been on her side. Layne had been fortunate to get out when she did.

While she stood in her backyard staring, the flames reflected in her eyes as her home and everything inside began to be burned into ash.

CHAPTER TWENTY-SEVEN

All that she had worked for had been in that house. She sat there across the street on the edge of the sidewalk and stared at the burning ruins. The FDNY had arrived and was slowly working the house fire under control with hoses from several trucks.

The smell of the fire hung heavily on the air, her clothes and even her hair as a reminder of the events that had just transpired.

That bastard had robbed her of everything that those walls held. Layne shut her eyes. It wasn't just the material belongings that were lost to the blaze; it was all the intangible memories that went with it.

"I'm not a good guy, and you're not a good girl."

Joey's voice echoed in her mind from the day he first set foot inside that house.

"No, watch! This is the part where he drops the entire plate of food on his date!"

Trashy television girl nights with Rebecca alongside tacos and margaritas.

"It's yours, Layne. You've earned it."

The way her father dropped the keys into the palm of her hand the day he bought the house for all the hard work she had done for the family business.

All of it was on its way to being nothing but charred wood and ash now.

"Layne?" Liam's voice prompted her to open her eyes. He half jogged over to her. "What the hell happened?"

Her fingertips quickly swept away a rogue tear from underneath her eye. "What are you doing here?"

"The company handling the fire alarm system had my number on file." He looked over at the extent of the ongoing damage to the property. "Fuck."

"Yeah." She had the same damn sentiment.

He stood there silently, staring at the destruction with Layne while she sat there doing the same. There was nothing but the sound of the fire roaring and the water pouring from the hoses trying to contain it. Emergency lights from all the firetrucks continued to reflect off the windows of all the surrounding houses and parked cars on the street. Nearby nosey neighbors peeked out from their houses to watch.

The sound of tires squealing against the pavement could be heard at the end of the street. It was followed by a set of headlights as a car rounded the corner and sped up to the other end of the street, where all the emergency vehicles were parked.

The black car quickly pulled off to the side as close to the fire engines as it could get. The lights went dark, and a car door was shut as a voice yelled out. "Layne! LAYNE!"

Immediately, she pushed away from the ground to get up onto her feet after hearing Joey's emotionally charged voice. When her eyes caught sight of him, he was trying to push past three firefighters toward the blaze that had been lit with the intention to consume her.

"Joey!" She took off running towards him. "Joey!"

Hearing her call his name, he shoved off the hands of the first responders, trying to keep him from charging into her house. Joey stopped struggling with the men standing between him and her house when he heard the sweetest voice call his name again from the other direction. When he caught sight of her, he immediately sprinted toward her.

When they met in the middle of the street, she threw herself up against him. Her arms wrapped around his neck, and her face burrowed into his shoulder.

He caught her as she flung herself at him, his arms lifted and held her tightly as he pressed his face into her hair. He didn't care that she smelled like singed daisies from the smoke and ash. He only cared that he would still have more days to wake up next to her intoxicating scent that reminded him of summer rain on a hill full of daisies.

Layne wrapped her legs around his waist, refusing to let go of him. No matter how closely she held herself against him, it wasn't close enough. Her body shuddered as the floodgates behind her eyes burst open. His shirt soaked up the tears from her eyes and muffled the sounds of her sobs. Her hands clawed at the shirt on his back, scrunching it up in her hands as she held herself to him.

Joey protectively placed a hand on the back of her head as he hushed into her ear. "I've got you. It's okay, Layney."

She choked on her own words as she tried to explain everything that had happened. "I-it was Eric. He saw you on the cameras, and… and he was furious. I tried, but—"

He stopped her right there, holding her tightly in the safety of his arms. "Shh. I'm here; nothing is going to happen to you."

After what felt like the longest release of emotional turmoil, she lifted her face to look at him. The tears had left their red marks down her cheeks. Visible was the bruise and slight swelling at her temple where she had taken the hit that had rendered her unconscious.

He immediately gave her several kisses of reassurance, not just on her lips but across her face to replace the salty tears. Joey was careful to kiss even more tenderly around the visible injuries.

Layne used one hand to hold onto the back of his neck as her other came up to brush away the strands of hair from her face. The raw abrasions from the cuffs were still fresh on her skin and stung with each flex of her hands.

She sniffled, trying to recover from the emotions that were still taking their toll on her after the evening's events. "How did you know to come here?"

Joey pressed his forehead against hers, his hands still protectively holding her to him. "I heard it over the police scanner. I recognized the address and…" His voice trailed off, unable to finish what horrible thoughts had entered his mind.

Realizing that he had run straight for the inferno taking over her home, she frowned at him. "You ran towards the house. That was stupid; you wouldn't have even made it to the stairs."

He looked her directly in the eyes and shook his head. "Layne, I love you. I would have let the flames take me straight to hell to pay for all my sins before giving up on you."

Her lower lip trembled as she released a few fresh tears from her eyes.

Her lips kissed him several times from hearing him speak those words to her.

A sarcastic voice interrupted what should have been a sweet and tender moment. “Yeah, right.” Liam chimed in, overhearing the private conversation. Her brother always had spectacular timing to decide to open his mouth and subject everyone to his assholery.

Joey’s eyes lost their warmth as he looked over at Liam. Gently, he set Layne down on her feet. He stepped up to Liam, looming several inches taller than the younger O’Reilly. “Do you have something to say?” The sharp edge of his tone indicated that Liam was walking on very thin ice.

Liam scoffed and didn’t back away. “I do. You’re full of crap. If Layne didn’t have her head all fucked up by your inability to stay out of her pants, our family wouldn’t be in this mess! You don’t give two shits about her.”

He forcefully shoved Joey to add emphasis to his words. The second Liam put his hands on Joey, it set off an immediate reaction. Joey grabbed Liam’s shirt and pushed him back roughly into a parked car. There was no hesitation as Joey’s fist crashed into Liam’s jaw.

“You’re a fuckin’ shitbag!” Joey’s words yelled back at him.

From there, Liam began throwing punches back, and the two of them began wrestling with one another. Layne stayed out of the way and watched, knowing Liam could use a little tough love from someone other than her for once.

Joey landed a few more body shots on Liam, who wasn’t anywhere near the same weight class by comparison. It was all too easy for Joey to keep the upper hand while they both wrangled with one another.

Finally, after several minutes of jabs and hooks exchanged, Joey landed one last hit across Liam’s face, sending him to the ground. Liam landed on the ground and rolled onto his side while groaning from the ass-kicking Joey had just handed him.

Breathing heavily, Joey wiped his mouth with the back of his hand, noticing a small smear of blood from one of the few half-ass hits Liam did manage to land. “I swear to God, if you ever disrespect your sister and all she’s done to fix your fuck-ups again, I will not hesitate to make sure to break your jaw so bad it will have to be wired shut for months.”

Layne walked up to Joey, placing a hand gently on his flexed bicep, still tense from the scuffle. “Let’s just go. I can’t be here anymore.” She gestured to the fire, still contrasting against the night sky as it consumed what was once her home. The exhaustion of everything she had been through was evident in her voice.

There was still an intensity in Joey's stare at the spoiled brat writhing on the ground. Finally, he noticed Layne's hand tugging at his arm, and he nodded in agreement. Joey wrapped his hand around hers, intertwining their fingers as he led her back to the Challenger he had arrived in.

Once they were both inside the car, Layne latched her seatbelt and then looked over at him. "Did you mean what you said?"

He raised a brow at her. "The next time he opens his mouth, Layne, I am not holding back. Someone needs to make him learn that there are bigger fish out there that don't give a fuck."

"No, that's not what I was talking about." Her emerald hues looked at him with the weight of all the evening's emotions in them.

Realizing what she was questioning, he turned in the driver's seat, and his hand reached over to take hold of her face. The warmth of his palm against her skin made her want to melt into his touch.

"Every damn word of it, and I never plan to let you forget it, either. You are everything that makes me want to continue breathing. I love you, Layney." Joey leaned over and made sure she felt every ounce of his words as he pulled her into a tender kiss.

CHAPTER TWENTY-EIGHT

"You're a real stubborn pain in my ass, you know that?" Joey sighed as he watched Layne shove another box into the corner of O'Reilly Manor's master bedroom.

She smoothed back a piece of hair from her face. "There's more space here than your place. No one is forcing you to move in here with me." Layne stated it matter-of-factly.

Joey wrapped his arms around her waist and drew her against him with a smirk. "Did you think that I was going to let you out of my sight?"

Layne pushed herself up onto her tiptoes to lightly kiss him. "No, and that's why I knew I'd get away with doing things my way." She smirked right back at him. Her hand patted his solid chest before she slid out of his arms.

Thankfully, she had some extra belongings in her old bedroom there in the house she grew up in. She had never moved them into the now-condemned property that had been her home for the last several years. Not to mention, between Joey and Rebecca, they both made sure that she had everything else she needed.

His eyes watched as Layne moved about the room, adjusting things to the way she wanted. Her ponytail swayed back and forth with each step. The way her hips moved just begged for his hands to grab them. When she bent over to grab another box off the floor, his cock stiffened at the sight of her magnificent ass that needed his hand, leaving red marks on it.

Joey was two steps away from acting on his desires when his phone began to ring in his pocket. He grumbled quietly as he answered it. "Yeah?"

After lifting the box off the ground, Layne turned at the sound of Joey speaking to see him taking a call. She prayed it was the call they had been waiting on. The call would reveal all of Eric's secrets and the green light for Joey to proceed with the hit.

Her eyes watched every shift in his movements as he listened to the person on the other end of the phone. One hand came up to rub over his forehead, the tattoos on his fingers flexing with each movement.

"What do you mean there's been a small issue?" The tension in Joey's voice indicated that whatever he was hearing on the other end of the line wasn't what he had hoped to hear. "I'm not going to wait for-fucking-ever. Figure it out, or else I'm making my move whether the client wants me to or not."

The call ended, and Joey forced his phone back into his pocket as he finally looked over at Layne with conflict and frustration in his eyes. "There were some issues with the integrity of the data. They're rerunning a few things, but the client is now getting gun-shy."

She put the box back down on the floor and walked over to him with a frown. This wasn't the news either of them wanted to hear about Eric. "Look, Eric's not going anywhere right now. He's in too deep, especially trying to sort through all of my business contacts he took over. I doubt he's going to take that big of a financial hit just to up and take off."

Layne rubbed her hands along his sides, hoping to ease his stress some.

He shook his head. "I'm sure by now he knows there were no casualties in the fire, thanks to the damn paper. Eric isn't going to just shrug this off and forget that you still exist, and he isn't getting a hefty life insurance payout."

"I know, but I've got you here with me. Do you think Eric is good enough to take both of us on? I'd like to see what army he would have to send." She tried to put Joey's concerns to rest, that waiting just a little longer wouldn't be the end of the world.

Seeing that Joey still wasn't feeling at ease, she grabbed his hand and tugged. "C'mon, I have something to show you that should make you feel a little bit better."

Joey's brow lifted curiously but didn't hesitate in allowing Layne to lead him out of the master bedroom. They both walked down the hall until

Layne led him downstairs. Eventually, she stopped at a closed door with a giddy smile on her face. "Are you ready?"

She swung open the door, and the motion triggered the lights to pop on, revealing what was in the room. The lights illuminated the room to unveil several black leather movie theater seats across from a large screen in an entertainment room designed for residential use. Fiber optic star ceiling tiles lined the ceiling, and theater-style wall sconces added to the atmosphere.

Layne pulled him inside with her so he could see the entirety of all the room had to offer. "This has always been my favorite room in the house. There are reclining seats, a professional-grade sound system, a snack station, and you can watch just about anything in here."

She wasn't exaggerating either. The room even contained a smaller version of a popcorn machine that you could find at the actual movie theaters.

He had never had the chance to fully explore O'Reilly Manor while Layne's dad was still alive, but he was pleasantly surprised to see that this room existed. Ever the typical guy, Joey imagined all the sports games he could watch in here.

Layne stopped and turned to him. "Oh, and my favorite part about this room?" Her eyes twinkled in mischievous delight as she was about to share some big secret. She leaned in and whispered to him. "It's fully soundproof. You can make me scream as loud as you want in here."

She grinned while pressing her teeth into her bottom lip as her eyes looked up into his while all the dirty thoughts in her mind ran rampant.

Joey immediately forgot about the disappointing phone call as Layne shared that little fact with him. His hand took her by the back of her neck while his other hand dropped down to grab a handful of her ass. His gravelly voice dropped into a possessive growl. "I'm going to need to test that out."

Excitement tugged somewhere deep inside of her between her thighs as she recognized the feral look in his eyes that he gave when he had her in his sights. He released her ass and began walking her back until she was against the black wall. Leaning forward, he rested his forearm against the wall as his mouth barely drifted over the side of her neck. "But first, you're going to do something for me."

Playfully, she bantered back. "Oh, am I?"

"Mmhmm. You're going to be a good girl for me." His hand wrapped around her throat, applying momentary pressure before releasing and running his hand down the center of her body. His fingers stopped at the top of the leggings she had on.

"That is unless you don't want to feel me here." His hand slid down a little further over her pants and pressed his fingers against the apex of her legs. With his fingers finding her weak spot, she quietly gasped out at the aching need flaring up.

"Or maybe, even here." His hand slid further back between her legs until his fingers pushed against the hole of her ass. "The way you've been shaking your fuckin' ass at me all damn day makes me think it needs to be taken."

Layne's body squirmed under his touch as her need for him escalated. Very quickly, she realized she would agree to do anything this man wanted her to do if he would just take her as he pleased. Her hips pressed against his touch as her hands pulled on his tee. "Joey, I need you to stop teasing me."

Slowly, he dragged his fingers back along her crease until his hand moved away from her entirely. "Uh-uh. You're not the one calling the shots right now."

She groaned as a sense of electricity in her body was lost the second he severed contact with her body.

"Strip." That was all he commanded of her before stepping back to give her enough space to comply.

The urge to just rip all of her clothes off in record time was overwhelming, but she knew that Joey couldn't resist a good show. While her shoes were the first to come off, she took her time with everything else. Her fingers lifted the bottom of her shirt and peeled it up away from her body, exposing one inch of flesh at a time.

After the black and gold lace bra underneath was revealed, she pulled the shirt up over her head and dropped it to the floor. She trailed her fingers down over her body before turning her back to him. Layne's hands reached back to find the hook of her bra, unclasping it with one smooth movement. She looked back at him over her shoulder to see that he had taken a seat in one of the theater-style chairs.

Her eyes met his as she smiled seductively. Her fingers slowly dragged the straps of her bra down over each shoulder. The bra joined her shirt on the floor. Keeping her back to him, she hooked her thumbs on the waist of her leggings and shimmied her hips a little extra for his viewing pleasure.

It must have been just the right move because she heard him groan in delight as he sat there behind her, his hand resting on the bulge pushing against the fly of his jeans.

Layne tugged the stretchy material down over the swell of her ass, bending over as she did so. It became quickly clear she was still being his good girl and abiding by his no underwear rule.

"Fuck, Layney…" His voice sounded out of breath.

She remained bent over for a few extra seconds so he could get a good look at her body before she stepped out of her pants. Layne straightened back up and walked over to him, inviting herself to straddle his lap on her knees.

"Was that what you wanted from me?" Her hands ran over the tops of his broad shoulders and up his neck until her fingers got lost in his hair. Her exposed tits and their stiff peaks were right in front of his face.

He rubbed his hands over the bare skin of her legs up over her hips before they grabbed her at her waist. "I want everything from you. You're too goddamn perfect not to indulge in everything your body has to offer." Joey latched his mouth onto her nipple, sucking hungrily on it. His tongue circled the stiffness while tasting her.

Her hands tightened their grasp on his dirty blonde locks of hair as she held his head up against her. She moaned out as his teeth nipped and prompted a pleasurable pain while the harsh scruff around his mouth brushed against her skin's softness.

Joey moved his mouth over to her other breast, being sure to give it an equal amount of attention. This time, however, he moved a hand between her legs and plunged two fingers deep inside of her.

Her body's dripping arousal made for easy entry and smooth movements as he began pumping his digits into her. She tilted her head back as a moan was drawn out of her. Her chest rose and fell with each sensation he thrust onto her body.

He took his mouth off of her to admire the sight of how her face moved as she felt the pleasure he was giving her. "Such a good girl getting all nice and wet for me, Layney. I bet your pussy is begging for me to give it a nice hard fuck, isn't it?" He circled his thumb over her clit, causing her hips to buck against his touch as she cried out.

She could barely put coherent thoughts together while his fingers continued to dive deeper into her. "Yes! Yes! I need you."

He pulled his fingers from her with a smile. His hand grabbed her jaw and pulled her face down to his so he could get a taste of her mouth. Overwhelmed with desire, it felt like he had consumed her soul with the kiss.

When he breathlessly broke the seal of their lips, he nodded behind her. "Go get on your hands and knees for me. I want to admire your sweet ass while you take all of my cock."

Layne complied, getting herself down on the floor as he asked like a lioness in heat. She heard the sound of his clothes hitting the floor, and soon the strength of his hands pulled on her hips to yank her back so she could feel his dick against her opening while he kneeled behind her.

Her body ached to feel him inside of her, prompting her to push back against him to get what she wanted. "Make me scream for you. Please."

"Oh, that's not going to be a problem." He smirked as he sank the hard thickness of his length into her. Once he was fully inside her, with her cheeks up against him, he groaned at the depths of her tightness that wrapped around him.

She yelled out in relief as he finally gave her what her body was craving from him. Joey drew back and rolled his hips back in again as he moved in and out of her pussy. Each stroke of him deep inside of her brought her closer to release.

Joey slammed himself harder into her as he felt her body tensing up in anticipation of her climax. "That's it, Layney, I want you to tell me who this tight cunt belongs to when you come."

With her hands holding herself up on the floor, she felt the shaking in her limbs as he continued to ram into her. She clawed at the carpet underneath her, and her body felt an explosion deep in her core as she screamed out. Her cries were drawn out as she clenched down onto him. "You do, Joey! You do! God! Yes!"

He growled as he felt the wet warmth of her cover his cock. "That's right. And that's not the only thing I'm going to own."

Joey pulled out of her, his fingers briefly diving back inside of her body, prompting another squeal from Layne. He ran the slickness of his fingers between her ass, working one inside the tight hole. His finger pushed and stretched her using her own cum to make the entry easier.

Her heavy pants from her orgasm were slowing, and now a new sensation was pressing inside of her. Before she could give it more thought, Joey's cock filled her soaked pussy once more, making sure he was well-coated by her body's wetness.

His finger was removed from her ass before he pulled his dick from her. Then, he lined himself up with the hole he hadn't yet taken.

She glanced back at him breathlessly as she felt the rounded head of his cock line up again, this time at a much tighter entrance. "Joey, you're not going to be able to fit."

He devilishly smirked at her. "Oh, don't worry, I will fit just fine. Now be a good girl, and let me finally fuck this ass."

She swallowed down a little bit of her apprehension before letting her trust in him take over. Layne nodded to give him the go-ahead.

With her body's natural lube still covering his cock he began to inch himself into her. Joey moaned out at the immediate tightness enveloping him, being sure to refrain from going too quickly to start.

Layne gasped lightly at the initial discomfort as her body had to stretch to accommodate him. The full sensation of him pushing into her backdoor for the first time had her hands trying to grasp at the carpet. With each push forward that he made into her, he allowed her to adjust before continuing.

"That's it, Layney. You're doing so well taking each inch of my cock in your sweet ass." He groaned as he pushed into her further, nearly to the hilt. "Mm, you feel so fucking good and so goddamn tight." His voice was strained from the way her body had to stretch around him.

After the full length of his member was seated inside of her, he sighed at the sensation. Layne moaned at the fullness he was providing her, finding it brought on a whole new and different level of pleasure.

"Joey, God, you feel even bigger when you're in my ass." She pushed her hips back against him, letting herself find enjoyment in having him take her body this way.

He pulled himself back until just the tip of his cock remained inside of her and pushed back into her, this time with one smooth movement. A feral moan escaped past her lips as she felt him fill her back up. Her hand reached down between her legs, and her fingers rubbed over her throbbing clit that was aching for attention.

Joey's hands tightly locked onto her hips as he began with slow thrusts before picking up the pace. The sound of their bodies slapping together filled the room. He grunted each time he shoved his dick into her, and she groaned at the way her body felt perfectly designed for him.

Layne's fingers worked over her small bundle of nerves, quickly working up to another orgasm as he fucked her ass as though he owned it, and own it, he did. Her body came to the familiar ledge of glorious release. Panting hard, she opened her mouth to tell him she was going to come, and instead, all that came out was another scream of ecstasy.

As Layne's climax tore through her, Joey whimpered while clinging to the last bit of control he had. “Fuck!” Following her over the same cliff of satisfaction, he cursed as he fully shoved himself deep inside her tight hole, and his seed shot forth violently inside of her ass.

Moments later, they were both a hot mess on the floor; Joey still buried inside her while his chest was pressed up against her back. His mouth kissed the crook of her neck while his warm breaths melted against her skin. His hand caressed over the side of her body lovingly.

Layne lay there with him, feeling a sense of satisfaction that had gone beyond anything she knew possible. She knew that he was her everything, and yet she still couldn’t bring herself past the other edge of fear to say those three words to him.

CHAPTER TWENTY-NINE

Despite the fact that they were waiting impatiently for word back on the data to be reevaluated by Joey's associates, Layne couldn't complain too much. It allowed the two of them to enjoy spending time together.

Earlier in the day, they had each gotten a workout in, with Joey helping Layne refine some of her skills that would be useful against someone significantly larger than her - which was most people she encountered. After their training session, they had another type of work-out. The type without any clothes.

Layne heard a knock at the door, prompting her to go answer while she was on her way to the kitchen to grab another round of drinks for both her and Joey. When she looked out the side window, nobody was to be seen standing out front. She opened up the door, and there was a bouquet of black magic roses wrapped in black and burgundy floral paper.

What should have been a welcomed delivery for most other women, Layne's face fell at the sight of them. She leaned over and picked them up, bringing them back into the house. Setting the unexpected gift on a side table, she plucked out the card from the center.

Her fingers opened up the black envelope and pulled out the crimson card. Flipping it open, something fell out onto the floor. The black ink was sprawled across the inside in neatly written words.

You fucked around. Now, you're going to have to play my game with my rules. - Eric

When Layne bent over to pick up the fallen contents from the floor, she saw it was a piece of hard plastic. Turning it over in her hand, she immediately noticed the face on the driver's license. Rebecca. Her heart couldn't have sunk faster if it had been tied to a twenty-ton anchor.

"No…" The words were hardly above a whisper.

"Who was at the door?" Joey asked from the sofa in the living room while the television had a replay of the NHL Winter Classic on.

She dropped everything onto the floor and pulled her phone out, immediately placing a call to Rebecca's number. Layne ran into the office she had been sharing with Liam, pulled out her gun, and checked to see that it was loaded as she waited for her best friend to answer. After it rang several times, it went to voicemail.

"Damnit!" She tried calling again as she tucked her pistol in the back of her pants as she left her office and nearly ran Joey over now that he was coming to check on her.

The concern in his eyes was heavy as he saw the frenzied look on her face. "Layne, what's going on?"

Ring, ring, ri—

The call was answered, and she was quick to blurt out her friend's name with panicked hope. "Rebecca?!"

A sinister and all too familiar voice spoke on the other end of the line. "This is Rebecca's answering service; she is currently unavailable right now."

"Eric, you motherfucker! I swear to God, if you have so much as looked at her wrong, I will put a bullet in each of your fuckin' eyes, then I will rip out each of your pathetic little balls and shove them into your eye sockets." Her body was shaking from the anger filling her up.

"My, my. There's no need for violence, little harpy. I just wanted to get to know your friend a little better. She means so much to you; it only seemed right that I make an effort to see how strong of a friendship you truly have." Eric's tone taunted Layne, and it was working.

Pinning the phone between her shoulder and her ear, Layne went to the coat closet and began digging through the various clips and rounds available in their stock. "Put her on the phone." Layne gritted her teeth, picturing all the ways that she was going to make Eric suffer the second she laid eyes on him.

Overhearing enough of the conversation, Joey gathered a bag and began filling it with his own selection of supplies. He grabbed his mask, shoving it into his pocket for now.

Eric chuckled darkly. "Only if you ask politely."

She took the phone back into her hand, squeezing it until her knuckles were white with tension. The temptation to just toss it down on the ground out of frustration was overwhelming. Yet, that wouldn't get her very far. Layne put the phone back up to her ear and fought through every insult she wanted to unleash on him.

Not hearing anything, Eric prompted her again. "I'm waiting."

"*Please*, put Rebecca on the phone." Her words weren't pleasant, indicating she was struggling with his request.

A dark chuckle could be heard in response to her ask, "I'm not sure that was nice enough. I know you can do better than that."

She shut her eyes to find a part of her deep down inside that she could summon enough of what he wanted to hear. "Eric, I would really appreciate it if you could be so kind as to let me speak with Rebecca. Please."

There was a pause on the other end before Rebecca's voice, riddled with fear and panic, spoke up. "Layne! Layne, please help!"

Simultaneously, there was relief her bestie was alive and heartbreak that this nightmare was actually transpiring. Layne took the small window of opportunity to speak quickly. "Listen to me, Rebecca. I am not going to let anything happen to you, I promise. Just hang in there, please. I will get you out of there as soon as I can. He's not going to—"

It was unclear how much Rebecca heard as Eric responded with a cruel and mocking tone. "You have such a habit of making promises. Are you sure you can keep that one?"

Impatiently, she snapped at him. "Just tell me what you're looking for."

"I thought you knew by now. I want you, my little harpy. All to myself." Eric made it sound damn obvious and simple.

"You let her go unharmed, and you'll have me." As Layne spoke those words, Joey's attention was caught as he looked over at her and shook his head. He had a warning in his eyes.

Eric made a half-assed attempt to sound apologetic. "It's not going to be that easy, I'm afraid."

"Then, make it that easy. I'm not going to play games with you." So many thoughts ran through Layne's mind. Mostly, they involved torture and death if Rebecca shed even a single tear because of this psycho.

"But you are if you would like your friend to remain unscathed. Meet me at Smitty Fitness Center in an hour. Leave your side piece at home. I know he's already standing there, ready to fight your battle for you, but that is not the game we are going to play." The health club formerly known as Smitty's was shut down earlier this week thanks to some repeated health code violations. That meant it was left to be a dark and deserted playground.

Without hesitation, she responded. "It's a deal."

The phone beeped as the call ended. Layne pocketed the phone and gathered the remainder of the arsenal she intended to bring.

"What did he say?" Joey finished stocking up the bag full of bloodthirsty goodies.

"Does it matter? He has Rebecca. He has the one person in my life who hasn't signed up for any of this." She walked up to Joey and looked up at him, her hand reached up and lightly rubbed the side of his face over the stubble on his cheek with an apology in her eyes.

"Layne." A subtle warning hung on the way he said her name, not even trying to sugarcoat it.

She pulled his face down to hers as her lips captured his. Her tongue soaked up the taste of his mouth. Layne wanted to be able to remember this moment with him in case she never got the chance to experience it again.

Joey grabbed her shoulders and pulled her back. "Whatever you're thinking, you're not. You know as well as I do that he's going to be playing by his own set of fucked up rules. He's just trying to lure you into a trap."

"I know." She gave a sad smile as her emerald pools memorized every feature of his face. A quiver tugged at her chin, and tears were pricking at her eyes. "I love you." Her voice cracked as her heart got caught in her throat. "So much. More than I thought I could ever love anybody. You have always had my heart, and there isn't anything in this world that can change that."

Hearing her say those three powerful words for the first time provided just enough of a split moment where he was caught off guard that Layne could make her move. The electric crackle was the only thing that gave it away when she pressed the taser into his ribs.

Immediately, he flinched before his body seized up as it soaked the electrical shock and dropped to the ground harder than a bag of bricks. He yelled out, cursing as his muscles locked up during the time the metal probes were in contact with his body.

"I'm so sorry, Joey." Genuine remorse hung on her words, but she knew that this was the only way that she could buy herself enough time to go take care of business without him compromising her ability to focus on what needed to be done.

Layne dropped the taser into the bag of goodies Joey had assembled and stepped around him before he was able to recover. She left him lying there on the floor as she left to save the person who had always been there to support her in her life.

CHAPTER THIRTY

The fluorescent sign above the building was no longer lit up, but you could still make out the bubbly outline of a bodybuilder next to the dark blue words "Smitty Fitness Center." Layne stared up at the sign with her bag of fun slung across her body.

She had done a quick change of clothes in her car in the designated flat lot across the street into an all black ensemble. If Eric wanted to play his games, she was going to play hers.

Her hand reached into her pocket and pulled out a small piece of black cloth. She slid it over her face, covering the lower half. A familiar emblem was stamped across the front of the fabric, one mimicking Joey's skull-faced mask. The only difference was that this one had orange and green ribbon criss-crossed across the teeth, imitating stitches keeping the mouth shut.

Layne walked around to the side of the building, finding the side entrance already propped open with a dumbbell for her. Undoubtedly, it was Eric's invitation. Well, here went nothing.

She pulled out her favorite baby Glock and stepped foot in the darkness of the abandoned building. The only thing lighting her way was the dim red glow of the EXIT signs.

Quietly, she stepped one foot in front of the other as she kept her hands on her gun in a two-handed grip. Her green orbs darted to the right, then to the left as she looked for anything or anyone that might jump out at her.

As she walked further into the establishment, she felt something underneath her boot. It didn't crunch. No, it was something much softer that gave away under her weight. If she hadn't been on high alert, she wasn't sure she would have noticed it otherwise.

Layne knelt and placed her fingers on the floor where she had just stepped. Locating the object, she picked up the bulb and realized it was the head of a now partially squished rose. The silky texture of the petals between her fingers gave it away as she examined the shape of it.

Eric was being a fuckin' dramatic bastard.

Dropping the floral prop back down to the floor, she stood back up and returned her hand to her weapon as she continued to advance through what appeared to be the cardio section with all of its machines lined up in neat rows.

Her ears perked up as she heard the sound of classical music playing lightly over the gym's speakers. He was definitely being a fuckin' dramatic bastard.

Layne wasn't sure what she should be prepared to see or hear, but she did know that she was mentally prepared to do what needed to be done if she was going to get Rebecca out of there alive. Whatever the cost was going to be, she was prepared to pay it in full with interest.

She had only been inside of Smitty's a few times before, and it was a couple of years ago. Her recollection wasn't particularly spectacular with remembering how this joint was laid out. However, she did remember that it housed many of the standard amenities. It had an indoor pool, an extensive weight room, group fitness studios, and a spin room, in addition to all the typical features of locker rooms, saunas, and tanning beds.

Bang!

A gunshot rang out and shattered the illusion that danger wasn't immediately present. Layne immediately dropped to the floor. The sound of the impact was on the other side of the room, indicating that she hadn't been close to being on the receiving end of it this time around. Deciding not to be a sitting duck, she pushed herself back up onto her feet and burst into a full run.

Bang! Bang!

She flinched, her arms automatically raised and shielded her head as her legs propelled her forth as fast as they could. Layne ran into the first room that she came across. Dashing inside, she immediately crouched behind a corner, trying to silently catch her breath. Tightly, she pressed herself up against the wall, her hands readjusting her grip on the pistol.

Eric's voice came over the speaker from the ceiling, interrupting the background music. "What a good little harpy, you did so well at following directions by coming by yourself. Let's play a little game. If one of my men finds you first, you come along quietly. If you find me first, then you and your friend will be allowed to go on your way."

Layne hated games. She hated them even more when it was clear the odds weren't in her favor.

He spoke up one final time. "Welcome to my playtime." The loudspeaker cut off.

She leaned her head back against the wall and steadied her breath. Quickly, she had to strategize on the fly. The darkness was both an asset and a hindrance, and she needed to take the path he didn't anticipate her to take.

In a barely there whisper, she cursed under her breath. "Fuck me." She needed to commit to a decision and do it quickly.

Finally, she made a move and got back up and moved away from the wall, waiting for a bogeyman to lurch out of the shadows at her. The second she stood up, though, the game's rules suddenly changed. Light after light began flickering on throughout the center. The weight room she was in was no exception.

Eric's voice rang throughout the place once more. "Oh, I did forget to mention that I don't like losing." Of course, he didn't. Lunatics rarely did.

Layne needed to move quickly now that it was likely eyes would quickly be on her. As quietly as she was able to manage, she scurried through the weight room to the door on the far side. With its blocky, rectangular symbol adhered to the front, she knew it had to be the men's locker room.

She pushed the door open silently to be greeted with yet another seemingly empty area. Making each turn carefully, she kept her eyes focused to avoid any surprises. When she made it to the back, past the showers, there was a second doorway with the strong scent of chlorine and other pool chemicals floating in the air surrounding it.

Using her body, she pushed open the door slowly to take a peek into the pool area. The coast was clear from the limited angle she had. Continuing to emerge from the locker room, she nudged the door open a little wider with her shoulder.

The pool itself had taken on a swamp-like green color, presumably from the lack of chemicals being used to maintain it after the center shut down. The surface of the water was eerily still and glasslike.

Suddenly, the door was pulled open on her by an unknown man. Instinctually, she straightened up and rammed the rest of herself into the door to give it enough momentum to smash into his face. He shouted out as he released the door and put both hands over where it connected with his face.

Layne aimed and fired off a shot into his stomach. The acoustics in the pool area seemed to amplify the sound of the shot enough that she may as well have used an air horn to announce her location.

The man who was struck in the stomach by her bullet dropped to the tiled floor, and before his cry of pain could continue, she re-aimed the lethal end of her gun at his forehead and silenced him.

With a heavier set of breaths coming from her, she had less than a few seconds before she heard a pounding echo through the pool area from up high. The muffled yells of her name were shouted. When Layne looked up, there was another floor up where offices overlooked the pool. Behind the large glass windows was Rebecca, with her hands bound together in small fists banging against the glass.

Her friend was suddenly pulled back away from the window, and Eric appeared there with a shit-eating grin etched across his face. In his hand was the receiver of a phone, and his voice came over the speakers once more.

"You're not very good at hiding, little harpy. I'm disappointed."

Layne flipped him off with her non-dominant hand, and her eyes set in a hard glare. Then, she saw three men emerging from various points around the pool.

"If I were you, I'd ditch your toys and let my boys bring you up here to have a chat about what to do with your friend. Alternatively, you can do things the hard way, and I will just have to pass the time up here with Rebecca. I've been telling her all about my favorite room in my house while I've been waiting for you." The way he spoke promised terrible things no matter which path she took.

Layne dropped her duffel to the floor with a light thud. She tossed her gun down on top of it carefully.

"Good girl." The words he spoke didn't have anywhere near the same impact on her as when Joey said them to her.

Though he couldn't see it underneath her mask, a small smirk twitched at the corner of her lips, and the glimmer of rebellion reached her eyes. She had him right where she wanted him: feeling confident.

Two of his crew members came up beside her, each grabbing an arm painfully hard. They led her away from the pool area and took her up a set of stairs right outside the humid room that led to the office one level up. The sole asshole that didn't have his hands on her separated from the group and took up the lead ahead of them. Eric must have been worried if he had four of his men ready to take her on, minus the one she left in a bloody puddle outside the locker room door.

When the office door opened, she immediately scanned the interior of the office. Her escorts filed into the room with her, and the door lightly clicked shut after the last of them. Inside, there were two desks, one wall of large floor-to-ceiling windows overlooking the indoor pool, a television mounted on the wall, some filing cabinets, and a sofa.

The sofa is where Rebecca was seated with Eric next to her, his arm draped across her shoulders like they were old buds. Her hands were in her lap, visibly trembling, while the wrists were secured tightly with duct tape. Her blue eyes were red from tears that had been shed.

Her voice shook as she looked over at Layne. "Layne, I'm sorry…"

Layne shook her head at Rebecca. "Don't worry, you're getting out of here." Her eyes darted to Eric, who had an arrogance wrapped around him.

He reached up to Rebecca's face and took a handful as he squeezed her cheeks in his hand. "She's just as cute as a button, isn't she?"

"Drop the theatrics, Eric. You got me here. Release Rebecca, and we can talk things over." Her voice was emotionless despite the rage running rampant inside of her that he dared to lay a finger on her friend.

He laughed outright and dropped his hold from Rebecca's face before standing up from his seat there on the sofa. Eric approached Layne, stopping directly in front of her, and waved off the two guys with their aggressive grasps on her.

"Theatrics, you say? Let's not throw stones here, Layne." His finger reached up to hook on the top of her mask and lightly began to tug it down. Before it got halfway out of position, she abruptly threw a fist at his smug face.

Her knuckles smashed into his cheek before his men were able to react quickly enough to snatch her back. Unfazed by her attack, Eric grinned as his fingers rubbed his face where she made the connection. "There's the little harpy I know and love. You've got so much fight in you."

He stepped up to her as she pulled against the grasp of the two brutes restraining her. The fires of violence lit up in her eyes. Eric's hand yanked the skull mask the remainder of the way down her face. "It will be so much fun breaking your spirit." Then, his fist thrust harshly into her stomach.

The blunt pain caused her to grunt out and double over. Immediately, a wave of nausea rolled through her, causing her to cough and gasp for air simultaneously.

Eric nodded to his two men as they released their hold and dropped her to the floor. Layne placed a hand on her stomach as she winced. Before she could fully recover, Eric's foot connected with her ribs in a kick that sparked another type of pain as Layne cried out and rolled in on herself. Immediately, she knew he had injured one of her ribs from the sharpness of the pain accompanying each breath.

With her hands hidden underneath her body, she covertly located the previously planted mini switchblade inside the waist of her pants. She encased it in her grasp while she was curled up in the fetal position.

Rebecca shot up from her seat. "Stop it, asshole! Leave her alone!"

One of the three hired hands inside the office shoved Rebecca back down onto the sofa to prevent her from interfering. His gruff voice barked instructions at her. "Shut your cockhole, blondie."

Eric knelt and grabbed a handful of Layne's hair to lift her head so he could look at her face. "Let that be a lesson of what happens when you step out of line. It seems that you didn't learn anything after being left to burn. At first, I was furious that you hadn't perished in the fire. I stood to inherit a pretty penny from the insurance policies you signed."

Through clenched teeth, she struggled to breathe through the pain, including the pain that came with every breath she took. Her eyes met his, reflecting the resilience and stubbornness she was born with. Hell, if he was going to be the one to snuff it out. Layne gritted her teeth and managed to push words out of her mouth. "What the fuck do you want, Eric?"

"Oh, you already know what I want." An amusement dangling on his words before he released his hold on her hair.

She swallowed down a little more pain and nausea and nodded her head. "Okay, I'm all yours. Me and everything that I come with." She propped herself up on one arm while the other hand remained on her stomach. Her eyes met Rebecca's across the room, and then she looked up at Eric. "But she gets out of here unharmed first."

He gave a drawn-out sigh. "Promises, more promises, and all of them fucking lies. That's all I've been getting from you, so how am I supposed to take you at your word now, hm?"

Layne groaned through the pain as she chuckled. Slowly, she pushed herself up onto her feet, wincing but fighting through the pain.

Eric didn't share the same amusement in whatever was going on in Layne's head. "What's so funny?"

"You. You were so desperate to get me here. So desperate that you kidnapped my best friend and went through all of this trouble. I'm the one thing you can't buy, and it pisses you off. You make business deals all the time, yet you can't even close a deal on a real woman." The pain still lingered on her face despite her amusement at the situation.

The flicker of rage on his face as she bruised his ego was paired with an angry snarl, predictably so. She braced herself as he grabbed her by the back of her neck with a painfully tight grip and dragged her over toward the large windows overlooking the pool.

Eric pressed the side of her face up against the glass, her cheek flattening against the smooth surface. The warmth of her breath left a small circle of fog on the glass. Layne braced herself with one of her hands against the window.

Her eyes caught a small detail down below. The bag of goodies she had left at the poolside when Eric's men grabbed her was nowhere to be seen. She suppressed the smile that wanted to pull at her lips.

"Do you remember when we first met? I made it clear that one day, you'd beg for my soft touch." Eric's mouth roughly sucked on her ear and gave it a hard nip before he hissed into it. "I'm going to be cashing in that bet."

His mouth and the words that came out of it made her stomach twist into more knots. "One request?"

Intrigued, Eric tilted his head some. "Hm?"

"At least look me in the eyes like a damn man. I don't beg for cowards."

He spun her around to face him, slamming her back up against the window. His cold eyes looked to penetrate deep into her soul. "That is one request I will grant because I want to see your face as I take you past your thresholds and into a whole new world of pain. The very same world that I thrive in."

Her eyes met his, and she smiled sweetly at him. "I want to see your face, too." *Click.* The switch of the blade in her hand flicked open and then sank into his upper stomach, getting lodged just underneath his ribs.

The look on his face was everything she had hoped it would be as she kept the knife held deeply embedded into his gut. Her green gemstone eyes didn't look away from him, even when the door was nearly knocked from its hinges as it got kicked in.

CHAPTER THIRTY-ONE

With his skull mask drawn over his face, Joey unleashed a flurry of chaos the second he kicked in the door. Layne shoved Eric to collide with one of the men coming to his aide. The two men fell to the floor together.

With two guns drawn, Joey easily dropped one of the other two with a single shot. However, the smarter one of the bunch was already using Rebecca as a shield. He shuffled, keeping his hold steadfast on Rebecca as his insurance that he wouldn't meet death today.

"Rebecca!" Layne stepped forward but stopped when she noticed the man had a shaky grip on a gun against her friend's side. Joey's eyes never left the most critical target, which was the man threatening the innocent young woman.

Eric remained on the ground groaning as the knife remained stuck in his midsection. However, Layne sensed the movement of the one jackass she had knocked Eric into. He made the unfortunate decision to take a run at Layne.

She hunched down, lowering her center of gravity using the man's height against him as he attempted to tackle her. Using his momentum, she deflected his attack, sending him careening into the cheap metal filing cabinet, where his head collided with the sharp corner before dropping motionlessly to the floor.

The maneuver caused her to wince and curse at the harsh reminder of her injured rib that continued to be a bitch and protest rather loudly inside her body.

When she looked back at the situation with Rebecca, Joey was slowly stepping to the side to make sure he maintained enough space to not spook the man into doing something stupid. As the man edged towards the door, seemingly with his ticket out of there, he smiled, feeling more confident.

The man yelled at Joey and her. "I will shoot the bitch if you follow me! Stay back!" Layne didn't doubt that this man was going to make good on his word. He was so on edge; they were lucky he hadn't already pulled the trigger by accident.

"Just be calm." Layne's words were meant for both Rebecca and the man threatening her wellbeing. She came up next to Joey, her hand sliding to the back of his pants, finding an extra firearm there that she helped herself to.

The man backed out of the open door, roughly jerking Rebecca with him out the door. Layne glanced over at Eric lying on the floor, suffering, and then at Joey. He already read the conflict in her eyes between dealing with Eric and saving her friend.

Joey softly spoke to her. "Go get her. I will take care of things here."

Trusting him to do as he said, Layne bolted for the door leading out of the office. Her feet ran down the steps as fast as they could before she lept over the bottom two. The painful thought of losing someone who was closer than a sister outweighed the physical pain of Layne's injuries getting aggravated by her movements.

She set eyes on the man dragging Rebecca away. Layne raised her gun but then realized she didn't have a clean shot. "Damnit!"

Layne ran after them as they quickly moved alongside the pool. She shouted at them to get the guy's attention. "Hey, asshole!"

He turned, and the tiny window of opportunity opened up as he exposed himself and gave Layne just enough of a space to comfortably fire off a round into his head. The impact caused him to fall back into the pool with a ceremonious splash. Simultaneously, the man's falling body pulled Rebecca off balance, and she also fell into the slimy water.

Knowing damn well that Rebecca didn't have use of her hands and had never learned to swim, Layne dropped the gun and dove in after.

Meanwhile, upstairs in the office, it was just Joey and Eric. Joey had Eric up on his feet in front of him with his bicep wrapped around Eric's throat in a tight hold. Joey's hand twisted Layne's knife deeper into the wound she had made.

Roughly, Joey spoke into his ear. "I have been waiting a very long time to snap your fuckin' neck. There is nothing more that I would like to do right now than feel the breakage of your C2." So many violent thoughts of Eric's demise were filling Joey's head. The way this man had thought he had a claim on Joey's woman had him seeing red.

Eric gasped for air as the hold around his throat made receiving oxygen a struggle.

"What was that? I couldn't hear you." Joey gave the knife another push in a new direction. Joey's arm eased up just enough to hear the yell of pain that pulled a pleased smile across his face. He wished he could spend all day up in that office, finding new ways to spread the pain across Eric's body. Despite his wishes, he wasn't going to risk leaving Layne to fend for herself very long.

Panting from the onslaught of pain wracking his body, Eric's strained words were barely audible. "You're no…better than me."

Joey ripped the knife out of Eric's body. "Maybe not, but Layne is. And, I plan to be the man who sees to it that it stays that way." He heard the gunshot from downstairs, and it served as a reminder that he had better places to be than letting Eric take another breath.

Eric coughed, the blood leaking from the corner of his mouth. "She'll never—"

One bloody hand grabbed the back of Eric's skull while his other grabbed his jaw and cut off Eric's words with onc sharp forcc, fracturing a cervical vertebra. He released Eric's body, letting it fall to the floor lifelessly.

"Fucker."

Joey's client be damned, Eric was never going to leave here alive if he had anything to do with it. He stepped over the shitbag's corpse. Quickly, he ran downstairs to track down Layne and, hopefully, an unharmed Rebecca.

The previously still water was now showing signs of being recently disturbed, indicated by the ripples on the surface. A tint of red from the blood seeping from the last of Eric's men swirled unnaturally in the already swampy-looking water.

Layne shoved Rebecca up to the surface as her legs burned under the weight of her kicks to get them both back up for air. Her hand reached up and grasped onto the pool ledge to pull herself up with her other arm around Rebecca's waist to get her above water as well. Rebecca gasped as the air finally greeted her lungs.

Joey ran over and immediately hoisted Rebecca up out of the water to sit her on the floor next to him. She coughed and took several deep breaths for air. After seeing she was okay, he turned his attention to Layne.

With a pained sigh of relief, Layne hooked both her arms on the wall and rested her forehead against them while trying to catch her breath from rescuing her bestie from a watery grave. Layne was the only one here who ever needed to have experienced that.

Each gasp for oxygen prompted a sharp jab from her very pissed off rib.

"Come on, you too." He grabbed Layne, lifted her from the water, and set her on her feet. His hands held onto her face as he stared at her with a light smirk. "What is it with you and water?"

With the water dripping down along her face in tiny rivers, she gave a small laugh followed by a groan as she placed a hand onto her rib. Before Joey could get himself all fussed over it, she shook her head to head him off. "I will be fine."

He pulled his mask down so he could capture her lips with his to help ease some of her pain. It was a small gesture but one he could offer at the moment. When he pulled back, he leaned in and whispered into her ear. "You're going to have a lot of making up to do after that stunt you pulled tasing me earlier." He kissed her temple with a grin.

Rebecca sat up, having recovered enough oxygen to get back to her sassy self. "I hate to break you two up, but I could use a little help here." She raised her bound wrists.

Layne's attention was finally drawn back to Rebecca, helping her onto her feet. "Sorry." A sheepish smile appeared on Layne's face, having nearly gotten lost in Joey's words.

Joey pulled a knife from his pant leg. Taking Rebecca's hands, the tape was quickly severed.

Immediately, Layne tugged Rebecca into a big hug. "I'm so sorry you got pulled into this. It should have never happened."

Rebecca pulled back and looked at Layne with her stern mama bear face. "Stop that. Don't you dare apologize for something a mentally unstable creep did."

Layne's mouth pulled down into a frown, still letting her guilt weigh on her.

"You know what you can apologize for?" Rebecca eyed up her best friend.

Layne raised both of her brows, wondering what else she was going to bring up in the moment.

Rebecca motioned over at Joey. "Not introducing tall, dark, and handsome over here. How the hell can I do my obligatory best friend due diligence if you keep these things to yourself?" She gave a little wink to Layne.

The light tease chased away some of the guilt as she glanced over at Joey. "Rebecca, this is Joey—*the guy*. Joey, Rebecca." Her hand motioned at each of them.

Rebecca scanned Joey with a suspicious eye. "Oh, so you're the one? Hm. Well, just know that the jury is still out on you."

Joey grinned at how much spunk Rebecca had. He shouldn't have been surprised, given anyone lucky enough to have Layne in their life needed to have a bit of a spark.

Before Rebecca could give Joey the third degree, Layne looked at them both. "We should get the hell out of here."

Nobody argued with that plan of action. While they were walking out, Layne looked over at Joey as a question nagged at her. "How did you know where I was?"

He smirked. "I can't give away all my secrets. Although," he reached over to take a look at the soaked mask down around her neck, "it looks like I'm not the only one keeping secrets."

After getting Rebecca back home safely, Layne met Joey back at O'Reilly Manor. She parked her car out front. The Beamer had been the one thing that had been spared from the fire, all thanks to the inability of people to read a damn sign that said not to block the driveway.

Layne turned off the engine and sighed as she leaned back in her seat. It had been a hell of a night. She tried to summon what little energy she had left to get out of the car.

One final sigh, and she opened the car door. That's when she remembered that Rebecca had written down the name of a doctor who could squeeze her in for a quick look at her rib. Layne had insisted that a doctor wasn't necessary, but Rebecca threatened to never make her famous berry oatmeal bake for her again if she didn't agree.

She opened up her console and saw the note sitting right on top. However, something else caught her eye. Layne had completely forgotten that she had left the blue envelope she had found in her dad's paperwork in her car. She reached in and pulled it out to take inside with her.

Joey was already waiting for her when she walked in the door, though she still had her eyes focused on the envelope in her hands with her name written across it. She opened it up and unfolded the papers inside. Her eyes looked over the contents with the expectation that it would be nothing important.

When Joey saw her jaw drop and her expression go wide-eyed, he walked over to her side to see what she was looking at. "What is it?" His eyes scanned over what she was staring at on the first page before he muttered. "Holy shit."

CHAPTER THIRTY-TWO

To Layne's surprise, it had taken much longer for the NYPD to be alerted that there were decomposing bodies inside Smitty's Fitness Center. Apparently, no one had been checking on the abandoned property on any sort of regular interval.

There was a pitiful investigation done by the police. After the realization that Eric Ellis had been a major player in the underground sex trafficking world thanks to an anonymous tip from someone by the name of Cowboy, there was little public outrage to look into what transpired inside the gym that night. It was assumed that the dangerous criminals of the world took out the trash living in their own backyard. They weren't entirely wrong.

Layne had been more than happy to celebrate her status as Eric's not-so-grieving widow. Particularly since it turned out that the insurance policies and his assets went to her by default. She bet he had never expected that one. Needless to say, finances were looking up for the O'Reilly organization.

As for the documents left for Layne by her father? Layne and Joey decided to keep that to themselves for now. There was no sense in rocking the boat…yet.

Several months had passed, and on this particular night, Joey stepped inside O'Reilly Manor at nearly three in the morning. He shrugged his jacket off and hung it up in the coat closet right near the front entrance.

In what should have been a minor job that night, it had taken longer than expected. The house was expectedly cast into pitch darkness, indicating that Layne was already in bed fast asleep.

Quietly, he made his way upstairs and to the master bedroom. Pushing the door open, it only gave the slightest of creaks while swinging on its hinges. He walked over to the bed they had been sharing nearly every night for the past couple of months.

His hands reached behind him, grabbed the back of his shirt, and pulled it up over his head, exposing the muscled physique underneath that was home to all the tattoos he had. Joey walked over to her side of the king-sized bed to check on her before he planned to hop in the shower to get cleaned up.

As he reached out to feel for Layne, his hand felt nothing but the cold sheets. His hand patted the mattress, finding no one was there in the bed. Sighing, he hoped she hadn't fallen asleep in the office again. He had carried her upstairs to bed on several occasions as a result of her spending hours diving into figuring out damage control of the failing criminal empire bearing the O'Reilly name.

Joey headed back downstairs to check the office. A glimmer of light was shining from underneath the door. When he walked inside, he was surprised not to find her asleep on the desk with her head on top of the keyboard.

As he approached the desk, a small but powerful body rammed into his back, knocking him forward unexpectedly. Slender arms wrapped around his throat, and bare legs around his waist. Fortunately, he was easily able to upright himself. The arms around his neck squeezed threateningly, and a sultry and demanding voice whispered into his ear.

"It's just you and me now, handsome. I'm only going to ask my questions once, and you're going to be a good boy and answer them."

He inhaled the familiar scent of daisies after a rainstorm. His hands grasped onto Layne's legs, wrapped around him as he smirked. "Is that right?"

"Mmhmm." She responded as her hand spread out and ran over several of the tattoos covering the front of his chest. "Where were you tonight?"

He tensed at the question before he walked over to the desk with her still clinging to his back like a little monkey. "I told you I had a job to wrap up."

She slid down off of him, placing her feet firmly on the floor. Layne's hands spun him around to face her. "That's not what I heard."

Joey looked down at the sight before him, his eyes lighting up in excitement at what he saw. Layne stood there wearing a pair of black panties with a matching bralette. Her long locks of chestnut hair hung down freely in loose waves around her shoulders. However, it was the dark and twisted mask stretched across her face with the green and orange threads crisscrossed over the skull teeth that sealed the deal on his cock quickly jumping to full attention in his pants.

"Doing a little stalking of your own?" He lifted a brow at her curiously.

Layne nudged him back until he voluntarily sat on the edge of the desk. Her hands grabbed his knees and pushed his legs apart so she could stand between them. "I believe I asked you a question. Are you making me ask twice?"

A grin stretched across his face in amusement at being on the receiving end of inquiries that were typically his. "No, I wouldn't want to do that." His hand reached out and tugged that black mask down over her face to expose her full and currently pouty lips. "You want to know where I was?" His thumb traced over her bottom lip slowly.

She gave a small nod in response.

He moved his hand up to slide over the side of her face until his fingers wrapped around the back of her neck while his thumb stroked over her cheek softly. "Seeing someone about a deal I made."

That answer didn't quite satisfy her if the look in her eyes was any indication.

He pulled her head in closer as his lips met with hers. Joey's mouth lovingly claimed her mouth slowly and sensually to ease whatever unfounded concerns she had. When he relinquished his sweet hold on her and drew back, he presented her with what was in his other hand. In the center of his palm was a small black box made of satin.

Layne went still as she saw what was in his hand. Her eyes stared at the closed box for a few seconds and then darted back up to look at his face, seeing his eyes set on her.

"I have never wanted anyone the way that I want you. Since the night I first saw you sitting inside McGregor's, I was immediately hooked. There are days you drive me fuckin' insane, but those are the days where I want to be your everything the most. I don't care what battles we have to face, but we will be the storm that everyone should prepare for. I love you, and I would die a thousand painful deaths for you."

He pulled open the box, revealing an eye-catching, thin platinum band with a sparkling oval diamond at the center, surrounded by a black rhodium-plated collar with black diamonds. A small emerald to match her eyes was set at both the top and the bottom of the diamond in the middle. "Will you marry me?"

Layne stood there, not even looking at the uniquely gorgeous ring but looking at his face in shock.

"Don't make me ask twice, Layney." He did his best to mask the slight uptick of anxiousness in his voice.

Her bottom lip trembled slightly, followed by a large smile as she threw herself up against him. Layne's lips crashed onto his as she devoured the taste of his mouth. Her response came out between several kisses. "Yes!" *Kiss*. "I love you." *Kiss*. "Yes."

A wave of relief washed over him as he welcomed her onslaught of affection and returned it with his own. His tongue slid its way into her mouth as he savored all of her taste. After several moments of their lips wrangling together, Joey pulled back with a smile. "Let's get this ring on you before another guy thinks he can take a shot at what's mine."

After removing the ring from the box, he lifted her hand to slide the small piece of metal onto her finger. "There, a perfect fit."

Layne smirked playfully at him. "Much like something else." Her hands dropped to the belt on his pants. Her fingers unlatched his belt and yanked. It slid from the belt loops with the tail whipping around until it was freed. She dropped it down to the floor.

That's when Joey possessively wrapped an arm around her waist as he got up off the desk. With a single arm around her, he lifted her and turned to have her take his place on top of the desk where he had just been seated. His hand took hold of her chin while grazing her lips with his mouth as he spoke in the low and husky tone that always set her insides on fire. "Be a good girl and spread those legs for me."

Her breath caught in her throat as he gave that demand. Layne's lips parted slightly as she did as she was told. "I need you." The words barely came out above a whisper.

Joey shoved his dark cargo pants down, taking his boxer briefs with them. Unleashed was his large, hard cock, ready to go. His smirk was full of dark desires and promises. "You're going to get me." He stepped up to her while his hand gripped and twisted the bralette in his fist. "Every damn day."

Before her gasp could fully be released from her mouth, he pulled her forward by the flimsy lace containing her breasts. A searing kiss locked onto her, and his hands pawed at her chest, sliding the straps of the bralette over her shoulders and the remainder of it to her waist.

Layne feverishly returned his kisses, imagining their life together. In a rush of anticipation and excitement, she shoved the lace undergarments off her body. Her mask was pulled off from around her neck and tossed to the ground.

He lowered himself to capture one of her feet in his hands and began sowing a garden of kisses leading up the length of her leg. Layne leaned back on her hands while sitting there on the desk as his mouth worked its way closer to her core.

When his mouth finally made it to the top of her leg, he licked a long line along her inner thigh. She whimpered as he edged closer to where she needed him. Layne needed to feel his mouth consuming her arousal like it was the damn fountain of life.

The strength of Joey's hands pushed her thighs even wider as he licked his lips. "You better hold on tight, Layney. I'm going to fill myself up on the taste of you."

That was all the warning she got before he was burying his face against her pussy. Layne immediately surrendered to the pleasure he brought her. Her hands knocked several items off the desk as her body reacted to his mouth.

His mouth brought her over the edge into sexual bliss several times before he pulled her off the desk. Layne's head was delightfully clouded with pleasure as she smiled at him. "Somebody has an appetite tonight."

Joey gave her a smirk. "Only for you." He carried her over to a chair, where he took a seat with her in his lap.

With his cock teasing at the opening of her sex, Layne leaned in and kissed her way over the shadow of facial hair along his jaw until she reached his ear. "You should hold on; you're not the only one who is going to get their fill tonight." She lowered her body down onto him. Her hands held onto the sides of his body, one of her hands covering up the 'Chaos Addict' script tattooed along his ribs.

His hands landed on her waist as he groaned in approval of the way her pussy took him in. He looked into her eyes, getting lost in them as she began to move her hips to ride his cock.

The two of them tangled themselves up in carnal pursuits there in the office until the sun began to filter in through the windows, and they ended up together on the floor. Both of their bodies were covered with a mix of sweat and arousal.

Joey lay there with his arms wrapped around her, staring up at her face as she lay on top of his chest. "You'll always be mine, forever."

Layne stared down into the face of the one man who had gotten past the walls surrounding her heart; she smiled happily. "You'll always have me, forever."

EPILOGUE

When Layne walked into Cassidy's Cave, the upbeat music was pulsing throughout the entire strip club. The place was packed with primarily male patrons looking to get their dicks hard by watching a bunch of girls remove one article of clothing at a time while flashing smiles of fake interest.

In the dimly lit space, several small stages cluttered the floor; the main stage was at the back, and two birdcage-style platforms hung from the ceiling. Glitter was everywhere. It looked like there had been a reverse harem of unicorns that had all jacked off all over the joint.

Joey was at her back, scanning the room for any sign of Liam. His hand rested on the small of her back to confirm his presence there with her after not getting past the doorman nearly as easily as Layne had with a flash of her pretty smile.

It didn't take long to pinpoint Liam's location. He was making a spectacle of himself over at a VIP table surrounded by no less than four women who were employees of this establishment, evidenced by their lack of clothing. Easily, Liam had probably dropped a head-spinning amount of money on this night out.

Liam stood up with his shot glass in the air and yelled. "Shots on me!"

Layne groaned. "For fucks sake." She didn't want to deal with this, but she was going to have to. If not her, who else?

Joey leaned down and spoke into her ear. "Can I just take him out back and give him a dose of reality?"

She tried not to let the smile fully tug at the corners of her mouth at the thought. As tempting as the offer was, she knew that this was going to require more finesse and less brute force. After shaking her head to decline Joey's request, she walked through the crowd, avoiding men tripping over themselves to get a better view of their visual entertainment.

Her brother leaned over and wrapped an arm around one of the girls, planting an aggressive kiss on the side of her face before whispering something into her ear.

Layne had been told by one of her associates that he had been here since they opened up six hours ago. Based on his noticeable level of intoxication and disheveled appearance, she fully believed it. His shirt was half untucked from the waist of his pants, and the top few buttons were left undone enough to bare his pale chest in front of all his monetarily compensated admirers.

When Layne got to the table, she began picking off one girl at a time while Joey stood back and didn't get in her way like the smart man he was. He leaned against the wall with his arms crossed in front of his chest while he casually observed. Joey still wished Layne had let him knock some sense into her brother. The night was still young, though, so perhaps there was still a chance.

Liam was too busy guiding one of the dancer's hands onto the crotch of his pants when he finally noticed Layne physically moving one of his admirers from the table to make a path closer to him.

"Well, look who it is! Come to join me in the celebration?" He lifted a half-empty bottle of vodka that was easily worth a grand.

"Li, you've done enough celebrating for the entire club. Let's go." She motioned with her hand for him to stand up.

"Don't be such a stuck-up bitch. Our business is on the way to being back on fuckin' top!" He tugged the girl to his right, closer to his side. "Right, baby?" His drunken stupor caused him to forget that Layne was standing right there trying to have a conversation with him as he began to make out with the girl hanging onto his arm.

The only thing that would make this situation worse is if Kristill were here to curse him out and cause an even bigger scene. Thank God for small favors from the universe that she wasn't here.

Layne's hand grabbed the girl's arm and pulled her up to her feet.

"Here, take this." She shoved a hundred-dollar bill into her hand and shooed her away.

Predictably, Liam had an angry outburst like the manchild he was. "What is your goddamn problem, Layne?!"

Tiredly, she sighed. "I'm not doing this here with you, Liam. Let's go outside and deal with this."

"You're not the damn boss of this family." Liam snorted at the ridiculous thought of it.

It was clear this was going to be a battle. Layne attempted to soften her tone. "That's what we need to talk about."

He shook his head, not seeing that there was anything to discuss.

She was losing the little patience she had for his bullshit. "Liam, get the fuck up. *Now.*"

"What the fuck ever." He pulled his wallet out and dumped a wad of cash on the table amongst the various shot glasses and empty bottles.

Layne looked over at Joey. "Watch him while I close things out here and make sure he doesn't do anything stupid." The last thing she needed was ill will towards the O'Reilly name now that a new era was on the horizon.

She looked at Liam and gave him a stern look. "Stay here, keep your mouth shut, and your hands to yourself, or so help me, Li, I will call every club in the five boroughs and have them blacklist you for life."

She turned and walked away to go to the bar to speak with the owner to make sure she smoothed things over for any troubles Liam may have gotten himself into. Layne pulled out a credit card to cover any of the miscellaneous charges and idly tapped it against the bar top while she waited.

"You were looking for the owner?" The steamy and smooth voice came from behind her. When she turned, she was met with a man who looked to be in his early thirties, far younger than she would have expected for a strip club owner. Not to mention, he had these light brown eyes that were like freshly melted milk chocolate that could lure you in with as much of a wink.

Layne lifted an eyebrow, not hiding her surprise that this guy wasn't who she was expecting. Most strip club owners she had met were sleazy and creepy old men. No, not this one. He was dressed semi-casually, with a white dress shirt with the sleeves rolled up to his elbows, exposing the cords of his muscular forearms, and a pair of lightly distressed jeans. It was hard to tell with the lighting and the gel in his hair, but he looked to be an ashy shade of blond.

He extended a hand out to her, the top of his hand was inked up with tattooed letters that spelled out 'WRATH' across the tops of his knuckles. "Name's Gage."

She gave a light smile as she took his hand and gave it a quick shake. "Layne. Look, my jackass brother had a table over there," she motioned in the direction of the table that his back was to, "and I don't know what type of trouble he's caused tonight, so I just wanted to make sure I clear everything out."

Without even turning to look at the table she referenced, he responded quickly. "It's taken care of." He grinned at her.

Tilting her head in confusion at him, he continued. "He's lucky to have a sister that cares enough to help him out. Loyal siblings are a rarity. Besides, it means I got the pleasure of meeting you." A charming smile spread across his face.

She grinned and shook her head at how thick he was laying it on her. "Thanks, but I don't like owing favors." Favors were very dangerous things.

Gage leaned over and whispered to her. "I won't tell if you won't."

That's when Joey came up to Layne's side. "Liam is in the parking lot puking his brains out. So help me, if he pukes in my car, I'm going to make him lick it all up." The irritation was weighing in hard on his voice.

Joey glanced over at the man Layne had been speaking with and went as still as the dead. Tension locking in across his body. His cocoa-brown eyes swiftly shifted as he hardened his gaze.

A large smile came over Gage's face, accompanied by a chuckle of amusement. "Look who it is. After all these years and all the places, I didn't expect to run into my big brother tonight."

Stay Tuned for ***Incoming Layne Shift***

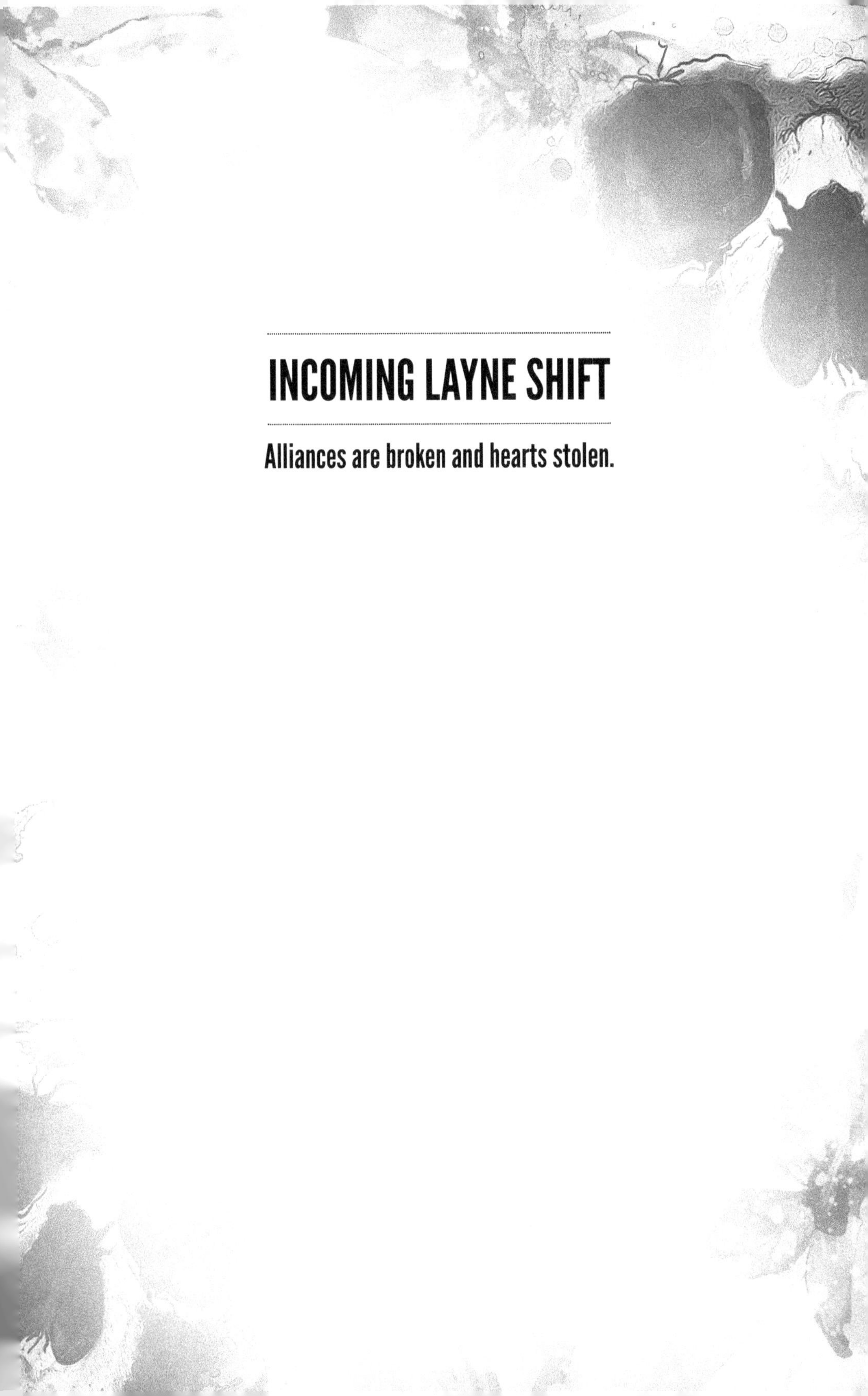

INCOMING LAYNE SHIFT

Alliances are broken and hearts stolen.

To any man who has gone through the process of tattooing his cock…
I learned some things writing this book.

Thank you for jacking up my Google search history.

OFFICIAL PLAYLIST

Below The Belt (ft. Set It Off) - Point North
Body Bag - I Prevail
Brand New Numb - Motionless In White
CONCRETE JUNGLE - Bad Omens
Dirty Thoughts - Chloe Adams
Fire Up the Night - New Medicine
Iris - DIAMANTE, Breaking Benjamin
Kiss from a Rose (ft. Kayla King) - No Resolve
Legends Never Die - Halocene
Punching Bag - Set It Off
Royalty - Egzod, Maestro Chives, Neoni
Song #3 - Stone Sour

EPILOGUE

Wherever You Will Go - The Calling
Your Guardian Angel - The Red Jumpsuit Apparatus

The official playlist can be found on Spotify.

CONTENT & TRIGGER WARNINGS

All trigger and content warnings can be found on www.sadiewinchester.com.

CHAPTER ONE

Continued from Layne Closure Ahead

A large smile came over Gage's face, accompanied by a chuckle of amusement. "Look who it is. After all these years and all the places, I didn't expect to run into my big brother tonight."

Joey's back was straighter than a steel rod, and his chest puffed out defensively. His arm reached out and possessively guided Layne a step behind him as his eyes remained on Gage.

Layne stared at the two men, *two De Luca men*, in her presence. Once Gage dropped the bomb that Joey was his brother, she couldn't unsee it. Their eyes had the same warm brown hues. Their facial structures held similarities that one often would expect between siblings. Both had darker shades of blonde hair. Shit, even both of them had a charm that rolled off of their smiles with ease.

Her eyes darted between them both in shock as she noticed Joey's reaction didn't give off any warm and fuzzy vibes. He never told her that he had a brother, when speaking about his childhood, it had always sounded as though he was an only child. Not once did he mention having any siblings. The way he was looking at Gage right now gave her the impression he had wished that was the case.

"Layne," Joey calmly spoke, "go wait in the car."

She blinked several times. "I'm not—"

Joey cut her off, "I'm not fuckin' asking twice." His words didn't have the usual playfulness to them, causing her to flinch at the harsher tone.

Gage attempted to lighten up the tension in the air between them. "She's welcome to stay, and we can have a few drinks together." He made the mistake of reaching out for Layne's arm.

Without so much as the blink of an eye, Joey snatched up two handfuls of Gage's crisp white shirt and forcefully shoved him. "You don't get to fuckin' touch her!" He released his hold after the strong push of his little brother, which resulted in Gage stumbling back several steps.

Regaining his footing, Gage lifted his hands harmlessly with a smirk. "I didn't mean anything by it. Relax." He chuckled, entertained by Joey's overreaction. His gaze shifted back to Layne, who stood there bewildered and unaware of the history between them. He gave her a sly wink.

Whether or not he knew the subtle move would push Joey's buttons wasn't obvious. What was clear was that Joey wasn't going to put up with it. Years of pent-up rage rumbled to the surface. He lunged at Gage, colliding with him, and they both crashed into a nearby table. A few scantily clad girls shrieked in response to the fight breaking out between the two men.

Upon impact with the table, drinks immediately spilled everywhere while Joey and Gage wrestled with one another. After they both rolled off the table and hit the ground, both of them had a fistful of each other's shirts as punches were thrown.

Both men appeared to be evenly matched with one another. Neither of them were gaining the upper hand in the scuffle. Layne stood back, unsure of how or if she should intervene. If Joey's life appeared to be in danger, she wouldn't have hesitated, but this looked more like brothers hashing out their issues.

The rest of Cassidy's Cave occupants seemed to ignore the battle between the two, rolling around on the floor as if this was nothing but a typical brawl at the club.

Joey rolled on top of Gage, pinning him down as he drew back his fist decorated with the skull tattoo. Seizing the opportunity, Layne grabbed his arm with both of her hands, knowing she needed to if she was going to have a chance of putting an end to this.

"Stop, Joey!" Her fingers dug into his arm, pulling back on it to avoid it continuing its path downwards towards Gage's jaw.

Luckily, he had enough awareness of Layne's presence to not lash out at her as well. Feeling her tug on him again, his heated glare remained on his brother but gave in to her insistence to put an end to the altercation.

He got up off Gage, speaking between clenched teeth, "I don't want to ever see your face ever again." Joey slid his arm from Layne's grasp forcefully. His bloodied hand from his split knuckles dropped to snatch a tight hold of her hand.

The younger De Luca partially sat up on an elbow and used his thumb to wipe away a small stream of blood coming from the corner of his mouth as he watched the two of them. Well, it was more along the lines of watching Layne's ass in those skintight jeans she had on. Fuck, that perfect ass practically had his name on it.

Breathing heavily while recovering from the skirmish, Joey tugged Layne along with him on his way out of the strip club. Her steps were doubled up to keep up with his long strides. She looked over at his face, the tension still pulling at his expression in hard lines.

Once they were all in the Challenger, with Liam drunkenly passed the hell out in the backseat, the silence was damn near suffocating.

Unable to take it anymore, Layne spoke, "Joey, you never told me you had—"

His eyes never leaving the road ahead of them, he stopped her right there. "We're not talking about this." The topic of his brother was immediately off-limits.

Both of her brows lifted in surprise that he thought his statement was going to prevent this discussion from happening. It may have put a halt to it for now, but that was only because they had just pulled up in front of Liam's studio located on the outskirts of Tribeca.

Layne sighed irritably and got out of the passenger seat. She pushed her seat forward and leaned in the back, giving Liam a jab to his arm. "Wake up, jackass."

A sharp snortle came from Liam as he shifted his position in the back. She wrinkled up her nose, and her fist pounded into his bicep once more, this time harder. There may have been a little of her own frustration behind that second hit.

His hazel eyes half-lifted open as he glanced around, grumbling at the inconvenience.

She shook her head and stepped back from the open door. "We're here. Go drink some water and put your ass to bed."

Liam's hand rubbed over his auburn hair, which was already thoroughly disheveled as he tried to shake off enough of the intoxicated slumber to get himself out of the backseat.

Once she saw him get inside the upscale residential building, Layne got back into the car. Her fingers massaged over her forehead, recalling how this evening hadn't gone as planned. From the call about Liam going on a rager at the adult entertainment venue to the drama between Joey and his brother, which Layne never knew he had.

With dread filling her voice, she spoke, "I'm going to have to tell him soon." It was clear that she wasn't looking forward to hashing out more shit with Liam.

Joey scoffed and sarcastically replied, "I'm sure he's going to take it *so* well." He pulled away from the curb to begin driving them back to their home—O'Reilly Manor.

Her green eyes stared over at him. "About as well as you took having a conversation with *your* brother?" She didn't hide the annoyance over his decision to conceal Gage's existence from her. Their late-night conversations had been filled with talks about everything and anything, and he had failed to mention something as simple as having a sibling. It had old feelings of distrust whispering in the back of her brain.

Joey's hand readjusted its grasp on the steering wheel, holding it a little tighter. "Just drop it, Layne."

When did she ever just drop things because she was told to? "No."

Before he got the opportunity to make some comment about him asking twice, she continued, "Don't even start that crap with me, Joey. What the hell was that back there at the club?!"

He reached over and finally decided that he was done with silence and turned the volume knob up to blare the music to avoid any actual conversation between them. The heavy rock tunes filled the car.

While driving back uptown, Joey fought through each of the painful memories at war inside of his head from nearly ten years ago.

Rosie giggled as she ran her hands across the smooth and unmarked skin of Joey's bare chest while he stood there in just his jeans. "You're being so bad! Gage is going to be home any minute."

He gave a devious smirk. "So? Let him see who really knows how to get your pussy wet." His hands continued their descent over her body towards her little white shorts.

Joey leaned in, whispering into the hot, young blonde's ear. "Nothing is going to stop me from giving you the hard fuck you deserve, Rose. Gage is going to have to learn how to share."

He gave a hard blink at the thoughts creeping up of what led up to a horrific day that had been burned forever into his skull. His jaw clenched even tighter, still recalling each detail of Rosie's sun-kissed skin and the sound of her voice when she tried to sound serious but instead sounded as threatening as a kitten mewing.

Out of the corner of his vision, he snuck a glimpse of Layne. She sat there with her arms crossed in front of her chest, watching out the window as each street passed. The street lights flashed across her fair skin as each one passed, reflecting the blank expression she wore when she tightened the screws on her temper. He knew that look on her face too well. She was pissed, and he couldn't blame her.

When they got back home, Layne went inside ahead of him. She didn't bother to wait for him to follow behind her.

After he locked up the front door, Joey found her inside the kitchen with a cold beer in her hand. The way her lips connected with the opening of the bottle, he thought about all the other ways those plump lips could be put to better use.

Layne fully avoided eye contact with him as she leaned back against the counter and took another sip of the hoppy pale ale. Her tongue slipped forth and ran over her lips afterward to collect any remaining beer on them.

Joey stepped up in front of her, caging her in place as he set his hands on the counter on either side of her. His eyes had a soft burn to them as he peered down at her. "I'm sorry."

Refusing to look at him to help maintain her resolve, she shook her head. "No, you're not. You're thinking about getting your dick blown."

He sighed but didn't argue her assumption that had been right on point.

She pushed away from the counter, but when he didn't move his arms, she pushed against them. Instead of allowing her to pass, he slid an arm around her waist, drawing her up against him.

Joey's hand eased the beer from her hand, bringing it to his mouth and chugging it down. Leaving the now-empty bottle on the counter behind her, he took her face by the jaw to look at him.

"And you're thinking about blowing it." A smirk eased over his face as he soaked in the way she made her irritation look irresistible.

Her insides were beginning to melt as she was forced to meet his eyes. "You're not getting out of this so easily."

Gently, his hand turned her head to expose the line of her neck. Joey leaned over, bringing his mouth up against her fair skin. The short and bristly hairs of his stubble scratched at her as his lips worked over the sensitive flesh, kissing and sucking at it. His teeth pressed into the skin, applying a moderate but brief amount of pressure.

Layne exhaled a light moan as he worked his magic against her neck. Her hands came up to his chest, digging her fingers into the soft cotton of his tee. "I mean it, Joey." Her words had lost their edge to them as her eyes fluttered closed momentarily while his tongue grazed along her throat.

He released her jaw so he could grab her hand and bring it up against the zipper of his pants to feel the strain his hard cock was putting on it. "You can mean it all you like, Layney. Hell, you can even be pissed, but you're going to take my cum down your throat like a good girl."

The heat of her anger was spreading elsewhere and forming a desire between her legs. Her hand rubbed over the bulge pushing against the front of his pants.

She pushed him back against the pantry door behind him with her other hand. Layne's eyes locked onto his own with a steamy gaze. Her hand roughly jerked on his pants as she tugged them open. She may have been pissed, but she was going to seize this opportunity.

After her petite hand retrieved his throbbing cock from his dark boxer briefs, she dropped down onto her knees in front of him. His hands immediately came down to bury themselves in her silky hair. Her long, dark locks draped over the various lines of the tattoos and dried blood across his fingers.

Now at eye-level with his member, she could see the precum glistening as it spilled over the head of his cock. Her tongue snaked out and licked away the clear liquid from him in one smooth motion. "You better hope that I choke on your cock and forget that you owe me an explanation."

Feeling the velvety stroke of her tongue against his head, he groaned, "Fuck." His grasp on her head tightened. "Suck my cock with that mouth of yours, and we can talk afterward."

Noticing a slip in his initial stance on having a discussion, she grinned and pulled his length into her mouth. Sucking on him roughly, she didn't waste time drawing him back farther towards her throat. Her head slid back and forth against him eagerly.

He moaned out above her as he watched himself disappear into her mouth. "Christ, Layney, slow down. I want time to enjoy this."

If she didn't have a mouthful of him, she would have smirked, but instead, she hummed against him, causing his body to tense up from another spark of pleasure. She continued at a swift pace as her mouth worked around every inch of him.

Joey's hands attempted to slow her down, but each attempt was met by her tongue dancing along the bottom of his cock and effectively distracting his efforts.

Her oral skills were sending him quickly into overdrive, his moans growing more intense. The buildup of pressure of his arousal was quickly nearing its breaking point. "Layne, ugh. Take it easy…"

When he told her to ease up on him, that's when her hand cupped his balls in the palm of her hand and gave him the money look. Her vibrant green eyes peered up at him through her thick eyelashes as she remained kneeling in front of him.

Seeing her staring up at him like he had the only dick in the world she could ever want, he whimpered right before he exploded. His hips pushed forward, shoving his cock deeper into her throat as thick ropes of seed erupted. Joey released a loud groan while he continued to spasm inside her mouth.

Layne swallowed each mouthful as he came for her. She felt a sense of pride and satisfaction in her efforts. If he had been a good boy and took the time to have the conversation with her about Gage, she may have drawn out the way her mouth sucked him.

Once the tension eased in his body, she pulled her mouth away and got back onto her feet with her swollen lips in a victorious smile.

She used her fingertips to wipe away a few drops of his seed and her saliva from the edges of her mouth, sucking her fingers clean afterward. "Now, are you going to tell me what the deal is with your brother?"

CHAPTER TWO

Post-blowjob version of Joey was a little more at ease. But still, he stood there staring at Layne as he tried to find the words to respond to her tireless crusade to find out more about Gage.

He tucked his half-hard cock back into his pants, closing up shop with a zip and slip of the button.

"Well?" She pressed him again for a response.

His hand rubbed the back of his neck before he gave a robust exhale. "It's a long story, Layne. Just take my word for it that we're both better off never seeing him again."

She rolled her eyes at him, unsatisfied with his response.

If he didn't want to be exiled to sleeping in Layne's childhood bedroom surrounded by pink frills tonight, he realized that he needed to do better. "Alright." He dropped his hand from its hold on the back of his neck.

"Gage and I had a falling out about ten years ago. One thing led to another, and people got hurt." It was the short and not-so-dirty version of what happened. He stepped closer to her, his hands rubbing over her arms reassuringly. "I just don't want history to repeat itself."

Layne pursed her lips together at the thought of how his so-called long story managed to be summed up in a few sentences. Her eyes searched his face, finding small traces of pain lingering beneath the surface of his coffee-colored eyes.

Dropping the tension in her shoulders slightly, she closed the distance between them with another step. Her arms wrapped around his waist as she looked up at him. "How can you expect history not to repeat itself if you don't tell me what to look out for?"

Joey's hands gave both of her upper arms a light squeeze. "As long as he stays the fuck away, it won't repeat itself."

"With everything that's about to change in our lives, I can't have you keeping things from me. You keep telling me you're all in, but you won't tell me what happened a decade ago?" Now, her tone was shifting to reflect some of the hurt she was feeling from him not trusting her with whatever it was that had him avoiding a few simple questions.

His mouth found her forehead, planting a delicate kiss. He hated that she was feeling any sort of way about the trust they had rebuilt between themselves. It had not been an easy road to pave. Layne had worked so hard on herself to allow him inside her heart again, and he didn't want to shatter it all again. If he did, he wasn't sure that she would ever come back from it. Truth be told, he wasn't sure he would either.

"An innocent girl died," he tried to keep his voice even and emotions withheld. "A woman, actually," he clarified. "Her name was Rose." Rosie had been twenty-three, Gage twenty-two, and Joey had just celebrated his thirtieth birthday.

He stood there trying to find the words to explain how this all went down, struggling to disconnect emotionally enough to explain.

Gage punched a hole in the bedroom wall. "What the fuck, Rose?!"

"Babe, please, just listen." Rosie implored as she pulled her shirt down over her perky and naked breasts. Her hands tugged her white shorts up her thighs. She frowned as she walked over to him after fastening the button at her waist.

Joey sat there in Gage's bed, leaning back against the headboard with an arm tucked behind his head, not even making an effort to get up.

Rosie frowned as she took Gage's hand, squeezing it tightly before raising it to her light pink lips to lay several tender kisses on his unpainted knuckles. "We talked about this, remember? Keeping things open, an open commitment."

While Rosie was looking at Gage, he was looking over at Joey, who was failing at suppressing his shit-eating grin.

"I didn't expect you to turn around and just drop your pants and bend over for him*!" Gage gritted his teeth while he gave a deadly glare at his brother.*

"Gage," Joey finally spoke up, "don't be mad that she has good taste." He smirked at the additional thought of how sweet her cum had been on his tongue.

A small rumble emanated from Gage, his fists clenching at his sides as he made a step toward the bed where Joey so casually sat with a sheet just barely covering his lap.

Rosie sidestepped in front of him, both hands resting on top of Gage's chest as she looked up at him pleadingly. "There's enough of me for both of you."

With Gage's light brown eyes staring his older brother down, he shook his head. "You just love stirring up chaos, don't you? You're fucking addicted to it."

When Joey returned from the silence of his thoughts, his eyes were met with Layne's concerned expression while they both stood there in the kitchen of O'Reilly Manor. He couldn't put into words the memories that had just crossed his mind.

"It was a business deal gone bad. Gage takes risks he shouldn't. The odds could be stacked against him a thousand-to-one, and he would still think he has a shot. He doesn't think about what the hell happens when the other guy doesn't give a damn about the odds."

He shook his head, already feeling the simmer of fury starting up in his blood as the sequence of events unfolded in his brain.

"You're up." Joey hooked his thumb in the direction of the bathroom, still warm from the steam lingering after his shower. A towel was wrapped around his waist, and droplets of water still scattered over his freshly bathed skin.

Gage nuzzled up against Rosie's side while they lay there in the king-sized bed that barely fit all three of them. "Are you sure you're not going to join me?"

She gave the sweetest of laughs. "You both have left me barely able to use my legs after all that. All I want to do is stay here and take a nice long nap." Rose smiled and leaned over to lovingly kiss Gage. "Go clean up. I'll be right here when you get done."

Joey tossed his damp towel over the arm of a chair and snagged a pair of underwear, quickly pulling them on to avoid the chill of the air.

As for Gage, he smiled at the beautiful blonde before him and nodded. "Okay, but not before I get you some water and something to snack on. Can't have our girl not getting the care she needs to recover." He pushed the sheets off his lower body and rolled out of bed.

Gage yanked on a pair of boxers and left the bedroom to go retrieve water and some fruit from the kitchen down the hall.

While Gage was focused on his mission for sustenance, Joey grinned as he partially climbed onto the bed with one knee and leaned over to steal a kiss from the woman lying there in complete satisfaction. "You're amazing. I could die a happy man right now."

The heartfelt moment between them was interrupted by the sound of the front door of the shitty apartment they shared in Jersey City being busted open. Immediate shouting filled the small space.

Joey sprang into action, pulling his semi-automatic from the nightstand drawer. "Stay here," he ordered Rose. He ran to assess the situation, but as he made it to the bedroom door, several men in ski masks barged in with weapons drawn.

"Hey..." Layne's hand was resting on the side of his face, lightly caressing her fingers over his week-old scruff. She tried to lure him back from whatever was going on inside his mind.

He finally released a breath he had been holding far longer than he should have.

"We don't have to do this tonight." She saw the struggle he was going through trying to explain his animosity towards his brother. It was clear that this wasn't an issue that ran only skin-deep.

Joey shook his head. "No. You need to know." He cleared his throat, summoning the words to casually describe what transpired that broke the relationship between Joey and Gage De Luca.

"Gage fucked over the wrong person. One day, Gage, Rosie, and I were hanging out at Gage's place. We were all ambushed. We never had a chance to adequately defend ourselves. We fought like hell, but they ended up taking Rosie. She was payment for what Gage had swindled his business partner out of."

He paused as his hand came up to remove Layne's hand away from his face so she couldn't feel the agitation tugging at his jaw as he internally relived what happened next.

Twenty-four hours was all it took for Rosie's return, and even then, it had been too long. Rosie's suffering lasting more than one millisecond was an unbearable thought. Twenty-four hours after she was taken from the apartment, her body was dumped from an unmarked van in front of a veterinarian's office. It was a cruel parallel to how she was treated—like nothing more than an animal instead of the angel she was.

She was still clinging to life when she was found that morning by the receptionist opening up the office. Barely alive was still enough to give Joey and Gage hope.

Both of them were there at the hospital, one on either side of her as she lay unconscious and attached to all the machines. A tube shoved down that dainty little throat of hers as a means to keep her breathing. The sight had been straight torture.

As Rosie's lifeline grew fainter, the anger brewed hotter between both of the De Luca boys, some of it misplaced and targeted at one another. And when her heart could no longer tie her to this earth? Chaos and Wrath were born amidst her loss.

Joey swallowed down the memory, keeping it safely tucked away. Clearing his throat, he shook away the unsteadiness of his voice. "She died from the injuries she sustained. The doctors said it had been injuries consistent with what you would find in third-world countries where captives are beaten and assaulted within an inch of their lives, but never to the point of death. Merely, an ongoing lifetime of torture at the hands of monsters."

She wrinkled her forehead in sympathy, unable to imagine what the poor girl had gone through. "I'm so sorry." Layne knew those words could never ease the pain, but despite Joey's attempt to keep his emotions detached, even she could see how Rosie's death made a lasting impact on him.

He shook his head. "If Gage had been smarter and stopped to think about his actions, it would have never happened. He knew better, but he continued to be reckless anyway. That part of him will never change, Layne."

"This is all your fault, motherfucker!" Gage shouted back in Joey's face. "You were the one that inserted yourself into Rosie and I's relationship. Then, when push comes to shove, you just let them walk out of there with her!"

One of Joey's hands pushed against Gage's shoulder. "My fault?! You decided to play stupid fuckin' games with the wrong people! I did what I could, but I couldn't help get her back if I was a goddamn corpse! I don't recall your unconscious ass being much help either." The sharpness of his words cut through the air.

Gage half-laughed in disbelief. "I would have died for her. I loved her, and you only wanted to fuck her."

Even ten years later, those wounds still wept.

CHAPTER THREE

Last night had been draining on multiple levels, and this afternoon wasn't shaping up to be much better.

"I think it's better if you're not here." Layne looked at Joey as they both stood there in the office located on the first floor of the home they shared. On the exterior, she may have looked confident and at ease, but internally, her apprehension was coiled tightly with her nerves fraying.

He squeezed her shoulders, seeing straight past the multiple walls she had raised all around her. With a nod, he agreed, not liking it, but she needed to hold her ground on this. "Feel free to pop one in his ass if he gets too far out of line." It's what Joey would like to do to Liam regardless of being given a reason or not.

A smile cracked at the corner of her mouth. Joey grinned, seeing a glimpse of one of the things that made his life worth living—Layne's happiness. His thumb and finger took her by the chin and drew her lips into a drawn-out kiss. It was a brief stint in his own personal heaven.

She could feel herself beginning to lose her control over the tough exterior she had spent all morning building up as his mouth took over hers. Layne had come to terms with the fact that Joey was capable of getting past all her defenses with so much as a damn look. However, today, she couldn't afford to have her vulnerabilities on display like a highway billboard.

As much as she didn't want to end the affectionate moment, she eased her face away from his. "Get the hell out of here before I end up a puddle on the floor."

He smirked at her and whispered in her ear. "I will have you begging to be a puddle later."

Layne's cheeks flushed slightly with heat at the thought, and she smacked her hand against his chest. "Go already!" Her teeth pressed into her bottom lip, trying to suppress her smile.

Joey finally listened to her and left O'Reilly Manor to go take care of some business matters of his own. Word had gotten around that his masked alter ego might have had a hand in disposing of one very disliked mayor who had just stepped down from his position. Contracts were rolling in left and right, providing a steady stream of income.

Liam arrived twenty minutes later. He walked into the office they had been sharing ever since Layne had moved into their father's house after hers was burned down by that dipshit ex-husband of hers, Eric Ellis.

A pair of designer sunglasses remained over his eyes to protect his hungover ass from being blinded by life itself. He had a coffee in his hand as he looked around at the rather empty space. "Where is everybody?"

Layne sat in the chair behind the desk, the blue envelope from her dad she had discovered months ago in her hands. "I told everyone the meeting was canceled today."

Her brother walked over to the desk, and a brow lifted above the top rim of his shades. "Why are you in my chair?" He set the paper coffee cup down on the desk. "And, you what?" His voice was still hoarse from the drunken binge he had engaged in yesterday at the strip club.

"I told everyone we weren't meeting today." Thanks to more financial stability and a few trusted associates, Layne had managed to get the O'Reilly family's business dealings back on track. There was still a lot of work to be done, but at least they were slowly rebuilding their workforce again.

"Why the fuck did I come down here then?!" He yelled at her and then winced as his escalated volume prompted a harder pulse of his headache.

Ignoring his attitude, "Because you and I need to talk, Liam." She stared at him without giving away how apprehensive she was about this entire encounter. "It was driving me insane that you haven't been able to access our primary account."

He groaned in annoyance about this bullshit being brought up again. "For fucks sake, Layne. I will get to taking care of it when I get to it. I have a bunch of shit on my plate right now."

She shook her head and pulled her phone out, dialing the banking institution's number and placing it on speakerphone so he could hear for himself. After a few prompts, a female representative came on the line.

"Thank you for calling Sandy Island Financials. How may I help you today?"

Layne sat back in the chair and motioned for Liam to go ahead and get this taken care of.

He rolled his eyes and placed his hands on the desk. "Yeah, I can't access my damn account. Something is fucked up on your end of the system; this is the fifth time I've called."

She quietly scoffed and shook her head; it was more like the second time he had called.

The banking rep, who sounded like someone's sweet little grandmother who baked cookies every morning, took Liam's personal information. After several long moments, she responded with an apologetic voice. "I'm sorry, Mr. O'Reilly, but you don't have access to that account."

Liam gave a huff. "Someone over there obviously made a big fuckin' mistake."

Layne leaned forward and interrupted Liam before he went on a tirade, stating how important he thought he was. "I'm sorry, I know you said my brother doesn't have any authority on the account, but could you check to see if I do?"

"Of course, I will just need your name and a few other pieces of information to check." The lady seemed pleased to be dealing with someone who wasn't ready to berate her for doing her job.

After taking all of Layne's information, it didn't take long for her to check it against the account. Layne's green hues never left Liam's face while they waited.

"Ms. O'Reilly, yes, I see here you are the sole authority listed on the account. Is there a transaction you would like to make today that I can help you with?" Now, wasn't that funny? Liam had zero control over the accounts their father had left behind.

As much as Layne wanted to flash a snarky grin at Liam, she refrained since she was trying to handle this situation with as much grace as humanly possible. "No, that's all. Thank you so much for all your help." Her finger tapped the phone screen to end the call.

Liam's face was riddled with confusion. "What the hell? Why didn't you tell her to put me on the account instead?!" He pushed away from the desk and began to pace as his irritability increased.

Her eyes tracked each step he made, knowing that this was about to go from bad to worse. "Li, it's not just the account."

He paused and looked over at her, his jaw hanging open slightly. "What the fuck do you mean it's not just the account?"

She handed the blue envelope over to him, containing everything he needed to know. It held everything she found out months ago and had opted to keep close to her chest until things settled with the business. Going from being on the verge of collapse to freshly stabilized, Layne hadn't wished to shake up the mix too soon.

Angrily, he yanked it from her hand and pulled the contents from it. His eyes quickly read over page after page. The documents contained their father's final wishes and distribution of assets, including some that were never known to either of his children. It was all dated the day before his passing. Layne had full control of all the O'Reilly enterprises.

As Liam stood there soaking in the information, she was predicting a volcanic eruption. When it never came, it was more frightening than if he had flown off the handle.

He finally tossed the collection of papers onto the desk. "You think these mean anything? Nobody is going to listen to you. You don't even have a damn clue how to run things."

She stood up from her seat, her temper prickling at the length of her spine. Layne's gaze hardened as she stared at his body language. Then, it finally hit her. "You knew, didn't you? You've known this entire damn time?!" Her anger was spreading to her limbs now.

His silence and lack of denial said it all. Rounding the end of the desk, she scowled at him. "You've got to be fucking kidding me, right? You knew, and you didn't say anything?"

He shrugged at her. "I knew you couldn't handle things. You're too busy playing house." His dislike of Joey living there or even existing grated on his nerves.

Not taking the bait on his dig on her personal life, she stuck to the topic at hand. "Dad didn't seem to think so. We were on the brink of utter devastation for months, and you kept telling me to keep out of it! We had one foot in the grave, and you still chose to be a selfish asshole?! Even now, we are just barely coming out of that hole that you put us in!" Each word that exited her mouth grew more heated.

The nagging ache of his head didn't stop him from barking back at her. "All of this belongs to me, it always has!"

"Not anymore, it doesn't. Either you can accept that and help, or you can get out of my way." She was willing to give Liam the chance she never got, but hell if she was going to let him think he was going to continue as the head of this organization.

He gave his answer to the idea of sharing leadership by laying his hands on her. Liam shoved her back hard enough that had the desk not been behind her to brace against, she likely would have landed on her ass on the floor.

Layne charged back at him, returning a shove using every ounce of her body weight behind it. He only budged a couple of steps, but she didn't stop there. She gave him another push and immediately followed with her right hook, colliding precisely on target with the hinge point of his upper jaw. The impact knocked his sunglasses square off his face.

If she hadn't been so pissed off, she would have immediately recognized the pop of pain in her hand. Thank God for adrenaline surges.

Liam's face got rocked by her strike, and it only took him a moment to recover and take a swing right back at her. She dipped down, causing his hand to swipe above her head. When she stood back up, she drove her fist up into his stomach.

He doubled over and heaved. Last night's hefty overindulgence of booze had left his stomach queasy, and her fist assisted in pushing it over the edge as he coughed and expelled whatever was in his stomach onto the floor.

Layne stepped back from him, shaking her hand as that second hit didn't get the full benefit of adrenaline that the first one had. She clutched onto her trembling fist, which was now feeling the intensity of the injury it had sustained upon that first punch.

Her brother coughed and spit out the last bit of vomit onto the floor. He used the sleeve of his shirt to wipe off his mouth while glaring at her. His breathing was ragged while he spoke through the continued waves of nausea, "You should have just stayed in your own damn lane."

She bent over to look at him, resting her good hand on her knee. "Well, it's my highway now. So, you can get off at the nearest goddamn exit." Straightening up, she walked over to the office door. Layne shook her head, leaving him there to contemplate what he wanted to do. Either he was going to answer to her or could fuck off.

Now, the real work was going to have to happen. There was a new face to the O'Reilly faction, and she was going to take back the respect and power that had been lost since the death of her father.

CHAPTER FOUR

Trying her best not to wince in pain while wiggling her fingers, she inhaled sharply instead. She sat on the edge of the examination table in the makeshift in-home clinic that only those involved in the city's criminal underground knew about.

It looked like the room must have been a sewing room in its past life. The strip of wallpaper bordering the top of the walls had vintage-looking spools of thread and silver needles sprawling across it. The colors were faded maroons and olives, indicative of an era long gone.

Instead of smelling like a typical sterile medical office, it smelled like cranberry and spice, reminiscent of the holiday season. The basket of potpourri probably had a lot to do with that. In a way, it made seeking medical attention a lot less overwhelming. It could even be considered cozy.

Dr. Patricia Kimmel continued her examination of Layne's right hand, which was now swollen and bruised, within hours after using it to strike Liam down.

Layne had been using Dr. Patty, as she preferred to be called, for years, especially when it came to injuries that required a no-questions-asked policy. The last thing that was needed was nosey doctors asking about the frequency of injuries sustained by her or anyone else who did work on her behalf. Layne still wasn't sure how much Dr. Patty knew about the O'Reilly business matters, but the woman never dared to ask.

It was the way that Dr. Patty scrunched up her broad nose in disapproval that made Layne uneasy about the forthcoming diagnosis. After landing an explosive hit to Liam's face, Layne suspected something had gone haywire by the snapping sensation in her hand surrounding her ring and pinky fingers, followed by numbness. That was before the swelling even began.

"How bad is it?" She asked the doc, hoping for news that her worst suspicions wouldn't be confirmed.

Gently setting Layne's hand down, she shook her head, her loosely held bun loosened up even further with the movement. Dr. Patty shoved her square-framed glasses up on top of her head of black hair that showed signs of silvery grey streaks coming in. "It's a boxer's fracture, Layne. You'll need to get this immobilized to start allowing it to heal properly."

Layne groaned in annoyance. Of course, of all faces to break her hand on, it would be Liam's. Not to mention, Joey was going to lose his shit.

"How long before it's all healed up? Three weeks?"

The older woman gave Layne a stern look. "Try two to three months. Minimum. Especially if you want to regain full use of it."

While the doctor gathered some supplies to wrap up Layne's hand, Layne grimaced at the thought of any part of her not being fully functional for that length of time. She had too much going on professionally not to be physically on top of her game.

Layne hopped off the table after her hand was shored up in a soft black splint with her ring and pinky fingers stabilized together.

"Oh, don't forget to take these as needed for the pain." Dr. Patty handed her over a bottle of painkillers. Layne's mouth went dry as she stared at the bottle that was just freely given to her. Her mind went back to that dark spot she had been in after her father's funeral, where she relied on the numbing effects of prescription medication.

Layne nodded at her briefly. "Thanks." She pocketed the pills into her leather jacket. They felt like they carried the weight of a two-ton bag of bricks. Despite the pain stemming from her fifth metacarpal, she wasn't sure she could bring herself to allow the relief to enter back into her system.

She began to leave when Dr. Patty lightly touched her arm. "Before you go," the look in her eyes shifted into those resembling a concerned mother. "Please, be careful out there. As much as I know you don't like coming here to see me, I also don't want an increase in our visits. There's been something brewing in the air, and I don't like the feel of it." Well, that wasn't ominous at all. For a woman who relied on science, it was out of character for her to tap into unsubstantiated gut feelings.

With a partial smile tugging at her lips, Layne shrugged casually. "You know me, but I will do my best to avoid any more visits for a while."

When she finally left the modest home that housed Dr. Patty's unlicensed medical practice, she pulled out the plastic pill container and looked it over. The temptation was literally in the palm of her hand, staring her down. It whispered such beautiful promises to her like a devil on her shoulder. She squeezed her palm around the cylindrical object and cursed under her breath.

As she passed by a trash receptacle on her way back to her car, she chucked the pills inside. It was going to be a shitty and painful couple of months.

Layne sat in the backroom of McGregor's after texting Joey to meet her there for a quick bite to eat for a late dinner. She hoped that being in a somewhat public setting would help keep his reaction to the turn of events on the milder side. Thanks to her ownership interest in the pub and the seedy nature of its patrons, there was a lot of discretion as to what transpired there.

When she saw Joey walk in, wearing a rugged pair of jeans and a slate gray shirt under his leather jacket, she lost her train of thought of how she was going to explain to him how she ended up with a broken hand. His blonde hair was a bit out of place, which usually was an indication he had just removed his motorcycle helmet.

He laid his eyes on her, immediately noticing the black brace on her hand. His cocoa-colored eyes filled with darkness. Striding over to her, he gently lifted her arm while his muscular body vibrated with the need to inflict violence on her behalf. "What the hell happened?" The tone of his voice indicated he was ready to go break the hand of the motherfucker responsible, or worse.

Attempting to brush it off, she murmured, "It's not that bad." She eased her arm out of his hold, but it only prompted him to look her over for any other potential injuries she may have sustained. His hands roamed over her body only to find nothing else to feed his desire to inflict suffering.

"I'm fine, Joey," she attempted to reassure him again. "It's just a minor fracture from trying to put Liam in his place. It was worth it."

Not seeing any other obvious wounds, he sighed and drew her in with a hand on either side of her head and laid a kiss on her forehead. "How did he take the news?"

She shook her head. "He already knew."

"What?" His voice dropped in disbelief as his hands fell to the tops of her shoulders. "What do you mean he already knew?"

Trying not to get herself all riled up again, she took a deep breath. "He's known. He's known this entire goddamn time that everything was supposed to be under my control."

"Two-faced, selfish motherfucker, I'm going to fuckin' kill him!" Joey stepped back from her and began to pace across the floor. His fingers combed through his long-cut dirty blonde hair as he wracked his brain on all the ways Liam tallied up a long list of shitty deeds.

Layne retrieved her glass of golden ale with her left hand, the engagement ring on her finger lightly tapping against the glass as she did so. Her eyes watched as Joey worked through his thoughts and feelings. Taking a few sips of the beer before setting it back down again, she finally decided to try to get him to settle down.

"Look, he can either get on board or not. The guys I signed on to work the daily operations know who is calling the shots. The few who pretended to respect Liam's authority will go where the money is." And the money was definitely not in her brother's hands. Eric Ellis's inheritance, liquidation of assets, and life insurance payouts were to thank for that.

Out of habit, she went to prop her hand on her hip but hissed as the pressure elicited a sharp burst of pain in her hand despite the brace. She dropped her hand down to her side, trying to control her exhale through the discomfort.

It was the sound of her reaction to the pain that shook Joey from his spiraling thoughts. He paused mid-step and turned himself to head back to where she stood. He looked down at her, his brown eyes holding a soft command to them. "Sit."

His eyes were met with her own delicate green hues. "I don't need to—"

"Shush." His finger trailed across her lips. "Did it sound like I was asking? I will force your ass in that chair if I have to."

A glimmer of mischief reached her eyes as her mouth formed a small smirk while she thought about him making good on his word. It made other parts of her body ache in such delicious ways.

Joey's hands dropped to her hips, firmly grasping them and guiding her back until she was at a chair. His tone dropped to a light rumble. "Layney, sit down."

It wasn't difficult to follow his orders, the way he had spoken them had made her legs weak. Her ass found the seat of the chair, and now her head was tilted up at a greater angle while she stared up at him.

"Good girl." His hand brushed over her cheek before he rewarded her with a gentle yet brief kiss. "Stay here while I get us some food." Before he left, he slid his jacket from the fit shape of his upper body, draping it over the back of his chosen chair. The short sleeves of his shirt allowed all the designs of his tattoos sprawling over his arms to be on display. All the rich shades of red roses stood out against the darker ravens and skulls.

He disappeared for a few minutes to head out to the main area and put in an order for food with John, Sean's backup, when he had the night off. When he returned, she was still where he had left her but nursing her beer as her only option to self-medicate.

"What did you get me?"

Joey grinned and pulled his seat up closer to her. "The same damn thing you always get."

Layne smiled. "Cowboy burger, medium-rare, extra bacon, and barbeque sauce on the side?"

He rolled his eyes as if he didn't have her very specific order memorized by now before he nodded. "Yeah, and I told them I didn't want to hear you bitch about it being overcooked again."

With her injured hand useless and throbbing with constant pain, she kept it resting on top of her thigh. Joey took notice of how much she was babying it. "What did Dr. Patty give you for the pain?"

She shook her head. "Standard shit that will knock you on your ass for a week. I just tossed it in the trash."

With a sigh, he leaned over and squeezed her thighs reassuringly. "You can't just sit here and suffer. I won't let you go down that dark road again, but there's no reason for you to constantly hurt." Watching Layne being in pain was one of the few things that had him feeling like it was worse than death itself.

"I didn't want to risk it. Besides, with Liam now being on notice that he either is with me or he isn't, there's too much to let my brain get all foggy. Then, there's all the work that's going on with trying to reestablish power in the city." Layne did her best to brush it all off as no big deal. All that she had said may have held some truth behind it, but the biggest factor was her prior history of using painkillers to take care of more than just the physical pain.

Before he could try and convince her otherwise, John came over with two plates of food. Layne's burger and Joey's cluster of buffalo wings. Their conversation paused while he delivered the food to their table before he left again.

She felt Joey's eyes on her still, despite their food having arrived and sitting in front of them. She held half of the messy burger in her left hand while she stared back at him. "What?"

He smiled deviously at her. "Nothing. If you're not going to take anything, I'm just thinking of all the other ways I can make sure you feel good." Joey reached over and slid his hand along her inner thigh. "I want your body aching for far better reasons."

Putting her burger back down on the plate, she gave a playful frown. "You know, now that you say something, it really does hurt. *A lot.*" He was one drug that she didn't ever want to break the habit of.

"Oh? Well, I can't have that. I have just what you need." He rose from his seat and took her uninjured hand, leading her back to the men's bathroom.

Once inside and ensuring there were no other occupants, he locked the door. His hand settled on the small of her back and pulled her back to him, not allowing her to stray too far.

Joey pressed her back up against the door as his face dropped down closer to hers. His eyes were full of lustful thoughts and intentions. His hand wrapped around her throat just under her jaw. "You remember the last time I had you in a bathroom all to myself?"

Layne whimpered at the memory. How could she forget? She had been out on a date before Joey ambushed her on the way to the ladies' room. His hand had brutally brought her to the cusp of an orgasm that had threatened to leave her entirely undone, and then he abandoned her there on that ledge. It had left her in an epic state of frustration.

"Mmhmm," she responded, already breathless just from having his fingers curled around her neck. It drove heat down into the pooling sensation of desire in her core.

His smirk showed off how much he knew his actions were affecting her. "Good. This time, I'm going to show you just what I really wanted to do to you that night."

A chill of excitement flooded across her body. Her lips parted in speechless awe. Joey took advantage of her open mouth by claiming it with his. Immediately, his tongue dove inside to seek out her own.

He stepped up against her, letting her feel the heat coming off of his body and the way his jeans were failing to conceal his arousal. When she tried to grab onto him, she forgot about the restricted use of her hand. The movement drew a protest from the fresh injury, and her gasp of pain got swallowed up by the kiss they shared.

Joey pulled back, releasing her throat, his hands carefully guided both of hers away from him. "You're going to keep your hands to yourself. I want to show you exactly what you do to me simply by standing here looking so fuckin' beautiful."

Her teeth bit into her lower lip while she grinned. "I can't make any promises."

His hand slid up the back of her neck, getting lost in the tangles of her chestnut waves of hair. Closing his fist around a handful of it, he tugged her head back as his lips dragged up along her throat. Once his mouth was at her ear, his gravelly whisper came forth. "If that's the case, I can't make any promises I will let you come all over my cock like I know you want to."

A delicate little moan came from her at the mere thought of how badly she wanted him buried deep inside of her. Her hands fought the urge to latch onto him again.

Joey nibbled along her lobe for a second, waiting to see if she was going to adhere to his instructions. When she refrained from putting her hands on him, he smiled and pulled her by her hips until he had her positioned at the counter where all three sinks were lined up.

His hands spun her around so she was facing the large mirror on the wall behind the sinks. Layne met his eyes in the reflection before she felt his hand run up along her spine. It gradually placed pressure on her until she was hinged at the hips and bent over the edge of the counter.

Joey's fingers hooked onto the side of the black leggings she was wearing and rolled them down past her thighs. He squatted down with the motion, the warmth of his breath caressing over the bare skin of her ass before he laid several kisses across it.

The fact that she was still going without panties had his dick twitching excitedly in his pants. It was simply knowing he would have immediate access to her pussy without so much as a damn piece of string that passed for women's underwear these days.

As he laid those kisses across the roundness of her behind, she felt his hands glide up the backs of her thighs. Her knees quivered in response, threatening to give out at any moment.

When he stood up, he slid his hand between her legs, allowing his fingers to stroke along her slit. "You're goddamn soaked, Layney." He gave a broad smile while he single-handedly began to undo his belt and open up his pants.

She pushed her hips against his fingers, craving more. "Joey, stop fucking around. You know I can't take it when you tease."

He pushed two of his fingers into her, Layne's arousal allowing for smooth entry. "Don't lie, Layney. You can take a hell of a lot. I've seen this cunt of yours take anything I've ever given it." Joey's fingers slid in and out of her, drawing out the sweet sound of her moans with each movement.

Layne stayed glued to her place, bent over the counter while his fingers stroked those parts deep within her. When he removed his hand entirely, her moan dissolved into a whimper. Before she could protest, Joey had his cock out of his pants and shoved deep into her pussy in one quick movement.

Her body gripped around his length from the second he entered her. Joey groaned as his dick immediately throbbed as her walls encased him. He grabbed her at the waist and began to fuck her from behind, her ass presented to him like the prettiest little gift of encouragement to keep going. He moaned out, "Mmm, fuck…"

"Yes, God, yes!" Layne let the pleasure quickly take over her body, allowing everything else to fade away from her mind.

Joey continued to slam into her tight cunt, each thrust of his hips becoming more urgent and full of need. "Beg me for my cum, Layney. I need to hear how much you want your pussy filled with it until it's dripping down your damn legs." His voice grew breathless as his desires began to approach the apex of pleasure.

Her body trembled at the sound of his words. Each stroke of his cock deep inside her body, pushing against her sweet spot, had her coming more and more unraveled. With the mirror in front of her, her eyes looked up at his image reflected in it.

"Joey, please, I need your cum deep inside of me. I need to take all of it." Her gaze witnessed his heated expressions, and it had her quickly losing herself. All of Layne's body tensed up as she shook from the violent orgasm that ripped through her as she screamed out.

The moment she spilled over into her climax, Joey gave several more frantic thrusts into her as he breathlessly moaned out at the sensation of her body's warm fluid coming over his rigid cock.

He growled out a curse as he gave one final slam of his hips up against her, driving his length fully into her before his seed erupted. Each spasm of his cock releasing more of his cum until he finally felt the sigh of satisfaction settle deep in his chest.

Layne dropped her head down until she felt the cool counter against her cheek. Still panting after that explosive release, she couldn't even manage to get her words into a coherent sentence. "I… Wow. Everything."

What broken hand? The sea of ecstasy made it feel as good as new.

CHAPTER FIVE

A few mornings later, Layne rolled over in bed, expecting to find a large, warm body next to her. Instead, she was just met with the small mound of the cold white bedding Joey had tossed aside.

She frowned as she opened her eyes and found a small piece of paper left on his pillow.

Have to pick up a package for a client. Be back in an hour to have my breakfast. - Joey

P.S. I'm never late.

Layne grinned in giddy anticipation, damn well knowing that between her thighs was going to be ready for him the second he walked in through the door. He had been finding creative ways and sneaking in every opportunity to distract her body from the pain of her fractured hand.

She slid out of bed, wearing a cropped light blue camisole with a matching pair of shorts. After taking care of a few things in the bathroom, she left the master suite and went downstairs to find a cup of coffee left on a warmer for her.

It looked like he was doing his best to stay in her good graces, and she wasn't complaining about it. The coffee was only a small gesture in comparison to how he had been trying to help her organize and restructure how she took over the operations of her family's business. The stressors of her new role, plus the added injury to her hand, had been leaving her already short fuse even quicker to blow.

Liam had been radio silent since their blowout, likely licking his wounds and having a pity party for himself between Kristill's legs. After he puked all over her office floor, she had to toss the maid a little extra money to come in on her day off to clean up the mess he had left behind. Layne could handle some bloody violence, but vomit? Hard pass on the sour smell alone.

Before Layne could let the first drop of caffeine hit her lips, the doorbell echoed throughout the house. She set the mug back down on the center island in the kitchen before leaving to answer the door.

When she swung open the front door, an unexpected face greeted her on the other side of it. She blinked a few times at the scruffy-jawed man with eerily similar brown eyes as Joey.

Gage stood there with a broad smile at the sight of Layne answering the door in her pajama set and her long brown locks of hair in wild waves, indicating she had gotten out of bed not too long ago. "Well," he licked his lips as his eyes wandered, "good morning, love."

Layne stared at him in both surprise and confusion as to why he was standing there on her front step. "Gage? What are you doing here?"

His hands were tucked in the front pockets of his dark blue jeans, and a pale green shirt that seemed one size too small for the ripped lines of his upper body. A long chain hung from his neck. At the very end of the chain was a small coin-like charm with the spread wings of an eagle and the letters *SPQR* at its base and a laurel wreath curved around the outer edges.

The short, dark blonde hair on his head was styled casually to appear as though very little effort and thought had been put into it. His smile reflected how at ease he was feeling enough that he attempted to step inside without an invitation.

Having gotten used to the soft brace on her right hand, she immediately put her left hand against his chest to put a halt to his advance into her home. He didn't press onward, but he did look down at her hand and grin. Taking his hands from his pockets, he wrapped one around her fingers and examined the platinum and black rhodium diamond ring on her slender finger.

"My brother give this to you?" He lifted a far too curious brow.

She ignored his question. It was none of his damn business. "You haven't told me why you're here. How did you even know where I live?"

Finally releasing her hand, he raised a finger to her while a hand slid into his back pocket. When he pulled it back out again, he held her credit card between his middle and pointer fingers. "You dropped this the other night at the club. A few online searches, a few questions asked of chatty ex-neighbors, and here I am."

Despite that, he was now smiling oh-so-proudly, Layne plucked her credit card from his hold and kept her eyes full of suspicion. "Thanks."

Gage leaned over to attempt to catch a glimpse of what lay just past the front door of her home. "Nice lookin' spot. Looks like Joey traded up."

She stepped to the side to try and block his view of the interior of her home. Though, it was a moot point given how he easily saw right over the top of her head, given his towering height that matched Joey's. "Why are you still here?"

He chuckled and raised both hands in front of him innocently. "Settle down, sweetheart, I'm just being friendly."

"The fuck you are." She leaned over and slapped her credit card down on the thin side table to the left of the door before she crossed her arms in front of her chest.

Amusement sparked in his eyes as he leaned one forearm against the doorframe. His eyes noticed the way her arms pushed her breasts together in that cute little camisole she had on. "Oh, there's a bit of a brat in you. Now, I get it." It seemed his brother's taste in women hadn't changed much.

"Get what?" Her patience was quickly running out as she released a sigh of frustration. "I swear to God, is there a gene in your family that causes you to be irritatingly arrogant and cocky?"

He laughed in response to her observation. The way he did so had a deep and rich tone to it that seeped in past her barriers. It made something inside of her flutter with excitement. Layne quickly tried to pitch those feelings to the side and focus on how he had interrupted her morning coffee.

His charming smile didn't leave his face as he rubbed his hand over his jaw in thought. The sunlight glinted off of a few silver rings decorating his fingers and also highlighted the inked letters 'WRATH' just above his knuckles on the back of his hand.

The way he was now staring at her while he did it was getting her even more flustered. Layne shook her head. "Alright, congrats, you've found me and returned my card. Either move along, or I will—"

Gage shoved his way inside, firm hands catching her off guard when they grabbed just below her shoulders and moved her to the side. "Hey!" She squawked. His foot kicked the door shut behind him.

After his hands released her, he began to wander deeper into the house. His head nodded to himself as if he was impressed with what he was seeing. He stopped right outside the dining room, which was currently a mess with plastic liners, buckets of paint, ladders, and various other tools. The memory of Mick's death there needed to be erased along with the outdated decor.

Gage motioned at all the hardware. "Doing some renovations? You know, I'm pretty good with my hands, or so I'm told." He smirked at her.

Layne strode after him, her bare feet padding quietly against the tiled floor of the main hall. Fuck the pain in her right hand; she shoved his shoulder with it to turn him partially to face her as her left hook came at that smug face of his. If he wanted to invade her home, he was going to get an unwanted visitor's welcome.

He gave a brief look of surprise as he pulled his face back before she could make contact. Gage's grip wrapped around her left forearm, twisting her around until he had her back pulled up against the front of him with her left arm twisted behind her back. The strength of his other arm wrapped across her and squeezed tightly.

"Take it easy, killer." He chuckled.

Layne wriggled in his hold. "You have no idea." She wouldn't mind adding him to her body count at that moment, even if he did smell like an intoxicating combination of spices and soothing vanilla.

Gage leaned over and gave her a quick peck to her cheek before letting go of her, nudging her forward away from him. "So, where is Joey? I was hoping to catch up, make amends and all that shit, then maybe even bring him into a business deal I'm working on."

She took a few steps forward when he released her, then spun around to glare at him. "What makes you think I know where he is?"

He waved off her question. "You're going to play that angle? My brother doesn't start getting hot and throwing punches over a one-nighter. Though, I am surprised he was willing to get on one knee." He shrugged at the thought of Joey popping the question to any woman. Maybe the woman standing in front of him was that great of a lay. He wouldn't mind taking a tour of everything she had to offer to see what had Joey getting all possessive over.

"He's not here." As if on cue, the front door creaked open. Joey stumbled in, his hand clutching onto his side. A large patch of red soaked into the white fibers of his shirt, and his blood covered the hand he was using to apply pressure to the area.

Layne looked over her shoulder at the sound of the door opening. When she saw him trudge in with a grimace on his face, her face fell, and her heart sank right along with it.

"Shit," she uttered as she ran over to him. Her hand grabbed onto his arm, though she wasn't sure what good it was going to do if he fell. His weight was easily twice her own and would take her right down with him, and hard. "What the hell happened?!"

Joey groaned as he looked up at her, trying to brush it all off. "Son of a bitch brought a cracked-out friend thinking he was getting out of handing over the package..." His eyes caught sight of Gage standing off to the side.

His pain turned to anger with the flip of a switch. "What the fuck is he doing here?!" He tried to straighten up but immediately doubled back over again as pain shot through his body. Layne stumbled under the weight as her arm tried to at least keep him upright.

She shook her head. "Don't worry about him right now. I'll shoot him on your behalf if I have to. Let's get you in a chair."

Gage snorted. "Hopefully, your aim is better than your swing." Then, seeing the struggle between the both of them, Gage took pity and approached. "Move," he commanded as he encroached on Layne's space at Joey's side.

It only took a brief moment for Layne to assess that Gage didn't have any malicious intent in his eyes before she allowed him to take her spot. He took up Joey's non-injured side, wrapping Joey's arm around the back of his shoulders to help take the burden of the weight.

Layne left to grab a chair out of the dining room, returning to meet Gage and Joey halfway across the foyer. She set the chair down in front of Joey. "Here. I will go get supplies." Moving quickly, she disappeared to gather any first aid supplies they might need.

Gage eased Joey into the chair. Immediately, Joey let out a sigh and leaned back. With Joey's jaw set in a hard line from both the searing pain in his side and his anger, he leered at his younger brother. "What the fuck is wrong with your hearing? Have you gone deaf in the last ten years and didn't hear me when I told you to stay the fuck away?"

Squatting down, Gage began to peel back the shirt to try and see how bad the damage was underneath. When Joey didn't move his hand to allow him to take a look, Gage sighed. "I heard you, but you think I give a shit? At least let me check this out and see how much of a pussy you're being right now." He had seen his fair share of wounds from fights breaking out in the various establishments where he worked as head of security over the years.

"Fuck you." Joey relented and eased his hand away to allow Gage to further lift the bottom of his shirt up to expose the injury.

Despite all the blood surrounding the area, making it difficult to determine the full extent of the damage, it was obvious that the slash was the deepest, right above the waist of his black pants on his side.

Layne returned, a bin of various medical supplies in her hands. She knelt at Joey's side to see the laceration for herself. Her emerald hues looked up at Joey, silently saying everything she was thinking. His stubborn ass should have called. He should have been more careful. The last thing she wanted was to lose him.

She pulled out disinfectant, but Gage plucked it out of her hands. "No offense, but I think someone who has full use of both hands automatically makes me more qualified." He motioned to the black brace on her right hand.

Joey grumbled but didn't protest, allowing Gage to proceed.

Almost an hour later, Gage removed his gloves after applying a bandage to the freshly stitched wound. During the course of the hour, Layne had tried to break the awkward tension between the two of them every so often by asking Joey questions but only received one or two-word responses.

"All set." Gage stood and offered a hand to help Joey up out of the chair. It was either hard-headedness or pride, but Joey pushed through the pain, still very much present, and stood from his chair on his own accord.

Layne gently hugged Joey's uninjured side as she looked up at him. "Why don't you go upstairs and get some rest?" Seeing the distrust painted over his face of leaving her alone with Gage, she rolled her eyes. She reached up and grabbed his face to turn and look at her. "I can handle getting him out the door."

As a means of reassuring him and maybe even sending a message to Gage as well, she stood on her tiptoes and brought her lips to Joey's.

Kissing him long and slow, she allowed the taste of him to linger in her mouth. Once she felt some of the tension in his body fade, she pulled back with a sweet smile, promising more to come.

After Joey was upstairs, Layne turned and looked at Gage as the sweetness of her smile shifted into a conflicted look between gratitude and sheer irritation he was still lingering. "Thank you for helping."

Gage grinned, finishing her unspoken thoughts, "But, get the fuck out?"

She tried to hide the smile pulling at the corners of her mouth, but she wasn't quick enough, and he caught sight of it. He already knew from that glimpse that he wanted to see just how big of a smile he could get out of her in the future.

Layne walked him over to the door. He turned after stepping foot onto the front step to look at her. "I still need to talk to him about a few things."

Scoffing at the thought of Joey willing to entertain the notion of having another talk with Gage, she shook her head. "Good luck with that."

Trying to re-engage his charm and smooth-talking, his eyes looked into hers. "Well, that's what you are - luck. I'm sure you can find a way to convince him to come down to Cassidy's and have a chat. What do you say, lucky charm?"

"Why would I do that for you, of all people? After everything that's happened between the two of you." She didn't make any effort to diminish the skepticism in her tone.

He tilted his head slightly with a curious note in his words. "And, just what did he tell you happened?"

She crossed her arms in front of her chest and gave a small shrug. "Everything I needed to know."

"I very much doubt that, but my offer applies to you as well. If you ever want to know what you're in for, come see me." He gave her a harmless smile.

"Bye, Gage." She shut the door in his face.

Layne turned and looked at the main staircase that led upstairs. A small voice in the back of her head wondered what else there was behind the animosity between the two De Luca brothers.

CHAPTER SIX

Finally, after several weeks of pain and torture for them both, Layne's hand was free of that godforsaken brace. In her opinion, it had wreaked enough havoc and inconvenience for a lifetime. While her hand wasn't fully healed yet, per Dr. Patty, she at least had full functionality of it again. She just had to promise she wouldn't go around punching anyone else until it was completely healed. It was a tough sell, but she agreed she'd do her best.

Joey's knife wound was healing up nicely. As much as neither of them wanted to admit it, Gage had done a good job stitching up the laceration. As a precaution, Dr. Patty also provided some antibiotics. Nobody wanted to drop dead from an avoidable infection; this wasn't the Middle Ages.

The forced downtime allowed her to continue laying out strategy and resilience plans for the O'Reilly organization. She had a newfound appreciation for all that her father had been in charge of. Having not been raised to take on this role, she felt lost more often than not, but no less determined to reestablish the respect her last name used to demand.

Layne found herself in the office standing before the most senior associates who worked for the O'Reilly faction - who now worked for her. She had been meeting with all of them in smaller groups, but now she had all of them in the same room with her to make sure her message could be heard loud and clear. She wanted to be able to stare at all their faces to make sure nobody was missing the memo. From here on out, it was Layne in charge of how things operated. Nothing was to be done without her being made aware of it. The way things operated under Liam's piss-poor leadership would no longer be the standard.

Bringing all her boss bitch energy, she looked at the faces of the group of men with eyes on her. All of them came from various backgrounds but had one thing in common: criminal intelligence. Could she have hired every thug looking to make a quick buck to beef up her workforce? Sure. But she didn't want just anyone executing her vision for this organization; she wanted people who knew what the fuck they were doing.

"With all that said, anybody who disagrees can see themselves out that door right now. I am not going to tolerate disloyalty, inadequacy, or excuses. If you can't or won't put everything on the line to honor all this enterprise stands for, then get the fuck out. My dad set forth stringent expectations for all those who reported to him. You can expect that those standards have now been raised when you report to me." It wasn't going to be easy taking back power across the city, even more so knowing that all the other factions would consider her an emotionally weak female undeserving of respect.

The fierce green of her eyes shifted as she scanned each of the men there in the room with her, looking each one in the eyes while assessing their body language to determine how reliable and trustworthy they might be in the long run. The only person missing was her brother. The invitation for him to take a spot reporting to her had gone without a response. It seemed someone was still feeling a bit butthurt that he might have to take orders from Layne for once.

When no one made a move to leave the room, she nodded and leaned back against the edge of her desk. Her arms crossed in front of her stomach as she got comfortable. Layne began to dish out instructions to have her crew make the first moves under her reign.

First up was Jonathan, the most diplomatic of the bunch. He had worked in politics, covering up scandals and making illegal deals behind closed doors for years. He wasn't much of a fighter, but he could talk a deaf man into listening. "Jonathan, you go rub elbows with the other faction heads and try to smooth things over with the change in leadership. Make it clear that what was flying the past few months is no longer the case. Anyone who has a problem with that can take it up with me directly, and I will be more than happy to paint them a very clear picture of what I won't be tolerating."

Next was Ethan. He had nearly as much of a temper as she did but a far more intimidating stature. The man was built like one of the NFL's top defensemen. He had started his career out as a professional bodybuilder competing in fitness competitions until he branched out into shakedowns for whoever gave him the largest commission. "Ethan, you take your guys and begin cracking down on overdue payments. I don't want there to be a single penny still owed to us."

Finally, one of her favorite hires was Sammy. He was a perfect blend of both Jonathan and Ethan. A smooth talker, but the man could get damn scrappy in a fight. Either he was brawling his way out of shit situations or using his words to manipulate others. "Sam, please see to it that Diego is relieved of his duties at the Brass Mirror. I can't be having someone operating that site who can be easily bribed by someone like Eric Ellis." May the bastard be rotting in hell. "I need someone with a backbone running that operation."

One of the others, Thomas, stood from his seat. He was well into his fifties and had seen some shit during his time served in this industry. She had determined anyone with that level of wisdom would be an asset as an advisor and mentor to the others. "Layne," his tone full of caution, "this isn't going to be a smooth transition given how weak the O'Reilly reputation has been."

She nodded. "I'm aware. That's why I'm doubling down on everything. If anyone thinks they're going to find themselves getting second chances, you can make it clear in no uncertain terms that I have a one-strike policy. Don't pay? I will take what you owe and more in any way I see fit. Ignore the boundaries of the O'Reilly territory? You will be struck down without hesitation. I'm not here to play games." Lord knew that she couldn't afford to fuck around.

Skeptically, Jonathan looked at her. "That goes against all the rules of engagement we have with the other factions, politically speaking."

Layne gave a harsh laugh that rattled the atmosphere. "You mean it goes against the unwritten and outdated rules? What good were those rules when I was being shot at when this business was circling the drain? Fuck their rules. I'm making my own now."

She shook her head in irritation, recalling all the struggles over the past year when she should have had all of this under her control and not under Liam's inept ass.

"Anything else?" She glanced around the room, waiting for anyone to speak up. When she was met with heads shaking and a lack of affirmative responses, she waved them all off. "I want reports coming back on everything; I don't care what time of day it is. If it can't be spoken over the phone, you better be knocking on the door."

Her hand waved off the men that she had hand-selected to be the foundation of building a stronger O'Reilly empire than had ever existed before. Money may have gotten them in the door, but now she would see just how much money talked when it came to them taking action on her behalf.

The men filed out of the room gradually, some chatting amongst themselves about more mundane things like sports and financial markets. Finally, it was just Layne left there in the office, and she felt like she could drop the façade of being a confident and fearless leader.

She stepped away from her desk, walked over to the window, and peered outside at the traffic coming and going down the street. Her brain felt fried, and her lack of personal engagement on the front lines of the business had left her feeling useless. Getting lost in her thoughts, she hadn't even noticed a presence coming into the office.

The strength of Joey's arms wrapped around her waist from behind. It was at Layne's behest that Joey not be part of her meetings with her leads. This business was already too male-oriented; if he were to participate, they would be too quick to look to him and ignore the little lady in the room. She needed to build the foundation first that she wasn't just a pretty face pretending to be the head of a criminal syndicate.

Layne leaned back into him and allowed a sigh to escape. "I was never prepared for this. Liam always got the insight on how to run things."

"Look what good that did him. He had his chance." He didn't hide how unimpressed he was with her brother on both business and personal levels.

She was on the same train of thought. "That's because he's a fucking idiot."

Turning her around by her hips, Joey looked down at her with a grin. His hand cupped her chin. "And that is what will set you apart from how he handled things." He lowered his mouth onto hers, coaxing her into a more at-ease state.

When their kiss broke, he smiled at her lightly. "There is another matter of business we need to discuss, Layne."

She furrowed her brows together, wondering what other details needed to be ironed out that she must have overlooked.

"You're not just running side jobs for Liam or your dad anymore. You're running the whole damn show." He set his jaw in a hard line as he thought about the harsh reality he was going have to admit to out loud.

"That puts a massive target on your back. As much as it pisses me off to say it, even I have my limitations on what I can do to keep you protected. We need to consider seeking out someone who can professionally see to it that you're safe when I'm not around."

Her face fell at the thought of anyone other than Joey hovering over her every move. "And you're going to trust another human being to do that?"

Now, it was Joey's turn to frown. "I didn't say it was going to be easy finding someone, but it has to happen. I will check around and see if anyone is worth talking to about the job."

Not being on board with this idea, Layne shook her head. "I have always been able to take care of myself. I'm not going to just trust some stranger breathing down my neck and hope that they have my back when it matters most."

To prove a point, Joey knocked her feet out from underneath her while pushing her back. Instead of letting her back hit the floor, he caught her with his other arm. With his spare hand, he pointed his index and middle fingers at her forehead. "Bang."

She tried to mask the surprise on her face as she stared up at him, but her slightly wide eyes gave it away. Her hand pushed his fingers away that were aggressively pointed at her. "Are you planning on taking me out yourself? Playing the long game and finally finishing the job for Franzetti?" Layne narrowed her eyes at him.

He pulled her back upright onto her feet. "No, but it's people like me that I'm worried about, Layne. Do you think they're going to give a shit about where you are or who you're with? You'd be lucky if all they do is fire a single round into you. I wouldn't be able to live with myself knowing I had the chance to put safety measures in place to prevent it."

The stubborn side of her wanted to fight him on this and tell him he was wrong. She pressed her lips together, ready to push back on the issue, but her phone began to ring in her pocket, disrupting her from debating with him. "This conversation isn't over yet."

She stepped away from him as she pulled out her phone and answered it. "Yes?" Layne stopped mid-step as the caller spoke in her ear. "What?" She was pretty sure she had to have heard the person on the other end of the line incorrectly. "Oh, for fucks sake. I will be right there. No, don't do a damn thing."

Layne pressed the red button on the screen to end the call. Returning her phone to her pocket, she balled her hands up into fists and pressed them to her forehead as she shut her eyes tightly. She wanted to scream at the top of her lungs in frustration. Instead, she muttered, “I’m going to kill him.”

After approaching her, Joey lightly tugged on her wrists to pull her hands away from her face. “What is it?”

She opened her eyes and shook her head in disbelief. “Liam got his stupid ass arrested.”

CHAPTER SEVEN

For the sake of avoiding any unnecessary entanglements with Joey accompanying her to the police station, she left him behind while she handled this on her own. With Joey's criminal record and history with the department, the last thing she needed was for them to receive any unwanted attention or harassment.

As for Layne, the only charge formally tied to her record was an old misdemeanor of public lewdness after a night of drunken debauchery on her twenty-first birthday. It resulted in a slap on the wrist and a wink in her father's direction.

When she arrived at the 1st Precinct of the NYPD, there was a lot of foot traffic outside the primary entrance. A podium was set up, and surrounding it were several officers in their blues, various media outlets with cameras and recorders, and what could only be assumed to be assistants, civilians, and other interested parties.

A woman with short, ashy blonde hair that was a little too long to be considered a pixie cut was standing at the podium. From the appearance of her dress blues decorated with extra stars and service stripes, it was the Chief of Department of the NYPD.

The woman's voice carried a warm yet commanding tone. "Spearheading this new initiative, it is my honor to introduce you to New York's newly appointed Police Commissioner, Vincent Saito."

There was a round of applause from the surrounding crowd as a man in his late forties approached the podium in a navy suit paired with an unoriginal white collared shirt underneath. His shiny black hair was just long enough to comb over to an off-center part. From the slight slant of his eyes and his skin tone, it appeared that he had a mix of both Asian and Caucasian heritages.

Everything about him was clean-cut and nearly too squeaky clean to be any sort of appointed official. This guy looked like he spent weekends coaching his kid's soccer team, feeding the homeless, and honing his golf skills on a country club green.

He shook hands with the Chief and gave a sparkling smile to the people, and if there had been a baby present, he probably would have kissed it, too.

Stepping up onto the curb towards the back of the crowd, Layne paused and began to watch whatever bullshit this guy was about to spoon-feed everyone.

Commissioner Saito repositioned the microphone in front of him before resting his hands on the edges of the podium. "Thank you, Chief Graham. It is with great pleasure that I would like to announce this city's greatest step towards cracking down on organized crime. With increased funding from an anonymous donor and partnership with the Federal Bureau of Investigation, I am proud to announce the Unwind and Un-organize Initiative."

Layne raised a brow as she crossed her arms in front of her, her interest piqued. Every new commissioner that was appointed always rolled in with vows to do things differently. Each one of them ultimately just made a show out of their empty promises.

She listened intently to the man speaking to the masses about how he was going to crack down on organized crime in Manhattan. It was mostly the same shit she had heard before from law enforcement: more training, zero tolerance, and supposed accountability.

After the rundown of specifics on this new plan that was going to be implemented across the city over the next twelve months, Commissioner Saito began to take questions from overeager journalists.

One woman raised her hand high, trying to capture the attention to be called on. When the Commissioner pointed at her, she gave a hopeful look and an excited smile. "Commissioner, as we all know, there is a concern about officers being swayed to look the other way and investigations being swept under the rug. Criminal behavior doesn't just stop at the front door of the NYPD. How are you proposing to put an end to that?"

To his credit, the new guy on the block took a moment to look thoughtful before selecting a response from a likely preplanned list of answers. "We hold all our officers and detectives to a high standard of integrity. If there is any reason to believe that integrity has been compromised, I will personally ensure that those involved will be harshly reprimanded." Yup, same old bullshit.

It would take time for any of this to get past all the red tape and bureaucracy, but Layne added the mental note to keep an eye out for any potential headaches this could all bring. It wasn't just a worry for her but for all the rampant and corrupt underground criminal factions.

Deciding she had enough of listening to all the political grandstanding, she walked around the sea of people until she squeezed by enough to get into the main entrance of the precinct.

Once inside, she went through the mundane and drawn-out process of trying to get information from the clerk sitting at the front desk. After having to repeat Liam's name nearly three times, present her identification twice, and be given the stink eye, she was finally escorted back to the holding area.

Despite Layne having triple-checked, she had removed anything that could be construed as a weapon from her body before arriving, a small pang of paranoia nagged at her after she went through the metal detector. Fortunately, the machine remained silent, and the officer guided her to a cell that held several men, one of whom was her disheveled-looking brother.

From the state of his hair, he must have been tugging at it and leaving it sticking out in every direction. He was in a pair of jeans and a loose-fitted tee, all of which had seen better days. Clearly displayed across his face was the stress of his situation.

"You have five minutes," the officer warned her, but when she looked at the man's hands, he subtly flashed his five fingers twice, indicating she had ten minutes. Corrupt cops were one of her favorite assets during times like these. Layne nodded in acknowledgment before stepping up to the bars, keeping Liam from being a free man.

The second he saw her, he stood up from the small bench and quickly approached. His hands each wrapped around a bar as he looked relieved to see her. "Layne, finally, you made it."

She stared at him, and while her face may have appeared emotionless, she was anything but. Layne wanted to tear him a new asshole for the stupidity of getting himself locked up.

Beginning to pitch his story, he blurted out the start of his excuse. "This is all a big fuckin' mistake."

Layne shook her head in disappointment. "Shut up, Liam. I don't want to hear another word from you until I'm done saying what I came down here to say."

Liam's hands tightened up on the bars in front of him while his lips were tightly pressed together in a strained effort to keep his words to himself.

"You know what some of the charges they have pending against you are? Assault of a police officer, driving under the influence, possession of a deadly weapon, resisting arrest. Oh, and the real cherry on fucking top? Bribery. Were you just trying to see what they could throw at you?" The second he opened his mouth, she lifted a finger to indicate she wasn't done speaking yet.

"Since you're unlikely to get out of here on a Desk Appearance Ticket, let me put this clearly for you so there is no mistaking what I will and won't be doing. I will not be posting bail for you. You can go to your arraignment and pray that the judge forgot his anti-senile pills that day. I will make sure that you don't have the dumbest fucking attorney show up to represent you." She stared at him without any hint of jest in her expression.

He gave a shake of the bars in his grasp before hitting one with the side of his fist. "Fuck you, Layne! You know damn well that Dad would have already gotten me the hell out of here."

Her eyes widened in disbelief before she scoffed. "Oh, really? What good would that do you, hm? You'd just turn around and do it all over again. Dad *knew* he fucked up with you. That's why things are the way they are right now, with me once again cleaning up your fuck ups. Only this time, you're not getting back the chance to sabotage it all again." Sometimes, the best truth was the harsh truth.

The anger in his voice rose as he glared at her from within his cage. "You need to bail me out! It's my damn money, too." He clenched his teeth so hard she hoped his face got stuck like that, or he cracked a tooth, preferably both.

Remaining the calmest she felt in years in dealing with her brother's bullshit; she shook her head again at him. "No, it's not. You spent every last dime on pieces of ass and who knows what else. We nearly lost everything! *Everything*, Liam. As far as I'm concerned, you don't have a penny to your name until I say you have earned it. If this is the lesson you need to learn to get your ass to that point, so be it."

Her feet brought her a step back from the cell, maintaining eye contact with Liam as he seethed at her with a deep-seated sense of loathing and hatred at that moment. She didn't care if he never spoke to her again after this, she was tired of his messes and inability to take responsibility for himself.

"I will let Walt Elkins know you will need representation at your hearing. It's the best you're going to get from me." Walt was the latest addition to Layne's growing team of assets. He was an expensive lawyer to keep on retainer, but his track record was noteworthy. Enough so that she felt confident that Liam wouldn't get raked over the coals, even if he did deserve it.

She let out a tired sigh. "When you do get out, come find me. If you want any part of this business, this bullshit has to stop."

Layne turned on her heel and walked back down towards the end of the hall, where an officer opened up a door that led out of the holding area. The echoes of her brother's voice reverberated off the walls and into her ears.

Liam yanked on the unyielding bars again, this time with explosive frustration. "Bitch! I hope you fucking get eaten alive out there! You won't make it a month in this business without me! The others will never give you any more respect than they would a damn whore!"

When he noticed that his outburst wasn't capturing Layne's attention, he unleashed a raw yell. "Fine! Go! Go fuck that freak, but he's only with you for the money and power! He will be nothing but a goddamn cum stain on our name, just wait and see!"

She paused at the doorway, her back to Liam as he hurled those last vile words. Layne gave a hard swallow, trying her best to deflect the pain of the verbal attacks. One would have thought she had learned to ignore her brother's wielding of words as weapons by now.

In a perfect world, she had always hoped that with enough time, maturity, and healing, he would find his way to being a better person. She didn't expect anyone who worked in the realm of underground violence and crime to be a saint, but she did expect more from someone she shared a bloodline with. Maybe it was a lot to hope for, but a small piece of her had tried to hold onto that optimism for as long as she could.

With every bit of self-control she had left, she locked her jaw shut to prevent spewing forth her thoughts, which were not meant for public ears. Especially not when she found herself in the middle of a police station.

She glanced over at the officer waiting for her to leave through the open door. Steadying her voice to hide how shaken she felt inside, she nodded at the man, "Thanks."

Layne left the holding area, left her brother, and had to tell herself that this all would pay off in the long run. A girl could dream, right?

CHAPTER EIGHT

Her boot-clad foot slammed into the stomach of the poor sap lying on the cement floor in front of her. "Then, he says I'm not going to make it a *month*!" It wasn't clear if she was recounting the visit with Liam to the victim on the receiving end of her brutal kicks or to the watchful man at her back.

She huffed as she felt suffocated by the black mask stretched over her face. The heat of her breath trapped behind the fabric created a sheen of sweat across her face. Layne couldn't imagine how Joey made a habit of wearing his for long periods of time. The rest of her donned all dark clothing from the slim-fitted pants with enough stretch to allow for movement and a black tee underneath a jacket.

Ever since she started making moves to lead the O'Reilly organization, Joey had insisted she take some precautions to protect her identity. It wasn't the big baddies that worried him, but also the saints of the world looking to help the so-called good guys. Honestly, she just figured Joey got turned on seeing her wear it.

As a result, she had been doing her best to remember her similarly styled skull mask that covered the lower half of her face from the bridge of her nose down over her chin. The white toothy smirk of the skull had crisscrossed ribbons in orange and emerald colors to honor her Irish descent.

Layne brushed a strand of her dark chestnut hair away from her face, attempting to incorporate it back into her ponytail as she exhaled an aggravated sigh.

The man in front of her was sniveling as he rolled back and forth with his arms wrapped around his stomach. “I swear, I don’t know nothing about no deals between Russ and Italo,” he cried out pathetically.

This worthless low-life was supposed to have information on Russell Spencer, the same jackass that had worked with one dead Andrew Correlli and thought the O’Reilly legacy should be defunct by now.

Word on the street was that Russ had been working with a mid-grade crony, Italo Giorgi, to assemble a meeting of the minds of various criminal units across the city. Layne hadn’t been extended an invitation, and she doubted it was an oversight. She was pretty damn certain that Russ was still hung up on their last discussion where she promised he would make the top of her shitlist if he crossed her again. The difference now was that she was the one in charge of O’Reilly Enterprises, and he had to answer to her, not to her jackass brother.

She had come here to personally extract some information from this piece of shit after one of her more reliable resources had suggested he was potentially useful. So far, she hadn’t gotten anything from him except vague non-answers. “That’s not what I fucking heard.” Her temper was already at full flare before this idiot made the decision to lie to her.

Behind her, also bearing witness to Layne’s attempt at relieving some stress while demanding answers, was Joey. His face was concealed by the very mask he had worn when he had first encountered Layne after Franzetti’s goons had abducted her and brought her down to the docks.

He leaned back against the exposed steel beam of the third floor of the warehouse, which was currently under construction. The bulk of his muscled arms crossed in front of his chest as he stayed out of her warpath. From head to toe, all six-foot-two of him was dressed in black. The collage of tattoos on his arms were covered by the long-sleeved black shirt, and his broad thighs were in a pair of cargo pants with a utility belt around the waist.

At the root of his reasoning for being there were mostly good intentions in ensuring her safety now that she was leading the charge at the top of the O’Reilly ranks. The less honorable side of him just wanted to get his dick hard by watching her sport that dark mask and bring a grown man down to his knees. It did something primal to him, knowing that lesser men bowed before her and begged. Yet, he was the only man capable of getting her to drop to her knees before him. Call it ego, alpha male bullshit, or whatever else you'd like, but he got off on all of it.

He spoke up, "Look, man, this isn't looking good for you. I'd just tell her what she wants to know." Joey was hoping it would help the man have a moment to see the light to the path of his salvation.

Layne squatted down and pulled her Glock from the back of her pants, yanking on the slide to make it clear it was hot with a round in the chamber. The man stared at her with wide eyes that let you know he was one hiccup away from shitting his pants.

While trying to maintain an even tone, she stared right back at him. "We've been at this for over an hour. You need to give me something to work with here. A name, a place, some chick that overheard something in the middle of a blowjob. Help me out."

The man perked up a little bit and nodded his head quickly. "Oh! I know someone who might know something."

She rolled her eyes, hoping this wasn't going to be another trail to another dead end. "And…?" Layne urged him to continue as she gave a slight wave of her gun for him to continue speaking.

"Italo has a girl. She works at this fancy nudie bar. Um… uh… Katie's, n-no, Cassidy's Cave! That's it! He gets a private room with her every Thursday night. Does a lot of his meetings there, too." He nodded in excitement with his eyes full of such hope that he had given Layne something to go on.

Layne glanced back over her shoulder at Joey at the mention of Gage's strip club. It's not where either of them wanted this trail to lead to. Looking back at the quivering rat of a man on the ground, she pushed her hands against her knees as she stood back up. "Was that so hard? Thank you."

The man breathed out in relief. A false sense of security claimed him as he relaxed back against the floor.

Without warning, Layne fired a single shot that found a home directly in the man's temple. He had never seen it coming. At least he had died without fear, that was more than some people got.

She went through the motions of ensuring her firearm was safely tucked away again. Her right hand curled into a fist and stretched back out several times as the kickback from the shot drew an ache in protest. The freshly healed fracture still did not leave her without its occasional reminders.

Joey didn't even flinch at the sound of the gunshot echoing inside the room full of exposed beams, stacks of sheetrock, and scaffolding. He came up to her, easing her gaze away from the body on the floor. "Look at me, Layney."

Even with his fingers guiding her by her chin to look away at the price this man just paid so she could have her information, her eyes struggled to tear themselves off the morbid sight.

"*Layne*." This time, the demanding depth of Joey's voice asserted itself more forcefully to draw her attention. Her eyes finally looked up at him. The hypnotizing darkness of his chocolate hues drew her back from what was going on inside of her head.

The violent edge her voice had possessed over the past hour had eased down into something softer and more delicate. "I couldn't risk him tipping anyone off."

He tugged down his mask now that it was just the two of them there. "I know. I would have done the same thing." Joey's fingertips traced along the trail of ribbon across the front of her mask until he found the edge and eased it away from her face.

She became more aware of her breathing as her body recognized the tender trace of his touch. "Joey, now isn't the time..." her voice apologetic, ready to wave off whatever advances he was about to make.

He leaned down, and his hands grabbed her right underneath her ass and lifted. His cock was already straining to be free from the confines of his pants. Getting her back up against the beam he had been leaning on earlier, he had her legs naturally spread for him to press himself up against her center.

His fingers roughly dug into the backs of her thighs. "The hell it's not. I want nothing more right now than to fuck you after watching that."

Layne's hands grabbed onto the top of his wide shoulders, feeling the muscles rippling underneath as he supported her weight. She groaned as his hardened bulge pressed against her core.

After she wrapped her legs around his waist, linking her ankles together, his hands glided up her sides, rough palms sliding up underneath her shirt against the smoothness of her bare stomach.

With a lustful blaze in his look at her, his hands stopped just short of the bottom of her satin bra. "Go ahead and tell me." His husky tone bore the weight of a dare in it.

Her body not only felt like his hands were lighting her on fire but incapacitating her. Layne's emerald eyes looked right back into the depths of his. She was hardly able to swallow down her own saliva that was pooling in her mouth at the thought of what was positioned at the apex of her thighs.

"Tell you what, Joey?" She asked, genuinely wondering what he wanted from her besides a good hard fuck.

He inched his mouth closer to hers, leaving just enough room for a single breath. "I want to hear you tell me you're going to stop being my good girl and taking my cock any time I want to give it to you." Joey's hips rolled up against her to make it unquestionably clear what he planned to give her, whether it was the time for it or not.

If any words were spoken in the universe that could have caused her self-control to self-combust, he had just spoken them. Her heart rate was picking up speed, and the dead body on the floor no longer registered in her awareness.

With a sharp inhale at the push of his body, reminding her pussy how much it was throbbing, she shook her head while her teeth bit into her lower lip.

The tiny gesture of how she drew in her lip only increased his need for her. Closing the gap between their mouths, his lips connected with hers possessively. His teeth then sank into her bottom lip to draw it away from her own bite. Sucking on her lip to savor her taste, he lingered there for not nearly enough time for either of them.

"That wasn't an answer. Are you going to stop being my good girl, Layncy?" His hands grasped onto her ribcage, his thumbs caressing over the delicate skin just below the swell of her breasts. It was all too easy to feel how quick and shallow her breaths were in reaction to him.

Layne caught herself shaking her head again and was quick to push the words out. "No, I will always be your good girl."

A sensual growl of approval escaped past Joey's lips when she confirmed what they both already knew. His mouth came to the side of her neck, lavishing it with electrifying kisses as one of his hands slid over the cup of her bra. His fingers pulled the cup away from her breast so he could wrap his hand around the mound of her flesh.

Layne's hand slid along his shoulder and up the back of his neck as she tilted her head back until it was pressed against the beam behind her. The soft pink lips of her mouth parted as she let out a quiet moan of approval.

Joey pushed himself roughly against her core despite the clothing on each of their bodies. His hand pushed her body down so she could feel how hard his cock was for her. As his mouth consumed the taste of the skin of her throat, his fingers took the stiff nipple of her breast and twisted it between his fingers. His hips still slowly trying to dry-fuck her.

Her arousal was soaking through her panties as she felt the desire reaching peaks that had her other hand dropping down to frantically pull at the button of her pants. Before her fingers could dip inside to provide some self-provided satisfaction, Joey's hold set her breast free, dropped to grab her wrist, and pulled it up above her head.

He raised his head from her throat, his lust-drunk expression drawn across his face. "Not yet. I have first dibs on that wet cunt of yours, Layney."

Fuck. She had some idea of how much Joey got turned on while she worked, but this was a whole new level of his domineering side, and she was here for it.

"Then fucking take it." Her voice was breathy as she leaned forward and crushed her lips against his hungrily. She was met with his tongue pushing past her lips to invade her mouth. His hand tightly held onto her side inside her shirt while his other dropped her wrist and grabbed the side of her face. His fingers curled around the back of her neck, keeping her head exactly where he wanted.

The ding of the elevator on the other end of the wide-open space echoed through the air. No one should have been in the building at this time of night. Yet, here they were, loaded with weaponry and keeping company with a rapidly cooling body on the floor.

Immediately, their faces split from one another. Layne dropped her legs down from his waist as Joey set her on her feet. His fingers made sure the first thing he did was pull Layne's mask up over her face as a measure to keep her safe, no matter the cost.

"This way." His hand latched onto hers tightly, pulling her in the direction opposite of the elevator doors. By the time they got to the door leading to the stairwell, he had his skull-faced mask also back in place.

Running over to the door to the emergency exit with Joey, she slipped into the stairwell first, with Joey close behind her. Her feet quickly carried her down the steps, his heavy set of boots sounding off quickly behind her.

When the fresh night air washed over them as they exited the building, she saw Joey's black sports bike parked right where he had left it in the alley just several feet from the door they just emerged from. He jogged ahead of her, snagged the sole helmet off the seat, and tossed it at Layne before mounting the bike. His hand retrieved a pair of protective riding glasses from his thigh pocket, sliding them over his eyes. A second later, the purr of the engine filled the air.

Her hands caught the helmet, immediately pushing it down over her head. Her hand grabbed onto his hard bicep as she hopped on behind him. After her ass was in the seat, Layne's arms were tightly wrapped around his waist as she adhered herself to his back.

As Joey pulled out of the alley, Layne looked, and her gut filled with both dread and relief as they sped by the front of the warehouse they had just fled from. Two NYPD patrol cars sat out front with their lights flashing. There was no way that they were there by coincidence. Someone had tipped them off.

CHAPTER NINE

Inside the modest apartment belonging to one Rebecca Zappa, the two girls hung out in the cramped living room. The limited space was filled with papers scattered across the coffee table, boxes of samples of various wedding paraphernalia, and a laptop off to the side.

Rebecca rapidly tapped the top of her pen against the pad of paper while she mulled over the thoughts inside her head and stared down at the doodles and diagrams in front of her.

Layne lay across the dark brown leather sofa with her head supported by the arm of it, a bottle of beer hanging out in one hand while the other rested on top of her stomach. Her hair swept up into a messy bun on top of her head, a comfy pair of black leggings on her lower half, and a distressed scoop-neck turquoise tee hanging off of her upper body.

"You know," Layne spoke up, "does it *really* matter where the flowers go?" She turned her head to look over at her best friend. This entire wedding planning was all Rebecca's jam and not something Layne had given second thoughts to. Did people actually care if flowers were low on the table or up on a pedestal? She didn't.

Her blonde bestie's jaw hung open after a small gasp, her pen immediately ceasing its movement. "Of course it does!" she exclaimed. She set the pen down on the pad with a dramatic sigh. "I'm not going to let you downplay your own damn wedding day, Layne. It's going to be extravagantly beautiful, perfectly executed, and all you need to do is show up and say, 'I do.' You deserve it after all the shitstorms you've had to endure."

Rebecca knew better than to bring up the horrific circumstances surrounding Layne's first marriage—if one could even call it that. Signing papers that were questionably legal with Eric had been nothing but a cold and emotionless business transaction. She knew that Layne deserved better than that. Even if she still had minor reservations about Joey, she could agree that he had been taking care of Layne more than any man ever had. That was no easy feat.

After taking a small sip from the amber lager, Layne gave a light smile at the notion of seeing Joey standing across from her, ready to commit to being in her life forever. The thought of seeing him dressed in a tux, in a church of all places, began to remind her of the last time he had gotten all cleaned up for her. A memory where she ended up on the hood of his car left a heated desire beginning to pool in her lower stomach.

Disrupting Layne's thoughts was the sound of the front door to Rebecca's apartment giving a small click as the handle turned and swung open. Joey pushed his way in with several bags of food in his hands. He nudged the door shut behind him and carried the bags over to the nearby kitchen table, where he unloaded all of them.

"When you said you ordered lunch, I didn't expect to be picking up an entire damn buffet." He griped as he shoved his sunglasses up on top of his head to rest on his slicked-back dark blonde hair.

Rebecca gave the biggest smile ever, trying to exude as much innocence and sweetness as possible. "You're the best. It wouldn't be girls' lunch without options. Besides, we both know that Layne needs the reminder to eat every once in a while before she gets too cranky." That earned a piercing glare from Layne at the minor dig.

"Does that mean I'm officially out of the doghouse?" He raised a brow at her.

She gave a shrug of her shoulders and a playful grin. "Ninety percent there."

Joey looked over at Layne, who was lazed out on the couch. "She's a tough one to win over." He nodded over at Rebecca before coming over to the end of the sofa where Layne's head was resting.

"Nearly as tough as you are," he murmured as he leaned over her. His hand ran along Layne's throat until it cupped under her jaw to tilt her head further back so he could greet her mouth with an upside-down kiss. The several-day buildup of scruff on his face was lightly abrasive against her skin.

The magnetic draw of his mouth left her wanting more as her back arched slightly at the sensation. It wasn't until Rebecca cleared her throat that the two of them wrapped up their moment of affection together, leaving Layne with a sheepish smile on her face.

Joey rounded the edge of the couch and took a seat at the end where Layne's feet were, lifting them momentarily to lay them back down in his lap. "How's the planning going?"

That earned him a rolling of eyes from both girls for different reasons, but it was Layne who chimed in first. "She's in full, level five-thousand wedding planner mode. At this rate, I expect members of a royal family from a country I've never heard of to be attending." Her snark and sass were in full swing.

Rebecca, on the other hand, shook her head in denial and looked at Joey for backup. "Help me out here. I've already explained to her that showing up to the courthouse and having a kegger afterward is not only *not* what she deserves but sends the wrong message socially."

Layne shifted, so she was now propped up on her elbow. "There's nothing wrong with that plan!"

"Except it's not what you want." Rebecca fired back quickly. "Do you want me to go into the many in-depth conversations we've had over the years? I will be more than happy to share your extremely detailed dream wedding plans involving Jackson Holloway in the ninth grade. *Including* the wedding night."

Her eyes widened. "Oh my God," Layne groaned as she sat up. "Don't you dare," she warned before looking over at Joey. "Look, you've even said it yourself, it's a piece of paper."

Suddenly finding himself in the middle of this, Joey sighed and looked over at his future wife. His incredibly stubborn future wife. His hand gave her foot a gentle squeeze. "I did say that, but that was different."

Goddamn, if he didn't want to bring Eric Ellis back from the dead just to snap his neck all over again for the number he had done on Layne. The bastard never deserved to have his name next to hers on that marriage certificate.

He straightened up in his seat, directing his eyes right at Layne. "Layney, I want you to have the day you deserve. I want everyone to know that you get the best of everything, including the best of me. Let's show the world that we aren't paper-thin." He let those words sink in for a moment.

When she began to show signs of backing down, the tightness easing away from her shoulders and a softness flittering across her eyes, Joey flashed her a smirk. "Although, I am interested in what you had in mind for the wedding night."

Layne sat up, grabbed one of the throw pillows tucked against her side, and tossed it at him. "Not a damn chance!"

He easily dodged the square pillow with a chuckle. "We'll see."

After an afternoon of planning, well mostly of Rebecca laying out options and drawing out opinions from Layne, Joey drove Layne back home.

"Have you heard anything about Liam?" He glanced over at Layne in the passenger seat while they sat at a red traffic light.

Looking up from scrolling through some messages on her phone, she shook her head. "Only that he had his arraignment hearing. He was denied bail, so he will have some time to sit and think about his actions behind bars. Walt thinks it was a politically driven decision by the judge." She shrugged, trying to appear unfazed and indifferent.

"You still did the right thing, Layne. Sometimes, the best thing is to be in lockup. When I did my time at Rikers, it was shitty, but I fucking learned what I needed while I was there." It had been a hellhole of an experience for Joey, but it gave him the resources and contacts to learn some of the best tricks of the trade. Not to mention, it made him smarter, so next time, he wouldn't make the same fuck ups.

She felt a deep breath fill her lungs before she released it, trying to absorb the words of reassurance he was attempting to give her. "I know. I just had hoped things would be different, ya know? It's only him, and I left in this family, and I expected more."

The light turned green, and Joey proceeded, taking them towards their destination. "Blood makes you related, not family. Liam hasn't been your family since I've known you." Perhaps a harsh iteration of the truth, but from the outside peering in on the O'Reilly household, Liam only gave a shit about one person—himself.

Trying not to dwell on the topic, she shifted things over to the subject of another troublesome sibling. "So…" Her voice trailed off as she tried to find the best way to broach the topic.

Joey glanced over at her briefly while trying to maintain his focus on the road. "So?"

"I think it's a good idea if you hang back tonight." She did her best to keep it sounding as much of a neutral decision as possible. It was Thursday, and if luck was smiling upon them, Italo would be at Gage's strip club for a weekly private dick rub.

Immediately, his upper body stiffened in the driver's seat. His hand jerked the steering wheel and cut off several other drivers before pulling off to a side street where he double parked the Challenger. "You've lost your damn mind. Not happening." His chocolate eyes looked over at her, full of unyielding assertiveness.

The sudden maneuvering of the vehicle and near collisions nearly caused her a heart attack and shook all her efforts to keep her voice calm. "Christ!" She glanced around at where they were parked on the street before staring back at him. "You really think that you can hold your shit together if Gage is there tonight? Honestly?"

He reached over, his hand curled around the back of her neck to make sure he had her full attention. Joey wanted her to hear his words loud and clear. "Gage isn't my concern. You are, and you aren't going there without me. Do you understand?"

The warmth and the strength of his hand on the back of her neck had tingling sensations coursing down her spine and spreading down each of her limbs. His words carried the weight of a man who was hellbent on getting his way.

"Don't make me ask twice," he added.

She nodded at him. He accepted her acknowledgment by leaning over and briefly locking his lips onto hers to ease away the sternness he had thrust upon her moments ago.

"Good," was all he said afterward before he sat back in his seat.

Great, it looked like they were both going to Cassidy's Cave tonight. She just hoped that Gage wouldn't hinder their efforts and Joey could keep his personal shit with his brother on lockdown.

CHAPTER TEN

As it turned out, Thursday evenings weren't very popular at the strip club tucked away into the outer edge of the Hell's Kitchen neighborhood. It was just shy of one o'clock in the morning, and a bouncer wasn't even posted outside the blacked-out glass door.

The neon letters above the entrance were a symbolic mixture of what you'd find inside, with 'Cassidy's' in a swirly pink feminine font and 'Cave' in more masculine blocky blue letters. The color combination was reminiscent of a tuft of cotton candy you would purchase at a fair. Though, the treats inside this establishment were much more carnal.

Layne held the door open long enough for Joey to follow in closely behind her. The second they stepped foot inside, the heavy scent of various floral perfumes and freely flowing booze was overwhelming. Music played in the background, something sensually upbeat with a husky-sounding female singer that Layne didn't recognize.

Dancing half-assed to the tune was one platinum blonde on a circular stage before a sole male patron seated at a table in front of her. Given several empty cocktail glasses at his table, a gold wedding band laid next to them, and the sullen look on his face, the poor guy looked like he had been having a day.

At the bar was a scantily clad bartender, wearing nothing more than a black bra filled with a pair of obviously fake tits and a pair of hot shorts that may as well have been painted on. She was leaning back against the liquor display behind the bar, and right next to her, standing at the cash drawer, was a now familiar figure.

Gage had on a pair of faded blue jeans that were fitted just enough to do justice to his tight and drool-worthy ass. A black dress shirt covered the hard muscles of his upper body; the sleeves rolled up to his elbows, showing off several tattoos, which included several roses. He counted a wad of cash in his hands and tucked it back into the drawer before pushing it shut.

The woman bartender nudged Gage's arm and said something to him, prompting him to turn around. Setting his deep brown eyes on Layne first, one side of his mouth lifted as he gave a cocky smile. His sights shifted to Joey standing next to her, his smile then faltering ever so slightly.

He left his spot behind the bar and approached the two of them. "You finally convinced him to bring his stubborn ass down here?" His brow lifted curiously at Layne. Gage's arms crossed in front of his chest; it became clear he was wearing a white tank underneath the dress shirt where the silver chain of his necklace hung just underneath.

Joey didn't waste time in responding. "We're not here to see you." His voice strained to keep things as amicable as possible.

"Really?" Gage looked around at the sparsely populated club and then back at Joey. "Not too many other people here to see." He grinned at Layne. "Just couldn't stay away, could ya?"

Over his cocky attitude, she brushed off his question with a roll of her eyes. Layne hoped there was at least one other customer there. "Are any of your private rooms occupied?"

Something entertaining must have crossed Gage's mind as he gave a sinful little smirk while his eyes briefly surveyed what Layne was wearing. The way she wore her ensemble had his cock coming to life inside his jeans. It wasn't just what she had on, but it was the way her black pants fit her toned legs and wrapped around her hips. The curve of her body up to the swell of her breasts in the snug black long-sleeved shirt with a low scooped neckline had his thoughts sinking south quickly.

Layne's dark hair was woven into an intricate French braid, leaving Gage with thoughts of wrapping his hand around the tail of it and pulling until she submitted to him. He would happily occupy a private room with her, given the chance. It made him wonder just how much of a brat she would be in the bedroom or if she knew how to behave when given a thick and hard reason to.

"Just one, but we can make it two." He finally responded to the question with playfulness dancing across his words.

Joey gave a growl, earning him a look from Layne to simmer down. He shifted his stance, his arms flexing under the moment of tension. He had opted to wear his go-to outfit for his jobs, the all-black tactical attire that made him more easily blend into the shadows. The only thing that was missing was his mask—for now.

She approached Gage, painting a sexy little smile on her face as she stared up at him with her best big ol' innocent doe eyes. "Gage," she spoke with a gentle voice as her finger trailed up the center of his chest. The tip of her finger ran along the exposed skin below his collarbone until it hooked under the chain of his necklace. Twining the cord of metal around her finger, she pulled it into her grasp so she could pull him forward to come closer to her face.

Her face was inches away from his as he voluntarily leaned down at her beckoning. "Does it look like he's the type that wants to share?" Layne referred to Joey, standing just a few steps behind her. "Just tell me who is in the private room."

Layne's question earned her an unexpected chuckle and an amused grin from Gage. He weighed the risks and benefits of taking advantage of the proximity to those deliciously pouty lips of hers, ultimately deciding to bide his time. "Oh, you'd have to ask him about that one." His eyes flicked at Joey with a wicked grin.

The response had Layne's hand loosening up on the chain enough to allow it to fall from her fingers as she hadn't foreseen that answer to her question. Her lips separated partially in confusion and the inability to find the words to respond.

Gage straightened up, putting some fresh air between them before he pushed any more of Joey's buttons tonight. "It's one of my regulars, Italo Giorgi. Comes here every week. Brings a few of his buddies, and my girl, Danielle, provides the entertainment. He's usually in there 'til nearly three in the morning most weeks."

Joey's hand came onto Layne's shoulder, grasping onto it possessively, sending an unspoken message to his brother. "Clear the club, Gage." A fierce look in his eyes made it clear that this wasn't a request. The fewer witnesses they had, the better.

She stood there assessing the tension between the two men before stepping away to scope out the club to get a count of who was currently present outside of the private room.

When she returned, the two guys were still standing where she had left them. She arrived within earshot only to hear the tail end of the conversation between them.

"Layne isn't Rosie," Joey said. "She's—" his words cut off sharply once he noticed Layne approaching. Whatever else he had intended to tack onto the end of that sentence was left unsaid.

Despite what he thought, Layne had overheard enough for the seed to be planted in her mind about whatever was going on during the conversation she had interrupted. However, they weren't here to talk about past issues. She had business to take care of.

Her emerald hues stared at the two of them. "Are you two done here? I have shit to do." The words spewed forth more harshly than they should have.

"Sure," was all Gage responded with before he stepped away. He dismissed the few remaining employees on the clock, which in turn prompted a very disappointed and sad middle-aged man who had been the sole recipient of entertainment during this slow evening.

Layne didn't look at Joey while she tried to focus her brain on Italo and what was going on in that private suite. Who else was in there? What information was she going to be able to extract? What did Rosie have to do with anything that Joey and Gage were talking about?

After all was said and done, Gage returned with confirmation. "That's everyone."

The second that Layne made a move to head back toward the private room, Joey's hand stopped her. Easily, his hold swallowed up her elbow in his grasp, ceasing her from continuing forward. Her eyes glanced down at his inked hand and then his face, wondering what the hell he was doing.

His other hand reached into her pocket and retrieved one last important item. "You don't know who else is in there." When he lifted his hand, her mask hung from his fingertips.

She snagged the mask and began to stretch it across her face. "Oh, good. I wouldn't want anyone to mistake me for Rosie." Layne knew she shouldn't have jealousy over a dead woman she hardly knew a thing about. Yet, there was something in the way Joey had spoken her name to Gage that still had her insides twisting with insecurity.

Layne pulled her arm from his grip, not bothering to wait for any sort of reaction to her bitterness. She stormed off to the area where she had noticed the private rooms where only one door was visibly shut. At least she could put her feelings to good use; it would make things much easier.

While the urge to just kick in the damn door was strong, there was no sense in expending extra energy on making a dramatic entrance. She twisted the doorknob, and much to her surprise, it fully rotated, indicating it remained unlocked.

Right as Joey was approaching with his own dark mask now in place, she swung open the door to reveal the occupants inside.

Well… fuck. There were four people inside that room suddenly staring back at her. That didn't include who Layne assumed to be, Danielle, given she was the only one with tits out and a strand of yarn for panties. Taking a good look at each man cramped into the room on the velvet sofa, she didn't recognize any of them. Each of them wore cheap and grungy clothes, indicating they weren't rolling in the big bucks. Low-level thugs.

Layne leaned her shoulder against the doorframe, using her small and innocent size to look as unassuming as possible. Behind her back, she spread out four of her fingers and gave them a wiggle. It was the signal to Joey of how many potential threats she saw before her. "I'm Danielle's replacement for the evening. Which one of you assholes is Italo?"

When she was met with silence and uncomfortable stares, she shrugged and pushed away from the doorframe. "The strong and silent types, eh? I can work with that." She motioned for Danielle to come closer. When she did as she was told, Layne gave her one more instruction. "Go home."

The dancer hesitated, so Layne repeated herself more firmly. "Get the fuck out." The woman with a face full of makeup and glam nodded and slipped out of the room.

That's when someone finally found their voice and stood up. It was a lanky-looking man who had spent too much time underneath a tanning bed. "Yo, what the fuck, bitch? You into some kinky-ass shit with that mask or somethin'?" He squared his shoulders and thrust his chest forward to look like he was something titillating to look at.

She made sure to keep her eyes out for any other movement, but knowing Joey was out of their sight a few feet away, she had very few concerns.

Finally, she decided it was about time to stir the pot and see which one these asshats were going to react. "I told you, I'm looking for Italo. Actually, I'm looking for any one of you who might have been talking to Russell Spencer. Does that name ring a bell?"

Ding, ding, ding! That was the winning ticket. The second Russ's name was dropped, they all began to scatter like roaches running back to their hidey holes when the lights got turned on.

It was the man who first stood up that reached her first. The skinny bastard tried to push her out of the way, and instead, her hands latched onto him and propelled him into the hallway headfirst toward a wall. Upon contact, he was dazed and dropped to one knee.

Two more guys ran out behind her, encountering the looming presence of Joey. He clotheslined one who fell to the floor like a sack of potatoes, then grabbed the other by his throat before greeting the center of the man's face with a harsh punch. The impact shattered the bones of the guy's nose.

The last one? He ran by Layne just as she was bending over, grabbing a fistful of the first man's hair and slamming his head into the wall one more time. Her eyes caught sight of the straggler who darted past her. "Damn it, we got a runner!"

Without a second thought, she released Mr. Crispy-Fried Tan guy who was now blessed with a massive headache. She immediately chased after the last guy, who at least had the sense not to run toward Joey. Layne could appreciate his decision to take the opposite path. Joey was nothing less than fearfully intimidating, even without his mask on.

While securing zip ties on the wrists of both of the men he had incapacitated, Joey looked up to see Layne rounding the corner out of his sight in pursuit of the fourth man. "Gage!" he barked over his shoulder for his brother.

Layne sprinted as fast as the short length of her legs would go. The man she was chasing after was quick but not agile. He slowed down each time he had to shift the movement of his feet to avoid running into various pieces of furniture and other obstacles as they entered the back storage area of Cassidy's. It allowed Layne to cut down the distance between them.

There was a backdoor exit straight ahead of them, and if he made it out that door, he was going to be likely as good as gone. Before she could make a final push to get close enough to him to prevent that, a metal bat swung out straight into the man's gut. The attempted escapee lost all the breath in his lungs at the unexpected strike that came from off the side and left him lying on the floor.

She tried to skid to a stop right as Gage came into view, wanting to avoid running right into him. He tossed the piece of sports equipment off behind him, figuring this guy was as good as down for the time being.

Immediately, he held his hands up, catching hold of Layne as she failed to slow her momentum in time to prevent the collision with him.

Her small body landed up against him without so much as shifting his weight on his feet. Gage grinned proudly at her as his hands remained locked on her arms. "Do I get a token of your appreciation for coming to your aid?"

Still trying to catch her breath from the chase, her eyes looked up at him in disbelief that he thought he deserved anything other than a thank you. "*Please*. I would have had him."

He leaned over and whispered in her ear, looking for any excuse to get closer to her. "Keep telling yourself that, sweetheart." Even with a little bit of sweat gracing her skin, he took note of the scent of her perfume lingering underneath it. Gage could already imagine how amazing the mixture of daisies, rain, and her sweat would smell on his sheets after giving her a night filled with his type of pleasure.

The scent of spiced vanilla invaded her senses, with Gage leaning in so close to her. She squirmed in his hands to avoid the temptation to lean in and let herself get wrapped up in it. Her arms eventually broke free of his loose hold. "If you want my appreciation, you can drag his ass back to the others."

Layne didn't wait for him to agree, she just began walking back to where things had kicked off just outside of the private room. Gage pulled the man who thought he was running out of here to his feet and dragged him back to where Joey had the other three all in their zip tie constraints. He shoved the attempted runaway towards his brother to take care of.

"Have any of them said anything useful?" She eyed the collection of lowlifes before her. Gage hovered at her backside as Joey stood on the other side of the group.

Joey tightened the last tie and gave a shove to the fourth man to join the rest of his comrades on the floor. "No, just a lot of pissin' and moanin'."

From behind Gage and Layne was the sound of a door swinging open. Shit, none of them had checked the bathroom. A man wearing clothes with a little more class emerged from the men's room. He was dressed in a pair of khakis and a dark purple polo.

Layne spun around to fully give the man her attention while Gage just peered over his shoulder. She started to step out from behind Gage to take care of this new situation.

There was little time from the moment the new guy came out from the restroom to the point where he saw the gathering of his pals on the floor, a woman and man both masked up and the club's owner.

Gage tried to keep his voice friendly. "Italo, man—shit!"

That's when things took a turn for the worse. Italo immediately withdrew a gun from the back of his pants, raising it in Layne's direction.

Then shots rang out.

CHAPTER ELEVEN

Italo squeezed the trigger with the intent to eliminate one of the masked individuals closest to him–Layne.

The second the jerkoff had revealed the firearm, Gage saw it being lifted in line with where Layne was. Gage stepped toward Layne, who was fortunately still within his arm's reach. Protectively, he wrapped his large arms around her, drawing her in tightly to his chest as he turned his back to Italo so his body curled over Layne's petite form like a shield.

He ducked down, covering as much of Layne's body as he could, paying particular attention to her most vital parts, like her head and upper body. Tightly, using his strength, he clutched onto her like a man fearful of losing a rare treasure to the depths of the ocean.

She had no time to react from the moment Italo became an active threat and when she was suddenly yanked into Gage's tight embrace. It had happened so quickly that all she could ascertain was that she was cloaked in safety. While the protective hold that Gage had on her was damn near suffocating, it was far better than suffering a potentially fatal gunshot wound. One experience in the whole being shot department was more than enough for her.

Layne felt Gage's body flinch around her as the sound of the bullet bursting into flight echoed in the air, her hands were pinned between their bodies, not allowing her to grab for anything defensively. Being pressed so close to his chest, she couldn't see shit. All she could do was huddle up with him and listen to the sound of his heavy breathing. Quickly after the first shot, that's when she heard a second round fired, which caused a slight ringing in her ears and was followed by a heavy thud.

It all felt like it transpired over the span of minutes, but it had only taken mere seconds. Even as panic set in at the sound of a body hitting the floor, and she began to struggle and push against Gage, he didn't allow her a single inch of freedom.

Once Gage looked up, Joey was holstering his pistol, and behind Gage was one less regular patron of Cassidy's Cave.

Joey immediately came over to where Gage was crouched down, his arms locked around Layne. He met eyes with his brother, not needing to say anything as a look passed between them. It was a look from Joey that held something with the least amount of hostility than it ever had in recent history with Gage.

His voice held a gravelly texture to it as Joey spoke. "Let me see her."

Layne was still squirming against Gage's chest, only easing up as she felt Gage pull her up with him as he stood. He loosened his arms from around her, allowing her to create space for herself. However, Joey didn't give her the chance as he immediately pulled her into his arms, surrounding her with the familiar woodsy scent of sage and leather.

The hug was brief but just enough to erase the concern from them both. Joey pulled back and looked her over. "Are you okay?"

She nodded and did the same inspection to Joey to confirm he was equally unhurt. "I'm fine."

Now that the adrenaline-filled moment was over, Gage looked at his arm, which had a burning sensation nagging at him. As he moved his arm to take a look, he gave a quiet hiss of pain, noticing a small tear in the curve of the shoulder of his shirt. "Goddamnit, this was a new fucking shirt," he grumbled.

Gage undid the series of buttons on the dress shirt until he peeled it from his torso. It revealed the white tank top that clung to each line of his bulky muscles and exposed the series of tattoos creeping up his arms. The lines of ink curved into images of roses and various sharp-edged weapons.

He inspected his shoulder, where there was a small wound, a line of blood creeping from it. Thankfully, it was only a graze. If he hadn't pulled Layne to him, it was quite possible she would have been struck down. He would accept this minor inconvenience over the thought of her perfect body being damaged.

When Layne noticed Gage stripping his shirt off and revealing where

Italo's bullet must have skimmed past him, she had a mixture of feelings fill her up inside. Guilt that he had put himself in harm's way for her and awe that he hadn't even thought twice about it. Sprinkle a little gratitude on top of all that, and she found herself seeing him through a slightly different lens. That lens especially didn't look half bad when she saw how the thin fabric of his tank top adhered to his fit form and the cut of the muscles of the steel-like biceps that had been clenching around her moments ago.

Interrupting her thoughts while her eyes had been lost on his younger brother, Joey spoke. "Now that we're down a lead," he motioned over to Italo's still body, "hopefully, these four are feeling chatty."

Layne looked over at the group of men all on the floor with their hands bound behind their backs. Some looked worse for wear, especially the one with the smashed nose courtesy of Joey's fist.

Killing Italo was not in the plan for tonight, and it put a major hitch in her plans. She tried not to be pissed about it, given they didn't have much of an option when guns were drawn. Pulling away from Joey's hold, she walked over to the group of men, all with different expressions on each of their faces. One still looked to be in pain, another looked defiant, one appeared to be terrified he would be shot next, and one was in shock and mentally checked the fuck out.

"The first one of you to give me something useful about Russ Spencer will be the only one walking out of here with both legs intact." Her eyes narrowed at them dangerously; she wondered who was going to break first.

Layne had been pleasantly surprised that the man who had appeared full of steadfast contempt was the first to crumble. He had sung like a canary the second Gage had fetched her the metal bat he had used earlier, and Layne used it to give a love tap to the lackey's kneecap.

Ended up that Russ had been working with Italo to begin setting up a series of intimidation tactics on known businesses that either supported Layne or straight up were on the outer edges of her territory. Of course, Italo needed the help of pettier criminals who were willing to engage in violent acts for less of a monetary incentive. That's where all four of these men came in.

She had made good on her word, leaving the man's legs uninjured. He only left the strip club with a broken arm and a promise from Layne. If he so much as tattled to Russell, there was no place he could hide that she wouldn't be able to track him down and creatively find more ways to impart pain on him.

The other three? None were so fortunate. Each of them left still sucking air into their lungs, but they all earned a bashing of their legs to have them hobbling or crawling out of there.

Layne locked up the front door after the last of them was gone, exhaustion weighing down on her. The two De Lucas were stationed at the bar, giving her the space to carry out her methods. Gage had offered to assist, but Joey convinced him that Layne was more than able to take care of this on her own while they sat back.

Tossing the bat to the side, she removed her mask and walked back to where Joey and Gage were standing, noticing each of them tracking her movements. What she noticed pressed against the zipper of Joey's pants wasn't unexpected, given how he felt about watching her assert herself. It was the outline at the front of Gage's pants that she hadn't expected to notice, and it was incredibly difficult not to have her attention drawn to it.

Well, shit, that was a hell of a sight to see in front of her. Trying her best to ignore that she had seen the dually magnificent sight that had her imagination swirling, she took up a seat on one of the stools.

Joey reached behind him, grabbed a glass of whiskey, and handed it over to her. It earned him one of her delightful smiles. "Thanks." She took the glass from him and wasted no time in emptying its contents into her mouth, swallowing down the burn happily after all of tonight's events.

Gage leaned back against the bar top on his elbows. "I took care of Italo. His body won't be found until someone takes a fine-tooth comb through whichever landfill he ends up at." One perk of Manhattan was the metric tons of trash the city generated got transported to one of many sites, some as far as South Carolina or even overseas in China.

She nodded, impressed that he was willing to help clean up their mess. Layne set her empty glass down on the bar. "I appreciate it." Her emerald eyes looked at his exposed shoulder. "How's your arm?"

He shrugged indifferently. "I'll live. Not the worst I've ever had, and the ladies love a good battle scar." Gage winked at her.

Joey poured another finger-high amount of the amber booze into Layne's empty glass. "Layne," he started with an even tone that sounded like he was about to discuss a trivial matter. "Gage and I were talking."

She sat up straighter in her seat, not liking how guarded he was making his voice. Anytime he started a conversation with such calm, it usually meant she wasn't going to particularly like what he had to say.

"About what?" She turned to set her gaze on Joey, who was now removing his mask and shoving it into his pocket. He rubbed his hand down over the front of his mouth, knowing that this had the potential to be met with a lot of resistance. It also had the risk of Layne trying to send him to sleep on the couch.

He offered her the refill of whiskey, but she refused to take what was only being handed to her to help ease the impact of whatever he was about to drop on her. Joey slowly inhaled and set the glass to the side.

"We already talked about you needing an extra set of eyes on you. I don't want to trust just anyone looking out for you. I need someone I can rely on, and finding anyone in this business that even comes up close to the caliber of protection I need for you…"

Joey didn't even have to finish his thought before Layne jumped to the conclusion. Her eyes darted to Gage, who, to his credit, wasn't wearing a smug smile for once. "Are you kidding me? Gage?!" She shook her head. "No." This should have been a point-blank decision from her and the discussion done with.

"Layney—"

She cut him off before he tried to pull out his charm to smooth this over. "Ever since he's come around, all you've been doing is telling me how reckless he is, and you don't want him around. Now, you're doing an entire one-eighty on that?"

Gage nodded. "She has a point. I'm about as reckless as you are." The sarcasm was in full swing on his words.

Joey shot his brother a glare before stepping up to Layne, taking her face in his hands. "It's just for the time being. If he does anything to give me pause, he's gone." He pressed his forehead to hers, lowering his voice. "You don't have to like it, but I'm not asking you to. I'm telling you, this is what has to happen."

Met with Joey's face in close proximity to her own, she gave a small frown, displaying her dissatisfaction with his decision overriding her own. His ass was already in the doghouse from his comment to Gage earlier, and now he was dropping this bomb on her, and she wasn't happy about it.

"Hope you find the couch comfortable to sleep on." She grumbled, knowing trying to argue with him on this was going to be pointless. It would have resulted in hours of back and forth, eating up energy she didn't have to expend.

Joey's lips pressed onto hers with a heat to melt away her agitated demeanor. When he pulled back, he smirked at her. "Couch is going to be just fine when you're underneath me taking my cock all night."

His words sent a spark of desire straight down between her legs, distracting her from realizing how soon she was going to always have a De Luca at her side.

CHAPTER TWELVE

All of Layne's abdominal muscles down the length of her torso were on fire. Her forearms were pressed firmly into the gym mat underneath her, supporting the weight of her body. The short span of her body was suspended in a rigid plank inside the home gym around the corner from the kitchen.

Her forehead donned a scattering of sweat droplets as she squeezed her eyes shut. She had to have been holding this plank for at least thirty minutes. Her body was beginning to tremble as her muscles felt pushed beyond fatigue.

When her eyes opened to take a peek at the timer between her wrists, she was sorely mistaken. The last bit of air in her lungs was forced out in a huff as she dropped her body down flat onto the mat with a groan. Almost two minutes. Her hand slapped the timer off as she laid her cheek against the cushy texture of the mat.

Layne lifted her head to look in the mirror affixed to the wall ahead of her. She saw Joey's reflection where he was seated on a weight bench at the back of the room. He finished the last shoulder press in his set before he set the heavy dumbbells down. "You're thinking about it too much." He said it like he knew exactly what was going on inside her head.

She groaned as she continued to lay there. "What else am I supposed to be thinking about when my stomach won't stop screaming at me?"

Joey stood and walked past her to the mini fridge filled with bottles of water. Her eyes watched each movement, appreciating that he had done his workout in a pair of navy gym shorts, sneakers, and nothing else. All of his tattoos were exposed for her to admire as they sprawled across the hard muscles of his body, which were currently coated in a light layer of salty perspiration.

While he pulled two bottles of water out of the fridge, Layne shifted her position so she was up on her knees and sitting back on her ankles. Her hand reached out to take the water Joey offered her. Twisting the cap off, she welcomed the sting of the icy temperature of the first sip filling her mouth before being swallowed down.

The only other thing plaguing her mind besides her abs being on fire was what had been said at the strip club the other night. "We still haven't talked about the night at Cassidy's." She finally initiated the topic that she had been unable to just let go of. Lord knew she had tried to forget it, but the words spoken between the two men replayed over and over in her mind.

Joey had already chugged nearly all his water down in a matter of two large gulps. "Gage is going to be your shadow when I'm not around. There's nothing else to talk about." Perhaps it was wishful thinking that Layne wouldn't press the issue about the other elephant having a tea party in the room with them.

"You know damn well that while I disagree with it, that's not what I'm talking about." She pushed herself up onto her feet. "What did you mean that I'm not Rosie?"

He sighed and sucked down the last little bit of water before tossing the bottle a few feet into the open trash can. "Nothing, Layne. It's self-explanatory. You aren't her." Joey did his best to play it all off as nothing but a matter-of-fact observation he had made.

He must have thought she clunked her head and suddenly was stupid enough to accept that explanation. Her eyes narrowed at him as her temper kicked up a notch. "Don't fuckin' go there, Joey! You don't just drop the name of a dead girl randomly and make a comparison like that for the hell of it. What did you mean by it?"

There was nothing but silence from him in response, and the tension in the air was palpable. Layne locked her eyes on him, waiting for him—begging him to explain himself.

Losing faith, he was going to clue her in; she began to walk away from him toward the door. "You know what? If you're not going to tell me, I will be spending enough time with Gage, and I'm sure he'll be more than happy to share."

As her hand started to draw the door open, Joey rushed over to her, shoving it back shut again. The look on his face was a flurry of emotions ranging from panic to desperation and even agitation. "I don't get why you're so hellbent on this. It's all shit from the past. I'm doing my goddamn best to let past shit go with Gage, so why can't you just drop it?"

Her hand jerked on the door again, and to no avail, it remained shut as his hand made sure of that. "Because I see the look in your eyes when you say her name. Because there's clearly something I'm not being told. Call me fucking crazy, but I thought it's reasonable to expect you aren't going to be keeping any more secrets from me." Her anger pricked at the back of her neck in response to the emotionally charged topic at hand.

Joey looked down, and for the first time, she saw a pinch of shame in that handsome face of his. "Because it's not fair to you." His voice lost its edge as his fingers pinched the bridge of his nose while gathering his thoughts.

"She was our girlfriend." The proclamation was seemingly harmless on its face, and it left Layne wondering why the hell he had been so hesitant to say something.

"Who was dating her when everything happened?" Layne didn't quite put it all together on his first attempt at an explanation.

The depths of his cocoa eyes pulled up from looking at the floor, and when they connected with hers, he made it clearer. "We both were."

Oh. *Oh.* She hadn't been expecting that. Any responses she had expected to say to him hadn't been prepared to learn that he and Gage had been seeing her at the same time. Her mind began to jump through a series of thoughts and emotions. Rosie had been with both the guys, and at first, that unveiling was a surprise. Then, Layne was filled with something that was an even bigger shock. She found herself envious and thought about how Rosie had been one lucky bitch.

Furthering down the web of thoughts, she thought back to her first meeting with Gage and the fight that broke out. Joey's possessiveness had come exploding at an all-time high. After mentally going through the story of his history with Gage, she was able to fill in some of the gaps and unspoken truths. Fast forward to their most recent meeting, where the odd response from Gage about asking Joey about sharing suddenly made sense.

All the puzzle pieces clicked into place in her brain, and she was unsure of how long she had been standing there stuck inside her head. What does one even say to this? Joey must have been having his own internal string of thoughts, and fortunately for Layne, he spoke up first.

"Layney." He reached out, taking hold of her arms gently. "I didn't want to say anything because I didn't want you thinking—fuck, I don't know." Joey found himself frustrated that he couldn't cohesively put together a decent explanation for her. He wanted to give her what she deserved to hear without leaving her full of disappointment in him. Even worse? He couldn't fathom losing the trust she had in him.

Out of all the emotions that were rolling through her, anger wasn't one of them. When she looked up into his face, she found herself looking for answers. "Did you love her?"

His Adam's apple bobbed in the center of his throat as he gave a hard swallow. "Gage will tell you that I didn't, but I did, in my own way." He moved his hands up to draw her face into his hands. "Not in the way that I love you, though, Layne. You are the spark that keeps my heart pumping blood through my veins."

She shook her head at him. "You don't have to defend your feelings, Joey. I will always be here making sure that you know you will always have my heart." Layne wrapped her arms around his waist, stepping up against him. "I will love you so hard for the rest of your life that you won't ever have to worry about losing that spark."

When Joey saw the curve of her lips as they lifted into a smile, he fell into a sense of ease and relief. His mouth sought hers out, and before he could fuse their lips, Layne pulled back with a smirk. "One question, though."

His brow arched at whatever was nagging at her brain. "Hm?"

Layne's eyes looked at him, full of curiosity. "Did you both… at the same time?"

He responded with a dark chuckle. Coyly, he responded to her, "Did we both, what?" Oh, he was going to make her say it just to see her reaction.

It could be counted on one hand the number of times Layne blushed from a mere thought. Now, here she was, fucking blushing. The spread of pink on her cheeks made her either want to hide her face from him or punch him so he didn't get the chance to see how flustered she was.

Joey could have made her life all the easier by stating the question for her, but he was enjoying seeing the warm blush spread over her fair cheeks. He began to walk back toward the weight bench, tugging her along with him. He dropped his hands down onto her hips. "You're going to have to be more specific, Layney. Now, be a good girl, and don't make me ask twice."

With his hands now locked firmly on her, he spun her around so her back was to him and the bench in front of her. Joey used a hand to bend her over so that her firm ass was nudged against the front of his shorts, where it was clear his cock was very much coming alive with excitement.

She had nowhere to run and hide from her discomfort at the question niggling at her. Her teeth scraped over her bottom lip as she looked back over her shoulder at him. "Did you and Gage both have sex with her? Together?"

His eyes filled with a mischievous twinkle, and his grin spread wider. Joey's fingers stretched the material of her workout pants down over the curve of her ass until she was bared to him. "Mm, of all the questions you could ask, and you want to know if she got stuffed with two cocks?"

Not releasing his tight hold on her, he dropped down to his knees behind her. A growl rumbled in his chest as he saw just how wet she was talking about him and Gage sharing Rosie. He leaned forward, his tongue dragging along her slick pussy, drawing in a long line of her taste into his mouth.

Layne moaned out as his tongue snaked out and sampled her arousal. "Yes..." Her hands grasped onto the edge of the bench her forearms were resting on.

There was a slight saltiness that enhanced her sweetness from the left-over perspiration from her workout that had made it to her center. He groaned out, "Fuck, Layne. You're the best-tasting post-workout I've ever had." His hands grabbed her thighs, spreading them wider for better access to her needy cunt. Joey hungrily put his mouth on her again, this time his tongue diving inside her.

The swell of pleasure immediately had her squirming against him as she made a sound of approval of the sensation. One of his hands left her thigh and found her throbbing clit. With just one swipe over it with his finger, she wanted to collapse down on him.

He swirled his tongue inside of her tight pussy to collect more of her flavor before he pulled back enough to talk. "She got whatever amount of cock she wanted from us." Joey's finger circled over her highly charged nub again, extracting more gorgeous moans from her throat.

She felt her knees shake underneath the weight of pleasure collecting low in her stomach and expanding throughout the rest of her body. Layne cried out as she felt Joey give one last lick of her folds before his presence and his touch both left her momentarily.

Before she could whimper as the sinful sensations ceased in her body, she felt Joey behind her again. Now, he was standing, and his shorts were down at his feet. The swollen head of his cock teased her entrance.

"Fuck, Joey, I need you in me," Layne begged with a neediness to chase back after her release again.

His hands braced her hips, holding them steady for him. "Just me, or are you thinking about how it'd feel to have more than one dick inside of you?" Pushing forward, he began to invade her pussy with his hard length. Her body tightly encased each inch of him.

Out of desperation to be filled with him, she tried to push her hips back to take all of him. Joey held her still so that he had full control of how much of him was inside her perfect cunt. "You can say it, Layne." His words were filled with encouragement.

Her breaths came out quicker as he took his entry nice and slow. Listening to how his words were spoken instilled a sense of confidence and safety to confess. Layne nodded. "I'm thinking about how good being filled up would feel."

Joey moaned out behind her as he sank into her until he was pressed flush against her round ass. His cock glided into the warmth of Layne's body, which felt like the closest thing to heaven he would ever get. Hearing her admit to getting turned on by the thought of getting two cocks had his dick hard as steel.

Her body rocked forward gently as he seated himself inside her. She cried out, enjoying the full sensation his size always gave her. Joey pulled back and thrust back into her, this time more vigorously. "Fuck, yes!"

All the thoughts of the many combinations of how two guys could ravage her already caused her to succumb to her body's trembling. The cusp of her orgasm swiftly approached as Joey began to ram himself into her.

Getting lost in his thoughts, he envisioned Layne as she was now but with her pretty mouth filled with dick, swallowing down a large load of cum while her pussy got filled. The imagery had rekindled a desire in him that he hadn't felt in years. His hips slammed against Layne over and over as he replayed those fantasies in his mind.

The sound of their bodies smacking against each other filled the space of the home gym; Layne was now screaming out in absolute ecstasy as her climax took her body hostage. Her release exploded as she came hard and furious for him. Her vision blurred at the edges from the instant state of immense bliss her body fell into.

Layne's inner walls squeezed Joey's dick so tightly he swore he would be lost inside her forever. He gave a raw growl as his cock pulsated before his seed shot deep inside her body. He gave small grinds up against her ass as he continued to fill her up with more of his thick cum.

After several moments of heavy breaths filling the air and the cloud of intense orgasms subsided, they were both seated on the floor. Layne was settled into Joey's lap with his arms wrapped lovingly around her waist. He kissed along the line of her exposed shoulder. She leaned back against his bare chest in total contentment.

"You will always and forever be mine, Layne. Don't you ever forget that," he murmured against her skin. Even if he were to ever share her, that would never change.

CHAPTER THIRTEEN

After their—ahem—post-workout stretches, Joey informed Layne that the following day, he had to drive out to Newark over in Jersey for the day. That meant Gage was going to be stepping up to the plate. She wasn't sure if it was better or worse now that she knew the truth about Rosie.

Up in the master bedroom, Layne yanked her forest green shirt down over her head and torso. Her hands retrieved her long tresses out from underneath the top, allowing them to fall freely over her shoulders. "I could just go with you." She glanced at herself in the full-length mirror on the back of the bedroom door to make sure her outfit was up to her standards. Being the face of a criminal empire meant being aware of one's image.

The long-sleeved shirt clung to her body, accentuating every curve, including a peek of her cleavage from the sharp v of the neckline. The dark hue of the green helped to make her eye color pop amongst her other features. The hem of the shirt stopped just above her belly button, revealing the fit muscle tone of her stomach. Layne partially twisted, pivoting her hip to check out her best asset in her low-rise jeans. The swell of her ass proudly showed off all the hard work and squats she did to maintain it.

Joey's hands wrapped over her shoulders as he came up behind her. He brushed her hair to the side, revealing the length of her neck. Lovingly, he laid a path of kisses from the crook of her neck up to her ear. "These aren't the type of people that welcome outsiders. Especially ones with a goddamn ass that begs for some dick." His mouth captured the bottom of her ear lobe, teasingly sucking at it before he drew his lips away from her skin. Those dark brown eyes of his glanced down to admire the plunge of her shirt and the view of her supple cleavage.

The strength of his cut arms wrapped around her and squeezed. "Besides," he continued. "It's a good opportunity for you and Gage to get to know each other a little better. See if he's up to the challenge of keeping up with you." He smirked at her, knowing damn well Layne wasn't an easy assignment to keep tabs on.

Layne turned in his arms, coming face to face with him with a grin. "So, does that mean I can hop a ride on the back of a bike with some stranger to ditch his ass?" Her hands slid around and grabbed a handful of his ass as she recalled how their first date kicked off.

His hand came up below her chin, his thumb running across it, barely tracing along the bottom edge of her lip. "If he fucks up that badly the first day on the job, I will beat the shit out of him. And if you pull that crap on him…" Joey's voice held the edge of a soft warning. "I will find your ass and take you somewhere secluded where no one will ever find us."

"A vacation? I accept." Her smartass comment was coupled with a playful grin.

Before Joey could get more than a grumble out, the doorbell of O'Reilly Manor pierced through the air of the house.

"Probably Gage." He looked down at his watch. "Asshole always runs at least five minutes late. I will meet you downstairs." Joey leaned over and brushed his mouth over hers quickly before leaving to go down to the first floor to let his brother inside.

When Joey pulled open the front door, Gage stood there with a smile and a pair of aviator sunglasses on his face. "Hey. Reporting for duty." He mockingly gave Joey a salute.

"Come inside, you're late, jackass." Joey was taking a big but calculated risk by letting someone other than himself watch after the woman who meant everything to him. It didn't mean he had to be happy about it, either.

When Joey stepped back from the entrance, Gage came inside, his hands tucked into the dark tan pants he was wearing. "I have to admit, I never expected you to be living the swanky Upper Eastside life."

"Shut up." Joey was already sensing a headache approaching with his little brother making stupid comments. He pushed the front door shut and moved to stand in front of him. "Ground rules."

Oh, this was going to be good. Gage didn't typically have rules set for him; he was the one who set them. With an amused smirk, he pulled his sunglasses from his face and hung them on the neck of his black long-sleeved tee. He looked directly at Joey. "I'm all ears."

With all seriousness in his face, Joey stared at Gage. "What she says goes. The only exception is if it involves you taking your eyes off of her, do you understand me? If she has so much as a papercut when I get back, I swear, Gage…"

The younger De Luca chuckled and raised a hand to stop Joey's impending threat right there. "Relax, I basically took a goddamn bullet for her. I think that should earn me a little trust, yeah? Besides, keeping my eyes on her—" he paused his words as Layne appeared on the stairs. "Not going to be a problem." Damn, the sight of that woman had him ready to face a firing squad for her.

Layne made her descent down the staircase, her ankle-high boots giving quiet little taps against the floor. She had chosen a light jacket to go over her shirt, making it easier to conceal several weapons on her body.

Noticing Gage's lustful gaze past him, Joey turned to see Layne approaching them both. He took another quick look at his watch, realizing he needed to get on the road soon unless he wanted to be late. His hand gripped firmly onto Gage's shoulder, pulling him in so Joey could whisper, "Follow the fuckin' rules for once."

"Sure, boss." Gage's smile didn't falter while his focus was trained on Layne.

When she got to where they both were, she saw Joey whispering to Gage. She was pretty sure it was some threat having to do with keeping her out of harm's way. After releasing Gage, Joey turned to her, his expression softening partially, but a sternness remained present in his eyes that reminded her of pools of melted chocolate.

"You. Behave." A simple instruction. His hand reached behind her neck and pulled her in close. While upstairs, he had been brief with his affections; he took his damn sweet time now - whether it be for show or not. His other hand dropped down to grab a handful of her sweet ass, possessively squeezing it in his hand.

The way Joey's lips claimed her own had her gasping for breath, only for his tongue to glide into her mouth, where it wrestled with her tongue.

He didn't want that moment to end, so he soaked up as much of her taste as he could in the few seconds he had to spare.

Once he released his hold on her, Joey smiled gently. "I mean it, Layne."

Layne crisscrossed her finger over her heart with a grin. "Stop worrying so damn much."

After gathering his jacket and a duffel, Joey was out the door to take care of some contract business matters forty-five minutes away in the next state over. It left Layne and Gage standing there in the foyer of her home, staring at one another.

"So, princess, what's on your schedule for the day?" He didn't make an effort to move, waiting for her to feel like she was the one in charge. Gage had all day to figure out all her inner workings, and he was looking forward to it.

Before she had even come downstairs, she knew this day was going to go one of two ways. One or both of them were going to choose violence, and with him calling her 'princess,' it seemed he was intent on sealing his fate.

Recalling Joey's words to her to behave, she slowly filled her lungs with more oxygen to find some sort of inner peace or some bullshit like that. Layne exhaled the worst of her temper and settled on providing him a bitchy look.

"I have a few stops to make to check in with a few of my family's most loyal clients. You should be able to hang back and keep your space." She dug into her jacket pocket a moment before she tossed her car keys at him. "You're driving."

Gage caught the keys with one hand without missing a beat. He examined the blue and white luxury logo on the key fob before dropping it into the safety of his pants.

The moment Layne went to walk past him, he jutted an arm out in front of her, blocking her path. "You're going to have to do better than that."

Her feet stopped short, so she didn't walk right into his massive arm. "Excuse me?" She notched up a brow along with her attitude.

"I'm going to need names and places. I may be the new guy on the block, but this isn't my first gig. Joey may have his rules, but so do I." His tone was assertive, but it still had a pleasantness to it. It was irritating as hell.

Gage's past experiences in dealing with seedy businessmen weren't just limited to cash transactions. During the infancy of Cassidy's Cave, he couldn't afford bouncers and had the pleasure of removing rowdy patrons himself and keeping his girls safe. Even outside of that scope, he had a few stints watching some spoiled brats with pervy stalkers—and fucking a few of them, too. The spoiled brats, that was.

Layne rolled her eyes; these De Lucas and their goddamn rules. She crossed her arms in front of her chest. "How do I make this easy enough for you to understand? I am not a wilting flower that some underboss has hired you to follow around while she gets her nails done. I am the fuckin' be-all and end-all of my damn business. You don't make the rules here, I do."

It took a hell of a lot of restraint on his behalf to suppress the laugh that was tugging inside his ribs. From his perspective, Joey had no problem setting rules for her. He wondered how well she followed them. She had a damn firestorm of an attitude that stirred excitement in his pants at the challenge it presented. "You this bossy in bed, too?" He gave a devil's grin at her.

Today was going to be a long one if he kept this up. "Too bad you'll never find out."

"Are you sure about that? You seemed to be quite content when I had you in my arms at the Cave." He leaned in, making his words softer, "Admit that you enjoyed being so close."

Refusing to admit to anything, her arms dropped down from her chest, and her hand shoved his arm out of her way. It didn't take much effort; Gage allowed her to make a path for herself. "McGregor's is first on the list." This man was going to drive her insane before the day was over. She led the way to the garage where her car was parked.

Gage smugly smiled to himself as he trailed behind her. It seemed little Miss Be-All, and End-All could submit when led down the correct path.

CHAPTER FOURTEEN

The office that stored all the administrative crap for the Irish pub, McGregor's, was located directly above the bar on the second floor. It could barely be called an office, though, it was merely a cramped room the size of a walk-in closet with hardly enough room for one person, let alone two. It had a vintage wooden desk with rickety drawers underneath it, a miniature window to allow a small rectangle of light inside, a short stool that often remained tucked under the desk, and creative storage solutions cluttering the area.

Now that O'Reilly Enterprises had a decent amount of workers, she could have left the more menial tasks like checking books to some of the guys further down the chain. However, there were a few long-time supporters whom Layne liked to keep the relationship strong with. McGregor's and its owner, Sean, was one of those VIPs.

Layne stood in front of the worn desk. Her finger flipped to the next page of the book that contained all the cash records. Slowly, she ran her finger over the line of each transaction, mentally calculating the incoming and outgoing cash flows for the past month. Nearly every transaction was appropriately labeled.

At her back, Gage was squeezed in behind her. He was close enough that she could feel each breath he exhaled while he hovered over her. The scent wafting off of him, spicy and warm vanilla notes, suffocated her senses so that she no longer noticed the musty smell of the ancient building that was strongest there on the second floor.

Not taking her eyes off the numbers written on the page, she spoke up, "You could stand right outside the door instead of hovering over me like an assassin is going to pop out from one of these drawers." She shifted uncomfortably as she tried to find herself more space.

Sure, he could have given her the extra two feet of space, but where was the fun in that? He grinned as he watched over her shoulder as she continued her financial examination. "Can never be too cautious, ya know? I gave my word that I would protect every part of your body from suffering any harm." The deep register of his voice quieted as he spoke slower, "Every. Last. Inch."

She slapped her palm down on the current page of the accounting records she had been reviewing and turned her head to glare at him. "Can you not?"

His lips curved into a smirk that suited his face, drawing his mouth up in a way that she was sure had girls everywhere ruining panties. "Just doing my job. You're all mine to watch over today."

Layne gave an exasperated sigh as she spun around to face him fully, doing her best to still leave a little room for the grace of God. "You can do your job damn well while not invading my space. Just because you may have a history of playing nicely in the sandbox with Joey doesn't mean it automatically makes you entitled."

His face shifted to one of delightful surprise. "So, he finally told you about Rose?"

As Gage leaned toward her, his hands planted themselves on the edge of the desk on either side of her. Layne did her best to keep her back rigid while holding her ground as her eyes stubbornly stared at him. "We talked about it." She prayed that the sound of her racing heart couldn't be heard.

"That sounds promising." He nodded to himself, seemingly impressed at this new development.

She scoffed at his ability to feel so full of certainty. "Get over yourself."

Finally, her hand made contact with his chest. As her hand applied pressure to try and give herself some space, she could feel the strength of the muscles tensing just beneath his shirt. When her thoughts strayed to pondering what his broad chest looked like without his shirt, her hand immediately recoiled like she had been burned by a lump of hot coal.

The sudden jerk of her hand off his chest had him casting a quizzical look at her before it faded back to the amusement of her reactions to him. His hand captured hers and placed it back on his chest, dragging her palm down between his pec muscles. He didn't stop there; he moved her touch further down over his rippling abs.

With her breath caught somewhere between her throat and her heart, at the last moment, she jerked her hand back before it made it down to his belt buckle.

Quickly, she spat out, "I don't have time for this. Please, get the hell out of my way." Layne was now impatiently waiting for him to decide if he was going to take his foot off the gas pedal of flirtations.

Gage held his stance there before her for another heartbeat before he took two steps back, dropping his arms down at his sides. "Sure thing, lucky charm." He could still feel the ghost of her touch along the center of his body, and it sank even lower to his cock.

He still managed to grate on her nerves with his snarky little nicknames for her despite complying with her request. Layne knew she needed to get some space to douse the flames he had stoked inside her with some water instead of pouring more kerosene on it.

Before heading back downstairs, where Sean was restocking the bar, Layne grabbed this month's accounting records off the desk. When she arrived on the main floor with the book in hand, she dropped it on the bar top in front of him. "The numbers are off."

For as long as Sean had owned the Irish pub, she had never known his books to show as much as a penny difference. However, this month, his books were reflecting a discrepancy of precisely six-hundred and eleven dollars and twenty-four cents. The entry in the book had her initials, 'L.O.,' next to it in the accounts payable column with no detailed description.

Thankfully, McGregor's wasn't even open to the public yet for another hour and a half, so there were no prying ears to overhear this rather sensitive topic. Sean ran his hand over the back of his neck, trying to look ignorant of the oversight.

Gage had followed Layne downstairs, resting against the edge of the bar with his elbow. Still thinking about their moment upstairs, he wondered about the current state of her panties. He could see the appeal his brother had in her. She was a strong little spitfire who didn't take any shit. In this line of work, it was rare to find a woman able to hold her own.

"Is there?" was the only acknowledgment of the accounting error Sean gave.

Layne frowned at him. "Sean…" her voice lost some of its edge as she stared at the man who wore his age poorly. The crows' feet at the corners of his eyes were more pronounced, his hair donning a little more white, and the restlessness in his soul, as seen through his eyes, was heavier.

"Sean," she repeated herself. "You're off by over six hundred dollars. Where did it go? There's nothing here in the books, and I sure as hell didn't sign off on it."

Using a bar rag, Sean wiped his fingers off before wringing the towel between his weathered hands. "Must have been these old eyes and rattled brain." The lie on his tongue caused Layne more distress than it should have. He quickly followed up on his excuse, "Let me double-check the entries tonight after closing."

She reached over and laid her hand on top of both of Sean's. "If it's anything but your eyes, I need to know. You've been a great asset to my family since I was a little girl."

Layne recalled the way she used to carelessly run through the pub while her father checked the books or held private meetings. Often, she had gotten underfoot and received a scolding from her father. A much younger Sean had been there to soften the stern tone of Scott O'Reilly and made a Shirley Temple with extra cherries to help lift her spirits. Now, even as an adult, when she was aggressively hungover, it was something she craved.

Sean gave a half-smile at her before pulling his hands away so he could remove the book from the top of the bar. "Layne, you've been like a daughter that I never had. I have always respected and honored your family."

His words rang true with sincerity and honesty, but there was something about the way he looked at her that reflected a soul in despair. Layne withdrew her hands and nodded, hoping that after closing, she could sit down with him to figure out these numbers.

"I will be back by tonight after closing." She watched Sean secure the spiral-bound book containing the financials behind the bar. Layne looked over at Gage and nodded toward the door. He straightened up, pushing away from the edge of the bar, and joined her after she said her goodbye to Sean.

After they got back to her silver BMW, she placed her hand on the passenger door's handle. Before pulling on it to open the door, Gage was there with his hand on top of hers. The sunlight illuminated the intricate linework of the blossomed rose on the back of his left hand.

"Allow me." The soothing tone of his voice was like silk against her soul.

From an outsider's perspective, it appeared to be a chivalrous gesture. From Layne's perspective? It felt like an excuse to encroach on her space again. Her emerald orbs looked up at him, trying not to allow her breath to get caught in her throat again.

Layne slithered her hand out from underneath his palm, allowing him to swing the door open for her. Once she was settled in her seat, he closed the door for her before getting in on the driver's side.

She pulled out her phone and noticed a few messages from Joey, a smile immediately spread over her face.

JOEY

How are things going?

I may be a little later than I thought tonight.

I would rather be there with you than waiting on these assholes.

LAYNE

I haven't strangled him...yet.

Be careful and don't do anything stupid. I love you.

JOEY

Always and forever.

When Gage got in the car, he was watching as Layne's fingers tapped across her phone and the way her guard came down as her smile indicated she was likely texting with Joey. It was a glimpse past the hard exterior that she usually had wrapped around herself.

Layne looked up to see Gage sitting there watching her. The protective exterior snapped back in place as she shoved her phone into her pocket. "What?"

He sat up straight in his seat with his head held high. "Where to, your Highness?"

She shook her head. "Will you stop with the damn cutesy names?"

Gage relaxed his posture and smirked at her, hearing the irritation in her voice. "Just trying to see what fits you."

"Just fucking drive. 15 East 7th Street." Her hand waved him on, and when he complied, turning his attention to the road ahead of him, she couldn't help but allow her eyes to linger over his profile.

Casually, he was sitting back in the seat with one hand on top of the steering wheel, the rest of him appearing at ease as he navigated each street on the way to the next location. His right elbow was on the center armrest as he hung his arm over the edge of it. The tattooed word on the back of his hand was in plain sight: WRATH.

"Wrath? Who the hell gets that tattooed on their hand?" It seemed a pretty interesting message to make part of yourself forever.

Gage smirked to himself as he shifted in his seat. "You'd be amazed at what types of tattoos I've gotten over the years. This particular one just happens to be a promise I've made."

Growing more curious, Layne's eyes roamed over his body while he drove. What other tattoos were hidden underneath all those clothes? "What type of promise?"

His voice grew more solemn. "To repay anyone who ever takes something from me again." In particular, to whoever had a hand in plucking his precious Rose from this lifetime.

All this time, he felt her eyes roaming over him, and he suppressed the urge to look over at her and acknowledge it. The one thing he couldn't suppress was the way his cock twitched between his legs, knowing he had her attention.

It didn't take much for the day to get away from them after several more stops checking in on a few establishments. There had been a variety of places on Layne's agenda, including a convenience store, a commercial real estate office, and the Brass Mirror.

After receiving several updates from Joey, it was clear that he was going to be lucky to wrap things up before the next morning's daybreak. Gage was far too happy to hear that his duties were still required well past the time frame he had expected.

Since it was beyond closing time at McGregor's, Layne figured she might as well get this awkward discussion out of the way with Sean to see if he was able to track down the accounting error she had discovered in his books.

Standing outside of the pub, she stopped and looked at Gage. "What are the chances of you staying out here so I can have this talk with Sean privately?"

He seemed to take a moment to mull over the response before he flatly responded. "None." Gage grinned as he leaned in with his hand on the small of her back. "But, after this, I will take you home, and you can tell me how close you want me." The innuendo was poorly hidden as the words held a husky purr to them.

"Keep dreaming." She stepped away from him and pulled on the front door to McGregor's. It didn't budge, the deadbolt already being turned. It was unusual for Sean to lock things up, knowing she was stopping by. Fortunately, she had a copy of the key.

Flipping through each of her keys, she found the correct one and twisted it in the deadbolt. Letting herself inside, the place was cast in an unsettling pitch black. Sean had known she was coming, why would he have closed things up and left? Her hand reached over and flipped on the light switch that she knew was just to the left of the entrance.

The bar area lit up and exposed a horrific site before her. Bar stools were broken and cast aside, tables on their sides, glasses shattered, all the photos on the walls destroyed, and ultimate destruction had left no part of the front room of the pub untouched. Aggressive and angry red spray paint stained the back wall where the iconic McGregor's handmade sign and logo were still proudly on display.

Sprawled in all caps was a very clear message: BACK OFF BITCH. YOU'RE NEXT. Layne had a sick feeling expanding in the pit of her stomach. She carefully stepped over the trash scattered across the floor. "What the fuck?" Her words were barely audible, even to herself.

Gage's head was on a swivel as he took in the devastating state of affairs in the same bar he had been in just earlier that day. "Layne, I don't like this." He kept close to her.

She chose to ignore him as she called out, "Sean? Sean, are you here?!"

When she made it to the back of the main area where the back room began, she reached a hand out to flip the switch to turn on that section of lights. Gage saw it before her brain registered the grotesque sight awaiting her discovery.

Despite his iron-like grasp snagging her backward and turning her into him, it was too late. The horror had already been captured by her vision. Sean's body hung from a blood-stained rope in the center of the backroom where her family had conducted so many meetings and negotiations over the years.

Adding insult to injury, Sean hadn't only been hanged but vertically ripped open, leaving a sickening display of gore and guts pouring down the front of his body. Layne's brain had trouble reconciling the terrifying and grisly image, but once it did, all she could hear was her scream ripping through the air. It couldn't have been Sean, it couldn't have been real, and it sure as hell couldn't have been a random and meaningless act of horrendous violence.

"Fuck." Gage's hand clasped to the back of her head, making sure she didn't turn back to see any more than she already had. He had seen some sick shit before, but even with his iron stomach, this was one for the top of the charts leaving even him queasy.

Layne's scream against his chest made him ache to take away what she had just seen, wishing he could erase this memory for her. She may have been one hell of a badass woman, but she still had a soul deep inside of her that could hurt.

When her voice couldn't find any more sound to expel, her body began to tremble in his arms. Her form felt like it suddenly had no bones to support it, and Gage's strength was the only thing to prevent her from collapsing onto the floor.

"We need to get the fuck out of here." His arms easily supported her as he tried to walk her back to the front door. When he noticed her feet were unable to coordinate her movements, Gage leaned down and scooped her up with her legs draped over one arm and his other supporting her across her back. "I got you. Up you go, baby."

His hold was steadfast as he quickly navigated the destruction and got them both the hell out of there. If he could have driven without releasing his secure hold on her, he sure as shit would have done it. Instead, he managed to slide her into the front seat before taking up his spot behind the wheel.

Layne doubled over in her seat, trying to fight through her heavy breaths as her face got buried in her hands. She had no doubts that the threatening note had been meant for her. The problem was figuring out who she was pissing off badly enough for them to send the type of message that was now burnt deep into her brain.

CHAPTER FIFTEEN

She found herself sitting on the edge of her king-sized bed in the master bedroom, staring into a glass half-filled with straight Irish whiskey courtesy of Gage. The amber tones were muted by the darkness of the room, save for the one small lamp lit up on one of the nightstands.

Gage had driven her back home, stopping at least once so she could wretch up the contents of her stomach. He had stopped being the aggressive flirt long enough to hold her hair back away from her face despite her protests that she wasn't inept. After getting her back to O'Reilly Manor and settled upstairs, he kept a watchful eye over her.

Layne watched the drink's small ripples in her unsteady hands as her brain tried to eliminate the grotesque imagery of not just the hanging of someone she knew but the exposure of his insides as well. Victims who found the end of the rope were nothing like how movies portrayed it. It was a far more disturbing sight, with eyes bulging from their sockets and darkened by all the broken blood vessels. This is why she preferred simple shootings; they were quick, to the point, and not messy. What she had seen tonight probably had Eric Ellis beaming with pride in whatever circle of hell he was in.

Sean's death felt not just tactical but deeply personal, and she had no doubts that whoever was responsible had wanted to make sure Layne also felt the pain. They had accomplished their goal. This attack, combined with the night at the warehouse where the cops had been tipped off during her interrogation of the loose-lipped lowlife, she was certain someone was determined to keep a target aimed at her back.

Having heard the front door slam shut downstairs, Gage stepped out of the room, softly shutting the door behind him. The sound of heavy boots running up the steps at a fast clip suggested that Joey had just made it back from Newark in record time after Gage had reached out.

There was some hushed conversation right outside the door. Layne could hear bits and pieces as Gage filled Joey in on what had happened during his first day on protective duty.

"It was a literal bloody shitshow, man," Gage explained to Joey. "I got her out of there as quickly as I could, and she's holding up, but…" The words trailed off before the door opened up, and Joey walked in first.

With Joey's face full of concern, he approached her quickly, dropping down to both knees before her. His hands reached up to take hold of her face. "Layney, I'm sorry I wasn't there, but I'm here now." When his lips met with hers, she felt the love in them, but she couldn't summon the energy to return the gesture.

Gage stepped into the room, quietly bringing the door to a close as he gave them space. He was unwilling to leave his post, knowing first-hand what Layne had seen and the intentions behind it.

Her eyes hurt, dry from the tears that had already depleted any moisture from them. She continued looking into her glass like it was going to provide some answers or, even better, induce selective amnesia.

Joey used the firm hold on her face to try and shift her face so her eyes would fall on him. "Layne, look at me." His voice tried to hold a firmness but fell too soft. He could have tried to use his standard line on her to try and get her to do as he asked, but it would do no good in the state she was in.

He dropped his hands to rest on her thighs, rubbing them reassuringly. "We will find out who did this, and it will get handled. I can't do anything until I know you're still here with me." Joey was met with silence from Layne. That's when Gage came up next to Joey.

"Here." Gage's hand guided Layne's hands, holding the glass of whiskey up to her mouth. "Open up." His words demanded compliance from her. Joey may not have wanted to push her, but he was going to try things his way.

However, when she still failed to react to the edge of the glass pressing against her lower lip, Gage took it a step further. His hand slid up the back of her neck, grabbing a handful of her silky locks and tilting her head back slightly. "What did I tell you? I told you to open those pretty lips and drink for me."

The order finally sank in past the volume of her thoughts, and her lips parted while Gage guided the angle of the glass to spill the heat-filled booze into her mouth. Once a generous amount was given to her, he eased the glass from her hands. "That's better," he murmured.

Layne swallowed the mouthful down, and only then did Gage release his hold on her richly colored chestnut hair. As the warmth filled her body from the mouth down through her chest and into her core, she finally was able to see past her recollections of the evening and into Joey's eyes.

"I don't understand…" Her voice cracked as it tried to fend off the emotions placing pressure on it.

Joey's forehead pressed to hers as he showered her with several more kisses. Despite how terrible it was, he was thankful that Layne hadn't been there when the attack had transpired. "We will figure it out after you get some sleep, let's just get you to bed." He looked over at Gage with an earnest display of grateful fortitude in his eyes, speaking all the thanks that was needed. "I will call you tomorrow."

Whatever remained in the glass Layne had been holding was immediately slung back and swallowed down by Gage. He shook his head stubbornly. "I'm not leaving her side. Not after tonight." It wasn't about how Layne fired up a desire in him, but the compulsion to make sure that both she and his big brother got through this fucker of a storm.

Both sets of similarly shaded brown eyes stared at one another, neither of the guys saying anything as something silently passed between them before Joey turned back to Layne. "C'mon. It's late," he said as he took note of the time on the clock on his side of the bed. It was half past four in the morning, and sunrise would be here all too soon.

Joey selected a set of pajamas for Layne to change into, one of his favorite things to do for her when she was having a rough day. It was a simple pair of pink cotton shorts she owned in the softest material he had ever felt and a corresponding cropped cami with a lace trim neckline.

While she was changing in the bathroom for privacy and while Gage was bound and determined to spend the night, Joey stripped down to nothing but his boxer briefs. Layne emerged from the bathroom in her sleepwear; her hair swept up into a high mound of a messy bun on top of her head.

Joey's arm wrapped around her shoulders and guided her into the bed, making sure the covers were pulled up to her waist as he joined her. She laid on her side to face Joey, immediately curling into his chest. The warmth of his body and his familiar scent eased the heaviness tugging on her soul while her eyes closed.

Sunrise came, and late morning arrived. Layne stretched out in her bed, having felt an immense sensation of safety and security throughout the hours she had allowed herself to sleep. The invasion of multiple scents wrapped around her senses: sage and leather with the essence of warmth from a spiced vanilla.

Her head rested in the crook of one large arm, a large hand rested on top of her hip while she lay there on her side, and another hand curled around the dip of her waist. When her vibrant green eyes fluttered open, still weary from sleep, she saw Joey's slumbering face before her. Her head was nestled into the bend of his arm, and his painted hand planted securely on the swell of her hip.

As she stirred, she felt the other arm draped over her waist, drawing tighter. She rolled onto her back and glanced to the side opposite of Joey to find Gage on her right and his arm steadfastly around her midsection. He lay there shirtless with the bulk of his upper body fully visible and only adorned with the silver chain around his neck that carried the round SPQR medallion he always wore. The white sheets shielded the lower half of him.

Gage's chest had fewer pieces of inked artwork than Joey's, with most of his designs creeping up from his hands onto his shoulders. There were roses of various styles scattered between the designs of many sharp-edged instruments ranging from daggers, swords, javelins, and others. Between the two of them, it was a delicious sight to wake up to and easily one she could get used to.

Feeling Layne's movement there in bed, Joey lifted his head from the pillow with half-open eyes. Joey's hand moved up to her jaw, turning her face to look at him. He greeted her with an adoring kiss; his lips massaged over her own until she forgot all about the other man sharing the bed with them.

The kiss grew deeper as Joey pressed himself up against her, letting her feel his excitement quickly growing against her lower stomach. Her leg draped over Joey's hip as desire grew more intense between her legs.

Feeling a shifting of movement behind her, it brought her back into reality. Layne pulled back from Joey's mouth, though he was reluctant to let her break the connection between them.

"Don't stop on my account." Gage chuckled, his arm giving Layne a squeeze at her waist.

Noticing the conflict in Layne's eyes, Joey glanced over at Gage, trying to warn him to tread carefully before he looked back at the woman he had fallen so deeply in love with. "Your call if you want him to stay, Layne." All she had to do was say the word, and he would shove his brother's ass to the curb with or without clothes.

With the choice being hers, she couldn't help but let her thoughts wander back to what had transpired after hours at McGregor's. Wincing at the scenes locked into her memories, the only part of the recollection that eased it was the way Gage had taken care of her and gotten her home. Layne needed something to get her past the fresh hell of those thoughts, and after hearing Joey talk about the way he and Gage shared a bed with Rosie, she was excited at the potential.

Gage scooted closer to her, making himself flush against her back as he whispered into her ear. "Better choose wisely, kitten. I am not for the faint of heart." The press of his erection was already prodding against her ass.

Layne swallowed hard as she tried to think past the arousal soaking her pajama shorts, having forgone any panties. Feeling two cocks already pressed against her body was sending it into a heated overdrive. She glanced back over her shoulder at Gage, who was still leaning in close, and then she looked at Joey, who maintained a neutral expression to avoid swaying her decision.

With a little smile full of mischief, she gave her response, "He can stay." The moment she gave her decision, Joey was ready to lean in and devour the taste of her mouth, but her hand on his bare chest right below his shamrock tattoo put an end to that. "I have conditions, though."

Immediately, Gage's eyes darkened with lust, and his smile twisted in amusement. "Lay 'em on me."

Layne rolled onto her back, squeezed between them both as she looked over at Gage. "Joey comes first. It stops when I say it stops. The second the two of you start bitching or fighting with one another, it's done. I'm not going to be caught up in some masculine tug of war."

He raised both brows as he shot a look at Joey. "She's adorable when she thinks she's going to be in charge." Gage traced his fingers along her arm until he found the engagement ring on her finger. There was a moment of admiration for the piece of jewelry wrapped around her before his fingers traced back up along the length of her arm.

His hand drifted over her shoulder before curling around her throat, his thumb stroking along the side of her neck. "Don't worry, you can keep wearing his ring on your finger. I just want you wearing my collar around your neck." Gage's dirty little smirk crossed his face.

CHAPTER SIXTEEN

Layne's legs pressed together as she felt the immense amount of excitement building between them as Gage's hand labeled with the word 'WRATH' wrapped around her throat. Her eyes felt heavy with lust while her chest rose and fell with a quicker tempo. The thin material of her cami allowed the stiff peaks of her nipples to be visible and straining against the fabric.

Gage bowed his head so his lips barely brushed against the side of her face while he whispered to her. His hand slid up along the length of her throat until his fingers firmly took hold of her jaw to keep her head still. "But first, I want to watch how you fuck my brother."

As if on cue, Joey's hand eased Gage's hand from Layne's face, replacing it with more of a loving touch as he cradled her face between his palms and leaned down to lock his lips onto hers.

She wondered if all of this was truly happening or if this was all some sort of intense sexual fantasy playing out in a dream. The only thing she knew for sure was she didn't want to wake up if that was the case. Her arms wrapped around Joey's neck as her hands ran over his upper back. The movement of her lips against his started off heated but only grew more scorching as he hungrily delved his tongue into her mouth.

Joey's arm slid underneath her, pulling her upright with him until they were both on their knees there in the middle of the oversized bed with Layne's back to Gage. Both his hands explored her toned body paying particular attention to the well-rounded ass he loved so much. He grabbed a handful of each cheek as he moved his mouth down to her bare shoulder, planting several tender kisses against her skin.

"You ready for me, Layney?" Joey murmured against her shoulder while his hands kneaded each globe of her ass.

"Mmm…" Her hands moved down over the chiseled strength of his upper body, her fingertips tracing over the images on display before her. First, the raven wings that led up onto the side of his neck. Then, the blood-stained shamrock over his heart. The final one being graced by her touch was the 'Chaos Addict' words along his side.

She gave a playful smirk at him. "Maybe." Her hand slid between his body and the waistband of his underwear, immediately, she felt his hard cock straining in the confines of the boxer briefs while her hand wrapped around it. "It seems you're ready for me, though."

Gage laid back, tucking an arm behind his head as he watched the two of them engage one another. An intrigued smile never faltered from his face. His hand dug into his boxers, finding his throbbing erection, and began to give himself slow and long strokes. From this view, Layne's ass had the most delectable heart shape to it, even in those tiny shorts she wore.

Joey groaned as Layne grabbed a hold of his cock. His need for her grew more frantic as his hands came to the bottom of her cami and pulled it up. She was forced to release his dick as she lifted her arms to be stripped of the shirt. Her ample breasts were revealed as the camisole was pitched onto the floor. Before he continued, he quickly shoved his boxer briefs down to reveal each magnificent inch of his length. The precum glistened at the head. The sole article of his clothing fell to the floor, where it joined her top.

During her distraction with Joey, she recalled that Gage was still there in bed with them. She looked over her shoulder, her glistening green eyes admiring the sight of him laid out with his hand inside his shorts, very clearly working over himself. His eyes focused on her while he did so.

A hand came to her chin, turning her focus back to Joey as he grinned at her. "Didn't he tell you to do something?"

In response, she bit her lower lip as a smile tugged at the corners of her mouth. Layne pushed her hands against Joey until he lay on his back. She hooked her thumbs onto the sides of her tiny cotton shorts and worked them down over her hips. After wiggling them off her legs, she climbed on top of Joey, leaning over to engage him in a fiery kiss.

Teasingly, she rubbed her center against Joey's cock, letting him feel just how much her body wanted this. The slick arousal that had been worked up left a trail over his skin.

He groaned against her mouth as his hands massaged over her thighs. "Fuck, Layney, you're so goddamn wet." Joey's hips pushed up against her pussy, hoping to quench the thirst of his dick.

Layne reached between her legs and guided him to her entrance before slowly lowering herself onto him. Her wet desire provided a smooth entry as she moaned out, his size began to stretch her inner walls. "God, Joey, why do you always feel so good inside me?" She took a moment to adjust to his size before teasing him; her hips moved in a slow grind.

She had been so focused on Joey that she failed to realize that Gage had gotten up out of bed. It wasn't until she felt movement behind her and a pair of hands grabbing onto her hips that she was aware he had found another angle to watch the show from.

Behind her on his knees, Gage gave a low hum of approval as he looked over her backside while his hands took control of her hips. The heat of his mouth, when it made contact with the back of her shoulder with a single kiss, made her core melt even more. "I need to hear more of those beautiful moans coming out of your mouth."

As Gage knelt close behind her, she could feel his excitement prodding at her back, indicating he had ditched his boxers before coming over there. Her body felt full of electrical sparks, with Joey buried deep inside of her while Gage had only given the softest of kisses. It was inundating her senses.

With Gage's tight grasp of her hips, he forced her hips to ride Joey's cock. He took ultimate control of each movement right down to the speed and pressure. Layne's hands braced against the cut abs of Joey's stomach as she immediately was crying out in pleasure at the sensation mounting to a quick new height.

Joey's fingers dug into Layne's thighs as his gravelly voice groaned out. "Fuck. That's a good girl, Layney." His breathing turned into soft pants as he watched Gage put his hands on Layne from behind to manipulate her body on top of him.

Layne began tensing up with her nails scratching against Joey's stomach and her hips involuntarily fighting against the rhythm Gage was setting for her. Before she could hit her climax, he abruptly stilled her body. She exhaled a breathless whimper.

"What was one of your conditions?" Gage smirked, knowing damn well that he had Layne on the very edge of a sexual explosion. Yet, here he was, playing the sexual puppet master and orchestrating each part of her performance.

She whimpered again as she tried to catch her breath, her orgasm that had been so close began to slip out of reach. "J-Joey comes first."

"That's right. That means I don't want you to come until he fills your pussy, do you understand me?" Gage left another kiss on the back of her other shoulder, this time while he waited for her to answer him.

She furrowed her brows together. "That's not what—"

The man at her back took a handful of her messy bun and tilted her head back so he could see her face. "Do you understand?" Gage's words were sterner this time as he cut off her words.

Layne gave a breathy response as she briefly looked into Gage's eyes, which looked like saucers of steaming coffee. "Yes." His hold on her hair released, and his hand returned to her hip, where he drove the movement once more.

Joey had always been dominant with her, but Gage was on a whole new level, and Layne couldn't help but find herself falling hard for it. Joey's hips thrust up into her as he felt how tight her pussy was squeezing around him. He moaned out, "Mm, you like taking my cock like this, don't you Layney?"

All she could do was nod between each of her gasps for air between her moans, struggling to adhere to Gage's instructions.

To push the limits even further, Gage slid one hand off her hip and down to the front of her, where his fingers found her swollen clit. "You better remember what I told you, baby girl." His fingers rubbed quick circles over the sensitive bundle of nerves, nearly sending Layne careening off the highest cliff.

She shrieked out as her body shook with the effort not to be overcome with the immense amount of pleasure that seemingly filled each vein inside of her. Her hands squeezed tightly onto Joey's sides while she shut her eyes tightly, trying to maintain anything resembling control.

With the intensity raging inside of Layne's body as she fought against giving in to her release, Joey yelled out as her slick walls squeezed so tightly around him that he wasn't sure her body would ever let go. "Jesus fucking Christ, you got her choking my goddamn cock!" He gritted his teeth as the pressure of her body caused the build-up of pleasure to speed up towards its ultimate goal.

Hanging by a damn thread, she desperately looked at Joey. "P-please… I need you to come." Each of her words strained as she begged between heavy pants while Gage's assault on her clit continued.

Seeing Layne's face overcome with a losing battle of control and hearing her beg to fill her with his cum, Joey tipped over the edge as he shoved his hips up. The full length of his cock was as deep as it would go inside of her. He roared out as his orgasm tore through him, and he shot a massive load of his hot seed up into her.

Gage smirked, and he continued to use his one hand to direct Layne's hips to work over Joey's cock as it continued to empty into the depths of her cunt. His thumb and forefinger gave a hard pinch to Layne's clit. As he predicted, she completely unraveled.

The peak of her pleasure came to its breaking point as it pitched her into utter ecstasy, leaving her feeling nearly blind or somewhere beyond this realm. Her moans devolved into screams and curses of the purest pleasure. Gage slowed the movements of her body against Joey but didn't halt them so she could ride out her orgasm fully.

Each moment that passed while the high of her climax took its toll on her had her body releasing all the tension that had built up. Gradually, the intense sensations began to fade.

Hearing just how hard her orgasm struck her, Gage's cock was leaking precum down his thick shaft. His own needs caused it to throb and ache, nearly painfully so. He relinquished his hold on Layne, and she immediately slumped forward on top of Joey, where they were both a sweaty and panting mess together. A few barely there kisses were shared between them.

Layne was pretty sure she wasn't even alive any longer, she would have bet money on it. It wasn't too long after she started to recover that Gage pulled her back upright. His hands pulled her off Joey and dropped her onto her back. With how loose the entirety of her body felt, she moved with the ease of a ragdoll.

"You know what happens when you follow directions?" Gage's eyes brimming with tremendous need and desire as he took in the sight of Layne's naked body splayed out before him. Damn, her body hit all the right marks from her perky and round breasts, the flatness of her stomach, the way her hips curved, and how fucking hot her swollen pussy looked as Joey's cum slowly leaked from it.

Getting her first sight of Gage without anything but his necklace around his neck and a few rings still adorning his fingers, she gasped slightly as her eyes trailed down over the bulk of his muscles. When her eyes lowered to drink in the sight of his lower half, she was greeted by one hell of a surprise.

He had a tattoo on his lower stomach that began right as the V of his body ended. A branch of laurel followed the cut of his V at the front of each of his hips. The red plume of an ancient Roman soldier's helmet began a few inches below his navel. The bold design of the profiled helmet continued south until a wooden plaque with the Roman Legion initials 'SPQR' was etched right at the base of where his cock protruded from his body. Much to Layne's shock and intrigue, the tattoo continued to cover every delicious inch of his dick with a design of three broadswords intersected with one another on the top and sides of his shaft and the two branches of laurel appearing to twist and follow down along the underside of it.

Gage positioned himself to kneel between her legs and gave her a few moments to take a full look at the artwork decorating his body. It was a guilty pleasure of his, watching initial reactions to the location and design of the tattoo he wielded on his lower half.

Once he had given her sufficient time to get a good look at him, he lowered his body down on top of her. His face was intimately close to her own.

Layne slightly turned her head to snag a look over at Joey, who was watching with a grin as he was still trying to recover from his round with her.

"He had his turn with you," Gage spoke to her gently as his hand turned her head back so he could stare into those enchanting green hues of hers. "Now, I want you looking at me."

He had intentionally avoided kissing her up until this point, wanting to reward her for behaving for him. Gage took his time memorizing the features of her face while the backs of his fingers caressed over her cheek. "Damn…" The beauty of the woman lying underneath him had him trying to remember how to fucking breathe.

"What?" Layne asked in a whisper.

"You're gorgeous." Gage pressed a kiss to her mouth, slowly acquainting himself with the delicious taste that greeted him.

At first, Layne was reserved and hesitant, but that quickly all dissipated as she got lost in his lips, passionately returning the gesture as her hand held onto the back of his neck. When he drew back, he grinned at her. "I need to hear you tell me, Layne."

Looking up at Gage, it took a moment to register what he wanted from her. She sweetly smiled at him. "Gage, I want to watch you fuck me with those swords drawn on your cock." Her legs spread wider for him to get easier access, solidifying her words that granted him permission to take claim of her body.

Gage gave her another firm kiss before he supported himself above her enough that she could see his hard cock pressing up against her entrance. Layne peered down to see the tips of the swords begin to figuratively pierce into her as he gave a slow push inside her body.

Layne's hands held onto his bulky biceps, and she moaned out as her body accepted his thick member. Everything at her core was already so sensitive, feeling him enter her was quick to stir up intense feelings of pleasure.

He pushed himself deep into Layne until the tattooed swords completely disappeared inside her pussy. He groaned at the tightness of her slick walls, appreciating what Joey had likely been feeling when he had control over Layne's movements earlier.

Watching his little brother slide himself between Layne's legs and hearing the sweet song of her moans, Joey found himself swiftly growing hard again. He rolled over closer to them, lying on his side as his hand grabbed his dick.

Fully seated inside of Layne, Gage bent down and gave her an electrifying kiss. He drew his cock back out to the tip before pumping it into her again. He swallowed her moan with his mouth while his tongue pushed past her parted lips.

He created a rhythm of thrusting into her, getting rewarded each time with the sounds she made. She squirmed below him, writhing as her body's desire escalated quickly. Her legs wrapped around his waist to draw him deeper into her.

"God, yes!" Layne's hips found a rhythm matching Gage's as he continued to ram himself into her. The speed of each thrust increased in tandem with the carnal pleasure they were both experiencing.

She began to feel the head of his cock pounding against that sweet spot deep within her body. Her hands squeezed tighter on Gage's arms while she tried to fight the growing swells of the orgasm hovering on the horizon. She shook her head as she looked up at him. "I c-can't, I can't hold it back."

Knowing she was so damn close, Gage grinned at her. "I don't want you to, baby. You go ahead and come all over my dick while I keep fucking this cum-filled pussy of yours."

Joey fisted his cock, pumping it while he saw how Layne was being such a good girl for them both. Keeping one hand stroking his length, he leaned over and took a mouthful of her bouncing titty that was just calling out to him.

With Joey suddenly sucking on one of her stiff nipples, his tongue relentlessly swirling over the peak, she fell into her release hard. "Ah! Fuck, yes!" Her pussy clenched down onto Gage, clinging to his cock with profound need as her walls pulsed with her orgasm.

Despite how her body tried to still his thrusts, Gage pushed on in pursuit of his release. "Fuck, baby, that's it." He clenched his jaw after a few more shoves into her before groaning out loudly as he gave one final hard movement into her body, shooting off ropes of cum into her.

Gage remained in her to the hilt as he tried to catch his breath. Looking down at Layne, he saw her slowly melting into a puddle, her legs releasing from his waist down onto the bed, and on her left breast was Joey giving one final tug of her nipple with his teeth before releasing it.

Joey's hand worked his erection harder and faster, seeing Layne was fading quickly from her orgasm, he was going to get himself in her one more time. He shifted so he was sitting by her head. His hand eased her face to the side. "Layney, open up and be my good girl. I want to see you take a third shot of cum and swallow it down. Are you going to do that for me?"

She wasn't sure what was beyond cloud nine in terms of hazy feelings, but she was pretty sure she was there. With Joey turning her head, she saw his hand quickly jacking himself off right beside her.

In response to his question, she opened up her mouth for him. Joey growled in excitement as he shifted himself so he could work himself into her mouth. "That's my fuckin' girl." It was only a few moments before Joey hit his second release, and he came into her mouth.

Layne swallowed the hot seed down despite fighting the exhaustion wearing on her. Joey pulled out of her with a sigh of satisfaction. Having her take his cock and watching her take Gage's afterward had brought his fantasy to reality. He never wanted to lose his memory of this. God willing, this wouldn't be the last time Layne was shared between them.

Gage withdrew himself from the sticky mess of fluids leaking out of Layne's used pussy, proud of his contributions to that amazing sight between her legs. It looked like a damn masterpiece that deserved to be framed and hung up in his bedroom.

While Gage temporarily disappeared to the bathroom, Joey laid down and drew Layne into his arms. He kissed her temple several times while squeezing her tightly in his arms. "I love you so damn much."

When Gage returned, he placed a glass of water and a bottle of ibuprofen on the nightstand. "For later." He had no doubts that Layne would be feeling the resulting soreness from the activities within a few hours.

He joined Joey and Layne in bed, placing a hand on her hip to let her know he was right there while his older brother cradled her.

Besides feeling thoroughly worn out and feelings of satisfaction beyond anything she had ever experienced, Layne was pretty sure that she would never want to be without either of these men in her bed.

CHAPTER SEVENTEEN

Truth be told, Layne could have slept another hour or two if it hadn't been the grumbling of her stomach demanding she feed it. When she opened her eyes and lifted her head from the pillow, her bed was completely empty. Zero De Lucas to be found.

She lay there a minute longer, a smile forming on her lips as she thought back to what had transpired. Her toes curled against the sheets as she recalled how intense her feelings had taken her hostage.

Finally, she decided that tracking down some food was going to be priority number one after she hopped in the shower to wash away all the dried bodily fluids smeared between her thighs.

Layne scooted to the edge of the bed, and the movement gave a small protest of soreness between her legs. She saw the water and the ibuprofen that Gage had left for her before they all passed the hell out. Deciding it wasn't a half-bad idea, she went ahead and swallowed a single dose down.

After a shower that left her feeling refreshed, she left her hair down in dark and damp waves around her shoulders. Layne pulled on a pair of black joggers to go with a distressed tee that had a wide-scooped neckline, causing it to slip down off one shoulder.

While the guys had been the perfect distraction, her thoughts began to come back to her as to the sight she and Gage had stumbled upon at McGregor's. The erratic letters spray-painted on the wall communicated the message in no uncertain terms. Sean's body with a large and gaping wound while dangling there from the rope was meant to drive home the point of how serious the threat was.

When she got downstairs, she heard two familiar voices as she approached the kitchen. Entering the spacious area designed for someone with far better cooking skills than she possessed, Joey and Gage both turned to look at her. Each of them displayed their own unique signature smile. Gage's had a rugged yet boyish charm to it, while Joey's smile always seemed to have an edge of mischief tugging at the corners of his mouth.

Joey had on a pair of his navy sweats and a white tank clinging to the trim muscles of his torso. As usual, each of Joey's tattoos flexed with his movements, creating a show that she could watch for the rest of her days and intended to. As for Gage, while he had on a pair of jeans, he was missing a shirt. The cut of each of Gage's large muscles was on full display, while the necklace he always wore hung down in the center of his chest.

The sight of them both made her mouth water, and her mouth wasn't the only thing getting wet. It was a quick reprieve from the more serious thoughts floating around in her mind seconds ago.

"There you are." Joey approached her, one hand resting on her hip while his other slid into the soft chestnut locks of her hair. He greeted her with a kiss that had a fiercely possessive love behind it.

After he pulled away, he stepped away to rummage through the fridge. That's when Gage stepped up to her next. His hands came up to her face, and before he made a connection with her lips, he spoke in a low voice to her. "Did you take the ibuprofen I left for you?"

Layne nodded her head. "Yes."

Gage smiled in approval, but he still hovered his mouth over hers. "You forgot something."

When her eyebrows shifted in confusion while her emerald pools stared up at his face, looking for an indication of what he meant.

He brought his mouth to her ear while he whispered, "'Yes, Sir.'" The emphasis on the way he added the title to it sent a heat barreling deep to her core. Gage drew back to face her again. "Try again, lucky charm. Did you take the meds I left for you?" If she wanted him in on this little arrangement, he was going to make his expectations known.

The way his eyes felt like they were watching the burn of lust warming her soul had her willing to say any goddamn thing he wanted. "Yes… Sir."

After addressing him the way he demanded, Gage gave her the kiss he had been withholding from her. His mouth gently caressed her lips as the expanse of his hands cradled her face just underneath her jaw.

Gage grinned happily after he eased away from the kiss. "Just had to make sure you'd be as much of a good girl as Joey said you would."

That earned a snort from Joey, who pulled out a sub from the fridge and began laying it out on a plate for Layne. "I said she's a good girl when I want her to be. I never fuckin' said that you'd get the same treatment."

"Hm, seems she's a quick learner." Gage flashed a wink at her before he walked back over to where there was an open bag of chips on the counter. He leaned back against the counter and dug into the crinkly bag for a handful of the salty snack.

With both of them talking about her, she shot them a sassy look. "If you both keep talking about me like I'm not here, I'm not going to be anybody's good girl."

That earned her a chuckle from Gage. "Oh, I'll be looking forward to that." He enjoyed dishing out punishments to bratty bad girls.

Layne walked over to where Joey was pulling the last of the paper from her sandwich. "Tell me that's for me. I'm starving."

Joey nodded at her and kissed her cheek as he pushed the plate towards her, not before giving a smack to her ass for her smart-ass comment, though.

After both of them watched her devour the roast beef sandwich in record time, Joey was the first to bring up the sensitive topic of what happened at McGregor's. "Layne, we should talk about what happened at the pub."

She raised a glass of water to her mouth, washing down the last of her sandwich. "I agree." Both Gage and Joey blinked at her unexpected response. Layne brushed off her hands over the now empty plate and continued, "I'm pissed—no, I'm fucking livid. When I find out who is responsible, they're going to learn real damn quick. If they want to fuck with me thinking I'm going to be scared off, they have another thing coming. This is one bitch that is going to come out, play the damn game, and win."

Layne was tired of people being ripped from her life, one tragedy after another. One of the other factions had to be at play here, and she was bound and determined to find out which one thought they were going to fuck with this O'Reilly. Her father, Scott O'Reilly, would have never tolerated this type of attack, and Layne wasn't going to either.

Her eyes looked at both of them, "I'm going to meet with the head of every damn faction in the city myself. Someone is going to give me answers." Layne's voice was firm but surprisingly calm.

Gage popped one last chip in his mouth, chomping down on the crunchy round quickly. "I like this plan. Let's do it."

It was Joey who gave an irritated sigh at Gage's enthusiastic response to what seemed like a reckless plan. He tried to be the voice of reason for all their sakes. "We've got an unhinged psychopath here. Before we shake up a hornet's nest even further, let me try to see what information I can shake out of a few sources."

She wasn't swayed off course by Joey's attempt to dissuade her. "I've already texted Jonathan, telling him to start setting up the meetings. I'm not backing off just because some coward wants to make a move behind my back." Russ was at the top of her list of suspects, and she was willing to put money on it that he was involved one way or another.

Gage had to take off shortly after their discussion with Layne. It was one of the most popular nights at Cassidy's, Eat Me, Greet Me night. All of the girls got candy necklaces, and with every purchase of a lap dance, each patron received one as well. The concept was devilishly simple: the candy could be eaten off of its elastic string wherever the necklace was placed on the other person.

Layne was doing what she did best, burying herself in work to avoid letting her mind wander too far into the darker depths of her soul. She had been holed up in her office all afternoon, making back-to-back phone calls to faction heads.

She sat in the office chair, her feet propped up on the edge of the desk as she leaned back with her phone to her ear, listening to the thick Russian accent of Alexei Kuznetsov.

"Pchelka," he sighed as he called her 'little bee' in his native tongue. "I am a very busy man."

Her fingers were buried into the hair on the top of her head, growing tired of political dances through minefields of oversized egos.

"And I'm a very busy woman, Alexei. In fact, I'm going to be even busier once I find out which of your men took shots at me several months ago." Layne's voice grew heated with irritation.

There was a long pause before he responded to her. "I told you, none of my men had any involvement. Was big misunderstanding."

She sat up in her chair, dropping her feet back down to the floor. "*Misunderstanding*?" Her harsh laugh at his minimization of the incident cut through the air. "If you want to avoid any *misunderstandings* when it comes to who feeds the hand of your vodka distributor, I would highly suggest that you find fucking time in the next week to make room for some drinks with me."

It sounded like Alexei pulled the phone away from his mouth as he yelled at someone in Russian. With the very limited knowledge she had of the Russian language, Layne only caught a word here or there—both swear words. As he returned to his conversation with her, he had a much softer tone. "Alright, pchelka. We shall talk, yeah?"

Feeling a sense of relief wash over her, she finally cracked a smile. She wrapped up the details with him before hanging up and tossing her phone onto her desk in front of her. There were knots embedded in her muscles all over her body, knowing the uphill battles she was fighting daily in the criminal underworld. This entire situation surrounding Sean and McGregor's added to the already heavy load.

The door to her office creaked open, and Joey popped his head in, no longer hearing or seeing her on the phone, he fully stepped inside. "Hey."

She lifted her gaze off the phone lying there on her desk to see him walking over to her. He came to her chair, turning it to face him so he could take her hands and urge her out of her seat.

Layne smiled sweetly at him. "Hey."

Joey could see the stress locked tightly into her shoulders. He released her hands and began to knead his fingers into the compactly coiled muscles around the base of her neck. "I wanted to talk."

She groaned and closed her eyes, giving in to the nearly painful manipulation of the stubborn knots his hands were trying to work out. "Mm, I already told you my plan. If it makes you feel better, I will let you or Gage come to the meetings with me."

"Let?" He raised a brow at her choice of words. Joey's fingers stopped their massage, and his fingers grabbed ahold of her chin. When she opened her brightly colored eyes at the interruption of his hands' work, she saw him with a heated gaze.

His face came in closer to her own as he spoke with his voice on the edge of a growl. "Make no mistake, Layney, one or both of us will be there whether you allow it or not."

The way he slowly spoke the words to her had her heart beating a little quicker inside her chest.

Joey wasn't going to fuck around with her safety. In a perfect world, she should have been perfectly safe having talks with the other faction heads as the head of her own criminal enterprise. However, he didn't trust any of those fuckers, not after they all had basically left her for dead when Liam was fucking shit up. "Do you understand me?" The seriousness weighed hard on his words.

Layne gave a small nod. "Yeah."

"Good." His mouth closed the gap between them, stealing a kiss from her to reassure her that he was still going to be her shadow whether she liked it or not.

After he pulled back, he gave her shoulders a squeeze. "That's not what I came to talk to you about, though."

His hands trailed down her arms. "I need to make sure you're good with how things are between us and Gage."

She glanced down, feeling the spread of the heat on her face at the way both the guys had taken care of her upstairs. Layne licked her lips before biting into her sheepish smile. "Joey…" Finally, she looked up at him. "I'm good. I'm a little surprised, but I'm good with all of it."

He dropped his hands onto her hips and grinned. "Surprised?"

She gave a soft chuckle. "I didn't expect you to be okay with any of it. You beat the shit out of a guy for dancing with me at a club, or did you forget about that?"

He grumbled, remembering the way the little punk had been putting his hands on Layne. The ass-beating had been justified. "That was different." Joey pulled her in closer by her hips.

Layne didn't look very convinced, so he further explained himself.

"I never want another man laying a hand on you. No other man deserves to hear how it sounds when you come. I never want to hear you screaming out any other name but mine."

She tilted her head as his words seemed to contradict everything that had transpired upstairs between them and Gage. Before she could question it, he raised a finger and pressed it to her lips to prevent her from speaking.

"The only exception is Gage. He is the only one who ever gets the privilege. Whatever the two of you do together is up to you. At the end of the day, you're still going to be all mine." Joey had shared all his favorite things with his little brother growing up, why should this be any different? Especially when Layne was able to get double the pleasure from it. Anything she wanted, he wanted to be able to provide it for her.

Joey removed his finger from those sultry lips of hers. Layne's hands ran up the front of his chest, her fingers enjoying the feel of hard muscle underneath them. She smiled lovingly at him.

"I will always be yours, Joey. But, two De Lucas?" She grinned. "You're both going to keep me a very busy girl."

A devious grin spread across his face. His hands roamed past her hips and gripped tightly onto her ass. "Just wait until I make you my wife, Layney. Gage is gonna have to fight for his turn with you."

He suddenly lifted her, tossing her over his shoulder. It caused a shriek from her as she was grasping onto the back of his shirt while staring down at his ass. "Ah! Joey!" After the unexpected change in her position, she giggled while he walked out of the office with her, carrying her up the stairs, planning on giving her a taste of what was to come after they said, 'I do.'

CHAPTER EIGHTEEN

Gage looked at himself in the mirror, running a hand down over the light beard he was growing in. Fuck, he was a handsome bastard. His hands came down to the midnight blue suit jacket, straightening it out on his large frame. He left the top few buttons of his white dress shirt undone. Underneath the jacket, he had two handguns holstered. Two were better than one, right?

He reached into the pocket of his matching blue dress pants and retrieved his keys. Layne would pitch a fit if he was late, and Joey would throw punches if he was. Leaving his condo in Hudson Yards, he arrived at O'Reilly Manor about twenty minutes later.

Before he stepped up to the front door, it opened, and Layne emerged. He gave a large smile, seeing her all dressed up for her meeting with Kuznetsov. She had on a pair of smokin' hot black boots that stopped right above her knees. The black dress she had on nearly looked painted onto her athletically fit body and all of its delicious curves. The long sleeves had cutouts exposing the tops of her shoulders. His cock was already beginning to stir to life, especially when he saw the decorative chain around her waist that was useless in serving its purpose as a belt. Fuck, he was going to have fun with that later.

Joey stepped out behind her wearing his black tactical pants and shirt, indicating he was on his way out to take care of his more violent business dealings for the evening. He leaned over and drew Layne into a deep kiss, thoroughly enjoying the taste of her mouth before he pulled back. "Try not to piss off anybody too much tonight." His eyes darted over at Gage, silently expressing the same sentiment towards his younger brother. The last thing he wanted to find out was that the two of them both lost their tempers.

Layne smirked. "Never." Her hands dropped down to his firm ass giving it an appreciative squeeze. The way his pants hugged his behind was something she wished she could stare at all day long. "I would like you to come back in one piece. So, be careful and don't go getting yourself killed, okay?"

He grinned. "Never gonna happen." Joey looked over at Gage and gave him a nod. "She's all yours." They clasped hands and gave a brief hug with a hand patting each other's back.

After Joey left in his Challenger, Gage gave her another appreciative once over with his light brown eyes before walking her to his vehicle. Layne abruptly stopped as he led her to the doorless, busted-up army-green TJ Jeep Wrangler with a tan hard top. "Are you kidding me?"

He hopped into the driver's seat and smiled at her. "What? It's a classic."

"It looks like a death trap." She was pretty sure that it was stubbornly clinging to the last moments of its life as she heard Gage turn the key, and the engine rumbled and sputtered.

"Put your ass in the seat, Layne."

She shook her head and climbed in, adjusting her dress to keep it secure around her thighs. Layne made sure her seatbelt was strapped securely around her body. They put doors on cars for a reason, and here she was, tempting fate in the open vehicle.

He reached over and grabbed the seatbelt, and gave it a firm yank with a bit of mischief in his eyes.

"Gotta make sure you're tied down."

In what seemed like such an innocent gesture of double-checking the seatbelt, his words sank deep to her core, imagining a series of intense scenarios, all leaving her aching between her thighs.

Seeing a tint of pink appearing on her cheeks, he chuckled to himself before sitting back in his seat and pulling away from the curb.

When they arrived at the agreed-upon nightclub, Alexei had his favorite table reserved for the occasion. Layne and Gage were escorted through the maze of tables tucked at the back of the establishment. The man guiding them was of average height, had a shiny bald dome of a head, and the personality of a paperclip.

He led them both to a table in the back corner where Kuznetsov rose from his seat, having a guard flanked at either side of him. Alexei may have been a small player in the game, but there was plenty of potential to turn him into a useful ally.

The man standing to greet her looked every bit his age and was approaching his golden retirement years. His goatee was showing the grey, overwhelming the light brown, and the same mixture of the two colors occurred on his shortly cropped hair. The lines around his eyes and across his face spoke to the toll the hard years had taken on him.

Alexei's suit was grey but almost looked silver with the sheen of its material. He gave her a polite smile as he opened up his arms. "Pchelka, so nice to see you." He leaned in to wrap his arms around her while pressing a brief kiss to both of her cheeks.

Gage visibly stiffened in his stance as he watched Alexei's every move. Polite greeting or not, he didn't like watching another man touch even breathing on her.

Layne returned the greeting, not looking to offend the man she hoped to get information from. "It has been a while, hasn't it?" She gave him a light smile.

The Russian gestured for her to take a seat as he took his own across from her. "Last I recall, you were just barely a woman, and now look at you. You are like a beautiful blossomed flower." He grinned at the sight of a matured Layne in comparison to what he remembered her as when she was a young lady still trying to grow into all her curves.

He motioned with two fingers for the man on his right to pour a drink for Layne from the open bottle of premium vodka sitting on the table.

Layne sat in the chair, crossing one slender thigh over the other, not bothering to glance behind her to ensure Gage was nearby. The scent of his delectable spiced vanilla cologne gave his presence away and provided her reassurance. Her hand reached out and took the glass full of vodka and raised it slightly in Alexei's direction, "Vyp'yem."

He did the same in return, echoing her toast in his native language before drinking from his glass. Layne sipped the vodka, which by far had to be one of her least favorite drinks of choice.

"I appreciate you taking the time to meet with me," she began, "I don't think it's any secret what I want to discuss with you. I'm sure you've already heard about what happened at my favorite little watering hole."

With his glass still hanging from his fingers, he extended his hand to one of his men, and with a snap, there was a cigar being handed to him. After getting it lit, he sat back and let his mind ponder over his carefully worded response. "Yes. Word travels quickly. You know who is responsible for such a disrespectful act?"

She gave a small shrug. "I have my suspicions. I was hoping that maybe you'd help to confirm them." Her eyes stared at him to reflect the serious nature of her inquiry.

He laughed before taking another puff from his cigar, blowing the smoke up into the air above the table. "Me?" He smiled in amusement. "Pchelka, you must think me a fool. If I knew, I would be wise to keep my mouth shut, just as you would be wise to heed such a stern warning."

Layne drew another sip of the vodka into her mouth. "Alexei, don't fucking play games with me. Your little weasels have their hands in a little bit of everything; I'm sure somebody knows something." That earned her an irritated grunt from one of Kuznetsov's guards apparently, he didn't like being called a weasel.

Still donning his smile, he shifted his gaze over her body. "I might know a thing or two. For a price." He ran his tongue over his lips like a wolf eyeing up a lamb.

She could feel his eyes trying to burn a hole through her clothing and what lay underneath. Now, it was her turn to laugh. "Oh, who is playing who for a fool, now?"

He shrugged casually. "Everyone must pay for something, yes?"

While he wasn't wrong, but Layne wasn't about to earn a reputation for fucking every faction head in the city anytime she needed something. She stood, causing not just Alexei's guards to shift into a state of readiness but Gage tensed up in his stance.

Layne stepped over to the Russian, bending over at her waist while leaning down to bring her face up close to his. Her words melted into a sultry whisper. "Oh, Alexei." She drank down the rest of her vodka and placed the glass between his legs on the seat of his chair.

It took everything Gage had not to intervene and tell Layne to stop playing with goddamn fire. She was toying with a very dangerous man and teasing another—him. The way she was bent over, the hem of her dress was threatening to reveal what lay underneath, forcing Gage to swallow down a groan. He mentally reminded himself what his purpose was here, and it sure as hell wasn't sinking his cock into her in the middle of the club.

She pressed the side of the glass forward between Kuznetsov's legs, bringing it up against the package bulging against the crotch of his pants. Layne's lips found his ear, where she whispered something only meant for his ears. It prompted Alexei to visibly shift in his seat.

Layne straightened up, leaving the glass where it was on his seat. "I want a name." She stared down at the man seated before her.

He cleared his throat. "I once told your father that you would make a nice printsessa for one of my sons. I misjudged. You are more like your father than I realized. I think you will find the answers you are looking for over at a little souvenir shop across from the Empire State Building." He placed his serving of vodka down on the table.

Her look turned dark as she got the answer she was looking for. "Thank you."

As she stepped away from him, his hand suddenly grabbed her wrist. Layne looked down at his tight hold on her, his grasp engulfing the narrowest part of her arm. She flexed her arm, pulling on his hold as she looked up to see his eyes.

"Be sure of your actions, pchelka. You do not want to lay judgment on the tiger only to be bitten by the snake." He released his hand from her.

She sat there thinking about his words and nodded. "Of course." Layne wasn't quite sure what he meant by the cryptic saying, but she wasn't going to let anyone in this city destroy her—tiger or snake.

Leaving the nightclub, she approached Gage's Jeep with determination in her steps. Before she could climb in, his hand grabbed her arm to turn her to face him. "What did you say to him in there that made him change his mind?"

Layne smirked. "That I knew his interests didn't lie in bedding the O'Reilly in front of him, that he would need to take a trip to visit Liam in Rikers Island to get his fix." Her devious little smirk grew before she added, "And that if he didn't give me what I wanted, I would cut his balls out, place them in a glass, pour his shitty fucking vodka over them, and make him drink it all."

"That's fucked up." Gage stared at her, knowing he should have been shocked, but found himself even more turned on knowing how she could hold her own in the big leagues.

"I know." She slid her arm out of his hold and got into the Wrangler.

After Gage joined her in the vehicle, he took a look at his phone and sent a text before tucking it back into his jacket pocket. He drove them back to his condo just south of Hell's Kitchen.

"What are we doing here?" She lifted a brow as he parked in the underground garage of a newly constructed building that laid residence to condos that were larger in square footage than the average American home. "Joey said he would meet us back at Cassidy's after he was done."

Gage didn't say anything when he hopped out of his seat and came over to her side. He reached over and pushed the release of her seatbelt, easing it off of her. "I told him there was a change of plans."

Her words held both irritation and suspicion. "What change in plans?" She hadn't been made aware of any changes, and she didn't like she was kept out of the loop. Layne got out of the Jeep and stared him down intently.

He took her jaw into his hand possessively. "Told him you were being a goddamn tease, and you were going to learn what happens when you shake your ass at me like that." His words were firm and laced with lust-ridden intentions.

CHAPTER NINETEEN

When they arrived upstairs at Gage's 24th-floor condominium unit, Layne was shocked to discover it was far different from the apartment Joey used to have. This was downright fancy as hell.

There were floor-to-ceiling windows in the primary living area upon entry that she imagined provided an impressive amount of natural light during the day. The furniture appeared to be high-end pieces, with a large cream sofa with navy throw pillows, a round coffee table in front of it, and an impressively large television mounted on the wall.

Gage slid out of his suit jacket, exposing the dual shoulder holster holding twin nine-millimeter semi-automatics. He tossed the jacket over the back of the couch before taking a seat. He leaned back as his eyes followed every movement Layne made.

"Layne," his voice husky and laced with need. "Come stand in front of me."

Maybe she was still riding her attitude and sass from her earlier conversation with Kuznetsov because she smirked at him. "Trying to be bossy now?" However, she still complied and walked over to stand in front of him, her hands perched on her hips.

His eyes narrowed at her, but he didn't respond to the question. Instead, he gave another order to her. "Turn around and bend over."

Oh, so he did think he was going to be the boss now, didn't he? She grinned as she felt excitement travel down her spine until it reached between her legs. After dropping her hands from her hips, she slowly spun around until her back was to him. Layne bent over halfway before looking back at him. "Satisfied?" The back of the dress still kept her body tastefully covered, barely.

"Not even close, baby. I want you touching your toes. Let me see that perfect ass of yours that you were so quick to taunt me with earlier."

She drew her bottom lip between her teeth, lightly biting it before continuing to fully bend down. The back of her dress crept up her backside until most of her ass was entirely exposed to him.

With his cock reacting to the sight of her holding that position, he contemplated plunging himself into her right then and there. He convinced himself to hold off; he wanted to teach her bratty side a lesson. "You realize how much I wanted to toss you down on that table tonight and spread your legs, not giving a fuck who saw? I would have drunk shots of vodka off your pussy before shoving my dick in you."

Layne had heard her fair share of dirty talk, but Gage's mouth was in a league of its own. The thin strip of her thong was very quickly getting soaked from her arousal as his vivid description had her aching from her core.

"Now, take off those panties and come sit on my lap." His palms rubbed down the length of his muscular thighs. Gage focused on keeping his hands to himself so he didn't get hasty and grab hold of her. There would be plenty of time for him to have her whenever it suited him, but tonight he had other intentions.

Her fingers hooked onto the sides of her thong, tugging them down her legs, and stepped out of them. After she straightened up, she brushed some of her dark locks of hair away from her face. Her face was flushed from all the blood that had rushed to it from being bent over for him.

She walked up to him, taking her spot and straddling his hips as her dress rode up past her hips to reveal what lay underneath. As she sat down on him, she could feel his cock trapped in his pants, begging to be freed.

"Mmm, you're doing such a good job listening. That's what I want from a good little submissive." Resting his hands on top of her thighs, he shifted his hips under her weight that rested on top of his erection. He didn't need to glance down to know her arousal was leaving its mark on his pants. She fucking wanted his cock in her as much as he needed to give it to her. "I want to see what else is mine underneath this dress." Gage ran his tongue over his lips, his hunger for her increasing.

Layne unhooked the decorative chain from around her waist first, dropping it onto the cushion next to them. Then, she pulled at the bottom of her dress, sliding it up until it was fully stripped from her body. Her fingers found the hooks of her bra and popped them free, letting that last piece of her clothing fall to the floor. The only thing remaining on her body were those over-the-knee boots she had been wearing all night.

Gage stared at the sensual buffet in front of him; he forced his arms back to rest along the back of the couch as he sat there. If he continued to lay his hands on her body, he knew there would be no stopping himself.

"Are you always this demanding?" She playfully asked him while her hands rubbed up the front of his chest, enjoying the feel of the solid wall of muscle under his shirt.

Allowing her hands to explore his body, he grinned at her question. "You haven't seen demanding yet. After the way you behaved tonight, taunting me with your ass, you're going to fucking find out. Consider yourself lucky I've shown as much restraint as I have."

"Oh, poor Daddy Gage, couldn't handle a little tease?" Layne playfully chided him with a fake pout. The attitude with this one was strong tonight.

His hand immediately found its place on her throat, pulling her face towards his own. "Don't. Play. With. Me." Gage's breaths were burdened with his desires as he fiercely stared at her. God help him with this woman that was driving him and his cock wild. With his hand on her throat, his imagination was drifting towards what his cock would feel like deep inside of it. How would her gags sound? Would her stunning eyes tear up?

Layne's gasp was nearly tainted by a moan when his strength took hold of her. Softly, she spoke, "Whatcha going to do about it?" Her hips rolled against the bulge of his pants to add a little extra tease behind her provocation.

His hand dropped from her neck, and he growled in response to her body grinding up against his already throbbing dick that wanted to find its way deep inside her. Wrapping an arm around her waist, he stood with her, walking over to one of the many windows that overlooked Midtown.

Gage put her down on her feet. He spun her around and bent her over so that she was revealing herself to the skyline of the city just on the other side of the massive window. "Don't move."

Layne gave a cheeky little smile but obeyed him, holding her position there.

He took off his shoulder holster, laying the equipment down on the coffee table next to them. His fingers yanked his shirt from his pants before undoing each button down the front until he could slip it off from his body.

Stepping up to her side, he ran his hand down her back and over the curve of her ass, enjoying the softness of the skin underneath his fingers. "You're going to count for me."

Her eyes tracked his movements, admiring the sight of him shirtless. "Count what?"

Smack!

A harsh sting of his hand coming down on one of her ass cheeks had her jolt from the sudden impact.

Gage smiled as the red outline of his hand graced her flesh. "If you want to show this hot ass off, you can do it for all of New York to see." His hand rubbed over where he had smacked, easing some of the heat of the strike. "But, you're gonna do it with my handprints all over it, so there is no mistaking who this ass belongs to. Do you understand me?"

The warmth of the smack against the curve of her behind wasn't the only heat in her body; her core was growing hotter with desire for his touch over more of her body. She nodded. "Yes, Sir."

He gave a grin filled with satisfaction at her response. "Now, fuckin' count until I've decided you have earned my cock." On the same spot he had just swatted her, his hand came down on it again.

Layne squeaked out, "One."

Gage brought down several more spanks on the beautifully fair skin, watching as it glowed an angry red with his large handprints. He waited between each one for her counts, and about halfway through, he switched to her other side. A total of six on each cheek plus one extra for all her sass.

He leaned over and pressed a kiss to the beautifully marked skin when he was finished. "You did so well, baby."

She was still bent over, breathing heavily, caught between the line of pain and lust each time his hand made contact with her.

Gage pulled her upright to face him. With gentler hands, he drew her face in to kiss her affectionately. Layne melted into the kiss, her hands landing on top of his chest to explore each cut and line of the strength of his body.

As the kiss grew deeper, Gage walked her back to the elongated chaise section of the sofa, refusing to break their connection as he did so. His hands quickly unlatched his belt and opened up his pants to drop them down to the floor.

With an increasing need for her reward from him, she pulled away from his mouth and laid herself back on the large section of the sofa. Layne smiled as she parted her legs for him, letting him see just how worked up he had her. The light pink folds between her legs soaked with her arousal.

Her eyes sparkled as she watched him dispose of the rest of his clothes. The grand reveal of the swords tattooed on his swollen cock had her hand dropping down between her legs, her fingers finding her sensitive clit and beginning to circle it. A moan slipped from between her lips. "I need you to take my pussy, Gage."

He didn't think his dick could grow even harder than it was, but when he saw Layne begin to play with herself, he damn near exploded. Smiling, he knelt on the cushion between her legs, positioning them against his shoulders.

His hand pulled her fingers away from her nub and slowly sucked the taste of her body from them before letting her go. "You better ask nicer if you want me stretching out your tight cunt with my dick."

Gage's hand went down the length of her boot until he found the zipper and slowly eased it off her foot. Doing the same with the other as he admired Layne's body laid out for him, waiting and begging to take him inside her.

She squirmed as she saw him hovering closer to her entrance. "Please, Sir, fuck me with your cock."

"Much better," he grinned and grabbed ahold of her legs up against the front of his chest. He placed a few soft kisses on each of her legs, making her wait just a little longer. "I could stare at your body all night long, watch as you stay wet with anticipation of having me shove myself balls-deep inside of you."

Layne whimpered as he continued to deny her of the thing that she yearned desperately for. Her legs pulled against his hands, which held them still. She was pretty sure she would lose her sanity if he didn't get inside of her soon.

As much as he was enjoying watching her ache for him, he had his own hard need for her. Gage rubbed the tip of his cock over her clit, relishing in how Layne cried out at the brief contact. Before she could beg for him, he lined up and pushed inside of her, making those swords disappear in her body.

Immediately, he groaned out in pleasure in unison with Layne's loud moan as he filled the tight space of her primed and ready cunt. At that point, he couldn't hold himself back as he leaned over, forcing her legs over his shoulders, and he began to drill into her roughly. Watching as his movements had her beautiful breasts bouncing, he groaned out appreciatively.

The sensation of him shoving inside of her sent her into a tailspin. Ecstasy began pulsing through her veins, and her voice, saturated with pleasure, filled the room. Her hand squeezed onto one of his that was braced on the cushion while her other found the back of his neck.

Gage showered kisses all over her body, starting at her shoulder and working his way up her throat until he found her mouth. Each time she moaned against his lips, he felt his dick fiercely ache with more desire inside her.

"Ah! Gage! Yes!" Her already tight walls began to squeeze even more around him as the peak of her pleasure built up to its breaking point. With stars floating across her vision, she cursed out, calling Gage's name as she came.

"Baby, that's fuckin' it, come for your Daddy," he growled into her ear. As Layne got lost in the depths of her pleasure, Gage couldn't fight his own anymore, and he gave a final thrust into her as his cum shot out like a damn bottle rocket.

Panting and resting his face up against the side of her neck, he gave tiny kisses. Despite having asserted his dominance over her and having her submit to him, deep down, he knew that very quickly he was the one becoming a slave to her. He was damn sure that no matter what Layne asked for, he would give it.

CHAPTER TWENTY

She balanced on the chair as she reached up to hang yet another framed picture on the wall of McGregor's. It was one of what felt like hundreds of photos she had reframed after the pub had been trashed the night Sean's body was discovered. So many of the framed images had been broken and scattered. Some of the actual photographs hadn't been salvageable, but she had saved what she could.

The walls had always been covered in snapshots of patrons from across the many years, and she sure as hell wasn't going to allow this incident to dishonor that part of Sean's heart and soul.

"Layne, we can have someone else do this." Joey chimed in from behind her. He watched as she stubbornly stood on her tiptoes to stretch to reach the nail on the wall just a few inches out of reach.

"No. I need to do this. They're holding Sean's wake here tomorrow, and hell, if I'm going to let this place look anything except as it should. Besides, I want to send a message to whoever did this." She grunted as she cursed her short legs.

Not waiting to watch her fall and break her neck, Gage wrapped his arms around her legs and lifted her so she could make the next few inches to hang the frame from the nail. Once the frame was secured, he softly dropped her onto her feet while keeping his arms around her.

"You're not going to send much of a message if you fall off a chair and break yourself." Gage gave her a gentle scolding before patting her on the ass and letting go of her.

She sighed quietly, knowing that he had a point. "That was the last one anyway."

Joey came up to her, turning her to face him. "It looks great." He leaned down and gave her a loving kiss.

While moving the wooden chair she had been using back to the table it had come from; Gage glanced over at the two of them. "How did the rest of the meetings go with the other families?" With things at his strip club picking up thanks to some porn convention in town, he had been unable to accompany Layne to several of the meetings she had with the other faction heads. Joey had happily stepped in to play the big, bad, masked man at her side.

Layne shrugged. "A few of them feigned ignorance. Two of them outright didn't want to get involved, which leads me to believe they're in Russell's pocket. Kuznetsov seemed to be the most willing to help. The rest of them seemed supportive, but who knows when push comes to shove where they'll land."

"What time is your meeting with Russ tonight?" Joey checked his watch, wanting to ensure they would have enough time to prepare.

"Ten o'clock. He said he'd text the location to me an hour ahead of time." Layne readjusted her hair, pulling it back into a loose ponytail at the back of her head.

"Gage, be ready to go by eight." Joey didn't want to run the risk of a last-minute time change when the ball was in Russell's court. "I trust this fucker as much as I'd trust the devil himself," Joey muttered.

Gage gave a nod back to Joey in acknowledgment. "For this? My schedule is wide open." Already hearing of the history between Layne and Russ, hell, if he was going to pass on the opportunity to be there.

She stared at both of them. "It's a courtesy meeting, not a beatdown. So, both of your asses need to settle down." Layne had no intentions of confronting Russ Spencer tonight if he was behind her troubles. She preferred to let him think she didn't know better while she gathered her resources behind the scenes.

That earned her a look from both the guys. Joey was the first to step in close to her, his hands cupping her face. Within seconds, Gage was at her back, and his hands grabbed a firm hold on her hips. The combination of their two scents mixing around her while she stood in the middle of a mouthwatering De Luca sandwich was fucking intoxicating.

Gage's voice whispered in her ear, "We have to keep our lucky charm safe, so you better settle *your* ass down." The hum of his words prompted goosebumps to rise over her skin and her lips to part slightly.

Joey smirked as he watched Gage get the subtle reaction out of her. He pressed his forehead to hers so that she would be forced to stare into his eyes, which could have commanded the stars in the sky to rearrange themselves. "You want to rephrase that, Layney? It almost sounded like you were trying to tell us what to do."

She was frozen between them, disarmed by the proximity of their bodies to hers and held captive by their words. Layne swallowed down any smartass comments. Despite her independent nature, she hoped these men would never relinquish their protective hold on her.

That evening, Layne received the text at precisely nine p.m.

RUSS

Bethesda Fountain

LAYNE

We will be there.

RUSS

Bringing your lap dog?

She gritted her teeth at Russ's snide comment, making a jab at Joey. Her fingers typed a response that initially had some colorful language before she decided to delete it. Instead, she took the high road.

LAYNE

Can never be too safe.

See you soon.

"He wants to meet at Bethesda Fountain in the middle of Central Park. It's a public spot, but at this time of night, it's pretty isolated." That was the nicest way of saying that anyone who had a care for their safety avoided Central Park when the sun disappeared, and the fountain was no exception.

Joey finished tightening his belt around his waist. "How romantic," he sarcastically responded to the divulged location of choice. He made sure he had his skull mask in his pocket.

Stepping out of the bathroom, Layne noticed Gage had chosen to mirror his brother in choice of outfit. Both of them had on all black, from the boots to the utility pants and black shirts.

Seeing the expression on Layne's face, Gage gave a goofy grin. "If I had known that dressing like this would get that look out of you, I would have ditched the expensive suit from the get-go."

Joey smirked and tossed a second mask over at Gage. "Wait until you see her face when you put this on."

Catching the mask out of midair, Gage looked over the design and chuckled, "Nice."

She was beginning to feel naked without her mask to round out the trio, but Layne reminded herself tonight wasn't about kicking asses and getting herself in trouble. It was all about having diplomatic discussions. It was the whole reason why she was dressed in a dark-washed set of jeans and an ivory blouse underneath a black jacket. Her chestnut hair was half pulled back, so it stayed out of her face.

Call her skeptical, but she wasn't showing up without a firearm tucked in the back of her jeans. Joey had said it best earlier; it would be easier to trust the devil than it would be to trust Russell Spencer.

Since they were using the Challenger, Joey demanded he drive. He had seen the condition of Gage's Jeep and Layne's lack of parallel parking skills. Upon arrival, he ended up parking a short distance from the terrace that overlooked the fountain. Both the guys stretched their respective masks across their faces, concealing their handsome features.

Gage's mask didn't mirror the toothy grin of Joey's skull design. Instead, his artwork resembled a demonic smile with splashes of red, misshapen teeth, and canines that were far too long and curved to be human. Joey had been right, the look on Layne's face when he put on the mask had been one of a woman about to pounce on a mate. He noticed the way she tried to hide her body's subtle reactions, her thighs pressed together firmly, and her hands grasped onto her arms tightly while her tongue wet her suddenly dry lips.

Reminding herself this was like any other discussion she had over the past few weeks, Layne drew in a deep breath to prepare to switch to the woman who both deserved and commanded respect while standing tall at the top of her empire's ranks.

Both masked De Lucas fell in line behind her as they walked across the terrace to the large circular fountain with amber lights barely keeping it illuminated. There waiting for her at the north side of the fountain was one cocky-looking Russell Spencer. He had three men of his own keeping him company.

He smirked as he took note of the masked guards behind Layne. "Two lap dogs?"

She didn't need to hear the light rumble from Joey to know he was irritated at the dig, the prickling heat of his anger perking up could be felt in the air.

"I wouldn't worry about them. It's the bitch who bites." If Russ wanted to draw parallels, she would be more than happy to fire verbal shots right back at him.

Russ chuckled as he approached her. "I quite remember that spirited bark of yours, Layne. Tell me, is that why we're here tonight? Our interactions in the past would have me believing you're returning to yap at me. Have you come here to disrespect my livelihood?" He tilted his head curiously at her.

"Depends, have you been disrespecting mine?" Her eyes stared threatening daggers at him.

A mild smirk pulled at his mouth. "Let's take a walk." Seeing the uneasy shift Gage made, he held a hand up in his direction while looking at Layne. "Tell your pack to stay; I would prefer we be out of earshot for such sensitive discussions. One can't be too careful these days."

Layne looked back at the two masked men at her back and gave a small gesture for them to hang back for now. Turning her attention back to Russ, she gave him the all-clear, "Lead the way."

He gestured to the other side of the large fountain where the spilling of water into its base pool made sure that no one could overhear their conversation. She walked with him to his chosen spot, still within sight of both their sets of security detail.

"You must think I don't have ears on the streets, Russ. You haven't been particularly quiet about whatever problems you have with my family." She got straight to the point.

Russ nodded in agreement. "Liam couldn't pick up the slack, and this isn't the line of work where a woman should be left in charge."

"Someone stepped foot in my territory and left me with a hell of a threat, Russ." Her eyes assessed every movement he made, from how often he drew a breath to how he blinked his eyes.

"I'd tread very carefully, Layne. It almost sounds like you're insinuating I had something to do with it. That would be in poor taste to come here and start hinting at something that could start a war."

She gave an indifferent shrug. "From the tone of your voice, it sounds like you wouldn't mind if there was one."

Russ grinned and reached out to touch her arm. She drew it back from him, not caring for him to so much as trace a finger on her jacket. He got the hint and dropped his hand away from her. "I won't argue that I have had my eyes on your territory for some time, but don't be mistaken in believing I'm the only one."

They stood there talking for another twenty minutes before returning to their initial meeting spot. Most of the conversation was full of useless back and forth, with Russ trying to come off as innocently not having his hands in the pot of shit this time.

"Oh, Layne?" Russ called out to her before she turned to leave.

She turned to look at Russ. "Yeah?"

"This business is cruel and unforgiving. I wouldn't want to see you or anyone you care about end up beaten to near death and then dumped at the nearest animal clinic in hopes of quick euthanizing."

Gage had been prepared to leave, but as Russ gave his parting advice, he was immediately triggered by memories of the past. He stepped forward. "What the fuck did you just say?" His blood was boiling in his veins and turning his vision red with rage.

Russ was unfazed as one-half of Layne's security seemed to take issue with his comments. "I said I would hate to see her treated like a stray, beaten and discarded like an unwanted animal."

Both Layne and Joey had been prepared to leave when Gage suddenly broke rank with them. Not initially picking up on Russ's comments, Joey was taken off guard by his brother's sudden shift.

After Russ repeated himself, it sank in for Joey. *Rose*. Her poor, battered, and tortured body and the way it had been dumped at the veterinary office. "Fuck," he uttered before bolting for Gage.

"You sick fuck! I will fucking rip you apart!" Gage lunged at Russ. Joey managed to grab hold of him, yanking him back from making a deadly mistake. It seemed he was just in time as each of Spencer's men were already reaching for their weapons. Joey's strength struggled to contain the threat of Gage's wrath getting loose.

Layne knew that if this outburst got the best of Gage, this meeting would end up poorly for them all. She ran over to put herself right in front of him, her hands coming to his chest to try and capture his attention. "Hey! Look at me!"

He continued shouting over Layne's head. "You destroyed her! I will send you straight to fucking hell after what you did!"

With her hands balled up in his shirt while Joey grunted to restrain his little brother, she yelled at him. "HEY! Not here! NOT HERE!" Her eyes filled with concern seeing how quickly this could go tits up if Gage's recklessness got the better of them all.

Finally noticing Layne's boldly colored eyes wide with panic, he stopped trying to charge at Russ. "You watch your goddamn back! I will end you!" He allowed Joey to pull him back, stumbling a few steps until he voluntarily turned around. He shoved Joey's hands off him as he headed back toward the car with Joey close on his heels.

Layne looked back at Russ, who appeared riddled with entertainment as he spoke up, "Better keep those dogs on a leash, Layne."

"You just worry about your damn self, Russ." She glared at him briefly before quickly jogging to catch up with the guys who were already halfway back to the car.

CHAPTER TWENTY-ONE

Layne squeezed into the backseat behind Joey, who slid in after her to take his seat at the wheel and start up the engine.

Scooting over to the center seat so she could look at both of them, she primarily focused on Gage, who was already sitting in the front passenger seat. "What the fuck was that?!" She shouted at him.

Gage was shaking his head, seething as the anger rolled off of him in waves. His fist punched the dash several times. His other hand yanked down his mask as he glared at Joey. "He fucking had a hand in it! You're just going to let him walk away?! That motherfucker deserves a one-way ticket straight to hell!"

Joey removed his mask, tossing it down forcefully into the cupholder between the front seats. His hands rubbed over his face, trying to think past Gage's yelling in his ear.

She did her best to get Gage to bring it down a notch as she leaned forward and reached a hand out to touch his cheek and turn him to look at her. Layne wasn't sure what the hell had Gage ready to go on a goddamn bender, but she needed to find out.

It took a lot of coaxing from her to get him to take his eyes off Joey while his breathing remained heavy from the aggression flexing all over his body. "You need to calm down." Her words were stern.

Dropping his hands down onto the wheel, Joey put the Challenger in drive and began to head back to O'Reilly Manor. "Layne, put your seatbelt on." His eyes glanced back at her in the rearview. He wasn't driving particularly aggressively, but hell if he wasn't going to make sure that she was safely secured in the event of an unforeseen accident. As far as Joey was concerned, Layne was the most precious piece of cargo in the vehicle.

Ignoring him, she kept her eyes on Gage as the softness of her fingers stroked over the coarse hairs of his short and dark blonde beard. "Gage, look—"

In unison, both De Lucas cut off her words while shooting demanding looks at her. "Put it on!" It seemed that Gage also had a vested interest in her safety.

She sighed and sat back in the seat, dropping her hand away from Gage's face. After she drew the belt across her body, latching it in, she wanted nothing more than to stick her tongue out at them both childishly.

Keeping his eyes on the road, Joey finally gathered enough of his thoughts. "We don't know it was Russell."

"The fuck we don't. Who the hell makes that type of comparison except someone who has first-hand knowledge of some incredibly dark shit?" Gage sat back in his seat, trying his best not to assault the dashboard again. "Did you see the smug look on his face?"

"He always has a smug look on his face; it's a permanent affliction." She chimed in from the backseat. "The two of you need to fill me in on what the hell is going on." If Russ was potentially involved in something more than conspiring against her becoming a force to be reckoned with in this city, she needed to factor that into her next move.

She was met with silence.

"Oh, for fucks sake. Pull over."

When Joey didn't immediately make a move to pull the car off the road, she slammed her hand on the back of his seat, giving it a good jostle. "I SAID PULL THE FUCK OVER!"

Her temper and intolerance reached new peaks that must have surprised even Joey, who didn't hesitate to pull over to the side of the road. Layne released her seatbelt and cursed this godforsaken two-door vehicle. If she could have easily climbed out, she may have done just that and walked her ass the rest of the way home.

Instead, she leaned forward over the center console and looked at them both. "Both of you listen to me very clearly. I'm tired of the damn looks you keep giving one another while you decide to keep shit to yourselves. You both signed up for this, so I'm going to need you to respect that I have a business to run that requires me to have all the cards laid out in front of me. If you don't want to do that, then I will get out of this damn car right now."

With both sets of eyes staring back at her, shocked expressions plastered over their faces.

"Well? Are you going to fill me in or not?"

Out of the corner of her eye, she saw Gage's hand adjusting himself in his pants, clearly thinking about filling her up instead. Then, she glanced down at Joey, who hadn't even bothered to hide his erection, creating a tent between his legs.

Exasperated, she murmured, "Jesus, help me." Layne was sure that trying to get through to both of them was going to require her to come up with more creative ways so their brains didn't immediately drop into their dicks.

"I don't think Jesus is your type," Gage smirked. It was the first indication that his vengeful mood had simmered down a little. Joey stifled a laugh in response with his hand, trying to subtly hide his grin at his brother's comment. He didn't want Layne murdering him in his car, which was his pride and joy.

Sombering up a little, Gage turned more in his seat so he could fully face Layne. "You're right, baby, but I'm not talking about it here. Let's get home first 'cause I'm going to need a damn drink for this." He leaned over and heatedly captured her mouth with his, trying to ease away her frustrations.

Joey's hand reached over and eased her face away from Gage's so he could also apologetically share a loving kiss with her. "Layney, we will share what we know, okay?" He didn't want to jump to conclusions about Russ's statements, but Gage's instincts very well could have been on the right path this time.

She straightened herself up, still riled up from the way they had always been dancing around some giant elephant in the room while she was around. "Thank you."

After getting settled back in her seat, safely belted in, Joey drove the rest of the way back to their home.

Once inside, they all got more comfortably dressed and gathered in the living room. Layne sat down on the sofa in a set of midnight blue shorts with a matching white and navy zip-up hoodie. Joey took a seat next to her, drawing her into his lap while he wore a pair of basketball shorts and nothing else.

Gage entered the room wearing a pair of grey sweats borrowed from

Joey and his tightly fitted black tank. The sweatpants were Layne's favorite pair Joey owned, and seeing them on Gage, she could agree that they were, without a doubt, the world's best sweatpants.

In Gage's hands, he showed he came bearing gifts, three glasses, each filled with bourbon poured over a large sphere-shaped piece of ice. He handed off a beverage to both Layne and Joey before easing himself down onto the sofa. His hand pulled Layne's feet into his lap. Both men felt more at ease having a physical connection with her.

There was a moment while she sat there that she wondered if this was how she could envision a random weeknight with both of them. Something as mundane as lounging on the couch together, simply enjoying one another's presence without worrying about what was going on outside their little world. It was a bittersweet fantasy, something that she wasn't sure would become a reality given all the risks they all took on the daily.

It took a few sips of the mahogany-colored liquor before Gage finally eased into the topic at hand. "You already know about our relationship with Rosie, but I don't think we've been clear about the details of what happened."

Layne sank back against Joey's chest, his arms squeezing around her like she was his security blanket to clutch onto.

Gage continued to talk, trying to keep his voice even as all the memories of the past came to the forefront of his mind. "She wasn't just beaten, but the men who took her chained her to a pole and treated her like they were breeding a fighting dog." He strained to get the words out loud enough.

His fingers ran through his hair at the difficulty in revealing what had been the most painful twenty-four hours of his life. "The medical reports said she had trace amounts of pentobarbital in her system—the same drug they use to euthanize animals. Between that and the beatings, she never had a chance of waking up."

Joey nuzzled his face into the back of Layne's neck, inhaling deeply the scent of her soap still clinging to her skin. He quietly chimed in, "They sent pictures of what they did to her."

She sat there, not realizing how tightly she was holding onto her untouched glass of bourbon. It was clear that what had happened to Rosie ended up deeply scarring both of them. Her heart ached that they both had to endure such a horrific nightmare. It pissed her off that anyone had so viciously not only inflicted this pain on them but had accomplished it by taking it out on an innocent soul in the process.

Raising his glass to quickly consume the rest of his drink, Gage looked over at them. "I know Russ had his hand in it. I don't know how, but my gut is telling me that fucker knows something at a minimum."

If all of this was true, it made Russ an even bigger target on her list than he already was. She tried to sort out everything she knew about Russ's business affairs, his interest in keeping her from coming into her own power base, and what she had learned from several other criminal underlords throughout the city.

"Joey said that all of this was all over a bad business deal? Who was it with?" She hoped maybe that would lead them to get answers if Russell was involved or not.

Joey tensed at her back, not giving her much comfort in whatever answer she was about to get. "I know what you're thinking, Layne. That maybe we can use them as leverage, but it's a dead end."

She looked back over her shoulder at him. "Tell me who." Her voice lowered slightly with the weight of her demand on her tongue. Dread filled her chest, making her question if she truly wanted to know the answer.

Recalling how they had agreed to tell her all the details they hadn't yet revealed, he held himself to his word. "Eric Ellis."

Her eyes damn near fell out of her head. "What?!" She pulled her feet out of Gage's lap and shifted around to stare at Joey in disbelief. "Why wouldn't you tell me that?!"

After placing his glass on a side table, Joey's hands rubbed over her arms. "Because it doesn't matter. He's gone, and there's not much to learn from a rotting corpse, Layne." Not to mention he hated bringing up the asshole's name.

Gage sat forward, resting his elbows on his knees. "I asked him not to. When Joey told me about your experience with him, it was clear the history I had with Eric had nothing to do with your encounters. At the time when this all happened, Eric was still working the small deals in Jersey City, nothing like the type of shit he got into by the time he moved here."

She frowned, still not liking that they both had kept this from her, even with her best interests at heart. "So, why do you think Russ is involved if the deal was with Eric?" Layne looked over at Gage, hoping he would fill in the gap.

He answered, "Eric had already left the state, and he didn't have the manpower, he had to contract it out to somebody."

She considered his response and thought it through. "So, you think that he had Russ doing his dirty work for him?"

Gage nodded.

She sat there thinking over everything she had learned about Eric. Were there any ties to Russell that would support Gage's theory?

Her mind drifted back to the audio recording where the pervy Andrew Correlli had been speaking with Eric.

"Good. Now, make sure that you go make good on our arrangement and go make friends with Russell for me."

Eric hadn't just been playing Layne, but he had been playing Andrew and Russell both. It could have all started with hiring Russell to take the hit on Rosie years earlier on Eric's behalf. Then, in a play to manipulate Layne, Eric sends Andrew as the pawn to a known associate—Russ Spencer. If Layne had lashed out at Russ, there would have been no skin off Eric's back at the end of the day. Instead, he had her dispose of the middleman linking these two assholes together.

The fucking manipulative bastard was juggling backstabbing everybody and anybody. Even from the goddamn grave, he was still fucking with her life.

CHAPTER TWENTY-TWO

Joey knocked on Rebecca's door with one hand tucked in the front pocket of his jeans before dropping the other down to slide it in the other. Layne was stuck getting all her hired hands to dig into more information surrounding Russell and his connections. How deep had Eric's influence sunk into the dark underworld of New York's criminal organizations?

The door swung open, and Rebecca gave a welcoming smile. "Hey, you made it just in time, I just got back." She had been out watching the children for the family she nannied for while the parents had a brunch date together. Layne had always said that punctuality had always been Joey's thing. She wasn't kidding. Rebecca stepped back, opening the door wider to let him step inside her apartment.

"Thanks. You said you had some stuff for Layne to look at for the wedding?" He shut the door behind him. His eyes surveyed the inside of her apartment that she always managed to keep clutter-free, except for all the various wedding-related items she held onto for Layne.

Rebecca nodded as she walked over to a stack of boxes she kept in the corner of her quaint living room. Each box was meticulously labeled and organized. Samples, favors, flowers, music selections, brochures, and color swatches. "Yeah, she still needs to decide whether she wants the Kelly Green or the Hunter Green for the chair sashes."

He lifted a brow. "Aren't they both just green?"

She rolled her eyes and shook her head. "No! You see, Kelly Green has a little more—you know what? Never mind. She just needs to pick one. Tell her that I think the Hunter Green is more aesthetically pleasing, but the Kelly Green fabric feels nicer." Rebecca dug into one of the boxes, pulling out a small plastic bag containing two fabric swatches.

Joey smirked. "You know she's going to close her eyes and pick one at random, right?"

She hated to admit it, but she knew he was likely right. Rebecca groaned at how difficult of a bride Layne was turning out to be. "Don't tell me if she does."

As she extended the samples over to Joey, her facial expression changed slightly. One that Joey was having a hard time deciphering. He may have been able to read Layne in an instant, but he hadn't yet been able to interpret the many expressions of her best friend.

He pocketed the samples she handed over. "Is there anything else?"

Rebecca stood there quietly, debating with herself before deciding that it was a topic of conversation worth bringing up. "Do you have a few minutes so we can talk?"

Joey shrugged. "Sure."

Rebecca headed over to her kitchen table and pulled a chair out for herself. Joey followed behind but remained standing, unclear of whatever was weighing on her mind. If something was bothering Layne's bestie enough to bring it to his attention, he was interested in hearing it.

Fidgeting with her fingers in her lap, she looked at him. "I know I occasionally give you a hard time." She grinned at her choice of words. "Maybe more than occasionally."

He grinned knowingly. "I wouldn't expect anything less."

She nodded. "It's just… Layne has been my best friend since we were in elementary school. I always knew her family was different - that she was different. She has never been one to back down from a fight. I remember she beat the crap out of the first guy who ever broke my heart."

Rebecca softly laughed at the memory. Poor Kevin had been on the receiving end of Layne's anger in front of the entire high school in the auditorium. "She got suspended from school for a week, but she had said it had been worth it to see the regret and embarrassment on his face after getting his ass handed to him by a girl."

Joey smiled, imagining a scrappy teenage Layne putting some kid in his place. "Sounds like her." Part of him wished he had known Layne in both of their younger years; it would have allowed both of them to spend even more of their lives together.

Sitting back in her chair, her pale blue eyes looked over him. "You know how much she has been through. I don't think I've ever seen her as happy as she is when she's with you or even just hears your name."

Joey did his best to keep Layne happy, even with her challenging personality that matched his equally challenging temperament. "I'm sensing there's a 'but' coming."

She gently smiled at his accurate prediction. "*But*, I still worry about her. I don't pretend to understand what she's involved in, and she has never been one to allow me in so that I can understand it. All I know is that it carries a lot of risk. The whole thing with Eric was…eye-opening." That was putting it mildly. It was the first time that she got a front-row seat into just how much Layne stared danger in the eyes without fear.

He shifted in his stance, knowing that Layne had made it clear in no uncertain terms with him that she didn't want Rebecca to know more than necessary. After Eric had threatened Rebecca's well-being, he couldn't exactly blame her. Layne had tried to go as far as to entirely ghost her friend in the name of avoiding any other incidents. However, he knew that Layne needed Rebecca in her life. It had taken weeks of convincing on his part to persuade her that she needed the time with someone who wasn't in this line of work. Rebecca was the moral compass they all needed every once in a while.

Joey ran his hand over the back of his head, smoothing his dirty blonde hair down. "Look, Rebecca…"

She was quick to shake her head. "I'm not looking for the nitty gritty, Joey. I'm just pointing out what I do see." A concerned frown came over her face. "I'm just scared. I worry that one day…" Tears began to form in her eyes as her chin quivered. Quickly, her fingers swiped away the first two tears that escaped her blue hues. "I'm just scared I'm going to wake up one day to the news that my favorite person in the world is no longer in it."

Legitimate fear filled her face despite trying to push back the emotions tugging on her soul. She glanced down and shook her head. "Sorry, I-I just can't imagine not having her to call up any time something stupid comes up, like the hot mailman smiling at me or that I had a great day or even a shitty one." Rebecca sniffled and attempted not to break down entirely. "I would rather be helping plan this wedding than planning a funeral."

Joey furrowed his brows and walked over to where she was seated. He squatted in front of her so he could look at her face. Taking her hands into his, he gave them a firm squeeze. "I don't want you to be sorry."

His voice was gentle as he began to realize in his own way he shared the very same fears. "There isn't a single moment of my day that I don't worry about her. Even when I'm sleeping, keeping her safe is all I dream about." Taking a deep breath, he prepared to share with Rebecca some of his most vulnerable feelings. "I promise I will always do what I can to keep her safe and mostly happy."

Rebecca raised a brow at him at the last part. "*Mostly* happy?" She was ready to lash out at him for not wanting to keep her one-hundred-fucking-percent happy.

He gave her a knowing grin. "Have you met your best friend? She can be a real stubborn pain in the ass that doesn't even know what is good for herself some days."

She laughed out loud, knowing that he was spot on. Layne really could be her own worst enemy at times.

His hand patted hers. "I love Layne more than I could ever tell you or anyone else. There is nothing I wouldn't do for her. I can't tell you that her life will ever be without very real risk and danger. All I can do is promise you that for the rest of her life, she will never go a single day without all the happiness I can give her."

Rebecca full-on burst into tears after hearing his words. She pulled her hands from his so she could toss herself at him and wrap her arms around Joey's neck in a massive hug. She nearly knocked him over while he was balanced on the balls of his feet while in his squat.

"Oof!" His hand had to grab onto the table for a moment so he didn't lose his balance. He wrapped his other arm around her, squeezing in a hug full of reassurance.

She pulled back and eased herself back from him, her hands hastily wiping off the tears from her cheeks. "You tell her I went all mushy like this, I will kill you." Rebecca joked as she smiled at him.

Joey pushed his hands against his knees as he stood back up. "Your secret is safe with me." He winked at her.

Now that she had gotten all of that off her chest, she finally was able to move the conversation to something a little more lighthearted. She grabbed a tissue to dab underneath her eyes at the last couple of tears that hadn't dried.

"Layne still hasn't told me if you guys are going on a honeymoon. She keeps telling me it all depends on work." Based on the expression on Rebecca's face, she was none too happy with that response.

He smirked. "Don't worry, I will steal her away from the city for a little bit, even if she kicks and yells the entire way."

They sat and chatted with one another for another twenty minutes, going over a few minor details about the day of the wedding. Most of it related to things he could give an opinion on, like the freely flowing booze.

When he finally left Rebecca's place, he began jogging down the stairs of the apartment building while checking his phone for any new calls or messages.

There was one in particular that caught his attention. It was a text from Layne. When he opened it up, he was greeted by a selfie of her scantily clad body and her flirtatious smile. It looked like she had found the black lace piece of lingerie he had bought for her and had been hiding as a surprise. Underneath the picture, she had sent him another text.

LAYNE

Finders keepers.

You need better hiding spots.

Joey had to grab onto the handrail to prevent himself from tripping over his feet at the delicious distraction displayed on his phone. He quickly texted her back.

JOEY

Funny, that's what I always say about you.

I will be home in ten, you better be ready for me.

He had found the one woman in this world who could make him want for nothing and planned to always keep her.

CHAPTER TWENTY-THREE

It was the end of yet another successful night at Cassidy's Cave. Gage sat in his office, leaning back in his chair with a sigh as he rested his eyes. It was nearly two in the damn morning. He wasn't thinking about sleep, though. Instead, he had one particular image in his mind. The way Layne looked up at him while on her knees through her dark lashes, how her body moved while taking him in, and the sight of his handprints being left behind on her curvy ass cheeks.

His dick was quickly twitching in his jeans, growing harder with each thought of Layne and all the things he still wanted to do to her. Gage wanted to see her tiny hands bound together while laid out on his bed, begging to be taken any way he pleased. He pictured how his collar would look around her slender neck. All these thoughts had his dick raging with need. His hand drifted down to undo his belt and pants. Sliding his hand inside his pants, he took hold of himself.

Quietly, he whispered to himself, "That's it, baby. Beg for your Daddy." He groaned, imagining Layne's response in his head.

It wasn't long before his fantasy was chased away as he was rudely interrupted by a knock on his office door. Before he could call out to acknowledge the knock, Danielle poked her head in. "You have a second?"

Pulling his hand from his pants, Gage opened up his eyes and leaned forward in his chair, forcing her a smile like he wasn't just about to jack himself off. He scooted his chair in while he discreetly and single-handedly closed his pants back up.

"Yeah, what's up?" He shifted in his seat, trying to ignore the throbbing of his cock.

Ever since the night that Layne had come into the private room and interrupted Danielle's weekly gig for Italo and his guys, she had been picking up extra shifts to make up for the generous tips she was now missing out on. Gage had to admit, she was working extra hard around here. If half the girls would put in a fraction of that effort, he would be making bank on even their slowest nights.

Danielle walked in, wearing a pair of black hot shorts that left most of her ass hanging out and a white Cassidy's Cave crop top that barely fit over her fake tits. Like most of the girls he hired, she was extremely attractive and held up the strip club's reputation for having some of the best adult entertainment.

"Before I leave for the night, I was wondering if you need anything." She flipped the extensions of her long, bleached hair back over her shoulder. Her eyes drifted down towards his waist.

He stared at her and shook his head. "If you've already closed out all your tabs and helped clean up the tables, you're free to go." Gage wasn't an idiot; he knew that some of the girls had their sights on him. When they all walked around nearly naked, he had seen his share of wet panties and sexy innuendos directed at him. As a good business practice, he didn't lay a finger on any of them. After meeting Layne, he didn't even want to.

She tried to mask her disappointment that he hadn't even thought twice before responding to her. "If you need anything in here taken care of, I can help out." Her eyes glanced down to his lap again as she started to lean forward over his desk.

Another intrusion into his office followed before he could dismiss Danielle's advances, this time, it was a much more welcomed one. Layne walked in, stopping short as she had expected him to be alone.

Layne had on a pair of tight and heavily distressed jeans with strategic rips and tears across her thighs. Under the forest green jacket, she was wearing what looked like the top half of some lingerie. The black lace was flush against her skin and pushed up those nicely sized breasts of hers that she flaunted so perfectly.

Right behind her was Joey, who seemed equally as surprised at Danielle's presence. He wore a black leather jacket with a faded graphic tee underneath it. His jeans had a few minor spots of old motor oil, indicating he was likely working on his car while wearing them at some point.

Straightening up from her bent-over posture, Danielle glanced back at the two party crashers in disappointment. "Just give me a ring if you change your mind." She turned from Gage, walked up to Layne, and wrapped her arms around her neck in a hug.

Layne stood there awkwardly, unsure if she should hug the girl back. She opted for a light pat on her back as she looked over at Gage with a confused expression on her face. Secretly, she had hoped that one of them would save her from the bizarrely random gesture. Had this girl just gone from flirting with Gage to suddenly hugging her? And for what?

Danielle smiled at Layne after releasing her hold. "I wanted to thank you."

One of Layne's eyebrows perked up. "For what?"

"Oh!" She gave the fakest of giggles as she realized that it was unclear to Layne. "Ever since Italo and his gang stopped coming here, it has been such a blessing. They were a bunch of creeps. Honestly, they were shitty tippers with even smaller dicks. After you came that one night, they haven't bothered showing their faces again."

The twist of confusion on Layne's face increased as she tilted her head at the statement. Sure, she had interrupted Danielle's private party in that room, but she had been wearing her mask.

"Um. You're... welcome? I don't know why you think..." Layne shot looks over at Joey at her side and Gage across the room.

Danielle gave her a wink. "I would know these curves anywhere." Her hand slapped Layne's ass. It came so unexpectedly that Layne nearly jumped out of her boots as her eyes widened slightly.

The guys seemed to find humor in Layne's surprised reaction as they stifled their laughter. Danielle walked out of Gage's office, and Joey shut the door after she was gone. "It seems we're not the only ones that appreciate how fuckin' hot you are," he said as he moved over to the chair in front of his brother's desk and took a seat.

Layne was still a little weirded out by the entire encounter. Sure, Rebecca had given her ass a smack or three, but it had always been during drunken shenanigans. She shook her head, trying to reset her focus on why she and Joey were both here.

She approached Gage's desk, partially taking a seat by perching half her ass on it so she could look at both of them. "I heard back from Brandon." Or, as he preferred to be called by his hacker name, Cowboy. He had been a great asset to Layne after Joey had introduced them during their initial investigation into Eric's dirty work.

"He said that technology has changed so much over the last ten years there wasn't much to work with to confirm if Russell had a hand in what happened with Rosie. As for Eric," she swallowed down the nausea churning in her stomach at even saying his name. "His operations were still in their infancy, making them far more difficult to trace. He could have contacted Russ, but there's no way to be sure."

Joey's eyes still held a little bit of rage, knowing that Eric was still stirring up shit postmortem. He shifted his look to Gage. "Also, since Sean hated anything that left a trail, we don't have anything like cameras to rely on." Despite repeated requests from patrons to at least put a television in McGregor's, Sean had been a hardheaded son of a bitch and refused any bit of technology.

Gage ran his fingers through the shortly-cut blonde hair on his head as he tried to think of other avenues. "What about street cameras?"

Layne shook her head. "That area is jam-packed with people coming and going. It would be impossible to tell who may have been inside at any given time. We'd be pulling from an entire city's worth of straws."

"Fuck," Gage sighed. This wasn't the news he was hoping for. He really wished that Joey and Layne had just let him shove a gun down Russ's mouth that night at Bethesda Fountain. It would have solved a shit ton of his problems, or at the very least, would have made him feel better.

Joey propped his feet up on the edge of the desk, crossing his ankles. "The best we've got is what all of the city's top-tier criminal leaders have had to say." Which wasn't much.

The cocoa-colored hues belonging to Gage reflected a moment of realization of a new approach. "What about your brother?"

She wrinkled up her forehead. "What about him?"

"Would he have insight or something that could be a lead that we haven't already considered?" Gage looked so hopeful that maybe this was the key to it all.

It made Layne snort. "Liam wouldn't know good intel from his own ass."

"Is he still at Rikers?" Joey curiously asked since he hadn't heard Layne griping about her brother recently.

Layne shrugged, the lack of fucks obvious from how she did so.

"Probably, I guess? I haven't talked to him. I know he didn't make bail at his arraignment, and that was the last shit I had to give about it. Let him pay the piper."

"Alright, then back to square one. We keep digging." Gage still was sure that Russ had involvement in all of this. He sure as hell wasn't going to let history repeat itself and allow Layne to suffer the fate that Rosie had. He knew they were two very different women, but he never wanted to see Layne endure anything less than what a goddamn goddess deserved. A fuckin' dangerous goddess that deserved the gods of chaos and wrath at her side.

They all sat around and chatted a little longer, talking out some other unturned stones that perhaps they could turn over. Finally, Layne had decided all the iced coffee she had ingested earlier needed an outlet. She left Gage's office to see herself to the ladies' room.

Once Gage was sure that Layne was out of earshot, he looked over at Joey. "She's stressed. I don't like it." Layne would never admit it, but she would carry the weight of her world on her shoulders even though she had a hell of a support system to share the load.

Joey nodded in agreement. "Until this all gets resolved, I don't think it's going to get any better. She was talking earlier about postponing the wedding just until everything settles."

With an immediate opinion on that issue, Gage shook his head. "You didn't agree to that, did you?"

Dropping his feet back down to the floor, he could only shrug. "It doesn't matter if I agreed to it or not, Gage. She's hellbent and set on it. Rebecca even got involved, threatening to wear some hideous pumpkin gown if Layne didn't change her mind."

Nodding his head as he soaked this all in, Gage let the gears in his head spin. He suddenly smirked, thinking back to earlier when he had been alone with his thoughts. "You know what I think she needs?"

Scoffing, Joey was sure Layne needed a lot of things, but he didn't initially follow the mischievous look on his brother's face. He glanced over at Gage, who appeared to settle on a devious course of action. Finally catching on, Joey grinned. "You mean…?"

Gage nodded slowly, giving a large smile. "I do. I'm game if you are. Everything should be shut down up front, and everyone gone for the night."

"Fuck, yes." Joey's excitement was already building up. "Let's go get her."

Gage's hand dug into his desk drawer, retrieving something that just might come in handy. Shoving the item into his pocket, he stood from his chair, ready to give their girl the time of her life.

CHAPTER TWENTY-FOUR

When Layne came out of the ladies' room, she expected to cross through the main area of the club, where all the stages were spread out, and head back past the bar to Gage's office.

Instead, what she found when she approached the center stage was not what she had expected. Sitting on the edge of the circular platform with their legs dangling off the side were both Joey and Gage seemingly waiting for her.

The two of them looked at her with a hungry gaze. She slowed her steps as her heart began to beat a little heavier, and her breaths became a little lighter. "What's going on?" The suspicion tainted her voice.

"Be a good girl and come over here," Joey begged her closer with the gesture of his finger. He gave a devilish grin at her, knowing damn well his words would have her getting weak in the knees.

She walked over to the stage that was raised a few feet from the ground. It was a large circle with a silver pole in the middle, and the platform itself was painted black. The only thing that marred its coloring was the glitter that would likely be forever adhered to it no matter how much it got scrubbed and cleaned.

Layne stood before the two of them. "I thought we were wrapping up to go home."

Gage hopped down from the edge of the stage, landing on his feet with a gentle thud. He circled 'round her until he was at her back. His hand got wrapped up in a fistful of her silky brunette locks, and tugged her head back. “Not yet, baby.” His hand slid down over the front of her jeans and possessively grabbed between her legs.

Despite the thick material of her pants, her breath caught in her throat as her eyes filled with need when she saw Joey still seated there across from her, with desire thick in the air between them.

“Gage, she’s looking a little flushed. It might be a little warm in here for all that clothing.” Joey was down on his feet quickly after that and came to stand before her. He ran his hands over the top of her chest, sliding them underneath her open jacket. Slowly, he pushed the fabric away from her shoulders until it was falling down the length of her slender arms.

While Joey worked on removing her jacket, Gage kept his hand securely wrapped up in her hair while his mouth began to drag kisses along the side of her neck. He glanced down at the tops of the curves of her breasts that were now straining against the material of her lacy top with her excited breaths.

Layne moaned quietly, feeling the stiff bulge of Gage’s cock pressing up against her ass while his lips caressed over the most sensitive spots of her neck. “You both are going to be the death of me.”

Joey smirked as his hand rested on the side of her face. “No, Layney. We’re going to make sure you’ve never felt so alive.” His mouth possessively claimed hers while his hand slid onto the back of her neck to secure his hold on her.

With Joey’s hand grasping onto Layne, Gage relinquished his grasp on her hair and brought both his hands down to her jeans, where he undid the button and zipper. He pulled her pants by the belt loops until they were down around her ankles.

Gage tapped her left shin. “Foot.” When Layne shifted her weight off of her left foot, Gage was able to extract it from her shoe and shove her pant leg off. He repeated the gesture for the other foot until she was finally left in nothing but that revealing black top and a black g-string that kept her fine ass on full display.

As Gage rose up behind her, he found the round cheek of her ass too tempting not to indulge. He gave it a couple of delicate kisses before giving a playful bite to its fullness. After, he fully stood and began to strip himself down.

Feeling Gage’s teeth bite into her, she gasped into the kiss that Joey was still assaulting her mouth with. Her tongue was fighting for dominance with his and very quickly losing the battle. Finally, Joey broke the connection between their mouths. His hands grabbed her by the shoulders and turned her to face Gage.

Standing there only wearing his excited smile and a thick erection on full display, Gage didn't hesitate to take his turn, pulling Layne up against him as he shared a ravishing kiss with her. His dick pushed up against her lower stomach. She barely had enough time to catch her breath as she went from one De Luca to the other.

Behind her, she could hear Joey stripping down and clothes hitting the floor after being tossed. When he came up behind her, it was skin-to-skin contact as his hard cock pressed up against the line of her ass teasingly. His hand firmly grabbed her hip while the other slid between her thighs.

His fingers easily pushed past the string of her underwear until they stroked along her crease. Joey groaned out as her arousal quickly coated his fingers. "We're only getting started, and you're already fuckin' soaked. This wet pussy of yours is going to be put to good use, Layney."

Gage swallowed up her moan as Joey's hand teased along her sex. His grin spread into the way he kissed her before he drew back and stared at the beauty of her face, flushed with desire.

She was slightly panting from the quick and sinful turn of events that left her body full of intense need. Layne pressed her hips back against Joey's hand, wanting his touch where it mattered most. However, when his touch was removed from her body, she was left with a pout.

Taking her by the chin, Gage's thumb ran across her lips as playful darkness filled his deep brown eyes. "You're going to work for both of our cocks tonight, baby. Then, you're going to thank us for every orgasm we give you. If you do as you're told, we will leave you full of our cum. Do you understand?"

Layne's lips got distracted by the way the tip of his thumb traced over them. She opened up her mouth to draw his thumb in, lightly sucking on it.

From behind her, Joey's hand curled around her throat, lightly squeezing. He growled into her ear with a heated command. "I didn't hear you tell him 'Yes, Sir'."

She was already full of lust that needed to be released, her thoughts running on fumes as all her blood was rushing to other seemingly more important parts of her body. Layne's mouth let go of Gage's thumb. "Yes, Sir."

"Go get up on stage." Gage nodded at the one they had been seated on earlier. "Let us watch as you give us a show."

Both of the guys took their seats in chairs placed front and center. Layne smiled at them as she was more than ready to give them what they wanted, and maybe even more. She stepped up onto the stage, and fuck if she didn't need any more inspiration than what she saw before her.

Joey and Gage sat there, both completely naked and looking like a feast worth devouring for eternity. Both of their bodies were covered in their hard muscles, the intricate artwork canvased over their flesh, and two sets of chocolatey brown eyes watching her every move.

With the sensual music still playing over the speakers even after hours, it wasn't hard to find a rhythm as her hand grasped onto the metal pole. Her hips swayed as she engaged in a hell of a strip show for them. Her fingers coaxed the lacy top from her body. It was discarded by being flung at Gage's face.

Gage had his hand firmly wrapped around his thick cock while watching her body tease them both. Thank God she never became a stripper working at Cassidy's, he would have broken his no-touching rule a thousand times over. His hand caught her top, taking a moment to inhale the scent of her from it before tossing it to the floor.

Layne's breasts had now joined the show, her nipples in stiff peaks, showing how her body was enjoying this as much as they were. She suggestively grinded up against the pole with a come-hither look in her eyes.

Seeing Joey's hand also working over his large length, she worked her tiny bit of underwear down her legs. Using her foot, she flicked it over at Joey, managing to make the shot of a lifetime as it landed right around his cock.

Joey's face lit up like he had just won the damn lottery, and he was getting antsy in his seat, barely able to sit back and watch her much longer.

She saw the slipping self-control and decided to push both their buttons a little more. Layne got on her hands and knees, crawling to the edge of the stage. Her emerald eyes shimmered with the heat of several suns as she reached between her legs. Her finger found her clit, slick with her body's desires, and began to circle over it.

The first moan she let out had both men clamoring to join her on the stage. Gage barely made it there first as he pushed himself onto her, rolling her onto her back. His hands gripped each of her wrists, pinning them above her head. "Who said you could touch this needy little cunt of yours?" He smirked, looking down into her eyes.

"Seems like you need a reminder of who is responsible for all your pleasure, Layney." Joey stepped up onto the stage. "Give Gage a taste of that delicious pussy."

Changing positions, Gage laid on his back, already licking his lips in anticipation of the meal that awaited him between her thighs. "Sit and ride my face, baby. Show me how much you want to fill me up with your taste."

She was lucky she could feel her legs at all the way they both had her on the edge. Layne got herself on her knees, hovering her center over Gage's face.

"Goddamn, you smell delicious," he murmured before he pulled her the last few inches down to his mouth. Gage's hands quickly captured her hands behind her back, holding them tightly together. It forced her back to arch slightly, thrusting her breasts forward more.

Layne cried out as Gage didn't waste a moment in drawing his tongue along her folds and capturing the flavor of her need. Hungrily, he sucked on her throbbing clit like it was his last meal. Her body squirmed under the intense sensations, only encouraging him to continue.

Joey wasn't going to sit back and be excluded from the fun. Layne's mouth looked like it needed something other than the moans it was forcing into the air. He grinned and stepped in front of her, his hands grabbing her head. It forced her attention to him, her green hues staring up at him while heavy breaths pulled at her chest.

"Beg for my cock like a good girl. I want to hear how you want your mouth fucked while you get eaten out." Joey's eyes soaked in the sight of her with her hands restrained behind her while she had his brother tasting the sweet nectar of her body.

Gage's tongue was relentless in its pursuit as her hips drove against his face. The coarseness of his beard only intensified the sensations as it brushed against her most intimate parts.

With Joey's dick right there in front of her, pre-cum glistening over its head, she was quickly being launched towards her release. Her strained words made it very clear that she was approaching the slippery slope. "F-fuck my mouth, Joey… Feed your cock to me." Her words were saturated with the need to have both of them touching her at the same time.

On her next moan, Joey pushed himself past her parted lips. Her mouth opened up wider to take him while he kept control over her head.

Gage's tongue snaked up into her entrance, feeling the tight opening already quivering. The muffled cry above him made his cock painfully hard, knowing that she must have had a mouthful of De Luca. Squeezing onto her wrists tighter, his teeth scraped over her sensitive bud as he continued to use his mouth to leave no part of her hot core untasted.

Feeling the back of Layne's throat squeezing onto his tip, Joey groaned out. With her moans vibrating against him more frequently, he began to thrust into her, letting the feelings send his cock into a frenzy. "That's my fuckin' good girl. Suck my cock and leave a mess on Gage's face." He released a moan, "God…"

As Layne's body began to quiver, Gage took the opportunity to release both her hands so he could slide two fingers up inside her while he sucked hard on her little bundle of nerves. His fingers reaching deep up into her pussy and curling to press against the magical spot.

The second she felt her walls having to accommodate the new intrusion into her body, she got slammed with her climax. She screamed out in pleasure, but it got lost as Joey shoved his length deeper, pushing past her gag reflex at the back of her throat. It prompted her eyes to water, but she hardly noticed as wave after wave of her body's release overcame her.

Gage continued to push against that spot deep inside of her while she rode out her orgasm. When she came with such force, he got exactly what he had wanted from her as a stream of liquid filled his mouth.

Joey pulled out of Layne; his fingers wiped the leftover saliva on her chin. She gasped for air as her release began to slowly fade.

Layne was quickly shifted around as Gage moved her by her hips off his face. She was slid down the front of his body so her head could rest on his chest, which was also rising and falling after his oral efforts. She gave a sigh of satisfaction at the delightful high that had overcome her and had her head swimming.

Gage affectionately rubbed the back of her head to give her those few seconds to recover.

She stuttered out. "T-Thank you…" Her words barely above a whisper.

Gage kissed the top of her head. "You're welcome, but we're not done with you yet, lucky charm." His hands moved her again, this time so his still-aching dick was between her legs, rubbing against her slit.

His hands came up on either side of her neck while he kissed her passionately several times, letting her taste the remnants of her cum on his lips. "Go ahead and sit back on my swords," Gage smirked at her as his tattooed cock wanted nothing more than to be deep inside of her while she rode him, but this time not on his face.

While Layne was getting a brief reprieve from their affections, Joey stepped away to retrieve a small bottle of slippery and clear liquid from Gage's pants. The item Gage had retrieved from his desk drawer in anticipation of their dual conquest over Layne's body tonight.

Once Joey returned, he positioned himself on his knees between Gage's legs while he admired the view of Layne's ass facing him. His hand slid up along her back, making sure she remained laid on top of Gage so he had just the right angle.

Gage's hands ran over the sides of her slender body, feeling each curve along the way until his hands grabbed her ass and spread it wide for Joey's viewing pleasure. Layne pushed back onto Gage's cock, her tight entrance stretching around each inch while she sank onto him.

Layne moaned out as she got one of her holes filled up with one of her guys and another hole being prepared to take the other.

Joey took the lube and prepped not just himself but Layne as well. He knew that what was already going to be a constricted entry was going to be more so with Gage buried inside her cunt. "Layney, are you ready to have us both? I'm not going to be able to fucking hold back the second I'm in your tight ass." God knew it was one of his favorite places to take her, and she had taken him so well there many times before.

"Yes," her voice breathy with half a moan as she pushed her hips back, aching for them both.

"Good girl." He grinned and took his cock up to the entrance of her ass, and eased the first inch inside. Immediately, he could feel the difference in the amount of effort it was going to take and groaned. His hands grabbed her waist tightly to use her body as leverage as he shoved himself into her. Layne's gasps had a tingling sensation of pleasure at the base of his spine.

It wasn't just Joey who groaned out from the pleasure of having her while she was so full, but Gage did as well, as having Joey in her ass placed more pressure on his cock buried inside her pussy.

Layne heard them both, and her body was already trembling, something fierce as she cried out from being so full of De Luca cock. As promised, Joey didn't hold himself back as his feral side began to take over.

Working in tandem, Gage's hips drove up into her and helped her ride him hard while Joey kept his rhythm, ramming himself into her ass.

"Fuck!" All her moans drowned out the music playing in the background. Her hands clutched onto Gage's chest, his silver SPQR necklace getting tangled in her fingers and pulling against the back of his neck. His face painted in his own pleasure, struggling to maintain control of it.

Between his own pleasure-laden breaths, Gage looked up at her. "You're taking your two Daddies so well, baby." He groaned out the words.

Joey grunted as his hips smacked against her ass, his hands squeezing onto her waist tighter with each movement. "How's it feel to have two fuckin' cocks, Layney?"

Stars. That was it. Just stars and blinding light danced across Layne's vision. She had no clue if she even answered either of them as her body was taken elsewhere to another galaxy as her release smashed into her. She had never come so hard, even in her dirtiest fantasies.

As her body was wracked with ecstasy, she tensed up from her fingers down to the curl of her toes. It created a chain reaction as Gage's fingers dug into her thighs as he yelled out, and his seed shot out of him like a missile. Joey's hips shuddered as he gave one more harsh thrust into her ass, his cock spasming as he also tumbled over the ledge of his release.

With heavy pants from all of them, Joey collapsed into the pile of tangled limbs with Layne and Gage. Both guys wrapped arms around her, showering her with kisses anywhere they could find a spot on her damp skin.

She closed her eyes, not wanting to move so much as a toe while she lay there in their embrace. Quietly, she mustered enough energy to whisper, "Thank you."

Gage chuckled and kissed her forehead. "Anything for you, lucky charm."

Nuzzling his face into the side of her neck, Joey brushed some hair away from her face. "I love you more than life itself."

Right outside of Cassidy's Cave, someone sat in the darkness of their vehicle waiting. How long were the two men and the O'Reilly girl inside going to stay there? What the fuck were they doing?

Just as the person's impatience was hitting an all-time high, the establishment's front door opened up, and all three of them emerged from the strip club. Layne on Joey's back, legs around his waist, and her arms wrapped around his neck for support as he carried her out into the parking lot. Gage fell behind for a second while he locked up the door before jogging to catch up to the other two.

They all walked to a black Challenger parked next to Gage's shoddy-looking Jeep. Staying glued to the older brother's back, Layne leaned over and engaged in a sultry kiss with the younger De Luca like the whore she was.

Fuck her and fuck them all.

CHAPTER TWENTY-FIVE

The three of them headed back to Hudson Yards since it was only less than a mile away, and the sun would be rising sooner rather than later. Exhaustion overcame them all, and they crashed right into Gage's bed together.

Layne had never slept so hard in her life. With Gage on one side of her and Joey on the other, she felt entirely at ease. All the stressors of her life took a backseat as she allowed herself to succumb to a state of utter relaxation. After several hours of slumber, when she began to wake up, Joey was still in bed with her. His hand was securely attached to her bare breast underneath the t-shirt that Gage had given her to sleep in.

She giggled quietly as she leaned over and laid a sweet kiss on his mouth while the growth of his facial hair tickled her skin. He must not have been sleeping as soundly as she thought because he suddenly gave a growl and yanked her closer to him while kissing her neck and nipping at her throat playfully.

Layne outright squealed and fell into a fit of laughter while squirming in his hands. "Ah! Joey!"

He rolled on top of her, pinning her down with his body with a sparkle in his rich brown eyes. "Good morning…" Joey's hips suggestively rolled against her, with his cock already beginning to harden in his boxer briefs.

Gage walked into the room with a smirk. "If you both are going for round two, I'm going to need more coffee first." He stopped at the side of the bed, wearing just his black silk boxers.

She cupped Joey's face in her hands and lovingly kissed him. "Maybe later. I am supposed to meet up with Thomas today for an update on what the pulse is across the city's factions. If something is being stirred up, there are going to be whispers, and I want to make sure I hear them first."

Joey squeezed her tightly with his arms before rolling off of her and onto his back. Tucking his arm behind his head, he sprawled out there amongst the charcoal sheets, with the sunshine filling the room and lighting up the lines of his collection of tattoos on his bare chest.

As for Gage, he smiled at her and leaned over, scooping her up into his arms. "You're not doing anything until I get you in the tub so you can recover a little more before you start your day."

Her hand held onto the back of his neck as she found herself quickly laying across his arms as he began carrying her to his master bathroom, where he had already prepared a bath for her. "I think I can handle a little soreness."

"Are you arguing with me?" Gage grinned teasingly and set her feet down on the tiled floor of the extravagant bathroom. It had a massive floor-to-ceiling window with a view of the Hudson River that allowed the bathroom to be drenched in natural lighting. A dark granite tub was inset into a rectangular base right next to the window.

"No, Sir." Layne smiled as she found herself in awe of the beauty of not just the design of the oversized bathroom but the view it would give her while she soaked.

His fingers lifted the edge of his tee from her body until it was completely removed. "Good. Go get in the tub, and I will bring you some coffee and your phone so you don't bitch you're not able to get any work done." He patted her ass lightly as encouragement.

She stepped into the warm water and gradually lowered herself down into it. "How well you know me," Layne smirked. Gage seemed to take to heart that despite how much he got enjoyment out of bossing her around between the sheets, he ultimately wanted nothing more than to spoil and take care of her afterward.

It was a few minutes later that she was alone in the bathroom, her mug filled with freshly brewed coffee in one hand and scrolling through her phone in the other. Gage had been right, the warmth of the water with a mixture of scented salts was gradually melting the soreness away from her body.

She sent a message to Thomas informing him that she needed to push back their meeting by at least an hour. After setting both her caffeine and her cell to the side on a dry ledge, she leaned back and got cozy. Her eyes couldn't have been shut for more than five minutes before her zen-like state was interrupted.

Gage was heard yelling from the other end of his condo. She couldn't hear his words, but he sounded livid. She opened her eyes and sat up in the tub hesitantly as she strained to hear the words he was shouting.

Layne got out of the tub, drying herself off before wrapping the fluffy, bright white towel around her body and securing it under her arms. She left the bathroom and made her way to where Gage's voice was growing louder.

"What the fuck do you mean the damn alarm didn't go off?!" His voice thundered in the kitchen. Joey was standing there sipping from his cup of coffee, leaning against the counter, waiting to find out more information about this not-so-pleasant phone call his brother had received.

Gage punched one of the kitchen cabinets with his balled-up fist. "I set it myself! It was fucking ON!"

She stepped into the kitchen, staring at the both of them for a few minutes before Joey noticed her. Setting down his mug, he walked over to her and rubbed her arms gently. "Something happened at Cassidy's last night after we left," he explained quietly.

Pacing back and forth, Gage listened to one of his managers on the other end of the line. He grabbed a handful of his hair in frustration. "I will get down there when I can." His words were slightly calmer but still vibrating with anger. He hung up on the caller and tossed the phone down on the counter. "Motherfucker!"

Layne grew worried and stepped away from Joey to try and ease Gage's fiery rage. Her hand rested against his tightly tensed bicep. "What happened?" Her eyes were full of concern as she peered up into his eyes.

Not wanting to misdirect his anger at Layne, he took several ragged breaths. "Someone broke into Cassidy's last night sometime after we left and before my manager came in to prep for opening later. The joint got completely ransacked."

Trying to think of a way to help, she rubbed his arm soothingly. "I'm sure if you pull the camera footage, it should at least show who it was, right?"

He swallowed hard, his jaw clenched as he was internally kicking his own ass. With a softer but still strained tone, he replied, "I turned them off before the three of us…" His words trailed off.

She frowned that the one thing that could have perhaps captured who was responsible was not available thanks to Gage's consideration and thoughtfulness of not evidencing their extracurricular activities together.

"I'm sorry, Gage. Look, we can go down there, assess the damage, and maybe try cleaning it up." She tried to share some of her optimism with him.

Joey placed a hand on Layne's shoulder with a gentle squeeze and patted Gage on the back supportively. "I agree with Layne. We will all go down there and take a look."

Layne nodded. "I will reschedule my meeting with Thomas for another day. I will see if I can get some of my men to come down and help once we know what level of damage there is. I just need to run home first and get a fresh change of clothes."

Gage tried to take a calming breath, his fury still simmering underneath the surface but remaining under control for now. "Alright. Joey, you take her home. I'm going to make some phone calls, and then I will meet you both over there in two hours." He leaned over and gave Layne a tender kiss. "Don't the two of you get into trouble when I'm not around to join in, okay?"

She chuckled. "I will make sure he behaves." Her emerald hues gave a playfully stern look at Joey.

After both she and Joey threw on their clothes from last night, they left to head back uptown. With both of them deciding that a shower wasn't optional, they got cleaned up and dressed, ready to do some potential dirty work that didn't involve exchanging bodily fluids.

Her fingers swept her long locks of hair up into a ponytail as her thoughts plagued her mind. "It can't be a coincidence that Gage's club was targeted. He got involved in my life, and now…" The first signs of guilt weighing in on her conscience began to seep through the cracks of her strong façade.

Pulling his shirt down over his head, Joey immediately came over to her and forced her to turn and face him. "This is *not* your fault."

"But isn't it? I could have said 'no' to all of this. I could have slammed the door shut in his face. It could have just been you and I against all five boroughs. Now?" Layne shook her head. "He shouldn't have to be targeted and potentially end up like—"

"Sean?" Joey finished her thought.

Layne hung her head and tried to swallow down the truths that clawed at the little bit of morality she had left. "Yeah."

Joey tilted her head back up with a finger under her chin. "We all chose this—together. We will get through this together. You already know how I feel about you, and I can tell you that Gage's feelings for you run just as deep. His stubborn ass may not know it, but I see it."

She swallowed past the swell of a lump in her throat, still struggling with allowing her emotions to get the best of her. "I don't want to see him or you get hurt because of me."

"Layney," he smiled and gave her several small kisses. "I wish you could see what I see right now."

Layne wrinkled up her nose. "What's *that* supposed to mean?"

Chuckling, he wrapped his arms around her shoulders and drew her into a tight hug. "Nothing you won't figure out eventually." Joey ran his hand over the top of her head, his fingers trailing along the length of her ponytail before kissing her forehead. "We need to get going if we're going to make it back over to Hell's Kitchen. God knows one of us is going to need to prevent Gage from lashing out at any fucker that looks remotely guilty."

She nodded in agreement. There was no reason to have Gage dealing with this on his own. Just as she was dedicated to being at Joey's side, Layne needed to make sure that Gage knew she wasn't going anywhere. She was just as much his as she was Joey's.

CHAPTER TWENTY-SIX

When they pulled up to Cassidy's Cave, the pathway to destruction was clear. Spray paint marred the exterior in senseless patterns, and spiderwebs of cracked glass adorned the exterior windows. Trash was strewn about the sidewalk right out front.

Layne wanted to believe the outside of the building was the worst of it, but realistically, she knew that the inside had to be far worse. She spotted Gage's Jeep already parked outside, indicating he was likely inside assessing what had transpired during the early morning hours.

She and Joey entered the strip club, and the sight they were greeted with was far beyond even their wildest imaginations. The club wasn't just vandalized, but it had been thoroughly wrecked. Holes were in the walls, shattered glass everywhere, and broken furniture—the whole nine yards.

This wasn't just a small-time crime spree or random strike. Everything about the sight laid out before them screamed intentional and deeply personal like a fit of rage. Flashbacks of what she had seen at McGregor's came rushing forth from her memory.

They weren't the only ones to show up. The bar manager, Rory, was cleaning behind the bar and disposing of busted liquor bottles. A couple of dancers were sweeping off the stages of scattered trash and debris. Even the dressing rooms had been struck by the looks of it as Danielle carried out a handful of colorful pieces of lingerie and dropped them into a large trash can.

Joey's hand came to the crook of her neck and squeezed affectionately to find comfort for them both. He stopped one of the girls on her way to take a bag of trash outside. "Where's Gage?"

The redhead gestured towards his office. "He said he'd be in his office making phone calls."

Layne didn't wait to head that way, stepping over piles of busted electronics and trash strewn about. The door to Gage's office was left partly ajar. Her hand slowly pushed it open wider so she could look inside. "Gage?"

His head shot up from its position on top of his desk. "Yeah, come in." He shook off the emotions that came with seeing the business he had poured so much time and energy into in such a state of disrepair.

With a frown partly filled with sympathy, she looked over at him while noticing the signs of distress in how he pushed his eyebrows up into his forehead. "It looks like you have a few hands to help out around here, at least."

Gage nodded and looked at both her and Joey. "This place belongs to the girls just as much as it belongs to me. It gives them a home in a sense." His fingers pinched at the bridge of his nose, trying to rub the worst of his thoughts away.

Joey shook off his black leather jacket and draped it over one of the chairs. "Where do you want us to start?"

The offering of help gave Gage some relief and perhaps even a smidgen of hope that they could salvage this place. "Fuck, I don't know. Anywhere you can."

With that simple instruction, they got to work. The three of them began to tackle the harder projects like busted speakers and closing several of the bathroom stalls until replacement sinks, toilets, and plumbing could be installed to replace anything that had been smashed.

Layne walked to the back door to grab a few more contractor bags for the guys. Danielle followed behind her. "Layne?"

Hearing her name, she glanced back at the girl while looking for the next box of bags that Gage told her had been back there. "Yeah?"

"Do you mind helping me? I took some bags of trash out back earlier, and they were too heavy for me to lift into the dumpster. I could use another set of hands if you don't mind." She looked at Layne hopefully.

Stopping her search for the bags, she looked at the door next to her that led into the back alley where all the dumpsters were located. "Sure."

"Oh my God, thank you! The other girls just told me to get one of the guys to do it. I guess they didn't want to get their hands dirty or whatever." She shrugged and walked out the backdoor, holding it open for Layne to follow.

Quickly following Danielle out back, the door shut behind Layne. Danielle stopped and turned to Layne before they reached the dumpster. "You know… I expected better."

Layne scrunched up her face. "What?"

That's when, from behind her, a hand clamped down over her nose and mouth, muffling her immediate yells as it yanked her back into a massive body. When she felt a sharp jab into her thigh, she initially assumed it to be a pitiful excuse for a knife. Following the impact was a burning sensation of something being injected into her. The drug rushed through her veins from her adrenaline, pumping her blood fast and hard.

Each of her limbs, despite her will to keep them fighting, grew heavier. As pervasive as Layne's stubbornness was, she couldn't fight the dissociative anesthetic disarming her body's ability to remain under her control. While her vision grew blurry, one of the last things she saw was Danielle's sick smile as she stood there with her arms crossed in front of her chest.

After her vision blacked out entirely, her body went limp in the arms of the man who had administered the needleful of the heavy dose of an anesthetic. The burly man easily scooped her up and hoisted her over his shoulder.

Noticing Layne's phone sticking out of her back pocket, Danielle approached and plucked it from her jeans. She pitched it down at the concrete as hard as she could, ensuring the screen got all smashed up and rendered useless.

"Get her in the back of the van before anyone starts missing her." Danielle gestured toward the grungy-looking van with some electrician's faded logo on it.

The man Danielle had hired was a good little listener and brought Layne's unconscious body to the back of the vehicle, tossing her into it carelessly like she was nothing but a bag of garbage being tossed into a dumpster to be disposed of.

After the crony got into the driver's seat, Danielle joined him, and just like that, they were gone before Joey or Gage could intervene.

Joey finished unscrewing the bashed-in paper towel holder from the bathroom wall and looked at Gage, who was looking at one of the stall's doors, which was crookedly hanging on its hinges. "Layne said she was bringing back another box of bags, right?"

With a sigh, Gage gave up on trying to come up with a plan for the broken door. "Yeah, let me go see what's taking her so long. The box should have been right there by the back door." He wiped his hands on the thighs of his jeans and left the men's room.

When he got to the back, he saw no sign of Layne, and the box she was supposed to get was sitting right there in plain view. Gage's gut began to form a knot of apprehension as his instincts immediately began to swirl like a cyclone inside him. Trying to be rational, he took a step out back to see if maybe she was throwing out some garbage or grabbing some fresh air.

After realizing she was nowhere to be found outside, his worries began to escalate. Before walking back inside, he caught sight of something on the ground. He bent down and picked it up. The back of the phone case had the image of chains forming the shape of a shamrock on it. Upon recognition that it was Layne's phone, his thoughts spiraled out of control. "Layne?!" He yelled as he spun around, looking for any sign of her, and when he saw nothing to quell his fear, he ran back inside.

"LAYNE!" He frantically checked the other rooms inside the club despite knowing deep down he wouldn't find her there. He looked anywhere and everywhere, even places that were illogical for someone to be found.

Hearing Gage's voice booming out for their girl, Joey came out of the bathroom, nearly crashing into his brother. "What's wrong?"

Gage was filled with a storm of emotions, his jaw ticking with anger at some unknown person and at himself. The guilt and worry only added to it all. "She's gone."

Groggily, Layne lifted her head that had been slumped forward, causing an ache along the back of her neck right into the base of her skull. Her brains felt so goddamned scrambled. Trying to lift her hands to her face, she found them unable to move. As her green eyes fluttered open, she noticed several ropes wrapped around her forearms, keeping her stuck to the uncomfortable metal chair she was sitting in.

Part of her just wanted to vomit after coming out of the fog of the ketamine dosage. She groaned and closed her eyes again. It was unclear if she took another nap or another minute or so passed by, but her eyes gradually opened again when her head was forced back by a grip on her hair. Layne found herself looking at the blonde bitch that worked for Gage at Cassidy's.

"What…the…fuck?" Her mouth felt dry as shit, and of all people to see in front of her, Danielle wasn't who she expected.

Giving a painful tug on Layne's hair, Danielle smirked. "Did you have a good little nap?" Her words came off her tongue in a mocking tone.

Progressively getting a little bit more of her wits about her, she winced at the pain tugging at her scalp on top of the headache that was making itself more known by the second. Hoarsely she spat out, "Fuck you."

The next thing she felt was a harsh slap across her cheek. The pain helped Layne shake off a little more of the grogginess. It had been a lighter slap in comparison to the experience of a heavy smack of a man's hand, but it still left a stinging sensation and a red mark on her skin.

Looking around the room now that she was trying to piece everything together, she discovered that it couldn't have been a space bigger than a single-car garage. The concrete floor had dirt and stains, and it was lit up with a single lightbulb in the ceiling. There were no windows and nothing else other than the bitch standing in front of her.

"You know what your problem is, Layne?" Danielle began to pace in front of Layne.

In response, she couldn't hold back a scoff, Layne could make a list of things that were her problems. Danielle was very quickly making her way to the top of that list. "Why don't you tell me?"

Giving Layne a hard glare, Danielle continued her thoughts. "You don't know when to give it up."

"A character flaw, I know. I give it up to Gage just fine, though." Yes, Layne was feeling fucking sassy despite not being in a position to be sassing anyone. It helped keep her head focused to push buttons and assess just how much of a threat Danielle truly was.

Mission accomplished, blondie's face turned bright red with anger, and stalked over to her, getting up in Layne's face. "You're a fucking slut who slept her way into power! You'd be nothing but a sex toy like the rest of us if you didn't go around opening your legs for anything that resembled a dick with money and resources!"

Danielle drew back a fist and unleashed it on Layne. The small hand connected with the corner of her mouth, Layne's teeth cutting against the inside of her cheek and spilling the taste of copper inside. Layne spat out the blood toward the floor.

Layne's face remained unfazed even as she was verbally assaulted with false accusations and physically assaulted with a pitiful punch. "Is that what you think I did to get to where I am?" Her words were dangerously calm. This chick was walking a very fine line between injury and death once Layne figured a way out of the whole being tied to a chair situation.

She was curious as to what the hell Danielle was on and who everyone was that she referred to. "I don't know what your game is here. If you're just pissed because some guy doesn't fawn over you or what. You clearly have some fucking mental issues, so why don't you clue me in as to why you're trying to take them out on me."

Danielle straightened back up and gave a broad smile. "I'm going to be the one that takes your place and snatches up all the power in this damn city. There's only room for one queen amongst all the kings."

Layne outright laughed; this girl was on some seriously good drugs with the lack of sense she was making. "Good luck with that. Who the hell is going to listen to some delusional stripper?"

Now, it was Danielle's turn to laugh. "You don't know? Oh, gee, this is awkward." Her voice made it clear that this girl didn't feel the least bit bad about any awkwardness.

She squatted down in front of Layne so she could watch her reaction. "I only took that job at Cassidy's, so I could keep tabs on Italo and his pathetic little crew. Then, you came along and disposed of him, and it was clear that it was worthwhile sticking around. You see, I have a vested interest in making sure Daddy gets his way if I'm ever going to rise to the top."

Layne had been good at controlling her face up until this point, but the more Danielle spoke, the more she realized this was far worse than a case of a psycho chick with jealousy issues.

With the confusion in Layne's eyes growing, Danielle smirked. "You didn't know my last name is Spencer, did you?"

That may as well have been the atomic bomb on Layne's brain. Everything began to snap into place as all the events that had transpired to this point were on rewind in her brain. The interest Danielle showed in Gage. Being present at all of Italo's meetings as the entertainment. Straight back to the day she had barged into the souvenir shop Russ owned to confront him about poaching Andrew Correlli.

Layne walked into the retail storefront, ignoring the girl at the cash register scrolling through her phone.

Even Alexei Kuznetsov had tried to warn her.

"I think you will find the answers you are looking for over at a little souvenir shop across from the Empire State Building."

She had thought he was referring to Russell's offices hidden in the back of that building. Not the girl who worked at the front counter. The very same girl that stood at the front of the store that day wasn't just someone looking to earn a few bucks; it had been Russell's daughter—Danielle. Fuck. This just went from being an inconvenience to being a goddamn crisis with potentially fatal consequences.

The realization left Layne speechless as she tried to sort through all the frantic thoughts in her brain. Even Alexei's cryptic words to her during their meeting were floating to the forefront of her mind.

"Be sure of your actions, pchelka. You do not want to lay judgment on the tiger only to be bitten by the snake."

She was snatched out of the things going on inside her head when the snake's hand grabbed her by the face. "Just wait until he gets here, he's going to be so proud to see what I have wrapped up in a slutty little package for him. I bet you'll even spread your legs and beg for him, too."

Layne didn't avert her eyes from Danielle's scornful face. "You have no idea what you've just done…" Her heart may have been beating faster than it should have, but she had never felt more sure of what needed to happen.

Danielle stood up, releasing her hold on Layne. Her eyes lit up with excitement. "Oo, is this where you tell me that your two boy toys are going to come save you? That they'll come here and save their damsel in distress?"

Layne shook her head. "No." She made direct eye contact with Danielle, a gaze filled with violent promises. "This is where I tell you that you've started a war. A war that I promised I would bring to your dad's front door if he crossed me ever again. A war he won't win."

It seemed that Danielle wasn't too concerned by the shrug she gave. The stupid girl was clueless about how the city's criminal politics were played. "In case you haven't noticed, you're not in a position to be doing much of anything. You would have been much smarter to start the war after I convinced my own boy toys to do a little redecorating at that little dive bar you love so much. I heard the owner put up a hell of a fight."

"You sick fuckin' bitch!" she screamed out. There was the temper flare that Layne was known so well for. She yanked at her arms bound by those ropes and thrashed in her seat, wanting to cover every inch of Danielle's face with the bottom of her boots.

Danielle cackled in amusement as she backed up towards the door. "You don't know the half of it. Maybe I will send my boys in here to teach you a lesson or three, a lesson for each of your holes. See you in a bit!" She blew Layne a kiss before she left the room, slamming the door shut behind her and clicking the locks in place.

Layne yelled out in utter frustration as she pulled at her restraints despite the pain it caused. This bitch needed to die, and Layne decided that it would be her life's mission to end it in a spectacularly glorious fashion.

CHAPTER TWENTY-SEVEN

Layne sat in isolation, tied to that chair for what felt like hours. Her thoughts were jumping all over the place. She was worried, not for herself, but for her guys. They had to know she was missing by now, and they were likely ready to burn the city down just to find her. It hurt her heart even thinking about what they were going through. God, she hoped that they weren't doing anything stupid that put their lives at risk.

Then, there was the person who was responsible for putting her here. It seemed that little Miss Spencer wanted to follow in her daddy's footsteps, or maybe she was trying to compete with Layne. Either way, she was a poor imitation of what strength and strategy looked like in this line of work.

She couldn't be sure how much time she had before Danielle made good on any threats of sending in a bunch of cowards to torture or assault her. The ropes that kept her bound to the metal chair were creating burns against her skin from all the attempts to wiggle free from them. Nonetheless, she kept working at them.

As she heard voices approaching the door, she rushed her efforts along. It seemed not quick enough as the lock shifted and the door swung open. Danielle's shitty face with too many layers of cheap makeup was the first thing she saw, followed by three men. Well, this was going to be a goddamn rager of a party, wasn't it?

There was a brief thought in her mind reflecting some self-doubt. Layne shoved it back down into the place where she fed her temper. This bitch wanted to make good on her threats? Layne was going to make good on hers.

Danielle damn near skipped in and was so full of happiness. "Did you miss me? I brought some friends to keep you company."

It may have looked like Layne was sitting there refusing to speak out of defiance, but what she was doing was making calculations. Out of the three men, all wearing cheap ski masks, she did quick assessments of their heights and builds and how that would translate into who was the biggest potential threat. One had a gun on his hip, and she'd pay a fortune in blood to get her hands on it. Of all of them, Danielle was the weakest link; she'd die last just so Layne could get satisfaction out of it.

"Cat got your tongue, Layne?" Danielle stepped off to the corner of the room. Did she have intentions of watching this all unfold? Layne hoped so. "If you're worried about dying, don't. I'm sure my dad will want to have a few words with you after I tell him about everything I've accomplished without his help. Then, afterward, he can watch while I do the job myself."

One of the men came up behind her and began working on untying the ropes that held her down to the chair. The other two stood in front of her, perversion clouding their eyes as they stared at her. It seemed they were feeling confident that three fit men could handle one fired-up Layne. Oh, they were going to learn some things today.

"I'm just wondering if you've figured it out yet." Feeling the ropes gradually loosening up around her, the adrenaline began amping up in her body. She was going to have one chance at making this happen.

"Figured out what?" She looked perplexed at Layne's statement.

"That you'll never be me. You'll never have what it takes. I didn't get where I am by shaking my ass; I got here by getting my hands dirty, even when I was at rock bottom. I don't rely on a bunch of cowards to do it all for me." One more shift of rope was all she needed; it would be just enough to get out of this damn chair.

Danielle rolled her eyes. "Oh yeah? Look where it's gotten you."

Layne smirked. "Right where I want and deserve to be." Then, there was the last bit of slack in the rope that she required. Before the ropes were fully removed from her body, she was able to push up onto her feet. Her foot kicked the chair backward into the man behind her. It sent the metal piece of furniture into him for just enough time to catch him off guard.

It started a scene of complete chaos, with the other two men lunging for her. She blocked a punch from the guy on her right before jabbing her elbow into his ribs, doubling him over. Layne immediately gave a front kick to the man on the left directly into his gut, forcing him to stumble back.

There was no hesitation for her to spin around, expecting the third guy to be coming at her from behind, which he was. She thrust her fist up under his chin, causing his head to sharply tilt back from the impact before she kicked him right in the balls, ensuring he was going down and staying down.

The arms of the man who had taken her elbow to his ribs locked his arms around her upper body. With the only other guy standing, mistakenly thinking she was being contained, he approached to strike out at her. He threw a punch that hit home right across her cheek. Now that he was close enough, Layne drew up both feet, kicking him in the chest and knocking the wind out of him. She pitched her head back, slamming it into her captor's face hard enough that he dropped her from his hold.

Layne spun around, and while the man was holding his face, she grabbed the gun from the holster on his hip.

Bang! Bang! Bang! Bang! Click.

Well, fuck her. The asshole hadn't kept his firearm fully loaded like a good little henchman.

She still managed to fire one shot to the chest of the guy who had brought it to the party, two at the man who was still writhing around holding his balls, and one at the last man. It was a fucking shame there hadn't been one bullet left for Danielle, who was standing there in the corner of the room, frozen by the obscene unfolding of events.

Already surrounded by three dead bodies, Layne breathed heavily, trying to catch her breath as she stared at Danielle. She tossed the now empty gun down on the ground. She spread her arms wide, welcoming Danielle to come at her. "Don't be shy now." Layne gave a winded chuckle with a hint of unhinged mental instability.

The slimy bitch made a run for the door. Layne grabbed the nearby metal chair and swung it at her, making contact right with her face with one of the legs. Danielle screamed out and fell back onto the floor from the momentum of the impact.

Layne tackled her the second Danielle tried to scramble back up onto her feet. They wrestled there on the floor, each of them trying to gain the upper hand with each punch that was thrown. Finally getting back on top, Layne grabbed a handful of over-processed blonde hair and put everything she had into smashing her fist right into Danielle's face. She didn't stop there; she followed up with at least four more until Danielle wasn't fighting back anymore.

Wearily, Layne stood up, her hand aching fiercely as blood dripped from her knuckles. "You wanted to start a damn war? Well, guess what, Danielle?!" Layne angrily yelled the question at her. "You started it with the wrong fucking family!" The sweet taste of blood pooled in her mouth. Layne spit out the blood from her mouth and down at Danielle. Hell, if she was going to be taken out by some fake bitch with a bad boob job.

Danielle groaned out in pain, barely finding it in herself to move, let alone respond with any more of her snarky comments.

Layne went over to where the rope was lying on the floor that had previously held her hostage. She picked it up and walked back to Danielle's battered body. When Danielle began to open her mouth to either beg or protest, Layne stepped on one of the bitch's hands before kicking her harshly in the jaw with her other foot. "Shut the fuck up."

All the feel-good and fuzzy emotions had left Layne the second she woke up in this room. Knowing all that Danielle was responsible for left Layne with nothing but the urge to inflict pain and death. Drawing enough length of rope, she leaned over and wrapped it around the girl's throat tightly before knotting it.

Layne dragged Danielle by that rope around her neck until they got to the door. The gagging and choking sounds fell on deaf ears. She took the other end of the rope and wrapped it around the door handle until Danielle was forced into a sitting position if she didn't want to strangle herself.

After securing the rope, Layne checked one of the corpses lying in a puddle of blood. She found a knife, and looking it over, she glanced back over at Danielle. "This'll have to do."

Feeling the weight of the knife in her hand, she looked at her target, who was now beginning to face the fear of death with wide eyes. Layne squatted down in front of her. Danielle didn't deserve any words of comfort or any parting one-liners before meeting her demise.

Grabbing the knife tightly, Layne slammed it into the hollow of Danielle's throat just below where the rope was wrapped tightly around her neck. The entirety of the blade sunk into her body, utterly destroying the esophagus and major arteries. It left Danielle choking on her own blood in her last moments until she all too quickly bled out.

Leaving the knife lodged in the throat of Russell's daughter, it was one of the few deaths Layne was more than happy to have on her hands. She pulled the door open, which took more effort than it should have, considering Danielle's body was still attached to the backside of it.

Now it was time to get the fuck out of here, wherever here was. Layne was quickly losing energy now that the rush of adrenaline was fading. Not knowing where she was or who else was there with her, she moved quickly and quietly. Navigating the only hallway that led her around a few corners, she ultimately came to an exit.

She stepped outside of the building, noticing how dark it was outside. It must have been considerably late because the only people she saw looked like they were working the street corners in search of a date.

Layne groaned when she didn't recognize the area. The building she had just come out of had signs saying 'Permanently Closed' plastered all over it. The original business logos had long been faded and almost entirely peeled away from the exterior.

Needing to be nowhere near this hellhole, she began walking. Exhaustion would have been welcomed by comparison to how she felt. Out of sheer desperation, she asked one of the hookers for her cell phone. The girl had been too quick to hand it over.

While dialing the only number she knew by heart, Layne caught a look at her reflection in a parked car's window. No wonder the girl hadn't argued, she had blood splattered across her face and clothes. Layne's split knuckles had stopped bleeding, but the stickiness of the dried blood remained. "Fuck…"

Layne listened to the other end ring only once before the gravelly voice answered on the other end, "Hello?" She collapsed down onto a bench, hearing the sound of heaven on earth.

"Joey?" She leaned over with her elbows resting on her knees as she sighed with relief. "Please come get me."

CHAPTER TWENTY-EIGHT

When she had spoken with Joey, he rapidly fired off what felt like a thousand questions. He asked her if she was okay, where she was, what happened, and more. Layne couldn't focus on answering any of them except the nearest intersection she was at. Everything was beginning to hurt, even her thoughts.

Within twenty minutes, both he and Gage had picked her up. The drive should have taken at least thirty, but Joey ignored just about every traffic law on the way. She was just over the New York State Line in New Jersey.

When they arrived, Joey nearly forgot to put the car in park before hopping out. The two of them smothered her with hugs and kisses despite the wreck she was. Gage had managed to stop Joey from hammering her with a million more questions. The important thing was that she was okay, and they weren't going to let her out of their sight until they had the full story of what transpired.

On the ride back to O'Reilly Manor, she laid across the back seat of the Challenger with her head in Gage's lap while his hand stroked over her head. For once, they hadn't harassed her about buckling up. Seeing the state she was in, they both didn't want to do anything more than allow her to find a little bit of comfort. Once they made it back to her house, they gave her the space she needed despite wanting to hover.

The guilt and fear had eaten away at Gage while she had been gone, and nobody knew where she was. If Layne hadn't been there helping clean up, she wouldn't have been in the wrong damn place at the wrong time. Conversely, Joey had simply been ready to start busting down every criminal syndicate's door and racking up body counts in search of her.

She stood in the shower for nearly forty-five minutes, washing all the filth and blood from herself as the hot water and soap stung the abrasions on her body. Afterward, she pulled on a pair of her favorite sleep shorts with a bralette. It was the only set of clothes she could get comfortable in with the way her body ached.

Now, she found herself sitting on the kitchen counter with both the guys staring at her. "I told you I'm fine, just tired." Her fingers pinched the bridge of her nose while trying to fend off the lingering headache.

Gage dabbed some antiseptic on her knuckles, eliciting a hiss of pain from her. "Sorry, I'm trying to be gentle, baby."

Joey frowned as his hand carefully turned her head so he could inspect what injuries she had now that the blood had been washed away. Every bruise, cut, and rope burn he saw notched up his anger one more tick. He knew that for each mark visible on her, she had to be hurting internally on top of it.

Taking a measured exhale, Joey turned her to look at him. "What happened?"

Layne shook her head. "I don't want to get into it. I just need my phone so I can call Thomas and—"

"Now is not the time to make me ask twice, Layne." Joey's voice grew heavier, and from the look of his brown eyes, they were ready to turn black with death.

She knew this was all going to go over like a damn lead balloon for both of them. Layne began to recount what happened, from being jumped in the back alley after Danielle lured her out there to waking up in the dingy room tied to a chair and Danielle's failed attempt to get her boys to do all her dirty work. All the while, Layne avoided telling the kicker of it all. If Joey and Gage both didn't already have all the reasons to lash out at Russell Spencer, this was going to be the breaking point.

Gage finished patching up her hand and laid a kiss lightly on top of the bandage. "Why? What the hell was her issue with you?"

"Besides being twisted in the head?" Layne paused, hating that they were at this point. She had both guys staring at her, looking for answers that would make all of this make sense.

The silence from Layne continued for a little while until Joey's agitation began to eat away at him. "I swear, Layne if you don't just spit it the hell out…" It may not have been the gentlest of prompts, but it was effective as he saw Layne's shoulders sink in forfeit.

She shook her head. "Her dad is Russell Spencer. She wanted to make him proud or some shit, I don't know."

"Motherfucker!" It was Joey who reacted first. Before he could storm off, Layne grabbed him by his belt and nearly slid off the counter if it hadn't been for Gage, who caught her before she did. He eased her down onto her feet while Layne refused to release her grasp on Joey.

"Dammit, Joey, wait!" She pleaded. "I don't think he knows, and I want it to stay that way. If shit is going down, I want plans in place. That's why I want to get Thomas on board so he can prepare the rest of the team."

He reluctantly turned back around. The desire to go visit Russ right now and destroy every bone in that fucker's body was right up there with, wishing he could resurrect Eric Ellis just to send him right back down to hell.

"Wait for what, Layne?! Wait, so another motherfucker can take a shot at you?!" All of Joey's pent-up frustrations and fears that had weighed on him during her disappearance were all getting unleashed. "I'm tired of waiting around! You could have died, and there was *nothing* I could have done to stop it. Do you even get that?!"

His words of anger were accompanied by a sense of misery in his eyes that he had been hurting, knowing that there had been the possibility of her life being ripped from him forever.

In response, her green hues began to glisten with unshed tears as she felt the pain in his words.

Gage interjected, speaking to his brother, "You're not going to do shit without me." Then, he turned to look at Layne. "And you're not doing anything until you get some rest." He wasn't going to add to the already emotionally charged situation with what he was feeling.

Now it was her turn to be irritated, but with how much her body wanted to crash, she couldn't even raise an argument with him.

Joey sighed, realizing he probably shouldn't have gone off on her the way he did. It didn't make anything he said less true, but his fears had come uncomfortably close to fruition. "Look, it's been a fucker of a time for all of us. Go get in bed, and we'll be up in a minute to join you." He agreed with Gage's determination that Layne needed to sleep and allow herself to recover after everything she had been through.

Maybe it was the 'we' in that statement that convinced her to listen or the fact that she could hardly keep herself up on her feet, but Layne nodded. "I'll be upstairs, don't take too long."

After Layne left the kitchen and went up to the master bedroom, it was Gage's turn to lash out with all the emotions that had been locked away to prevent Layne from getting any more riled up. His hand smacked the bottle of antiseptic off the counter angrily, sending it flying across the kitchen. "Son of a bitch! I fuckin' *knew* Russell was bad news. He and his entire goddamn operation needs to die."

Joey looked over at Gage, filled with a calmer variation of his rage. "This isn't going to be pretty. If she makes this move against Spencer, she is either going to get torn apart by the other factions or have half the city by the balls."

Slowly nodding, Gage ran his fingers through his hair in frustration that they both had come too close to having history repeat itself. "Then let's make sure she gets her seat on the throne she deserves to be on."

Layne thought she felt like shit when she had gotten back home last night, but when she woke up the next morning, all the aches and pains were tenfold. Her pride refused to voice the weight of her body's angry protests. She was moving much slower and fighting through it all on her own.

She curled up on the sofa, watching the morning news on the television with a cup of coffee held between her hands. Joey came up behind the sofa, leaning over and rubbing his hands over her shoulders lightly before kissing the top of her head. "You're up earlier than I expected."

"I couldn't sleep." She sipped from her piping hot morning routine in a mug.

He came around the end of the couch and took a seat next to her, resting his arm along the backrest behind her. "I have ways to help with that," Joey smirked at her playfully.

Lightly smiling, she leaned over into his side, soaking in the warmth and safety his presence provided. "Some of the best ways. Is Gage still upstairs sleeping?"

He shook his head. "He went out to take care of a few things. He promised he'd be back in a little while with food."

"Mm, I could use something to eat. I'm starving." Her stomach rumbled in agreement.

She leaned over to cement a kiss onto his mouth. Joey's hand wrapped around the back of her head to hold her in close for the kiss. Murmuring against her lips, he teased, "I got something for you to put in your mouth to hold you over."

She smiled against his mouth, and the kiss began to grow into something more passionate before getting interrupted.

The female news anchor spoke with a solemn voice, "Breaking news. This just in, several bodies have been discovered at an abandoned veterinary clinic in Jersey City. Police are investigating the incident and, at this time, say there are no leads. Maria is reporting live from the scene."

Layne pulled back from Joey to look at the screen, which showed the very building she had escaped. This time, it was surrounded by yellow crime scene tape, flashing lights, and an excessive amount of law enforcement.

The image of the reporter standing in front of the building had the same tone that all reporters seem to have, one which evokes seriousness with perfectly crafted sentences and a hint of suspense. "Thank you, Susan. I spoke with one of the officers earlier, and he said that there were four bodies discovered inside. Three of them died of apparent gunshot wounds. The fourth was of a woman who suffered in what was only described to me as a 'heinous act of disturbing violence.'"

Setting her coffee on the table in front of them with a groan, both of her stiff movements and a realization. "Fuck. I need to make a call."

"What is it?" Joey sat up, eyeing her.

Slowly, she eased herself up off the couch with a wince. She looked at Joey with eyes that reflected her anger at herself for making a stupid rookie mistake. "My fingerprints are all over the murder weapons, Joey."

He tried not to add to her worries with his own as he stood up. "We'll get it fixed. Your prints won't mean anything if there's nothing in the system to compare them to."

Layne stared at him, her face full of concern, not easing up any.

He raised both his brows. "When the hell did you get arrested?"

She gave a small smile, recalling the little she remembered about the incident. "Things got a little ridiculous on my twenty-first birthday. After the cops were called, the one Boy Scout in the group didn't like that I flashed my tits at him."

He smirked. "One lucky son of a bitch. I would have arrested your ass just so I could have you all to myself." Joey wrapped his arms around her and showered her with a few hungry kisses.

There was no fighting the smile and the way he could put her at ease. "Ok, ok! I have to call my contact at the crime lab to make sure that any prints that are lifted are determined to be inconclusive."

His hand rubbed over the curve of her ass. "One call, then you're mine for the rest of the morning until Gage gets back."

They both left the room, leaving the television on. The image shifted to the studio news anchor again to transition to another news story. A familiar face appeared in the upper right part of the screen while the woman continued her news coverage.

"In Midtown, another young woman was found deceased. Kristill Hendricks, twenty-four years old, was discovered by her neighbor after noise complaints about Hendricks' Chihuahua continuing to bark for hours on end. Sources say that the young woman had a history of drug abuse and prostitution, but police aren't ruling out foul play. More to come."

CHAPTER TWENTY-NINE

A war had been brewing, and Layne was now ready to kick it off. She had been spending the last couple of weeks making plans with all her associates. Danielle may have been the most recent primary aggressor, but the Spencer name would spread like cancer if Layne didn't take action to put an end to it now.

Russ knew what games he was playing, trying to encroach on the O'Reilly territory, and hell, if she was going to let him get away with it any longer. She had been too nice in trying to play politics. The time for sweet talking was over. She was going to send a message loud and clear to any factions in the city that supported him that she wasn't going to tolerate his bullshit any longer.

Joey and Gage both had her back in this endeavor. It didn't hurt to know if they wiped Russell from the playing board, with a little bit of luck, they would also get to unleash their chaos and wrath on the man responsible for Rose's death.

Layne sat on the hood of her car in the middle of an empty parking lot, looking at her crew of men who had shown up for this evening's strategized power play. She was dressed in all black, from her boots up to her long-sleeved shirt, and in her hand was her skull mask with its orange and green laces. Her hair crisscrossed into a French braid with matching orange and green ribbons running through it.

"Ethan, you take your crew and see to it that Russell's little souvenir shop with his office gets a hot bath in some gasoline." She couldn't wait to see that retail storefront burn down to its foundation.

Layne pointed at the man standing next to Ethan. "Sammy, go see to it that Russell's right-hand man doesn't see the light of day tomorrow."

She smiled as she got to the last of her senior associates gathered there with them. "And Jonathan, pay a visit to his favorite butcher shop and let them know we will be taking over all the accounts. If they have a problem with it, they can expect Ethan to show up there next."

Jonathan nodded at her, understanding the assignment, but he had some hesitation. "Layne, there's a lot more business in Russ's territory, this is a drop in the bucket."

She crossed her arms in front of her chest and sighed. "I know, but it will have to be the starting point. We can keep pushing until everybody learns a damn lesson of who not to fuck with in this city."

Standing back a few feet from Layne's car were both De Luca brothers. Each wore tactical black pants and black hoodies, ready to assist Layne in her role in tonight's endeavors. Joey had on his mask with its smiling skull jaw on it, and Gage wore his hellish demon mask across his face.

"Actually…" Joey stepped up to Layne's right with a phone in his hand and showed it to Layne. A familiar face was on the video call, smirking at her.

"Pchelka, why did you not invite me to the party sooner, eh?" Alexei winked at her. "I have my men on their way to visit a few other of Mr. Spencer's top clients. Consider it an early wedding gift."

Her eyes stared at Kuznetsov in shock and then over at Joey, who, even with his mask on, seemed to be beaming with pride at this little surprise he presented her with. "Thank you." Layne meant it for both the Russian on the video call and the sneaky asshole who had coordinated with him.

Then, Gage came up on her left also with a video call on his phone. "That's not all, lucky charm."

Layne blinked a few times as she looked at Gage, and on his screen were several faces she didn't recognize at all.

"I called in a few favors from some old friends from my days in Jersey City. They're going to help us out wherever we need them tonight." Gage explained to her, and one of the guys on the phone spoke up with a heavy Jersey accent.

"Don't let him fool you, he's a conniving asshole." The man joked with a hearty laugh. "Anything you need tonight, we got you."

She smiled and looked at Gage, moved that he had also gone out of his way to seek out extra help. God, she loved him. She loved them both so much. Layne offered her words of appreciation for Gage's friends before hopping down onto her feet in front of her car.

"Let's go give Russell the news." She dismissed the crew present with her and then turned to see Joey and Gage now side by side, ready to accompany her.

Joey stepped up to her, took the mask from her hands, and placed it over her face. "No matter what happens, I've never been prouder, Layney."

"Me, too." Gage came up to her side, and the three of them came into an embrace.

She smiled and patted each of them on their sides. "Alright, let's go before I change my damn mind and beg you both to take me home instead."

Each of their hands gave a swat to a side of her ass, with Joey chuckling. "You can beg us later."

They piled into her car, and Layne took the seat behind the wheel. She drove them all to Russell's house, which was on the Upper West Side. Parking down the street from the Spencer residence, she sat in the driver's seat for a second, running down her checklist and patting herself down to ensure she had her weapons all in place.

She took one more deep breath and nodded to herself. "I'm ready." Pulling out her phone, she shot off a text to Ethan to give him the green light to proceed burning down Russell's base of operations.

Layne got out of the car and began heading towards Russ's house. If she was going to do this, she was going to bestow the news on him herself. Joey and Gage stuck close to her, keeping an eye out for anything that might become a threat.

It was quiet in the neighborhood, which she had counted on, being that it was half past midnight. She jogged up to Spencer's front door and waited off to the side, glancing at her watch. Layne was waiting on Russ getting the call that his shop was on fire, given the yelling she heard from coming inside the house, he had just received the unfortunate news.

A few more minutes passed, and she nodded to Joey and Gage, who were across from her on the other side of the door, as she heard footsteps approaching from inside the house.

The moment the door opened up and Russ was ready to rush out to deal with the situation at his store, Gage rushed him and pushed him right back inside. Layne followed next, and Joey filed in behind her, shutting the door.

Alarmed, Russ yelled out as Gage's hand had a grip on his shirt, shoving him back against a wall. "WHAT THE FU—" His exclamation was cut off by Gage's fist colliding into his face.

A huge smirk pulled at Gage's mouth underneath the mask, it had felt exceptionally fucking cathartic to hit this motherfucker. Russ was stunned by the strike and was now glaring at the three of them. "What do you want?"

Layne pulled down her mask away from her face. "Hi, Russ." Her smile at him was full of confidence and fake pleasantries. "Hope you don't mind the late-night visit. I was just in the neighborhood and thought I'd swing by."

Joey did a quick check to make sure that there wasn't anyone else in the house before coming back to standby while Layne had her conversation.

Russ shook his head. "You stupid little bitch! Didn't you learn anything from the last time you came barging onto my property?"

She pursed her lips in thought. "Hmm, it seems not. It also seems you didn't learn anything either." Layne stepped in front of him, her striking green eyes staring at him. "I promised you a war. The sad thing about war is that it comes with casualties. Your psycho-bitch daughter was the first of what I imagine will be many more to come."

He made a move to come at her, but Gage shoved him back against the wall, and Joey stepped up to assist in pinning him there. With one hand on Russ's shoulder, Joey dug the end of a handgun up underneath Russ's jaw. "Give me the tiniest excuse to blow your fuckin' brains out."

The ding of her phone went off in her pocket, followed by another one and another. She pulled her phone out and smiled to herself. "You see, Russ," her finger flipped through a few messages on her phone. "I have my men all over the city tonight taking over your assets one by one."

He scoffed at her. "You don't have the resources."

She gave an indifferent shrug. "No, you're right about that. However, I had quite a few friends step up to the plate to provide some assistance. While you were so busy focusing on picking off my assets one by one, I was having talks with other factions. It turns out you're not as much of a well-liked guy as you seem to think."

Russ scowled at her and tried to maintain his confidence that this was all one huge bluff. "They'll all turn on you the moment you close your eyes. Even if they don't, my employees will feed your corpse to a bunch of rabid dogs."

She placed a hand on her chest, feigning the hurt of his words. "Oh, wow. That hurts nearly enough to make me change my mind." Layne shook her head and smirked. "Tell me one thing, Russ, who's going to give the order to come at me if I don't let you walk out of here tonight?"

Layne pulled up a photo on her phone from a message that had just come in from Ethan. She showed it to Russ, and the way his face fell and the color drained from his face had been worth all the stress and sleepless nights the past few weeks. There on the screen was a photograph of his second-in-command, lying in bed with two fresh holes in his head.

She turned off her phone and slid it back into her pocket. "What happens next is up to you, Russ. I have some questions that I'm dying to know the answers to."

"Yeah, like what?" He struggled to get comfortable with both Joey and Gage tightly gripping onto him and the ever-present threat of the firearm lodged up against his neck.

Watching his face carefully to see how his expression would change, Layne spoke casually, like they were about to discuss who won last night's hockey game. "When did you first meet Eric Ellis?"

The question seemed to throw Russ, unclear of where she was heading with this. "What?"

Gage tightened his hold painfully. "The lady asked a goddamn question." He said through clenched teeth.

Russell seemed to take a moment to count back the years. "It was well over ten years ago. Why the hell do you care about Ellis? He's fucking nothing but worm food now."

She pressed her lips together in a hard line, knowing the next question quite possibly had an answer that she didn't want any of them to hear. Not because she wanted to live in ignorant bliss but because she knew that it would be one that either confirmed years of pain and brought healing or left them at a loss with more unanswered questions.

"Did you take a job from him? One that involved taking an innocent woman and physically collecting a debt from her that left her for dead?" She swallowed hard as her chest tightened.

The reaction from him didn't satisfy Layne, and she stepped closer so her face was up near his. "Did you?"

"I tossed Eric a favor every now and again, so it's possible. If you're talking about some blonde cutie that my guys picked up, then yeah, she was easy money. Too bad she broke a little too easily, though, I had to ditch her to get her pussy sewn back up at the nearest vet." Each of his words lacked remorse.

Layne shook her head in disappointment and stepped back. "I am more than happy to let you walk out of here tonight, Russ. I want you to see how it's me taking all your assets from you and letting you get swallowed up by the rest of the scum in this city."

She looked at Joey and Gage, giving them both the look they had been waiting for. "But it's not about what I want. These two," she motioned to the masked men standing before him, "won't be allowing that to happen. They're going to be collecting a long overdue debt from you."

Joey shoved his pistol into his thigh holster so he could use two hands on Russ. They both yanked him away from the wall and dragged him through the house until they got to the kitchen.

Layne followed behind, watching as Russ cursed at all of them and attempted to wound them with insults. She leaned back against a wall and comfortably crossed her arms in front of her stomach. Her eyes were void of any empathy for the man who had scarred both her guys so many years ago.

What transpired next ended up being a kind ending to Russell Spencer's life in comparison to what he had put Rosie through. Both Joey and Gage took turns using him as a punching bag, allowing all their years of accumulated pain to be taken out on the man responsible for it. After that, things got a little more creative with the use of the garbage disposal, destroying each one of Russ's hands at a time. The heavy stainless steel fridge door was slammed against the man's head until the door itself broke.

Finally, just when Russ was losing consciousness from the brutal attacks, Gage tossed him to the floor and pinned him there underneath the weight of his boot. "Goodnight, motherfucker." He pulled out his semi-automatic and fired three shots into the back of Russ's skull.

Layne slowly released a breath as it all came to a bloody conclusion. Standing there witnessing them both avenge Rosie's murder filled her with a mixture of feelings. One of which had her understanding both the guys on a different level. Her panties were growing damp with desire and arousal as each of them unleashed their fury.

She hoped that tonight could help them both heal and find their peace.

More importantly, she hoped that this would be a clear message to anyone who fucked with her or anyone that she loved that Chaos and Wrath would follow. If anyone found themselves in the presence of Luck, may it be her good side.

CHAPTER THIRTY

The night they sent Russell Spencer to his grave had gone off smoother than even Layne had expected. While she didn't have half the city's criminal factions at her back as she had promised Russ she would; she was slowly building up her rapport and gaining respect from the other families across all of New York. There was still going to be a long way to go before she elevated herself beyond her father's legacy, but she was confident it would happen someday.

Alexei had made good on his word, and as a token of her appreciation, she guaranteed him a portion of the income she was drawing in from Russell's assets she had seized.

Several of Gage's friends had agreed to sign on to her team, willing to help be extra manpower whenever she needed it. Gage had managed to get Cassidy's entirely renovated and remodeled. No longer known as Cassidy's Cave, it was renamed to Cassidy's Chains. It was now being dubbed as one of the hottest new nightclubs, with a sexy twist, of course.

Rebecca had been hounding Layne with last-minute wedding details, ensuring that Layne wasn't getting cold feet and constantly reminding her that the big event was only a week away. While Layne hadn't outright told her best friend about her involvement with Gage, it seemed Rebecca had already connected the dots without forcing Layne to have the awkward conversation about her unconventional relationships.

Joey had gradually eased out of his contract work to help Layne manage her growing team of enforcers. He took a job here and there, but now his primary focus was training each member of her crew. If Layne was going to be successful, all of her associates needed to be able to tackle problems with ease.

Layne had decided to get her very first tattoo. It wasn't much in terms of size, but it fit her to a T. Across the back of her neck, in a black feminine cursive, was a single word:

Luck

The bottom of the 'k' swirled below the rest of the letters and dropped down into an upside-down shamrock, representing both sides of the same coin. Luck was neither inherently good nor bad and was always to be found in the eye of the beholder.

Gage had been hopping between his place in Hudson Yards and O'Reilly Manor, depending on the day. Both he and Joey kept Layne busy in the bedroom and out. Date nights rotated between one-on-one time and then all three of them. All of it felt so easy with both the guys, making her one lucky bitch.

Getting home from a rambunctious night out with two De Lucas who had their eyes on her, Layne laughed as she ran over to the stairs, resting her hand on the railing. "You both were on terrible behavior all night!" She kicked off her silver heels, so she was standing barefoot on the step in her little dark green dress.

Joey smirked at her. "Can you blame us? You have been giving that look where you bite your lip, knowing it goes straight to my cock."

Shrugging off his jacket, Gage tossed it onto the mounted coat rack, not giving a shit if it actually landed on a hook or not. "Not to mention, you've been talking back to me all night. All I've been able to think about is bending you over my knee and smacking your ass." He grinned deviously at her.

Layne flashed them both an innocent smile. "Well, you know the rules, only one of you gets me tonight. Guess we'll see who catches me first."

Both of the guys paused to size one another up before attempting to shove the other one out of the way before they both chased after their girl. Layne let out a shriek and ran up the stairs.

Joey doubled up steps going up the stairs, but Gage was quick behind him. Once both men were at the top, Layne was already dashing down the hallway toward the master bedroom.

Gage pulled at Joey's shirt to yank him back to get the lead. He ran like his life depended on it and quickly gained on Layne, an arm scooping her up around her waist and pulling her back against him. He growled into her ear. "Got you."

He got her into the bedroom, kicking the door shut behind him. "Sorry, man, you'll have to wait 'til tomorrow morning!" Gage yelled back at his brother as he released his arm from around Layne. His hands tugged the back of his shirt over his head as his eyes filled with lust and something else more mischievous.

"Dammit!" Joey sighed on the other side of the door. "You two better at least try to keep it down this time!" While disappointed, he also had taken a few liberties during dinner with his hand up Layne's dress and buried it between her thighs, taking advantage of her lack of panties. If Gage wanted to gloat, he intended to make him pay for it and watch as he fucked Layne on the kitchen table tomorrow morning during breakfast.

Layne giggled as she did that damn lip thing again. She backed up until she flopped down onto the edge of the bed, leaning back on her hands. "Going to come here and claim your prize?" Her eyes sparkled with excitement as she watched him reveal his bare chest.

He didn't make a move. Instead, he beckoned her over with his finger. "Get over here and get on your knees, baby."

Still feeling quite sassy, she smirked while crossing one leg over the other, showing she had no intentions of listening to his command.

"You've already racked up a good number of punishments for tonight, are you sure you want to add a few more?" His dick had been hard all night every time she taunted him, and she was only adding to the number of times he was going to have his payback for it. His mind came up with several ways to teach his bratty lucky charm that he was in charge when it concerned that pretty pink box between her legs.

She shrugged at him coyly. "You're dealing with one of New York's most dangerous women right now. How lucky are you feeling?"

Gage laughed and walked up to her, his hand coming under her chin and tilting it so she looked up at him. "Go ahead and try me."

Layne suddenly made a move to grab his arm to pull him off balance and take control of him. It hadn't been a full-out effort, but even if it had, she knew that Gage would have overpowered her any day of the week. He easily avoided her half-assed attack on him, grabbing hold of her and pushing her back onto the softness of the mattress. He flipped her over onto her stomach and pinned her down with one hand.

He got between her legs; his other hand came up underneath her, pulling her hips up so she was ass-in-air for him. Gage groaned as his fingers shoved the dress up her body until it was bunched up at her waist, revealing her bare ass being offered up to him. "What do you tell your Daddy when he's got you right where he wants you?"

Her hips pushed back against the front of his jeans, moaning as she felt his large cock begging to be freed. "I will take your cock wherever you want to bury it, Sir."

"Mm, that's right." His fingers traced down over her slit before pushing three deep inside her wet entrance. "Did you think I didn't notice how Joey fucked you with his fingers throughout dinner? I wanted nothing more than to pull you under the table so you could wrap your lips around my dick."

She squirmed and moaned out as the heat in her core began to pool when he inserted his fingers into her wanton pussy. The silver rings on his fingers rubbed at her opening for extra stimulation. "Please, yes!"

Gage pumped his fingers into her harder, luring her closer to her release. Just as she glided along the fine line of falling into a world of ecstasy, he removed his fingers with a grin. He took his time sucking the taste of her body from each finger while he began to open up his jeans with his other hand.

Layne whined as he left her hanging there on the edge of what had promised to be a hell of an orgasm.

He got up off the bed and shoved both his pants and boxers down, stepping out of the rest of his clothes. All of his tattoos spread across his body were on display, especially the Roman helmet and corresponding swords that were drawn over his length.

Layne took the opportunity to sit up so she could lift her dress over her head and fling it to the side. She crawled over the edge of the bed in front of Gage, sitting back on her ankles while she rested her hands on top of her thighs. Her beautiful doe-eyes looked up at him, full of need.

"You're going to get more than just my cock tonight." He smiled at her and leaned over, taking her pouty lips hostage with a deeply held kiss.

Layne's hands reached up to hold onto both sides of his bearded face, moaning with a desire for him. She urged him to come down onto the bed with her, dropping a hand to wrap around his swords, stroking him encouragingly.

Gage moaned, feeling her hand working him from base to tip. Before they got too carried away, he pulled his mouth from her and leaned over to pull something out of the nightstand on the side of the bed he often slept on. "Turn around for me, Layne."

It was the way he said her name that grabbed her attention. She released her hand from his cock. Reluctantly, she moved her position so that she had her back to him while she sat back on her ankles again.

"Let me see your tattoo, baby." Another request came from him, and she complied, her fingers gathering up her length of chestnut tresses, holding them away from the back of her neck.

The bed shifted as Gage joined her on it. Soon, his hands were placing a cool strand of metal around her throat. The gold necklace fit comfortably around her neck. Hanging from the clasp at the back was an extra two inches of chain that had a small sword charm dangling from the end of it. After it was secured on her, he leaned over and laid several kisses across the nape of her neck.

Layne's fingertips drifted over the front of the piece of jewelry with a smile, having not expected a seemingly random gift from him. Her hand released her hair, letting it fall back down beyond her shoulders.

Gage's hands turned her around to face him, his face full of warmth as his light brown eyes filled with love for the woman he saw before him. "This is my collar for you. It's my promise that I will always be here to take care of you, no matter what. You will always be my lucky charm, worth protecting with my life. This isn't a symbol that you're mine but that I'm yours. I love you for all that you are, and I will be yours for as long as you'll have me. Just know that next week, when we're all in that church together, Joey may be saying the vows out loud, but I will be saying them with my heart."

She melted as she saw Gage lay out his feelings for her. Layne's heart swelled as his love for her filled it even more. "Gage De Luca, I couldn't possibly love you any more than I do right now. You make my life complete; you and Joey both make me the happiest woman to ever exist. I don't want to picture my future without either of you in it." Layne wrapped her arms around his neck and pressed herself up against him, passionately taking hold of his mouth with her lips.

He embraced her, laying her back until he was on top of her. His tongue slid into her mouth to greet hers, stroking over it in a sensual dance. His hands explored her body; his palms kneaded her breasts as her stiff nipples pressed into his touch. Gage's mouth left hers to travel down her throat; his teeth lightly tugged at the collar around her with a playfully possessive growl.

His hands held tightly onto the dip of her waist, ready to move her at the drop of a hat. The coarse hair of his short beard dragged against her skin while he continued to kiss down the length of her body, stopping partway to draw each nipple into his mouth and circle it with his tongue until the sound of her moans graced his ears.

"Where do you want my cock first, lucky charm?" He smirked as he looked up at her.

Layne lifted her head from the pillow to look down at him. "First?" She smiled excitedly, hoping she had heard right.

"There's no part of you that isn't going to feel me tonight, baby." He lowered his mouth down to her pussy that glistened with her arousal. "You're not going to come until you are begging me to take one of your tight as fuck holes. I want to hear how needy you can be." His tongue dragged over her sex, just barely flicking her clit, prompting her hips to twitch at the small shock of pleasure.

Gage made good on his promise, dragging her to the edge of pleasure time and time again. For every time she had run her bratty mouth at him that night, he was sure to taunt her body by always keeping her release just out of reach.

Finally, he turned her over with her ass raised for him to take as he saw fit. His hand slapped her ass harshly for the last bit of sass she had given him. Not waiting for her to acknowledge the heat of the smack, he plunged his rock-hard cock deep into her pussy.

She cried out in relief as he rammed himself inside her, filling her up. He pounded into her, his hips making contact with her with each thrust. "Fuck, baby, I've got your pussy a wet mess, and I'm nowhere near done with you yet." His hand reached down and grabbed a handful of her hair, pulling. "Now you can come like a good girl."

The words barely needed to be spoken; just feeling him stretching her tight walls had her knuckles turning white as she clutched onto the sheets of the bed. Layne screamed out as the intensity of her release tore through her body.

Gage spent the rest of the night making sure that he had her in that constant state of utter satisfaction until he couldn't hold back from spilling his cum into her.

Once all the noises coming from the bedroom upstairs quieted, Joey silently crept up to the second floor. Pushing the door open to their room, he looked inside and saw Layne and Gage there in bed, passed out in each other's arms. He joined them, bringing his chest to Layne's back so that he could be lulled to sleep by the natural scent of her body's arousal mixed with her perfume of rain-kissed daisies.

He never would have thought that anything would be so perfect as the three of them being bound so closely together. This was a feeling he couldn't ever imagine letting go of, not if he had anything to say about it.

EPILOGUE

Rebecca smoothed out the train of Layne's dress after they both stepped out of the white limousine in front of the Cathedral of St. Mary, the catholic church where Layne had grown up attending Sunday School. Her bestie made up the entirety of the bridal party as Layne's Maid of Honor. Rebecca was done up in a simple pale green dress, with her light blonde locks cascading down in loose curls.

Layne stood there staring at the steps laid out before her leading up into the religious institution. Given all the egregious sins she committed on any given week, it was rather ironic that she was about to step foot inside a church and have a priest bless her union with Joey in any shape or form. By all morals and religious standards, both of them were destined for an afterlife full of fire and brimstone.

Already, she could feel her heart picking up its pace; she knew the two men whom she loved unconditionally were waiting just beyond the doors for her. A part of her wanted to run straight into both their arms.

She looked up at the clear blue sky, seeing a few birds soar on by, careless and free. Everything about today felt peaceful, calm, and perfect. All the worries about having a rainy day were behind her.

Her bestie placed a hand on her bare shoulder. "You can do this. He loves you, Layne, and I know you'll spend every day loving one another for the rest of your lives. Just take a deep breath and let everything and everyone else fade away."

A soft smile crossed her face as Layne gave a small nod in response to the encouragement. Rebecca was right. Once she was on the other side of those doors, there were only going to be two points of focus pulling at her heart. She was going to pledge her life to loving both of them with all she had.

Holding tight onto the bundled stems of her bouquet's mixture of traditional white roses and the less traditional green hue of Bells of Ireland, Layne took the first step towards the stone steps that led the way to the entrance.

Once inside the church, the large and ornate double doors leading into the nave where all the guests were gathered were shut, blocking her view of what awaited her. Those doors were separating her from the two most important men in her life.

She swallowed hard, feeling the nerves vibrating all over her body with anxiety. Irrational thoughts flooded her mind. What if he hadn't shown? What if she couldn't say the words? What if this was all a dream?

Rebecca gave another fluff of the short lace train of Layne's dress before coming around to stand in front of her with a smile full of love and eyes glistening with proud tears. "You look absolutely gorgeous and deserve every bit of this happiness. I will be upfront, cheering you on. Just one foot in front of the other, okay?" She leaned over and hugged Layne.

Moments later, Rebecca disappeared beyond the doors. Layne knew there was classical music playing just inside, but she couldn't hear it over her thoughts. She wondered if her dad would have been proud and walked her down the aisle to give her away to commit her life and love to a man like Joey. She knew Liam wouldn't have.

Breaking free of her thoughts, she noticed a little old woman had her frail hand on one of the doors and was waiting for Layne to indicate she was ready. After getting a small smile from Layne, the elderly woman nodded to the man standing behind the other door. Simultaneously, they drew the doors open, revealing the sight down the length of the path she was about to walk.

The aisle was lined with flowers in various shades of green. Light poured in through the massive stained glass windows. The rows upon rows of pews filled with guests all on their feet with their eyes all looking at her. Layne could have sworn the church was void of any guests at all because her eyes immediately found her entire universe standing up by the altar. The pianist began to play a romantically slow version of *Wherever You Will Go* by The Calling.

Joey stood tall, his hands clasped in front of him. The rich hues of his brown eyes stared at her. His dirty blonde hair was neatly styled and locked into place, and his scruff precisely trimmed. He was wearing a black tux that fit against each of his muscles and paired with a white shirt and black tie just underneath the jacket. The wings of his neck tattoos playing peekaboo just above the edge of his shirt's collar.

At his side was the other half of her heart, Gage—Joey's Best Man. His tux mirrored Joey's, except instead of a white shirt, it was all black. Gage had a hand holding onto the top of Joey's shoulder supportively and to perhaps prevent him from running to Layne to scoop her up into his arms halfway down the aisle.

The first thing Joey saw when he saw those doors open was a goddamn Irish angel. He was pretty sure that if he was ever allowed to pass through the Pearly Gates, this was exactly what he would see waiting for him. His heart damn near stopped for what felt like hours as he drank in the stunning sight, slowly walking down the aisle, moving closer and closer to him.

Layne's long chestnut locks were drawn back from her face and off of her bare shoulders. Her hair was all pulled into a loose bun at the nape of her neck, with a couple of small decorative white roses tucked into the top of the bun. The scripted letters of her tattoo, 'Luck' on the back of her neck, was on full display. Her sparkling emerald eyes left the window to her soul wide open for him to see right into everything that made her the woman Joey adored.

Her strapless white dress was a seamless blend of lace with a sweetheart neckline. Scallop-edged lace arm bands hung loosely around her trim biceps, the body of the dress hugged her petite figure and perfectly clung against the curves of her hips. Across her mid back was a band of matching lace in a design similar to the pattern of butterfly wings.

Around her throat was the thin gold chain Gage had given her just last week. She had refused to take off his discreet collar, keeping it on served as a reminder of all his promises to her. While he wasn't the man being recognized by church or state as Layne's soon-to-be husband, that necklace was his vow to have and to hold her all the same.

Joey was rendered breathless, his heart swelling so much he swore it would burst through his chest. Next to him, Gage was grinning like a damn fool at the beauty nearly at their end of the aisle. He nudged Joey to go get their girl as she reached the steps that led up to the space where they stood in front of the altar.

Layne's eyes never left Joey's face as her heart moved her feet down that aisle. Rebecca had come to ease the bouquet out of Layne's hands before Joey joined her at her side, extending his hand to her. She placed her hand in his, watching as his tattooed fingers curled over her hand as he guided her up the steps where they could turn and face one another.

The priest began to speak, and the ceremony commenced, Joey's hold on her hands being a constant reassurance of his devotion to her happiness. Soon, they were exchanging rings and saying their vows out loud to one another. Layne shifted her eyes to Gage every so often so he knew he was included in every promise she was making.

The man cloaked in holy robes addressed Layne, "Do you, Layne Nicole O'Reilly, take this man to be your lawfully wedded husband?"

She gave the widest smile at Joey. "I absolutely do."

The priest then shifted to look at Joey. "And do you, Joseph Elliot De Luca, take this woman to be your lawfully wedded wife?"

Joey squeezed Layne's hands tightly in both of his. "I do. She's mine, always and forever."

Before the officiant could complete his statement declaring them both joined in holy matrimony, Joey jumped the gun and immediately pulled Layne into his arms, crashing his lips onto hers. Layne's hands held onto the sides of his face as her mouth welcomed him, her tongue eagerly pushing past his lips to sensually dance with his. It most definitely was not a chaste kiss that most couples engaged in before such an audience.

Several drawn-out moments passed before there was a stern clearing of a throat from the priest, prompting the newlyweds to separate themselves just enough to regain their composure while they both donned giddy smiles.

"I now present Mr. and Mrs. De Luca."

Layne looked over at Gage, giving him a subtle wink. Joey wasn't the only Mr. De Luca she was tied to.

After Layne and Joey walked back down the aisle together, the formalities continued at the front of the church. Greeting all the guests on their exit from the holy building, they shook hands and shared hugs with some of New York's wealthiest and some of its most corrupt.

Once everyone cleared out, Gage nodded at them both. "I will tell the driver to meet us out front so we can get this party started." He smirked before heading out the front doors.

Joey grinned at Layne as he wrapped his hand around hers. "C'mon."

He began leading her back into the expanse of the empty nave now that everyone had gone on their way.

She giggled as she had to quickly move her feet to keep up with him. "What are you doing? We have to get to the reception."

"I'm not waiting for tonight." He pulled her toward the altar.

Layne couldn't help but wrinkle her nose in confusion at the nonsense he was spouting off. "For what?"

He turned her around and pressed her back against the altar in what was probably going to be either the most holy of acts or the most unimaginable sin. Feverishly, he kissed her, bringing his body up tight against hers. His hands began bunching up her dress in his hands, exposing the lean length of her legs.

She gasped as he made it suddenly clear what his intentions were. If he was willing to go to hell, she would dive off that cliff with him any day of the week. Hell or high water, right? Overcome with desire for him, her hands pulled at the belt of his pants, her fingers going to quick work to open up his pants that were already under tension from his stiff cock.

Layne switched to helping gather all the fabric of her dress for him while Joey pulled his length out of his underwear.

He reached down and hoisted her up, separating her legs to wrap around his waist. "Hold on tight, Layney. I'm going to make sure that with God as my witness, you're screaming out His name while I fully make you my wife." Joey sinfully smirked at her as he lodged her back against the altar for support.

Her hands held onto the back of his neck as her breaths grew heavy with anticipation. She leaned over and stole a kiss from him, breaking it for a moment to whisper, "You better make it worth at least ten Hail Marys." She grinned at him, closing the gap between their lips once again.

Joey growled against her mouth as he lined up and sank himself fully inside of her. Hearing her decadent moan into their kiss, he began to hastily thrust himself inside of her. Every fiber of him needed to feel her cunt clenching around him.

Grasping onto him tightly, Layne moaned out at the movements as he needily shoved his cock into her. His arm tightly wrapped around her waist with his other around her back. He began to lay kisses along her throat with his labored breath, heating her skin while he worshiped her body.

Layne's fingers dug into the back of his neck as he furiously continued to lay his claim on her tight pussy. "God, Joey, yes!" Her body was already hanging by a thread, knowing they could be discovered at any moment.

His mouth dragged over the front of her chest, giving a bite to the top of her cleavage that was threatening to spill over the top of her dress. Layne tilted her head back as she panted hard, trying to suck in oxygen between her moans of pleasure.

His gravelly voice spoke against the tops of her mounds, "I never want to forget this moment, Layney. You'll always be my good girl, no matter what." He groaned as he felt the swell of his cock began to throb, his release threatening to explode into her.

She cried out as suddenly she was overcome with the surge of pleasure that burst from her core. Right as her body squeezed down around Joey, he shuddered as he drove himself even deeper into her. He yelled out against her neck as he shot his cum far into the depths of her body.

They both remained there in each other's arms for several minutes. Layne provided him with several delicate kisses as they both tried to find some level of composure. After gathering themselves, they walked back out of the church to the top of the stone steps, hand in hand. Layne's cheeks still flushed from their consummation, her eyes shimmering with boundless love.

Gage was at the curb, leaning back against the side of the limo with his arms crossed in front of his chest, shaking his head. He knew that look of satisfaction from a mile away. He muttered to himself with a smirk, "Horny motherfuckers." He fully intended to get his fill of Layne in the limo on the way to the reception. His cock hardened in his pants, imagining her dripping with their cum for the rest of the night.

There were still some guests lingering and chatting on the sidewalk who hadn't made it back to their vehicles yet. The reception didn't start for at least another forty-five minutes, leaving everyone a little time to get where they needed to be.

Layne smiled as she used one hand to lift the front of her dress as she began walking down the steps with Joey's skull-tatted hand firmly holding onto her other. She had never expected to ever be filled with this much love in one lifetime, and she was looking forward to basking in all of it for years to come.

"Hey, Layne!" A voice shouted out to her while she and Joey were midway down the steps. The familiar voice of her brother was recognized before she even saw his face. Liam stepped past a few of the guests, his face full of a deadly cold calm. He raised his hand, and at the end of it was a forty-five-caliber pistol.

Crack!

Time stood still.

Gage began to push off the side of the limo.

Joey instinctively stepped in front of Layne.

Before there was any time to comprehend what was occurring, Layne felt the impact of the hard stone steps against her back. Joey's weight was on top of her, his back against her chest. She squirmed underneath him, struggling to get out from his expansive body that had shielded her own.

Liam paused with an evil smirk smeared across his face. He may not have struck his intended target, but he had hit the next best thing. Upon seeing Gage reaching into his jacket for a weapon of his own, Layne's brother shoved the nearest wedding guest out in front of him before turning and darting down the street. There was no hesitation as Gage took up chase after him.

Squeezing out from underneath Joey, Layne sat on the step as he lay there at her side. His hand clutched onto his chest. Panic rose in Layne's throat, the stark contrast of red quickly spreading across his white shirt. Joey winced as he gasped for a breath of air.

"Joey! Shit! God—No." Layne stammered out. Immediately, her hands pulled open his shirt and pulled his hand away from where it was clutching. Blood leaked from a hole in his chest, having torn right through the shamrock tattoo overtop his heart. Instead of inked blood leaking from the design etched into his skin, warm liquid seeped from his body. Her hands pressed down firmly over the wound despite the trembling in her body. It was all pouring out of him so quickly, her hands getting coated.

Tears spilled from her eyes, streaming down her cheeks until they fell off the edge of her face. Layne's lips quivered as she sobbed out while staring down into the pain-riddled chocolate hues, looking back up at her.

"Layne…" His voice trying to provide her some comfort.

She shook her head fiercely. "No, don't you dare. Don't you fuckin' dare. Please." Layne's heart went from feeling like it could have burst from happiness now to feeling like it was imploding on itself.

Joey coughed lightly as he raised a hand to her face. "It's okay."

"It's not… It's not okay… I'm not okay…" Both of her cheeks shone with her flood of tears while her hands held steadfastly on his chest, getting covered in the deep crimson from his body.

He offered up a weak smile to her before swallowing hard at the pain radiating from his chest. It had all been worth it. She had been worth it. Even overcome with grief, Layne's beauty gave him comfort in those moments.

As Joey's eyelids grew heavy, Layne screamed out at him while laying herself down over his chest, wishing she could pour all the love she had ever felt for him into his wounds to mend them. She would have given everything in that moment to trade places with the man who had always completed her soul.

"I love you. Always and forever, remember? I can't do this without you, I never could." Layne kissed him several times, tasting the saltiness of her tears that were dripping over her lips. Those three words should have been enough; she desperately wanted them to be his salvation.

Heavy sobs wracked her body as she noticed his skin paling. She clung to him with every hope that she had. Her words were broken from her tears, unable to sound out any of the millions of words she wanted to say to him. Her repetitive professions of her love muffled against his chest. She didn't care that her dress would be forever stained with his blood. It all meant nothing without him.

His voice hardly above a whisper, "I'll always be yours, Layney." Joey's hand rested on the back of Layne's neck, holding her close while she clutched onto him, repeating herself over and over.

"Don't leave me, please don't leave me." Her words overflowing with pain she wouldn't have wished on her worst enemy.

Gage had lost Liam fairly quickly after he hopped into a getaway car that had been waiting around the corner for him. Returning to the church, he was now jogging up the steps to the heartbreaking sight. Others had begun to gather around the tragedy, including Dr. Patty, who was already working her way through the crowd to try to assist. "Layne, I need you to move," the physician said as she tried to gain access to Joey's body underneath his grief-stricken wife.

Despite Gage's own emotions stinging in his eyes, he ran over to Layne, not caring who he knocked out of his path. "Baby, you need to let the doc do her work." The words pushed past the ache of his own heart. His hands tried to ease her from her position there on top of Joey. When Layne refused to budge, it took all of Gage's resolve to use his strength to pry her away from his brother's wounded body.

Layne unleashed a raw scream of protest, "NO! I'm not leaving him! No! No! No!" Her body fought against Gage's hands, trying to stay there with Joey, wishing she could go wherever he went, even if it meant the grave. Her tears never slowed their march down her face as she refused to take her eyes off of the man she so fiercely loved. That bullet had been for her, and despite it physically striking Joey, it had still managed to assassinate her heart.

Her broken sobs interjected through her screams of the worst pain anyone could ever feel. Losing the battle with herself, her struggles in Gage's arms began to slow until she didn't even have the strength to stand on her legs. He lowered her down as he felt her weight grow heavier in his hold and sank down onto a nearby step, drawing her into his lap.

Gage rocked Layne in his arms, doing what he could to be the cushion for her emotional blow. His eyes were wet with the tears he was struggling to hold back for her sake. He had promised to have and to hold her, and that meant being Layne's strength while she was in this state of utter devastation.

Joey had wanted to say so many things to her, but they got lost somewhere along the way as his pain began to ease and the world around him began to fade to black. Hearing Layne's voice replaying over and over in his mind until the final thing to linger across his senses was the faint scent of daisies after a warm summer rain. Maybe there would be a spot in Heaven for him after all.

How does it all come to an end? Find out in…

Chaos *Luck* Wrath

CHAOS LUCK WRATH

Alliances are broken and hearts stolen.

For all the good girls. Don’t ask twice.

OFFICIAL PLAYLIST

A Grave Mistake - Ice Nine Kills
Adrenaline - Zero 9:36
Adrenalize - In This Moment
Black Hole - We Came As Romans, Caleb Shomo
Cold Blooded - Of Virtue
Come Undone - Bad Omens
Death Wish - Royale Lynn, Danny Worsnop
Fight Fire With Gasoline - Self Deception
Hallelujah - No Resolve
Hell And Back - Self Deception
Here's My Heart - SayWeCanFly
In The End Mellen Gi Remix - Tommee Profitt, Fleurie, Mellen Gi
It's Got My Name On It - Tommee Profitt, Sarah Reeves
Limits - Bad Omens
Qwerty - Mushroomhead
RATATATA - BABYMETAL, Electric Callboy
Scarlet - In This Moment
Thank You For Hating Me - Citizen Soldier
There's Fear In Letting Go - I Prevail
Throne - Bring Me The Horizon
Without You - My Darkest Days

Watch Me Burn - Michele Morrone
Wrong Side of Heaven (Acoustic) - Five Finger Death Punch

The official playlist can be found on Spotify.

AUTHOR'S NOTE

What a wild ride this has been! I kicked off the Broken Alliances series with my debut novel (Stay In Your Layne) and never expected it to evolve into a four-book series. Becoming an author has been such an incredible experience that has forged amazing friendships with readers and authors alike.

To everyone who has stuck with me throughout this series, thank you so much. It means the world to me that not only have people read Layne's story, but have continued to follow it throughout four books. For something that had been just a silly little story in my brain to turn into something others can enjoy, that truly amazes me.

It is never too late to shoot for the stars and I hope that you all follow your own dreams regardless of what anyone tells you.

Much love (and smut),
Sadie

CONTENT & TRIGGER WARNINGS

All trigger and content warnings can be found on www.sadiewinchester.com.

Chapter One

THE AFTERMATH

Continued from Incoming Layne Shift

A hand waved in front of her face. "Miss?" The man dressed in a cheap gray suit stood in front of her. The emptiness of her emerald eyes stared ahead, not seeing the man or the hospital waiting room they were both in.

Layne sat there in her soiled wedding dress; sections of her hair had come loose from their previously pristine position in her bun, and Joey's blood stained everything, including what was left of her heart.

Chaos

This was what her life consisted of; it was how he entered her life.

Luck

Both good and bad followed her everywhere; it was how he managed to save her from herself.

Wrath

Equally, her affliction and what she planned to inflict on the world; it was what put him where he was now.

Gage returned with a bottle of water in one hand and a cup of coffee in the other. Seeing the middle-aged man in front of Layne, he immediately rushed over, setting both beverages down on the table next to the set of seats where Layne was. "Hey, hey, hey! What the fuck are you doing, man?"

The man frowned as he looked up at Gage. "Detective Adams. I need to ask Ms...." He checked a notepad in his hand. "Ms. O'Reilly, a few questions about what happened in front of St. Mary's today."

Before Gage could tell him to get lost, Layne said her first semi-coherent words since leaving the church steps, "De Luca." The tone of her voice was cold, flat, and empty, much like the rest of her felt.

"What?" The detective looked over at her, being caught off-guard by her sudden decision to speak up.

"My name. It's Layne...De Luca." Her eyes finally moved slowly through the sludge of emotions they were drowning in to settle on the man looking for answers on the day's catastrophe.

The man cleared his throat. "Oh, um, yeah, so, I'm really sorry, but it's standard protocol that we get statements from witnesses as soon as possible while everything is still fresh. The remaining witnesses have been less than cooperative. I was hoping you could provide some clarity."

Layne's voice continued to remain soft and monotone, "I didn't see anything." She had seen everything, and she continued to see it on replay inside her mind. A fresh set of tears welled up in her eyes as she squeezed them shut, expelling them onto her cheeks.

The detective frowned again. "I'm sure there must have been something that stood out—"

That's when Gage interfered, placing a hand on the detective's shoulder with a solid grip. "Now isn't a good time. She said she didn't see anything." He knew that was bullshit, they all had seen it.

He took a few steps away from Layne, guiding the detective with an arm around his shoulders as he lowered his voice. Several moments later, Detective Adams handed over a business card to Gage and went on his way. The card was immediately dropped into the trash.

Gage came back, picking up both beverages and sitting down next to Layne. "Baby, you should at least drink something. It's been hours."

When she said nothing, he leaned over to whisper in her ear, "I told you to do something; is this how you show me you're listening?" It was his last-ditch effort to get any level of reaction from her. It failed. He frowned, lowering his forehead to her shoulder while his lips kissed her arm lightly.

With her eyes still shut, flashbacks of the day were on a continuous loop in her head. The love and the pain. He told her it was okay, and yet nothing was. The second a sob started to crawl from her chest into her throat, she opened her eyes, shook her head, and stood.

Choking down the sob, she looked at Gage. "I wanted a lot of things from him, but I never wanted him to sacrifice himself for me. I'd rather give myself to all the monsters lurking under my bed at night than to have him do what he did." Truth be told, those monsters were already poisoning her thoughts and beckoning her to surrender herself to the darkness calling to her soul. Without Joey, the fire within her was slowly being snuffed out.

Looking around at the piss-poor attempt of the hospital to look warm and welcoming, all she could see was despair and pity. "I can't be here." She wasn't sure where she could go to find her escape, but sitting for hours inside this waiting room wasn't it.

Gage's hand reached out and wrapped around her wrist. "Layne…" He wasn't sure what he could say to her to make this better because he was feeling just as lost inside.

Before she could pry his grasp off of her, a doctor approached. It was a woman in her late fifties wearing dark blue scrubs that gave a boxy appearance to her body. "Mrs. De Luca?" She looked at Layne with eyes full of empathy, likely mastered from countless depressing conversations with families of patients.

Layne looked up at the doctor who was now standing in front of her. This was it. This was the moment she didn't want to be present for. She had played it out in her mind a thousand times over in the past hour alone. She could hear the words over and over that, yet again, someone was sorry for her loss. He was dead and gone with no chance of ever coming back to her. She would be told that the doctors did all they could, and it still wasn't fucking good enough.

"I'm Dr. Monroe; I am the surgeon who worked on your husband." She pulled a tablet from under her arm.

Hearing someone refer to Joey as her husband made Layne's heartache burn even deeper. Gage's arm was suddenly wrapped around her shoulders, holding her firmly as they both braced for impact.

The doctor tapped on the screen several times as she drew in a deep breath to share the news. "He is currently in our Intensive Care Unit. I was able to extract the bullet from his chest and repair the tissue." She continued to go into the finer details of what had been done during the surgery, using her tablet as a reference point, but Layne was still stuck on her first sentence.

"He's in the ICU?" She stared at Dr. Monroe and wondered if this was her mind playing games on her. Had they renamed the morgue?

Dr. Monroe nodded. "He lost a lot of blood, and he's not out of the woods yet, but he's extraordinarily lucky the bullet barely nicked his heart. If it had been only a hair to the left, it would have been fatal."

Layne's body was involuntarily shaking like a leaf, and her lungs felt like they couldn't get enough oxygen. The renewed wave of hope had come from nowhere and crashed down on her. She didn't even feel the rolling set of tears on her cheeks.

Gage hugged Layne into his side, feeling the same relief and hopefulness upon hearing the doctor's words. "When can we see him?"

Dr. Monroe tucked her tablet back under her arm. "We'd like to monitor him for a little while longer to make sure he's stable after surgery, but I will have a nurse come get you when you can go to his room."

Whatever else was said, Layne couldn't have told anyone because her mind was solely on seeing Joey for herself. What if the doctor had gotten patients mixed up? Maybe she was mistaken, and Joey was lying in a cooler with a tag on his toe.

About forty-five minutes later, a nurse came to lead Gage and her into a room located in the heart of the trauma ICU. When she entered, it smelled so sterile and not at all like the leather and sage she wanted to be greeted with. When she approached the bed, she saw him lying there unconscious and quite pale. Tubes provided him oxygen and drained excess fluids from his chest, IVs provided his body with medications, and monitors constantly checked his vitals.

Her hand covered her mouth, stifling a sob. Gage squeezed her shoulders reassuringly as his body released some of the tension it had been harboring since they had arrived at the hospital.

Layne stepped up next to the bed, carefully taking hold of his hand while her fingers trailed over the side of his face in disbelief. Touching him and feeling his warmth made it real. He was still here with her, and he hadn't left. His life hadn't been robbed of him in the name of Layne's survival.

Her words shook with the weight of her tears still on them. "You listen to me, Joey motherfucking De Luca. I swear to God, if you die on me now, after all this, I will hunt your soul down and never let you hear the end of it."

Gage joined her at Joey's bedside, lightly patting his brother's shoulder. "You've always been a stubborn son of a bitch." He tried to make the commentary light, but his own emotions were getting caught on the words.

She stood there watching every breath he took into his lungs. Each minor movement of his body had her attention. When it was clear she wasn't letting go of his hand, Gage brought a chair over to her so she could sit. Layne rested her head on his arm, both of her hands steadfastly clutching onto the familiar skull tattoo on his hand.

"Hey, Layne!" The crack echoed in the air. Joey's weight on top of her. His cocoa-colored eyes were full of physical and emotional pain.

"Hey, Layne!" Liam's voice filled with nothing but hatred.

"Hey, Layne!" All her sense of security was shattered.

"Hey—"

She startled awake, lifting her head from the edge of Joey's bed to see the nightmare wasn't entirely over. Her heart was galloping a little harder in her chest to the point she could practically feel it in the back of her throat.

"Layne," Gage's voice repeated her name for a third time. His hand lightly rubbed the exposed skin of her upper back to ease her out of her nap.

Groggily, she responded, "Yeah?" Her fingers rubbed the slumber from her eyes as she tried to erase the fog that had settled over her. Glancing up at the clock on the wall, she had only managed to snag an hour of rest.

He had a large paper bag in his hand. "Rebecca dropped off some clothes for you to change into." She hadn't been allowed beyond the nurse's station since she wasn't considered immediate family, but Rebecca had met Gage for a few minutes to get an update and to see what else she could do.

Layne shook her head. "No." Her eyes looked at the unchanged, slack expression on Joey's face. "What if he wakes up and I'm not here? What if he… and I'm not?" Her fears were getting the best of her and making her unable to say the morbid alternative.

Gage squatted down next to her, a hand soothingly rubbing over her thigh. "Baby, he's not going anywhere in the next ten minutes." He offered her the bag with her clothes in it. He had already changed out of his tux and into a set of casual jeans and a solid blue t-shirt that his buddy had dropped off while Layne had been catching some rest.

Layne stared at the bag for a minute, then sighed as she stood from the chair. She leaned over and kissed Joey's mouth softly. "I will be right back, okay?" There was no telling if he could hear her or not, but it made her feel better to think he could.

It took what little strength she had in her to release Joey's hand and grab the bag instead. Gage stood and motioned in a direction across the hall. "The nurse said there's a bathroom right over there you can use."

After Layne left the room, Gage plunked down into her chair. One elbow rested on his knee while the fingers of his other hand roughly ran through his cropped hair. "She's hurting, Joe. Hell, I'm hurting. If you check out, you'll be taking her with you. You gotta pull through this for all of us." His emotions tainted the last few words that passed through his lips.

Finding the easily marked bathroom, Layne stepped inside. She stared at herself in the mirror. The day had begun with her looking and feeling her prettiest. Now, her eyes were swollen and bloodshot from the tears, her makeup smudged into dark circles around her eyes, her hair frazzled, and the red bloodstains still marred her fair skin.

Mentally, peeling off her wedding gown had been the most painful part of the process. The weight of the fabric should have been a relief when it fell to the floor, but her body still carried an incredible emotional load. Looking in the bag of clothes, Rebecca had done her typical thing. Not only did she pack two outfits, but she had tossed some spare toiletries in there as well. After scrubbing any speck of dried blood from her body and washing her face, she brushed out her hair, putting it in a ponytail.

Layne chose a pair of black leggings, slip-on sneakers, and a lavender tank with a dark purple zip-up hoodie overtop. She shoved her dress into the bag, unable to get it to fit fully, so the skirt was cascading out the top like a fountain of tulle. Why was she even keeping it? It had to be bad luck to keep something that you wore when your husband took a bullet for you, right?

Emerging from the bathroom, she came back to Joey's room. She dropped the bag onto a small sofa that doubled as a sleeping space. As much as she hadn't wanted to leave and try to put herself together, Gage had been right to urge her to do it. It left her feeling slightly more human and briefly chased away some of the darkness consuming her thoughts.

Gage got up from the chair, his eyes red from the few minutes he had to allow the day's events to sink in. He walked over to her and wrapped his large arms around her, giving a near-crushing hug. "You look gorgeous."

Her partial laugh fell flat. "Liar." Her arms wrapped around his waist, and she let him hold her for the amount of time they both needed. "How is he?" It seemed a silly question since she hadn't been gone all that long.

He pulled back and turned to look at his brother. "Still here, just like I told you. You should go get yourself something to eat. There's a cafeteria down on the first floor."

Immediately, that was a hard pass for her, and she shook her head. "I'm not hungry." It felt like she was being chased away from Joey's side, and her defense mechanisms began to rise up in protest.

Cupping her face, he stared at her. "I need you to eat. It's not going to do anyone any good if you pass out 'cause you're too damn stubborn to take care of yourself."

Frowning, she pulled her face back from his hold. "I'll be fine."

He groaned in annoyance that this was going to be a battle. "Sitting here refusing to do anything but stare at him isn't healthy. Joey would be kicking your ass right now for forcing the question to be asked twice." The moment the words flew out of his mouth, he instantly regretted it.

Layne's hurt came bubbling back up to the surface, and she pulled back from Gage.

"I'm sorry, you know I didn't mean to…" His eyes were apologetic as he reached out for her, but she kept herself just out of the reach of his hand.

Her eyes shifted to where Joey was lying. His condition hadn't changed since they arrived in the room. It was neither better nor was it worse. "I'm going to go get some air. Call me if anything changes."

She reluctantly left the room in search of some space to clear her head. When Layne got past the sliding glass doors that led outside, she was greeted with a small breeze filled with cool air. Finding a bench to sit on, she stared up at the sky, letting the one question fill her head. Why? Why was this happening to all of them? Why did Liam have to do this? Why hadn't it been her?

There should have been unparalleled rage directed at her brother, and she was sure, at some point, it would rear its vicious head. Right now, the only thing she felt was small, lost, and shattered, all thanks to the crippling grasp of fear her brother left her with.

Chapter Two

SPARKLESS

Should she have walked out on Gage the way she had? No, but her mind was all over the place right now. Emotions were erratically jumping from one point to the next without any logic to guide them.

She mindlessly flipped through hundreds of messages left on her phone while sitting outside the hospital. The senior associates of her crew were looking to her for their orders, Rebecca was checking in, and some of her allies were sending their fucking useless thoughts and prayers. Layne didn't have any answers for herself, let alone anyone else. The messages went unanswered. Before she tucked her phone away, a new text popped in.

GAGE

Are you okay?

LAYNE

What do you think?

GAGE

Please, come back up here.

We're in this together, and I can't help if you won't let me.

Layne wanted to ask him why she should bother returning to that cold and depressing hospital room, but she realized that she wasn't the only person in pain. Gage found himself watching his big brother struggling to live just as much as she was.

She spent several more minutes convincing herself to go back inside. Yesterday, she would have kicked her own ass, but today? She had lost that spark that made her want to put up a fight.

"You are the spark that keeps my heart pumping blood through my veins."

Her eyes squeezed shut, expressing a few more silent tears as the pain tore into her heart a little more, and the memory of Joey's words drove into her shattered soul.

"I will love you so hard for the rest of your life that you won't ever have to worry about losing that spark."

Inhaling a shaky breath, she mentally scolded herself for perhaps loving him too fiercely. If he hadn't been so wrapped up in loving her back, maybe he wouldn't have stepped in front of her. Alternatively, she wondered if this was happening to her as punishment for having not loved him enough. Maybe getting fucked at the altar in church could have been God's tipping point, too.

Quickly, her fingertips pushed the tears off her cheeks as she readied herself to go back inside. Every muscle in her body felt triple its weight, making the process of standing more challenging than it should have been.

On her way back through the main entrance, a vaguely familiar face was just leaving and captured her attention when he spoke up. "Ms. O'Reil—I mean, Mrs. De Luca?" Detective Adams smiled apologetically.

She stopped in her tracks to look at the man, struggling to recall his name. "Hi…"

He saved her from having to fumble for his name. "Detective Adams, we spoke earlier."

Right. When she was wallowing in the thoughts of her husband's presumed death, he had been interested in getting her retelling of the tragedy.

"I'm sorry, I don't have anything that can help you." The verbal apology was the best he was going to get out of her. She simply didn't have enough energy to muster up a fake smile for the sake of appearing polite.

The detective immediately shook his head. "No, I understand. I just wanted to make sure you got my contact information in case you do have anything you'd like to share." Though he had previously given it to Gage, he had a suspicion it wouldn't get passed along. He dug into his suit jacket, pulled out his business card, and extended it toward her.

Hesitantly, Layne took the white piece of cardstock from him. She gave it a glance front and back before sliding it into the pocket of her black pants. "I already told you that I didn't see a damn thing." Irritation started to rise in her voice.

He nodded at her. "Just hold onto that in case you ever need it." His face filled with empathy before he added, "I hope your husband makes a full recovery."

Layne muttered, "Thanks," before she turned and left him standing in the entryway as she found her way back upstairs to join both her guys waiting for her in the ICU.

When she walked into Joey's room, Gage wasn't present. The only other person in there was a nurse who was changing out one of the bags hanging from the metal stand next to Joey's bed that dripped into his IV. The young raven-haired woman was about Layne's age and gave a polite smile. "I will be out of here in just a second."

"It's fine, do what you need to." Layne went over to the empty chair at Joey's bedside, plunked down into it, and the nurse was out of the room as quickly as she had stated.

Both of Layne's hands took a tight hold of Joey's hand at his side and rested her face on it while she closed her eyes. She quietly whispered, "I feel like I've given you all the spark I have left in me, and it's still not enough."

The swell of emotions crept up on her again, and she buried her face into the cheap hospital-grade blankets as she suppressed a sob. Her shoulders shuddered as they soaked up the cries and screams she wanted to unleash.

A hand came to the back of her head reassuringly. "It'll always be enough, Layney." Joey's hoarse voice spoke through his grogginess as he opened his eyes to see her clutching onto his other hand while visibly upset.

Her body stilled, wondering if she had fallen asleep again or if she had just devolved into hearing things. When she lifted her head, she saw his heavenly brown eyes staring at her. She choked on another sob, but this time one of gleeful disbelief.

"Joey!" She released his hand and immediately stood to lean over and smother his face and mouth with her kisses of relief. The tears that were still fresh on her face fell onto him as she pressed her face up against the tattooed bird wings on the side of his neck in an attempt to latch herself onto him in a hug.

He lightly returned her kisses but struggled to hold back his winces of pain as she leaned against him. His hand rubbed her back reassuringly. "I told you it would be okay." Joey's last couple of words fought through a groan of his body's reminder that he had been shot in the goddamn chest and undergone a major surgery.

Hearing the discomfort in his voice, she eased up off of him. "I didn't hurt you, did I?"

Shaking his head in a lie, he gave her a light smile. "Never."

Using the bottom of her sleeve, she dried her face off until just the red splotches left behind from her tears remained. Her glossy hues stared at him in disbelief that he was awake and talking. Before more questions could be asked, the door opened, and Gage walked in with a handful of snacks.

Not only was Gage surprised to see Layne had returned, but Joey was awake. He juggled the food in his hands, nearly dropping an apple to the floor. "Hey, man! Fuck, you gave us a hell of a scare."

He set the food down on a small table quickly before going to the side of Joey's bed opposite Layne. Relief filled his face as he looked at his brother and bent over to give a partial hug with a gentle pat on Joey's shoulder. Joey's hand returned a tap to Gage's bicep.

Layne smiled, unable to come to terms that this was real as she looked at both Gage and Joey. Finally, she pulled herself away enough from Joey's side to ease back into her chair, her fingers lacing with Joey's. "How are you feeling?"

"Like I got shot." He smirked, seemingly, he hadn't lost his sense of humor.

She rolled her eyes and tried to suppress the smile, still tugging at the corners of her mouth. "Thanks, smartass." Layne sat there, simply staring at him, overcome with gratitude that he hadn't been eliminated from her life.

The three of them sat there talking about everything and anything except for the person responsible for the assassination attempt on Layne. She didn't dare to even think his name and instead opted to focus all her thoughts and energy on Joey's road to recovery.

"When you get back home, I'll make sure we have plenty of your favorite snacks stocked up and whatever else you need," she reassured him. He wouldn't be leaving here for a little while, but having him back home with her was something she could look forward to.

Being happy to just be on this side of the dirt, Joey grinned as he watched Layne make plans for all of them. He had a second chance at a life together with her, and hell if he was going to waste it.

Gage took a sip from his bottle of water. "I hate to bring the mood down, but before we start making too many plans, we should talk about the obvious here." His eyes looked at Joey first, looking for his agreement.

After a deep inhale, Joey winced as he sat up a little straighter in his bed, fumbling with all the fucking tubes and wires attached to him. "What do we know?"

Her eyes darkened with a glare at Gage for bringing up the topic she had been actively avoiding. "We don't need to talk about this." Layne knew she couldn't ignore this forever, but she wanted to stay in this bubble of happiness a little while longer.

Joey couldn't pretend to understand what she was going through, given her brother was responsible, but he did recognize the signs of her internally shutting down if they didn't tread carefully. "Layne, you can't ignore what he did."

Gage chimed in with his opinion, "We don't know what the hell else Liam is up to."

She lashed out with a spark of anger for the first time since the incident. "I'm not fucking ignoring it! I'm going to take care of it!" Immediately, her sharp tongue and even shorter temper had her sinking down into her guilt.

The past twenty-four hours had taken its toll on her. The sleep deprivation, the highs and lows, and all the stressors that had her running on fumes by this point. Layne put a hand to her forehead and dragged it down over her face as she squeezed her eyes shut in frustration.

"Layney..." Joey's soothing voice spoke her name, attempting to pull her back from spiraling.

She didn't make a move from her current position as her thoughts began to swallow her whole.

Standing from his seat, Gage came up behind her, rubbing his hands over her shoulders. "Look, now that Joey is awake, why don't you get some rest, and we can pick this up later, hm?" He leaned over and laid a kiss on the back of her neck directly against the curves of the shamrock inked into her skin.

Stubbornly, she shook her head. “No, I’m fine.” She had been using that word a lot, and it was the furthest thing from the truth. Layne didn’t want to rest knowing her idiotic brother was out there, knowing her nightmares would taint her memory of what should have been the happiest day of her life.

“Come here.” Joey’s hand tugged on her wrist, drawing her hand away from her face. When she opened up those beautiful green eyes, they were shaded by sheer exhaustion. He didn’t have much room to shift, but he gave her enough so she could at least perch on the edge of his bed. His arm pulled her down to his side, his strong arms squeezing her tightly.

Layne lay there in his embrace, wishing she could bottle up the feeling of him for eternity. Remaining vigilant of his injury, she laid her arm across his stomach. His hold on her helped to relieve some of her tension.

Joey pressed several kisses across her temple. “Go home, let Gage take care of you, and get some rest.”

“I can’t,” she murmured against him.

“Yes, Layne, you can. I need you to. I didn’t fight like hell for you to run yourself down.” His fingers lifted her face by the chin. “You’re going to need the rest. When I get out of here, my cock is going to be making up for lost time.” He grinned playfully before he closed the gap between their mouths. Passionately, he locked his lips onto hers like he hadn’t tasted her in years.

It was enough that when she finally came up for air, she was already looking a little more amenable to listening to reason.

“I love you. We will be back as soon as we can, okay?” Layne stole one more kiss from him to hold her over until they returned.

While she pulled away to gather her things, Joey looked at Gage. “Don’t—”

His little brother cut him off, “I know. I’ve got her.”

Gage waited for Layne to collect her things before leaving the room with her.

Once the two of them left, Joey exhaled and leaned back. His brows pinched together as he winced in pain, his hand lightly resting on top of his chest. He had done his best to mask the injury’s toll on him for Layne’s sake, but holy fuck. This brush with death and coming to terms with his own mortality had him seeing things in a very different light than he had ever before.

Chapter Three

TROUBLES & BUBBLES

Gage decided to bring her back to his condo in Hudson Yards. There was too much uncertainty surrounding Liam to take the chance of going back to O'Reilly Manor. On the way, Layne texted Sammy to let him know that she needed him to get her home secured. Everything had to be checked from attic to basement, all the locks changed, and the entire residence secured better than Fort Knox. There was no telling what else Liam may have had planned.

After unlocking the door and pushing it open, Gage held a hand out to stop Layne from entering. "Wait."

She drew up a brow at his sudden change of mind. "What is it?"

He gave her his typical smile filled with boyish charm. "I know things didn't go as planned yesterday, but if you're going to have the De Luca last name, I'm going to do right by it."

Before she could ask him what the hell he was going on about, he bent over and scooped her up into his arms. Turning sideways, he carried her into his unit over the threshold.

Layne giggled as her hands clutched onto him. "Are you really that superstitious?"

"When it comes to you, Lucky Charm, I'm not taking my chances." He grinned. Continuing to hold her in his arms, he carried her back to their bedroom and into the master bathroom before setting her down on her feet.

He twisted the faucet on the dark granite tub, filling it with steamy water. Tapping a switch on the wall, he activated the feature that kept the tub at a warm temperature.

Gage stepped over to her, his eyes melting into soft brown hues. His fingers slid the zipper of her hoodie down. "Layne, I want to take all your worries away for a little while."

As his hands pushed the sweatshirt from her upper body, she felt her breaths fill with the familiar heaviness of desire. Her body began to ease as the scent of the oils and salts in the bathwater began to fill the air with eucalyptus and mint.

He hooked his finger onto the thin gold chain of the discreet collar he had bestowed on her, pulling her closer to him. His lips drifted across the side of her face until his mouth was at her ear, whispering, "Let me."

Her hands came to the front of his chest, fingertips exploring the curve of each of his muscles underneath the cotton t-shirt. "I don't even want to remember where I am when you're done." She pleadingly gazed up at him with her eyes still reflecting the pain of tears long since dried.

"Baby, the only thing I need you to remember is how goddamn good my cock feels stuffed inside you." His finger released the thread of metal around her throat and grabbed her by the back of her neck. Gage's lips crashed against hers, kissing her hungrily.

Each of their hands worked at removing the other's clothing. Layne's hands shoved Gage's shirt up hastily until she couldn't reach up any further to get it over his head, and he assisted in yanking it the rest of the way off. He, in turn, lifted her shirt from her and relieved her of her pants and underwear in one downward motion. Layne's fingers popped the clasp of her bra, dropping it to join the pile on the floor.

Now free of all her clothes, she eagerly pulled at his belt until it gave way, and she worked his zipper down over the large size of his cock, already trying to spring free. Layne's hand slid into the front of his boxers, seeking out his stiff length. Grabbing him, she worked her hand down to the hilt of his swords and back up to the tip.

The deep groan of his voice echoed against the tile walls of the bathroom. The way her fingers curled around his thick cock, firmly working over each inch, had him spiraling into thoughts of the rest of her body squeezing around his dick.

Falling prey to her distraction, he nearly forgot his place. He smirked and grabbed her jaw. "Did I give you permission to touch my cock, baby?

Are you so fuckin' needy for it that you forgot how to get on your knees and beg for me?"

Layne pouted and tried to kiss his observation of the minor infraction away as her hand continued to stroke him. He wasn't having any of it, though. His hand took the length of her ponytail around his hand and tilted her head back before she could try to distract him any further.

Gage grinned, dropping his other hand to remove her grasp on his solid length. "It seems you need a little reminder, don't you?"

"Yes, Sir," she purred.

"Hands on that towel rack and stick your ass out for me." He took his hands off of her to motion at the stainless steel bar that currently had two white body towels folded over it.

Layne looked over at the bar affixed to the wall and smiled. Without arguing, she nodded and walked over to it, her hands yanking each towel hanging from it onto the floor. With some sass in her movements, she curved her hands around the cool metal before she bent at the waist and pushed her ass backward.

Seeing her in a position that he could easily sink himself into, he gave another groan of approval. He quickly finished the job of removing the rest of his clothes. Despite the temptation to just ram into that perfectly tight pussy of hers, he had other plans. He walked over to one of the drawers of the bathroom vanity and reached inside, retrieving one of the few gifts he kept for such an occasion.

Standing at her side, he smirked knowingly at his intentions. His hand reached behind her, dragging a cool metal object between her thighs, coating it with her arousal. "You know what happens when you don't keep your hands to yourself, baby?"

She moaned quietly, feeling the smooth object drag along her slit. Her eyes begged him for something more to sate her lustful appetite. Layne shook her head in response to his question. "No."

"I'm going to make sure you keep them busy." With the small plug now coated in the wetness from her body, he dragged it to her tight back entrance. Gage slowly pushed the acorn-shaped toy into her until it was seated deep inside of her.

Her hands tightened around the rack as she groaned out, feeling the plug gradually stretching her while it was worked inside. It took much more effort to accept Joey into her ass, but the sensation of the toy now inside of her provided an equally welcomed sensation.

"Good girl. You like taking it in your sweet ass, don't you?" His cock was throbbing as he inspected the flare of the metal base between the rounds of each cheek. He gave a hum of approval at the sight.

"Yes, it feels so good." Layne began to straighten up but was met with Gage's hand against her back.

"Oh, you're not done learning your lesson yet, Lucky Charm." His sinful desires prompted the corner of his mouth to pull up into another smirk. Backing up one slow step at a time until he was at the edge of the bath, he sat on the ledge of the rectangular inset that surrounded the infinity pool-style tub in the middle of it. His eyes never left the gorgeous sight of her partially bent over for him with her ass filled with the toy he had filled it with.

He leaned over and turned off the running water that had the tub at their disposal whenever they got around to it. Right now, there were more pressing matters requiring his full attention.

He gave his order, "Come for me. If you want to use those hands for something, you're going to use them on that greedy cunt of yours. I want to watch as you get yourself off."

She hadn't even made a move yet, and he already had a grip on his hard cock, fisting it in long strokes.

Layne peered over her shoulder back at him. "But I'd rather have you." Her eyes lowered to the sight of his swollen dick in his hand, her body aching for it fiercely.

Sternly, he spoke to her, "Baby, I can take in this view all damn day, but you better hope you come before I do if you want any of this."

Holding her position at the towel rack, she dropped a hand between her legs and stroked her fingers over her clit, slick with her desire. Her first moan pierced the air. The tips of her fingers began to rub circles against the sensitive bundle of nerves, prompting her body to fill with pleasure. "Mmm…" Imagining Gage's rough hands coursing over her body, she got lost in the sensation of her fingers working her body over hills of pleasure.

Hearing Layne's moans of self-derived excitement, Gage took his time with himself with each stroke. His cock grew harder as he witnessed every movement she made. He couldn't wait to fuck the ever-living daylights out of her the moment she made herself come.

Layne began to ache for the sensation of her inner walls stretching around a hard cock. Her fingers slid back and pushed two deep inside of herself. She started slowly, working them in and out before picking up the pace with the climb of her needs. "Ohh, Gage," she moaned out as her body began to tremble, knowing he was watching the intimate affair she was having with her body.

He released a low growl in excitement as he watched her slim fingers push inside her tight pussy. "Fuck, baby, I wish you could see how fuckin' delicious you look right now. Your ass filled and your fingers fucking your hot little pussy."

Her hand squeezed onto the towel rack tighter, threatening its stability in the wall, while her hips engaged in a sensual dance with her fingers shifting inside the depths of her core. Having the plug buried inside of her ass while she did so made her crave release all the more.

Layne's knees began to quiver as her peak neared. Driving her fingers inside of her and curling her fingertips, she cried out as her pleasure spilled over the edge and the warmth of her orgasm covered her small digits.

Gage moaned out as his hand squeezed his dick, pumping it harder as he watched Layne make herself come. There was something about making her get herself off that filled him with a heated sense of satisfaction.

She slowly came down from the high of her release, panting as her hand fell from between her thighs. Her body remained bent over, hanging by the one hand that refused to let go of the bar it was latched onto for dear life at this point.

"What a good job you did, baby. But now," he let go of his cock and stood from the edge of the tub before quickly closing the space between them. His hands took her by her waist and pulled her upright with her back against his chest. Gage's hand slid up around her throat, squeezing around her necklace to capture her attention. He growled a whisper into her ear, "It's my turn."

Gage grabbed the hand she had just fucked herself with and sucked her flavor off of each finger. The taste of her body was considered an extra reward for himself after refraining from interrupting that hell of a show she had just given him.

Layne gasped as he possessively took hold of her, feeling his cock pressing against her and making her flush with a renewed flame of desire. The heat of his breath against her neck as he uttered those last few words to her had her feeling like putty.

Dropping his hand away from her throat, Gage pushed her up against an empty space on the wall, using his large and muscular body to keep her held there. His foot kicked her legs apart, giving him more access to her heated cunt. His fingers dipped between her legs to her slick folds, spreading them as he positioned the head of his cock at her entrance. Taking hold of her hands and lacing their fingers together, he pinned her palms against the wall above her head.

She whimpered as she felt him so close, yet not inside her. “Please,” she begged.

Holding her hands tightly, he didn’t need to hear her say more. He thrust himself deep inside of her, getting his dick encased in the warmth of those tight walls. Gage let his primal side take over, not waiting after he pulled back and rammed himself into her again. Aggressively, he kept pumping his cock into her.

Layne cried out as his length pushed against the tightness of her body, delightfully stretching her with his size. Her hands squeezed around his fingers while his body began to feed her pleasure. “Fuck! Yes!” She tilted her head back against his chest, letting him rip away any thoughts of all the negative events that had transpired.

Gage bowed his head down, deeply inhaling the sweet scent of her skin as his mouth roughly sucked at the flesh on the side of her throat. His heavy breaths scorched her skin while he gave her the fucking they both deserved after surviving hell together. When he observed a red patch left behind on her neck from his mouth’s efforts, his teeth proudly nipped at it. He panted through his groans as his hips furiously worked at slamming himself into her body.

Both of them needed this stress relief, a way to let go of everything that had been weighing heavily on them. Layne’s body clamped down on Gage’s cock as she cursed out when another orgasm tore through her, leaving her gasping for air as her body squirmed between him and the wall in front of her.

“That’s it, baby, fucking come all over my cock.” His husky voice dropped low as he kept pushing his dick into her, driving past the tensions of her release, trying to lock down around his length. Grunting through his efforts, his rhythm began to struggle.

She pressed her forehead to the wall as she tried to float back down from her spike of ecstasy. “Gage, I want you to come in my ass,” Layne murmured with the last bits of energy she had left in her, hoping he’d hear her.

Oh, he heard her, and he damn near lost control of his climax. He pulled out of her, withdrawing his hands from hers. His fingers found the base of the plug still secured inside her ass and eased it out of her. “What my Lucky Charm wants, she’s going to get.”

Only having one goal, he discarded the toy onto the floor and shifted her position away from the wall to bend her over. With his cock freshly coated in her cum, he pushed the tip into the puckered hole that had been stretched by the plug. "You ready, baby? This is gonna be quick and dirty." The expanse of each of his hands grabbed a handful of her ass cheeks to steady her body in anticipation of his full entry.

Her palms pressed to the floor as she stood there, already reveling in the initial push of just the round head of his cock in her. Layne nodded her head, "Mmhmm."

Gage sank his cock deeply into her, his fingers digging into her as his grasp tightened. Groaning loudly as he felt the reluctant stretch of the muscle wrapping around him, he felt a tingle travel down his spine. "Fuck!" He withdrew and thrust into her again, yanking her hips back to meet his own. He repeated himself while he moaned out, "Fuck!" He said it several more times, with each frantic and hard shove into her body.

Her body bounced with each impact of his hips, driving his length into her ass. The swell of pleasure had her moans joining him in a sexual symphony.

As he warned, it didn't take long before there was a final plunge of his dick into her. He yelled out, and his throbbing length released the pressure that had been building up. Ropes of cum shot from the tip, filling up the tight space he was nestled into. His hips rolled up against her with each spurt of his release. Heavily panting, he remained seated inside of her as he looked up at the ceiling and closed his eyes for a second, feeling the satisfaction of ecstasy wash over him.

Gage gradually regained his composure, his heart still pounding away inside his chest. Sliding out of her, he happily grinned, seeing his efforts leaking from the hole he had just fucked like a goddamn animal.

He eased Layne upright and turned her to face him. Her face was beautifully flushed, and her emerald hues filled with sated desire. His smile stretched broadly across his face. Gage rested his hand on the side of her face, his light brown eyes taking a mental snapshot of what heaven on earth looked like.

"Have I told you how much I love you? That felt amazing." Layne stood on her tiptoes to lovingly kiss him, to which he pulled her up against him as he met her mouth with a more tender hunger. Allowing some time for them to linger in the moment before he broke the kiss, he leaned down and scooped her up into his arms.

Layne was carried over to the tub, where Gage carefully stepped in and lowered them both down into the steamy water. He shifted her so she was seated in his lap and leaning back against him. She sighed in total relaxation, closing her eyes while she rested her hands on his broad thighs.

They sat there together in the glow of the sunset coming in through the massive window to their right as it dipped below the skyline of the city. Gage took his time making sure that he lathered every inch of her body with soap, washing away all their sweat, fluids, and burdens. It was the best therapy ever for them both.

He leaned back against the side of the tub, willing to hold her for as long as she needed. "Baby, I could spend all night like this with you." He gently kissed the back of her head, hoping he'd always be able to take away her troubles.

Chapter Four

NO NEWS

"I'm dying," Joey grunted. "The food here tastes like Layne cooked it." He tossed the plastic fork down on the tray in front of him. The plate housed what could only be described as slop in a shape that might resemble the food it was supposed to be.

"Fuck you!" Layne's hand smacked his leg at the offensive statement.

It had been a little over three weeks of listening to Joey bitch about still being stuck in the hospital. If it wasn't the food, it was the bed, the lack of anything to do, and most importantly, the lack of sex. At least his chest tube had been removed, and he had been transitioned from the Intensive Care Unit into a regular room as of last week. It granted him a little more freedom and space.

Joey winked at her. "My cock is right here. Mount up, Layney." In response, he got one of those eye rolls from her that made his sexually deprived dick begin to perk up.

Gage laughed as he looked over at Layne and shrugged. "Baby, you have many talents, but cooking is definitely not one of them. There's a reason why Rebecca is always stocking up your freezer with meals."

Layne pointed a finger at Gage. "Don't you start." Her eyes went back to Joey as he sat there in his bed, and she took another bite from her granola bar. After swallowing, she sternly spoke to him, "I told you, you're not getting anything until you're cleared for physical activity. I don't need my last memories of you to be performing CPR on you while your dick is still in me."

Sitting on the spare seat next to a circular table across from Layne and Joey, Gage smirked with pride. "Don't worry, bro. I've been keeping her pussy busy for you." He was all too happy to point it out.

Glaring at his brother, Joey grumbled and shook his head. Other than the moment inside the church, he hadn't even been able to give his wife a proper fucking, and it was leaving him with the worst case of blue balls. He would rather go down drowning in Layne's pussy than via gunshot, that was for sure.

Intentionally, he changed the topic. If they continued talking about sex, he would be tempted to say fuck it and jerk off right there in front of them both.

Approaching the topic cautiously after Layne's last blow-up over her brother, his chocolate-colored eyes looked at Layne, trying to keep his gaze above her shoulders. "Any news on where Liam is holed up?"

She pulled her legs up onto the chair she was sitting in at Joey's bedside as she nibbled at the nut and oat snack in her hand. Shaking her head, she spoke with clear frustration, "No. There's been nothing from the guys on tracking him down. He's gotta be hiding out somewhere. I had Ethan check out his old place down in Tribeca, but it doesn't look like it's been touched since he got arrested." At the same time Ethan had scoped the place out, he had helped her coordinate getting Liam's crap out of there and into storage for the time being.

Gage raised a brow, "Do we even know when he got out? I thought he didn't make bail."

She shrugged. "I didn't think he did either, but both the court clerk and Department of Corrections aren't being cooperative in giving me any information."

Joey blew out a breath of air angrily. "Motherfucker better be prepared when I get out of here. I don't care what rock he is hiding under; I'm going to track his ass down."

Pulling a knee to her chest and resting her chin on top of it, she looked over at him. "And do what, Joey? Give him another chance to finish the job?" She frowned, hating that they were in this situation at all. Despite being her little brother, Liam had shattered the last of her shaky bond with him the day he aimed his weapon at her.

Quickly replacing Joey's feeling of horniness was his rage at the little shithead. "I don't give a fuck, Layne! Sitting here and doing nothing keeps you an open target."

Lifting her chin off her knee, she reflected the irritation right back at him. "I'm not sitting here and doing nothing! Jesus Christ! I've been trying to juggle business, worrying about you, and this entire fucking Liam disaster. What else do you want me to do, huh? If he was smart, he has left the damn country already." Wasn't that wishful thinking?

Deciding to play referee, Gage got up from his chair and walked over to them. "Alright, let's just chill the hell out for a second, okay?" He looked at Layne. "We know you've got a lot going on; nobody is suggesting you handle this all on your own." Then, he turned to Joey. "She's not going to be a target as long as I've got eyes on her. We'll find him."

Just as she was going to tell Gage she didn't need him constantly keeping eyes on her, the same nurse with the dark hair Layne had met up in the ICU walked in with a bright and bubbly smile on her face. "Hope I'm not interrupting; I just need to swap in some fresh fluids." Her hand motioned to the bags leading into Joey's IV.

Joey nodded, "Yeah, go ahead." It would at least give him the opportunity to simmer down a little.

The conversation between the three of them paused with the nurse now present. The general public didn't need to be privy to the plotting and conspiring of her brother's ultimate demise.

Layne felt her phone vibrating in her pocket. She reached in for it and pulled it out, seeing an unknown number on the screen, not an uncommon occurrence given the clientele she worked with. "I need to take this." There was a strong hope that maybe one of her associates had uncovered something useful.

She stood from her seat and walked away from them both, keeping her back to them. Layne stopped and stood at the small table where Gage had left the last half of his lunch, his wallet, and his keys scattered across it. Answering the call, she placed the phone to her ear. "Hello?"

A dark and harsh voice spoke quietly, "Don't say a damn thing. I would hate for one of the nurses to fuck up and introduce a deadly air embolism into fuckface's vein." Liam's voice on the other end of the call sent a chill down her spine.

Glancing back over her shoulder, the nurse was seemingly having a pleasant conversation with the guys. Layne looked back down at the table in front of her as she placed a hand on her hip and bit her tongue. She wanted nothing more than to lay into him with all the hate-filled words she could come up with.

It was clear he knew precisely where she was and who she was with. She couldn't be sure if he was bluffing or not, but after almost losing Joey once, she wasn't going to take the risk of it happening again.

When she said nothing further, Liam continued speaking. "We need to meet and talk." He gave a thoughtful pause before continuing, "Unless you'd rather I find someone else worthy of paying the price on your behalf since your freak of a husband didn't have the good sense to die?"

Layne's body tensed from head to toe with her anger. Her hand squeezed tighter onto her hip to prevent the trembling from her emotions from being visible while adrenaline surged to prompt her heart to gallop in her chest. She tried to swallow down the knot in her throat, but no matter how many times she attempted, it remained lodged there. "Just give me the details." She had chosen her words carefully to not draw any attention from Joey or Gage to the conversation.

The malicious chuckle on the other end of the line made her want to put her fist through a window. Liam responded to her request, "Thirty minutes, House of the Chinese Dragon. Have the good sense to come alone and don't be late, okay? We are long overdue for a little brother-sister bonding time. I would hate to feel like I need to make good on my promises to finally get you to listen."

Being familiar with the restaurant, she knew it would be a tight time-frame to make it down there in half an hour. She didn't even have her damn car here since Gage had insisted on driving her all over the place. "Sure thing."

Before Liam hung up, he left her with a short and artificially sweet goodbye, "See you soon, sis."

Keeping the phone to her ear even after Liam ended the call, she turned around and walked past the guys. On her way by, she pointed to her phone and then out to the hallway to indicate she was going to finish the call right outside Joey's room. She got a nod from each of them in acknowledgment before disappearing from their sight.

Not long after Layne stepped out, the nurse's pager went off, and she glanced down at it. Quickly, she finished up her work of swapping out some bags and making sure that Joey's vitals were all on point before she presumably left to see the next patient.

Joey rubbed his hands over his face tiredly. "I can't sit in this place any longer. It's driving me fucking insane. Not being able to see or touch Layne any time I wake up in the middle of the night is a damn nightmare."

Gage sighed, "I told you, I've got this. Did they give you an idea of when you're being released?" He leaned back against a wall comfortably.

Shaking his head, Joey responded, "If all continues to look good, in the next two weeks. Apparently, I've been healing like a fucking badass." He proudly smiled. "The doctor said on the 15th, I think." Then, it hit him, his smile faded, and he groaned. "Fuuuck." He tilted his head back against his pillow.

Gage's eyes widened with a bit of concern at the sudden shift in Joey's demeanor. "What is it?"

Joey frowned and pulled his head upright again. "That's the anniversary of Layne's mother's death." His fingers combed through his dirty blonde hair. "Goddammit. I have to be out of here before then."

He saw the look on Gage's face, which indicated that while he was empathetic about the gravity of the day itself, his brother was clueless about what it meant for their girl. Joey further explained, "She's going to be a fucking wreck that day, she always is. I'm talking about drinking to find the bottom of the barrel and then some. With everything going on, I have to be there for her this time."

"We'll figure it out, man. I'll talk to the doctor, get him to clear you, and we can both find a way to keep her…preoccupied that day." Gage paused and looked at his watch, "She's been on the phone for twenty minutes."

"Fuck, I hope that means it was good news." Joey shook his head, feeling doubtful.

Gage walked over to the round table where all his belongings were. He grabbed a bag of gummy bears and then paused, tilting his head. "Huh."

Joey raised a brow, "Hm?"

His brother turned with a puzzled and concerned look on his face. "My keys were right here." Gage patted the pockets of his jeans to make sure he hadn't put the set of keys back in them. Each pocket turned up empty.

"Fucking hell." He dropped the bag of gummies down onto the table and jogged out of the room into the hallway. He saw nothing but medical staff and visitors milling about. There was no sign of Layne.

Jumping to the same conclusion as Gage, Joey cursed and shoved the sheets off of himself as he got out of bed. He ripped the tape off where the IV fed into the back of his hand, then pulled the line out. There wasn't even a wince at the pain, which paled in comparison to everything else he had already been through.

If Layne took off, it wasn't for anything good, and Joey wasn't going to wait until he was discharged to get the hell out of this godforsaken hospital. They would have to detain him against his will and have all of the New York Army National Guard posted at the door.

Chapter Five

KUNG PAO CHICKEN

The entire drive into Chinatown had been riddled with enough stress to leave her sweating by the time she finally parked Gage's Jeep. The damn thing had been making a rattling noise inside the dash the entire trip, driving her fucking insane when her nerves were already on edge. He had enough money to live in a ridiculously swanky condo in Hudson Yards but couldn't let go of a rusty piece of shit Jeep? Luckily, he had reinstalled the doors on it after listening to her bitch for an hour about her hair getting whipped around and tangled into the worst knots she had ever dealt with in her life.

Before she left the hospital, she turned off her cell phone to force all calls to go straight to voicemail. She would have to answer to the guys later about taking off, but this was her decision to make. Layne already saw the price Joey had nearly paid, and hell, if she was going to drag either of them further into this shitshow. Liam was her brother, and that made it her problem.

Layne walked down to the little Chinese restaurant half a block from where she parked. The House of the Chinese Dragon was tucked between two other retail spaces. On one side of it was an Asian grocery store, and on the other side? It was what could be called a massage parlor with a very ill-reputed area of expertise.

This wasn't a randomly selected takeout place. Their father, Scott O'Reilly, had made a tradition of taking them here whenever there was something to celebrate. It didn't have to be good grades or a birthday, but he was known to bring them down here after winning a fistfight, closing a deal under the table, or even after their first kill. It was a way of finding comfort in family and food.

As she stared up at the sign written in two languages with the image of a dragon sprawled over the top of it, this place no longer brought the joy and nostalgia it once did. Having her baby, Glock, tucked into the back of her jeans made her feel less anxious but didn't seem to prevent her palms from feeling clammy. She wiped them against the sides of her pants one more time before walking inside the restaurant.

It maintained a rather eye-catching and spacious interior for in-house dining. The little Buddha statue by the door was the first thing she recognized when she entered. Music lightly played in the background like little chimes being struck to mimic cheerful sounds of nature. Inside was just as she recalled, lots of red and black splashed across the decorations and multiple pieces of artwork of dragons in various styles. At the back corner table—her father's favorite—was Liam.

Reminding herself that they were in a public space, she hoped that it would be the one piece of security that would allow this to be as fruitful of a discussion as it possibly could be. Was Liam stupid enough to start a gunfight in public? She was hoping not, but after what transpired on her wedding day, she wouldn't put it past him.

Layne walked past the other tables, most of them full of hungry patrons. Once she was within three feet of the table, Liam looked at her with an at-ease smile. She didn't bother giving him one in return. He may have been happy to see her disregarding all the red alarms sounding in her head, but she wanted nothing but to come in here with a stick of dynamite to shove up his ass.

He looked the way he always had in some ways but different in others. His smug fucking face was laced with signs of an ugly heart turned black. His auburn hair was no longer in a messy heap on his head but smoothly styled with an off-center part. Liam's hazel eyes seemed darker in an unsettling way, with less of the green popping through the brown. The clothes he wore now looked like he owned a Fortune 100 company. The black tie paired with his custom designer suit was screaming for her to tighten it until he choked to death. Did he think he was Dad? He was far from it, in her not-so-humble opinion.

"I was beginning to think you weren't going to show. You had two minutes to spare." He took a slow sip from the small ceramic cup in his hand, swallowing down the serving of green tea. "Are you going to sit or just stand there glaring at me?"

Layne pulled a chair out for herself opposite him and plunked down into it. She crossed one leg over the other and crossed her arms in front of her stomach. "Nice suit. A little out of your budget, though, isn't it?" She had been monitoring all the cash, including what was set aside for Liam before he had gotten arrested. His name wasn't listed on any of the accounts, so he had to be getting funds elsewhere.

He grinned at her as one of his hands ran down the smooth material of the jacket. "You like it? I reached out to Dad's old tailor, and he hooked me up."

So, he really was trying to emulate Dad, wasn't he?

"Where did you get the cash?" Her voice was flat in an effort not to let her emotions boil up to a full rage just yet. Flipping the fuck out and scaring all the innocent bystanders was not going to be in her best interest.

He sat back in his seat; his eyes remained on her. "Well, no thanks to you, I had to make a few business deals of my own. Knowing that Dad left everything to you, I took a few proactive steps to ensure that I had some rainy-day funds. I made a few friends, did a little negotiating, and kept those important details to myself." Liam shrugged like it was as much of a common practice as opening a savings account.

There were so many questions she wanted answers to, with the biggest one being whether he wanted his body buried or cremated. Layne sat there, looking far more casually dressed in her jeans and snug-fitting black button-up blouse. The loose waves of her chestnut hair hung down a couple of inches past her breasts. The light above the table caused Gage's gold necklace around her neck to shimmer subtly.

"What's the point of all this, Li?" The first hints of pain tainted her words. She shook her head in disappointment. It wasn't just him she was disappointed in, but herself for somehow never seeing it coming down to this. "The money was there, all you had to do was work for it. I didn't ask for a whole hell of a lot from you."

The corners of his mouth twitched in amusement. "You think this was about money? Cute, Layne. Real cute." He set his cup of tea down on the red linen tablecloth. "Where do you want to begin? For starters, Mom dies, and you shack up with the man responsible for it."

Her facial expression slipped, indicating her surprise at his knowledge of Joey's involvement in their mother's demise. In turn, Liam grinned menacingly as he continued to explain, "Yeah, I know all about it. After realizing you were falling to your knees for our masked friend's dick, I did some research. It wasn't easy, but I see why Dad never traced it back during the hiring process. That fucker has some friends in high places."

He shifted in his seat with a smirk, "Did you know that he was fucking the former mayor's daughter at one point before blowing her dad away on his way out the door? I bet the cum was still freshly smeared over her thighs. Sheesh, he knows how to pick jobs with benefits. I'm almost jealous."

She recalled a contract Joey had taken and executed on the retired mayor back after Eric Ellis had been eliminated. He wouldn't have betrayed her, would he?

Layne gritted her teeth, trying her best not to take anything Liam was saying to heart. There was no telling if he was lying out of his ass or telling the truth. Even if he was being honest for once, she was never ignorant of what type of work Joey often was contracted for. Yet, that little tidbit about the mayor's daughter refused to be unheard.

She shook her head and pushed her chair back to stand up. Liam smirked. "You may want to sit back down until I'm finished." He jutted his chin in the direction of a table near the door. "You see that man in the Yankees cap? All he has to do is make the call, and my contacts at the hospital will make sure that there is an unfortunate incident of gross medical malpractice."

He motioned at another table closer to them. "That one there is always looking for a reason to strangle a pretty face to death. When he heard you nearly drowned once, you should have seen how quickly he nearly busted the zipper of his pants with his erection. The way he's been looking at you since you walked in the door, I would say he might even have a crush on you."

She glanced at both the referenced men. The Yankee fan's face was obscured by the shadows of his location in the restaurant while he had his nose buried behind a newspaper. As for the other man, she was sure to remember his face in the event she ever saw that fucker again. Begrudgingly, she sat back down. This time, she let her anger and hatred start to seep into her eyes, no longer trying to host a composed front. "Fucking talk quicker then," Layne spat out impatiently.

Liam was more than happy to draw this out as long as he wanted, knowing he had her full attention for as long as he wanted it. "In addition to your poor taste in men, you ended up fucking me out of a very beneficial deal with Eric Ellis. I stood to take control of several of his business ventures, plus one more for every baby he knocked you up with."

God, she was thankful she wasn't ordering food, or else she would have projectile vomited across the table at the thought of procreating with Eric. She wasn't looking for any offspring with anybody, and Liam was a prime example of why birth control was a life necessity.

"I knew one day you might find evidence that Dad left you everything, but I never expected you to seriously try to take control of it all. I'm glad I began making plans to ensure I could take back what has always been rightfully mine." With the way Liam was now glaring at her, this was the part that burned him up the most. Layne had what he wanted and what he thought he deserved. How toddler-like of him.

She shifted in her seat, refusing to interrupt him and draw this out any longer than necessary.

Liam continued droning on, "Did you know that Kristill had this special ability to suck the information out of just about anyone? Quite literally, her blow jobs were that phenomenal. I'm kind of regretting my decision to kill her when she threatened to tell you everything." He had the nerve to look remorseful.

"I digress, though. Based on her talented efforts, when I found out you would be beating the crap out of some fucker for information months ago, I thought having her tip off the cops would get you busted and thrown behind bars." He shook his head with disappointment that it hadn't gone that way at all.

"I had to change up my strategy after that. Thanks to that beautifully sloppy mouth of hers, the judge granted me release on my own recognizance. After that, it was smooth sailing, dropping a few pennies into several pockets to keep it all very hush-hush. I wanted our reunion to be a surprise. Shooting your husband instead of you was just a happy little accident." His smile was filled with anything but warmth upon his last statement.

Layne leaned over in her seat after she memorized every damn word he was saying to her. She spoke through her clenched jaw, "Fuck. You. You're a goddamn embarrassment to our family name."

Her brother sat there for a second in silence before he also leaned in closer from the other side of the table, lowering his voice. "As the Upper East Side whore, who really is the embarrassment here?"

The temptation to reach back for her gun and off him in the middle of the restaurant was growing by the second. She ran quick calculations on the likelihood of ending up in prison without either Joey or Gage, and it wasn't odds she wanted to take. But hell, if it wasn't an enticing thought.

Layne eased back into her seat. "Why the hell am I here, then? What do you want?"

Seeing her back down from the edge of her temper, ready to explode, he also sat back. "Everything. Every asset, every dollar, and all the damn respect that I've been owed. If I get that, I'll give you a once-in-a-lifetime opportunity to leave New York and never come back."

He was the worst fucking liar. "Why don't you just try shooting me again? Because you're not getting any of those things from me." She had clawed her way from the bottom to get where she was. Layne wasn't about to give it up because her brother suddenly found his balls and showed up to the game.

"Oh, believe me, Layne, I will, and I won't miss. I'm being gracious enough to try and make this as peaceful of a transition as possible. Now that you know how serious I am, I'm hoping you will come to your senses." He plucked up a fortune cookie off a plate in the middle of the table and cracked it open. Pulling the little paper message out, he barked out a laugh. "Shit, it seems that even my fortune knows I'm destined for greatness."

When Liam tossed the rectangular piece of paper at her, she rolled her eyes and looked at the message typed on it, 'There can only be one crown found through greatness in forming unexpected alliances.' Well, this was the biggest piece of vague bullshit she had read from an all-foreseeing cookie.

Her brother checked his phone before tucking it into the interior breast pocket of his suit. "As much as I would love to stay here and discuss this further, I have some clients who are waiting on me. I will be in touch but just know one more thing. If you start taking too long to come to terms with this, I won't hesitate to forcefully take everything you have one asset at a time. If it comes to that point, I will find more creative and personal methods to persuade you to cooperate."

Liam got out of his seat and straightened out his suit jacket, smoothing his hands over the front of it. He came over to her side, placing one hand on the back of her chair and the other on the edge of the table. Bowing his head down, he whispered to her, "I heard Rebecca is still single; do you think she still has that middle-school crush on me?"

That was the tipping point. Her anger spilled over the edge, and she began to rise from her seat, ready to break her hand on his face a thousand times over. Her brother anticipated as much and grabbed her roughly by the back of the neck, forcing her back down into her seat.

Keeping his words quiet, he snarled into her ear. "Fucking try me, Layne. I've made a lot more friends than you even realize. I could blow your damn brains out right now, then sit down for some kung pao chicken, and nobody here would blink a damn eye."

She winced as his grasp on her painfully tightened. Just when she thought maybe her head would pop off her shoulders like a broken bobble-head, his hand released her, leaving a red mark behind on her fair skin.

He straightened up and gave her a pleasant smile like they just had the best time catching up. "This was nice; I'm looking forward to our next chat sometime soon. Enjoy the rest of your day, sis." Liam nodded to the two men he had drawn attention to earlier, and both got up from their respective tables. The three of them left the Chinese restaurant, leaving Layne behind.

Layne sat there hoping to feel a sense of relief now that he was gone, but that sense of dread never lifted.

Chapter Six

CONFESSIONS

Layne sat there inside Gage's Jeep, staring at her phone cradled in her palm. The logo popped up on the screen as it powered back on. Moments after it booted up, the backlogged text messages from the group chat between her, Gage, and Joey began to pour in.

GAGE

Where are you?

JOEY

Answer your damn phone.

GAGE

Layne?

Baby, we need to know you're safe.

JOEY

Layne, so help me.

Where the fuck did you go??

Give us something to work with.

GAGE

You don't get to get up and ditch us like you're the only one capable of making decisions in this relationship!

THIS IS FUCKING BULLSHIT!!

That's when the texts stopped coming in from Gage. Joey had sent several more repeating things he had already said. It had been the only thing they could do without more information on her whereabouts. Gage tended to be more patient with her, so the fact he had lost his shit in the chat had her shrinking down lower into a darker headspace than she was already in.

Layne leaned forward in the driver's seat, resting her forehead against the worn and faded leather-wrapped steering wheel. She tried to rein in all the competing emotions of guilt, stress, fear, and anger. She knew that leaving without saying a word to either of them was less than fair, but risking their lives thanks to her brother's newfound penchant for retribution was also unfair. Seeing Joey on the cusp of death was an image that would never leave her and one she never wished to see again.

Her phone began ringing in her hand. Lifting her head upright, she saw Gage's name sprawled across the top of the screen. She frowned, preparing to get an earful. Her finger swiped, and she answered, "Hey, I'm okay." She figured reassuring him she wasn't lying dead in an alley somewhere probably was at the top of the list of things to say.

Waiting for Gage to scream or even say anything at all felt like an eternity.

He blew out a breath of air into the phone. "What the hell, Layne?" His tone wasn't loud or angry but was full of a wearisome relief.

When she wasn't greeted with the same level of aggression he had reflected in his last texts to her, she hoped it meant he would give her the chance to explain herself.

"Look, I'm sorry I didn't say anything. I can explain, but I can't talk about it while you're still there at the hospital. Tell Joey I didn't have a choice or time to spare." The last thing she wanted was for either of them to think that she had worried them without good reason. "I can come back to the hospital to pick you up, then fill you in." Not knowing where Liam had prying ears, Layne didn't dare risk saying anything out loud about his continued threats directed at those she loved the most.

Gage responded, "Don't bother. I got a ride back to your place; I hoped maybe you'd show up here. Just… Just come home, and we can talk about it. I'll let Joey know you're alright."

She nodded, even though he couldn't see it. "Thanks. I'll be there in twenty."

When Gage hung up with Layne, he shook his head, still pissed off. He had the call on speaker so Joey could listen as they both stood there in the living room of O'Reilly Manor.

"She better have a damn good excuse for this shit." He looked over at Joey. The last time she had gone missing had been at the hands of the she-bitch, Danielle Spencer. That had been enough hell for him to endure for years to come.

Joey perched himself on the arm of the sofa, arms crossed in front of his chest. "Let me deal with it when she gets here." His hand lifted to pinch the bridge of his nose as the sound of her voice had given him hope that whatever had pulled her away left her unscathed.

Shaking his head, Gage shoved his phone into his pocket. "No, this is a problem for all three of us." He let his thoughts begin to unravel and get the better of him again. "Fuck! What was going through her head to take off like that? Is she trying to get herself killed?"

All Joey could do was shrug as he was wondering the same things as his brother. He knew Layne, he knew her weak spots, and that meant Liam likely knew them as well. If he had anything to do with what had drawn her out into the open, he feared this wouldn't be the last time.

Finally, Joey stood up from his spot on the sofa and walked over to Gage. "You can't push her too hard until we know what happened. She'll push back and then shut down entirely."

Gage didn't like it, but he knew the last thing they wanted was for her to feel like she wasn't safe to confide in him and Joey. They both loved her deeply, more than life itself, and their feelings for her had no contingencies. If she was getting pulled into a shitty situation, they were going to dive into it with her. The tricky part was getting her to understand and accept that.

The entire drive back uptown, Layne was caught up in her thoughts. Was it worth fighting this battle with Liam? What were her options when the risks involved some incredibly hefty costs? What went on when Joey took his contracts? The second her doubts about Joey's loyalty to her heart sprang up inside her mind; she felt a pang of guilt for even questioning his faithfulness. But…

She parked the Jeep out front and walked up the porch steps slowly. Each step was slower than the last as she approached the front door with dread of the conversation she was going to have with Gage.

Pushing the door open and walking in, she called out, "Gage?" She shut the door behind her.

"I'm in here," he called from the living room.

Layne walked through the foyer and into the living room, where she saw him sitting on one of the ottomans that paired with an oversized chair. He was leaning forward with his elbows on his knees. His tender eyes looked up to gaze at her, still reflecting the pain of her disappearance and the disappointment in the lack of her trust to confide in him.

Her face fell, and her heart crumpled as she saw the way he was still struggling with what she had done and put him through. She began her heartfelt apology, "I'm so, so sorry, Gage. I couldn't…"

That's when a hand came and grabbed her hip from behind, turning her around to come face-to-face with Joey.

"Couldn't what, Layney?" He guided her backward until the wall was flush with her spine, and he was leaning into her space with his other hand braced against the wall.

From the light scent of soap and the sight of his dirty blonde hair still damp, he must have just gotten out of the shower. The rest of him was dressed in a pair of jeans and a long-sleeved crimson tee. It had been far too long since she had seen him in anything from the bland and unflattering hospital gown.

Her eyes widened in disbelief that she was seeing him standing there before her in the home they shared. He should have still been in the hospital; he wasn't slated to be released for a couple of weeks. Blinking several times through the shock of it all, she glanced over at Gage, who was now getting up off of the ottoman to join them both.

Joey's hand left her hip and cupped her jaw, turning her attention back to him. "Eyes on me. You couldn't what, Layne? Couldn't be bothered to tell us where you were running off to? Couldn't care less what the hell we would think? Go ahead, explain to us what you couldn't do."

Layne's mind was still stuck on processing his presence before her. "They discharged you?"

Gage spoke up from a step behind his brother, "He discharged himself when we didn't know where the fuck you were."

She pitched herself forward into Joey's chest, wrapping her arms around his waist as immense relief overcame her. "Thank God!" Her eyes squeezed shut tightly as she inhaled the hint of leather and sage that had been missing the entire time he had been a patient at the hospital. Having him home again gave her back a little peace of mind.

The very sudden and emotional reaction had been unexpected. Joey had been ready for her to barrage him with her headstrong attitude about why she had done what she had. He had been prepared to hear her tout something along the lines of being capable of defending herself in dangerous situations. He hadn't expected her to fall victim to a softer set of emotions.

His arms embraced her upper body, holding her close despite the lack of answers about her whereabouts. Joey sighed, and his voice softened as he pressed a kiss to the top of her head. As angry as he was about her choices, it felt good to wrap his arms around her again without all the excess medical equipment getting in the way.

When she was ready, she pulled her head from his chest with her stunning green eyes soaked with her recently shed tears. She sniffled and rushed to erase them from her face with the backs of her fingers. "Sorry..."

"Baby," Gage moved to the side of them. "Don't be sorry; we just need to know what the hell happened." His hand came to the small of her back and gently rubbed it to help soothe whatever feelings had those pretty little eyes tearing up.

She shook her head and looked down. Without hesitation, Joey's fingers captured her chin and tilted her head back up. The concern was painted across his face. "There's nothing the three of us can't figure out," he assured her.

"I underestimated Liam." She went to lower her face again, but Joey's hold on her chin prevented her from hiding herself from either of them. "This is all my fault; I should have seen the signs. He's been making moves since God knows when. At this point, I'm beginning to question whether or not he has been plotting shit since he was born."

At the mention of Liam, Gage's jaw tensed, and his eyes darkened with fury. "Please tell me you didn't take off on us to go meet up with him. Not after what he did."

Layne didn't need to say anything. When her eyes looked at Gage apologetically, it had him grumbling under his breath, "Son of a bitch."

Joey shot a hard glance at Gage, warning him to keep himself in check. Then, he looked at Layne and ran his fingers along the side of her face before sliding them into the depths of her brunette locks. "None of this is your fault. If I ever hear you say that again, I will wash your mouth out with my cock every night for a month straight."

He pulled her mouth up to his before whispering against her lips, "And before you get too excited about that prospect, I should add that it won't be getting buried in other parts of you afterward."

Closing his grasp on a handful of her hair, he remained painfully close to the pale pink of her lips. "Do you understand me, Layney?"

As quiet as a mouse, she uttered her response, "Yes." It was hard to tell if Joey was bluffing or not, the man had yet to show any amount of restraint when it came to fucking her. However, she enjoyed his cock in her too much to find out just how much he was willing to stick to his word.

"Good. Now," he released her hair and leaned back away from her without ever gracing her with the kiss she had been expecting. "Go sit your ass down and tell us everything."

Both her brows lifted the second he retreated from her. "You're not even going to bother giving me a kiss?"

"If I put my mouth on you right now, the only discussion that will end up taking place is going to be you screaming out my name." One thing Joey didn't have was an infinite amount of control. After a few weeks of going without so much as a hand-job from her, he barely trusted himself to be in the same room as her without yanking her pants down and jackhammering into her.

When she looked over at Gage for some level of backup, he merely shrugged at her. "Don't look at me, Lucky Charm. You're going to have a lot to answer for when I get my hands on you."

Great. She knew she had some explanations to make, but she hardly expected to have them both keeping their distance from her in the interim.

Layne took up a spot in the center of the couch. They both followed, and while Gage seemed to prefer standing, Joey sat across the way in a plush armchair. Both sets of brown eyes were on her, patiently waiting for her to lay everything out on the table.

She started from the moment that Liam had called her and walked them through everything up until the time he left the House of the Chinese Dragon. Neither of the guys interrupted her, though, at some points, it looked like Joey was going to put his fist through the glass coffee table in front of him.

"I couldn't risk it, not knowing whether or not he could actually follow through on his threats." Layne sank back into the couch now that she had retold the entire incident.

Gage squinted his eyes in confusion, trying to follow Liam's logic. "Wait. Besides the part where he's a whiny bitch unable to cope with you being in charge, part of this whole damn thing is because he's pissed thinking that Joey executed a contract on your mom?" He scoffed in disbelief.

She shifted uncomfortably, as did Joey. It wasn't a topic they often discussed. They had talked about it enough times to work through the painful realities of it. Layne had gotten to a place where she was able to redirect the blame onto the man who had given the orders, Michael Franzetti. If it hadn't been Joey, it would have just been someone else.

Noticing the awkward silence that fell upon both Layne and Joey, Gage blinked several times in disbelief. He looked at Joey. "Seriously? That's fucked up."

Joey cleared his throat to try and push past the lingering guilt over it. "It was long before I knew Layne." There wasn't a day that passed where he didn't regret that entire fucking contract.

Shifting his attention back over to Layne, Gage now better understood Joey's insistence about being there for Layne on her mother's death anniversary.

Layne busied her hands with a strand of her hair between her fingers as she thought about what else Liam had said about Joey's past. It was something she had deemed unnecessary to bring up during the rundown. "Yeah, so, that's about it. He left it pretty fuckin' vague on when he expected me to get my affairs in order. It could be tomorrow, or it could be three months from now, for all I know."

Standing, Joey pulled out his phone from his pocket and began texting quickly. "I'll get Brandon working on seeing what he can find out about the two other guys that showed up to the lunch date with Liam." After several more taps of the screen, he sent the request over and returned the device to where it came from.

Having a better understanding of why Layne had done what she had, Gage came over to sit next to her on the couch. "Baby," he placed a hand on her thigh. "I'm sorry I lost it. I know you want to make sure everybody is safe, but you can't do that when you don't have someone watching your back."

"He's right, Layne. This can't be an ongoing thing. If Liam knows hanging this threat over your head will lure you to him, he will keep playing that card for as long as he can," Joey piped up, also rising and joining them on the couch on the other side of her.

She looked at them both, wondering how she got so lucky. Two men who loved her to a fault. Two men who would never rest when it came to her protection. Two men who were way too close to her to have any sense at all. Layne wondered how soon her luck would turn bad if she didn't start playing some Russian roulette.

Chapter Seven

HELLO & GOODBYE

"Joey! Fuck! Joey!" Layne cried out as his hips slammed into her again.

After they discussed Layne's little disappearing act to have a chat with Liam, it seemed the air shifted around them quicker than an approaching hurricane. When she leaned over Joey to place her gun and its holster on the side table, his most primal instincts had taken over. The way her body brushed against him in that innocent movement, the light curve of her back that led over her ass which was all but short of presenting itself in front of him, and the quiet groan she made as her arm stretched to reach over to the table on his left. Joey's restraint promptly left the building.

His cock had dictated that it find itself deep inside of her with such an urgency that when he grabbed Layne, the startled look on her face drove him even further into a frenzy. He had tossed her onto her stomach on the sofa and yanked her pants down enough to expose the sight of her pussy that he would happily risk a torturous death for. Joey barely waited for a breath after opening his jeans and pulling out his aggressive hard-on before he shoved himself inside her like a man who had been stranded in the goddamn Sahara, and her body was the oasis he needed to survive.

Layne felt his hands tightly gripping her hips for dear life as he rammed his steel-like cock into her. Her pleasure immediately blindsided her, leaving her moaning out intensely without so much as a chance to ask him what he was doing. His rough entry had her cunt aching as it stretched around him. Yet, all of it was welcomed after the medically mandated hiatus.

He hadn't been the only one that had missed this. While Gage had been more than happy to tend to all of her needs, he still wasn't Joey. Each De Luca had their own particular flavor, and she couldn't handle not having a little bit of both swirled together in her life.

Standing in front of the couch, Gage was giving his brother the moment to satisfy himself with Layne, but he was sure as hell staying for the show. His hand was fisting his cock as he watched their girl get her pussy claimed in a moment of heated passion. "Goddamn, baby," he groaned. "You're taking Joey's cock so well." His brother sure as hell wasn't going easy on her, but Layne still welcomed him with open arms, er…legs.

Kneeling behind Layne while he roughly fucked her from behind, Joey groaned out. "That's right, Layney." He panted hard at the physical exertion on his still-recovering body. He growled, pushing at his limits, "Take this cock like my good fucking girl." Despite getting winded, he didn't give a damn if his heart exploded, he was going to get his fix of her one way or another.

Each harsh thrust into her had her body lurching forward, only to have Joey's grasp pull her hips right back against him. There was no escaping the mounting pressure that was building deep inside her core. Every collision of their bodies had his dick crashing against her sweet spot.

Her hands clawed at the cushions underneath her as her body trembled with the rapidly approaching climax. She whimpered his name as she teetered right on the border of divine release.

That's when Joey smirked and sank himself into her again. "You better show me how much you enjoy getting fucked by your husband while Daddy Gage watches." His hand reached down to grab her hair enough to turn her head so she could see Gage handling his swords in a smooth corkscrew motion.

Joey rolled his hips into her again, watching her face as it showed signs of slipping right off the ledge of ecstasy. Her vocalized orgasm filled the room and was music to his damn ears. His cock was throbbing, and he had barely made it this far along without blowing his load, so when he felt Layne's walls clamp down around him, he knew he was done for.

Her body pushed and pulled at him simultaneously as she fell into the crashing waves of her release. She wasn't even sure what words poured out of her mouth or if they were even words at all.

With Layne's body coming for him, Joey hastily got the final few thrusts into her before he joined in the blissful state of relief. His dick pulsed as he filled her depths with his hot seed.

When it was all said and done, Joey was still trying to catch his damn breath. It felt like he had just run a marathon—untrained. Oh, but it had been worth it.

His hand patted Layne's ass after he pulled out of her with a satisfied sigh. He fell back onto his ass and let the couch give him the rest he needed.

That was Gage's cue that he was up. He came over to her and eased her from the couch, not intending to make her well-worked cunt take any more dick today. He smiled at her and got her down on her knees in front of him, his thick cock in front of her face already primed by the efforts of his hand.

"Alright, baby, let me see you swallow my swords." Gage grinned at her, his thumb tugging at the bottom of her chin to draw her mouth open.

Late the following night, the three of them showed up at Rebecca's apartment. Layne was doing her best to ignore the soreness from Joey's pounding into her yesterday as she walked. Firmly, she rapped her knuckles against her best friend's door.

There was the sound of the scurrying on the other side of the door, Rebecca called out, "Be right there!"

Layne's heart already ached that it was coming down to this, but it was in everyone's best interest. She couldn't afford to be selfish when Liam was out there ready to prey on anybody who held value to Layne.

Rebecca turned the lock from the other side before swinging the door open. Her face was full of emotion as she saw Layne standing there, mirroring the same feelings. Joey and Gage stood at Layne's back, giving the girls enough space to greet one another.

"Are you ready?" Layne looked down at a few bags sitting just right inside the doorway. Maybe if she just focused on the checklist of things in her head, she could avoid turning both of them into a sappy puddle of emotions.

That all went out the window as Rebecca immediately grabbed onto

Layne and squeezed her into a hug that was tighter than life itself. Layne rested her head on Rebecca's shoulder as she shut her eyes, returning the hug equally tight.

"I told myself I wasn't going to cry," Rebecca gave a half-hearted giggle overtop a partial sob.

Layne sniffled, trying to ignore the tears welling up behind her closed lids. All Layne could do was nod, afraid that if she said anything, she would lose her already shaky composure.

When Rebecca pulled back, she noted Layne's fingers were already trying to erase any evidence of the tears that had begun to slip from her green hues. She frowned, not liking the way this situation had Layne in such a pained state.

"I shouldn't be leaving you like this," Rebecca tried to push back on Layne's demand that she pack her bags and indefinitely go live with her mother several states away.

Immediately, Layne straightened up and snapped her guarded exterior back into place. "Rebecca, you are getting on the train, and don't you dare say otherwise."

Her best friend's voice wavered underneath the weight of the thought of abandoning someone whom she held such a tight bond with. "I want to be here for you." The blue eyes looking at Layne right now were filled with the pain of the unknown, swirling with concern and sadness.

Layne stood there in silence as she tried to find the words to make her friend understand why it was necessary for her to suddenly pick up and leave. The breath of her inhale was rocky but managed to smooth out when it was exhaled. "I don't know what is going to happen. Liam is no longer who I thought he was; he has threatened everyone and anyone in my world. I'll be damned if I let you get caught in his crossfire. I can't deal with him when I'm worried about who will end up as collateral. I won't do it, Rebecca."

Frowning, Rebecca still felt a sense of disbelief that it was all coming to this. Liam may have been the asshole little brother, but it was hard to imagine that he would fall this far down the path of depravity.

Joey spoke up, trying to give them both a gentle reminder, "We need to get going if we are going to make it there on time."

Following up on that, Gage came to the doorway. "I'll get your bags."

After collecting Rebecca's luggage, they all went back down to Joey's car. Rebecca climbed into the backseat first. Before Layne joined her, Gage paused her with his hand on her shoulder.

"It's only temporary." He ran his hand up along the side of her neck before stroking his thumb across her cheek tenderly. It killed him to see Layne making the difficult decision of parting ways with a piece of her heart, not knowing what was going to happen after this was all done and over.

Layne stared into his gentle eyes, and she wanted more than anything to believe him. "I hope so." She ducked into the backseat.

After each of the guys took up the seats up front, Joey drove them to Penn Station. The air was thick with silence the entire trip. Rebecca reached over and held Layne's hand tightly. It was the only communication needed between them.

Once they were inside the busy train station, Layne stood in front of Rebecca. "I know there's a lot up in the air right now, so I want you to take this." She reached into her coat pocket and pulled out a thick envelope. "It should be more than enough to pay the bills for a few months."

Rebecca shook her head adamantly. "Layne…I can't take this." Her hand pushed the envelope back toward Layne.

"No, you can. Please, Rebecca." Layne reached over, grabbed her friend's hand, and placed the money-filled envelope into her palm. "It's the least I can do for uprooting you away from your life here so suddenly."

Reluctantly, her friend accepted the wad of cash safely secured in the envelope. Shoving it into one of her bags, she gratefully looked at Layne. "I plan on giving every dollar in here straight back to you when I come back."

Forcing a light smile past the looming goodbyes quickly approaching them, Layne leaned in for one last hug. "And I will still argue with you when you do."

A barely coherent voice came over the speaker system, announcing the boarding for Rebecca's train. Rebecca squeezed Layne even tighter than she had earlier. "Be safe."

Layne responded with as much reassurance as she could muster, "I always am."

"Fucking liar," Rebecca quickly retorted with a grin.

They both shared a soft laugh to overshadow the grim truth.

Releasing the woman she considered a sister, Layne shooed her with her hand. "Get outta here before you miss your train."

Drawing in a breath to find the courage to go through with this, Rebecca looked at the two men standing close by. "You two better take care of her." She wagged a finger at them threateningly.

Joey grinned. "Don't worry, Rebecca, she's in good hands."

"As long as she listens to us for once," Gage smirked, then shot a look at Layne.

Rebecca put on her bravest face, readjusted the strap of her bag over her shoulder, and pulled her miniature suitcase with her as she took the first steps towards the stairs leading down to the platform. Before she was out of sight, she looked back at Layne and blew her a kiss.

Without a second thought, Layne blew one right back. She didn't want to imagine if this was her bestie's last memory of their time together, but Layne sure as hell hoped it would be a positive one.

She stood there long after Rebecca disappeared down the steps to get on that train down to Baltimore. "Now is your chance to join her if either of you want a ticket out. I'm not going to ask either of you to stay here with me, knowing how messy this is going to get."

Layne knew it was a long shot, but she wished they would both take her up on the offer. If she didn't need to worry about either man's safety, maybe there was a chance she could keep her head screwed on straight.

"Always and forever, Layney. You're not getting rid of me that easily." Joey's hand slid across her upper back to rest on her shoulder.

Gage's hand did the same and rested on her opposite shoulder. "You're my Lucky Charm, that's not something that you just leave behind. I'm afraid you're stuck with me too, baby."

She slowly nodded. "Okay, then. Let's find out what other fucked up plans Liam has."

Chapter Eight

FAMILY DISPUTES

Layne groaned, rubbing the heels of her palms over her eyes as she sat at her desk. It was nearly three in the damn morning. She knew she was burning the candle at both ends but couldn't find it within herself to give a fuck and surrender to her body's demands for rest. Time was of the essence if she was playing catch-up on whatever strategy Liam had been concocting for months if not years.

She had snuck out of bed in her black joggers and matching cropped camisole, leaving Joey soundly asleep while he caught up on his still much-needed rest and recovery. Despite his reassurances, he was nowhere near back to his prime after the shooting.

As for her other love, Gage was likely wrapping up at Cassidy's Chains about now, the recently renamed strip club-turned-night club. Whether he intended to come back here or just crash at his condo was always a toss-up on any given night.

After speaking with her senior advisor, Thomas, earlier in the evening, it was noted that the relations between her alliances were getting dicey. Contradicting reports were coming in about who did and did not support Layne after the misfortune of events the day she and Joey were married. Some factions thought Liam's move was ballsy enough that perhaps he was a worthy connection to side with. Regardless of Thomas' words of comfort, this would all blow over in time; she didn't feel any less stressed out. All her hard work to get where she was, and now Liam's emergence was fucking it to hell and back.

Now, here she was listening to Jonathan, her prized political negotiator, about how another faction was refusing to do so much as keep their eyes or ears open for Liam and whatever crew he was working with. How was it that no one could tell her the extent of what he had managed to pull together underneath her nose? He had gone dark, and nobody knew a thing? She found that fucking hard to believe.

"There's nothing I can do about it," Jonathan apologized for the umpteenth time on the other end of the phone that lay on top of her desk on speaker. He continued, "The Holskis are claiming that they don't want involvement in a family dispute."

"*Family dispute?!*" she shrieked. Great, just fucking great. Another flakey-ass criminal organization was going to turn a blind eye. Trying to reel herself back in, she lowered the volume of her voice. "Keep putting pressure on them, make whatever negotiations you have to. I don't care what the hell it costs, we can't afford to lose support right now."

After their goodbyes, Layne hung up and pushed away from the desk. She walked over to the window that overlooked the street out front. It was as empty as the room she was standing in.

Alone with her thoughts, she got lost in the web of hypotheticals being woven in her brain. Were any of them going to be left standing at the end of this? Could she pull the trigger to end her brother's life? Maybe if she gave herself up, Joey and Gage would have a chance at survival.

Her train of thought was interrupted as her cell phone began ringing from its position on her desk. Layne rushed over and answered, "Yes?"

Silence.

"Hello?" Her voice carried the crankiness from her lack of sleep. She double-checked to make sure the call was still connected before she repeated herself.

More silence.

She turned her back to the door so she could perch her ass on the edge of her desk. "Oh, for fucks sake," she was prepared to hang up until she heard the silence breaking on the other end.

Liam's laughter echoed in the receiver like he had just delivered the world's funniest punchline. "Jesus Christ, Layne. You sound stressed. You should learn to let loose a bit. Go get a massage or some shit."

If she hadn't been dealing with high blood pressure before, she sure as hell was now when she heard him on the other end of the line.

"What the fuck do you want?" she muttered tiredly.

"Just checking in on my big sister, making sure you're doing okay. Is that a crime?" Liam nearly had her convinced for a split second that he gave a damn.

Looking at the clock hung on the wall, she forced out her exhale. "Given what time it is, yes."

"Hmph," Liam seemed to take offense. "I guess I will get straight to the point. Have you decided if you're going to be surrendering control of all your assets to me?"

"I've been a little busy. I know this might be difficult for you to understand, Liam, but running this business requires a lot of work. So, if you'd—"

The phone was taken right out of her hand. When she gazed at the thief, Gage stood there with fire blazing in his eyes as he put the phone to his ear. She had never even heard him come in.

His massive hand looked like it was about to crush her cell as his body filled with palpable tension. "Look here, shithead. You come fuckin' near her again; I will kill you. You call her again, I will kill you. You so much as mention her name, I will kill you. Do you get my drift?"

Layne dropped down onto her feet from her seat on her desk and attempted to pry the phone from Gage.

Easily keeping it out of reach from her, he pointed at her and then the chair aggressively. He mouthed the word 'sit' with such force she nearly heard it shouted from his thoughts.

Slowly, she sank into the office chair as she waited for Gage to conclude his talk with her brother.

Gage was greeted with Liam's sniggering. "Oh, you must be the other one I've been hearing so much about. Couldn't find a woman of your own, so you had to settle for passing my sister back and forth between you and your brother? Seems real fuckin' pathetic if you ask me."

The twitching in Gage's jaw was visible despite the dim lighting of the office. His anger was rolling off of him and very quickly filling the room. He responded through clenched teeth, "That's a lot of big talk from a little fucking man."

Liam's cocky attitude danced along his words, "Tell *Layne* she better start making up her mind on what she wants." His emphasis on his sister's name was clearly intentional after Gage's threat. "I've got far less patience than she does, and I have my eyes set on taking back a lot of things that belong to me."

Before Gage could snap back, the call went silent as Liam disconnected. He looked at the phone before dropping it down onto her desk. "Goddamn asshole!"

Layne sat there staring at him, unsure of what to say to ease him down.

The brown hues of his eyes were filled with the darkness of his current mood. "I don't want you fucking talking to him again. Not without Joey or me present. God knows what bullshit he's going to start filling your head with. Do you understand me?"

He rubbed a hand over his short blonde beard, the frustration painted all over his face. His eyes shifted to Layne when she began to get up from her seat. "Just go upstairs and get to bed, it's late." There wasn't much pleasantry in his voice as he ordered her to leave like a child being sent to bed.

Trying to provide a level of comfort, she softly spoke as she reached out a hand to his tensed arm, "Gage—"

Jerking his arm out of her reach, he raised his voice. "What?!" The sharpness of the word cut through her as it bounced off the walls of the room. "I don't need you to be a brat right now!"

Gage was normally her source of comfort when things were stressful, but hearing him lash out at her made her second-guess all she wanted to say. She shook her head, deciding it wasn't worth saying anything at all. Instead, she pushed past him on her way to leave the office.

After seeing the hurt he inflicted reflecting in her eyes, his face softened, and a pang of guilt struck his heart. "Layne, baby..." He only needed to break into a light jog for his longer legs to catch up to her shorter strides. His hand gently took her elbow before she was able to get past the office door.

He gently pulled her up to him. "I'm sorry. You didn't deserve that."

She wiggled her elbow from his hand, doing what she did best, and withdrew from uncomfortable conversations and feelings. "It's fine. I'm going to bed like you told me to." The attitude saturated her tone, indicating all was not as fine as she wanted it to seem.

He picked up on it, seeing right through the veil she was trying to hide behind. "No, you're not. You're going to bed because you're pissed." Gage frowned at her, realizing that they were all dealing with short fuses around here, and he was no exception.

Layne tried to laugh it off as a ridiculous notion, but it fell flat and unconvincing. She crossed her arms in front of her to help bolster her defenses that she was holding her shit together. "Whatever you say, Gage."

God help him, he wanted to shake her by her shoulders when her stubbornness flared up like this. Instead, he opted for a different approach and smirked at her.

His hand slid up the front of her throat. "That's right. When your Daddy tells you to do something, you do it." Gage's voice dropped into a low and gravelly tone that made her knees weak.

Her eyes lifted to meet his, struggling to maintain the heat of her anger. "I'm not in the mood." Her voice was already betraying how much his touch was taming her temper.

Gage brought his mouth to her ear as his grasp on her tightened slowly, "Did I ask if you were in the mood? Be a good girl and meet me in the movie room in five minutes." His lips nibbled at the bottom of her ear lobe before he pulled back and released his hand from her neck.

She felt him give her ass a nudge of encouragement to get moving. Still irritated with his outburst at her, she huffed but turned slowly and left the room. Despite the temptation to ignore his request, she opted to hit the bathroom before going to the room that housed the scaled-down movie theater.

He was there waiting for her, lounging back in one of the double-wide leather recliners with a remote in his hand.

"If you're expecting to get laid, you've got another thing coming," she warned him.

A goofy grin spread across his face. "If *you're* expecting to get laid, *you've* got another thing coming," he parroted back at her. His hand patted the vacant space next to him.

Tilting her head in confusion at his comments, she warily approached. Climbing into the seat to his right, she drew her legs up onto the recliner with her as she got comfortable.

Leaning over, Gage's arm wrapped around her shoulders and drew her in close while his left hand grabbed a blanket and draped it over both their laps. Using the remote, he turned on the digital movie projector, illuminating the screen with the opening credits of Layne's favorite movie.

Seeing that he finally gave in to watching her favorite cult classic from the eighties with her, a small piece of her attitude faded away.

Reclining the oversized seat back, he squeezed her against his side, allowing her to rest her head on his shoulder. "Comfy?" He smiled lightly at her.

Layne nodded. It was hard not to be comfortable when he was securely holding her, and the faint scent of his toasted vanilla cologne was wafting over her.

"I shouldn't have yelled at you," his apology was full of remorse for the hurt he inflicted on her. The only pain he ever wanted to bring her was the type that was paired with intensely gratifying pleasure. His hand rubbed over her arm soothingly.

Not hearing her jumping to forgive him, he realized he had a little more work to do.

Lightly sighing, he ran his hand down over her side. "The thought of ever watching you slip through my fingers would have me battling the darkest of demons. I may not deserve you, Layne, but I will never stop fiercely loving you."

She tilted her head to look up at him as he made his heartwarming profession to her. His words were so full of raw honesty backed by his love that Layne couldn't help but allow the rest of her anger to melt away.

Her hand reached up and pulled his face down to hers, accepting his apology with her lips connecting to his. Her tongue easily pushed into his mouth, exploring the addictive taste of him.

Falling into the sweet caress of her mouth against his, he knew all the bruises to his heart from years gone by were well on their way to fading for good, and it was all due to the woman currently in his arms.

Layne's lips drifted from his after several tender moments, her hand stroking over the side of his scruffy cheek. Without the obstruction of her defenses, her eyes shimmered despite the only light coming off the movie screen. "If I ever slip through your fingers, it's because I feel most at home in your heart."

Relieved that there was still hope they could make it through the ongoing nightmare Liam pitched them into, Gage showered her with several more kisses to erase the invisible wounds his words had created after the rare moment of losing his temper.

Once they both settled back on the cozy dual recliner, it wasn't any longer than ten minutes before Layne was lulled to sleep with the movie still playing on the big screen in front of them. Gage's hold never fell away from her as she passed out, listening to the sound of his heart beating in his chest.

Chapter Nine

GASOLINE

After Sean's grotesque passing, McGregor's no longer held the same atmosphere and appeal it used to. Maybe Layne was just projecting her feelings, but the joint used to hold a sense of home and belonging that had seemingly been torn from it. Sean not only had been the face everyone saw behind the bar but his dry humor and work ethic turned the joint into a safe haven for many.

With such a presence now missing, Layne had a hell of a time finding the right owner to replace the man who had been the backbone of this establishment for as long as she had been alive.

It had been sheer luck that Jillian, Sean's niece, was looking to move back to the city. She was every bit of a spitfire that Layne was. Turned out she had experience managing a bar in the rougher parts of Chicago for several years. But when Jillian got homesick, she put up the dive bar for sale and decided the Big Apple was where her heart was.

At first, Layne was wary of Jillian's ability to turn a blind eye to the seedy business transactions that occurred at McGregor's Pub. However, in the first week that she was running things, it was made clear she was a perfect fit.

Layne and Ethan had been meeting to discuss business as usual when a disgruntled drunk not only disparaged Ethan's favorite waitress but refused to leave her a tip. Layne's senior enforcer didn't take kindly to it and, in a move of stupidity, ended up stabbing the man's hand and pinning it to the table with a steak knife. It took everything Layne had not to do the same to Ethan for his lack of awareness and unsound judgment.

Jillian's reaction had been outrage, but not because a member of Layne's crew had just blatantly attacked one of the patrons. No, she had been pissed because of the mess the drunkard's blood left on the table. Ethan had been made to apologize to Jillian and forced to clean up after his moment of indiscretion. Layne had never seen the table so shiny and clean in the entire history of McGregor's.

Currently, with the anniversary of Shannon O'Reilly's death only days away, Layne was checking the accounting records earlier in the month than usual. This was going to be the first year that Layne didn't show up to her favorite pub for her annual inebriated shitshow.

While Jillian seemed to fit in with the rest of the criminally inclined crowd, Layne didn't feel comfortable exposing the more vulnerable side of herself. This year, with Sean's presence no longer there, it would just add to the dark hole she planned to dive into.

"What are you looking for? Those are the books from months ago," Joey asked as he sat back in his chair with a bottle of cheap beer in his hand.

After the day Layne had suddenly taken off from the hospital, Joey and Gage had made it clear that she wasn't going anywhere without either of them. She would have been more agreeable to a thousand papercuts than having her guys risking their lives for her. But arguing with them had gotten her nowhere; the stubborn assholes dug their heels in just as much as she typically did. Only they used it to their advantage that there were two of them and only one of her. So here Joey was, keeping a watchful eye over her.

Layne had dragged the box of records down from the second floor to a table in the back and was now combing through each of them. "Trying to figure out if I'm as crazy as I feel," she responded with heavy distraction lingering underneath her words that indicated she was mostly talking to herself.

She flipped another page, scanning each line for the very thing that had raised red flags the day Sean was killed.

Joey's hand reached out and stopped her from turning another page. The skull on the back of his hand was staring right at her. Layne looked over at him, "What are you doing?"

"You've hardly said more than a few sentences to me since you got back from meeting with Liam." His look grew serious as he tried to read through the masked expression on her face.

She rolled her eyes. "I disagree." Layne attempted to pry his hand from the book, but he was determined to leave it there. She would have had better luck trying to lift a two-ton vehicle than getting him to budge.

Taking a measured breath, he shook his head. "Sentences that revolve around you moaning out 'God, yes, Joey' don't count." He set the beer bottle on the table in front of him, wiping the condensation it left on his hand on the thigh of his jeans.

Not that he was complaining about both of them getting their insatiable fixes of one another, but she had been incredibly more guarded than normal. It was her raising of defenses that he knew so well that had him the most concerned about what was going on in her head. If her thoughts were spiraling, he needed to put a stop to it.

With a blank look on her face, Layne stared at him, waiting for him to say more. When he refused to back down, she let out a huff. "I'm just trying to figure shit out. The sooner we can resolve this fucking situation with Liam, the sooner we will all get back to normal." It wasn't a total lie, but it wasn't the thing that had been chewing away at her typically steadfast foundation.

It didn't seem that Joey was buying what she was selling as he inched his chair closer to hers. When she attempted to lean back, his hand was suddenly on the back of her neck, forcing her to stay right where she was. "Layney, I was shot in the goddamn chest, not bashed over the head. Do you think I can't tell when you're putting up your barricades? I'm going to give you this one chance to answer my question. What has you pulling away from me?"

The way he asked that question of her tore a little hole in her heart. He may not have been a man who wore his emotions on his sleeve, but she knew him well enough to hear the pain in his words. Her hand came up behind her neck to rest on the back of his hand, which was refusing to let her run and hide from this conversation. After several unsuccessful attempts of her fingers to peel his grasp off of her, she finally dropped her hand back into her lap.

Seeing his lips part to follow up on his unanswered question, she quickly let the words tumble out of her mouth. "I wish you had left the city the same night that Rebecca did."

Joey's hand loosened up its hold on her. "What?" His hand shifted from holding onto the back of her neck firmly, now to gently cradling it. The rich tones of his brown eyes reflected a series of emotions, including one that made her feel guilty for even voicing her confession.

"Please don't look at me like that." She frowned. "I can't think straight with you around. I don't know what to believe anymore, and I can't stand that it was you bleeding all over the church steps that day when it was supposed to be me."

At first, she wasn't sure if he was pissed at her honesty or if he was simply in disbelief that she laid it all out for him. Perhaps it was both.

Deciding to leave the heavy conversation there, she pushed her chair back to get up from her seat. His hand fell away from her neck when she stood. It wasn't more than a fraction of a second before his hand wrapped around hers, ensuring she didn't walk away from him.

He pulled her closer until his other arm drew her down to take a seat on his thigh. "Layne, I want you to listen to me." Both his arms wrapped around her waist, holding her securely.

"I know what you're going to say." She braced herself for him to tell her she was being ridiculous and that she needed to suck it up and deal.

He scoffed. "Are you going to shut the hell up and let me talk?" Joey paused, waiting for her to decide if she was going to let him get out what he needed to tell her.

After a few seconds, he continued, "Do you feel this?" His hand lifted hers to rest on his chest directly over his heart. The light pulse of the muscle circulating blood throughout his body thumped against her palm. "You're the only one that will ever have the power to make it stop beating. That's the only thing you ever need to believe."

Feeling the strong beating beneath her hand it grounded her anxious thoughts. Layne leaned over and pressed her forehead to his, trying to focus on the steady rhythm of his heartbeat. "That's what scares me. You're caught up in all of this mess because of me."

"And I would do it all over again. The day I sat down next to you on that stool over there," he pointed over at the line of stools up against the bar, "was the luckiest day of my life."

"Look at you being all sentimental," she teased lightly.

Joey grinned at her, taking her face with both of his hands. "Now, this is the part where I'm going to tell you to suck it up. You're better than this. Don't try to put out your fire because you're worried about me or anyone else. I want you to pour fuckin' gasoline on that bitch."

A smile cracked at the corners of her mouth.

It was the way her lips curved that he saw the piece of her that had been shaken up after his brush with death beginning to fade to make room for the feisty Irish girl to return. "Speaking of sucking things up, I have something else you can use your mouth on while you're at it," his words lowered into a growl.

Immediately, her hand smacked his shoulder. "You're an ass. You should have quit while you were ahead." She laughed.

He smirked, "There's my girl." He pulled her face to him as his lips possessively locked onto her own.

Layne's hands balled up his shirt as she leaned into the kiss, passionately wrestling with him for control. Her need for more of him escalated quickly as she shifted from being perched on his leg to straddling his lap with her body grinding against him.

It wasn't until Jillian cleared her throat, standing in front of their table with her arms crossed, that Joey and Layne halted their actions.

"You two almost done here? If not, God created these things called alleys you can go fuck in." Jillian motioned at the side door that led outside to the nearest said alley. "I would like to get these books back upstairs before I leave for the day." Her eyes dropped to the accounting records Layne had been perusing.

Biting her lower lip with a sheepish grin, Layne was definitely considering going outside to continue what they had started. Her thumb swiped below Joey's bottom lip, wiping away a bit of leftover saliva from their heated exchange.

She looked over at Jillian as she eased off of Joey's lap and back into her seat. "I am almost done. Just give me a few minutes to finish going through this book, and then we'll be outta here."

Jillian nodded, "Mmhmm," before walking away. She was not entirely convinced the two lovebirds would be able to keep their hands to themselves long enough.

As Layne tried to focus back on the records, her eyes stole a glance over at Joey. Damn, getting through the last few pages of this book was going to take every bit of effort and self-control she had in her. He was sitting back in his chair, legs spread with his hand casually resting on top of the bulge that pushed against the fabric of his jeans.

Telling herself that she could manage to keep her hands to herself for another five minutes, she forced herself to look back down at the book in front of her. Intentionally, she placed an elbow on the table and pressed her fingers to her temple to feebly attempt not to be distracted by him. Where were a set of damn horse blinders when you needed them?

She flipped to the next page, and when she got midway down, she paused. Cocking her head to the right, she blinked a few times.

Abruptly, she popped up from her seat. “This!” Layne snatched up the book, strode over to the bar, and dropped the book down onto the counter in front of Jillian.

She tapped aggressively at the line item that had captured her attention. “Do you know what this is??” With wide eyes, Layne hoped her hunch was correct.

“Um,” Jillian looked down at the transaction that was being brought to her attention. “Your initials next to a payment for $611.24?”

Layne shook her head. “Yes! But it’s really not. Have you had any other transactions like this since you’ve been here?”

Now, the woman was beginning to believe some of the rumors of Layne’s unhinged behavior, given how she wasn’t making much sense right now. “No, you take your cut straight from the cash reserves.”

“Exactly!” She slapped her hand down on the bar. “Son of a bitch! Fuckin’ Sean knew I’d question it.” Layne unleashed a laugh that bordered on the brink of insanity now that she finally had a breakthrough and not a damn breakdown.

Joey came up behind Layne, laying a hand on the small of her back. “Question what?” He raised a brow, wondering how concerned he should be at the suddenly erratic behavior.

She pointed at the page again. “L.O. Those aren’t *my* initials. Sean made sure that I never had my shares recorded in the books. It *has* to be Liam! It would explain how he was getting funds without me or anyone else noticing.”

Layne cursed under her breath at both the ingenuity of it and whatever other heinous acts Liam must have resorted to in order to get the money out of Sean. If it had been anybody else checking the books, it would have likely gone unnoticed.

That’s when the thought struck her. She only checked the books for a few long-standing clients and left the rest to be checked by the lower ranks of her crew. “Fuck…” Layne pulled her phone out of her pocket, quickly dialing up Ethan.

“Ethan? I need the books checked for every damn client of ours for the last few months. If any of them have records with my initials next to them, I want to know.” She paused, listening to his response before cutting him off, "I don't care, get Jonathan or Sam to help you. Get it done, and don't tell anyone else what you're looking for." She tapped the red circle, ending the discussion.

God help her if she discovered any of her clients were still actively funding Liam's ventures. They would see firsthand just how hot her fire could burn.

Chapter Ten

BOGEYMEN

Same fucking day, different fucking year. Shannon O'Reilly's death would always live on inside her daughter's head. Of all the fucked up things Layne ever witnessed, she couldn't get past the sight of her mom getting into the car on that fateful day. The vibrations that reached inside the house as the explosion went off would never be unfelt. The burst of light as the flames ignited wouldn't ever be extinguished in her mind. The instant when her mother was no longer whole could never be pieced back together in her heart.

Lying on her back, she stared up at her ceiling fan as it made rotation after rotation. The air in the bedroom shifted slightly with each movement of the fan blades cutting through the air. Despite having redecorated the master bedroom upon moving in, this was still the very same room her parents used to retire to at the end of a long day.

"Mom!" Layne bounded into the bedroom on a Friday night after coming home from Rebecca's house. She launched herself onto her parents' bed, bouncing gently against it after landing on her stomach. Her hands propped her head up under her chin while her legs idly kicked back and forth.

Shannon sat there in bed with a book in her hands, reading glasses perched on the tip of her nose, and her beautiful mane of chestnut hair in a loose braid hanging over her shoulder. She lifted her gaze from the words on the page to her ten-year-old daughter with a smile. Her fingers pulled the thin-framed glasses from her face and rested them between the pages of the novel she had been enjoying, titled "Deadly Bonds."

"Layney, how many times have I told you not to throw yourself onto the bed like that? You're bound to break the frame one of these days." Her mother scolded her gently, still upholding a loving smile.

Layne rolled her eyes at the comment she had heard time and time again and blatantly ignored it. Instead, she dove right into her reason for barging into the bedroom in the first place. "You're not going to believe what happened at Rebecca's tonight." She pushed herself up onto her knees, sitting back on her feet as she began to dive into the story.

With childlike excitement, Layne wildly spilled all the details of the eventful evening. "So, we were playing outside on Rebecca's front steps. She was being so bossy again and wouldn't let me pick what game we were gonna play. She was going to go back inside, but that's when Tilly got out the front door!" Layne's hands dramatically moved with each explanation, especially as she mentioned that her best friend's Scottish terrier made an escape attempt.

Her mother gasped, appearing fully invested in the story her daughter was telling. "Oh my, Layney! Did you get Tilly back?"

Layne popped up onto her feet on the bed, ready to continue explaining while standing on the mattress. However, with a stern look from Shannon and a gesture to sit back down, Layne dropped onto her butt with a mild bounce.

"Yeah, we got Tilly back, but she almost ran out into the street! I ran to go get her, but some nice man managed to scoop her up. He had the COOLEST motorcycle. It had a skull sticker on it and everything!"

Layne grinned as she remembered the stranger. The tall man with the dirty blonde hair had been parked right out front of her friend's house. When he heard both girls shrieking for the little black dog to come back, he stopped what he was doing to snatch up the pup before it ran by him towards the open street filled with oncoming traffic.

He carried Tilly back to Layne, squatting down in front of her as he handed the furry runaway back to her with a polite smile.

"After he gave Tilly back, he told me to be careful and all that jazz, but I'm smarter than that. I wouldn't have run out into the street after her. I told him that, too." Layne declared her intelligence proudly as she wrapped up the retelling of events.

Shannon's smile faltered slightly, forcing the curve to remain on her lips, but the hint of concern filled her eyes. "That was very kind of him,

Layney. But come here for a second." She waved her hand at her daughter to scoot closer.

When Layne crawled over to sit next to her mother in bed, cuddling up against her side, Shannon pulled her into a close hug. "I'm happy that Tilly is okay, but I want you to realize something that I know you might not fully understand. Not every stranger who does a good deed is a good person. Daddy's job can make a lot of people upset sometimes, and we should always be careful who we trust, okay? Even if they seem nice."

Her mother leaned over and placed a kiss on the top of Layne's head. "Now, why don't you go get your pajamas on, come back here, and we can watch a movie together before you go to bed."

Layne remembered that night so clearly. She and her mother cozied up in bed together, laughing at a silly movie until Layne conked out. It had all transpired in the same room she found herself in now. No matter how the paint changed, how the furniture got replaced, or the different voices echoing in the air–these four walls would always contain the bittersweet past.

Being stuck inside her memories, Layne could still hear the sound of the explosion as her mom's existence was wiped from this earth months later. Layne wondered if her mother felt anything. Had she known she was getting blasted to pieces? Was there fear of death? What pain had she suffered? Did she have any regrets?

This year, Layne had so many other thoughts weighing on her as she wondered about how things would be if her mother were still alive today. Would she be supportive of Layne's relationship with Joey and Gage? Would Liam be the same homicidal lunatic he had turned into? There were so many questions she didn't have answers to and never would.

She sighed as she remained there in the empty bed for another fifteen minutes while getting lost in the whirlwind of emotions. Layne assumed that at least one of her men was in the house if not both of them. Joey had been adamant about keeping eyes on her with Liam off his rocker. Gage was being equally protective. The two of them took turns at her side, no matter where she was. She couldn't even shower in peace, but that was because both of the guys had other intentions besides her safety.

If she got up out of bed, she could immediately start raising her blood alcohol levels. Yet, the blankets weighing down on her were very convincing in their efforts to dissuade her from leaving their captivity.

Deciding that caffeine and booze made a better tag team than some Egyptian cotton bedding, she kicked the sheets off herself.

Trudging downstairs in her dark blue boy shorts and gray tank top, she grumbled when she entered the kitchen and saw the coffee pot empty. "What the fuck…"

Layne began to go through the process of preparing a pot of coffee so she could at least pretend to be a shell of a human being today. About the time she hit the button to kick off the brew cycle, she looked around the kitchen. It was quiet. Why had no one made coffee this morning? Where were the guys?

She poked her head around a corner, "Joey?"

No response.

Walking down the hall and to the bottom of the stairs, she called up to the second floor, "Gage?"

Silence.

Shrugging with indifference, she shook her head and walked back to the kitchen. Their presence, or lack thereof, wasn't going to alter her self-destructive agenda for today.

Noticing there was enough coffee in the pot for a single cup, she grabbed a mug and filled it halfway with the wake-up juice. The other half was filled with the good stuff: whiskey. For good measure, she added a splash of Irish cream.

Armed with today's breakfast of champions, she headed back upstairs. Once she returned to the bedroom, she slowly sipped the bitter beverage in her mug as she flipped through her phone, finding no messages from either De Luca brother.

"Whatever." She tossed her phone down onto the bed carelessly. Why should she care if they were going to listen to her and actually leave her alone for the day? Last night, she had threatened them both that she would give up sex for Lent if they interfered with her plans for today. That in and of itself would be the greatest gift they could give her as far as she was concerned.

Before she could take her coffee into bed with her, an unusual sound came from downstairs. It sounded like something had fallen, or had it been knocked over?

Placing the mug on her nightstand, she went to pull her firearm from the corresponding drawer, only to discover that it wasn't where she had left it. That was…odd.

Another crash of something downstairs. She tiptoed to the door, straining for any other sounds that would give her a clue of what was transpiring on the first floor. When she heard nothing further, her bare feet carried her down the hall to the top of the stairs as she peered over the railing, looking for anything out of place.

Waiting another moment, she continued to investigate while slowly creeping down the steps. Her paranoia began to grow louder inside her head; anxiety sped up her pulse. On one hand, her brain was yelling at her for stupidly walking closer to potential danger, unarmed. On the other hand? It was telling her to stop overreacting and continue towards the source–it was likely nothing at all. As for the teeny part of her brain that thrived off of danger, it was getting excited like it was the damn Fourth of July.

Her feet met the cool tile at the bottom of the stairs. There were no more sounds, no bogeyman was jumping out at her, and all she was met with were thoughts of her ridiculous imaginings.

The tension in her shoulders finally released, visibly lowering them into a state of ease. This damn old house had too many noises.

Layne turned to go back upstairs, only she was stopped by the looming presence of not one but two bogeymen.

Layne yelped at the sudden appearance of two men clad in dark clothing who had managed to creep up on her. She practically jumped out of her skin at the unexpected sight after settling into a false sense of security.

The man closest to her immediately grabbed her by her arms with a firm grip to prevent her from running off or wildly swinging fists. As her initial shock wore off, her eyes finally observed the obscured faces of the two intruders. One mask with a toothy skull across it and the other with bloody demon canines. Both were unmistakably familiar.

These fuckers had her heart racing inside of her chest, thinking that someone had broken into O'Reilly Manor.

As she opened her mouth to bitch them both out, Mr. Tall-Dark-And-Skull-Masked, who had his hands on her, lifted her and tossed her over his shoulder with ease. Her barely covered ass was up close to his face. His gloved hand gave it a hard smack that echoed across the foyer.

"What in the fuck?!" she yelled out. "Joey, I swear to Christ!" Her hands pushed against the flexed muscles in his back.

As she began to protest loudly, that was when Mr. Demon-Couture-Mask approached. He pulled something from his pocket.

"Open up, baby." His brown eyes glimmered in excitement. Excitement that she was not currently sharing with either of them.

She wrinkled her nose up as she often did when she was riled up. "Gage, I will fu—"

Her words were cut off as he shoved a ball gag into her mouth, securing the straps around the back of her head. He made sure that it was tight enough to remain in place but as comfortable as one could hope for.

When her hands instinctively lifted to pull the gag out from between her lips, they were ensnared by Gage's hand while his other pulled a set of steel cuffs from Joey's back pocket. With expertise, both of her wrists were detained by the metal rings.

Neither of the guys could understand her muffled ramblings and grunts, but their imaginations filled in the gaps. Layne was less than thrilled they had interrupted a day where she wanted everyone to leave her the fuck alone while she wallowed in misery and obscene amounts of booze.

Gage patted the side of Joey's arm. "She's set."

Joey adjusted her weight on his shoulder. "Be a good girl, Layney, we're going to go take a drive."

Based on the way she smacked her hands against his lower back, she wasn't planning on following directions. He was more than happy to let her throw her fit; it gave him all the more reason to remind her how to be a good girl for them both.

Joey chuckled as he carried her into the garage, where his Challenger awaited them.

Gage got into the backseat first, then helped pull her into the back with him. He was careful not to bump her around too much. However, Layne didn't make it easy for either of them.

Wrapping his arms around her, Gage pulled her into his lap while Joey took up the driver's seat. He smirked behind his mask, knowing his already hard cock was pressing right up against her ass.

"Relax. Today, we're going to make sure you're going to be very well taken care of," Gage whispered into her ear.

The engine of the car began to purr as Joey started it up before pulling out of the garage. His eyes glanced up at the rearview mirror to take a look at Gage and Layne. Thank fuck for the heavily tinted windows. He couldn't imagine being pulled over and explaining to an officer that this was just a casual kidnapping of his wife in an effort to make her day better.

"Layney, I better hear you behaving back there." Joey grinned to himself, trying to consciously pay attention to the road. It wasn't a long drive down to the docks, but his dick was telling him that it wasn't a short enough trip.

With one arm remaining latched around Layne's waist, Gage pulled his mask down enough to use his teeth to yank off one of his gloves. Using his now bare hand with the WRATH tattoo across the back of it, he slid it down over her stomach until it passed underneath the waistband of those tiny boy shorts she had on.

Layne's breath caught as she felt his finger stroke along her crease. She melted back against him.

Gage let out a groan as he felt how much her arousal was coating her already. "Baby, you're so damn wet. Are you getting off on being taken hostage by us?" His finger stroked a circle over her clit.

Her hips pressed down into his lap as her moan vibrated against the silicone sphere lodged between her lips. Layne's ass pushed further against the excitement of his cock.

Hearing that first moan, Joey's hand adjusted his erection in his pants, beginning to regret his decision to be the driver. "That's a good girl, you let Daddy Gage work your cunt." Fuck, he hoped he didn't crash the car before they arrived at their destination.

Skillfully using his fingers, Gage continued to massage circles over her sensitive bundle of nerves. Each movement drew another velvety moan out of Layne. Her ass continued to grind against him, teasing his dick and driving him to stroke her quicker.

The way her heart was pounding in her chest before they left the house had been from the surge of adrenaline. Now, it was the rise of pleasure saturating her body. With her hands bound in front of her at the wrists, she pushed Gage's hand further into her panties, wanting his touch inside of her. Her thighs parted, allowing him more access to her heated core.

Chuckling, Gage pulled his touch back up to her clit. "Mmm," he growled into her ear. "It seems like you've had a bit of an attitude adjustment, Lucky Charm." His fingers made tighter circles over her slick nub, listening to each of her moans grow heavier with the need for release.

Layne whimpered as she felt her climax drawing closer, but still just a breath out of reach. Just as she thought he was going to leave her dangling on the edge, Gage finally dove his hand lower to shove two fingers deep inside of her tight pussy. Curling his fingers, he had no difficulty finding the sensual spot that would have her coming undone.

She cried out as her pleasure spilled across her body, squirming against him as she came. Gage's arm tightened around her so he could selfishly take delight in the way her body writhed in his hold. Each of her loud moans was dampened by the obstruction he had placed in her mouth, only making him harder at how her ecstasy couldn't be fully silenced.

"Fuck, baby. Coming so soon?" He wiggled his fingers inside of her tauntingly to extend the clutch her orgasm had on her. "We haven't even gotten started." Tauntingly, he pushed his hips up, driving the solid bulge of his cock against the center of her ass.

She panted hard as she laid back against his chest, her breaths being forced past the sides of the gag. Layne shut her eyes, allowing herself to bask in the afterglow while Gage kept his fingers buried deep inside of her. Every so often, she could feel him move them, prompting her body to respond with delightful little shivers across her skin.

Joey found himself placing more pressure on the gas pedal as Gage had their girl already unraveling between her legs.

Chapter Eleven

HAPPY ANNIVERSARY

Arriving at the docks, the tires caused a crunching sound of the gravel underneath the rubber as the car rolled to a stop. Joey parked the Challenger right in front of the same abandoned building where Layne had first encountered the darker side of his occupation. It was the very same day he made the best decision of his life, the day he decided to let her go free instead of carrying out Franzetti's contract on her head.

Joey exited the car, with Gage helping to ease their girl out of the backseat and back over Joey's shoulder. Securing her with one hand, Joey reached into the pocket of his black tactical pants with the other. He grabbed a set of keys and tossed them over to Gage, who snatched them from midair and unlocked the building, allowing his brother to enter with Layne first.

With less resistance in the afterglow of her orgasm, Layne kept herself steady by holding onto the back of Joey's shirt. She still wanted to give them both an earful for interfering with her plans for today, but it was pointless to try when they couldn't comprehend her past the gag firmly lodged in her mouth.

The door clicked shut behind the three of them once they were inside. The interior of the building hadn't changed much from a few years ago. It still looked just as abandoned but with more cobwebs and the same musty and ancient office furniture.

Layne was slid off of Joey's shoulder and down onto a chair, wrists still held captive by the handcuffs Gage had slapped on her. Being upright, she could more easily see a few of the differences in the room from the last time she had been in it. The air mattress on the floor was the most obvious addition, and next to it was a cooler.

They didn't bother securing her to the chair, both of them confident in their abilities to prevent her from running off. The bigger threat was how much she was going to lash out at either one of them before they were done here. Further validating their confidence, when she went to stand up, Gage came behind her and pushed down on her shoulders to get her ass back in the seat.

The boots Joey was wearing softly thudded against the floor as he double-checked several of the locks and windows before circling back to stand in front of her. With his face still obscured by his hallmark skeleton mask, his eyes were truly what gave his lust-filled intentions away.

Gage's hands remained pressing onto her shoulders to keep her in one place; the way his fingers massaged the muscles of her upper back, he was doing his best to relax her.

Joey leaned over with his hands braced against his thighs as he stared at Layne. "It's not often anyone gets second chances, Layney, but when the opportunity presents itself, I've learned not to turn it down. Do you recognize where we are right now?"

Not bothering to fight the obstruction in her mouth, she simply nodded at him. How could she forget anything about the fateful day he entered her life? It was the day their story began.

"Good." His eyes glanced at Gage, and he gave a curt nod. The gesture prompted his brother to loosen up the straps of the ball gag until it was removed from her mouth and returned to Gage's pocket. If she got mouthy again, it would be easily accessible.

Layne opened and closed her mouth several times to ease the ache from her jaw. Her cuffed hands came up to wipe the trail of saliva away from her chin. "This is fucking ridiculous. I told you both last night that I just wanted to be left alone for one goddamn day."

Gage's hand wrapped itself around her hair and tugged her head back. "Baby, it's not your turn to talk yet." He leaned over and pressed his mouth to hers with a softness that was in stark contrast to what would look like a rather grim sight to an outsider: two masked men holding a woman hostage in an abandoned building.

After that tender kiss, Gage smirked at her. "But if you prefer one of us to fill your mouth with something other than the gag, we will be more than happy to oblige."

When Gage eased up on Layne's hair, her attention was drawn back to Joey. He moved his hands to the top of her bare thighs while squatting down in front of her. "Now, be a good girl and tell me what I want to know." His hands squeezed onto the tops of her legs, digging in firmly with his fingers to make sure he had her attention.

"If the question is if you're both in such deep shit right now, then yes. You better pray when I get these cuffs off that both of you are miles away." She rolled her eyes with a fierce attitude and shook her head at their audacity of going to this extreme length. On a day when she always woke up in a foul mood, they hadn't exactly made it any better. Well, except the orgasm on the way here hadn't been half bad…

Joey laughed. "There's the part of you I love the most. All the attitude and confidence behind your words, even when you're not in a position to be pitching threats."

He leaned in and whispered into her ear, "Do you think I don't know you well enough to be several steps ahead of you? I bet you were confused when your gun wasn't in the nightstand drawer earlier, huh?" He had already been shot once by an O'Reilly; he wasn't looking to make it two-for-two when they caught her off guard at the house earlier.

She huffed out a breath in frustration. "You know today of all days is my one day for myself. It's not about you."

Tugging his mask down, Joey leaned down and dragged several rows of kisses up over the soft skin of her inner thigh as he inched closer to her center. His thin layer of scruff brushed against her body as he murmured, "That's where you're wrong, Layney." His hands forced her legs apart wider as his final kiss was pressed to the damp fabric of her boy shorts.

Behind her, Gage tossed his mask and gloves down onto the floor. Each of his large hands ran over her shoulders and down onto her chest until he slid them into the top of her tank top. His palms found her firm and round tits and began to knead them in his grasp.

Layne quietly fought the moan her body wanted to respond with at both of their touches. The weight of her desire began to impact her breathing as her heart sped up and her core pulsed with desire. Her damn body was trying to betray her again.

Continuing, Joey pulled his face away from between her legs to peer up at her, "Today is about me, it's about you, and going forward, it's going to be about the three of us." The warm pools of his espresso eyes were full of certainty and promises. "Are you going to be a good girl for us? Today can be all about allowing us to worship every fuckin' inch of your body until you've come so far undone that there's nothing left of you for us to take. All you have to do is say the words, Layney."

Still, with his hands down the front of her tank top, Gage's fingers pinched her stiff nipples, twisting them between his fingers. It elicited a gasp from her as her body shifted under his touch. Each tug at her body had her hardheaded attitude faltering.

While Layne was struggling to be amenable to the new terms of what this day was going to be about, Joey's hand commanded her attention as it grabbed under her jaw.

"I asked a question, you know what happens when I ask twice," his gravelly voice deepened into the cusp of a growl. His other hand dropped between her legs, grabbing at her thinly covered pussy.

Lustful thoughts were already filling her eyes as one set of hands continued their exploration and play of her breasts, but when Joey introduced his rough handling of her body, all she could think about was hunting down her next release.

Layne's full lips parted in anticipation of the gasp pulled right out of her. Losing a battle she wasn't sure she even wanted to win, she whispered, "Make me your good girl." Her voice was breathy from the shameless desire that had eaten away her self-control.

Joey smirked before sliding his mask back into place; his eyes glanced at Gage, who pulled back from Layne, bearing a grin brimming with excitement at the playtime they were all going to have together.

She was promptly pulled to her feet as Joey lifted her arms above her head and lowered them around his neck. Her cuffed wrists ensured that she wouldn't be escaping the proximity of his body.

Coming up behind her, Gage put his hands to better use by yanking her boy shorts down from her hips until they fell to the floor. Once his job was done there, he left to find the bag he had dropped off in a corner earlier.

Impatiently yanking at his belt, Joey's hands opened up his pants before pulling out his impressively-sized dick that ached to fuck the everloving shit out of her. His hands grabbed onto the back of her thighs and hoisted her up until her legs wrapped around his waist.

Layne's arms tightened around his neck as her ankles locked behind him. His cock was already teasing the slick entrance of her body. She stared at his mask-covered face as he walked with her until her back hit a wall.

"Don't hold back," she instructed him. If either of them wanted to make today not about her emotional wreckage, it needed the physical intensity to shatter the mental barriers.

"Oh, I wasn't planning on being gentle, Layney. I plan to fuck you like I just stole you." He drove his cock roughly into her, proving his point. He groaned as he felt her tightness squeeze around him.

She tilted her head back against the wall as she loudly moaned out as he forced her body to mold around him. Her nails clawed into his upper back, finding any part of him to latch onto.

His hips drew back and pushed into her again, the head of his cock attempting to spear straight through her. The way her arousal warmed his cock, he wanted nothing more than to forever live buried deep inside her.

Despite the mask covering the lower half of his face, she could still feel the heat of his breath against the skin of her neck as he panted with his efforts. Equally, her labored breaths were expelled as she continued to voice out the intensity of the pleasure he was giving her.

"You should have taken my dick just like this the first time we were here together." His hands squeezed onto her legs tighter. Allowing his lust to drive his movements, he sped up his thrusts to keep fueling both of their needs. Roughly, he claimed her body, his hips nearly bruising in their intensity as he used his strength to take her.

Barely able to keep up with her breaths between her moans, she gasped at the thought of if she and Joey had caved to their desires the same day they had met. "I-I… I would have never given it to you."

She groaned out as the tip of his cock stroked over the sweet spot deep within her core. With every shove of his hard length into her, he was pulling at the string wrapped around her release, getting closer to unraveling it.

Lifting a hand, Joey tugged his mask down and then snatched up her throat in his grasp. "Don't lie to me; you would have let me fuck this insatiable pussy of yours however I wanted."

His lips feverishly kissed her lips, swallowing up her moans hungrily. The strength of his hand squeezed around her throat, placing enough pressure to have her feel the slowing of blood on the way to her brain before releasing the hold. Joey repeated the process of squeezing and releasing several more times as his hips drove into her.

With the power of his thrusts jolting her against the wall, her body quickly ramped up towards its climax. "Fuck, Joey! I-I'm gonna come!"

Her body was already wildly squirming against him as her insides trembled.

Joey dropped his hand from her neck down to her hip, where his other hand joined it, steadying her body so he could continue fucking her even harder there against the wall.

He growled into her ear, "You're gonna suck your cum off my cock when I'm done with you. You better be fuckin' hungry." His teeth caught the bottom of her ear lobe, giving it a possessive nibble.

The metal links holding her wrists together pulled against the back of Joey's neck as her body tensed around him. His words were just enough to pull the trigger to fire off her orgasm. The walls of her pussy clenched onto him as her release spilled over his cock, coating every thick inch of him.

Gage was finishing the last few touches of his setup over by the air mattress when he heard Layne's screams of ecstasy as she came for Joey. Listening to her moans while Joey had her wrapped around his dick had been a sweet form of torture. He was more than ready to have his turn with her, and the way his erection was fighting against the confines of his pants had him tempted to reach in and take the matter into his own hand.

As Layne's high began to clear enough that she wasn't holding Joey's dick hostage inside of her, he pulled back, fighting the urge to blow his load into her pussy.

Joey groaned as the cool air outside of Layne's body met the wet skin of his cum covered dick. Moving quickly, he let her down on her feet and ducked out from the circle of her arms. He grinned, urging her down onto her knees, "Show me how much you enjoy tasting yourself on my cock."

Layne sank to her knees, her hands holding the fabric of his boxer briefs away from his dick, still standing at full attention. Her cum shone against his skin, mixing in with his clear precum leaking from the tip of his length.

Her tongue snaked out and stroked a long line along the underside of his cock. The flavor of her mildly sweet juices mixed with the taste of his flesh.

With one hand braced against the wall in front of him, Joey dropped the other to the back of her head. "Layney," he groaned as his cock twitched when her tongue made contact with him. "You better not be fuckin' teasing me down there." He tilted his head to look down at her.

She smirked and looked up through her dark lashes at him. "Would I ever tease you?" The hint of snarkiness tainted her words.

His hand fisted her hair. "Open up, smartass," he ordered.

Opening up her mouth wide, she drew him into her mouth, sealing her lips around him. Sliding her mouth down over his length, she taunted him with the dance of her tongue.

The sensation of her sucking on him while her tongue did its wicked movements had Joey hissing out a string of curses. Layne's head bobbed back and forth along his cock, cleaning him of all the evidence of her release.

Trapped in pleasure's passage of time, it didn't feel like long before Layne's throat was squeezing around him, prompting his hand to firmly push her head even closer to him as he groaned loudly, "Fuuuck!"

Several thick spurts of his seed shot down into her throat, quickly filling up her mouth before she swallowed his release.

Layne slowly pulled her mouth from him, sitting back on her feet as she looked up at him with swollen lips, flushed cheeks, and a satisfied smile.

Heavily breathing, Joey weakly smiled at her before leaning over and helping her onto her feet. He pulled out a key to her handcuffs and popped them open, releasing her wrists from the steel bracelets.

Joey's finger and thumb held onto her chin gently as he looked into her eyes. To think he had been so lucky to fall head over heels for the woman in front of him on this day a few years ago had him wishing for nothing else in life.

He leaned over and lovingly captured her lips momentarily before whispering against her mouth, "Happy Anniversary, Layne."

Chapter Twelve

FOUNTAIN OF YOUTH

After the tender moment shared between them, Joey glanced over his shoulder at Gage, who had given them space for Layne's first fuck of the day and certainly not her last.

Noting that his brother looked ready for his shot, he looked back at Layne and smirked, knowing that her day with them was only beginning. They promised her that they would make this day about the three of them together. That was a promise they planned to deliver–in spades.

Gage approached, taking Layne's hand with his. Without a word, he led her over to the air mattress. "Baby, now it's your Daddy's turn to take care of you." He stopped at the edge of the makeshift bed and faced her. His hands grabbed the bottom of her shirt and lifted, removing the last piece of her clothing. It left just the golden chain of his collar around her slender neck.

His boyish smile spread across his face as his eyes trailed over her fit figure on display before him. Everything about her captivated him, from the currently tousled locks of chestnut hair hanging down past her shoulders with the ends brushing past the sides of her perky breasts to the petite figure that was home to the unique soul that called to his own. Tying it all together was her captivating set of royal emerald eyes that glowed with every ounce of her spirited personality.

Her hands went to the zipper of Gage's black hoodie and began to slide it down. When his inked hand with the rose on it halted her about halfway, she looked up at him with confusion clouding her face.

Lifting her hand to his lips, he gently kissed each of her fingertips. "Not yet. Take a seat." He nodded over at the air mattress.

Layne hesitated, wondering just what his intentions were. The man standing before her didn't budge as he patiently waited for her to comply. She got down onto the mattress, feeling the air shift underneath her weight, Layne crawled to the center and took a seat while leaning back on her hands.

He stepped to the cooler and retrieved a partially frozen bottle of water from it. Gage removed the top and discarded it into the depths of the room, where it rolled off to join other random debris left behind in the abandoned building.

Joey took up a seat in the chair Layne had been in earlier while he recovered from his efforts with their girl. Slowly, he began easing out of his clothes, starting with his boots, while he casually watched the interactions between the two in front of him.

Kneeling between her ankles, Gage beckoned her with his finger to lean closer to him. When she did as she was told, her arms hanging down between her thighs, he placed two fingers under her chin and tilted her head back slightly. "Part those lips for me, baby. I can't have you getting dehydrated this early on."

There he was—her caretaker—always making sure she was in a healthy state, whether it was physically or otherwise. Layne smiled at him and opened up her mouth. Gage slowly poured the frigid liquid into her mouth until there was enough for her to swallow down. He repeated the action until he was satisfied she had consumed enough.

"Thank you, Sir." Her eyes sparkled as she gave him her full attention.

Gage proudly smiled that his bratty Lucky Charm was actually using her manners for once. "You're welcome, baby. Now lie back so I can quench my thirst."

Partially leaning back on her elbows, she rubbed her leg suggestively against his hip with a grin. "Last I checked, you are a bit overdressed for the occasion."

It seemed her good behavior was short-lived as her inner brat made an appearance. He grabbed her leg that was rubbing up against him and yanked her forward several inches so she fell the rest of the way on her back.

Dragging the bottom of the cold water bottle down over her abs, he watched as she sucked in her stomach in response to the icy sensation against her skin. Gage continued the movement south and noticed her breath cease momentarily as the chilled plastic hovered closer to her center.

"What were you saying? That *almost* sounded like you were trying to tell me I don't know what pleases my girl." A devilish smile crossed his lips.

Layne lifted her head to watch as the frigid object threatened to come into contact with her heated folds. "Gage, that wasn't—"

With his grip still firmly on her leg, he lowered the bottle down over her pussy, immediately finding gratification in how her squeak interrupted her protest. "Is that how you address me?" He removed the bottle from her sensitive flesh.

She dropped her head back down onto the mattress as she blew out a breath of air. Shaking her head in response, "No, Sir."

Gage smiled, released her leg, and gave her inner thigh a pat. "Better. Go ahead and spread your legs, baby. I want to make sure I don't leave any part of you untasted."

Biting her lower lip to prevent herself from making another sassy remark, she parted her legs enough for him to have all the access to her body he could want.

The dark brown hues of his eyes soaked in the sight before him, filling up with a desire to have her falling apart at his doing. He leaned down, his lips just barely brushed against her folds as he spoke. "Your pussy is gorgeous when it's so swollen after taking Joey's cock."

He held onto her hip with one hand while his other hand remained on the plastic bottle with frosty condensation forming on the outside of it. Gage's tongue came forth and ran along her crease, reveling in the taste of her arousal.

Layne moaned out quietly, needing more contact from him as he took things slowly. When she thought he was going in for another lick, she felt the sting of the ice-cold water running over her clit. Her hips instinctively jerked at the unexpected sensation, but Gage's strong grasp kept her steady.

As she gasped in surprise, she felt an immediate warmth from Gage's mouth, sucking the water from her pussy. There was a drastic change from cold to warm that had her body reacting to a new type of tortuous pleasure.

Hearing Layne react favorably to the temperature play, he hummed in approval against her core, drawing out another satisfied moan from her. Gage's mouth drank away the chill thoroughly, allowing himself to feast on her body. He continued the cycle of spilling the water over her body's most sensitive areas before melting away the bite of the cold using the strokes of his tongue.

The back and forth of him pulling her sensations to both ends of the spectrum had her in a frenzy of whimpers and moans.

While his tongue swirled over her small bundle of nerves, working her up hard, he ditched his hold on the partially frozen bottle he had been holding in his hand. It fell off to the side and rolled a few feet away from the bed. Gage nipped at her clit, adding in another type of pleasurable pain.

She cried out, "Please, Daddy, I need to come!" Her hands tugged at the sheets on either side of her.

Knowing damn well his fingers and the silver rings on them, were cold as hell from holding onto the water for so long, Gage shoved two fingers deep inside of her for another added layer of contrasting sensations. The depths of her warm pussy heated his fingers while her body soaked the cold from them.

"Fuck!" she repeated several times. Layne shook as the opposing temperatures hurdled her into her release. The tight walls of her center locked down on his icy fingers in the process. Her back arched up from the mattress as her hips pushed against his face.

Gage continued to lap at her cunt while he thrust his fingers deep inside of her, the silver rings held the cooler temperatures much longer and rubbed just beyond the entrance of her pussy. The tips of his fingers eagerly stroked and pushed at the special area far within her. Not letting her orgasm fade off, he continued to use his fingers to fuck her while she was making the most beautifully feral sounds.

His voice thick with need, he glanced up at her, "Baby, I told you I was goddamn thirsty. Now, I'm going to need you to give me more to drink." With quick and deep movements, his fingers curled inside of her, keeping her ecstasy at its highest levels.

She could hardly breathe as each moan tore out of her throat. Her body continued to tremble and tense up with each of his movements. "I…I…" Before she could complete the thought into anything coherent, Gage latched his mouth back down on her clit, roughly sucking at it while his fingers continued to press into her.

Layne's eyes rolled back into her head briefly as she cried out, and her body crashed into another vicious climax. This time, as she came, a stream of liquid spilled from her body.

Swiftly, Gage removed his fingers and began to drink straight from her tap as the mild taste of her body's oasis delighted his taste buds. He swallowed down every last drop while she squirmed against the movement of his mouth.

When he finished, he lifted his head and saw Layne lying there heavily, panting with a sheen of sweat over her flushed body. He sat up on his knees and began removing his clothes. "Baby, I'm so proud of you. You taste fuckin' magical when you squirt for me." He was pretty sure he had been drinking from the Fountain of Youth while she had been falling into the abyss of obscene pleasures.

Quickly shoving off the last of his clothes from his body, Gage lowered himself over her, allowing the swollen tip of his tattooed cock to push against her entrance.

His SPQR medallion necklace hung down from around his neck, where it dragged over the length of hers while his hand stroked the side of her face. "And for being such a good girl, you are going to get a reward." He smiled down at the breathless expression on her face in awe of the beauty he saw lying there underneath him.

Layne's endless pools stared up at him, still clouded by the high of her releases. Her eyes glanced down the length of his body, drawing in the sight of his chest muscles flexing as he propped himself up above her. His cut abs were on display down to the start of the ink at the bottom of his V and led onto the broadswords painted over his hardened length hovering at the opening to her aching pussy.

"Eyes up here, beautiful," he instructed. When she complied and looked up into his tender espresso eyes, Gage slowly pushed himself inside her.

Her hands slid up over his large biceps, over the tops of his shoulders, and onto his upper back as she moaned out. The soreness between her legs fed into extra sensitivity as he stretched her cunt to fill her completely.

Barely audible, she whispered his name on the tail end of her moan, "Gage…"

"Yeah, Lucky Charm?" He rolled his hips into her, the head of his cock driving back into her.

Uncertainty was splashed across her face, and her mind began to drift into thoughts of events of the past despite the efforts of both her men. "I don't know if I can take much more."

"You're already trying to tap out on us, baby?" He lowered his mouth down to her ear and whispered, "C'mon, Layne, your pussy was made to take both of us. The way your cunt is wrapped around my dick right now tells me it wants to continue being used." He kissed her neck right below her ear. "Just keep your focus on what feels good."

Layne's fingers slid up the back of his neck, burying themselves into the short, ashen blonde hair on the back of his head. Her hips pressed up against him, encouraging him to keep going.

Gage planted several kisses along the length of her neck, his hips beginning to pick up the pace of driving himself deep into her. He groaned as her slick walls stroked him with each thrust.

He looked back over his shoulder at Joey, smirking, "How's it look watching me fuck your wife?"

Joey had fully undressed himself and was lounging back in the chair, his cock was already recovered enough and back to being half erect, watching and hearing Layne as she took Gage. He continued slow but sure strokes of his hand on his rapidly swelling dick. He grinned at his brother's question, "She still looks like she's missing something."

"Oh?" Gage turned his attention back to Layne. "Did you hear that, baby? He thinks you're not being worked hard enough."

Breathlessly, knowing she was flirting with the line of her body's limits with all their affections, she blurted out, "Fuck you, Joey."

That got her a chuckle from him in response and a stoppage in Gage's movements. Joey responded with a devilish grin, "If you're offering, Layney, I'm not about to turn it down."

Using the strength of his hands, Gage quickly rolled them both over onto their sides while still buried inside her. He grabbed her leg, pulling it over the outside of his hip. Swiftly, his open palm slammed down on her ass cheek, leaving a stinging red glow.

Giving a surprised squeak, Layne's hips pushed against him as she jolted from the spank he had just given her.

Smiling, Gage looked at her with delight. "One of these days, I'll be able to smack that sass out of you." Though, he secretly hoped it wouldn't be anytime soon.

Joey rose from his seat and strode over to a bag next to the cooler. Reaching in, he pulled out a bottle of lube, slathering it over his thick cock in preparation for diving into his favorite part of her–that round ass of hers.

Soon, she could feel the bed dip under Joey's weight as he joined the two of them, his hand came to the indent of her waist as he pressed his chest to her back. Gage's hard cock gave a taunting nudge deeper into her while Layne felt the steel-like erection from Joey nudging between her ass cheeks.

The stubble from Joey's face lightly scratched against the back of her shoulder as he kissed it. His hand slid over her stomach and upward to grab a handful of one of her breasts. His fingers pinched and rolled her nipple between his fingers.

The depth of his gravelly voice vibrated against her soft skin as he spoke, "Layney, I swear to God, I will never grow tired of fucking this perfectly tight ass of yours. Now, be a good girl and beg for both of your holes to be full. I know you can sound goddamn needy when you want to."

She moaned out as Joey's fingers toyed with her stiff nipple, and he teased her back entrance with the tip of his cock. "Please, I need both of my Daddies filling me up; I need to be fucked like your good girl." Her voice was heavy with her desire as her body ached to be full from the waist down.

Joey's hand left her breast and slid up to her throat, wrapping around it possessively. "I can't wait to hear you scream as we make you fuckin' come so hard that you'll never question who the fuck you are ever again." His hand tightened around her neck as his eyes flicked over to Gage with a nod.

Smiling as he saw Joey gear up to push into Layne's back entrance, Gage looked at their girl. "You're Layne motherfucking De Luca."

In a smooth motion, the head of Joey's swollen cock inched into the tight space of her ass. Sweeping over him immediately was the pleasure of her body squeezing around his throbbing cock, causing him to curse. He pushed into her until he was fully seated inside, the familiar tightness that came with their girl taking both their cocks had him reeling already.

As Layne's lips parted to moan out, Gage shoved two fingers into her mouth, forcing her moan to get cut off as she gagged on the two large digits. He groaned as it caused her pussy to strangle his cock, barely allowing him to draw back and drive back into her. "Fuck, baby, you better pray for your birth control. I'm going to fill you with so much of my damn cum that you'll be leaking for days."

In tandem, both De Luca men hungrily indulged in taking her body in a coordinated rhythm. Joey's hips bucked against her ass as he nipped at the side of her neck as his cock claimed her body. "You'll always be ours, Layney," he huskily spoke into her ear.

Both the guys used their hands to play with her body's ability to utilize oxygen. They alternated between Joey's hold on the outside of her throat and Gage's fingers trying to find the back of it; she gasped for air intermittently as they allowed moments of reprieve and recovery. Each time their hands took control, her body squirmed wildly between them as the sharp escalation of extreme pleasure overtook her.

The room was filled with sounds of bodies smacking against one another, heavy panting, and feral sounds of ecstasy as they all chased after their needs.

Layne's hand scratched over Gage's chest, clawing at it while yanking on the silver necklace he always wore. Her other hand had her nails biting into the back of Joey's hand on her. Her green eyes watering from all the breath play while they both continued slamming their large cocks into her with fierce determination.

Seeing a burst of starlight behind her eyes, she screamed out as her release tore through her very existence. Gage removed his fingers from her mouth, allowing them both to revel in the sounds she made. Her pussy had Gage's cock in a vise grip, and her ass locked down onto Joey's dick.

After she tumbled off the cliff into a state of unparalleled bliss, Gage roared out as his cock pulsed and ropes of his hot cum shot forth deep inside of her. Each spurt continued to fill her up until there was no part of her inside that wasn't drowning with his release.

Joey growled as he wrapped himself around Layne's back, his own climax erupting out of him violently. He whimpered as he filled her ass with his seed and was overcome with intense satisfaction in every part of his body.

All of them were still tangled up together, Layne sandwiched between the men who laid their claim to not just her body but her heart.

None of them had to say a word as they lay there listening to the heavy breaths and pounding heartbeats of one another.

Chapter Thirteen

IN CASE OF EMERGENCY

Perhaps it wasn't a five-star hotel and sex by candlelight, but the efforts both Joey and Gage made to diminish the morbid association that day held for Layne had been one for the books. Instead of attempting to pretend that it was any other day of the year, Joey reminded her that it had been the start of their story together. Gage's involvement gave her hope for the future that he was in this for the long haul to meet her every need.

Spending all their energy on carnal pleasures for a day in an abandoned building down at the docks may not have earned the label of being hopelessly romantic, but it was meaningful to the woman who bound them all together.

Several days had passed, and Layne still felt like every muscle in her body had been put through the wringer by both guys, not that she was complaining. Gage had insisted on treating her like a goddess worth pampering, knowing how much her body needed the recovery.

Sitting in the center of Gage's bed cross-legged with her laptop in front of her, phone to her right, and her earbuds lodged in her ears, she growled in frustration.

"Thomas, there's evidence he was fucking stealing from my businesses all this time. Liam's been stealing from *me*. I want to know why it's taken this long to get answers!" She swiped her fingers across the trackpad on her computer, scrutinizing every record available to her.

Listening to her trusted advisor spout off a million reasons why it so easily slipped under the radar was giving her a dull headache at the base of her skull. Her fingers smoothed away the wrinkles between her eyebrows that were evidence of her annoyance.

Her eyes lifted from her computer screen as Gage entered the bedroom with a plate of food. Quickly, she minimized one of the windows on the computer. The last thing she wanted was for either of her guys to ask more questions when they didn't need to know the answers.

Gage was wearing one of his slate gray dress shirts and a pair of jeans. Right above the left pocket of the shirt was embroidered silver thread with the initials 'C.C.' for his kink-inspired night club, Cassidy's Chains.

Approaching the bed, he set the plate down on the night table for her, a grilled chicken wrap and a handful of chips neatly piled on it.

Layne's hand shooed him away even though she couldn't recall the last meal she had eaten. At her dismissive gesture, Gage's face went stern.

She continued to focus on her conversation with Thomas, who explained further that Liam's whereabouts were still unknown, and they were no closer to figuring out his next moves.

"So, we've got jack shit? This is fucking unbelievable; it's *Liam,* for God's sake!" The heat of her words caused a shameful silence on the other end of the line. "Tell Sammy, Ethan, and Jonathan to meet me at the Brass Mirror tonight at eight, and they better have good fuckin' news." Her finger firmly tapped the end call button on her phone before plucking her earbuds from her ears.

It wasn't until Gage's hand gripped her jaw that she realized he hadn't left the room. His hand turned her head to face him.

"Open." He commanded as his other hand held half of the wrap he had brought her.

Still irritated with the lack of details on who her brother was coordinating with to have him feeling so confident in his ability to snatch back the family business, she pushed the wrap Gage was offering away from her face. "I'm not hungry. I'll eat later."

Not approving of her response, Gage kept his hand firmly attached to her jaw. "I wasn't asking," he paused before continuing, "unless you want me to find out just how much punishment your ass can take."

That had her attention as the stubborn look in her eyes faded to a softer and more wanton glow. Layne would be lying to herself if she didn't admit to flirting with the idea of defying him one more time just to see what sort of discipline he had in mind. The rumble from her stomach quickly chased away the bratty consideration.

Layne parted her lips, and Gage brought the sandwich to her mouth for her to bite into, smiling proudly. "That's my good girl."

When Joey and Layne arrived at her covert and elite gambling club, the Brass Mirror, it was packed with members obscenely wagering away their trust funds and generational savings. Each of the tables was full, seating the richest and dirtiest fucks the city had living in it. Scantily clad waitresses moved from table to table, taking drink orders and dirty one-liners with a smile.

Despite not barging into the room commanding attention, there was a large portion of eyes drawn to her when she stepped foot inside. There wasn't a single soul that didn't know who she was and her reputation for not putting up with anyone's bullshit when it came to the denizens of the criminal underbelly.

After Russell Spencer's assets were seized by her associates and he found a permanent home at the bottom of the Hudson River, Layne had a lot fewer issues with the other factions. Despite being one of the few females to have ever broken into the upper echelons, the other leaders rarely questioned how far she would go to back up her promises—or threats.

Joey's company tonight had been at his insistence. This makeshift casino was entirely under her control; anyone who tried to start shit here would have to be mentally unstable. Yet, it was an argument she lost the moment Joey had his hands on her. Goddamn, hormones were her weak spot.

His hand grazed across the small of her back. "I will be right over there," he tipped his head in the direction of the high-top table at the far end of the bar.

Layne smiled and nodded in acknowledgment. "I'll find you when I'm done."

Thank God he had been able to compromise on not being buried up her ass tonight, figuratively speaking. Instead, he was capable of granting her the space she needed to yell at these assholes who worked for her and were supposed to be finding out more information on her delusional sibling.

Scanning the room, she saw Sammy sit back in his chair at a poker table, unleashing a hearty laugh as the dealer shoved a pile of chips his way. The other men at the table with him all groaned, seeing the Full House laid out in front of her senior associate.

Sammy's cocky smile was full of pride as he sat forward to collect his bounty. "Sorry, fuckers, guess you just can't keep up with the pro," he said as he organized the slew of chips in front of him.

She came up behind Sammy, leaning over and plucking a few black chips off the top of the stack in front of him and pocketed them. When he snapped his head around, his hazel eyes were fired up, and he was ready to unleash a tirade of profanities at a woman touching his money. When he recognized Layne, his expression eased, and tensions quickly faded.

As one of the top men who worked for her, Sammy was used to Layne's high expectations and even higher attitude. He ran his hand over his slicked-back raven locks, realizing it was time to get to business.

"You're early," he pointed out. The light above the table glinted off the face of his Rolex on his wrist as he cashed out his chips and stood from his seat.

With displeasure in her voice, "And you were sitting here fucking off. Where are the other two?"

Straightening out the jacket of his black suit that matched the darkness of his hair, he shrugged. "Last I saw, Ethan was flirting with one of the waitresses, and Jonathan was yapping on his phone."

His mixture of brown and green hues shifted as he scanned the room for his partners in crime. Noticing Joey at the table near the bar, he gave a small nod in polite form to his boss's husband and got a nod in return.

"How's he feeling?" Sammy looked at Layne, the genuine concern painted over his olive complexion.

Not bothering to look at Sammy, she continued to keep an eye out for the other two. Layne answered his question, "As good as anyone can expect after giving death the middle finger."

Immediately, she picked out Ethan by his hulking size as he came out of the restroom. His fingers were buttoning up the last button of his gray vest over his white dress shirt. Close behind him, also coming from the single-person bathroom, was the head cocktail waitress at the Mirror.

Layne's green eyes locked onto Ethan's sapphire hues, and he immediately quickened his strides over to her. People parted like the Red Sea to avoid getting bulldozed by him on his beeline to her.

When he stopped in front of Layne, he gave a large smile, showing off his pearly whites, "Was just wrapping up… business."

She raised a hand to fend off any further details. "If you keep fucking every waitress at every damn place we do business, I'm not going to be held responsible for the fallout when they all find out about one another." Layne shook her head, trying not to picture the day ten women came after her lead enforcer. One woman scorned was bad enough, but a herd of them? He was just begging to get raked over the coals.

"What? Melissa's a sweet girl; we were just having a chat while she was on her break." Ethan smirked, knowing his lie was as plain as the sleeve of tattoos on his ripped arms.

Now that she had two of her three head honchos, she just needed to track down her top-tier negotiator, Jonathan.

"Why don't you both go grab the table in the back? I will see where the hell Johnny-Boy is." She pulled her phone from her pocket, but before she could even unlock it, a hand came onto her shoulder from behind.

"I think this still qualifies as fashionably late," Jonathan's voice smoothly spoke up as he came around to her side. Then, when he saw the pissed-off look on Layne's face, he winced, "Or not." He dropped his hand away from her and back down to his side into the pocket of his black dress slacks.

At the very back was a private room, though it wasn't very private as the room had glass walls on two of the four sides. The only level of privacy it offered was from eavesdroppers' prying ears.

Once they were all seated at the round table inside the cozy gathering spot, Layne sat back in the plush armchair and looked at the three men before her.

"I'm going to say this once. I expect fucking results, and I haven't seen shit from any of you except excuses," her eyes darted to Jonathan to shift the blame on him for all the piss poor explanations he had given her. "Horrible judgment calls," her gaze moved to Ethan, knocking his brash actions. "And a whole bunch of nothing." She stared at the last of the bunch, Sammy.

It was Sammy who tried to defend himself first, "Layne, there's not a trail to follo—"

Her hands slammed down onto the table in small fists as she rose to her feet and snapped at him. "He's not a fucking ghost! There's a fucking trail somewhere! I don't give a shit if you have to talk to every goddamn hooker in the five boroughs! *Somebody* knows *something*!"

Lord help her, she wanted to shoot the next person who tried to tell anything less than helpful to her current situation.

It wasn't just the lack of action and information that had her anger topping out, but the stress that, at any moment, Liam could strike again, and she wouldn't see it coming. He had already managed to take her by surprise twice; she didn't want to be caught off guard a charming third time.

Jonathan immediately went into mediator mode and raised both of his hands in front of him. "Let's just take a moment here to evaluate everything."

She tilted her head as she stared at her prime negotiator, a mostly clean-cut-looking guy. His dark brown was always styled into place, and just the faintest semblance of a goatee around his mouth.

"What's there to evaluate? I feel like a sitting duck, all I've got is twenty-four-seven security detail up my ass and the realization that Liam has been stealing from me. What part of that should make me feel good about where we are currently at, huh?"

Met with blank stares for a moment, all she could hear was her pulse roaring in her ears as her blood pressure rose in conjunction with her temper.

"What do you want us to do?" Ethan shifted in his seat as he posed the question to her.

Layne hung her head down as she shut her eyes, trying to think past her swirling emotions. Refusing to sit back down, she spoke through gritted teeth, "Someone get me a fucking name. The name of someone who can help me. I don't care who they are or where they're from."

When she lifted her head and opened her eyes, they were all still sitting there with solemn looks on their damn faces.

"NOW!" She barked at them, wondering what they were waiting for.

Sam was the first to push out of his chair and leave the room, followed quickly by Jonathan.

Ethan was slow to make his way out, stopping and whispering to her, "Liam always finds a way to fuck himself over; we'll find something sooner or later." Then, there was hesitation as his voice caught as though he was about to say something more.

Layne looked up at the broad and muscular man at her side. His longer locks of blonde hair hung down out of place in front of his eyes.

"What else?" she said defeatedly, expecting another dose of bad news.

Unsure of what lengths Layne was willing to go to or how desperate she was feeling, he hesitated in directing her towards a wild card. Ethan cleared his throat. "There's a high roller at table fifteen, the one that looks like he's had five too many plastic surgeries. He knows a guy that might be able to help."

The faintest glimmer of hope began to chase away her frustration. "What type of guy?"

"Just," he sighed, "a guy that I've heard that has methods that would have sent Eric Ellis crying to his mommy. Some Russian dipshit, not anyone I would want watching my back."

Of course, it was a deranged Russian—those assholes always seemed to have a screw loose. This bit of information sounded both promising and terrifying.

Seeing the gears turning in Layne's head, Ethan frowned and placed a hand on top of hers. "Only for use in case of emergency, Layne. I'm serious."

She gave a slow nod as she took it all under consideration.

"Thanks, E. I appreciate it." Layne offered him a light smile before he did the same and left her there with her considerations of what she should do.

Once she composed herself and pulled her big boss bitch panties on, she headed over to table fifteen. Sure enough, there was some man who should have looked old enough to be her grandfather, yet his face was stretched so tight that the jazzercise leotards from the eighties would have been jealous.

When she approached, she lifted a finger to the attendant at the roulette table, prompting a pause in action. Layne pulled up a seat next to the man Ethan directed her to.

Mr. Shiny Plastic Face glanced over at her and grunted.

Layne leaned against the edge of the table as she faced him. "I don't think I need to introduce myself. I need the name of someone who's known to get results, and I'm told you're the man who is going to give it to me."

The fucker laughed like she was running a standup comedy joint here. The other players at the table even knew that had been a mistake, and all seemed to lean back in their chairs.

Her cheeks grew warm with the flare of her irritation. Not in the mood to play fucking games with some rich asshole, she snatched the back of his head and slammed it forward into the table.

The impact had chips rattling and skittering in several directions. She made sure his face met the table two more times before holding his bloodied mug down against it.

She leaned in and harshly spoke to him, “The goddamn name. *Now*.”

Whimpering at the superficial damage she had done to his precious face he treasured so much, he stuttered out, “M-my… pocket, left pocket. His card is in my wallet.”

Pinning his head down, she went in search of the wallet. When she retrieved it, she opened it one-handedly, thumbing out a small black card from one of the slots. Layne released the gambler while she looked over the glossy cardstock with nothing but the initials ‘D.P.’ and a QR code on it.

“This him?” She showed the card to the man who was fumbling for cocktail napkins for the laceration above the bridge of his nose that was forking blood down both sides of his nose.

“Y-yes,” he muttered.

“Thanks for your cooperation.” Layne tossed the worn leather wallet onto the roulette wheel. After tucking the card away safely into her pocket, she motioned to a security guard to get the pathetic mess of a man out of her club.

Her eyes found Joey sitting at the table he had promised he’d be occupying. His soul-capturing brown eyes stared at her after the minor show of violence she had just put on. Layne’s heart both swelled and ached; he was worth every last emergency call and last-ditch effort. Hell, if she wasn’t going to make a deal with every devil, demon, and god if it meant preventing the two loves of her life from sacrificing themselves for her.

Chapter Fourteen

JOB OFFER

Sunrise. Sundown. Rinse and repeat. There had been no word from her trusted trio of associates, and it left her questioning whether doomsday would arrive sooner or later. There was no question it would arrive at some point.

Gage had forbidden her from talking with Liam, which had been easy enough since her brother hadn't bothered her since their last phone call. It was either a blessing or curse that she didn't have Liam chirping in her ear. But the silence? It was fucking unnerving.

Layne had kept the information about the unhinged Russian contact to herself. There was no need to get one or both De Lucas riled up over her consideration of involving a potentially risky third party. Not to mention, no matter how many attempts she made to get the QR code to work on the business card, it kept giving her various errors. They weren't your standard 404 errors when the webpage no longer existed; the errors had such foreign code to her that she was pretty sure she had been trying to break into the Matrix.

"Have you heard back from…" Joey grimaced before saying Brandon's cringy hacker name, "Cowboy?"

Layne pulled another dress from the rack inside the high-end clothing store, looking it over, she shook her head. "No, he said he should have something soon though. He's just running through the street cameras looking for any sign of Liam and his two miscreants coming or going from the Chinese restaurant."

She turned and raised the black satin cocktail dress for Gage to see. "Yes or no?"

Gage immediately shook his head and gave a thumbs down. "Baby, while anything you pick is going to look amazing on the floor, I think you're better off with something that makes you stand out in the crowd. Everyone needs to know that you're with me and to bow down to the fucking Queen of New York." He grinned proudly.

"You said the theme is 'Blackout,' and everyone was going to be wearing all black!" Layne exclaimed in exasperation as she roughly returned the hanger to the silver hook it came from. Black dresses blended in with a crowd no matter which way you cut it. This was one of the reasons she loathed dress shopping without Rebecca.

Cassidy's Chains was hosting its official Grand Opening party in a month despite already being open for business full-time. The party was invitation only, and Gage was determined to make it one hell of an upscale bash.

Smirking, Gage reached over and pulled another dress from the rack. "How about this one?" He waggled his eyebrows suggestively at her, looking oh-so-hopeful for her acquiescence.

Layne looked at the thin strip of fabric being marketed as a dress and placed a hand on her hip. "Are you kidding me? Wearing tinfoil would be more appealing." She shook her head and went back to flipping through the options in search of another black dress.

Gage chuckled and shrugged before returning the dress to where it came from.

Accompanying Layne shopping wasn't high on Joey's list of favorite things to do, but they had turned their group date into shopping, dinner, and a show. He leaned against a wall, crossing his arms in front of his chest.

Feeling his phone vibrate, a notification in his pocket, Joey dug it out and looked at the message that had just come in. "Jonathan says he might have something of interest."

She shifted her attention over to Joey; her curiosity was immediately piqued at the first sign of life from one of her worker bees. "Tell him after we leave here, we are heading to Qwerty for dinner; he can debrief me before we eat."

Clearing his throat, Gage chimed in, "*After* we eat. Anything related to your brother pisses you off, and then you bitch you're not hungry. So, he can tell you after you have something in your stomach."

With a frustrated groan, Layne rolled her eyes. "So, I can be pissed and nauseous throughout the show?"

"After dinner then," Joey confirmed, taking Gage's side as he texted the details over to Jonathan. If she was worried about the topic of Liam souring her mood tonight, he had plans to counteract that. Plans that involved having her squirming in her seat during the show.

His eyes glanced over at Layne, lustfully thinking of all the ways to make sure she was aptly distracted during the highly-rated acrobat show they planned to attend. It wasn't some family-friendly circus show, this one was advertised as quite the opposite, with darker themes of seduction and the magnificence of the human body.

Joey dropped his cell back into his pocket. As he was about to get comfortable against the wall, something caught his eye. He promptly walked over to a rack several down from Layne, selecting a dress from it, and he returned to them both.

"This one." The hanger dangled from Joey's fingers and suspended from it was a striking crimson dress.

Her eyes were immediately drawn to the beauty of the garment. While she thought it was stunning, it wasn't even close to the party's dress code. "Joey, it's red."

Gage immediately let out an appreciative whistle. "It's perfect." He smiled broadly, immediately falling in love with the shape of the dress. His dick was stirring to life in his pants, just thinking about how it would cling to Layne's body and how the color would match her spirit. Dress code be damned.

Despite her protests, both Joey and Gage refused to consider any other dress but the one Joey had selected. Once again, the De Luca brothers outvoted her.

After they left the store, they all had a delicious meal together at the oddly named upscale restaurant and microbrewery.

At the end of the meal, Jonathan arrived at their table. He stole an unused chair from the next table over and dragged it to the empty space between Gage and Layne.

Standing, Gage's hand took the back of the chair her associate brought over. "Take my seat."

The two men stared at one another in a battle of intimidation before Jonathan looked to Layne for her opinion. Gage didn't bother waiting for input from anyone; he immediately occupied the chair right next to Layne. He didn't give a fuck who the pretty boy thought he was; he didn't want anyone coming between him and his girl.

"Looks like you're taking Gage's seat." Layne shrugged.

Doubling down, Gage draped his arm along the back of Layne's chair and flashed a shit-eating grin.

With Joey seated on the other side of Layne, he smirked, knowing damn well he would have done the same exact thing as his brother. Well, maybe he would have done it a bit more aggressively and shoved Jonathan down into the seat.

Layne took a large sip from the frosted pint glass filled with a beer that had hoppy notes of citrus and pine. It carried enough of an alcohol content that she was feeling less tense than she had at the start of dinner.

Not able to wait another minute to hear whatever was discovered, she prompted him, "Spill it." Her eyes set on the man who was supposed to be a diplomatic guru and curator of navigating the toughest conversations.

Jonathan subtly wiped his palms against the thighs of his pants. "He purchased 430 East 84th Street."

She damn near dropped her beer. If it hadn't been for Gage's quick reflexes that took the glass from her hand and set it on the table in front of her, it would have ended all over the front of her blouse and jeans.

"Motherfucker," Joey grumbled, recognizing the address of the residence of one very deceased Eric Ellis. Layne had put the piece of real estate on the market months ago and recently off-loaded it with the acceptance of a generous offer.

The disbelief threaded through each of Layne's words, "What? It was sold to a corporation; it was plain as day on the settlement papers."

Her associate apologetically scrunched his eyebrows together as he looked at her. "SVO & Son Enterprises? It's just a placeholder, Layne. Liam's the sole owner."

Once again, her brother had flown under her radar. "Scott Vance O'Reilly and Son Enterprises," she muttered at the realization. This time, it was so blatantly under her nose that he had done it, she was pretty sure Liam's ego right now was the biggest it ever had been.

Gage's hand squeezed her thigh supportively. "He's fucked in the head, baby. He's trying to emulate your dad and live out whatever skewed sense of what could have been."

Joey looked over at Layne with pain and anger filling his eyes at how things were getting so much worse and not looking any better. He should have thrown Liam in the trunk of Shannon O'Reilly's car before it blew to pieces if he had been graced with the foresight to know how the youngest of the O'Reilly clan would haunt him so many years later.

Looking over at Jonathan, Joey cut to the chase, "What's he want with Eric's property?"

"Don't know. Your guess is as good as mine." Jonathan shrugged before looking over at Layne. "There's one more thing."

The way her stomach was beginning to churn, she was regretting the burger she had consumed twenty minutes ago. Her eyes narrowed at Jonathan, wondering what the hell else could be dumped on her.

"He…" her associate paused to choose his words carefully. "He called Sammy earlier. Sam didn't want to say anything to you, not after our meeting at the Brass Mirror. He made me swear not to tell you, but..."

Her eyes went from the warm green of a grassy knoll on a summer day to the shadowy moss on rocks at the bottom of an oceanside cliff. "Tell. Me. What?" Layne squeezed her words out past her clenched jaw as she leaned forward.

"Liam offered Sam a job." His visible discomfort as he shifted in his seat indicated that this wasn't a job involving doing grocery checkout at the supermarket.

A lump formed in Layne's throat, and both De Lucas on either side of her had their tensions inflating a thickness in the air around their table.

All eyes were on Jonathan; everyone on edge, waiting.

"Um, he turned it down, but… Liam offered Sam a well-paid spot on his team if Sam would, I quote, 'force his dick in you until you were broken and bleeding.'" It was clear from the shade of beet red that Jonathan's cheeks were now turning that he hadn't wanted to deliver this message either.

Gage nearly flipped the damn table over the second he shot up onto his feet, ready to brutally slaughter the messenger.

As the words sank in, Layne sat there feeling like the walls were closing in all around her.

Joey's rage followed closely behind his brother's, but he had the clarity not to take it out on Jonathan.

In the depths of her soul, Layne wanted to believe that those words never came out of Liam's mouth. Yet, all she could hear was her brother's twisted laughter inside of her head. She squeezed her eyes shut, trying to force all the thoughts back into a tiny black box inside of her where she never had to acknowledge they existed.

When her eyelids popped back open, Joey was ripping Gage off of her associate, who appeared so shaken that she would be surprised if he hadn't pissed his pants.

Getting in Jonathan's face, Gage spat out threat after threat, "If any of you fuckers ever consider laying a goddamn finger on her, I will fucking toss you into a bath of nitric acid and watch you rot!" He clenched onto the front of Jonathan's shirt, gave him several harsh shakes, and refused to let go.

She fought the urge to look around at the gawkers who were watching the scene they were causing in the otherwise tame atmosphere. Instead, she focused on reeling in her thoughts within the unraveling chaos in her small little world there at the table.

Attempting to force the trembling sensation in her limbs to cease, she got onto her feet. She put a hand each on Joey and Gage to draw their attention. Maybe it was the pleading look in her eyes or the draining of color from her face, but the hold on Jonathan's shirt was relinquished, and Gage allowed Joey to pull him back a few steps.

Her head was spinning, so when she spoke to her associate, who was sitting there wide-eyed, she wasn't even sure how much of what she said was intelligible. "Find out why—why he bought the house."

She backed up a couple of steps and grabbed her jacket off the back of her chair on her hurried exit from the restaurant. Gage followed directly behind her, leaving Joey glaring at Jonathan.

"The next time you have any information on that fuckface, you bring it to me first." There was no need for Joey to tack on an 'or else' to his demand, the deadly cold stare he gave was enough to make a corpse shiver.

Chapter Fifteen

LET THE GAMES BEGIN

The crisp air outside the restaurant had been more refreshing than the beer she had been drinking inside. The breeze swept away some of the panic that had been attempting to pull her under.

She pushed her arms into the sleeves of her cargo-style jacket, her hands pulling her long brunette tresses out from underneath the back of it afterward.

Layne remained standing out front, watching the hustle and bustle of the people on the sidewalk. The microbrewery, Qwerty, was basically in the center of the busiest section of Times Square. Even with the evening quickly falling over the city, the massive number of electronic signs lit up the area like it was high noon.

A pair of strong arms came down around her, pulling her back into the safety and warmth of Gage's chest. His face nuzzled into the side of her neck, lightly kissing over the soft skin and inhaling the scent of her soap.

"How are you doing, Lucky Charm?" His voice was just loud enough for her to hear but gentle enough not to come off as startling.

She swallowed down another piece of her anxiety. "I'm fine."

Gage's arms squeezed around her, wishing they could make everything right in her world.

Stepping outside right as Layne responded, Joey came around to face her. He cradled her face in his hands. "Layney, we all know that's bullshit. It's okay if—"

With a bit more forcefulness in her tone, she repeated herself, "I said I'm fine. If he wants to give me more reason to hate him, he's only making my life easier."

It was the answer she wanted them to hear, not the one she wanted to scream into the void. Trying to blow by the topic of her asshole sibling, she stepped out from between the two men. "We're going to be late for the show."

Allowing her to create space for herself, Gage dropped his arms from around her, and Joey's fingertips glided across her cheeks as she began to walk into the flow of foot traffic.

Layne led the way, with Joey and Gage quietly conversing two strides behind her. Both of them made sure they had a set of eyes on her back.

Joey leaned over, whispering to his brother, "Have you heard back from any of your buddies if they've discovered any other shifts amongst the other factions?"

Gage shook his head. "Nothing. Have you made the call?"

Inhaling deeply with a slow exhale, Joey also shook his head. "I'm trying to avoid it. It's a favor I don't want to ask unless we get desperate."

"Joe, this shit isn't going to de-escalate itself. He already tried to shoot her once."

Grunting at the memory of the pain of having a bullet lodged in his chest, Joey's hand rubbed the fresh scar over his heart. "Don't have to remind me."

They all passed by a set of doors that led from a theater. Timing as it was, a show was just letting out, and a sea of people came pouring from the double doors. The human stampede came between Layne and the guys, separating them further and obscuring Joey and Gage's view of their girl.

Joey yelled out, "Layne, hold up!" His words were lost over the sound of boisterous conversations of the audience that had just left the theater.

"Fuck," Gage muttered as he tried to push through the crowd.

When both guys got past the sudden surge of people, they still couldn't lay eyes on where Layne had wandered off to.

"She probably is still heading straight for the show's venue," Joey attempted to reason.

The two of them stepped off to the side, out of the flow of pedestrian traffic. Gage took out his phone and was in the process of pulling up Layne's location when a seemingly old homeless man with a Yankees ball cap approached them.

The strange man was hunched over and wobbly on his two feet. The brim of the cap shrouded his face, but visible was his peppered beard, which was unkempt and scraggly as it extended several inches below his chin.

With an unsure and meek voice, the disheveled man leaned in towards Gage, "P-please, excuse me. Could you spare some money? I could use some food."

Barely sparing the man a glance and irritated with the homeless man's shitty timing, Joey placed a hand on the vagrant's chest to stop him from getting closer to Gage. "Sorry, man, can't help." Joey continued to peer over at the phone in Gage's hand.

Gage's impatience grew by the second as he waited for Layne's blue dot to appear on the phone's digital map. Just as it did, the stranger tried to pull the phone from his hands.

"Maybe I could use your phone instead?" The strange man's strangely clean hands tugged at the device Gage was holding.

Defensively, Gage grabbed the dude's wrist and took back possession of his phone. He flung the man's hand away from him.

Angrily, Gage shouted, "Back the fuck up, motherfucker! What the hell is wrong with you?!" Jesus, he had never seen a homeless person so damn brazen before.

Joey huffed and, pulled a twenty from his pocket and tossed it at the guy. "Here, get the hell outta here asshole!"

The man fumbled for the bill and began to profusely thank them both, trying to shake their hands and grace them with all the blessings in the world.

When the crazy beggar went on his way, Joey looked over at Gage's phone. "Got eyes on her?"

With a nod, Gage zoomed in on her location and then looked up at their surroundings. "She should be right over there," his finger pointing towards the mob of tourists filling the heart of the popular sightseeing destination.

"Fuckin' Times Square," Joey muttered at the insanely busy area that made this place a nightmare to traverse.

Feeling the sudden herd of people behind her, Layne stopped and looked back. Her eyes were unable to locate either Joey or Gage. "Great..."

After feeling a figure knock into her shoulder, she stumbled a half step before a painful grip curled around her bicep. Her head spun around to face whoever was holding onto her, to be greeted with the face of the last person she wished to see tonight.

Liam's lips curled into a forced smile. "Keep walking." He yanked her close to his side.

Before she could protest, underneath the coverage of her jacket, she felt the unforgiving metal tip of a blade digging into her side. It was positioned perfectly between her fourth and fifth ribs, if he wanted to drive it into her heart, he easily could have.

Her brother leaned over and whispered into her ear as he led her farther away from her dutiful protectors, "At least fuckin' smile like you're happy to see me."

When her scowl didn't leave her face, more pressure was applied to the knife placed at her side.

Layne snarled as she mustered as much of a damn smile as he was going to get from her. "I'll be happy to see you when you're lying in a coffin."

As they walked into the thick crowd of the tourist area, he came to a stop right in the middle of the most densely populated section and also the most public. Times Tower, the twenty-five-story building with its iconic three-hundred-and-fifty-foot LED screen, loomed over them. The colors of the changing advertisements flashed across both their faces.

Her eyes quickly surveyed the busy surroundings. She scanned the area for Joey and Gage, assessed opportunities for a swift getaway, and noted the occasional police officer performing their public safety duties. Nothing was in her favor; Joey and Gage were lost in the crowd, the foot traffic was too thick and unpredictable, and murdering her brother in the middle of Times Square would be a publicity nightmare in the best-case scenario—battling homicide charges was the worst case. This was all assuming she wasn't stabbed to death first.

Keeping close to her, Liam's painful grip never let up. He kept his face inches from hers. "Did you get my message, Layne?"

She glared at him. "What message?"

Liam snickered, clearly getting off on the games he was playing that had been concocted inside his demented mind. "The message that there isn't anyone who I'm not willing to turn against you. Everybody has their price, and I have the funds to pay it."

"Go fuck yourself, Li. Not everyone in my inner circle can be bought." Trying to pull her body away from the threat of being stabbed was unsuccessful, and the tip poked through the thin layer of her shirt and then pierced the first layers of skin. Her hardened exterior faltered for the first time. Layne sharply inhaled as she winced, feeling the light tickle of a drop of her blood begin to drip down her side.

Her brother's face displayed wicked amusement at getting that brief reflection of her pain from her.

"Oh, you mean fuck boys one and two? Are you sure they're as loyal to you as they say?" He cocked his head at her, hazel eyes staring into her own and beating at the door of her soul's resiliency.

When she refused to respond, she was sure he was going to shove the blade between her ribs as the pressure continued to painfully increase.

"Check your phone." His weapon pulled back on the threat to impale her, but only just enough that she could breathe a little easier.

The urge to take her chances of making national headlines by blowing her brother away in Times Square was looking more and more appealing. However, she followed his instructions, and her hand slowly pulled her phone from her jacket pocket. Her eyes glanced down at the screen, where a notification from an unknown number was waiting for her.

"Go on, Layne, check your messages," Liam urged with nearly giddy excitement.

Using her thumb to unlock the phone and check the latest message, her fingers could barely conceal their trembling. When she pulled up the text, it only contained pictures.

The first picture was of a young woman in her early twenties with a large pregnant belly. Layne didn't recognize the girl at all. "So what? Do you need the birds and the bees to be explained to you?"

"Don't you know who that is? That's Mackenzie Pearce, the daughter of the tragically murdered Mayor Pearce. She's due with a baby boy any day now." The way Liam pretended he cared made Layne's disgust come to a head.

Her thoughts reeled back to when Joey had taken the contract on the retired mayor's head a little over eight months ago.

"You said it was an in-and-out job," Layne looked at Joey as he came into the living room, coming home later than expected.

He tossed his work duffle onto the floor next to the sofa, and his words came out strained with irritation, "It would have been, but apparently, his daughter was visiting for the holiday and was staying over."

Layne lifted a brow. "So, what did you do?"

Joey's hand pinched the bridge of his nose. "What the hell do you think? I took care of it–of her."

She blinked several times at him at his snippy response and uncharacteristically bad mood.

"I'm going upstairs to shower and go to bed." He left her there without so much as an apology or effort to smooth over his shortness with her.

Normally, after he finished a contract, he wanted nothing more than to curl up with her and relax. Not this time.

Coming back to the present with the image of the woman in front of her, she felt conflicted with all the things her heart knew about Joey and what her brain was trying to rationalize.

Liam lowered his voice to ask his next question, "How confident are you that he bothered using protection when he was fucking her?"

Layne pressed her lips together in a hard line, trying to combat the intrusive thoughts riddling her core with doubts. Joey had never bothered using a condom when he was with her, and since she was on birth control, she had never questioned it before now.

She tried to move past all the scenarios trying to infiltrate her mind by swiping to the next picture in the message.

The next image was of Gage and two attractive women inside his club. Looking closer at the surroundings, it was sometime after the renovations were done to convert Cassidy's Cave into Cassidy's Chains. Each woman was perched on one of his knees with his hands holding each of them around their waists. They were leaning in close to him, their fucking tits practically up in his face and their hands resting right on top of his damn crotch like they owned it.

Her brother frowned. "I'm sorry, sis. You deserve better. You can't possibly expect them to stick to one partner when you won't do the same." He watched as he saw the gradual decline in the faith of her two guys in her eyes filled with unshed tears.

Trying to come up with good reasons for the stories behind both pictures was becoming a losing battle. Her hand shakily turned the screen off, yet she could see both photos popping up in her mind still.

Sniffling back her emotions, her eyes looked at Liam, and shook her head firmly. "It doesn't change what you've done." Internally, she grasped for any straw of anger to chase back her rattled insecurities.

Liam shrugged and tapped the knife idly against her ribcage. "When you're ready to fall in line, I will be waiting. You had your chance to hand everything over to me and take your leave quietly. Now? Things have to get messy so that you can learn your lesson."

In the distance, over the dull roar of the crowd, she heard her name being shouted. Her attention was drawn away from Liam as she looked frantically for a familiar face or two. The first pair of chocolate eyes she met was Gage's, followed by the coffee hues belonging to Joey.

Realizing his time with Layne was up, Liam withdrew the threatening blade from her side and released his painful hold on her arm. No sooner had he done both of those things than he thrust the knife down into the muscle of her thigh.

Layne gasped as she felt the cold steel enter her leg, when she looked down, there was a goddamn pocket knife in her body. Well, fuck. That wasn't supposed to be there, was it? The searing pain quickly followed the sight her brain was trying to wrap itself around.

When she looked back up, Liam was already quickly blending back into the movement of people all around her. Ragged breaths escaped her as the pain and rage fused together in her veins.

Both her men had rushed to her the second they saw Liam leering over their girl. From their angle, they only saw a movement from Liam before Layne flinched and hunched over. The coward took off quickly thereafter.

"Layne!" Joey appeared at her side first.

Losing all sense in the hurricane of her feelings, she was already pulling out her Glock. Layne was prepared to empty her goddamn clip if it meant there was a chance of one bullet finding its way into Liam's skull.

Coming to her other side, Gage's hand abruptly shoved her arm back down, quickly pulling the firearm from her grasp and tucking it inside the front of his waistband underneath his shirt. He harshly whispered in her ear, "Hey! What the hell are you doing?"

"That fucking, son of a bitch, asshole!" The anger in her voice was enhanced by both the physical and emotional pain she was experiencing. She went to take a step to go after Liam, forgetting there was a fucking pocket knife stuck in her. Layne stumbled as the pain reminded her of that small but important fact.

Joey's hands caught her by her arm and waist. He looked down at Liam's parting gift and cursed under his breath. "Gage, we gotta get her out of here." He glanced around them, hoping between the both of them, they could cloak Layne's injury with their massive frames until they got someplace private.

Gage wrapped an arm around her. "Baby, just hold onto me."

She winced as the pain just seemed to blossom across her entire thigh now that her adrenaline was slowly fading. Feeling both of their hands on her, images flashed across her memory of the images on her phone.

"Don't touch me!" She snapped at them, shoving their hands away.

Seeing her lash out at both of them as they tried to help took them by surprise.

Her gaze fell back down to her leg, and the blood soaked into her jeans. "Fuck!" Layne groaned as her hand went to the handle of the knife, wrapping around it, ready to yank it out.

"Whoa, whoa, whoa." Joey took both her hands before she did something stupid. "Just stop, Layne. Look at me and fucking think for a damn second."

While she was directing her vicious stare at Joey, it was Gage who began tying the arms of his jacket around Layne's hips to cover the glaring injury before anyone else noticed.

As clouded as her head was, filled with a myriad of emotions ranging from highs to lows, Layne still recognized that she couldn't just stand there in her current state. "Call Jonathan and have him come here to pick me up and bring me to Dr. Patty's."

Gage tightened the knot of the jacket around her hips and looked over at Joey, hoping he wasn't the only one of them confused by her request for one of her associates.

Not seeing any indication that Joey knew what the fuck was going on, Gage reached over to try to hold her face. "Look at me, Layne," his tone soft in hopes she wouldn't verbally or physically lash out again. "Let us help you, baby. I don't know what happened, but we need to get you patched up."

The tug of emotions in her eyes was causing them to fill with watery frustration and pain. "I don't want you to do anything except call Jonathan and have him come get me." Her voice shook. Jonathan wasn't her first choice, but he was likely the next best one, given she knew he had been in the area after their discussion at the restaurant.

Joey's irritation was clear as he spoke under his breath, "This is fucking insane." Regardless, he pulled out his phone and called her associate as requested.

While he gave Jonathan directions, he and Gage assisted Layne to the nearest side street that was mostly out of the public eye. She stubbornly tried to refuse as much of their help as possible. Gage finally bit the bullet and risked suffering her wrath when he wrapped an arm around her waist and all but damn carried her the last few steps against his side.

Refusing to make eye contact with either De Luca brother, she silently leaned back against the side of a building while they waited for Layne's ride to arrive. Not accepting any further assistance, she used Gage's jacket to help stem the bleeding until she got proper medical attention.

Layne looked down at the knife buried in her left quadriceps. Her chin quivered as she saw the silver inscription lasered into the black handle.

J. De Luca

Chapter Sixteen

PATCHED UP

Her torn and bloodied jeans were in a pile next to her on the patient table inside Dr. Patty Kimmel's in-home clinic. Layne sat there in her underwear, furiously typing on her phone.

Jonathan was doing his best not to directly stare at his half-dressed boss, despite her obvious lack of fucks given.

"Are you sure you don't want me to wait outside?" He asked for the sixth time.

Growing more irritated every time he asked, Layne finally lowered her hands into her lap and looked over at him with exasperation filling her tone. "You want to be useful? Go outside and tell Joey and Gage to go the hell home."

The guys had followed Jonathan's car there to Dr. Patty's house, despite her repeated protests that her associate was more than capable of getting her there in one piece.

Unsure whose fury he would have rather endured in that moment, it seemed getting out of the room with Layne seemed the wisest decision. Jonathan took the opportunity and immediately scurried out into the hall.

A minute later, Layne could hear the front door close as he went to deliver her message. Did she really think either man lingering out front would listen to him? No, but it at least gave her a few minutes of peace with her thoughts.

She returned to tapping out a few more texts on her phone to her trusted techie, Brandon. From a short stool in front of Layne, the doctor glanced up at her and spoke without judgment in her voice. "You know as well as I do, Layne, that poor man is going to get an earful." She gave a soft chuckle.

Layne sighed. "His damn nervous energy was going to drive me insane if he stayed in here any long—" A hiss of pain escaped her lips as a fresh wave of pain coursed through her thigh.

"Sorry, all done." The woman in front of her finished wrapping the bandage around Layne's leg before getting up from the stool she had been perched on. With a light snapping sound, Dr. Patty removed the latex gloves from her hands and tossed them into a waste basket.

Silence filled the room, but it wasn't until Layne realized that Dr. Patty hadn't moved that she stopped her fingers' swift movements across the screen of her phone. The doctor was standing there with her hip cocked and a hand on her waist, looking at Layne over the tops of her glasses.

"What?" Layne asked in clear confusion as to why she was getting a stern look from her private physician. Granted, getting stabbed wasn't an ideal visit, though very few of her visits were routine checkups. Layne would like to think she had been a half-decent patient in not punching the crap out of the doctor when the knife had been dislodged from her leg.

Dr. Patty pulled the glasses from her face and perched them on top of her head. "I know the look of trouble in paradise, and I know you. Do you want my non-medical advice?"

"Are you going to give it to me anyway?" Layne had a feeling she knew the answer and expected to hear a long, drawn-out speech about playing nice in the sandbox, not being so damn stubborn, and how everything would be back to normal in a day or so. That was not the talk she got.

"Do they even know why you're pissed off?" She paused and then raised both her brows at Layne. "Do *you* even know why you're pissed off?"

The pointed questions weren't what Layne had expected. She took a moment to carefully mull over what she was asking, then frowned. Layne started to respond, "I…" but then she realized she didn't have a worthy answer.

Layne's eyes watched as the doc moved over to the sink and grabbed an item off the counter. When she returned, she held her hand out to Layne. Lying there in her palm was the pocket knife belonging to Joey that Liam had rudely embedded in her leg.

Taking the weapon from Dr. Patty, she gave a partial attempt at a smile. “Thanks.”

Lowering her now empty hand, she continued, “I don’t know Gage as well as I know Joey, but one of those men took a bullet for you. If that doesn’t speak to his character, I don’t know what does. So, whatever has you in a tizzy, the least you could do is clue them in on it. In all my years of practicing medicine, I have never come across a man who can read a woman’s mind except when it comes to one thing. Even then, it’s a rarity.”

Looking down at the inscription on the knife, Layne nodded. The truth was, both men had taken a bullet for her. Would they be capable of betraying her trust after something like that? What if they really had gone so far as to break their bonds with her? Maybe they both decided that if she got to indulge in more than one partner, then they should be afforded that luxury as well.

Pulling Layne from her thoughts, the woman spoke as she moved to the door, “Just something to think about.” She winked and gave a smile to Layne that was filled with kindness and warmth before leaving Layne to get dressed.

After dropping the knife into her jacket pocket, Layne was pulling up her jeans gingerly over her thighs as her phone began to ring. Answering, she pinned the phone to her ear with her shoulder as her fingers buttoned and zipped her pants. “Howdy, Cowboy. I’m guessing you got all my messages?”

Brandon spoke into her ear, and what he said had her straightening up and taking the phone into her hand. “What do you mean the QR code leads to a site that needs a password? It’s just a bunch of garbled nonsense when I pull the site up.”

Unsurprisingly, Brandon was better at this tech bullshit than she was and was able to sort through the code to find the access point. Apparently, said portal needed a password. That was incredibly inconvenient.

Great, now she needed something she didn’t have in order to contact a guy she didn’t know. “Okay, I will work on it. What about the two photos I sent over to you?”

She listened carefully as Brandon explained that the photo of Mackenzie Pearson was legitimate, it was even posted on the girl’s socials. He hadn’t been able to find anything out about the father-to-be, effectively leaving Layne still questioning Joey’s behavior when he was out of her sight.

There was some good news: the photograph of Gage was a complete fabrication, a good one but fake nonetheless. Fucking AI was getting better and better these days.

Cringing and feeling sheepish, Layne groaned at her idiocy for allowing Liam to fucking toy with her head.

Her hacker friend on the phone continued to give her updates on the other things he was working on, including finding out who had been with Liam at the Chinese restaurant. Brandon had been able to pull images of the two individuals and was cross-referencing their identities as he spoke.

She felt some of her stress melt away. "I appreciate the update. Let me know when you have a name or anything else useful." At least they were getting somewhere on finding out more about who was working with Liam.

As Layne said goodbye and hung up, she heard the front door of Dr. Patty's home aggressively slam shut, followed by heavy stomps approaching the exam room.

Swinging the door open, Joey burst into the room, his voice booming in the quaint space. "What the hell is going on with you?! I'm not taking fucking orders from Jonathan just because you're being too chickenshit to come talk to us yourself!"

She opened her mouth to say something, but he stepped up in front of her, continuing to yell so she couldn't get a word in edgewise.

"When the hell are you going to get it through your thick fucking skull that we are doing every goddamn thing we can to protect your ass and take care of you?! Instead, you keep fighting us tooth, nail, and titty on it!" He kept leaning in towards her with each word he shouted in her face.

In frustration, he let out a growl before continuing his venting, "You are the biggest pain in my ass! I swear to God, if I didn't know better, I'd think you have a fuckin' death wish!"

Layne had enough of his anger being hurtled at her that she finally snapped and began to toss it right back at him. She squared her shoulders, and her hand pushed at his chest as a warning for him to step back.

"Who the fuck do you think you are coming in here acting like you're not as big of a pain in the ass, huh?! You don't get to charge in here, ready to unleash hell on me because you don't like what I'm doing! I didn't ask for either of you to fuckin' hover over me, ready to protect me from a goddamn papercut!" Seeing that he hadn't budged from his position looming over her, she used both hands to shove him this time.

Joey's eyes widened before he pointed at her leg. "You call this a paper cut?!"

Gage came to the doorway of the room right as Layne was beginning to get physical with Joey. As equally frustrated with Layne as his brother was, he had still tried to talk him out of storming in here to wage a war none of them actually wanted. He made another attempt to intervene by firmly speaking up, "Both of you need to calm the fuck down."

With a glance at Gage, Joey sharply responded, "Fuck you! I am fucking calm!"

Layne scoffed at how clearly he was, in fact, not the least bit calm. "Get the hell out of my way. Gage can take me home."

When she went to shove him again, he defensively diverted her hands away with a firm push.

"Now all is good with him 'cause he's not the one calling you out?!" The anger still boiled beneath Joey's skin.

"At least he's not going around knocking up some girl while working a contract!" The words just fumbled out of her mouth before she could realize she was saying them. Sometimes her temper could be a heinous bitch.

Gage's eyes widened enough that they nearly fell out of his head while wondering if he correctly heard what Layne had just said.

Joey froze, standing there slack-jawed like she had just slapped him. His lips moved to try and find a response, but no words fell from him. Stunned by her accusation, he watched as Layne pushed past him and stepped around Gage to leave the room.

"What is she talking about?" Gage looked at his brother, hoping for clarification. He didn't want to murder his own brother, but if what Layne had said was true, he wouldn't hesitate.

Finally snapping out of trying to process what she had just claimed, he shook his head and stalked after her. "I have no fuckin' clue, but I'm about to find out," his voice calmer as he responded to Gage's question on his way by. Gage followed behind, needing the same answers.

Even fueled by her emotions, the fresh wound in her thigh had her moving slower than she would have liked. She had barely gotten to the front door when Joey ran up behind her and grabbed her by the elbow. He didn't let up when she rolled her shoulder to try and pull free from him.

Swinging her around to face him, Joey's confusion was quickly overriding the outrage he had been unleashing moments ago. "Layne! Have you lost your mind? What in the hell are you talking about?"

Her face was flushed, and she refused to meet his eyes. "Just forget it."

"Forget it?!" He caught himself beginning to relight the extremely short fuse he currently had going on. Taking a deep and steady breath, he did his best to ground himself. "Who is knocking up who?" It sounded ridiculous even to ask the question. He lowered his face down, trying to force her to look into his concerned brown hues.

Layne saw the doctor standing at the far end of the hall, overseeing the scene unfold. The look she was giving Layne reminded her of the one she had given earlier when she had asked what had Layne so upset.

She shifted her eyes from Dr. Patty to look at Joey, who was waiting for her to explain. Layne's emerald eyes were fighting not to fill with tears as she quietly said the name, "You and Mackenzie Pearson."

Joey wrinkled his forehead, becoming more perplexed. "*Mackenzie*?" The way he spoke her name was like it could leave an STD in his mouth. Good God, he wouldn't have touched that twisted bitch no matter how much she paid him.

Explaining further, "Yeah, I mean, it all makes sense. You were so damn off that night you came home from the job and refused to talk about it. You've never been that way after a job–ever." Layne shrugged defeatedly before attempting to pry herself out of his grasp again, only to remain unsuccessful.

He stared at her, trying to wrap his head around what alternate universe Layne thought they were living in. Then, Joey couldn't help it when a laugh bubbled up from his chest at the insanity of it all. He tried to hold it back, but the more his brain envisioned fucking Mackenzie, the next few laughs couldn't be contained.

Layne scowled at him. "I'm glad you find this fucking amusing, asshole." Taking his laughter as a sign of admission, she was damn near the point of kicking him in the balls to see if he thought that shit was funny, too.

His hand released her elbow only so he could take a firm hold of her face with both hands, looking her directly in the eyes. He failed miserably at containing his smile despite his efforts to be serious with her. "Layney, first of all, I'm not putting babies in anybody—not even you. I had that shit snipped years ago."

Seeing Layne's skepticism still etched over her features, he reassured her, "I will go jack off in a cup right now, and Dr. Patty can have it analyzed just to confirm that all I got are blanks."

"Fine, then you're not the father. Congrats." Her voice was completely flat and devoid of any emotion. It still didn't mean that Joey hadn't slept with the dumb hoe.

His thumb rubbed over her cheek, trying to stroke away her doubts. "Second, the reason I was in a bad mood that night wasn't because I had to come home to you after fucking someone else. It's because Mackenzie is a whack job, she's the one who hired me to take out her dad. She wasn't even supposed to be there that night. I was trying to get the job done, and she fucking grabbed my dick—twice." He shuddered at the memory. "Then, when I tied her up to make it look like a home invasion gone wrong–and so she would keep her hands to herself–she kept moaning like a beached whale and begging me to do weird shit to her."

Joey felt dirty even thinking about that night. "Layne, it was the worst contract I've ever taken because I had to deal with her." He was also certain if he had fucked the girl, his dick would have disintegrated into ashes from some undiscovered venereal disease.

Layne's cheeks began to grow hot as Joey began to explain away all her concerns about his faithfulness. All the concerns that had spiraled out of control in her mind, thanks to all the stress Liam's bullshit was causing her.

She sank her teeth into her bottom lip as she scrunched her brows together, realizing that maybe she had overreacted and her possessiveness over the two guys got the better of her. It wasn't like her to jump to conclusions, but nothing about what was going on in her life right now felt normal.

He shook his head at her and brought his mouth down onto hers lovingly to grab her attention for what he had to say next. "Not once since the day I met you has my cock been in another woman, and it never will be. You understand me?"

She nodded. "I'm sorry... Liam had mentioned it; then today, he showed me these pictures to try to show me you both aren't as loyal to me as I thought."

Gage stiffened hearing the source of all the lies being fed to her and grumbled, "That little prick doesn't have shit on me."

Her gaze shifted to settle on Gage while she frowned with embarrassment. "I thought he did; he sent me a picture of you at the club with two girls. It ended up being a fake, but it looked so damn real, and my head was already spinning by that point."

Pulling her into a hug, Joey gave her a hard squeeze and a peck on the forehead before he released her.

Gage took his place, capturing her chin with his fingers as he traced the bottom of her lip with the pad of his thumb. "Layne Nicole De Luca," he spoke with a playful sternness but still used her full name to emphasize how serious he was. "Until there is a day where you no longer want to wear my collar, you are the only woman that exists for me. If you haven't learned that by now, I may need to finally put you on my St. Andrew's cross."

He smirked at her, already thinking how she would look spread for him on the X-frame. Gage leaned in and affectionately locked his mouth onto hers to help wash away any of the fabrications and doubts Liam had tried to fill her head with.

When the sweet moment concluded, she suddenly remembered one more thing. "Oh!" Her hand dove into her jacket pocket and pulled out Joey's pocket knife. "This is yours." Layne offered it to him.

Joey perked up a brow, seeing that it indeed was his knife. Unnerved that Liam had gotten his hands on it and then used it on Layne, his jaw ticked as he swallowed his rage. He had been looking for that knife for several weeks and assumed it was hiding out somewhere in O'Reilly Manor.

Shaking his head, Joey nudged the closed blade back into her hand. "Hold onto it. I'll let you return it to Liam in whatever method you feel he deserves." He didn't want anything responsible for spilling Layne's blood in his possession.

Dr. Patty smiled as she watched Layne with the two men in her life who were bound to her with the utmost devotion. She knew the late Scott O'Reilly would have been so proud of his daughter, no matter how unexpected her life had taken a turn.

Chapter Seventeen

CHAOS

The vision of Layne was ethereal. Her dark brunette locks of hair were being caressed by the wind in a delicate dance. The sun illuminated her fair skin and the white wedding gown she wore. When she looked at him, her breathtaking emerald eyes sparkled as her smile made them shine even brighter.

"Why didn't you kill me, Joey?" Her words didn't match the visage of a goddess he saw before him. They were such harsh words said with such a delicate voice.

Joey stood there, reaching out for her hand. "What are you talking about? Layney, I love you. I would never hurt you." Somehow, her hand was always just out of reach of his fingertips, no matter how far he stretched.

Layne's face became flooded with glittering tears. "But you did. You killed me. You made sure I wasn't in that car. You have signed my death warrant every time you saved me."

He kept running for her, trying to close the distance between them. All he needed was to hold her. Holding her would make it all okay. Yet, no matter how fast his legs carried him, he never seemed to get any closer to her. "No, that's not true!"

Her sobs echoed in his ears. "You didn't save me this time, did you?" She looked down, and suddenly, crimson blood poured from several small holes in her chest. Holes which were created by bullets he should have taken for her. With profound sadness, she stared at her hands coated in the shiny red liquid of what should never have been spilling so freely from her body.

Joey yelled for her, feeling the painful burn of lactic acid in his legs and the ache of depleted oxygen in his lungs as he ran faster and harder for her. "NO! LAYNE!" He couldn't let her fall into death; he couldn't allow himself to lose her.

Just when he thought he could wrap his arms around her to pull her into the safe embrace of his hold, her body faded into nothing but cold.

The surroundings swirled and shifted, and now he was in the church they had been married in. At the altar were two coffins, one considerably smaller than the other.

When he approached the larger of the caskets, it remained open to reveal Shannon O'Reilly lying there in the peaceful slumber of death. He stepped over to the smaller casket, which had been left closed. Joey's hand reached out and began to lift the lid to see who was inside.

The top half of the coffin opened, and the horrific sight greeted him. A ten-year-old Layne was laid to eternal rest inside. She should have looked innocently angelic and perfect, and yet her body was bruised, and her skin was marred with damage.

The little version of Layne suddenly popped her eyes open like a creepy doll, staring directly at him. "You'll never keep me from my fate. I'm already lost."

He stumbled back, tripping over his own feet. When he fell, he expected to land on his ass—instead, the sensation of falling continued for far longer than should have been possible.

It was the jolt of startling awake from his dream that disrupted the images in his head. Joey's heart was thumping hard in his chest. Partially, he sat up as he struggled to catch his breath while he looked around the bedroom illuminated by the light of the early morning.

At his side and asleep soundly, curled up with her overstuffed pillow, was Layne. The blankets were tangled around her legs, leaving her bandaged thigh exposed to the air without the weight of the sheets on top of it. Her wavy locks of hair were held captive in a loose bun that had become half undone throughout the night.

Joey leaned over and gave the lightest of kisses to her bare shoulder so as to not wake her. He hovered close to her while he did so, drawing in the delicate scent of her body. The smell of freshly picked daisies that had been graced by the sun was what helped remind him that it all had been a nightmare.

He slid out of bed, nakedly walking around the room as quietly as his large form could manage before he located and pulled on a pair of boxer briefs. Joey took his phone off the charger and crept out into the hallway.

Allowing himself to stop tiptoeing after he was well past their bedroom door, he walked down the hall to one of the spare rooms on the second floor of O'Reilly Manor, where he locked himself inside.

There on the screen of his phone was a contact, someone he didn't want to ask a favor of. Gage had been right; there was no de-escalating the Liam situation. They were past the point of no return, and he needed to take measures with consequences be damned.

He pressed the call button and waited for someone to answer on the other end. When the bubbly receptionist picked up, Joey cleared his throat. "Hi, I need to speak to Commissioner Saito."

That afternoon, Joey found himself seated across from New York City's Police Commissioner, Vincent Saito, inside his personal residence on the North Shore of Long Island. As far as Layne was concerned, Joey was on a supply run, and Gage was left in charge of keeping watch over her.

The couch Joey was seated on was the brightest shade of white he had ever seen, and he wondered if it ever saw any use or if it just got replaced any time a stain sullied its blank canvas.

Vince held a short glass made of expensive crystal and filled with even more expensive bourbon in his hand. "Finally decided to cash in your favor, eh?" He raised the glass to his lips and swallowed down a large mouthful of the booze.

Joey rested his ankle on top of a knee as he sat back, trying to find comfort on the piece of furniture that he swore was stuffed with wood chips.

One of the household staff members Vince kept around to keep his home running smoothly brought over an identical glass of amber liquid to Joey. Taking it, Joey nodded politely and rested it on top of his knee.

"Seeing as I helped to pave the path for you to be in your current position, I figured now was as good of a time as any." Joey was keeping everything strictly business, refraining from bringing his private motivations into this discussion.

Vince may have looked like a minivan-driving soccer dad who went camping with his kids every weekend, but that didn't preclude him from being drawn into more sinister methods to get the results he wanted.

Idly swirling the remaining bourbon in his glass, the commissioner took Joey's words under his consideration. "Alright, I'll bite. What are you looking for?"

Trying to play it cool, Joey shrugged before laying it out there, "Where does Liam O'Reilly fall on your radar?"

The sudden laughter from Vince filled the massive space of a living room they were currently occupying. "Your brother-in-law?! Oh man, shit." His hand came to settle on his chest as he tried to gather his composure with a few more chuckles. "Fuck, if you were coming here to talk about anybody, I figured it'd be your wife." There were very few professional contacts who knew the unmasked version of Joey, and Vince was one of them.

Commissioner Saito snickered before he drew another sip of the bourbon into his mouth. Licking the flavor from his lips, he shook his head. "The O'Reillys have been on the NYPD's radar for some time. I'm pretty sure the Bureau even has their eyes on them."

It wasn't news that Joey was particularly happy to hear, but that's why he was here, wasn't it?

"Your wife is a real piece of work; ya know that?" He whistled in amazement. "The body count she's racked up over the past few years is astounding–according to my sources, anyways." Vince grinned as he sank back into the sofa.

Joey stared at the man who was drunk on power, the power that Joey had helped him achieve. "I'm well aware of my wife's indiscretions. I'm more interested in why the fuck Liam is still on the streets."

Tossing back the remainder of the alcohol in his glass, the commish finally engaged in the more serious side of the matter at hand. "Liam O'Reilly isn't enough of a headline-worthy perp to be focusing the NYPD's resources on. Don't get me wrong, he's not a saint, but from a political standpoint, he's nothing. Layne, on the other hand…"

Dropping his foot from his knee onto the ground, Joey leaned forward with a deadly threat looming in his eyes and a crushing grip on his glass. "You and I had a deal."

Before Joey got too carried away, Vince lifted a hand to halt him right then and there. "Relax. I'm not going back on my word. While nailing Layne would make for headlines of the century, she's not in any danger from my precincts." The press would have a field day with an attractive young woman in charge of an organized crime unit so violent that it made grown men shiver with either desire or fear.

There was no falling back into a sense of ease for Joey before Vince tacked on one little caveat, "But, I am not the only authority. As I'm sure you've heard, the FBI has helped us get the Unwind and Unorganize Program off the ground. It's only a matter of time before they realize she's not just a pretty face."

Joey consumed his entire serving of the oaky notes of booze in one go. He leaned over and set the glass on the coffee table in front of him. "Liam needs to quickly become one of New York's finest's top priorities."

"And just how do you propose I go about that without zeroing in on Layne, hm? They're from the same family. As you well know, where there is one family member with black blood, there are always more. Apples never fall far from the tree; you get what I'm saying?" The commissioner examined the empty glass hanging from his fingers as the sunlight shone through it in an array of refracted colors.

The hint of frustration reached Joey's voice as he made his point, "That sounds like it's your problem to figure out, not mine. Liam is his own person and responsible for his own actions. There's no reason you can't perform a sting operation focused on someone who shouldn't have left prison in the first place."

Chuckling at the irony, he pointed out to Joey, "Sounds like someone else I know." The commissioner's eyes looked pointedly at Joey before mulling over the idea of a sole sting op on Liam.

Vincent shifted his head from side to side, weighing every alternative. "I *could*. However, this seems like a hell of a favor to be asking."

Forcing to swallow his growl, Joey's eyes darkened with a glare. "Your biggest opponents to you taking up your current position have been silenced. Do I need to remind you what lengths I had to go to?"

Commissioner Saito leaned forward before laying out his counteroffer, "Here's the best I can do: I can look into it. Get his file reopened and turn it into an active case. It's not a quick turnaround time, though, these things need to be carefully curated." He motioned a finger at Joey's chest. "You know what would speed things up? If you suddenly recalled who put the bullet in your chest."

Well, that wasn't going to fucking happen. He wasn't about to get roped into a fucking political nightmare and put Layne in a position where her allies questioned her ability to keep her mouth shut. Openly working with the police wouldn't accomplish anything but put a strain on her business and both their livelihoods.

Joey stood and approached the man who sat comfortably in his politically powerful position with an air of arrogance wrapped around him. "If I hear the faintest whispers of Layne getting pulled into the scope of things, I guarantee you'll be waking up to a skull in your face in the middle of the fucking night."

Vince stood nowhere close to matching Joey's towering height. "Tread carefully, De Luca. Do you think you're the only one who can execute favors at my request?"

Narrowing his brown eyes, Joey chose his words carefully as he grasped the commissioner's hand in a firm handshake while laying his other hand on his shoulder and whispering into his ear, "Do you think I give a flying fuck about the sloppy assholes who pretend to be bumps in the night? They're pups trying to play amongst the wolves."

He patted the back of the commissioner's shoulder before pulling back and releasing his grip on the man's hand. "I'll be in touch."

Heading out of the room, he heard Vince shout out after him, "If the Feds get involved, it's out of my hands, and all deals are off!"

Joey prayed that it didn't come to that; he'd hate to try and take down the entire damn Government, but for Layne, he'd thrive in all the chaos.

Chapter Eighteen

LUCK

Using a small step stool, she pulled another box from the top shelf of a hallway closet where she kept some of her dad's belongings. She plunked it down on the floor with a huff. Layne sat down next to the box to see if there was anything in there that was useful in trying to predict Liam's next moves.

She lifted the lid of the box and was surprised to find nothing work-related. Instead, she found family photo albums from an era long before cameras were on phones, one where rolls of film had to be processed.

The maroon leather-bound album lying on top still had a thin layer of dust clinging to its front. She pulled it out and opened up to the first page.

Front and center was a rare impromptu O'Reilly family picture. Scott O'Reilly was in a pair of khaki shorts and powder blue polo, a grill filled with burgers and dogs behind him. Smiling proudly, his arm was wrapped around the waist of his vibrantly beautiful wife, Shannon.

The family's matriarch was in a flowy yellow sundress with a brown leather belt wrapped around her waist. Shannon's smile was as bright as the summer day when this photo was taken. Her hands were each resting on one shoulder of her two children standing in front of her.

Layne was giving the biggest, goofiest, and cheesiest-looking smile there ever was at about eight years old. Right next to her was a seven-year-old Liam, sticking his tongue out at the photographer.

Mick tried sputtering out words over his laughter, "L-Liam! Liam, stop sticking your tongue out like that! And Layne, sweetheart, can you give a nice-looking smile?" Their Uncle Mickey made one last failed attempt to wrangle the O'Reilly kids so they could get a decent snapshot during the summer cookout.

Giving up, Mick snapped the picture anyhow with a forced grin. The second he lowered the bulky camera, Layne and Liam went running off into the expanse of Mick's lush green backyard of his summer home.

Layne chased after her brother toward the swing set that was the largest she had ever seen. "Li, wait for me!"

She reached the ladder leading up to the slide at the same time as Liam, they both bumped against one another in an effort to be the first to climb up.

"Layne! I was here first!" Liam griped.

"I'm older!" Layne retorted.

Gaining the advantage of enough footing on the first rung of the ladder, Layne hurried up to the top. She made it down the slide with Liam following behind her moments later.

Not hesitating, Layne ran over to one of the two swings that swayed in the gentle breeze. She flopped her behind onto the blue seat, her hands wrapping around the metal chains that secured it to the wooden frame.

Just beginning to pump her legs to try and gain some momentum, an older child from one of the other families at the barbeque came up behind her and slammed his hands into her back. Layne was knocked right off the swing, landing face down in the grass.

The bully leered down at her like the little shit he was. "This is my favorite swing; girls aren't allowed to use it!"

As Layne pushed herself up onto her feet, Liam came barreling in and shoved the kid. "That's my sister!"

The two boys got into a shoving match while Layne ran back up the hill to tell her mom. The scuffle quickly ended when the boys were separated by one of the other parents in attendance, but not before Liam had landed at least one punch.

Scott took both of his children aside, and he praised Liam for all of his actions before sending him to get some ice on his hand. She stood alone before her father, who was down on a knee looking her in the eyes with disappointment.

"Layne," he started with a shake of his head. "Do you know what you did wrong?"

She frowned as the weight of his words sank into her soul. "No..."

"Not only did you not stick up for yourself, but you ratted out your brother. Don't you ever go snitching on your family again, do you understand me? That is not what O'Reillys do. I don't care what the hell he does; he's your brother, and you need to support him." Her father stood again, irritated with her choices. "Go on, get out of here. Go tell your mother to try to get those grass stains out of your nice clothes."

Layne slammed the photo album shut and tried to vanquish the echoing of her father's words in her head. She wondered if he would be so judgmental of her if he was alive to see what Liam was up to. Layne would like to think he wouldn't be, and not knowing for sure was the most difficult part of his absence in her life.

Sitting on the floor in the middle of the hallway, she took a moment to collect her thoughts. Her hand removed her phone from her back pocket as she brought up a name in her contacts. Layne sat there, allowing the judgment of her dad's ghost to berate her with whispers inside her ear.

Her thumb tapped the call button, and the screen suddenly reflected the damning words, 'Calling Det. Adams…'. The call rang once before Layne heard the footsteps jog up the main stairs at her back. She quickly disconnected the call before pushing herself up onto her feet.

Gage appeared at the top of the stairs and offered her a large smile. "There you are. Thought maybe you were going to try and get the slip on me."

She shoved her phone back into her pocket and shook her head. "No, just trying to go through some things. Miss me?" Layne smiled sweetly at him.

He wrapped his arms around her waist and pulled her up against the front of his body. "Always." Gage leaned over, and the warmth of his mouth washed over the length of her neck. He murmured against her skin, "You always smell so damn good."

She tipped her head back some as he lavished her with his kisses, a light purr rising from her throat. "Mmm, you're one to talk, Mr. Dolce & Gabbana." As much as she teased him about using such a fancy cologne, she couldn't complain about the way the spiced vanilla always perked up her senses.

His hand slipped underneath the shoulder of her shirt and pushed it down along with her bra strap, leaving space for him to continue to get a taste of her. He groaned, knowing that he had come up here for intentions not involving his cock getting some action.

"The way I want to bend you over that stepstool right now and pound into your pussy…" Gage wistfully sighed, his dick fully on board with the temptation as it grew harder in his pants. He pressed one more kiss to the faded scar on her shoulder from her old gunshot wound.

Gage pulled her shirt back into place. "But Sam is waiting for you downstairs."

"Mmm, duty calls then?" Layne's hands rested on his bearded face as she gave him a kiss, letting him know she appreciated all the things he had wanted to do to her. "Maybe afterward, you and I can have our own meeting, and you can convince me just how much you are the right man for the job."

When she went to put the box back onto the closet's shelf, Gage took the box from her and grinned. "I got it, short stuff." He winked at her.

Her hand lightly patted his firm ass in thanks before she quickly headed downstairs to have a much-needed discussion with Sammy.

Before putting the box back into the closet, Gage peered inside and curiously looked at the photo album right on top. Setting the box on the stool, he flipped to the first page, seeing the old photograph of Layne and her family.

He grinned, having seen that same cheesy smile from Layne on more than one occasion.

Flipping to the next page, the following picture wasn't nearly as heartwarming. The handwritten title 'Layne's 1st Broken Bone After Bike Collision With Liam' was above a picture of Layne with her right ankle in a cast and on a set of crutches.

She looked a little older than the previous picture, but not by much. The thing that caught his attention was Liam's smug face in the background, looking at Layne's bright pink cast. Even without knowing the full story, Gage had a gut feeling that the evil little shit was looking proud of his handiwork.

He closed the photo album before he worked himself up further into a rage. Gage securely put the box of memories back into the closet where it came from.

Downstairs, Layne walked into her office and saw Sammy standing by her bookshelf. His hands were tucked into his pockets as he shifted his stance nervously when she entered.

Based on his clothes, the dress slacks and a casual black button-up, her associate was trying to keep a professional but relaxed image. The tattoos crept up the front of his neck, meeting a silver chain clinging loosely around the base of his throat. “Sorry to drop in on you, Layne.”

“It’s fine.” She walked over to her desk and took her seat behind it. “Gage didn’t give you too much trouble, did he?”

Sam looked down in a rare moment of discomfort and shook his head. “Not more than expected.” He kept his distance from her while clearing his throat to try and make way for the words. “Look, Layne, I just wanted to let you know that I’d never…”

She cut him off, saving him the awkward words, “I know.” Slowly, she exhaled a tired breath. “Liam is doing what Liam does, pushing until he gets the result he wants.”

His hazel eyes looked at her with sympathy, seeing that all of this wasn’t without its toll on her. Somehow, dealing with people like Russ Spencer and other faction heads came with very little cost to her psyche. Sam may not have been a man with any sort of degree in psychology, but Liam’s actions were making more of an impact on her mentally than any other crime lord could.

“You’ll get through this.” He ran a hand over his thin beard, his fingers tracing over the outline of his mouth. “You just need to treat him like any other jackass that wants to come stomping all over your territory.”

She scoffed with a bit of a smile at how he simplified it. “But he’s not just any other jackass, Sam. He’s my brother. There’s no one else out there that has as many years of knowing what makes me tick.”

With a nod, he was willing to give her that point. “True, he may have years of knowing you, but you know what he doesn’t have?”

The urge to give a smartass comment as a response was all too tempting, “Fashion sense?”

That drew a chuckle from her associate. “You’re not wrong. But, even more importantly, he doesn’t have this.” He pulled his hand from his pocket and tossed an item onto her desk.

Layne leaned forward, reaching out and examining the small metal object in her fingers. Furrowing her brows together, she glanced over at him. “What’s this?”

Proudly smirking, Sam responded with words that were music to her ears, “A name.”

Flipping the rectangular box in her hand repeatedly, she finally noticed there was a latch. Popping the little spring mechanism, the container opened, and inside was an empty bullet casing. Layne picked it up, examining the shell between her thumb and forefinger, still unclear what this was supposed to tell her.

She read the words on the bottom of the casing, "Winchester 45 Auto?"

Sam shook his head with a grin. "Do you know what that's from?"

Well, she was guessing a forty-five-caliber pistol based on the imprinted text.

Knowing that he had her hooked at this point, he dropped the crucial piece of information. "That right there," he pointed at the casing in her hand, "is from the bullet that struck Joey."

Her expression immediately changed to one of disbelief as she stared at her associate. "What?" The question was so quiet that it sounded like she was posing it to no one in particular.

Stepping up to the front of her desk, he leaned over, resting his hands on the edge of it. "And as luck would have it, and with a little help from a friend, the three unique markings left behind from the fired round were able to be traced back to a gun. A gun that has been used repeatedly by a very slippery fellow by the name of Nicholas Orellano. So, the real question is, why would Nick allow Liam to borrow something so sentimental to him?"

The final question really wasn't a question at all. It hardly took any connecting of the dots to assume that this Orellano guy was somehow connected to Liam, perhaps even working with him. Her eyes lit up at finally getting a piece of useful information.

In an unusual and very rare show of girly emotion, she shrieked happily and popped out of her seat. Closing her palm around the shell, Layne clutched to it like it was a piece of treasure. She ran around her desk and threw herself at Sammy. Her arms wrapped around his neck as she gave him a huge hug.

Layne pressed a kiss to his cheek, not giving a fuck how unprofessional it was. He had just proven his worth by delivering this crucial tidbit to her.

Gage rushed into the doorway, having heard Layne's exclamation. Initially, all he saw was Layne up against her associate and Sam's hands on her sides. After the job offer Sam had been pitched by Liam, Gage was ready to beat the shit of the fucker for even breathing wrong at Layne.

Seeing Gage standing there, Sam immediately lifted his hands in the air off of her.

It wasn't until Layne pulled back with that goddamn cheesy smile plastered over her face that he thought twice about going into a blind fury.

"What's going on?" Gage's suspicion tainted each of his words.

Running over to him, Layne gave him several kisses before she showed him the forty-five casing in the center of her palm.

She explained, "Finally, a bit of luck."

Chapter Nineteen

WRATH

Gage had wrapped up closing down Cassidy's for the evening with a grumbling appetite in his stomach, and Three Stack Diner had the best grease-laden breakfast, especially at one in the morning. Bonus? It was located two short blocks from the club, making it an easy option for late-night chow.

He pulled open the glass door to the twenty-four-seven diner, the little brass bell chiming to announce his arrival as he did so. It was empty as hell in there. A lone waitress was rolling silverware at the breakfast counter, chairs were neatly tucked in at vacant tables, and you could hear the faint music of the local radio station playing.

The only occupied table was a large horseshoe-shaped booth filled with several guys, all appearing in their late twenties to mid-thirties. All of them trusted friends he had made throughout his business ventures, most visiting from across the river in Jersey.

"Damn, bro. Could you move any slower?" Devon griped at Gage, who was easing out of his seat behind the wheel of his naked Wrangler—doors and top all completely removed.

Pulling out a lockbox from underneath the driver's seat, Gage retrieved a semi-automatic and tucked it into the back of his pants. He shot a glare over at his buddy, who was coming along on this...business opportunity.

Jax climbed out of the backseat over the rear wheel well and jumped down onto his feet. "That's what happens when you get your dick tattooed." He had been the one person Gage had trusted his secret to, and it seemed it was a poor choice in judgment.

As Jax spilled the beans, it earned him the middle finger from Gage.

"Look, I'd like to see how quick you two are when your dick gets stretched out like goddamn salt water taffy and needles jammed into it for over an hour." Gage griped at his friends before joining the other two guys, Isaiah and Hunter, waiting on the sidewalk outside of a rundown rowhome.

Hunter raised a brow. "What are we talking about?"

"Gage had the bright idea to tattoo his dick," Jax smirked, finding any opportunity to spread this entertaining information amongst their group.

Isaiah cringed. "You know, I heard of a guy who did that, and he ended up with a permanent boner for life."

Devon shook his head. "Do I even want to know what you even put on it?"

Gage pulled out his phone, double-checking the address of the house they were supposed to be at. "You that interested in my cock, Dev?"

Laughing, Hunter shared his thoughts, "It probably says 'My Best Friend.'"

The rest of the crew joined with a few chuckles.

Rolling his eyes, Gage retorted, "Says the guy who still lives in his mom's basement and has struck out on the past five girls."

As the five of them took up space there on the sidewalk, a young blonde woman carrying a small bag of groceries approached. She had the sweetest smile as her eyes landed on Gage.

"Excuse me." She slowed her steps as she waited for them all to make space for her to get by.

Without delay, Gage stepped back. When his eyes met hers, he no longer gave a shit about the lingering discomfort of his healing cock. This girl had the most angelic voice he had ever heard, and it stole his words straight from him. His hand shoved Jax back to help make room for her to walk by.

An older woman still in her robe from the house next door came out onto the rickety front porch and shouted, "Rose! Did you remember my cigarettes?!"

While Gage was distracted watching the woman walking by them, Jax leaned over, smacking Gage's stomach with the back of his hand. He whispered, "Bet you'd like to impale that pussy with your swords… Vlad."

Interrupting his flashback, one of the men flagged Gage down like it wasn't obvious where they were all seated in the otherwise unoccupied joint. All of them were raucously chattering away with one another like a bunch of frat boys after a night of drinking and debauchery.

Once one of his friends noticed his arrival at the edge of the table, the rest of them all greeted him. Several of them shouted out, "Vlad!" welcoming him with giant smiles and laughter.

Rolling his eyes at his nickname that persisted over the years, Gage shook his head and took a seat at the unoccupied end of the booth as several guys scooted over to give him more space. After his pals found out about the three swords tattooed on his dick, he never was able to live down the nickname of Vlad the Impaler.

In total, there were five of them seated here, Gage included.

Everyone had their own beverages and plates in front of each of them. Flagging down the waitress sitting at the counter for a cup of coffee, Gage shared a few laughs at the jokes casually being tossed back and forth.

Jax, the friend he had known the longest, was sitting across from him. He caught Gage's attention. "How's business, man? I'm surprised you switched things up from the titty bar to just another nightclub."

Cradling the lukewarm cup of bitter coffee in his hand, Gage leaned back and shrugged. "It was time to switch things up." He lifted the mug to his lips, drawing in a mouthful of the stale beverage. Maybe it was just another nightclub to outsiders, but he liked to think that its kinky spin carved out a uniquely valuable spot for itself in the Big Apple. So far, the rebrand was paying for itself in spades.

The man to his right, Devon, shook his head and jumped in on the conversation, "Damn, dude. You were surrounded by pussy all day long, why would you give that up? I couldn't do it; I live for that shit."

All Gage could do was shrug. He knew damn well that he could have been drowning in women, and it still wouldn't have satisfied him the way Layne did.

"I know that look," Jax said as he smirked at the revelation. "Fuckin' bastard found himself a keeper."

Isaiah, the guy at the far end, laughed, "Nah, no way. Our Vlad? Pssh, I'll believe it when I see it. She'd have to be one of those innocent and naive starry-eyed aspiring actresses that move into the city every summer." Mockingly, he spoke in a high-pitched feminine tone, "Do you really think I have what it takes? Will you practice this kissing scene with me?" His voice dropped the imitation as he laughed.

Trying to deflect the inquiries into his personal life, Gage fired back at his friend. "Yeah, and when was the last time you got laid, assbutt?"

That got a series of elbow jabs, snorts, and chortling all around the table.

Jax's eyes drifted back to Gage. It seemed that everybody else was easily tossed off the scent by Gage's switch in gears, but not him. Though kudos to Jax that he had the good sense not to steer the conversation back.

After a few more minutes of bullshitting, Gage was prompted by his former roommate, Hunter. "So, you told us to meet you here to talk about business or some crap. You going to clue us in or what?"

Gage ran his fingers through his short blonde locks; it was now or never. "I'm having a Grand Opening party for the nightclub. I need extra security, people I can trust with my life." His eyes stared at every one of his friends there at the table with him. The heaviness of his gaze communicated just how serious he was.

While Gage knew people who were willing to help in this unsavory business and had helped him previously with Layne, this was different. Things were too close to home, and hell, if he was relying on just anybody to keep his girl safe.

All the guys shared looks amongst themselves, but it was Jax who spoke up first. "Whatever you need. You just tell me when and where."

The rest of his friends nodded in agreement, echoing the same sentiments. Isaiah was quick to reassure Gage he would be there to have his back, "If it weren't for you, my ass would have gotten jumped by those bikers at that bar in Atlantic City. I got you, bro."

Knowing he had to come clean with a few more important details, Gage shoved his now empty coffee mug away from him. "It's not me I'm worried about."

Jax declared his now confirmed suspicions, "I fucking knew it. It's a piece of ass, isn't it?" Feeling smug about his intuitions being on target, he smiled proudly.

Gage's eyes narrowed at his friend's assumption that this was over a one-and-done lay. "She isn't a piece of ass, and she can't know that you're there to keep tabs on her." He would never hear the end of it if Layne knew he was bringing in fresh faces to keep watch over her at the party in addition to himself and Joey. He'd like for the three of them to actually have a night to enjoy themselves without worrying about Liam's sick games.

Devon lifted his brows curiously. "It's one chick. No offense, Vlad, but it doesn't look like you've skipped the gym recently. So why do you need four of us to watch just one of her?"

That made Gage chuckle. Fuck, if these guys even knew how he would have difficulty trusting a goddamn army to keep Layne safe these days.

"It's complicated, just trust me when I tell you I will need you all on your A-game," he explained.

Slapping his hand on the back of Gage's shoulder, Hunter joked, "Aw, trying to make sure the little woman stays in line? You're getting soft on us."

Gage groaned; at this rate, he was going to need to protect his asshole friends from Layne if they behaved like this at the event.

He pulled out his phone and brought up a picture of Layne, laying it down on the center of the table so they could all lean in to see who needed the added insurance of safety.

The photo was a selfie he had snapped of them together while in the hot tub in her backyard one night. Her brown hair piled high on top of her head with a few strands hanging down loose around her face. The fluorescent pink straps of her bikini top contrasted sharply against her pale skin. Her left hand rested on top of his chest as she leaned in against him, pressing the side of her face up against his for the snapshot.

Each of the guys gawked as they stared at the beauty in the picture, a couple of them giving whistles of appreciation.

"Damn, man, I'd want to protect that, too," Devon commented.

Jax leaned in closer before giving an aggressive sigh combined with a groan as he noticed a small detail. "Oh, come the fuck on, man." He pointed at the pic, specifically at Layne's hand, that had her engagement and wedding bands on display. "Tell me you're not banging some guy's wife."

Shrugging, Gage was obviously unbothered. "I told you it was complicated. He's not who I'm worried about; he's well aware of everything that's going on. It's her shithead brother that's the problem."

"You screwing the brother, too?" Isaiah blurted out. Before Gage could correct him, Hunter smacked him upside the back of his head on Gage's behalf. "Ouch! What?" Isaiah initially looked confused as to what he said, then gave a goofy grin. "You never know who wants to be impaled by the mighty Vlad."

In disbelief of Isaiah's commentary, Jax muttered to himself while consuming the rest of his coffee. When he finally collected his thoughts, he gave a resigned sigh. "How much of a problem is the brother? Are we talking about a guy who talks big or one who brings all his low-life friends to come play?"

The memory of the pocketknife sticking out of Layne's leg and the bullet hole in Joey's chest had the emotions running hot through Gage's veins. Trying not to bend and snap the silver butter knife in both his hands that he hadn't recalled picking up, Gage's words came out strained. "The type who deserves the wrath of every damn horror in hell."

Chapter Twenty

SAFETY FIRST

"How's the leg?" Rebecca asked from the other end of the line.

It was on the edge of being a little too cool to be sitting outside in shorts, but it was worth the occasional goosebumps when the wind picked up. Layne looked down at her stab wound; it was just getting to the stage where it began to itch as it healed. Fortunately, Dr. Patty had only needed to do minimal stitching during the initial triage. The blade had felt like it created a foot-long opening when it had gone in but had only left about an inch-wide wound in its wake.

"It's healing. I've had worse," she responded, trying to minimize the incident. "Anything exciting going on down in Baltimore?"

With a giggle and a coy tone, Rebecca drew out her one-word response, "Maaaaybeee."

For a split second, Layne felt like she was living a part of her life that could be considered normal. This was just another talk with her best friend, and she could pretend for a little bit longer that they weren't hundreds of miles away from one another. She could also pretend that her life of crime and danger was nothing but a crafted storyline in a book.

The next thirty minutes were spent listening to Rebecca gush over her new beau. Some guy that shared many of the same interests as her and even had a decent taste in wine. She griped about him liking an opposing football team, but otherwise, he seemed like he was worthy of keeping around.

"Well, don't fall too hard for him until I get the chance to meet him, okay? I got to make sure he's good enough for my bestie," Layne playfully warned Rebecca.

Feeling a text come in from her watch, she noticed it was from her associate, Ethan. Real life was beckoning her back, it seemed.

"I'm sorry, Rebecca, but duty calls. I promise I will check in again in a few weeks, okay?" The apology was heavy in her voice.

The sadness clung to Rebecca's words, "I love you. Be careful."

"I love you more." Layne ended the call with a sigh. Promising to be careful would have felt like a massive lie. She wasn't going to make promises she couldn't keep.

She looked around the small square footage of the backyard of O'Reilly Manor. It was just enough space in a city where any amount of a footprint came at a premium.

Taking a few minutes to shift the gears in her brain, she looked at Ethan's message and smiled at the way he always attempted to lift her spirits.

ETHAN

Who is your favorite employee?

LAYNE

Depends.

What do you have for me?

ETHAN

Our latex-faced friend suddenly remembered a password.

LAYNE

Suddenly?

ETHAN

After becoming acquainted with the bottom of my boot.

Layne's lips drew upward into a smile. She could only imagine how quickly the man with the Russian contact's calling card cracked under Ethan's physical pressure.

LAYNE

Are you going to keep me waiting?

ETHAN

I want you to answer my question.

She rolled her eyes in minimal annoyance before she texted him the praise he was looking for.

LAYNE

You are my favorite employee.

Don't fuck that shit up.

ETHAN

I knew you loved me most.

Password: 12345

LAYNE

Seriously? 12345?

ETHAN

No, I was just making sure you were paying attention.

The password for real: pokayaniye777$SIYLLCAILSCLW

Holy fuckballs, that was a password. Layne copied and pasted that shit over to Cowboy immediately.

No sooner had she sent the password over to her tech guru than the sliding glass door from the house opened. She looked up, and her heart fluttered as she saw Joey step outside to join her.

"You planning on getting ready for tonight?" He asked as he crossed the brick patio to where she was seated on the lounge chair. "I know you take forever and a damn day." He grinned.

That's right, Gage's party was tonight. Gage had been supervising the setup for it all day. She had hardly seen him since he rolled out of bed this morning.

Layne turned, swinging her legs over the side of the chair to put her feet down on the ground. "Yeah, just wanted to finish a few things first."

His hand reached out, his fingers coming up underneath her chin and tilting her head back. Joey's eyes lovingly gazed down into hers. "Promise me something?"

The multitude of shades of green her eyes held were staring right up at him. "You know I don't make blind promises."

With a light touch, his hand trailed over her jaw and up onto the side of her face, his fingers tangling themselves in her hair. She leaned her face into the palm of his hand.

Joey stood there drinking in the sight of her melting into his hold. His mouth positioned itself in a knowing smile. His ask was so simple, and still, he knew nothing with his wife was ever simple.

"Try to have some fun tonight. Relax. No working and absolutely no worrying. Can you do that for me?" He leaned in, brushing his lips over hers to help sweeten the request.

It was a tall request that she wasn't sure she could give her word on, no matter how much she wanted to. "How can you ask me not to worry after everything that's happened? What if—"

He grinned at her stubbornness and cut her words off, "Don't make me ask twice, Layney." Joey pulled her up onto her feet, tugging her up against him.

Layne dragged her teeth over her bottom lip as she rested her hands on top of his chest. "But it's fun when I do."

His hands slid down her lower back and came to rest on her ass. Joey filled both of his hands with the full curves of her backside. "Get this ass inside and start getting ready before I make us both late to the party."

He looked down at his watch on his wrist. What the hell was taking her so long? Joey had been waiting out front of O'Reilly Manor for what felt like hours but had been more like fifteen minutes.

The front door opened, and Joey's cock hardened the second he laid eyes on Layne.

One dainty little foot after the other stepped over the threshold of the front door onto the front stoop. Her strappy black heels wrapped around her feet and crisscrossed several times over each ankle. Much to the delight of his dick, the rest of her lean legs were left bare.

Layne may have thought the stab wound on her thigh was an eyesore, but it didn't deter him from wanting to kiss and worship every part of her—scars included. The short length of the tight crimson dress had the smallest ruffle at the bottom hem that added an extra feminine flare to the style. It made him want to immediately plunge himself between her thighs.

He had known the outfit would be absolute perfection on her body when he had chosen it, but seeing it on her surpassed his wildest dreams. It adhered to every curve and line of her slender physique. The thin straps looked like he would be able to break them easily with just one pluck of his finger.

Layne's waterfall of chestnut locks of hair naturally hung down around her bare shoulders with a loose mohawk-style French braid down the center of her head.

The Challenger was already running in anticipation of getting them both to Cassidy's Chains ahead of schedule. He was so stunned by the vision he saw emerging from their home that his feet were left cemented to the ground until she was standing right in front of him.

She tried to steady her breath as she soaked in the sight of Joey dressed in a suit that he had no business wearing so well. The all-black ensemble was tailored to each swell of his muscles. The black dress shirt was left without a tie, and the top couple of buttons remained undone, leaving exposed the spread wings of the tattooed birds creeping up his neck.

"Every time you put a suit on—" she began, only to have her words silenced. Joey leaned in and crushed his mouth against hers. His lips nearly bruised her own with the intense need brewing behind them.

His hands roamed over her body, exploring it like he didn't already have every inch committed to memory. The spread of his palms ran down her sides, sliding back to grab at the spheres of her ass in appreciation before coming back around to travel over her hips.

Just as his hand dropped down past the hem of her dress, sliding between her legs, it took everything in her to bring him to a halt. Her hand grabbed onto his wrist as her thighs squeezed together to close off access to where he very much wanted to gain entry.

Layne's words were coming out breathlessly as she forced them past her lips, "You know it's Gage's night, and we promised we wouldn't be late." She wanted nothing more than to break the rules the three of them had set, and maybe she would at the after-party. However, she was doing her best to make sure that Gage also got his dedicated alone time with her.

Groaning in a mixture of disappointment and irritation, Joey knew damn well that he could press the issue and get past Layne's defenses with very little effort. However, they had agreed on solo nights so Layne could get some semblance of physical recovery while trying to keep up with all three of their needs. Given tonight was Gage's big evening, his brother had dibs.

Begrudgingly, he withdrew his hand, knowing it was going to be a long night watching Layne moving her body in a dress that looked like it was painted on. Gage better take advantage of their girl, good enough for the both of them.

She wasn't blind to the disappointment in Joey's eyes, but seeing as he was driving them to the club, perhaps she could find an acceptable compromise. Her hand patted his chest lightly as she walked over to his vehicle.

Joey drew in a deep breath, trying to convince his fucking erection to settle down. He turned and rushed ahead of her to open the passenger door before she got the chance.

Getting into her seat, Layne made sure she strapped herself in before he yelled at her for being reckless about her personal safety. It was going to be a twenty-minute drive in slow city traffic; she hardly expected any large-scale incidents where a seat belt was going to be required.

He rounded the front of the car and got settled before pulling away from the curb. "Remember what I said, Layne. We got everything covered, all you need to do is let Gage show you a good time tonight."

When Joey glanced over at Layne, she was unbuckling her seat belt. His jaw tensed, hating when she wasn't strapped in. "What are you doing? Put your damn seatbelt back on."

As they slowed for a red light, she gave a smile that said she was up to no good. Her hand ran over the large muscle of his thigh before reaching between his legs and rubbing over his cock that had only partially softened.

"Showing you a good time." Her hand gave another firm massage over the front of his pants before leaning over the console between their seats and working his pants open.

He shifted in his seat, his eyes darting between the mischievous woman now fishing her hand into his pants and the traffic signal ahead of them. "Layne, you need to be buckled up." His voice didn't sound convincing, and with one hand on top of the steering wheel, he wasn't making any effort to stop her with his other hand.

"Joey?" She pulled his long and hard length from his boxer briefs.

The light turned green, and he nearly forgot he needed to press the gas pedal to get the car moving. "What?" He looked down at Layne as her upper half encroached on his space.

"Shut the fuck up and drive." She smirked before she lowered her head and drew his dick into her mouth.

He groaned as his cock was suddenly buried into that tight and warm space past her lips. Joey's hand grasped onto the steering wheel tightly while trying to focus on the road.

Layne hallowed her cheeks while sucking on him like he was her favorite treat. Her lips applied added pressure in waves as she bobbed her head up and down on him.

Quickly, his spare hand roughly grabbed a handful of hair on the back of her head, guiding her movements as he cursed to himself.

"Fuck, Layney. You and your damn mouth." Joey pressed his hips up into her, feeling the tip of his cock greeting the back of her throat.

Her tongue swirled around his cock, taunting and teasing him as she made every effort to make sure that he had to work at maintaining his focus on the road.

Joey's palm circled the steering wheel as he made a turn that he had nearly forgotten to take. He was constantly torn between watching the road and sneaking glimpses of Layne with her ass in the air while her mouth worked him over.

With his release rapidly approaching, he gave a light growl as his hand pushed her head down on him. The way she gagged around his dick had him barely clinging to his control over his release.

"Ah, fuck! You better not waste a drop of my cum, Layney." His breaths grew ragged as he pulled her head back and forced it back down on his cock several more times.

His knuckles turned white from gripping the steering wheel so tightly. Feeling the tingle at the base of his spine, he pinned her head down on him right before his dick began pulsing. Groaning as his pleasure burst through his body, Joey's hips thrust up into her mouth as he came, shooting lines of his hot seed into the back of her throat.

Each swallow she made with him still buried inside her had him whimpering and working to catch his breath. His hand released her hair and slid down over her upper back.

"Jesus Christ." He sighed in satisfaction as he relaxed back into the driver's seat. It shocked the hell out of him that he managed to keep the damn car on the road this entire time.

Layne slid her mouth off of him, giving the head of his cock one final lick as she smiled proudly. She shifted back into her seat and pulled her seat belt across her lap.

"Couldn't have you feeling left out all night." Her eyes sparkled, complimenting the flush of her cheeks and the puffiness of her lips that were missing most of her lip gloss after her oral endeavors.

Joey gave her a relaxed grin before he pulled up to the building with a slate blue sign above it bearing the club's new name. Metal chains wrapped around each of the individual handles for aesthetics, and a line wrapped around the block of people waiting to get into Cassidy's Chains.

Before she could open her door, Joey reached over and took her by the back of her neck. With her face turned toward him, he smiled. "I love you." He leaned over and captured her lips in a tender and gentle kiss. If he had made the wrong decision so many years ago, it killed him to think that he would never have found his own piece of heaven.

Chapter Twenty-One

CONNECTED CHAINS

Inside the nightclub, most of the decor that had once screamed strippers and poles had been removed. The stages also had disappeared, except for the one designated for the DJ in the corner.

Along the walls were extensive lines of sofa-like seating with royal blue velvet cushions. Spaced out every couple of feet were small tables placed in front of it. Hung up throughout the space were framed photos of various kinky toys that included everything from your standard BDSM accessories to things a little more… adventurous, peculiar, and unusual.

The lighting was expectedly dim but was accented with the cool glow of blue lights placed around the seating areas, walkways, and bar. A curtain of thick metal chains hung in the entryway that divided the main area of the club where all the drinking and dancing happened to the hallway that led to the private rooms.

An evening of exclusive access to those rooms was available for a hefty fee. All of the photographs of toys and accessories on the walls of the main club area were made available for use and play. At your own risk and pleasure, of course.

Gage was standing in front of the industrial-looking bar, meeting with his extra security adds before the club officially opened up for everyone to file inside. It was the same crew of friends he had met at the diner around the corner a few nights back. Jax, Devon, Isaiah, and Hunter were all gathered in a loose circle.

Adjusting his earpiece, Jax looked at Gage. "I'll be doing rounds at all the points of entry to make sure there's only one way in here and one way out."

Hunter nodded and reassured Gage that they all had a plan in place, "Don't worry, Vlad. Someone will have eyes on her at all times."

While Devon began to reiterate some of the other minor details of the specific security measures in place, Isaiah smacked his arm several times with the back of his hand.

"Holy… fuck… Dude!" Isaiah's mouth was left hanging open as he stared at the front door.

Devon finally stopped speaking long enough to see what the hell Isaiah was gawking at. When his eyes followed the line of sight, he was also rendered speechless.

Turning his head to see what everyone was distracted by, Hunter raised both of his brows. "Is that…Joey? Your brother?"

Layne and Joey had just entered, being allowed to pass by the dedicated bouncer at the door. Joey's arm was wrapped around her waist, possessively keeping her close to his side. The two of them chatted between themselves as they drifted further into the club.

Isaiah, being the immature one of the group, chuckled. "Oh, man! You've got to be shitting me! You're banging your brother's wife, Vlad!?"

Gage's eyes narrowed. "Say that a little fuckin' louder, why don't you?"

It was Hunter who smacked Isaiah on the back of the head so that Gage didn't have to. "Why don't you ever shut up instead of saying stupid ass things?" He shook his head in annoyance.

To say it was a shock to all of them to see Joey there was an understatement, and that was without knowing the unique circumstances between the three of them.

Layne's eyes were drawn to the sight of Gage standing with several men, all dressed in your typical black security attire. It wasn't the crew standing around him that captured her attention; her eyes were fully focused on Gage.

The way Gage wore his black suit made her realize that she didn't see him dressed up nearly enough. A dark red shirt underneath the jacket complimented the same crimson red of her dress that she wore. Each cut of fabric hugged his bulky muscles, reminding her just how much strength he packed when he wasn't tenderly taking care of her.

Leaving Joey's side and crossing the room, Layne came up to Gage and smiled. "We made it."

Only a step behind her, Joey added, "Barely." He had a massive grin drawn over his face, still reeling from the blowjob he had gotten on the way there.

Locking his hands on her hips, Gage drew her up to him as his espresso hues admired the sight of her. "Damn." He let out a breath as he allowed himself to soak in every detail of how she showed up looking like a delicious goddess at his disposal.

Lowering his head, Gage slowly worked his mouth over hers, making sure she knew how much he approved of her arriving here looking like a snack he could quickly devour. A hand came up to her face, gently cradling her cheek as his tongue dove into her mouth, ready to get a head start on dessert.

Finally relinquishing her lips before he ended up bending her over the bar, he looked over at Joey. "Why the hell do you look so happy?"

Joey shrugged with a smirk, trying to remain casual about it. "It was a nice drive over here." His hand subtly dropped to adjust his cock that wanted to stiffen up at the replay in his head.

That got him a stern look shot from Layne as she looked over her shoulder. "*Nice*?" It had been a phenomenal blowjob, in her opinion.

Jax cleared his throat, drawing attention to the fact that he and the rest of the guys were still standing there. "We good here?" He looked at Gage for confirmation.

Gage nodded. "Yeah, we're good. The doors should be opening up in about ten minutes."

Fist-bumping a couple of the guys as they dispersed, Gage fully turned to Layne, lifting his hands to hold her face. "You have no idea how excited I am for tonight. I want everyone to know you're mine." He dragged a finger down her throat, tracing over the gold necklace she always wore–his collar that she refused to take off.

Smiling, he stole another kiss from her deliciously swollen lips.

The club music was blasting throughout the entirety of Cassidy's Chains. The bass could be felt through your chest and down into the floor. Everyone was packed onto the dance floor, dancing and having a good time. The drinks were flowing freely as every person seemed to be living carefree.

All the guests were dressed fully in black as the invitation had dictated, except for Layne and Gage. It made it easier to spot Layne from a distance through the crowded space. Not that Joey or Gage allowed her to get more than an arm's length from either of them.

Letting his brother have the majority of the time with their girl, Joey mostly kept an eye on things happening inside the nightclub. Hell, if he was going to let an evening out get ruined by fucking Liam and the war campaign he was on against Layne.

Despite Joey's giving them space, it didn't mean he and Gage hadn't pinned Layne between them during a dance or two. They let her feel both their cocks press against her like steel rods while both their hands explored her scantily clad body with the beat of the music driving each movement.

Gage had ditched his jacket early on, rolling up his sleeves to his elbows, exposing the corded muscles of his forearms. His tattoos sprawled up his arms until they disappeared under his shirt.

Layne had been pleasantly surprised to see a pair of black suspenders leading over the tops of his shoulders and down over the front of his chest. There was just something about the way the stretchy straps clung to his upper body that had her wanting to climb him like a tree.

She finished off the cocktail in her hand, having worked up to a solid buzz. Leaving the glass on a table, her hands grabbed Gage by his suspenders and pulled him back onto the dance floor with her. Layne's hips swayed to the beat of the music as she led him into the center of the crowd.

As she began to dance, she kept her body close up against him. The look in her eyes let him know that no one else in the club existed except him. Seductively, her lithe body rubbed up against him as the music seemed to pulse throughout her moves.

Gage's hand slid onto the back of her neck while the other slowly ran down her back towards the swell of her ass. His body moved with hers while he leaned over and began to drag his mouth over the side of her neck, where there was already the light taste of perspiration against her skin.

His hand glided onto her ass and gripped it possessively as he pulled her tighter against him. The roughness of his hand grabbing her sent a shock of arousal between her thighs as they continued their sensual dance together. Neither of them gave a fuck who saw them behaving like a couple of horny teenagers on the dance floor.

Layne purred in approval as she felt the hard press of Gage's cock against the front of her lower stomach. Arousal was already soaking her panties, leaving her craving more of him. Her hips pressed up against him, letting him know just how much she needed him.

He continued to grind his dick against her, letting her ache for him a little longer with a playful smirk. Gage kissed his way up to her ear, speaking into it, "Baby, are you ready to take my dick while I fuck your pussy?"

Her hands grabbed the front of his shirt, balling up the fabric in her hands. Moaning out quietly as he whispered to her, she nodded her head. "Yes, please." Layne's breaths were already heavy between her burning desire and her dance movements there with him.

Giving one last squeeze of her ass, he released it so he could grab hold of her hand. "I have a surprise, c'mon."

Layne lightly bit into her lower lip in excitement as Gage tugged her along with him, leading them off the dance floor. They walked through the curtain of metal chains, entering the blue-lit hallway with various doors.

He brought her to one nearly at the very end of the hallway, which had a reserved sign on it. Gage pushed the door open and allowed her to enter first.

Inside the private room was a very similar decor as the rest of the club, there was a small velvet loveseat and a table just big enough for a couple of beverages. Music from the club played from a speaker in the ceiling, adding to the ambiance. The room was cast into a warm glow from a few strategically placed red lights. The most notable item in there was the large x-frame in the corner.

Locking the door behind them for privacy, Gage spoke up from behind her, "I told you I was going to get you on my St. Andrew's cross."

She barely had enough time to take in the sight of the piece of equipment with its wrist and ankle straps before his hands snatched her by her hips and spun her around to face him.

Gage's finger came up under her chin to angle it up so he could look into those hypnotizing green pools of hers. He grinned and gave his command, "On your knees for me."

Layne had an intense ache between her thighs for him, and now, seeing him shift into his dominating side had her wanting to leap right onto him.

She lowered herself down onto her knees in front of him, never breaking eye contact.

He slid the straps of his suspenders off, letting them hang down at his sides as he began unbuttoning his dress shirt. All the while, he stared down at the beauty kneeling at his feet.

"Do you want to be fucked on my cross, Lucky Charm?" He yanked the bottom of his shirt out from his pants before removing it entirely from his upper body.

With her hands resting on top of her bare thighs, she spoke up with a breathy voice, "Yes, Sir." Her eyes watched as he bared his chest to her, his silver Roman legion necklace hanging down between his pecs.

He tossed his shirt over onto the sofa to his right. "Such a good girl, always wanting my cock," he praised.

Gage stood staring down at Layne, admiring the view as each breath she took had her breasts pushing against the neckline of her dress. "You know how hard my cock has been for you all night? I've been dying to get you in here. I was going to wait until the party was over, but then you had to go rub against me like you wanted to be fucked in the middle of the dance floor. I damn near bent you over and pounded into you for everyone to see."

Placing a finger under her chin, he bent over with a mischievous grin while appreciating the sight of her needy body waiting for him. "And you would have let your Daddy do it, isn't that right, baby?"

Layne was getting antsy just thinking about it, shifting her position there on the floor. Her knees parted slightly as her hand began to slide up the inside of her thigh towards her center. "Yes. I need you, Gage. Please." Her eyes were saturated with the need for the pleasure she knew he could give her.

He squatted and grabbed both of her wrists, making sure she didn't have a chance to touch herself. Pulling her up onto her feet, he clicked his tongue at her in disappointment. "Baby, you know you aren't allowed to touch yourself without my permission. You weren't thinking about doing that, were you?"

She whimpered, and it was music to his ears to hear how much she craved him. Her hands were in small fists as he held them up in front of her.

Swallowing hard, trying to get past the neediness in her voice, she begged him again. The intensity for which she had to have him nearly made her voice waver. "I'm so wet, I want your cock so badly right now."

Chuckling, he leaned in and gave her a delicate kiss. "Baby, you're going to need to do better than that." He backed her up until they were at the cross. His hands turned her so she was facing it. With ease, he latched each wrist cuff onto her, leaving both hands raised above her head.

Gage left her ankles unrestrained for the time being. His hands dropped to the bottom of her dress and yanked it up so that it was bunched up around her waist, leaving her round and firm ass exposed to him. His fingers hooked onto the sides of her thong and slid it down her legs until it was removed entirely.

As he stood, he ran his large hands over the backs of her thighs. Layne shivered in anticipation as she pushed her hips back towards him.

Fully enjoying seeing her like this, Gage smiled before his palm smacked down hard on her ass. The contact left a red mark on her fair skin that had his cock twitching in excitement.

"Tell me what you want." He began to undo his pants, no longer able to stand the way his dick was struggling against the confines of his pants.

"I want to be fucked by my Daddy. I want your cock showing me that I'm all yours." She squirmed while standing there, unable to move her hands as she felt her arousal beginning to creep down from her core.

Gage pushed his boxers down on his hips so his decorated cock sprang out. Layne wasn't the only one who was leaking, a clear liquid dripped from the tip of his cock. "Mmm, that's what I like to hear."

He stepped up behind her, his hand burying itself in her hair as he tipped her head back so he could see her face. "Baby, I'm going to make you feel so good tonight. I want the whole damn club to hear you."

Her lips parted slightly as she felt every part of her body yearning for him. Using just the rounded head of his cock, he rubbed it along her crease. With a tremble in her voice, she moaned out, only to have it devolve into a whimper again when he moved his dick away from her body.

"Fuck! Please!" She was pretty sure this was torture as she stood there being taunted and teased by him.

Letting go of her hair, he smiled and dropped onto a knee behind her. He finally locked her ankles into the soft cuffs attached to the bottom of the X.

"Be careful what you ask for, baby. Don't you dare come until my cock is in you, do you understand?"

Layne was quick to nod if it meant that she was going to finally be able to feel the pleasure he was withholding from her.

Another swat landed on her ass, echoing across the room. "You know the rules; I need to hear that you understand." His palm gently rubbed over the area he had just struck, easing away the sting across her ass cheek.

She winced lightly as the spank landed. "Yes, Sir."

"Good girl." His hand lightly patted her ass in approval.

Gage's hand dropped between her legs, his fingers stroking over her wet slit. Finding her clit, he massaged a few circles over it before running his fingers back to the entrance of her cunt.

Two fingers pushed into her nice and slow until the silver rings on his fingers were just barely inside of her. He groaned, feeling how turned on she was for him.

"Fuck!" She moaned out, finally getting the first run of pleasure through her veins. Layne's head dipped back as she gave herself over to the feeling.

His fingers pulled out of her before sliding in just as slowly as they had before. This time, he leaned over and pressed his lips to the back of her bare shoulder. His breath was warm against her skin as he murmured to her. "Does your Daddy know how to take care of you?"

She moaned out again, this time trying to push her hips down onto his fingers. "You always know how to make me feel so damn good."

"Mmhmm. Would I ever let my cock near any other woman?" He lightly bit the top of her shoulder.

Layne shook her head. "No."

"That doesn't sound like you're very convinced, baby." He plunged his fingers into her again, still keeping things at a slow and drawn-out pace.

Each breath she took was getting a little heavier while his fingers stroked inside of her. Struggling to concentrate with his fingers working her, she responded through a moan, "No, you're all mine. You only want me, and there isn't any other woman who gets to wear your collar except me."

Gage brushed her hair away from the back of her neck and laid several kisses over her shamrock and luck tattoo. "That's right, baby. You're my Lucky Charm, and you'll always have me and my swords. I would suffer every horrible and unimaginable form of torture if it meant being with you."

Being satisfied with her response, he rewarded her with his fingers moving more quickly inside of her.

She moaned out, her tight walls wrapping around his digits. The sensations began to grow sharply with each movement he made. Feeling her release approaching, she tensed up, trying to keep it at bay. "You're getting me close." Layne squeezed her eyes tightly to aid her control over her body.

Deviously, he smirked and slid a third finger into her. "Better not come, or else you're not going to get this hard cock that is waiting for your hot little pussy." He rubbed his dick against the inside of her thigh just to see how tightly she could hold on.

Her body was beginning to shake as she pulled on the restraints, keeping her limbs still. She cried out her next moan in a mix of pleasure and frustration in trying not to let herself cave. "I want to come! Please!"

Just when she thought she wasn't going to be able to take much more, Gage pulled his fingers out of her. She let out a sigh of relief that she could catch her breath. Her body began to relax as the edge of her orgasm began to distance itself slowly.

Gage grasped her hips with his hands after lining up his cock at her entrance. He sank his length into her slowly, wanting to bask in the way her body tightened around him until he was up to the hilt inside her.

"Fuck, baby. Your cunt takes me so well every damn time." He groaned into her ear.

Layne nearly melted against the cross the second he pushed himself into her. Her moan was full of satisfaction as he stretched her walls to accommodate his size.

He drew his hips back and shoved his cock back into her again, this time a little more forcefully. "You did so fucking well following directions. My little brat is finally learning that she gets rewarded when she does what her Daddy says, huh?"

Each movement he made had her unraveling at the seams. Waves of pleasure began filling her body, all coming from the way his cock made itself fit inside her pussy. "God, yes!"

Finding himself struggling with his urges, he grinded up against her ass, burying his cock even further into her. He panted as he rocked his hips forward, fucking her a little faster and a little harder.

She began to gasp for air as each thrust into her body spurred a jolt of pleasure that was ready to overflow. Being locked between him and the frame, she found herself unable to escape the mounting tensions in her body. "Ah! I'm gonna come!"

Gage slammed his cock into her, groaning as he feverishly began to chase after both of their releases. "Fucking come for me. I want my cock soaked by all of you." He continued to hammer himself in a frantic rhythm into her.

Her body locked up around him as she screamed out, pulling hard at each of the cuffs around her wrists as she came. Layne could barely draw in any oxygen between each shout of ecstasy.

Feeling her pussy squeeze onto his dick like it was a goddamn boa constrictor, he growled out a moan. Gage continued to fuck her through her orgasm, making sure he kept her in an intense and hazy state of bliss.

"Mmm, this pussy of yours is gonna get loaded with my cum soon, baby. Are you ready for it?"

She wasn't even sure that she was in a full state of awareness as she gave a weak nod. Breathlessly, she answered, "I want to be filled with your cum. Fuck, please."

With a shudder, Gage drove his cock hard into her as he roared out like a feral beast. His release struck, his dick pulsing as his seed fired out of the tip and into her well-fucked cunt.

He collapsed against the back of her, trying to catch his breath while inhaling the sweet scent of her body. "Jesus-fucking-Christ…"

Layne moaned quietly in agreement.

After taking a moment to regain himself, Gage reached up and unlatched her wrists, freeing them from the top of the cross. Pulling out of her, he made sure to do the same with her ankles, always keeping a hand on her to keep her steady.

He glanced up at her body while freeing her legs from the restraints and smirked. The sight of his cum was already beginning to leak out of her swollen cunt. "Damn, I could stare at you like this all fucking day."

She looked behind her at him with a sated smile. "You'll never hear me complain."

Gage swiped a line of the white liquid off her thigh with his fingers, then shoved them both back in her pussy with a smile. "My cum needs to stay right where it belongs." He winked at her.

Chapter Twenty-Two

GHOSTED

Emerging from the private room, Layne's hand was wrapped around Gage's as she stuck close to his side. He had spent nearly twenty minutes giving her appropriate aftercare and ensuring they didn't leave that room until he was convinced she had recovered enough.

They both made their way back into the main area of the club, where everyone was still partying the night away. Gage led her to the bar, where he ordered them both drinks.

As the bartender began crafting the cocktails, Hunter approached Gage, leaning in and whispering something into his ear.

Shouting over the thudding bass of the music, Gage pulled back and yelled, "What?!" Struggling to hear what Hunter was trying to tell him.

When his buddy tried to shout into his ear again, it was to no avail. Gage shook his head and gave a tug on Layne's hand. He nodded his head in the direction of his office, where things would be a little quieter.

Stepping away from the bar, Layne began to follow but then stopped short. She lifted a finger for him to wait. His eyes stayed glued to her as she released his hand and squeezed back through a couple of people to grab the drinks, waiting for them unattended at the bar.

Once she had the two glasses, she came right back to Gage. They made it to his office, with Hunter joining them. Closing the door for additional buffering from the loud party music, Gage took one of the glasses from Layne.

"What were you saying out there, Hunter?" He remained standing by the door.

Layne leaned back against a wall and observed quietly as she sipped her beverage, licking her lips at the sweeter-than-expected taste.

Hunter looked at Layne and then at Gage, wondering what he should say since it had been made clear that they weren't supposed to let Layne know their purpose for being there tonight.

"I was just trying to update you. Jax said everything has been all clear on the inside, and Dev said the same for the outside. No signs of… anyone." He shoved his hands into his pockets.

Picking up that this wasn't just typical security measures, Layne furrowed her brows. As she typically did, she inserted herself into the conversation. "What's that supposed to mean?"

Her eyes shifted to look at Gage as she tilted her head questioningly as she stepped away from the wall.

He cleared his throat, avoiding looking at Layne. "Nothing. Just making sure tonight went smoothly."

"Bullshit." Layne was now changing her stare to direct it at Hunter.

It wasn't an easy feat for a woman to make Hunter feel uncomfortable, but the way Layne was looking at him, he got the sense he didn't want to fuck around and find out with this one.

Gage saved Hunter from trying to explain himself, "Layne. It's not a big deal. I just wanted to make sure tonight went off without any issues."

"And by issues, you mean Liam." She cut straight to the point.

He looked at Hunter and waved him off with his hand. The man walked by them both, slipping out the door without another word.

She sighed as she looked at Gage, clearly frustrated.

Putting his untouched drink down on his desk, he stepped up to Layne. Both of his hands landed on her upper arms as he looked into her eyes. "Baby, I needed to make sure we had people I could trust."

"I have a team for this sort of thing, I don't need you bringing in fucking SEAL Team Six." She rolled her eyes.

He grinned at the comparison. "It's just for tonight. Though, if you keep scowling at me like that, I may see if they can sign on full-time." His hands rubbed over her arms gently.

"I swear to God, Gage, if I see them hanging around after tonight, I will kick your ass." Her finger jabbed him in the chest to accentuate her threat.

"Noted," he chuckled. "Now, let's go back and enjoy the rest of the party, okay?" He walked over to the desk and grabbed his drink, taking a large sip.

He coughed and scrunched up his face. "Fuck, this is definitely your drink. You and the damn ass water you call whiskey." Gage's least favorite liquor was whiskey, that shit burned like a motherfucker on a good day. The brands Layne enjoyed were some high-octane blends that left him questioning if she had any taste buds at all.

Layne laughed as she continued drinking Gage's cocktail. "Well, you're stuck with it now. I'm really enjoying your Negroni." Playfully, she stuck her tongue out at him.

He shook his head and took another sip, trying to get past the harsh bite of the alcohol. Swatting her ass with his hand, he nudged her towards the door. "Damn brat. Get out there before I give you something else to do with that tongue."

With a giggle, she opened the door and went back out to the club. Once they were back on the dance floor, Layne leaned back against Gage's chest as she suggestively moved her body against him to the pulse of the music. Idly, she sipped on the drink in her hand.

Her mind wandered as to what delicious trouble they were both going to get to once they got back to his condo. Gage's hand roamed over her body, wondering how he got so damn lucky with a woman like Layne. This night was turning out to be everything he had hoped for and more.

While she was lost in her thoughts, her eyes caught a face in the crowd. It startled her so much that she dropped her drink. Her body immediately went stiff as a board.

The music began to fade, the volume becoming more tolerable as it transitioned to the next song.

Gage straightened as Layne's glass shattered against the floor and splashed the beverage around their feet. He came around to face her, his face filled with concern. "Baby, are you okay?"

Layne craned her neck to try and look around him to see if she could catch another glimpse of the face she saw. "I…" She looked all around them, and she wondered if she had seen anything at all. "Yeah, I'm fine. I just thought…"

"You're as pale as a ghost, Layne." He also took a look around at their surroundings. He didn't see any threats, but he did see Joey over by the bar and flagged him down.

God, was she losing her mind? Her heart felt like it was leaping over massive hurdles inside her chest. She looked at Gage and tried to force an at-ease smile on her lips. "I promise I'm good."

Gage chugged down the rest of his drink, not liking the way she looked so spooked.

Joey wasted no time in forcing his way through the crowd of people when he saw Gage's hand wave him over. "What's wrong?" He looked at Layne and immediately got on the defensive, seeing how shaken she looked, even if she was trying to conceal it.

"Nothing is up." Layne tried to calm them both down.

"She just clammed up and dropped her drink," Gage explained. "I'm going to take her home." He set his empty glass on the tray of a waitress as she walked by.

"I will go update Jax and the rest of the guys, then meet you back at your place." Joey patted the side of Gage's arm. Then, he reached out and captured Layne's chin between his thumb and finger. "Seatbelt on," he demanded with a smile before he locked his mouth on hers firmly.

She happily accepted his kiss, returning it with one of her own. "It's a five-minute drive, and you both are overreacting."

The look they both gave her after that said it all. They had every right to be on edge, given everything all of them had been through. Her face fell as she slumped her shoulders in defeat.

Satisfied that Layne wasn't going to put up any more of a fight, Joey left to go find his brother's backup crew. Gage wrapped an arm around her shoulder and guided her towards the door.

Once outside, Layne looked at the cars parked out front. She didn't see his busted-ass Jeep anywhere. "Where did you park?"

Gage pulled out Layne's car keys from his pocket and pressed the remote start on the key fob. "Ran into a bit of car trouble when I went to leave this morning, so I took yours."

She couldn't hide the fact she wasn't surprised. "The Jeep wouldn't start—again?"

Leading Layne towards the silver BMW, he kept his head on a swivel. "Look, she's an old gal. Some days, she needs a little extra love to get movin'."

"For fucks sake, Gage, that damn Jeep has been revived from the brink of death five too many times." Arriving at her car, Gage made sure she was strapped into the passenger seat per Joey's instructions, five-minute drive or not.

He came to the driver's side, sliding in behind the wheel with the intention to be her chauffeur back to Hudson Yards.

She looked over at his profile while he focused on the road. At this time of night, the roads were mostly empty, making the trip rather peaceful.

Layne wondered how it was that she had two handsome men willing to go above and beyond for her. As irritated as she got with their protective efforts, deep down, it made her feel more valued than her family ever did. That feeling of being worthy was something her brother was slowly trying to destroy.

A few beads of sweat started to appear on Gage's forehead. He blinked his eyes several times as the traffic lights and their surroundings began to gradually shift in his vision. His hand came to his eyes, trying to rub the focus back into his brown hues.

Layne noticed his drawn-out blinks and the way he wiped the sheen of sweat from his head with the back of his hand.

"Gage, are you okay?" She reached over, placing a hand on his bicep.

His foot pressed the brake to roll to a stop for a yellow light. Layne's voice sounded so far away, like he was in an underwater cave. His breathing grew shallow while attempting to swallow the pooling saliva in his mouth, willing himself to stay conscious as he struggled to maintain clear thoughts.

Gage's hand dropped to the shifter, attempting to push it into Park but missing the knob.

Noticing that his eyes were fluttering, she cursed and shook his arm harshly. "Hey! Stick with me!"

Somehow, she heard the impact a microsecond before she felt it. An unexpected force slammed into the back of her car, launching it across the intersection and only stopping when the front of her vehicle collided with a pole. Another impact hit the backend again, crushing the Beamer further against the pole.

The hit was strong enough that airbags popped off after the first hit, providing a little bit of buffer from the way they both were violently jerked around inside their seats. Fortunately, seat belts kept her and Gage from suffering worse injuries.

Moments after the wreck, Layne was slumped in her seat with a small line of blood trickling from a minor head wound a couple of inches above her eyebrow. It was unclear how long she had lost consciousness in the aftermath of the incident.

Trying to open her eyes, she squinted at an imposing light shining directly on her face. The door on her side of the car was wide open, a presence looming there over her. Her head was pounding, and for a brief moment, she couldn't even recall where she was or what had transpired.

"What…?" Layne groaned as she turned her face away from the bright light. She lifted her hand to try and shield her eyes.

A hand roughly grabbed her by the hair, turning her so that the light continued to blind her vision. "Stupid little bitch," the faceless voice said with such an air of disdain.

The voice was rough like sandpaper, prompting all the hairs on the back of her neck to stand on end. It elicited fear to perk up from her gut, telling her to sound all her alarms. Yet, her body wouldn't coordinate the efforts on behalf of her head.

The flashlight came down harshly, striking her across the face. The hit knocked her back into her seat. Layne noticed Gage still in the driver's seat, slumped over the steering wheel, and passed out.

She winced, squeezing her eyes tightly with the pain radiating from the side of her face. The man who had been speaking to her cursed as he seemed to talk to himself, "Fucker and his timing." Something fell into her lap.

Turning her head back towards the man, Layne's eyes strained as they opened back up to see the outline of a man jogging back to a pickup truck waiting next to her car. Her body wanted to drag her into the dark of unconsciousness again, but she willed herself to try and see the person responsible before it did so.

Just when she thought she wouldn't be able to hold out any longer, the man turned and looked over his shoulder at her. A fucking evil smirk on his face. The same face she thought she had seen at the club.

No. Fucking. Way.

The man climbed into the heavy-duty pickup with front-end damage before it peeled off, the tires squealing against the pavement as it did so.

Her head was spinning through its haze as she tried to distinguish what was truth and reality. Did she simply hit her head hard enough to land in some mental ward where nothing was real anymore? None of this made sense, and that made her head ache even more.

Rolling her head to look back over at Gage, her hand shakily reached out. Her fingertips barely rested against his side in an attempt to provide comfort via touch for them both.

Joey's voice sounded miles away as he shouted her name. Hearing him, she knew she was safe—they both were.

She surrendered, and her eyes fell shut.

Chapter Twenty-Three

GAME

"I'm getting really sick and fuckin' tired of doctors and hospitals," Layne griped as she sat in a chair next to Gage's gurney in the emergency room. She removed the ice pack from her forehead.

After she had raised all hell refusing medical treatment, they were now just waiting on Gage's discharge papers after being stuck there for several hours. Unfortunately, coming to the ER wasn't ideal, but the NYPD was a bit too quick to arrive on the scene shortly after Joey did. It seemed the new brass was making a stink about response times.

"Baby, I wish you would have let the doctors check you out." Gage sat on the edge of the makeshift bed, looking about as worse for wear as she did.

She looked down at the cold pack that was doing little to alleviate her headache. "It's just a bump. I'm not the one who got roofied."

Joey pulled the small bag out of her hand and gently applied it to the side of her face where the flashlight had struck her. "But you were its intended victim," he countered.

As the stinging cold pressed to the tender spot on her face, she gave a light hiss of pain as she winced, trying to pull her face away. Joey's hand held onto the side of her head, preventing her from evading his efforts to alleviate the swelling.

"Since Gage doesn't remember shit, what do you remember?" Joey wanted to be pissed at his brother for getting behind the wheel and risking their girl's life, but there had been no way of knowing that the Rohypnol was in his system until he was already on the road. It wasn't until the doctors got Gage's blood work back that it was confirmed he had been inadvertently drugged when he consumed Layne's beverage.

Both sets of brown eyes were staring at her, begging her to recall even the slightest detail. She frowned, unsure that she had anything rattling around in her brain that was of any use. "I told you, I don't know what I saw. When we left Cassidy's, I had a pretty heavy buzz. The next thing I knew, all I felt was the car getting slammed into, followed by a bright ass fuckin' light in my face."

Gage held up a piece of paper that they all had read multiple times. "This note left behind in your lap doesn't even make sense. Are you sure it wasn't Liam?"

"I know my brother's voice; it wasn't his. Though I'm sure he had something to do with this." She leaned forward and took the piece of paper from Gage. Her eyes scanned over the words again.

Family First. Fucktoys Second.
Time to honor your commitments to this family.
430 at 830 on 227 for 611.

Frustration overcame her. None of this made sense. It looked like some cheat code for a game console. She was on the verge of crumpling up the note and tossing it in the trash when her phone began to ring in her pocket.

The familiar name on the screen popped up, prompting her to immediately answer. "Hey, what do you have for me?"

Cowboy, the technological genius, didn't sound like his typical giddy self on the other end of the line. "Hi there. Using the password you gave me for that contact of yours, I was able to coordinate a meeting for you."

Oh good, this was perfect timing to meet with a Russian who quite possibly was off his rocker. "Mmhmm. You don't sound like this is a good thing."

A slight pause before Brandon responded, "There's not much that creeps me out, but doing some digging on this guy… Well, just be careful, is all I'm saying. Does Joey know that you're meeting him?"

"No, and I expect it to stay that way for now." Her eyes glanced over at the man who had altered the course of her life forever. She wanted to tell Joey everything, especially given her shitty choices lately that had landed her in hot water with both of her guys. There's no way they would understand why she was doing this, though.

When her nerdy friend didn't respond, she prompted him, "You got it?"

"Yeah, yeah. I just," he sighed. "He'd want to know." He also didn't want to be on the receiving end of Joey's anger when he found out that he had helped Layne with this.

"There's a lot of things we all want, but that's not how life works. Anything else?"

Brandon was able to confirm that one of the men in the Chinese restaurant was indeed Nicholas Orellano, but all the scans of the second man in the ballcap were coming up with nothing at all: shit angles and no matches in public or private databases.

"Keep looking. Text me what I need to know, and I will take it from here." She ended the call with a tap of the screen and tucked her phone away.

Joey and Gage were both staring at her, expecting a recap of her conversation.

Gently, she eased the ice pack in Joey's hand away from her face. "Cowboy confirmed that Orellano was with Liam at the restaurant, but he said whoever else was with him is like trying to track down a damn ghost. He hasn't found anything so far."

"Our work is cut out for us then. We find Orellano and go from there." Joey was determined to make it as simple as that.

Seeing that Layne didn't readily agree, he rested a hand on her knee. "Layney, it's a step in the right direction," he tried to reassure her.

She frowned as she stared down at the note in her hand again. "It's always one step forward, two steps back, Joey. I feel like we keep showing up late to the party. We get a lead, and Liam is already three steps ahead of us."

Gage wrinkled his forehead in deep thought. "You need to stop trying to think like your brother and start thinking like Liam."

Layne lifted her eyes to look at Gage, overcome with confusion at his statement. Initially, she wondered if his brain was still half-drugged at the sense he wasn't making. "What?"

Lifting his brow, Joey also looked at Gage. "Yeah. What?"

Easing himself off the gurney, Gage came over to Layne, squatting in front of her chair. "If you stop approaching this like Liam is your family and start considering him like the violently unhinged asshole he is, the less predictable you'll be to him. I guaran-damn-tee you that he's been banking on the small part of you that remembers a time when he wasn't this warped."

It was hard for Gage to imagine that Liam wasn't ever this big of a psychopath, but Layne needed to see that any memories of Liam resembling a human being should remain in the past.

She sat there, letting his words sink in. The more she thought about it, the more she realized how much she was at fault for letting this situation get out of her control. If Liam wanted to go to war with his sister, he was going to be shit out of luck. Layne was going to bring the war to him as the judge, jury, and executioner of O'Reilly Enterprises.

Joey had driven them all back to O'Reilly Manor after escaping the slow as fuck discharge process, none of them wanted one another out of sight after everything that had transpired.

It had been late morning by the time they rolled in and crashed into bed together. Everybody got the hours of sleep that were much needed after being awake for nearly a day straight. Evening was rolling around, and that's when Gage turned over in bed, and his hand reached out to stroke over Layne's body. His fingers danced along a hard and abnormally large bicep rather than the slender one he had been expecting.

Lifting his head from his pillow, he opened his eyes to find Joey staring at him.

"Good morning, sunshine." Joey snorted.

Grumbling, Gage withdrew his hand quickly before stretching out his body. He felt like absolute garbage, despite all the fluids the hospital had given him trying to flush his system from the commonly used date rape drug. The car accident didn't do him any favors either.

"Where's Layne?" Gage groaned out his question past the unforgiving headache pulsing at his temples.

Tossing the sheets aside, Joey slid out of bed. "Probably downstairs, the way you were snoring like a broken chainsaw." He rubbed a hand over his face to try and erase the last remnants of sleep from his eyes.

Moments later, both guys came down to the first floor, each wearing just a pair of sweats. They followed the scent of freshly brewed caffeine coming from the kitchen despite the late time of day. Both of them came to a sudden halt as they saw Layne there, fully dressed and finishing off her cup of coffee. She looked ready to attack whatever was on her agenda. As far as they both knew, nothing should have been on her calendar for tonight.

She gently set her empty coffee mug into the sink before buzzing around the center island to snatch her phone off the charger on the counter.

"Layne? What are you doing?" Joey watched her with confusion splashed across his face.

When she didn't acknowledge either of them, Gage reached out and latched his hand onto her forearm to force her to take a moment and talk with them. "Baby, you look like you're ready to go somewhere."

Sighing like she had too much to do and not enough time, she stopped and looked at her two guys. "Yeah, I have a last-minute meeting I need to go to."

Joey's jaw immediately clenched as he suppressed his grumbling. "When were you going to tell us?"

She gently coaxed her arm from Gage's hand. "I know how this looks."

Gage lifted a brow at her. "Really? Because it looks like you were ready to bail without saying a damn thing."

Exhaling a short breath, she knew that this was going to be a hard pill to swallow for all of them, but better now than never. "Hear me out."

"Hear you out?" Joey grumpily replied. "We've been over this, Layne. Where you go, we go. End of story. Fuck, we can't even keep you safe when all three of us are together." Each word he spoke bearing more of his aggravation.

Layne stepped up to Joey and placed a hand on his bare sides, hoping her touch would assist in getting him to listen to her. "I know, but this is different. I have a shot at hitting Liam where it hurts and getting one step ahead of him. This is one meeting I can't risk anyone knowing about, so I need you both to stay here."

Gage's hand slid up her arm onto her shoulder. "You can't seriously expect us to—"

She cut Gage off, "I can and I do. I love you both more than life itself, but I can't be the leader I need to be with my head tied up in my emotions. You're the one who told me to stop treating Liam like my brother, and that's why I'm doing this. Liam expects me to be with one of you at all times. For all I know, he's got people watching who comes and goes from here. He's not going to give a fuck if one of you leaves to go to Mickey D's for a late-night snack. But more than one person leaving this house?"

She shook her head, imagining what lengths her brother was possibly going to in order to bring her down.

He hated to admit it, but he was starting to see her logic, and looking over at Joey's face, his brother also saw the point she was making.

Joey grabbed her face with both his hands. "I'm not budging on this, Layney." He was being a stubborn asshole, as usual.

As she went to look at Gage for support, Joey turned her face back at him. "Don't look at him, you're answering to me right now."

Her intoxicating green eyes were as calm as the sea before a storm. "You and I both know that I'm doing this with or without your permission. I promise you that I will take every precaution I can, but I need to take this chance. You wanted me to light my fire and let it burn, and I'm standing here telling you that I need a bit of oxygen to do that."

Staring silently into her eyes, Joey's conflict was clear.

Layne spoke in a whisper, "Please. I'm going to be late."

"Fuck," he cursed under his breath before pulling her face to his. Joey's lips locked onto hers as he hungrily kissed her.

When he pulled back, his hands were still tightly gripping her face. He forced his words out. "You fuckin' watch your ass. If the wind so much as blows the wrong damn way, you get the hell out of dodge. Do you fucking understand me, Layne?"

After she nodded, he dropped his hands from her face and wrapped his arms around her. Squeezing her tightly against him, Joey kissed the top of her head several times.

No sooner did Joey release her than Gage pulled her to him by the back of her neck. He pressed his forehead to hers. "Do you know what I'm going to tell you, Lucky Charm?"

She gave a slight smile. "To be careful?"

Gage grinned. "No, baby. I want you to go be a badass bitch, but when you get back here, your ass is ours." Using his mouth, he sealed that promise with a scorching kiss.

She let herself get lost in the way their lips wrangled with one another before easing away from him. Layne looked at both of them, knowing she had to do this for all of their futures if they were going to finally make progress.

Exchanging a round of 'I love you's,' she strode out of the kitchen. Her hand plucked Joey's motorcycle keys off the hook outside of the door that led into the garage.

Once inside the garage, she secured her designated helmet onto her head as she straddled the sports bike. Turning the key, she felt the purr of the motor between her thighs as the bike came to life.

Layne took one final look at her phone to confirm the details of her meeting. After she secured her phone in her jacket pocket, she pulled down the visor over her eyes.

Daniil Parshikov may be one unpredictable and possibly crazy Russian, but today, he was going to meet one bloodthirsty and pissed-off Irish Car Bomb. With any luck, they would both come out of this meeting as allies. If not, then she was prepared to burn this city to the ground to get what she wanted.

Both guys were left standing in the kitchen, looking at one another.

"So," Gage broke the silence, "are we just going to...?" He looked at Joey questioningly.

Joey stood there with a hand on his hip and the other on the edge of the counter, his jaw set in a hard line. He looked over at the time displayed above the stove. "I'm giving her a ten-minute head start."

Chapter Twenty-Four

SET

Zipping through traffic, Layne constantly kept an eye out all around her. It wasn't the concern of her guys following her but the paranoia that it was whoever else might have eyes on her back.

Constantly checking the mirrors, she twisted the throttle to speed up as the cold air whipped around her. Even with the black leather jacket zipped up over her upper body, the late autumn air cut into her. The dark blue jeans she wore did little to keep her legs warm as the temperature was rapidly tanking outside.

Layne's mind was racing just as fast as she was weaving through traffic and illegally splitting lanes. There were no guarantees in this business you could trust anybody. The only person she was going to be able to rely on today was herself.

Everything she had learned about this man, Daniil, was that he had grown up in this life much like she had. Rumors swirled about his family's involvement in some sort of mass casualty event, and that made Layne even more wary than she already was. It was one thing to take out people on the same level as you in this life and entirely another to be involved in wiping out civilians.

When she arrived at their designated meeting spot, she parked Joey's bike out front of the pretentious luxury hotel in the heart of Brooklyn. The building towered high, with the exterior appearing recently renovated. The valet stand was populated with clean-cut staff standing at full attention and ready to serve.

The doorman dressed in his blue and gold uniform gave a discreet nod of his head at one of the valet attendants. Eagerly, the young guy rushed over to Layne, trying to assist her off the sports bike decorated with various skull stickers.

Ignoring him, she swung a leg over the seat and stepped up onto the sidewalk. Removing her helmet, she smoothed her hand down over the french braid she had styled her hair. She hoped, with it being a short ride here, that she somehow escaped dreaded helmet hair.

Instead of passing over the key to the kid waiting to whisk her ride to a garage somewhere, she made sure the bike was locked. Joey would kill her if she allowed anyone else near it, let alone touch it.

Before the young kid could utter a word, Layne shoved a hundred-dollar bill into his palm. "Nobody touches the bike. Got it?"

Holding her helmet by the chin strap in her left hand, she glanced up at the name in golden script above the entrance: The Alderson Hotel. It may as well have just stated that this was a place to overpay for a subpar bed and ridiculous amenities that nobody actually used.

Walking past the doorman who held the door open for her with his mouth agape, she entered the grand lobby where the opulent decor continued to be constantly up in one's face. A few people dared to give her some dirty looks, and she couldn't blame them. Layne was sticking out like a sore thumb. Her face was sporting the car wreck's injuries, and she wasn't dressed for the goddamn Kentucky Derby like the rest of the rich assholes.

Crossing the floor to the elevators, she stood and waited for the next one to arrive to take her upstairs. As she stood there, a bellboy joined her at her side. He puckered his lips at her before grabbing the front of his pants suggestively.

Layne noticed the lewd gesture from the corner of her eyes and not-so-subtly shot him the bird, hoping he would get the hint. If she hadn't been worried about scaring the crap out of some little old lady, she would have been tempted to grab the bellboy by the front of his pants in an unpleasant fashion.

When the ding sounded and a set of doors opened, she boarded the elevator. The bellboy attempted to follow, but she extended her arm across the width of the opening. "Take the next one."

Layne would love to boast it was her charming personality that scared him off, but raising her arm lifted her jacket enough to reveal the high-voltage taser secured on her hip.

The taser wasn't the only weapon she brought with her. Various blades were concealed all over her body, her favorite Glock was tucked into the back of her jeans, and the high-impact helmet didn't hurt as an impromptu tool to inflict blunt force trauma if things went tits up.

After the elevator brought her to the sixteenth floor, she traveled down the hall and stopped at room 1621. Her knuckles rapped against the door demandingly, meetings like these didn't call for a delicate tap at the door.

While waiting for the door to swing open, she rested her hand on her pistol at the small of her back.

Each second that passed felt like years until, finally, the door swung open, and she saw a well-dressed man standing before her. The first thing she noticed was he wore his money well. While Layne may not have been your stereotypical Uptown girl, most days, she didn't look like she was hurting for funds. The only thing about her today that looked like it was hurting was the bruising on her forehead and cheekbone from the car wreck yesterday.

She hadn't known what to expect, but she hadn't expected him to look anything less than disfigured and crazy-eyed from the little she had heard of his reputation. Instead, he had that rugged and dangerous type of charm cloaked around him. Layne guessed that not every rumor had merit after all.

Skipping the pleasantries in favor of wanting to get down to business, "You going to let me in, or are you waiting to see if I shoot you?" she asked. She typically did a good job masking her nerves with her attitude, but given the past few months, her anxiety was at its peak.

He widened the door enough for her to barely pass. "You're not what I expected."

"I'm not what I expected either," she snorted, dropping her hand from the weapon holstered at her back and stepping past him into the room drenched in luxury items.

She set her helmet down on a small table as her eyes scanned the room for any signs of a potential ambush. Nothing seemed out of place, at least for a place of this caliber.

The room was laid out in three sections. Upon entry, you were greeted with a living area straight ahead of you and a kitchenette to the right–as if the wealthy elites who frequented this type of place actually cooked for themselves. To the left of the sofa in the living space was a door to a separate room where she could just barely see the corner of a bed inside.

Layne turned to face Daniil after hearing the door shut. "I don't trust you," she spoke with honesty as she watched each move he made as he stepped further into the room.

He cocked his head slightly. "Then, why are you here?"

"As much as it pains me to say it, I need someone that can't be trusted." Keeping the status quo of how she operated her business was getting her nowhere except closer to the grave.

He made a sound somewhere between a grunt and a chuckle.

Layne explained, "My brother has decided to make it his life's mission to either destroy me or drive me to insanity. So far, he's making good progress on the latter."

"From the looks of things, he's not doing too bad on the former." He motioned at the cut above her eyebrow and the bruised cheekbone she was sporting. Daniil walked by her to the small wet bar, where he retrieved a previously poured glass of alcohol.

Her jaw tightened as she tried to prevent her irritation from reaching her voice. "He's getting help, and I need to know how the fuck he's always one step ahead of me."

"What do you want me to do?" He sipped from the glass in his hand.

She stomped over to him after pulling a piece of paper from her pocket and slammed it down on the wet bar. "Find this asshole. I want to know everything he knows. I want to know everything from the moment he met my brother to the last time he jerked off." Her eyes flared with her rising temper.

Seemingly unrattled by her minor outburst, Daniil picked up the paper, unfolding it to reveal the name—Nicholas Orellano. Committing the name to memory, he dropped it back down onto the counter.

"I've heard you have quite the *personal* security team." As Layne's expression slipped in surprise that he knew anything about Joey or Gage, he added, "Did you think I would agree to this without doing some research of my own?"

He set down the empty glass after consuming the remainder of the amber liquid. "Why not allow them to do their job and take care of you?"

She rolled her eyes at the concept she had grown tired of since the day she was born. "There are complications."

He smirked. "It is not a very complicated concept for a man, or men, to take care of a woman." The innuendo quite clearly rested on top of his words.

Her shining green eyes narrowed. "My needs are more than taken care of. What I don't need is to be treated like an object incapable of making my own choices. If I wanted that, my life would be a whole lot fuckin' easier."

She nodded to the ring she observed on his left hand. "Is that what your wife wants, to be just another possession you have ownership of?"

Judging from the way Daniil's eyes darkened, Layne's words struck a nerve as she brought up his wife. She didn't feel the least bit remorseful. If there was anything she had learned, it was that nothing was off-limits when it came to this lifestyle.

She shook her head, beginning to wonder if this jackass was as good as she was told. "They're too invested. They're too worried about me to worry about themselves."

"Ah, so this is the problem, isn't it? You can't trust them, or you can't trust yourself. So which is it?" He posed the psychoanalytic question to her, and the way her face scrunched up said she wasn't taking it well.

"I never said that," Layne was quick to spit out.

He shrugged. "You didn't have to."

Patience was sure as hell not her strong suit, and right now, it was wearing thinner than a split hair. "Look, can you help me or not? For someone who supposedly knows how to get shit done, all I hear is a lot of damn bullshitting."

"How badly do you want the information from this man?" Daniil pulled his phone out, appearing to quickly fire off a message.

"I don't give a rat's ass if you want to pluck each hair from his head one follicle at a time or you simply beat the crap out of him. Whatever makes you happy and gets what I want from him." If it were up to Layne, she'd just shoot first and ask questions later. However, in this situation, she needed answers before any killing happened.

He seemed pleased that the options were limitless in the way he extracted information for her. "I don't hand out favors for free," he noted.

"Good, 'cause I don't accept handouts. Name your price, and I will make sure you will get it." She crossed her arms in front of her stomach, waiting to see how much this was going to cost her.

"$100,000," he said without so much as an ounce of hesitation.

Without the blink of an eye, she responded, "Done. You'll have it by tomorrow morning." There was no price too high to keep Joey and Gage from stupidly getting caught in the crossfire on her behalf.

"One more thing," Layne stepped uncomfortably close to him with a murderous look in her eyes with her hand digging in her pocket. "Tell him he can choke on this on his way down to hell." She grabbed Daniil's hand and pressed a small metal object into it.

After she withdrew her hand, left in Daniil's open palm was the same casing that housed the bullet that penetrated Joey's chest on their wedding day. Orellano may not have pulled the trigger, but he sure as hell put the gun in Liam's hand.

Daniil grinned as he held up the shell between his thumb and forefinger, letting his imagination conjure up all the creative ways to inflict this small piece of metal into his assigned target.

"I will contact you when it's done." He pulled his phone out again and looked at an incoming message. He raised a brow and looked at Layne. "Looks like you have company waiting for you downstairs."

When Daniil rotated his phone so she could see, there on the screen was a photo taken from the lobby of both Joey and Gage at the front desk, appearing to be asking questions.

"Oh, for fucks sake." She should have known better.

Pocketing his phone, Daniil walked over to the door and opened it for her. "Take it from me, no matter what you do, men like that will pay any cost for the right woman."

She shook her head as she grumbled angrily at their inability to follow simple instructions. Layne snatched her helmet off the table on her way to the door. "I'm about to hand them the fucking bill for not listening to me."

Daniil walked out with her, catching a ride in the same elevator down to the lobby. She was fuming as they passed each floor. When the doors popped open, they both stepped out.

Approaching the line of elevators were Joey and Gage. Both of them stopped short when they saw her and Daniil exit the elevator. Various emotions flickered over their faces from relief, surprise, suspicion, and their possessive jealousy over her.

Leaning in close to her, with Daniil's large frame blocking the view of both De Luca men, he whispered into her ear, "Here's the key if you need it." His hand slid the keycard to the hotel room into her back pocket discreetly. He winked at her before stepping back and gesturing to a few of his men seated in the lobby to take their leave.

Layne gave a brief nod, still seeing red that the guys had so blatantly went against her wishes when she was doing her best to keep them out of trouble. Her eyes stared at both her men's faces, trying to find the restraint not to shout and cause a scene there in the lobby.

"In the damn elevator. *Now.*" She ground out past her temper before turning and catching the elevator doors before they shut. Layne stepped inside and waited for Joey and Gage to join her, dead set on making them aware of how they fucked up.

Chapter Twenty-Five

MATCH

The entire ride back up to the sixteenth floor was in strained silence, with Layne's anger rolling off her like a summer storm. When the elevator doors slid open, she stalked down the hallway until she pulled out the keycard to open room 1621 and stepped inside. She didn't bother checking if the guys followed, she merely assumed that they would since that was what they were seemingly best at.

Once Joey and Gage were in the room with her, she slammed the door shut behind them.

"Who the fuck was that downstairs?" Joey turned to immediately jump onto the topic he was interested in most. Jealous? Joey? Never.

Layne stood there staring at both of them, her blood pressure spiking through the damn roof. She tossed the motorcycle helmet onto the table with such force it didn't bother staying and instead slid right off and fell onto the floor with a thunk until it rolled across the dark gray carpet. She didn't give a fuck about being gentle with much of anything right now.

Her hands jerked at the sleeves of her leather jacket, stripping it off and pitching it at a chair, revealing the white lace blouse underneath. With her temper being at an all-time high, coupled with her stress, the room felt sweltering.

Ignoring Joey's question, she tossed out her own, "How about we start with why the fuck you both are here? I told you both to stay back."

Gage crossed his arms in front of his chest, "We gave you enough space before we followed you here. Nobody trailed us."

"You don't know that!" she screamed at him, only imagining how all of this was going to blow up in her face if Liam got wind of what she was doing or who she was doing it with. "I told you both to leave me alone for a damn reason! What part of that did you not understand?!"

Barely clinging to any sense of calm, Joey shook his head. "You're overreacting."

That was probably the worst thing he could have said at that moment. "Do not talk to me about overreacting!" her voice remained elevated as she shouted at him.

Layne continued to lash into them, "You left me under the impression that you were going to do as I asked. I came here so that I could find a way to strike at one of Liam's top guys without him seeing it coming. I jumped through fifty goddamn hoops to set up this meeting, and you both were so willing to put it all in jeopardy!"

Leaning over to balance on one leg, she removed one shoe quickly, followed by the other. Both shoes were angrily discarded to the side, but not after contemplating throwing them at both of her guys like she was playing the milk can game at a carnival.

It was Gage who made the first step towards her. She glared at him with the weight of violence in her eyes, stopping him from approaching unless he wanted to feel her wrath next.

Gage raised his hands up innocently and retreated from the step he had taken towards her. "What about the risk you were taking? Did you consider that?" He offered an opposing viewpoint.

"I took this risk so you both didn't have to. The two of you have been so wrapped up in keeping me safe, and at what cost, hm?" She pointed at Joey. "You get fuckin' shot, and you," she pointed at Gage, "get drugged and into a car accident."

She knew neither of those things were their fault, but it had all been attacks on her that had caused them suffering.

Her chest was aching at the thought of how all these things could have ended poorly. The thought of losing either of them would wreck her soul, especially if it was because of their involvement in her life. Tears began to prick at her eyes.

Forcing her voice to remain steady, ignoring the emotions shining in her eyes like morning dew on a clover, "When does it fucking stop? When one or all of us is dead?" The words barely made it out of her mouth.

The air was thick with silence as she stared at both of them, her question going unanswered. Finally, Joey's shoulders relaxed, seeing past her anger and straight to the fear behind her rage. "Layney, I'm not going to apolo—"

"Shut up. Apologies aren't what I need." She plucked the taser from her hip and set it on the table before removing several knives that had been concealed underneath her clothes. The last item she drew was her firearm, the cool metal feeling comforting in her hand. Staring down at the semi-automatic, she shook her head, wondering how her life had spiraled so out of control. Layne needed to snatch some of that control back.

Her eyes lifted from the weapon in her hand to the two men in front of her. "On your knees, both of you." There was no uncertainty in her voice as she gave them both the order.

Slowly, Gage turned his head to Joey, looking for some indication that his brother had heard the same thing as him. The way Layne was holding onto the gun made him wonder if she was planning on fucking shooting them both.

Joey didn't take his eyes off Layne before he dropped down to his knees, his hands hanging down loosely between his thighs. He sat back on his feet, seeming all too willing to let Layne do as she wanted.

After seeing Joey lower himself, Gage mirrored the action and stared at Layne, trying to guess what was going on inside her head.

She walked around behind them and let them stew in their thoughts for a few minutes. Both of these bad boys could think about what they had done.

Setting the gun down quietly on the sofa behind her, she leaned over between them. Her hands grabbed them both by their sandy blonde hair and pulled their heads back so they were staring up at her.

"Dicks out," she demanded.

Clear from the expression that washed over both their faces, it had been an unexpected turn of events. Being able to catch them both off guard by her request had Layne's excitement at her core growing warmer by the second.

Complying, each opened up their pants and shoved at the waist of their underwear until she was greeted by the sight of both their cocks. Each thick length was growing harder before her eyes.

"Good boys," she purred out in praise. Her hands shoved their heads forward roughly as she released her grip on them. "Now, I want you both to show me how you stroke your cocks when you're thinking about me."

She straightened and watched as Gage took his swords into his hand and began to work in long, slow movements. Her eyes glanced over at Joey, and he was eagerly gliding his hand over his swollen cock at a slightly faster pace.

Layne leaned over and whispered into Joey's ear, "You might want to slow down. If you come, you lose. And I plan for us to be here for a little while." She smirked as he gave a quiet groan in response and pulled back on the pace of his hand.

Her teeth gave a light tug at the curve of his ear before she stepped between them, turning to watch their efforts. Layne's desires were rising within her, prompting her to give a hard swallow to maintain her composure. She could feel her thong quickly getting soaked with her arousal as they both submissively followed her orders. Having them jerk themselves off because she said so unlocked something in Layne that she wasn't even aware she enjoyed.

Gradually, her anger was melting now that she had them both finally listening to her. "Whose idea was it to follow me here?"

Joey piped up with a confession, "Mine."

That wasn't a huge surprise; her forever and always stalker. "Of course it was, you just can't help yourself. Can you, Joey?"

She stepped in front of Gage. Her fingers settled underneath his bearded chin, tipping his head back gently to look up at her. "Looks like you're up first."

Barely touching his skin, she trailed her fingers down the center of his throat slowly. Her slender fingers wrapped around his silver chain, peeking out of the collar of his tee, twisting it several times around two of her digits before tugging. "Up."

His hand fell away from his inked cock as he stood. Layne used his necklace like a leash, leading him to the armchair within Joey's sight. Turning Gage, she released his necklace and pushed him so he fell back into the chair.

Layne dropped down to her knees, shoving his muscled thighs apart so she could settle between them. Her fierce green eyes looked at Gage. "I want you to tell him how good I make you feel."

It took an act of God for Gage not to push his luck and give Joey a cocky grin that he was going to get some action while his brother remained in the doghouse.

Layne took hold of his hard dick, her grasp at the base as she angled him toward her. Lowering her mouth over the rounded head of Gage's cock, she sucked on him aggressively, refusing to be gentle. After taking several inches of his swords deeper into her mouth, Gage rested his head back against the chair and groaned out in pleasure.

"Baby, your mouth around my cock feels so good." His hips pushed up towards her with increased need. His hand slid onto the side of her head as her lips sealed around his swollen length. Resisting the urge to grab her hair and force her head forward, he clutched tightly with his other hand on the arm of the chair he was in. "Fuck, I love what you can do with your mouth."

Watching as Layne began to blow, Gage had Joey's need for any part of her body skyrocketing. His hand started to move faster over his dick until he remembered Layne's warning, forcing him to painfully ease up. God, he knew just how good her throat felt, and he would have done anything if it meant she would stop what she was doing and come suck his dick.

She continued to lower her greedy mouth down onto Gage, her tongue taunting the underside like a velvety snake. With each bob of her head, his hips pushed up to get rewarded with the tightness of pushing beyond her gag reflex.

His hand began to clutch harder onto Layne's head. "Fuck, Layne, yes. Make me come, baby." The desire was dripping off of Gage's words as his pleasure began to shift into a frenzied need.

The feeling was taken away all too soon after he mentioned coming. Layne slid off him, her hand gliding up to the end of his cock that ached for release. Her thumb rubbed over the head, mixing her saliva with the precum leaking from his tip.

Gage whimpered, "Come on, don't leave me hanging."

Layne smirked as she removed her hand. "I'll let you come when I decide you've earned it. You're still in trouble for going along with Joey's idea." She pushed herself onto her feet, leaving him there, wanting the one thing she refused to give him. His balls ached as she brought him so close to satisfaction, only to rip it away at the last second.

For a split moment, Joey felt smug that he wasn't the only one being toyed with by their girl. When Layne turned and approached him, he was certain that it was his turn in her mouth. However, when he started to get off his knees, she pushed him right back down again.

Lightly, she scolded him, "I didn't tell you to get up. You have work to do." His chocolate eyes stared up at her, begging so loudly for her touch he didn't need to verbalize it.

Her hands tugged her shirt up over her head, dropping it at her feet. Next, she shimmied out of her jeans until all she was left standing in was a blush pink bra and panty set.

Without looking behind her, she gave Gage his next order. "Gage, back as you were on your knees for me with your hand back on your cock."

Following instructions, her Daddy was behaving so nicely for her even though he was never the one in their relationship taking orders.

"Looks like someone is finally getting a taste of how it feels to be the sub," Joey smirked as he glanced over at Gage, who was no longer asserting himself as the Dom here.

Grabbing Joey's jaw, Layne turned his gaze back towards her. "And you're going to learn what happens when you run that bratty mouth of yours."

Taking two handfuls of Joey's hair to balance herself, she draped a leg over his shoulder while she balanced on the other. Layne gave a giddy grin. "My turn to feel good." She urged his face towards her waiting pussy.

More than happy to get a taste of her, Joey shifted the crotch of her thong to the side and dove into the sensual buffet that waited for his mouth. His tongue immediately lapped at her sweet arousal. If he ever ended up on death row, he'd want Layne to be his last meal.

She moaned out at the first contact, her hips grinding up against his lips. Each movement was a mix of sensations coming from the coarseness of his stubble, his punishing lips, and the firm flexing of his tongue. "Oh God, yes…" Her head tipped back as the sinful vibrations of pleasure coursed throughout her body.

Gage was left to watch and listen as Joey got to indulge in Layne's body, while he only imagined what it would be like to be balls deep in her while she made those delicious sounds. His hand squeezed his cock tighter at the thought.

Joey's hands came up to hold her steady, his fingers digging into her ass cheeks while he reveled in the taste of her cunt on his taste buds. Every moan she released drove him to taste even more of her.

The sensation of a groan of approval from Joey had her body beginning to shake as her release queued up. Gasping for air between her pants, she started to slip off that delicate edge. "Joey! Don't stop!" Her hands fisted his hair tightly to make sure he didn't draw back from her.

Taking advantage of her current state, Joey took it upon himself to inch one of his fingers into the tight hole of her ass, only far enough to send her careening into her orgasm.

She screamed out as she came, feeling her heated core bear down while her cum got devoured by Joey.

His scalp was nearly on fire the way Layne's hands were tugging on his hair, and it only fueled his need for her. She could ride his mouth like a fucking pony if it meant hearing her orgasm ricochet throughout her body like this.

Layne's breaths came out hard as she tried to reel herself back in from the ecstasy attempting to lull her into a sedative state. It was Gage's groans as his hand twisted along his cock that brought her mind back to dealing with these two. They both needed to learn their lesson of how to listen to her.

Her fists slowly unfurled to let go of Joey's locks of hair, pushing his hands away from her ass. Carefully, she removed her thigh from his shoulder and stepped back from him on shaky legs.

With the satisfaction still saturating her eyes, she looked down at him and tried to bite back her smile. "I didn't give you permission to touch my ass like that."

"It was worth it," he responded with a sly grin before he sucked off the taste of her from the finger he had used on her back door.

"We'll see if you still feel that way in a few minutes. Both of you, strip and get on the bed." No sooner had she said it than they were both rushing to shed all their clothes and wait for her in the bedroom.

Ditching her bra and panties so she was equally as naked, she followed them to the edge of the mattress and took a moment to enjoy the sight laid out before her. Both men were lying there, ready for her, with their cocks harder than steel in anticipation. All of their tattooed images on display across their flesh for her to admire.

She crawled onto the bed between them with a mischievous sparkle in her green hues. "For both of you not listening to me earlier tonight, neither of you will get to come. Joey, since you couldn't be a good boy, you get to watch me fuck Gage since he knows how to keep his hands to himself."

Before Gage could settle in and gloat, she issued her warning to him. "I'm fucking you for me, not for you. I'm the one in charge tonight. Do you understand?"

He still couldn't help but grin like a fool as he cheekily replied, "Yes, Mistress."

Layne straddled Gage's hips and roughly grabbed his arms, shoving them above his head. She looked over at Joey, "Make sure his hands stay right where they are."

Joey should have been a lot grumpier that he wasn't the one getting fucked, but at least he got a front-row seat to watching Layne take Gage's cock without the intention of giving him a happy ending. Seated near the headboard above his brother's head, he grabbed Gage's wrists and tightly restrained them.

"Damn, ease up asshole, you don't need to hold them that tightly," Gage complained as Joey intentionally went above and beyond the call of duty.

Before Gage could continue to bitch, Layne guided his thick tattooed cock into her tight pussy. He gave a husky groan as he felt himself disappearing into her.

She echoed the same level of pleasure, her face shifting as she felt the fullness deep within her. Rocking her hips, she began to ride him, beginning the chase for her own climax.

"That's it, baby. Show me how you can tame my cock," Gage moaned out.

With one hand planted on his firm chest, she clamped the other down over his mouth. "Mmm, Gage, I don't want to hear your filthy mouth right now."

Gage's restraint was slowly crumbling as he pushed his hips up to get his cock further up into her. His hot and heavy breaths got trapped under Layne's palm.

Wrapped up in her cloud nine of pleasure, Layne missed the exchange of looks between the guys. Just as she was finding her rhythm, the dynamics shifted hard and fast.

Joey released Gage's wrists, allowing him to roll over and use his weight to pin Layne underneath his body. She shrieked out in surprise at the sudden change of position. Taking advantage of her surprise, Joey captured her wrists, holding them in his firm grip as he kept his front-row seat at the head of the bed.

Not waiting for her to begin to yell at either of them, Gage began bucking his hips, ramming his cock into her. Each hard thrust jostled her body against the mattress as she moaned out, her full tits bouncing on her chest wildly.

"Did you really think I was going to let you dictate when I get to come, baby?" Gage huffed out between each of his movements as his dick slammed its full length into her repeatedly.

Her loud moans were strung together as she writhed and squirmed, her narrow wrists engulfed in Joey's hold that prevented her from gaining any leverage after this sudden mutiny.

Layne shook her head at Gage, "No."

With his Dom voice dropping a register, Gage dragged his lips over hers. "No, what?"

"No, Daddy!" she cried out as her orgasm was preparing to violently erupt inside of her.

"You better sing my favorite fuckin' song while you soak my dick with your cum, Layne." Gage firmly ordered her as he pounded into her body, their flesh smacking together. The tip of his cock was relentless as it jabbed at the especially sensitive spot inside of her.

The closer she got, the more she fought and trembled against Joey's restraint. Her toes curled as her legs began to kick at the mounting pressure that she was unable to escape.

Gage's hands clamped down onto her thighs. He had her legs pinned wide open as he watched his cock shine with the wetness from her body every time he withdrew it before shoving it back inside of her.

It only took a few more strokes of his dick before her cunt spasmed around him, and she ferally screamed out. Her release took her hard. It was taking everything Gage had not to unload into her right then and there.

"Fuck! Layne!" He groaned, continuing to try to hold his shit together, his own body on the verge of shaking. As Layne rode her burst of pleasure, her walls continued squeezing onto Gage's cock. Grinding himself into her depths, he tensed up as he yelled out as his seed flooded into her.

Panting heavily, Gage eased out of her and collapsed down onto his back at her side. Layne lay there blissfully like a well-used ragdoll. It made it easy for the guys to shift her so her back was on Gage's chest with his half-hard cock nestled against her ass.

Joey took up the space between her legs, draping them over the crooks of his arms. He had enough of the taunting and teasing she had done earlier; it was his turn to get his fix of her. The sight of his brother's cum slowly leaking from her pussy had his cock twitching as it felt like it was growing beyond the hardest he had ever felt it.

Breathlessly, she lay there with heavy eyes from the residual high her body had just surrendered to. "Both of you are shitty subs," she teased while lazily smiling.

Smirking, Joey used the round head of his cock to collect some of the escaped white fluid from her pussy and push it back into her entrance. "Layney, don't act like you don't fuckin' love it when we take any part of you the way we want."

Feeling him barely inside of her, she whimpered.

Gage's hands ran over her body, one traveling south to her clit and the other up over her stomach until he roughly grabbed her breast. He whispered into her ear from behind, "You've been a naughty fuckin' girl, baby. The second I'm fully hard again, you better prepare your tight little ass." His fingers pinched at her stiff nipple, causing her to let out a small yelp.

Seeing Gage's fingers begin to circle Layne's sensitive bundle of nerves, Joey slowly sank into her. Fuck, he loved how wet she was right now, and he wanted nothing more than to add his own cum to the mix. "I'm going to fuck the good girl back into you even if it takes me all goddamn night, Layne."

Between the two of them, Layne's antsy movements got her nowhere as they both focused on different parts of her body. Her body felt on fire from the overload of sexual stimulation she was receiving.

The way Joey pulled his cock back out so incredibly and intentionally slow had Layne whimpering at the loss of being full.

"What was that, Layney?" He smiled as he held his hips still, letting her yearn for him a little longer.

Gage's hand moved across to her other breast, twisting the nipple between his fingers. Everything they did to her body left her barely able to find words.

"I need your cock," she finally managed to let out in a heated whisper.

"You didn't want it earlier," he grinned as he gave her the shallowest little fuck as his hips made tiny thrusts at her opening.

She groaned desperately. Each tease of her body left her nearly in tears at the intense ache at her core. "Damn it, Joey, please!"

There was a rumble coming from Gage's chest against her back as he quietly chuckled at how much she wanted things her way.

Joey leaned over and locked his lips against her mouth, kissing her roughly. Her moans soaked into his mouth as she still wiggled between the two guys.

Barely separating their lips, Joey gazed down into Layne's eyes as a smile tugged at the corners of his mouth. "Layney, when are you ever going to learn? I'm always going to come for you. There is nothing you can do to stop me from making sure you always stay ours."

With that declaration, he drilled his cock into her, groaning out at how readily her body drew him in.

As Joey filled her greedy pussy and began to fuck some sense into her, Gage's dick was rapidly getting harder, being pressed against the warmth of her ass. It had his cock quickly recovering at the way she moved with each of Joey's pushes into her body.

Gage growled from behind her, "How's it feel when your bad boys take care of you, baby?" His fingers continued their massage of her clit. He whispered into her ear, "You'll always be ours, Layne."

Layne's body was trembling as she watched Joey's body take control of her own. No one could give her pleasure the way both of them did, whether they fucked her separately or together. As pissed as she had been that they could have fucked everything up today, a part of her, deep down, was glad they had.

She was theirs in every possible way. Now, her job was to make sure it stayed that way. Up 'til this point, Layne had been doing things all wrong. Instead of worrying about pushing them away to keep them safe, she needed to keep them closer than ever.

The three of them were the perfect match, and together, they would watch Liam's world burn.

Chapter Twenty-Six

UNIT 33

Waiting to hear back from Daniil on whether or not he was successful in his endeavors to track down and get information out of Orellano had been brutal. Each phone call, every knock at the door, any carrier pigeon, was a reason for Layne to perk up in her seat.

After her personal revelation at The Alderson Hotel, while she got her insides rearranged by the two men who had promised to be her everything, she had looped Joey and Gage in on how she had come across Daniil.

Expectedly, Joey had been pissed that Brandon had kept his mouth shut. Fortunately, Layne was able to soothe his anger down a few notches with a few sweet nothings and strokes of her hand before he marched downtown to scare the poor kid senseless.

Currently snuggled between her two large De Luca men on the sofa, she tugged the blanket over her lap as they watched the hockey game together.

"You've got to be kidding me! Where's the slashing call?!" Gage yelled at the television, raising his hands in the air.

Layne snagged another chocolate-covered rice cereal treat out of the bowl Joey was hoarding. The powdered sugar coating left a dusting on her fingertips after she popped the square into her mouth. Listening to Gage get all worked up like the referees on the ice could hear him through the television screen made her giggle.

"Makes up for the tripping call they missed earlier," Joey argued before he snatched up Layne's hand and sucked the white confectionary coating from her fingers.

Watching the guys bicker when their favorite teams played each other by far was one of Layne's favorite things to keep her mind preoccupied when they all weren't naked.

Her phone began to ring and vibrate against the coffee table. Not wasting any time, she leaned over to scoop it up into her hand without any hesitation in answering the blocked number.

"Hello?" There was a pause as she listened, sitting still as a statue. The way she tensed up prompted Gage to mute the game and Joey to put the snack bowl on the side table.

Her jaw tensed as she ground her teeth together when the caller laid the news on her. She squeezed the phone tighter in her hand, "I appreciate it, Daniil. Thanks."

Hanging up the phone, she shook her head. "Motherfucker."

Gage's hand squeezed her thigh. "What is it?"

Both of them were now staring at her with concerned eyes.

"I need to meet with Ethan, Jonathan, and Sammy. We've got a fucking problem." She tossed the blanket off her legs. It looked like this wouldn't be a night off from work after all.

After the wedding, Layne had paid some of her grunt workers to go to Liam's place, change the locks, and throw all his shit into a storage unit. Layne had been intending to go through her brother's belongings to see if there was anything of value but hadn't yet had the opportunity. The whole shitshow of her husband getting shot, getting stabbed herself, her Daddy getting drugged, her car getting wrecked, and trying to keep her illegal business ventures afloat was a major time suck.

She called up her top associates and had them meet her, Joey, and Gage there at Southside Storage for an urgent debrief. Joey lifted the storage unit's metal door; a single light bulb provided enough light to reveal the half-filled rental resting on a concrete pad.

"You think there's something in here that's useful?" Sammy asked as he walked into space with Jonathan and Ethan trailing close behind.

"I know there is," Layne said as she waited for all six of them to be inside before pulling the garage-style door closed.

Jonathan picked up a dusty bobblehead figurine before tossing it back into a box. "Looks like a bunch of crap to me."

Ethan sighed, imagining that this was going to be a long night of digging. "Do you have any idea of what we're looking for?"

Joey and Gage grabbed a chair, centering it in the open space.

Layne nodded. "I do, and it's right here." Her eyes scanned the interior of the unit before she looked at Jonathan. "Take a seat."

"What?" He blinked a few times as he pointed at his chest. "Me? Why?"

Joey grabbed Jonathan's shoulder and shoved him into the chair. "She said sit."

Her associate stumbled into the chair; the confusion was as clear as day creasing over his face. Both Ethan and Sammy looked at one another, mirroring the same cluelessness.

"I want to make something very clear." Layne pulled out her gun, tugging the slide back to load a bullet into the chamber. "I made it known when I took over the business that I would be setting some incredibly high standards. When those standards aren't met, it does not make me very happy."

She walked over to Jonathan and straddled his lap, putting the deadly end of the pistol right against his dick. Looking at her negotiator in the eyes. "Is there something you want to tell me?"

Ethan and Sammy took a few steps back, the look in Layne's eyes gave them enough warning not to interfere. Their boss may have looked like an otherwise sweet girl you'd meet on a night out, but she sure as hell had her father's commanding presence when it came to business matters.

Jonathan struggled to find his words, ultimately stuttering out, "N-no. No, of course not!" His eyes pleadingly looked to everyone else in the room there with them. "What the fuck is going on?" Looking for answers from anyone who would take pity. No one did.

Her hand grabbed his face with her other hand, squeezing it tightly so she could look at him. "I'm teaching a lesson in loyalty." She jabbed the gun harder against his junk.

"Layne! Jesus! Stop!" Jonathan's words mushed together by her fingers painfully digging into his cheeks. He began to push up from the chair, but Joey's hands shoved down onto his shoulders from behind.

Layne calmly gave her order to the other two associates, "Sam, Ethan, please make sure Jonathan stays put while we have this conversation."

Without hesitation, both guys came over and took Joey's place. She wanted them to see what happened when she was disappointed.

"Jon, you're a hell of a negotiator. You've helped close a lot of deals for me and smoothed over a lot of relations with other factions on my behalf. So, I want you to negotiate. Show me how good you are." Her hand released his face, but she kept her weapon right where it was. The urge to prematurely fire it off right then and there was incredibly tempting, given her newfound knowledge.

"You're fucking crazy! Negotiate what?" He had the nerve to look ignorant.

Her words were void of any emotions as she gave a nonchalant shrug, "Your life. Why I shouldn't blow your dick to pieces. I mean, I think it's pretty damn obvious."

Gage and Joey hung back, watching as Layne rightfully tormented the guy.

"Uh," was Jonathan's first word as he sat there with Layne sitting on his legs. "I love my dick. Like really love it. I don't want it shot to shit. Layne, I don't know what has set you off, but I swear I will do anything to help you out and make it right."

Was he kidding her right now? Layne rested a hand on the back of Jonathan's neck as she laughed darkly. "Holy shit, do you hear yourself right now?"

Nervously, Jonathan tried to read her laughter and gave a half-chuckle, trying to find humor in the situation to placate her.

"You should see your face right now." Layne smiled as she gave a softer laugh this time.

"Hah, yeah…" The bead of sweat on his forehead began its slow descent towards his brow.

Shifting back a few inches on his lap, Layne pulled the trigger. The bullet easily tore past the thick denim of Jonathan's jeans and straight into his cock.

Her other two associates simultaneously flinched and cringed; you could notice their legs flexing as they had fear struck into their own dicks.

Jonathan immediately jolted and howled out in agony. Layne's grip on his neck rotated to squeeze his throat, minimizing the sound of his yells.

"You are a fucking liar, Jon!" She yelled at him to be heard over his pain as the blood began soaking his pants, spreading outward over the crotch area. "You've been working for Liam this entire goddamn time! How are you going to make that right?!"

She moved the Glock, so it was now pressed against Jonathan's shoulder as he jerked and writhed, tears streaming down his face. "No, no, no, no!" His denial was on repeat, or perhaps he was in disbelief she had just put a bullet through his penis.

Glancing up to see the shock on the other two's faces, she began laying out everything she knew.

"No? No, you weren't helping Liam? You're telling me that you didn't tell him when I was at the hospital with Joey? You didn't feed him information about my every move? You sure that you didn't give him the heads up where I was having dinner down in Times Square?" Each recounting of all the puzzle pieces clicking into place made her anger tick up another notch.

Her face came up to his so close their noses were touching, and she didn't care how much spit came out with her words. "What about all my discussions with other factions that you were handling? Huh?! Did you fuck those up for me, too?! Is that why no one seemed willing to help me!?"

Jonathan cried out again, reeling from injury, filling his body with unimaginable pain. "Gah!! Pleeeeease!"

Layne pulled her face back to give a little more space. "I hate to tell you, Jonathan, but Nicholas isn't as tight-lipped as you thought. A friend of mine had him spilling everything he knew. Imagine my goddamn surprise when he told me one of my own fucking men was betraying me!" Layne was beyond pissed, and every word she spat out was laced with her dangerous venom.

When Daniil had called her to alert her he had tracked down Orellano, he informed her of everything that spilled out of the man's mouth. It had taken some extremely aggressive forms of persuasion, which the Russian had been all too happy to resort to. Nicholas had dropped Jonathan's name like a two-ton weight. He mentioned another man, but when questioned further, it was determined he knew nothing about Liam's other partner.

"What is Liam's plan, Jonathan? Hm? You better tell me something, or else I will make the pain you're feeling now seem like a mild headache." She dug the muzzle of the pistol harder into the front of his shoulder.

When it was clear he was too distracted to answer her question, she crashed the side of the gun across his face. "What's his plan?!" Her voice echoed against the walls of the small space of the storage unit.

She saw the defeat and surrender begin to peek through Jonathan's tough front as he sobbed. He choked on his words, "He…H-he wants you to," he gasped for some air between his fits of pain. "Meet at Eric's old place. It's on the note." He took several large breaths, trying to get through the intensity of the wound between his legs.

Layne thought back to the note left for her after the accident. *430 at 830 on 227 for 611.* The first number was the house number of Eric's old residence. The second must have been the time, followed by the date. However, her mind was drawing a blank on what the fourth number represented.

"What's 611?" she asked after being unable to figure it out on her own.

Jonathan shook his head. "I don't know." When she went to lift her pistol again, he screamed out, "I don't know! I swear! I just gave him info; I didn't ask questions!"

Well, that was fucking useless.

"Layne, I'm sorry." Oh boy, here came the apologies that she hated so much.

She got off his lap, pacing a few feet in front of him. "Who is helping him?"

"I told you, I don't know!" He brayed like a wounded jackass.

Bang!

Another bullet ripped through Jonathan, this time, it was the top of his foot. Layne looked up to see Ethan holding his gun out. "You piece of shit! If you don't start giving her answers, I will personally shove this gun up your ass and pull the trigger."

Color Layne impressed that Ethan was harboring the same amount of anger and resentment that she was. He was going to need a damn promotion.

Jonathan was now hysterically screaming, the words coming out of his mouth were a combination of nonsense and curses.

Layne's fingers rubbed across her forehead, trying to gather her thoughts past the incessant whines and whimpers as Jonathan's body became crippled from the attacks.

She tapped the side of her pistol against her thigh to help her think. Deciding that Jonathan was no longer of any use to her, she lifted the gun to aim it at his chest.

His eyes went wide, seeing that another shot was about to be fired. "Some old fuck! Real twisted!"

"Thanks. Your services are no longer required." Layne pulled the trigger, and the bullet found its home, lodged into Jonathan's heart, obliterating the critical muscle.

Sammy shook his head in disgust that out of the three of them, it was Jonathan who was working with Liam this entire time. "Layne, I had no idea…"

Sighing heavily, she nodded. "I know, nobody seemed to."

"Dickhead," Ethan said under his breath.

Layne returned her Glock to the holster in the back of her pants and pulled out her phone.

Gage raised a brow and came up behind her. "Who are you calling?"

"Liam," his name rolled off her tongue, drenched in disgust.

"Layney," Joey said with a warning tone.

"Don't worry, I'm making this short and sweet," she reassured both of them.

Putting the call on speaker, the other end of the line rang a few times before her brother answered.

"This is a pleasant surprise." Liam sounded far too excited to hear from her.

"Southside Storage, unit thirty-three. Come pick up your shit, motherfucker." Her finger tapped the end call button. A moment later, she sent a picture of Jonathan's hunched-over corpse to Liam.

The time of playing by her brother's rules was over. Now, she was playing by her own.

Chapter Twenty-Seven

ALWAYS & FOREVER

There wasn't a price Layne wouldn't have paid to see Liam's face when he received the picture of Jonthan's dead body. She hoped he shit his pants and was prepared for her to begin executing anyone else that got in her way.

Thanks to finding an unexpected ally in one particular Russian, her brother had to know about good ol' Nick's demise by now. May that fucker be suffering in hell alongside Jonathan.

With two birds down, she couldn't afford not to press forward, full steam ahead. Liam needed to feel the pressure to a point where he would royally fuck up. If he didn't make a mistake, she sure as hell wasn't going to stop until he did.

As for the note that her former associate had partially deciphered, it seemed they had less than a week before Liam expected her to roll up to the old Ellis residence and wave a white flag.

Good thing she didn't plan to surrender if things didn't go as planned. No, she would march over there beating her war drums for all of New York to hear if it came down to it.

Layne came downstairs wearing nothing but a black silk kimono robe overtop a silk lingerie set. O'Reilly Manor was expectedly quiet at eleven at night. With Gage meeting up with his friends to set up a plan to keep tabs on the perimeter of their home there on the Upper East Side, it was just her and Joey holding down the fort.

Joey had been stuck in the garage working on his car since dinner. It had been his way of busying his mind before he made the next strike in the early hours of the morning.

She quietly opened up the interior door that led into the garage and leaned against the frame as she watched him.

He was leaning over the side of the black Challenger, working on something under the hood of the vehicle. From this vantage point, she was happy to be standing there, appreciating the view of his jean-clad ass.

Joey's tee was draped over the seat of his motorcycle parked next to the car, leaving him shirtless and enhancing the already delicious sight. Each muscle in his back flexed as he worked.

Without turning to look at her, he spoke, "Eye-fucking me again, Layney?" Smirking to himself, he gave another twist of the socket wrench. Layne wasn't nearly as stealthy as she thought she was.

After being called out, she convinced herself that if she had been trying to be sneaky, he wouldn't have known she was there. Stepping onto the cool concrete of the garage floor, she was careful to watch where she walked to avoid tripping on any scattered tools.

"Was just seeing when you were planning on heading out." Layne stopped at the front bumper as she looked at him with gentle green hues.

He sighed and rested his forearms on the edge of the car, and looked over at her. She may have tried to silently admire him moments ago, but Joey made no such effort to conceal the way his eyes appreciated the woman standing there in the garage with him.

The silk robe was tied around her slender waist and draped over the rest of her petite figure. Its length fell to just above midthigh, making it unlikely she was wearing much of anything underneath. If he was lucky, she was wearing nothing at all.

Joey straightened up and tossed the wrench into the open toolbox next to the front tire. "I'm almost done here." He wiped his hands on the thighs of his stained pants, though it did little to remove the black smudges on his hands.

Crossing her arms in front of her stomach, her hands lightly grasped onto her elbows. "Everything all set for Liam?" The plan they had conjured seemed karmic, considering the last time an O'Reilly was executed. However, just thinking about some of the ways it could go wrong had Layne feeling incredibly uneasy.

Picking up on her restlessness and the concern settled in her stance, Joey stepped up to her. "It's going to be okay. You forget how long I've been doing this, Layne. I will head over to Eric's old place, install the explosives on the truck that Ethan says matches the description of the one that was involved in your accident, and hightail it the fuck out of there. With any luck, Liam will get what's been coming to him. If not, it will take out whoever is helping him."

"I know." The tension in her body didn't let up.

Sullied hands or not, he decided he couldn't hold back from using his touch to reassure her. Joey lightly wrapped his hands on either side of her neck just under her jaw, his thumbs caressing the lower lines of her face.

Cocoa brown eyes stared at her as he searched for what was weighing on her mind. "What are you really worried about?" he asked.

Trying to beat down her heart's emotions, she blinked back a few tears. War came with unexpected casualties, ones that you didn't get to pick or choose.

"Don't make me ask twice." He gave a small smile at her that didn't quite reach his eyes.

Filling her lungs with a heaping amount of air, she tried to steady her voice. "There's been a lot going on. When are we all just going to get a break and have a shot at normalcy again?"

His hands fell from her so he could draw her up against his bare chest, wrapping his arms around her upper body into a tight embrace. "We'll get our chance, I promise." If his new deal with Commissioner Saito held up, their opportunity would get here sooner rather than later. "Did you make the call we talked about?"

"Yeah…" The tone of her voice carried a mixture of regret and hesitation. Layne wrapped her arms around his waist as she rested her face against the warmth of his skin. Her cheek pressed against the scarred shamrock tattoo over his heart, the disrupted inkwork around the scar was a souvenir of him saving her life.

Joey's fingers smoothed back a few stray locks of hair away from her face. He hesitated as his words began to stick to the back of his throat, refusing to come out easily. Briefly, he shut his eyes tightly and kissed the top of her head, finding the strength to open up the last piece of him to her.

With eyes back open, he eased her face away from him so he could look at the woman who had changed him before he had even met her. "Layne, there's something I need to tell you."

Scrunching her eyebrows together, she wasn't sure what emotion she should prepare for. "About what?"

Immediately, his heart felt a pang of guilt, seeing that she was already hesitantly putting up her defenses. His large hands grabbed her face so he could make sure she saw the honesty in what he had to say.

"Layne, you are both my biggest regret and my greatest salvation. I never want to know life without you in it." In a rare moment, his eyes glistened as his sight remained locked on her. "There isn't a day where I don't regret all the negative impacts I've had on your life, but you saved me before you ever knew me."

As she began to part her lips to ask questions, his thumb sealed her lips shut. "Let me finish telling you what you deserved to hear long before now."

She stood there with her eyes filling with the heaviness of emotion as he began his final confession.

Joey's thumb rubbed across the perfect shade of pink of her lips. "You were never meant to be mine. Hell, you were never meant to become the woman you are now. I…" He braced himself for the moment he wished he could erase from his history. "You were supposed to be in the car with your mom."

Layne felt a whirlwind of confusion as she tried to wrap her brain around his words. "W-what?"

He frowned. "The contract was for both of you. I did months of surveillance, watching and waiting for the right time. The day I set the device on your mom's car, I realized I could never come back from taking your life before it even began. So, I made an anonymous call to your dad, threatening your life, knowing he would react by becoming even more overprotective."

Her eyes searched his face, noticing all the years of guilt coming to the surface. She struggled with the new revelation that her life could have been cut short at Joey's hands not once but twice. On the day she lost her mother, she couldn't understand why her parents wouldn't let her go out, and now it was all becoming clear.

Joey dropped his head down shamefully. "Layney, I'm so sorry I didn't tell you before now. It never felt like the right time."

Seeing a fresh line of moisture trail down his cheeks, she frowned.

"Hey," Layne said with gentle reassurance. "Look at me." Her fingertips came up underneath his scruffy chin to tilt his gaze back up to her.

His eyes met hers, expecting the worst of words to be spoken.

"I have learned to open myself up and lower the walls I have spent years building up because you make me feel safe. I have chosen to love you even knowing your past. You have always protected me, even when I didn't know I needed you to. That's not something I can be angry at you for." God knew she hadn't made his life any easier some days, but Layne wouldn't change their pasts no matter what she was offered in exchange.

No matter how you looked at it, Joey had spared her twice in her lifetime when he could have snuffed out her flame.

Her hands cupped his cheeks, her fingertips swiping away the pain expelled from his eyes.

Layne brought her mouth to his, kissing away all the doubts and regrets he had about his past. Lovingly, her lips pressed to his to do her best to put his conscience and soul at peace.

After feeling his body soften into her affections, she eased out of the kiss with a sweet smile.

Gradually, relief filled him, and Joey leaned in to steal another quick kiss from her. "You'll never know how much I love you, Layne."

Her hands slowly trailed down the front of the hard muscles of his stomach. When she spoke, her words were just one notch above a whisper. "Try showing me."

She didn't need to ask him twice. Joey's fingers purposely unknotted the sash around her waist as he began backing her up to the workbench at the far wall of the garage.

His hand slid up the back of her neck with a gentleness as his tattooed fingers embedded themselves into the depths of her silky chestnut hair.

As the sash came undone, the kimono fell open to reveal the forest-green lingerie underneath. Joey's desire for her still had a fiery edge to it despite the way his touch had become gentle.

Quickly, he cleared just enough space on the workbench for her ass before he lifted her and set her down on it. With his hands on her waist, he stood between her thighs as he took his time kissing her. First, it was reveling in the taste of her mouth; then, it was exploring across her jaw and down along her throat.

Layne dropped her shoulders so the silk material of the robe slid off her upper body, pooling around her as she let him spoil her with his affections. Quietly, she moaned as his tongue flicked out across the sensitive spot where her neck met her shoulder.

Her body was already reacting to their deep emotional and physical connection, her core growing damp with arousal. The tips of Layne's fingers hooked onto the front of his jeans, tugging him closer to her center.

When he pressed himself against her core, her breathing hitched at the sensation of his hard cock struggling against his jeans.

"Joey," she said, his name already sounding breathless. "I need you to fuck me."

His palms ran over the front of her bra, taking in the feel of her breasts held captive in the cups. He shook his head at her request. "I'm not going to fuck you; I'm going to do better than that. You're going to feel how deep my feelings run for you, Layne."

After his hands drifted behind her, he popped the clasp on her bra to free her rounded breasts and hardened nipples from the fabric prison. The stubble on his face brushed against her fair skin as his mouth continued its mission to love every part of her. From her collarbone, down over her chest where her heart was beating excitedly, each curve and peak of her breasts, and down the center of her stomach.

Layne's hands held onto his shoulders as he lowered himself down her body, continuing to slowly drag his lips across her flesh. Eventually, his fingers shimmied the thin straps of her thong away from her hips until it popped free and easily slid down her legs onto the floor.

For all the attention he was giving her, he passed by where she hoped his mouth would end up. Instead, he worked his kisses down one leg and then up the other. When he was finished, he straightened up and lifted her from the workbench, wrapping her legs around his hips.

Joey pecked her lips and smiled. "Don't give me that look."

Her arms wrapped around his neck to keep herself close to him, and she rolled those lively green eyes of hers. "What look?"

"The look where you get impatient and want my cock bad enough you don't realize you're pouting." He chuckled and walked with her out of the garage, carrying her through the house until they came to the living room, currently cast in darkness.

Carefully traversing his way through the room, he made it to the gas fireplace. Using one arm to support her against him, his hand reached out to flip a switch on the wall so that the soft glow of flames illuminated the room.

Arguing, Layne responded, "I don't pout." She pouted stubbornly.

He lowered them both down to the floor, setting Layne on her back. Joey kicked off his shoes to the side before he stripped himself out of his jeans and boxer briefs. The amber lighting from the fire at their side danced across his body, revealing the long length of his dick.

Kneeling between her legs, his hands ran up along her inner thighs. "Don't lie to me, Layney," he playfully teased her with a grin. His tongue ran over his lips as he looked down at her pussy. There was just enough light that he could see the gleam of her excitement across those pretty lips.

Whimpering quietly, she shifted her hips, her body ready to feel the pleasure of his touch.

Leaning down, his fingers spread her folds to expose her even further to him. Joey's tongue ran from her, opening up to her clit in a languid stroke.

It triggered a delightful shiver from Layne as she gasped out.

He continued to taste her arousal, his tongue progressively teasing her sensitive nub. Every contact made with her body was purposeful toward incrementally getting her closer to the cusp of an orgasm.

Nearing her release, Layne's hips rode against his mouth to seek out the key to her ecstasy. One hand grasped onto the top of his head while the other clawed at the soft area rug underneath her.

She was getting so damn close, and Joey knew it would only take one more graze of his teeth across her clit before she would be swept away in her release.

Opting to pull back, he shifted himself over top of her. Passionately, he kissed her, letting her taste the flavor of her own body on his tongue.

Positioning the tip of his cock at the opening of her cunt, he spoke against her mouth. "I'm yours, always and forever, Layne."

He took his time as he slid himself into her, basking in the feel of the slow stretch of her walls around his thick cock.

Layne moaned out at the gradual entry into her body, the pleasurable sensation being drawn out. Her hands ran over his shoulders onto his upper back as she held him close.

"Mmm, yes, Joey," her sweet sounds were made on the cusp of each of her breaths.

Continuing at the same pace, he pulled back out so the rounded head of his cock nearly popped free from her entrance. Then, he sank himself back into her.

Meanwhile, his face pressed against the side of her neck, inhaling the scent of rain-kissed daisies on her skin. He needed to be as physically close to her as possible while cherishing all of her body. Her breasts were pressed up against his chest, allowing him to feel the rise and fall of her lungs, seeking out oxygen while her heart pounded just beneath the surface.

Each movement of his hips built a slow burn of sensations inside her body. Layne's hips matched his movements, ensuring he was buried far into her at the base of every thrust.

Hooking her ankles behind him, she began to lose control of the sounds she was making. Each push of his cock into her had a deep spark growing with intensity inside her lower stomach that threatened to burn her alive.

Looking up into his eyes, she gasped for air after a long moan. "I love you. So much. Always and forever will never be enough time with you, Joey." Her hands never wanted to let him go.

He groaned, feeling the tight space of her pussy begin to bear down around him. "Layney…I'll always need to feel this way with you." Joey's words were rushed out at the end as his hips began to falter in their relaxed rhythm. His dick now rocked into her quicker and with more force.

Her fingernails dug into his back as she shuddered, and it felt like an eternity left on the cliff of her release. Then, there was nothing but a flood of warmth and a spike of sudden ecstasy as she cried out. Layne came hard, her body latching onto him as she surrendered to the carnally induced high.

Despite the way her cunt squeezed him tightly, refusing to let go, Joey kept rolling his hips into her, fighting the resistance. With an eager growl and several more thrusts, he felt the electricity ricocheting down his spine. Every inch of him pulsed as his cum was unleashed deep inside her, all too quickly filling up the home his cock had made for itself.

He continued to love all of her for several more rounds until Joey had Layne passed out contently in his arms as he lay there with her on the floor of the living room. Both of them were covered in each other's sweat and bodily fluids, and most importantly, their love for one another stained their souls.

Joey eventually carried Layne upstairs to their bedroom, tenderly tucking her into their bed. Making her understand the depth of his love had been his top priority. Now, it was onto the next—blowing her fuckin' asshole brother to kingdom come.

Chapter Twenty-Eight

BURN

"Layne," Gage shook her shoulder.

She mumbled something incoherent as she began to rouse from her slumber.

"Baby, wake up," his voice sounded urgent.

Layne finally rolled onto her back in bed, her body getting even more tangled in the sheets. "What is it?"

Gage hated that he was going to have to wake her for this, but he had waited long enough that his gut was at the bottom of the pit of despair somewhere.

He laid it on her, "Joey isn't back home yet."

Without coffee having her running on all cylinders, there was a little bit of lag as her brain began to process his words. She turned her head to the side to see the clock on the nightstand, showing it was shortly after ten in the morning.

The instant everything came together, she pushed herself up onto her elbows. "What?"

Fighting with the sheets tangled around her, she scrambled over to the side of the bed where her phone rested on its charger, pulling it from the cradle to scroll through any and all messages. Nothing from Joey.

Trying to grasp the seriousness of the situation, she asked Gage, "He hasn't called you?" Layne glanced over at him as she tried to avoid jumping to any conclusions. Internally, she was panicking like fuck.

He just shook his head as he looked at her apologetically, wishing he had a better response for her. There wasn't anything he hadn't already tried to eliminate as a reason for his brother having not made it back home after leaving to go set Liam's potential demise.

"Fuck." Layne scooted out of bed and grabbed one of the guys' spare shirts, yanking it down over her head. These days, it was difficult to tell which tee belonged to which of her men, not unless they had worn it and it held either the scent of toasted vanilla of Gage or the musky leather and sage of Joey.

She dialed Joey's number as she stepped over to the window, peering outside as she waited for him to answer. Her fingernail lightly tapped against the pane as her nerves began to fray.

Ring. Ring. Ring. 'The number you are trying to reach is currently unavailable; please leave a message after the tone.'

Layne hung up and redialed his number. Her eyes scanned the snowy landscape of a frigid February day just outside. Perhaps his car got stuck? The Challenger was shit in the snow. A million thoughts filled her mind as she hardly paid attention to the unanswered rings in her ear.

"Goddamnit, pick up," she whispered to herself.

Finally hearing the generic voicemail switch on again, she hung up and turned to face Gage and shook her head grimly. "Nothing."

Her stomach felt sick; this wasn't like him. "Fuck, fuck, fuck. Fuck!" She brought a hand to her forehead as worst-case scenarios began to bounce around inside of her head.

Gage came up and grabbed her shoulders; he kissed her softly. "Breathe. Let's just try to stay level-headed. There are still some good reasons why he may not be back yet." Internally, he was feeling anything but calm. He knew as much as she did that something had to have gone wrong, and the likelihood of his brother forgetting to check in was next to zero.

She stared into Gage's eyes that attempted to mask his concerns, but she saw right through it. Layne's lower lip quivered. "We almost lost him once, I can't even—"

"Sshh," Gage stopped her from going down that negative path. "There are a thousand explanations."

"All of which leads to Liam." She pressed her lips firmly together as she tried to see past her own spiraling emotions.

His hands grabbed her face firmly as he leaned in so their foreheads were touching. "Don't think like that," he sternly demanded of her. Both of them couldn't afford to be lost to their fears.

Layne's phone began buzzing in her palm. She glanced down and saw Liam's name appear–so much for avoiding their worst nightmares. Turning the screen to Gage, she said, "This can't be a coincidence."

Without waiting for Gage to provide alternative reasoning, Layne put the call on speaker. Putting on her best front, she steadied her voice, "What do you want, Li?"

Her brother darkly sniggered. "What do I want? More importantly, what—well…who do you want?"

She bit into her lower lip so harshly, trying to contain the rage that wanted to lash out at him that she swore she was going to break the skin. Unclear of how much silence had passed between them, she finally began assembling her strength to ask the question she needed an answer to. "Is he alive?"

Dramatically, Liam sighed. "Always with the dumb questions, Layne. If he wasn't, it wouldn't do me any good to try and get you down here, now would it?"

"Yes or no, Liam." The bile was rising quickly in her throat as she waited for a straightforward response.

Liam paused before replying to her, "Yes. For now."

The sick feeling temporarily waned as she at least had something to put her at ease, a sliver of hope. There was no telling if Liam was lying or not, but any hope was better than none.

Her brother continued, "You want him? You know where to come find him. Don't wait too long, though. When I get bored, bad things happen, sis."

She snapped, "Don't fucking threaten me, Liam." A heated and violent sensation was now flowing through her veins. "You want the O'Reilly empire to yourself? I will be fucking hand-delivering it to you." Her thumb smashed the red button on the screen to disconnect the call.

Gage opened his mouth to say something, but before he had the chance, she screamed and threw her phone across the room. It collided with her dresser, shattering the glass screen and falling to the floor. "Motherfucking piece of shit!"

Her chest rose and fell with the sheer amount of fury boiling up inside her. It wasn't until Gage grabbed her shoulders tightly and turned her to face him that she saw something other than blinding red.

"Look at me!" His grip on her continued to remain as firm as his voice. "I need you to keep your shit together, Layne. He knows that you're ready to run over there with guns out."

"Damn straight I am! He has six fucking holes in his body, and I'm going to put a bullet in every one of them!" Layne was prepared to go on a murder spree and take out anyone who got in her path. "This is it, Gage. I refuse to let him or anyone else fuck with our lives anymore. I'm *done*."

Nodding, Gage was on the same page with her but had to be the sanity check to make sure she didn't do something that got herself killed. While he was willing to spend an eternity in the afterlife with her and Joey, it wasn't something he wanted to start today. "Go hop in the shower; I will make a few calls and start packing."

Despite being amped up and anxious to get out the door, Layne showered and let her vivid imagination come up with every potential way of killing her brother. If Joey was anything less than unscathed, she would make her pain felt by all of the criminal factions in New York if she had to.

Getting ready to bring a war to your psychopathic brother's turf wasn't as quick of a process as she wished. Gage had been right in trying to get her to slow down and think things through. If he had let her leave right after that phone call, she would have left most of her arsenal at home so she could choke the shit out of Liam with her bare hands.

Instead, dusk was cloaking the city on a below-freezing winter's night. The snow on the roads and sidewalks helped cut through the darkness of the day's end.

Gage parked his Jeep in the church parking lot across the street from Eric Ellis's former residence. "This is it?" He stared at the massive corner property in disbelief. Valuing his life, he decided against asking Layne if Eric had been making up for lack of size in other areas.

"Yeah, Eric was a bougie asshole when he made the move here." Layne unbuckled her seat belt and swung open her door, hopping out onto the cracked pavement of the parking lot.

He hadn't been willing to say it, but fuck, Gage would have purchased the home in a heartbeat if it hadn't been for the bad blood associated with it. Now, he just wanted to see this gorgeous piece of architecture burn to the ground.

Layne had her hair pulled back into a simple ponytail and dressed in black from head to toe. Stretching her skull mask with the green and orange ribbons across her face, she looked over at Gage as he also got out of the Wrangler.

"Jax and his guys in position?" Layne questioned as she double-checked the weaponry hidden all over her body.

Gage nodded. "They're all set, just waiting on you, Lucky Charm." Whatever waited for them inside, he hoped that they had brought enough bodies to overcome it. There were eight of them, nine if Joey was in any type of fighting form. Truth be told, unless his brother was dead, he'd be prepared to inflict pain on anyone who stood in his way. Included in their headcount were Layne's top guys, Sammy and Ethan. Hunter had been sure to pick them up on his way here.

Her eyes looked across the street at the imposing home that stretched up three floors, four if you included the rooftop. Never did she want to step foot in this house again, but if it meant there was a shot of getting Joey back in one piece, there was nothing that would keep her out.

Before she could leave Gage to take the first steps on her own, he came up to her and adjusted her jacket over her body, making sure it fit snugly around her. "Baby, I love you. You are more than my stars and moon; you are my universe. Just remember what I said, okay?" He leaned in, tugging her mask down enough to fiercely kiss her, spreading his love for her into her soul through their mouths.

She nodded and echoed back to him what he had told her on the way here. "Headshots are permanent, everywhere else is an excuse to haunt your demons."

Trying to give her a proud smile, he coupled it with another tender kiss on her forehead. "That's my girl. We'll be in your shadow, okay?" His fingers adjusted her mask back into place.

It was now or never that she put an end to this feud with Liam. Taking one more deep breath, she blew it out harshly. "I'm good, promise. Liam will be finding his way to the grave tonight." Even if she had to go with him.

Gage's hand lightly patted her on the side of her face. He hated that he had to abandon her side, but there was no way that it was going to do any good to walk up to the front door with her. There was no question that there were bigger battles to fight on the other entrances around the property.

"Go ahead and make that asshole pay his debts." It took everything in him not to cling to her. If he knew he could whisk her away elsewhere, perhaps kidnap her to someplace safe, he would have done it. Joey would have wanted him to do it, but he couldn't justify abandoning such a major pillar in their lives. Layne would never survive it, and neither would he.

Layne tried to keep her voice void of any emotions that would make him feel uneasy, "I love you; I promise I won't stop fighting for all of us. Don't ever give up on me." If she was going to keep her head in the game, she needed to quickly eliminate all the mushy feelings. Yet, there was still the softness in her eyes as she looked at Gage one last time before jogging across the street toward the house that would be the end for at least one person tonight.

Her boots gave the softest crunch against the compacted snow as she approached the front door of the house she had sold only months ago. This place must have been home to some satanic rituals at some point, given the people it attracted. Not only was it associated with her ex-husband, but now Liam as well, so much for family bonds being the strongest.

Layne knew that Liam was expecting her, so there was no use in sneaking around. Hell, he was probably anticipating some of her crew to be in the area. The element of surprise may have been gone, but that allowed her insight into what he did or possibly didn't know. He knew she'd be coming, and she could rely on that information to drive her actions.

Her finger reached out and pressed the small gold button next to the door. A series of chimes sounded off deep into the house, being easily heard from right outside the door.

Scanning the exterior, everything inside the home looked dark and ominous. It was confirmed when the front door swung open, and she found herself peering into nothing but shadows.

Here went nothing. With a hand resting on the butt of her gun on her hip, she took the first step inside. Swallowing hard as her eyes fought the darkness, Layne glanced around with each advance into the main hall.

The last remaining clip of light from outside dissipated when the front door slammed shut. A voice bounded against the walls and echoed up into the height of the arched ceiling. It wasn't the words spoken that spooked her, but who was saying them that drove terror straight down her spine. All the hairs on the back of her neck were on end, and her skin became littered with goosebumps.

"So glad you could join us, Layne. It's been too long since we've had a family reunion." The male voice matched the one the night of the car wreck. With a clear head, she recognized it now. It didn't make any sense, but everything she thought she knew was wrong.

"How?" was all she asked into the darkness that surrounded her.

There was no response, only maniacal laughter.

Spinning around, she strained to hear any threatening movement that may have been approaching her.

A light flickered on, and she came face to face with a ghost. Layne gasped as her eyes widened at the familiar face. It was no longer her mind playing tricks on her; he was actually standing there before her. This motherfucker came back from the grave.

Her body went rigid before she said his name out loud, "Uncle Mick."

Chapter Twenty-Nine

GREATEST ACT OF LOVE

It sounded insane, even to her, to say the name of a dead man out loud. Every plan that she had plotted inside her head hadn't accounted for his presence.

With a cocky smile, he took a step closer to her. "Speechless? I guess death isn't the end after all." Each word he spoke sent a chill through her body like pointed icicles stabbing the strength of her resolve.

Layne pushed past all the questions clouding her brain and lunged at Mick, barreling her shoulder into his chest to knock him off balance. Despite the minimal light, she was able to grab hold of his shirt with one hand while her other drew her firearm.

Mick's bear paw of a hand was soon wrapped around her wrist as she struggled to aim the gun at the fucker who should have been buried six feet under. So much for headshots being permanent. Questions could be asked later.

As his upper body strength quickly overtook her, she thrust her heel up into his gut. Her wrist broke free from his grasp as they both stumbled back from one another. Aiming the weapon in his direction, she pulled the trigger to fire off the first shot.

With her finger squeezing the trigger, a force slammed into her head from behind. The bullet from her gun shot up into the darkness, missing its intended target. Her Glock clattered against the floor and slid several feet from her. Immediately, she dropped to the ground harder than a bag of cement. Trying to maintain her wits, she winced at the pain blossoming across the back of her skull.

Layne had been so distracted by Mick's resurrection that she hadn't realized there was another goon waiting to strike.

Weakly, she attempted to scramble onto all fours, only to have the rubber sole of a boot force her back down onto her stomach. Mick had a satisfied smirk stretched across his weathered face as he walked toward her.

"As I've always said, you're a stupid little bitch," Mick spoke with such disdain that she was certain that she'd be seeing either brimstone and hellfire or pearly gates soon enough.

Despite the sweet allure of unconsciousness wanting to drag her under, she stubbornly willed herself to keep her eyes mostly open. However, it was questionable how much she succeeded in those efforts as her recollection of the trip up to the former ballroom one floor above was spotty after she had been yanked to her feet.

When the double doors swung open to the expansive room, the lights from the chandeliers were blinding in comparison to the rest of the lack of lighting throughout the house. With one hand of the miscreant latched on the back of her neck and the other squeezing her upper arm painfully, she had nowhere to go.

Layne was still feeling wobbly on her feet, and as she looked at the occupants of the sweeping expanse of the ballroom, her remaining strength was ready to check-the-fuck-out.

There were hired hands all around the room, more than she wanted to give her brother credit for. At the center of it all, Liam was standing there with a stupid fucking glass of whiskey in his hand like he suddenly was the epitome of sophistication amongst douchebags. To his right, tied to an ornate gilded chair, was Joey.

Controlling her facial expressions was never a strong suit, and seeing half of her heart strapped down to the chair with obvious wounds to his face and bloodied clothes made it nearly impossible. There was no telling just how much of Liam or Mick's hatred he had endured in her absence. With the skull mask covering the lower half of her face, she considered it a blessing in this instance.

"Sis!" Liam exclaimed, like he was seeing her for the first time in years. "I am so happy you made it! Fuck, you certainly took your time, didn't you?"

Mick walked past her to join Liam at his side, wrapping an arm around his shoulders like a proud papa. "I told you, Liam. It just requires a little bit of patience."

Still being detained by the asshole at her back, she began quickly assessing the already dire situation. Her emerald eyes kept glancing over at Joey. His eyes were shut, and all she could do was pray to see them open one more time. Duct tape was not only covering his mouth but bound his hands behind his back and adhered his ankles to the legs of the chair.

"You got me here, Li. Congrats," she spoke up without looking at her brother. Layne took notice of several other men standing along the far walls. Even with her anticipated support on its way, they were still outnumbered.

She continued, "I guess this means you win." Her words lacked any level of sincerity.

The sound of her voice prompted Joey to open his eyes wearily. He was alive, and that in and of itself was motivation to keep fighting. If she had walked in here only to find him dead, she would have gone blind, unleashing the wrath of all hell's inner circles.

Sipping from his glass, Liam was all too happy as he smiled. "Oh, I've always been the winner, Layne. I've just been waiting to see how long you were willing to keep pathetically playing along."

Her eyes met Joey's, trying to convey reassurance to him with looks alone. It was interrupted when Mick stepped between them, breaking her line of sight.

Layne ground her teeth together as she glared at Mick. "How the hell are you even here?"

The man, who she could have sworn had been killed in the dining room of O'Reilly Manor, seemingly had an aversion to death.

Mick grinned at her before turning and walking to Joey's side, gripping his shoulder firmly. "Well, it seems your fucktoy here isn't as great of a shot as he thinks he is. You should have seen his face when I caught him trying to set an explosive on my truck last night." He gave a laugh reminiscent of a clown on crack.

He lifted two fingers to a spot just behind his ear, tapping a scar at the base of his skull by his hairline. "Call it a blessing from God, maybe even a damn miracle, but the bullet entered behind my ear here and came out just above my occipital bone. Head wounds bleed like a fucker, though, don't they?"

"And your funeral?" Layne inquired.

"A setup," Mick responded with a shrug like he was discussing the weather. "I had a real come-to-Jesus moment after that night. I realized with your dad withering away and Liam having no one to guide him; there was a real opportunity to see to it that the business remained in good hands. He's been so kind to make sure I've had adequate accommodations." Mick gestured at the room they were all in.

Liam added his side of the story, "You look as shocked as I was, Layne. When Uncle Mick showed up at my door, I couldn't believe it. He explained what really happened that night and how he wanted nothing but to see the family business thrive in the hands of its rightful owner. The only problem is you kept doing what you fucking do. You kept ignoring your place."

Taking another sip of the whiskey, Liam went to the other side of Joey and spat at the side of his face. "Then, you invite this asshole to live permanently between your legs and reap the benefits of a business that isn't his."

Joey grunted and pulled against his restraints in the chair. Layne's body tensed, waiting on edge for Liam to be stupid enough to do something that would force her to try to take on every fucking soul in this room by herself.

Chuckling, Liam looked at his sister. "To add insult to injury, you had to drag his brother into it. Speaking of which, I'm sure he's not too far. The great thing about Eric was he knew how to make a home a fortress, so my men will find him before he gets too far."

Liam looked at Mick like he was some savior. "Nevertheless, Mick has been guiding me and teaching me how to take back control of what is rightfully mine. If it wasn't for him, I may have eaten a bullet after Dad died."

If only.

Her brother continued to reminisce, "I was in a dark place, Layne. But once Mick helped me see my true potential, he made sure that my failed assassination attempt on your life became my advantage. He has been by my side nearly every day, ensuring that I never fail again."

Jesus Christ, Layne would have thought that Liam was ready to drop to his knees and start sucking Mick's cock the way he was placing the man on a pedestal.

The man she used to call her uncle had the largest shit-eating grin on his poorly aged face. "Layne, I'm rather hurt. It took until tonight to recognize me after all the chances I gave you. My years may not have been kind, but just because I was sporting a beard and a baseball cap, you still should have seen it. I expected better from you, sweetheart. Your dad would have been so disappointed."

Racking her brain for what she missed, she cursed as she realized that he had hidden in plain sight, starting with the day at the Chinese restaurant.

She looked over at her idiotic sibling, who didn't deny any of Mick's account of events. "Liam, you stupid fuck." She shook her head in disbelief. "Do you think he gives a shit about you? He betrayed our family. Once you're no longer of value, he will betray you, too."

Barking back at her loudly, Liam's face turned bright red, "Betrayed?! Let's talk about betrayal, Layne! How about not just you fucking the psycho who killed Mom but marrying him, huh?! How about your betrayal in trying to take over what belongs to me? FUCK YOU!"

Her brother's insults fell flat against her defenses. If he wanted to pitch stones in an attempt to hurt her feelings, he would need to try harder.

"I told you," Mick spoke knowingly as he walked to Liam, "She doesn't think she's done anything wrong. Typical woman, all wrapped up in her feelings. That's why women don't deserve to be in our position of power."

Glaring at Mick as he added his damn two cents, Layne was determined to make sure the next time he was shot, he wouldn't be able to come back from the dead.

"Oh, there are plenty of things I've done wrong. Starting with letting Liam get away with all his shit for this long," she confessed.

Gulping down the rest of the drink in his hand, Liam lazily tossed the glass to the side, where it shattered upon impact with the floor. He snapped his fingers at the nearest man willing to follow his unspoken orders. His lackey brought him a heavy length of chain.

The odds weren't in her favor, and she was beginning to think that maybe Gage and the rest of the crew ran into trouble down on the sublevel. Shitty odds never stopped her before, though.

Liam swung the end of the chain in his hand threateningly as he stalked towards her. "Time to pay the piper, Layne." Arriving in front of her, he wound up and whipped the chain at her. Instinctively, she raised her free arm to block the lash of metal.

As the links made contact with her left wrist, she embraced the pain and rotated her hand to wrap the chain into her grasp so he couldn't pull it back.

Simultaneously, the fucking cavalry finally burst through the doors, and Gage poured in with Jax, Devon, Isaiah, Hunter, Ethan, and Sammy.

The intrusion set chaos into motion, and unlike the rest of these assholes, she had learned to embrace chaos a long time ago. Layne jerked on the chain, circling her wrist, causing Liam to stumble off balance towards her, where her foot kicked harshly into his chest, sending him right back again.

The goon at her back had been distracted by her backup charging in, so when she bent over, she propelled him over her right shoulder onto the ground. She swung the weight of the chain, and it crashed right into his temple, knocking him out.

Gunfire erupted around her as her small army began picking off targets.

Layne immediately ran towards Joey, dropping to her knees and sliding a few inches towards his feet. She shook the chain from her wrist and withdrew the pocketknife Liam had gifted her with. It took nearly no time to slice through the silver tape and free Joey's hands and ankles, freeing him to rip the tape from his mouth himself.

Shoving the knife back into her pocket, she exchanged it for her gun, which she thrust into Joey's palm. No matter what Mick said, she trusted Joey's aim any day of the week.

"You okay?" There wasn't much time to have a long-winded conversation as she snatched up the heavy-duty chain from the ground.

Joey nodded. "You're late." He raised the gun and fired a couple of shots at the nearest threats.

She lightly scoffed, "It's your job to be on time, not mine." Layne grinned behind her mask as her eyes darted around the room, looking for Liam and Mick. Landing eyes on her brother first, he was ducking behind a column and returning gunfire as he began making his way gradually toward the curved staircase that led to the next floor up.

Before she could visually track down Mick, a few of Liam's hired hands ran at her and Joey. Despite the rough shape Joey appeared to be in, you'd never know it by the way he fought off the first attacker that made it to them.

Layne wielded the chain to smack it against the arm of a man who came at her. However, she fell forward as another one pummeled into her from behind. "Oof!" She hit the ground hard.

No sooner than she met the floor, the weight on her back was lifted. Gage easily jerked the man off her and shoved him toward Joey, who dropped him like a fly with one shot between the eyes.

Both De Lucas grabbed one end of the metal chain wrapped around her left hand and assisted in pulling her up to her feet as it felt like shell casings were raining down all around them.

Joey and Gage glanced down at the links in her grasp, the irony not lost on them that what should have been an item used to keep a person bound, their feisty shamrock repurposed it as a weapon.

With the others managing to hold their own, she searched for any sign of Mick. "Where did Mick go?"

Taking a quick glance around, Gage responded, "He's got to be here somewhere. We'll find him."

At that time, another wave of Liam's supporters swarmed into the room. *Fucking hell.*

The three of them immediately got put on the defensive, as everyone began utilizing whatever they had to survive. Joey emptied the remainder of the bullets in the gun Layne had given him before he began physically assaulting anyone who looked like a threat.

Wrapping the metal chain around some asshole's neck, Layne left it pinched around his throat, letting him choke to death before she moved on to the next person looking to die.

Layne caught sight of Liam as he cowardly made a run for it up the stairs several feet from where she was. There was no way he was escaping so easily. "No, you don't, little fucker," she murmured.

Using her small figure, she managed to push through a couple of guys as she ran for the stairs after her brother.

Joey tossed one of Liam's goons off him, slamming a fist into his cheek and knocking him to the ground. He looked up as Layne ran up the stairs two at a time after Liam. "Layne!!"

The shouting of her name prompted Gage to thrust a knee into the scrappy asshole he was dealing with before directing his attention to the same sight that had Joey barking out their girl's name.

"Devon!" Gage shouted, glancing over his shoulder at his friend nearest to him. "Need your help over here!" If they were going to chase after Layne, they needed to get past the group of men blocking their path.

Layne made it halfway up the stairs before she turned to look at both men. It was a split second or less, but her face softened with a silent apology clouding her green eyes. She tore her skull mask from her face, dropping it to the ground at her feet. Her perfect lips mouthed her love for them with those three little words before she continued her ascent up the steps, following Liam behind the door at the top.

Just like that, she was gone.

Chapter Thirty

DEATH IS NOT THE END

She chased Liam through the door at the top of the stairs. It led into the hallway on the third floor.

"Li! Get the fuck back here!" she shouted while watching him blatantly ignore her.

Her brother rounded a corner, and she heard a door slam shut. Quick to make the turn, she noticed a door that looked different from all the others. Panting from the pursuit, she pushed through it and saw a steep set of stairs that led to a single metal door that was just drifting closed.

Layne steeled herself as she followed, prepared for whatever showdown was going to happen with her brother. When she made it out the door, she got blasted with a gust of freezing air that whipped her ponytail around erratically. He had led her up to the roof.

The visibility of the night air was shitty, thanks to all the fat snowflakes that kept swirling around as they descended from above. Each flake that fell stuck to her chestnut hair and contrasted against the black of her clothes.

He couldn't have gone too far, and the moment she thought as much, he crashed into her side, knocking her to the snow-covered ground.

Without hesitation, she rolled and began swinging her fists at his face. Scrambling, she fought for the upper hand as they exchanged hits. Eventually, she was able to use leverage from her foot to create enough space between them so she could push herself onto her feet.

Liam got to his feet and stared at her with intense hatred. “You fucked up this family, Layne!”

Each of them was panting from the scuffle, their warm breaths visible when meeting the extremely cold winter air.

“Get the fuck over it,” Layne shook her head, and with every step closer he took, she took two away from him. “You have always been the one with the problem!”

Trying to keep tabs on each movement her brother made down to the flexing of the muscles in his arms, she reminded herself to also be aware of her surroundings. Her eyes stole quick looks at what was there on the top of the roof. Other than weathered patio furniture and HVAC systems, she had little to work with in the open space.

Liam angrily roared at her, “You’ve always tried to hold me down! Dad spoiled you and made you the fuckin’ favorite when it should have been me! You don’t deserve shit!” His hands wildly flailed as he shouted.

“You’re a goddamn spoiled brat, Li! You could have had everything! I overlooked so many of your faults in hopes that sometime you’d grow the fuck up!” She had always been willing to maintain what should have been a steadfast alliance with him, but his destructive behaviors ultimately obliterated any chance of that ever happening.

He charged at her, and when she turned to get out of his way, her foot caught on an old broom left buried under the snow. The trip sent her down onto her hands and knees, giving Liam just enough opportunity to grab her by the back of her jacket and yank her back onto her feet.

Forcefully, he shoved her forward into a large condenser unit. Layne yelped out as she felt the unyielding impact of the metal casing against the front of her body.

When he pulled her back to slam her back against it one more time, she extended her foot in front of her to prevent another collision. She pushed back with just enough oomph that she could duck and turn under his arm, forcing his grasp on her jacket to break. Her elbow jabbed into his side, eliciting a grunt from him as he stumbled.

Layne and Liam continued wrangling with one another, both their feet occasionally sliding against the slippery snow underneath their shoes. The ledge of the roof was getting closer, and Liam’s hand had found its way to her throat, latching onto it like the jaw of a rabid dog.

Fighting against the slowing oxygen and blood flow to her brain, her spine was suddenly bent backward over the partially raised wall that separated them both from a four-story free fall. Snowflakes fell into her eyes as she clawed at Liam's hand on her neck.

"Go burn in hell, sis! Don't worry, your shithead manwhores will be joining you shortly!" Liam's other hand was gripping the front of her jacket, and despite her struggles, her lighter body weight was getting eased off her feet as he began shoving her over the wall.

If she was going down, she was going to try and drag Liam with her. No longer fighting his chokehold on her, her hand fumbled until it found the pocketknife she had used to free Joey earlier. Without a second thought, she flipped open the blade and jammed it home into Liam's chest. It would have been sweet justice if she had struck his heart, but with her vision struggling under his choking grasp, she didn't get that lucky.

As the blade drove into her brother, his hands released her before she hit the point of no return over that wall. Layne gasped and coughed for air as her feet hit the ground on the side of the wall she was grateful to be on.

Drawing the short blade out of him, she angrily punched him across the face while he was still stunned. Her eyes stared at her ultimate betrayer as he slipped and fell to his knees with a hand grabbing at the wound in his chest.

Layne walked behind him, grabbing a fistful of his auburn hair. She jerked his head back so he was looking up at her. "I should thank you for hating me so much. You've made this so much easier." In a smooth motion, she slashed the edge of the blade across his throat, blood flooding from the critical arteries that she just severed.

There were some gurgling sounds before enough of Liam's blood stained the snow around him, and he fell into permanent unconsciousness. Seeing that he was well on his way to hell, she released her grasp on his hair and watched his lifeless body fall forward onto the ground.

She let out a relieved breath that it was over. Part of her mourned that it had to come down to this, something that could have been unavoidable if Liam had chosen a much different path in life. The other part of her was just happy to live another day without his constant attacks on her happiness.

Getting pulled from her thoughts, she heard the roof access door open up as Joey and Gage pushed through. Her gaze softened as she looked at them both, seeing the relief evident on their faces, seeing she was ok.

"It's over." She sighed and gave a small smile.

The familiar sound of a gun popping off echoed throughout the air. One, two, three quick shots went off in succession.

Joey went from a moment of intense happiness that Layne had finally ended Liam's pathetic existence to one of seeing his worst nightmare.

Layne's body jerked as all three shots landed on her chest, tearing holes in her jacket. The force knocked her down, her body hitting the ground hard.

While Joey's only instinct was to get to Layne, Gage's eyes followed the trajectory of where the gunshots came from. Standing across the way was Mick, smirking at the successful strike against the last of the O'Reillys.

Feeling the phantom pain of what it was like to have a single bullet enter his chest, it ached more painfully as three hit Layne's. With pain riddling his voice, he yelled out her name, "LAYNE!" Joey didn't give a fuck if he took a hundred more bullets, he only cared about the woman he loved that had just been gunned down in front of him.

Needing to eliminate the active threat, Gage retrieved his gun from his thigh holster and began firing at Mick, quickly working on emptying his last damn clip as he ran towards his target. "You motherfucker!!"

At least one of the bullets found its way into Mick's stomach, causing him to stagger. It gave Gage enough time to tackle him to the ground, using the butt of his gun to repeatedly smash into his face. This old shitbag deserved to feel his wrath before he died.

Making sure Mick stayed dead this time, Gage used the last bullet in the chamber at point-blank range between the man's eyes. That was a moment he wished he could relive over and over again. Instead, just the memory of it would have to suffice for Gage.

Arriving at Layne's body lying on its side, only a few feet from her brother's, Joey dropped to his knees next to her. She lay there still, nearly looking like an angel as the snowflakes clung to her dark eyelashes.

Horrified, Joey stared down at her, paralyzed by his fears becoming reality. Hidden behind her closed eyelids were the sparkling emerald hues he had fallen so desperately in love with. The pink, pouty lips he had kissed countless times were partially swollen and bruised from her altercation with Liam.

"Fuck, fuck, fuck. Layney!" Joey's hands grabbed her, trying to rouse her awake. His teardrops felt frozen against his cheeks as his panic set in. His hands began to tug at the busted zipper on her jacket from one of the bullet holes.

After the ringing in Gage's ears stopped from firing that bullet into Mick's shitty face, he could hear Joey behind him shouting at Layne. He got up and ran over to the two of them, kneeling on Layne's other side, across from Joey.

Losing Rosie had broken both Joey and Gage, and Layne had mended that wound; losing Layne would destroy them both beyond repair. Already, Joey was beginning to lose his shit as he fought with the zipper with trembling hands. Joey's voice cracked under the emotionally charged whisper, "Layney, you can't...*please*."

Gage swallowed against the lump forming in his throat, preventing him from getting any words out. Layne had to be okay, she was meant for so much more than this. Yet, he was terrified to see anything that said otherwise.

Pushing past his fear, Gage finally shoved Joey's hands away from Layne's jacket zipper and forcefully tore it open.

Joey straightened as he saw what lay underneath, sitting back on his heels. "What the..."

"Thank fuck..." Gage leaned over and laid his head on Layne's stomach as he blew out the breath he had been holding.

Underneath the jacket was a slim bulletproof vest that had a cluster of the three bullets lodged into it.

Sitting back up to look at her, Gage was grateful he had managed to convince Layne's stubborn ass to wear the vest tonight. Otherwise, he would have never forgiven himself.

Layne's eyes slowly opened as she stirred with a groan, "Fuuuck." She winced at the burning sensation against her chest. Despite the vest doing its job, it sure as hell did little to ease the sting of the impact that had stolen her breath away. She had a feeling the bruising was going to be quite the collage of colors.

Before Layne could make the effort to sit up, Joey pulled her upright and locked his arms around her. "Layney, you fuckin' scared the shit out of me." There wasn't much that frightened him, but losing her was a fate worse than death.

Her muffled voice spoke into Joey's chest, "If you keep squeezing me so tight, I'm going to die of suffocation." She groaned again as the aches and pains were screaming throughout all of her body.

Gage's arms joined Joey's as they both embraced her with the unspoken promise of their everlasting protection. "We aren't ever going to let you go, Lucky Charm."

Kissing the top of her head, Joey lovingly smiled. "You're ours, always and forever."

The priest stood between the two headstones as he spoke loud enough for all to hear, "Two young lives, lost all too soon. Liam and Layne O'Reilly, two vibrant souls who have gone home to be with the Lord."

Gage and Joey stood there next to each other in their black suits, gathering amongst the others who had come to pay their respects to the O'Reilly siblings.

Joey leaned over and whispered to Gage, "This is weird, right?"

Gage lifted a brow and whispered back, "Which part? The part where both of these coffins are empty? Or the part where the woman over there," he pointed at the dark-haired woman who had introduced herself as Nicole, "has been ready to jump your bones now that you're technically widowed?"

Layne had been extraordinarily clear that there was no way in hell Liam's corpse was being buried next to her unoccupied grave, and neither of them could argue with her. She had chosen to have his remains cremated and then dumped into a randomly chosen porta potty. Joey chose to pay his respects to Liam in the most appropriate fashion afterward. A little harsh? None of them thought so.

She sat in the back of Joey's Challenger and waited patiently as she observed the funeral services from behind the dark-tinted windows. Trying to pass the time, her hands fidgeted with the hem of the black dress she had chosen to mourn her life as the head of O'Reilly Enterprises.

Layne recounted the events that transpired the night she killed Liam. After both her men smothered her with their happiness to see she had survived Mick's final effort to destroy her, they continued their extraction plans. The intention wasn't just to get the hell out of that house of horrors but to remove them all from the insanity of her days of leading a criminal organization.

Instead, the business was left in Sammy and Ethan's capable hands. If everyone thought she had gone down in a blaze of glory, it gave the three of them a chance at something they never really had. It gave them a chance to enjoy time together without new and constant threats looming over them.

The most heartbreaking decision to make was deciding to keep as few people in the know about her survival, which included Layne's bestie. Joey had been tasked with making the call to Rebecca to gently break the unfortunate news to her. However, things didn't pan out as expected when she called bullshit on him.

One would have thought Rebecca was in denial, but the reasoning for her disbelief was pretty sound. Rebecca argued that Joey would have been in prison on numerous murder charges if Layne was truly dead–she wasn't wrong. In fear for his own safety at Rebecca's hands, Joey caved and added her to the short list of people who knew of Layne's true fate.

Ultimately, Rebecca decided to stay down in Baltimore, having found her own happily ever after.

There were still a few matters to wrap up before they could ditch the city life, but things were well on the way to finding new adventures to get lost in.

When the graveside service wrapped up, Joey and Gage both returned to the car, taking up the two front seats.

"Was it a nice service?" she asked, hoping that her funeral was exactly how she pictured it.

Gage smirked as he turned to look back at her, "Baby, if you're asking if shots of whiskey were passed around and everybody raised them in a toast to you…"

"Oh, come on! It's part of my final wishes, and nobody had the balls to at least honor that small request?" She crossed her arms in front of her chest, clearly disappointed.

Joey looked into the rearview mirror at her and smiled. "Layney, are you seriously going to be upset that your fake funeral didn't live up to your expectations?"

She rolled her eyes at the stupid question. "How else am I going to make sure that I get the funeral I deserve when I *actually* die?"

"Are you rolling your eyes at me?" Joey smirked and started up the engine.

Gage looked at his brother with a devious grin. "I think she is." He turned back around in his seat so he was facing forward. "We'll have to do something about that when we get back home. I have a new toy with my Lucky Charm's name on it."

They all headed back to Gage's condo in Hudson Yards. With Layne supposedly six feet under, the last thing they needed was anyone to spot her coming and going from O'Reilly Manor. It was a temporary living space, and as long as she had both De Luca brothers there with her, she didn't care where she was holed up.

Stepping inside the front door, Gage shed his suit jacket, draping it over the back of one of the kitchen stools. Joey unbuttoned his jacket as he went to the fridge, pulling out three bottles of beer.

Layne leaned back against the edge of the kitchen's center island and smirked as she looked at them both. "I have some news."

Both guys looked at her curiously; there wasn't usually anything that came as a surprise to either of them.

Joey popped the caps off of all three bottles before setting them on the counter next to Layne. "About what?"

With ease, Gage grabbed her waist and sat her down on top of the counter. His hands trailed over her hips down to the hem of her dress. Sliding his hands under the skirt of her dress along her bare thighs, he gave his boyish grin. "It better have to do with your lack of panties," he ran his tongue over his bottom lip, thinking about all the ways he could have her in the kitchen right then and there.

She smiled and shook her head. "Not quite." Layne pulled a small envelope out of her purse that was on the counter next to her. "It was bothering me that Liam's creepy and cryptic note never really made complete sense. He wanted something to do with 611, and it was driving me insane that I couldn't figure it out."

Taking a swig of his beer, Joey looked at the envelope in her hand. "I assumed he was just clinically insane and making shit up."

She began to explain about the day before they all had ended up going down to the former Ellis residence and how she had made her routine bank run. "While I was at the bank, the teller reminded me that there was a safety deposit box my dad set up in my name. It just so happens the number of the box is 611."

Taking the envelope out of her hands, Gage took a peek inside. "And this was inside?"

Layne nodded, unable to contain her infectious smile.

Reviewing the contents, Gage got excited as he saw the small object tucked inside, along with a sticky note. He handed the envelope to Joey, who also took a look, and his face lit up.

"Fuck, yes." He leaned in and lovingly kissed her. Things were looking up for the future.

Gage greedily pulled Layne's face away from Joey so his lips could seize her attention.

"It's going to be a hell of a Christmas this year," Joey set the envelope down as his mind began to pour over all the possibilities that awaited.

Layne giggled as Gage began to get carried away with his kisses that were now being showered over the side of her neck. Her eyes shone with true happiness as she had everything in life to look forward to. It was a happiness that she had never known before she gave her heart over to these two great men.

Despite everything they all had endured, finally, all three of them were going to get their happy ending. There was nothing more Layne could have asked for than to have her heart bursting with everlasting love and to forever share her life with Joey and Gage De Luca.

As it turned out, she really did have all the luck.

EPILOGUE

Layne POV

"So, that's my story. That's everything I have to tell." I look at the two agents seated across from me. Both of them have their jaws halfway to the floor. Perhaps I should have spared them a few of the more colorful descriptions. What could I say? Life is too short to spare the details of great sex.

One of the men straightens his already straight tie as a means to regain his composure. Clearing his throat, he stumbles over his first few words. "Ms. De Luca…"

"Mrs.," I correct him.

He tries again. "Mrs. De Luca, that… That was a very thorough recounting of events."

I smile sweetly at him, reveling in the fact he is so damn uncomfortable right now.

His partner begins pouring himself what must be the fifth cup of water he's chugged in the last hour.

"You asked me to give my version of events and spare no detail. Didn't you?" I smirk, knowing I damn well went above and beyond what the Unwind and Unorganize Program was looking for.

On the day I called Detective Adams to inform him of my potential interest in the initiative, I was surprised to discover the commissioner himself had told him to not only expect my call but prioritize it. The detective swiftly put me in touch with his federal liaisons.

Several discussions on the terms of my cooperation occurred before we ultimately reached an agreement. Now, here I was, giving these fuckers enough information to hit several criminal faction kingpins where it hurt the most.

Sure, I may have left out some details for those who were friends in the loosest definition of the word—allies, if you will. I'm not stupid enough to burn *all* my bridges. I don't have a crystal ball telling me if and when I will ever return to this line of work. The one thing I do know? This is it for me—for us—for now.

Mr. Tie-Straightener shuffles through a folder overflowing with multiple forms. "There is, um, just a few more pieces of paperwork to sign, and then you can be on your way."

Finally, his well-hydrated partner is put together enough to try and make light conversation. "How far along are you?" He nods at the large belly in front of me.

The asshole is brave enough to assume a woman is pregnant? I'm even more tempted to fuck with him. I barely resist the urge and give a glowing smile instead as I rest my hand on my bump. "Just entered my third trimester. It's twins, so each week from here on out is considered a win."

The man nods and seems to try and focus on the mundane details. "Any names picked out?"

I nod while rubbing my hand over the roundness idly. "Joseph Elliot, after the father, and we are naming our daughter Shannon Marie after my mother."

After pulling another form out of the folder, the man leading the discussion hands several pages over to me with a pen. "These all lay out the terms of your immunity and confirm you have fulfilled your end of the bargain by providing relevant information on the organized crime units here in Manhattan."

I read over each word, scrutinizing the way everything is phrased to ensure that the government doesn't end up fucking me over due to a typo.

Once I'm satisfied, I scribble my name at the bottom of each page before laying the pen on top of the stack.

"Is that all? It's been a long couple of days on my back." My wince as I shift in my seat supports my complaint. This entire process had been in play since the moment we realized the threats would never stop coming, not if my lifestyle didn't change. If I ever had a shot at living a normal life, I needed to take steps to create it for myself.

Both agents nod and stand from their seats. The one asking about my pregnancy is quick to help me onto my feet. Graciously, I accept.

"You have the utmost appreciation of the Federal Bureau of Investigation, Mrs. De Luca. Per the terms of your immunity agreement, a contact from our witness protection program will be in touch with you," he says as he walks me to the door.

"I look forward to it." With that, they make sure I find my way out of the federal building located not too far from the World Trade Center.

Right out front, waiting for me, is my ride. Gage smirks as he leans back against the side of the same shitty Jeep that just won't have the sense to finally up and die. I guess, in a way, I can relate as I continue to live my life, refusing to lie down and succumb to death.

He approaches me, reaching out for my belly. "Have I told you how hot as fuck you look? My cock is telling me that this needs to be an ongoing condition for you." Gage's hands cradle my stomach before he lays a kiss on it.

I roll my eyes at whatever breeding kink he has driving his dick wild right now. "Don't get your hopes up."

He follows up with a kiss to my mouth. "We'll see."

I climb into the Wrangler, struggling to get the momentum to put my ass in the seat, but with a little nudge from Gage, I am finally in and settled. My seat belt stretches across me to make sure all things precious to both of my guys are secure.

Gage jogs around to the driver's seat and gets in. "He's waiting for us."

Smiling, I can't wait to finally see his face. The Feds had been far too interested in Joey's criminal history and all the contracts he had taken from the moment he stepped foot in my life. To spare us both the risk of pissing off Uncle Sam, he has been keeping his distance and lying low.

It was a brief drive across the bridge into Brooklyn. I was all too ready to hop out of my seat the second Gage parked by the quiet little beach Joey and I had dubbed as our spot. His beloved Challenger was parked right beside us, and he stood on the beach watching the sun reflect off the calm water lapping at the shoreline.

To say I was running for him was the biggest overstatement of my life. This massive weight I carried on the front of me slowed me down tremendously. How did women do this more than once? I will never know.

Joey turned as I approached, and his face lit up. "Layney." His lovely brown eyes soaked in the sight of me. "Fuck, I didn't expect you to look this goddamn gorgeous." Clearly, he is pleasantly surprised at how well I wear the extra curves. I'd know that heated gaze anywhere.

My steps come to a halt in front of him. "Don't get any ideas." I grin and finally begin shifting things underneath my shirt while wrinkling my face up at the intense effort of it all.

His hand reaches out and takes hold of my chin. "We'll see." Those chocolate hues holding a promise within them.

These damn De Lucas and their hard-headedness when they get an idea in their heads…or cocks.

I welcome Joey's slow and intense kiss as he takes claim over my mouth, savoring each part of my lips before his tongue dives into my mouth. The kiss distracts the efforts of my hands underneath my shirt until, finally, I feel a sudden release.

Breaking away from his mouth, I let out a massive sigh of relief as the prosthetic belly falls to the ground with a ceremonious thunk. "Jesus, you have no idea how heavy and hot as balls that shit is." Makes me glad that I have no intentions of thrusting my lifestyle onto any innocent souls in the near future. No child needs to grow up in a life riddled with danger the way I did.

Gage catches up to us both and smiles. He leans over and picks up the rounded stomach from the ground. His hand dives into a small slit in the side, digging around for what is just underneath the surface.

When Gage's hand pulls back from the silicone, he holds a small electronic chip between his fingers. "How long do you think it will take before the Feds realize that the entire recording of your interview is useless?" He flashed an amused grin.

Thanks to Cowboy, he made sure that what I confessed to could never be used against any of us. His new girlfriend, Amanda, works in the costume design department for some theater production company on Broadway. She was kind enough to hook me up with the prosthetic to house the interference device. Who was going to question a pregnant lady?

The FBI may now know the names of major players and know who to focus on first, but without solid proof, nothing I said could ever come back to haunt me.

I shrug innocently. "Hours, maybe days." Either way, I expected all of us to be long gone before then.

Joey pulls out his car keys and dangles them in front of my face. "You're in charge of taking us where we're going now, Layne."

I reach out and take the keys into my hand, looking them over.

Smiling to myself, I can say that my decision has come easily. "I think it's time I leave this city behind. My time here is done, and I'm overdue for a nice, long vacation. How does someplace warm and sunny with plenty of booze sound?"

Joey smiles as he pulls my face to his with his hands. "I don't care where we go, as long as we're all going together." His lips caress over mine once more in a reassuring and loving gesture.

When I slowly pull away from the kiss and look over to Gage to gather his opinion, he responds by hooking his finger under the thin chain around my neck to tug me closer. The charming grin on his face says it all; he wants this change as much as the rest of us.

"You better believe that no matter where we go, I'm going to be there to correct your bratty behavior," Gage's tone makes it clear that his words are a lifelong promise. One that he seals with a playful kiss to my mouth.

After we all make it back to where both cars are parked, I turn and look at the Manhattan skyline. My eyes grow wet at the memories of the place I had grown up calling home. Letting go was proving to be more difficult than I anticipated, but I knew it was the right thing to do for all of us.

It's going to be a long drive down to the Florida Keys, but maybe I could learn to call the ocean waves and sandy beaches my new home. They say home is where the heart is, right? I am lucky enough to have the hearts of two De Lucas following me no matter where I go. And for that, I am so grateful.

My dad had left a key and address of a house located in Key West in my safety deposit box. I don't believe in fate, but I do consider it a sign that this is ultimately what he always wanted for me. Closing this chapter of our lives means we have all the unwritten possibilities ahead of us.

I will never stay in my lane, even now that I have found closure. Now, as my life shifts, I know that Chaos and Wrath will always and forever be on either side of Luck.

THREE MONTHS LATER

The oscillating fan in the small grocery store continues on its back-and-forth pattern of distributing airflow. I take a deep breath as I continue to stare at the line of products in front of me. Joey and Gage are probably wondering what the hell is taking me so long; I only came in here for one thing.

A woman stops at my side, nearly passing me before she backs up a few steps. When I glance over at her, she's seemingly smiling to herself as she looks at me with a glistening of tears in her eyes.

"Can I help you?" Not that I work here, but what else do you ask when someone stops to stare at you?

She shakes her head apologetically. "Sorry, you just remind me of someone who was a part of my life for a very long time. Someone who I had to recently say goodbye to."

My face softens, my heart reaching out to this woman who may have been a stranger but had an unexplainable sense of familiarity about her. Trying to put her mind at ease, I offer up some kind words, "Goodbyes are hard, but they provide the promise that something new is just beginning."

I reach out and give her hand a reassuring squeeze; it seems to provide her some solace as she gives me another sweet smile. "Thank you for everything," she says softly, returning the squeeze to my hand.

After she takes her leave, I'm left with my own words about beginnings as I'm once again looking at the shelf in front of me. I hastily grab a box at random and make my way to the checkout counter.

When I leave the store with my purchase in tow, Florida's humidity greets me. The island breeze is the only real thing, making it tolerable.

Crossing the parking lot, I climb into the front seat of Gage's Wrangler. After one too many tropical beverages on the boat this morning, Gage is squeezed into the backseat while Joey is behind the wheel.

"Get everything you need?" Joey looks at me curiously.

I nod and raise the bag in front of his view.

Gage leans forward between us with a giddy smile. "I'm feeling lucky."

I roll my eyes, of course, he is.

As Joey is pulling out of the parking space, another Jeep passes by us. Driving it is the same woman I had made a connection with inside the grocery store. She pops up two fingers on her steering wheel, giving Joey the signature Jeep Wave.

I watch as he gives her a smile with a hint of something grateful behind it as he returns the wave to her.

On the way home, I find myself lost in my thoughts as I look into the bag I'm holding in my lap.

There's only one question left.
Is the test going to be positive?

The End…?

ABOUT THE AUTHOR

Sadie Winchester is a romance author residing in the Pine Barrens of New Jersey with her husband, her son, and their two cats (Thor & Loki). She began her love for writing in high school, drafting stories on a popular internet platform.

The dream of writing and publishing a full-length novel first manifested a couple of years after she married the love of her life. However, it took a back burner as she focused on other adventures and goals. Finally, after becoming a mother and finding a way to rediscover herself, she was inspired by another new author to commit to this long-term dream.

When Sadie is not writing up her stories or getting lost in books, she is spending time with her family. She enjoys working out, cooking, visiting microbreweries, and binge-watching *Supernatural*.

You can connect with Sadie in the following ways:

SadieWinchester.com or Linktr.ee/SadieWinchester

amazon.com/author/sadiewinchester
facebook.com/sadiewinchesterauthor
goodreads.com/sadiewinchester
instagram.com/sadiewinchesterauthor
tiktok.com/@sadiewinchesterofficial
bookbub.com/profile/sadie-winchester

ALSO BY SADIE WINCHESTER

www.ingramcontent.com/pod-product-compliance
Lightning Source LLC
Chambersburg PA
CBHW070825020826
48982CB00014B/459

* 9 7 9 8 9 9 0 4 4 7 7 2 1 *